W9-AOX-641

Saffron Skies

Saffron Skies

A NOVEL

by
LESLEY LOKKO

**Doubleday Large Print
Home Library Edition**

Garden City, New York

This Large Print Edition, prepared especially for Doubleday Large Print Home Library, contains the complete, unabridged text of the original Publisher's Edition.

Copyright © 2005 by Lesley Lokko

All rights reserved. No part of this publication may be reproduced, stored in a retrieval system, or transmitted, in any form or by any means, electronic, mechanical, photocopying, recording, or otherwise, without the prior permission of the publishers.

This novel is a work of fiction. The names, characters, and incidents portrayed in it are the work of the author's imagination and any resemblance to actual persons, living or dead, is entirely coincidental.

Published by Doubleday Large Print, 401 Franklin Avenue, Garden City, New York 11530

ISBN 0-7394-5318-1

Printed in the United States of America

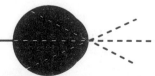

This Large Print Book carries the Seal of Approval of N.A.V.H.

For Vic

Heartfelt thanks are due to Christine Green, my agent and friend, without whose editorial brilliance and endless—repeat, endless!—patience this novel would never have happened; to Kate Mills, Helen Richardson and the entire "team" at Orion for their continued and fantastic support; to Alastair and Susan Cowan at Eastside Farm, Penicuik, for providing such a wonderful writing spot; to Patrick, for a thousand acts of kindness at all times, always; to all my London mates—Caroline, Cathy, Jonathan, Marko, Rahesh, Ro, Samir and Victoria—for staying so close, despite the distance; to the crews in Accra—"P," Sean, Yaw, Sally, "Sweet P," Elkin, et al.—for taking the plunge and coming back home; to Marko Jobst and Ceri Shields for their help and advice in moments of doubt; to Suzanne Szabo for her excellent translations; to Dietra for her wickedly sharp eyes and memory!; to Charles, as always, and to Vic, for his kindness, loyalty, encouragement and love.

AUTHOR'S NOTE

Saffron Skies is a work of fiction and although many of its locations have experienced events similar to the ones narrated, I have taken extreme artistic license with dates, persons and facts. I should like to emphasize that Mali, in particular, did not live through a coup d'état in 2002.

PART ONE

PART ONE

PROLOGUE
London, England
1974

Amber Sall squeezed herself into as little a ball as she could possibly manage, which, despite her height, was surprisingly small. She lay huddled in the space at the back of the downstairs shoe cupboard, trying to fit into the place where the vacuum cleaner usually went. The space was deep and dark, buffered from the outside world by the thick bank of winter coats and scarves that hung along the wall. It was the only place in the house where she couldn't hear the fighting. She could just about bear the shouting, Max's voice getting progressively louder, but she couldn't stand the crying. When her mother started crying, softly at first, then harder— huge, gasping sobs that tore through every room in the house—that was her signal to run from wherever she was to the cupboard. There, and only there, where the noise was muffled, would her heartbeat slowly return to normal and the panic in her chest subside. It was quiet inside, a thick, comforting kind of silence. She wrapped one end of a scarf around her face and began counting the minutes, hoping the fight wouldn't last too long. One, two, three . . . she'd reached nine when she heard a door slam followed by the sound of feet pounding heavily on the stairs. The front door banged shut loudly, panes of glass rattling against the frame. She held her breath, but there was nothing further. She sat very still for a few minutes, waiting to see if anything else would happen. Everything was quiet. Then she heard Max's car starting. The engine revved once, twice . . . and then he was gone. She breathed out in relief, pushed her way out of the cupboard and ran straight upstairs.

Her mother lay draped dramatically over the silk divan in the drawing room on the first floor. She turned a tear-stained face towards Amber as she burst into the room.

"Darling," she said thickly, "Max's gone."

"Yes, I know. It's only Monday," Amber said briskly. "He'll be back later, I expect. D'you want anything?"

"Just a hug. Give me a hug," her mother said, wiping back tears. "Come here, darling."

"No," Amber said firmly, eyeing the mascara running down her mother's cheeks. "You'll make my face dirty. I'll send Krystyna up." She turned to go.

"Will you ask her to bring me some . . . tea?" her mother called after her. Amber rolled her eyes. Tea? Brandy, more likely. She ran back down the stairs.

She found Krystyna, their affable Polish helper, in the kitchen, already preparing a tray for a routine that was pretty well rehearsed. Krystyna gave her a smile and a hug before disappearing upstairs with the tray and on it, a small silver flask. Amber grabbed her coat from the cupboard, picked up her homework and ran out of the house, slamming the front door behind her. She ran across the street, up the steps to Becky's front door and rang the bell impatiently. She wanted to be as far away as possible from the tensions at home.

Becky's mother opened the door and surveyed the ten-year-old girl standing on the doorstep, the scowl on her usually pretty face saying it all. She sighed. As exciting as it was to have the millionaire Max Sall living across the road from them, she did feel sorry for his children, especially Amber. Having Max for a father was difficult enough, what with his bizarre domestic arrangements—a wife and family in London *and* his mistress and daughter in Rome—but to have been saddled with an alcoholic, empty-headed mother like Angela . . . no wonder the poor child looked so miserable.

"Becky's upstairs, dear," she said, resisting the urge to hug Amber as she slipped past. She watched the girl run up the stairs two at a time. She hadn't said a word. Anyway, she thought to herself as she heard Becky's bedroom door slam shut, Amber wasn't really the kind of girl you hugged—even at ten, she was already far too self-contained, somehow, for that. She didn't need anyone's sympathy, she seemed to be saying, she could cope with things on her own, thank you very much. How different from Becky, her own daughter, Susan Aldridge often thought. The two of them had been best friends since kindergarten, more like sisters, really, but they were so, *so* different. Amber was a leader, a strong-willed, often bossy little girl, practical and serious to a fault. Becky was a dreamer, her head always in the clouds, a follower, always eager and easy to please. Susan supposed that was why it worked—opposites attracting, and all that. She closed the front door and walked down the corridor to the kitchen, wondering what to make for supper. Becky, she was sure, would eat everything that was put in front of her. It was Amber who was picky, with a list of *don't-likes* as long as her arm.

Upstairs, in the serene safety of Becky's room, Amber began to calm down. She hadn't said anything as she came through the door but at the sight of Becky's familiar belongings—books, dolls, scrapbooks, tapes, rolls of paper and hundreds of colored pencils, she slowly began to unwind. Becky didn't say anything either, just pulled out her shoebox of pencils and scraps of paper and pushed a pile across the floor. She calmly began preparations for their favorite game: paper dolls. Amber picked out a few pencils, half-heartedly joining in. In truth, it was really Becky's favorite game—she was so good at drawing, making up outfits and accessories . . . half the time Amber just sat beside her in silence, watching, awed by Becky's skill in dreaming up colors and patterns and turning flat, empty sheets of paper into a thousand outfits for both their dolls, none of them even remotely similar. She didn't know how she did it.

She watched Becky take a pair of scissors from the shoebox and begin to cut out a pair of dark grey trousers she'd just drawn. She liked the way Becky's long, auburn hair swung gently as she worked, concentrating on following the lines *perfectly*, not allowing the scissors to slip. Everything Becky did was neat and precise. Amber, whose own paper dolls looked as though they'd been torn, not cut, from the pages of the sketchbook, was envious. She looked around her. She loved Becky's room. It was full of the things Becky liked doing—drawings, little ceramic pots of pencils and paintbrushes, Becky's favorite pictures on the walls, clothes in wicker baskets, a coat stand full of her winter hats and her collection of ballet shoes . . . it wasn't messy, as such, it was just full. Full of life. It was so different from Amber's empty room. At home, a maid came in twice a day; once just after she'd left for school and again just after dinner, to put things away, tidy her drawers and make her bed. It was like living in a hotel, Amber complained to Krystyna. But Max's instructions to the staff were clear: keep the place clean and tidy. Amber knew it had something to do with the time he'd come back from a month-long business trip and found that she and Kieran hadn't had a bath in a week. It was a bet between them, the then eight-year-old Kieran tried to explain, to see how long they could go without . . . but Max was furious. After that, an army of staff descended on the house each day, cleaning, dusting and organizing things, keeping everything in the kind of order Max wanted and liked. Max, Max, Max. It was all about Max. Neither she nor Kieran ever called him "Daddy"—she didn't know why exactly. It would have sounded . . . silly. He was Max. Just as Angela was Angela, not "Mummy." Angela certainly never behaved like a mother. Mothers were soft, comforting women like Becky's mum, not the brittle, drunk and fragile creature they all knew Angela to be.

She looked at Becky's hand slowly begin to bring to life the clothes she was coloring in. A brightly patterned skirt; a flamboyant scarf . . . a tiny pair of high-heeled shoes. She sighed. She longed to be good at something, *any*thing. She liked the way everyone talked about Becky—*so good at art!*—but no one ever said anything about her. Other than how sensible she was and how well she coped. Well, she was tired of *coping*. She didn't even know what it meant.

≋ 1 ≋
London, England
1978

Amber woke early, dragged out of sleep by the fierce, leaden concentration of pain in her lower belly and the sound of voices downstairs. She lay very still, alternately being thrust above and below the threshold of the wringing, wavering pain. It was her first period. She knew what to expect—Becky's mother had told them both everything they needed to know—although she hadn't said much about it hurting so. But the pain in her stomach was nothing compared to the dread that crept through her as she heard Max's voice. *The last bloody straw*. She slid out of bed and crept into her bathroom. She washed herself quickly, found the packet of bulky sanitary napkins Mrs. Aldridge had given her, and put on a clean pair of pajamas. She was just about to climb back into bed when she heard a shout from down-

stairs, followed by the sound of glass breaking. Angela must have thrown something at Max. Or vice
versa. There was another shout, then the sound of
something being dragged across the floor. She
heard her brother's door open on the other side of
the hallway. She got out of bed again and opened
her own door, her heart thumping.

"What's going on?" Kieran asked, looking at her
with worried eyes.

"I don't know," Amber whispered, peering over
the balustrade. "I just woke up."

"I thought he was supposed to be in Rome. With
bloody Francesca," Kieran muttered.

"He came back last night," Amber said. "Mummy
wasn't expecting him, I don't think . . . she's been at
it since yesterday." She looked at Kieran. His face
was tight. He hated seeing Angela upset or hearing
the two of them fight. She sighed and looked away.
Although Kieran was two years her senior, to Amber
it often felt the other way round. She was the one
who had to comfort him when the fights got out of
hand. His face would close up at the sight of Angela,
bruised and hungover, pretending nothing had happened, that it was all completely, astoundingly normal—and then, Amber knew, it would take days to
coax him out of his furious, dark mood.

There was a final slam of the door, the sound of
a key being turned in a lock and then, mercifully, all
was quiet. Kieran turned and quickly walked back to
his own room. Amber watched him fumbling in his
dressing gown for the packet of cigarettes he always kept in his pocket. She stood at the top of the

stairs, a tight, cold feeling of fear creeping slowly through her veins. Something was going to happen; she could feel it just as she could feel the sharp, stinging cramps in her abdomen signaling another, different kind of change.

The next morning the house was unusually quiet. Krystyna didn't come to wake her. Amber stumbled out of bed, late for school. She pulled on her school clothes and ran downstairs. Angela was nowhere to be seen. Kieran had already left for school. She walked into the breakfast room apprehensively. Max was sitting at the table in his dressing gown, calmly reading the papers, as if nothing had happened. She slid into the seat next to him, careful not to disturb. "Where's Mummy?" she asked, as casually as she could manage, pouring milk over her cereal.

"Your mother needs a little rest," Max said, putting down the paper and looking at her. Amber swallowed nervously.

"Is she in bed?"

"Yes, for the moment. But she's going to go away for a bit, later on today."

"Away? Where?"

"Somewhere quiet." Max was looking at her closely. Amber blushed under his scrutiny. "And that's what I want to talk to you about."

"Are you going to live here now? Always?" The words were out before she could stop them.

"No, not quite." He smiled at her. And then dropped the bombshell. "I'm sending you to Rome for a few weeks. I'm too busy to be here all the time.

Kieran can stay here on his own but you're still too young. I'll arrange for you to have private lessons; it's nearly the end of the school year, anyway. Francesca and Paola will look after you." He turned back to his paper.

Amber's heart fell straight through her stomach. She looked at him in horror. She tried to say something, but the words wouldn't come out. *No!* she wanted to scream. *I'm not going, you can't make me!* A few *weeks*? With Francesca? And *Paola*? Her half-sister whom she hated more than anything or anyone in the world? She couldn't imagine spending an hour with Paola, let alone a few weeks. She sat in silence beside him, struggling with herself to speak. *No, I won't!* But you didn't say "no" to Max. You couldn't. Amber knew the rules. She bent her head, blinked back her tears and shoved a spoonful of cornflakes in her mouth. She'd known something terrible was going to happen. It wasn't Angela being sent away, it was her, being sent to Rome. Being sent to Francesca. And Paola. Sick with repressed rage, she scraped back her chair, mumbled goodbye to Max and ran to her room before Max could say anything more. Or worse.

Max barely looked up as Amber rushed out of the room. Despite his outward calm, he was fuming. He was furious with Angela. She'd done it again—he was about to leave for Eastern Europe to nurse one of his biggest deals to date through the delicate negotiation processes. He needed a clear head, free from the clutter and messy tangle of emotions that always seemed to surround his wife. He needed peace and calm, not *this* . . . the ongoing, boringly predictable drama in which she played the leading, neurotic role. He just couldn't understand it—he'd given her everything; she lacked for nothing. A beautiful home, plenty of money, two healthy children . . . anything and everything a woman could ask for—what the hell more did she want? He pushed his plate away from him, too angry to eat. He looked around the room at the elegant furnishings, the exquisite paintings on the wall, the fine bone china on which his congealing eggs and bacon sat, untouched. Yes, she had everything. It had been a long, hard slog to reach this point and now she wanted to throw it all away? For the price of a bottle of whisky? Max shook his head. It was beyond him. His gaze turned slowly away from the polished surface of the dining table and the artfully arranged flowers around him. The anger that had risen in him so suddenly dissipated, leaving him with an unfamiliar, inexplicable sadness. He pushed his chair back from the table and walked out of the dining room and upstairs to his study, his tread a little heavier than normal. He stood in the doorway for a moment, looking at his possessions spread around the room. His books; his favorite pieces of art and sculpture; the beautiful desk Angela had bought for him, years before . . . he walked over to it and sat down. He pulled open the drawer to his left. Inside, nestled in a bed of white tissue, was his most treasured possession: a dog-eared, battered-beyond-repair teddy bear. He stared at it, rapidly losing himself in the mists of time and memory. Within seconds, it seemed, he was back where he'd started, where everything had begun.

It was cold that morning in September 1939. The kind of cold that crept in under your clothes, surprising you with its dampness, signaling the end of summer. Nine-year-old Markus Salzman wasn't thinking about the cold, however—there were other, much more pressing concerns to worry about. His mother had been crying for days and no one would explain why. His father had disappeared the previous week and then suddenly returned the night before, looking ten years older. Markus was an only child: there was no one to share his worries with. Lotte, the housekeeper to whom he usually turned when Mutti was upset, or away, wasn't saying anything. She pursed her lips in that awful way she had and, apart from urgent, whispered conversations in the corridors with the kitchen staff or Joachim, his father's valet, said nothing. Nothing. It was left to him to try to figure out what was going on. Apart from the war, of course, that everyone said was coming—only a matter of days, that was what he'd heard sitting crouched down behind the closed drawing-room door the night before when his father came back, unannounced. His uncles were in the room, and their neighbor, the kindly Herr Finkelstein. He'd only caught snatches of a conversation he couldn't understand—*Kindertransport, England, Kulturgemeinde*—and he frowned, trying to make sense of it all. But before he could put any of the pieces together or at least remember enough of what he'd heard to run upstairs to his mother and demand to know what was going on, Lotte had found him and ordered him to bed.

So here he was on a cold September morning, struggling to pull on a pair of prickly woollen under-garments and wondering why he'd been summoned to the drawing room and told to dress warmly. He soon found out.

Mutti couldn't—or wouldn't—look at him. His father stood stiffly by the elegant drawing-room windows, gazing down at something unseen in the street be-low them. His favorite aunt, Berthilde, was crying softly in a corner of the room. Markus looked at them all, too astonished to speak. Go away? To En-gland? By himself? He blurted something out. *Aren't you coming? What about you? And Mutti?*—to which his father turned from the window and replied in a voice that even Markus could tell was forced and unnaturally cheerful. *We'll follow you. Soon.* It was, of course, a lie.

Everything had been arranged at the last minute. Harald Salzman, through the unexpected kindness of a German client, had managed to secure a place for his only son on one of the last *Kindertransport* trains leaving Germany, bound for Holland and then Harwich. Markus Salzman, aged nine, arrived in Harwich on 6 September, three days after the war had broken out. He remembered little of the good-byes at the station—huddled in a carriage with two hundred other crying, terrified children, the large windows of the German train pulled down all the way to allow the sobbing parents one last, lingering glimpse of their children before the train began its slow exit from the station. Germany, troops massing in the autumnal landscape, Holland, the port, the crossing . . . these passed before his unseeing eyes, making little lasting impression. He stepped off the boat in Harwich on an uncharacteristically bright and sunny day and discovered immediately that his understanding of the world, such as he'd experienced it to be, was of no use to him whatsoever in this new, unfamiliar place. He couldn't speak a word of the language around him. The one person he'd befriended on the journey across the Channel had disappeared almost as soon as they arrived. Markus saw him being led away from the train by an elderly couple—obviously delighted to see him—and that was that. He was utterly alone. He held in one hand a small leather case that his mother had hurriedly prepared for him and in the other, Solly, his little, dog-eared teddy bear that Aunt Berthilde had pushed through the windows at him as the train pulled away. He had no money, no address to go to, no names of people to look for, just a tiny folded-up piece of paper that Mutti had told him to hang onto, at all costs . . . and his bag. And Solly. *There just wasn't enough time*, his father shouted desperately to him, his voice whipped away on the wind and drowned by the sound of the departure whistle. *We couldn't arrange anything . . . not enough time . . .* it was the last time he heard or saw his parents.

*   *   *

He chose to forget. Six years at the Neasden Lane Orphanage in North London living in conditions he had only ever read about back home in Dresden. From his wealthy, cultured background where he had everything he wanted, whenever he wanted, he fell. He learned what it was like to live with hunger, a dull gnawing ache in the pit of his stomach that never went away, no matter how much food he and some of the other orphans managed to steal from the kitchens late at night; to live with cold, even in the summer; to close himself off from everyone around him and to forget everything about who he had been. Before. He learned English quickly and well, determined to rub out all traces of foreignness in his voice and manner. He was tall and handsome, charming when he wanted to be, arrogant and difficult when he didn't. He was quick-witted and sharp, despite the rupture in his schooling and the uncertainties of his new life. He became Max Sall and buried Markus Salzman. By the time he was nearly sixteen, the war had been over for a year and Max knew it was time to move on. He left the orphanage on a damp, rainy Monday morning with the same small leather holdall, a letter of recommendation to Sainsbury's from one of the superintendents, the folded piece of paper containing the three uncut diamonds his mother had given him and Solly, squashed somewhere between his one pair of decent trousers and two pairs of socks.

His first job was mopping up the floor in the butchery section at the Sainsbury's in Kentish Town. It was dirty, tiring work but Max couldn't have cared less. Anything was better than 24 Neasden Lane. He found lodgings on Baird Street in Camden Town; a single, narrow attic room with a shared bathroom on the landing below. Mrs. Mortimer, the overweight, overripe landlady took a shine to him, bringing him leftovers from the family meal downstairs when he appeared late at night; washing and ironing his one good shirt and even making breakfast for him on a Sunday, when the rest of her brood were out at church. Max was no fool. He lost his virginity to her one winter evening as Arthur, her ox of a husband, was listening to the wireless and the kids were asleep. She was an enthusiastic, if rather conventional, lover—afterwards, when she'd finished smoothing back her hair and tucking her shirt into her skirt, she turned to blow him a kiss. Max looked away. He couldn't stand the little gestures of affection. She'd got what she came for, hadn't she? And so had he, in a way. He was a man now. Sort of.

He lay on the bed after she'd disappeared down the stairs, smoking and contemplating his next move. Money. That was what it took, that was what it was all about. Money to get out of there, to get on in the world, to *make* it. He wanted to hear the faint chink of good china at the dinner table, to eat food carefully prepared by others, to lift the lid on a tureen of soup and let the aroma of meat, vegetables and spices waft through the air. He wanted to sleep on a firm mattress, with clean, freshly laundered sheets and to spend his days doing something other than swilling out blood and guts and watching Mr. Henderson, the butcher, carefully por-tioning out spam and shriveled sausages to hungry, patiently waiting housewives. He stubbed out his cigarette and rolled over onto his back, staring at the ceiling.

≈2≈
London, England

Becky looked at Amber's tight, unhappy face, wish-ing desperately that there was something she could say to cheer her up. She tried, but couldn't think of a single thing. She was as upset as Amber was. Go-ing away? For six whole weeks? She couldn't be-lieve it. Amber would miss Becky's fourteenth birthday party, as well as all the end-of-term events they'd been planning since for ever. She picked at her duvet cover sullenly, wondering how *she* was going to manage. They were inseparable. They'd been so ever since the day Amber had stood up for her in playschool, almost ten years earlier. One of the boys in their little group had pulled Becky's pig-tails and called her horrid names. Amber jumped up, stumbled over their plastic desks and thumped him so hard that tears immediately sprang out of his eyes. She'd been sent home by the teacher for her display of aggression but it had earned her Becky's undying admiration and affection. In return, Becky offered Amber a close, sisterly friendship, a kind of companionship she'd never had in the cold, lonely house in Holland Park.

Tucked away under the attic in Becky's room, playing together for hours on end, and later, talking or walking down Bayswater, going to the ice rink or looking at the clothes in the shop windows and discussing the boys in class, Amber felt normal, part of a normal family, like everyone else. Becky's great virtue, as far as Amber was concerned, was that she was *constant*. Not moody, like Max; not sullen, like Kieran; not willful, like Angela. Becky was always the same. Cheerful, generous with her affection and time and always willing to do what Amber wanted; they balanced each other perfectly. They were always in and out of each other's homes, although, as Angela's drinking became more and more pronounced, Amber would always try to engineer things so that it was Becky's house they went to after school, not hers. Not after that day when they'd crept into Angela's walk-in wardrobe to play dressing up amongst the hundreds of clothes that hung, still in their pristine, plastic sheaths and found Angela there, propped up like a rag doll, an empty whisky glass in her hand, clutching a mound of tissue paper and new clothes to her chest. She found it soothing, she murmured, slurring her words. *All the new clothes. So clean and fresh* . . . Amber yanked Becky backwards by the hand and ran downstairs, not stopping until they'd reached Becky's front door and she'd pressed the bell almost ten times before Becky's mother came to answer.

*   *   *

"Shall we . . . d'you want to go to the shops?" Becky asked tentatively.

"What for?"

"Well, you could get some . . . you know . . . clothes and things . . . for going to Rome," Becky suggested, trying, for once, to be practical.

"I don't *need* anything," Amber muttered angrily.

"I know, but . . . well, we can't just sit here all afternoon."

"Yes I can." Amber was sulkily adamant. Becky sighed. She knew better than to argue with Amber when she was in a mood. Sometimes, Becky thought to herself, Amber was just the teeniest little bit like her father. Not that she'd ever say it to her. Amber would probably reach across the bed and thump her. There was something about Amber's father, Max, that terrified Becky. He was about as unlike a father as anyone's she'd ever met. It was true he was good looking—tall, always well dressed, glamorous—and that he was rich and famous and everything but still, he was so remote and unapproachable and you never really knew what he was going to say when he did notice you. Although her own father paled into insignificance beside Max, Becky was actually quite relieved to have an absentminded, rather boring-by-comparison father at home, even if she did have to keep reminding him who the Osmonds were and why she liked Donny best. At least she didn't have to think about what to say to him before she said it. She looked at Amber rather uneasily until her mother called up to them: she'd made brownies for tea . . . didn't they want any?

Two doors up and across the road in their spacious, elegant townhouse, Angela Sall picked up the little silver flask and shook out the last drops of brandy into the empty tea cup. She looked around her. The drawing room was immaculate and silent. Krystyna had bought a large bunch of scarlet roses from the florist on the corner. They sat in a glass vase opposite her on the mahogany side table, their petals the only splash of color in the calm, white space. Angela felt closer to them, to their crimson, bleeding presence than to the neutral, off-white serenity surrounding her. The décor upstairs where she mostly lived had been Max's choice. She paused, her hand hovering on the little silver bell she used to summon her staff from downstairs. She needed a refill, a little pick-me-up, something to help her through the long, tedious late afternoon. She had no idea when her husband would be back. These days, she reflected somberly, she didn't seem to have much of an idea about anything. But it hadn't always been that way. Unlike Max, whom she was sure never wasted a second thinking about the way things had been, she could remember everything. Every single, little, precious detail. She could remember exactly when she'd first set eyes on Max—it was in her parents' country home in Wiltshire, the very day the Beatles' first hit single, "Love Me Do," was released. 5 October 1962. She remembered it because she and her sister, Mary Ann, were dancing around in the kitchen listening to it on the radio when the back door opened and a tall, striking young man walked in, a braided cap in hand. He was Lord Sainsbury's chauffeur, Mrs. Bambridge, the cook, told her. She and Mary Ann stopped dancing, giggling nervously as Mrs. Bambridge led the young man into the tea room at the back of the kitchen. She remembered his dark, dark eyes on her and the way her sister nudged her in the ribs and told her to stop staring. At dinner that evening with Lord Sainsbury and his wife, her eyes kept wandering to the kitchen to where the young man—Max, she'd found out his name—was eating supper with Mrs. Bambridge and her father's butler. They were staying the night; she heard her mother giving the housekeeper instructions to make up the Blue Room for their guests and the small room above the kitchen for the driver. She ignored her sister's looks of alarm and went outside after supper, ostensibly to take a walk in the gardens but really looking out across the lawn towards the kitchens to see if he might appear.

She was sixteen. Pretty, wealthy, horribly sheltered. She'd never been courted, never even been kissed. Well, not properly. Not in the way she'd have liked. She was desperate to get out of the unbearably stuffy circle of her parents, Lord and Lady Weymouth, and into what she called the *real* world—London, the big city—to hang out with the people and places she had heard about on the radio and seen on television. She thought she looked a little like the woman she'd seen on the cover of *Vogue* one day in the local newsagents, Jean Shrimpton, and although her mother certainly wouldn't let her buy the magazine, Angela spent hours trying to puff her hair up in the same way and secretly wore the palest pink lipstick at dinner.

"Angela?" Her mother's voice rang out across the gardens. She turned guiltily. "It's getting late," her mother called. "Do come inside before it gets completely dark."

"Coming!" Angela shouted. "I'm just . . . feeding the ducks," she added. She stifled a giggle. The ducks? She'd never shown the slightest interest in their well-being before. The ducks were simply part of the landscape, a necessary feature of the country life her father seemed to think a man in his position ought to enjoy. She sighed. That was it—that was the problem with her life, with all their lives. Her parents. The things they thought they *ought* to do, rather than what they wanted to do. Her mother, she was sure, absolutely hated the countryside and their enormous, draughty home. She hated wading around in Wellington boots with her carefully styled hair hidden under a scarf. She would have liked nothing better than to stay in London every weekend, in their Kensington villa, with all her bridge-playing friends, gossiping and drinking tea laced with gin. Angela knew all about those long afternoons. She disliked them almost as much as the long, boring ones spent huddled beside the fireplace in the drawing room at Haddon Hall.

"Good evening." A man's voice broke into her thoughts. She nearly jumped out of her skin. It was him! Max, the Sainsbury's driver, on the other side of the hedge.

"Oh. Gosh, you startled me." She was quite breathless. She tried to see his face in the deepening evening gloom.

"Sorry. I heard you say you were going to feed the ducks." He stepped forward from behind the hedge.

"Yes, yes. They're down there, by the pond. I was just . . . on my way."

"But what are you planning to feed them with?" Max asked her, looking down at her empty hands, smiling slightly. She blushed.

"Oh, I . . . I had some crusts . . . I must have left them behind. In the kitchen," she stammered.

"Of course."

He seemed to be mocking her. She looked down at her feet, unsure of what to say next. He had a way of looking at her that she found hard to bear. No one had ever looked at her that way before. Intensely, for one thing . . . and interested, or so it seemed to her. She was used to her father's reticence, his way of talking to his wife and two daughters as if they were really one being, his three women, rolled into one.

"Come. I'll walk with you. Perhaps we'll find something to feed them with on the way." She looked up and nodded. She liked the way he spoke—his voice was confident, polished, not like any of the other staff at Haddon Hall. In fact, it was hard to believe he was what her mother would have termed the "help." She'd never met anyone like him.

There was something wonderful and intense and alive about him; he looked and acted as though he didn't give a damn what anyone else thought. She liked that. It was exactly how she thought everyone should be. She slipped a hand through the arm he offered and at the first physical contact with him she felt herself begin to burn. She looked up at him and smiled. Max. She wanted to be near him more than anything else in the world.

≈3≈

Madeleine Szabo watched the two teenage girls walk slowly up the road, pausing every now and then to look at something in the window of one expensive shop or the other. She followed them at a discreet distance, the straps of her school satchel trailing behind her on the ground, wishing she had a best friend she could walk home from school with, stopping every now and then to admire an outfit or a new pair of shoes. She looked down at her own shoes—horrible, ugly shoes that someone had given her mother who'd promptly passed them onto Madeleine—and grimaced. They were too big for her and her feet slopped around in them like water in a pail. She looked up. The pair had disappeared into one of the shops. Madeleine stopped and glanced at her watch. It was nearly five o'clock. Her mother would be expecting her home any minute to help with supper. She ought to be going in the opposite direction, towards home, not away from it, and she really oughtn't to be following two girls from Radcliffe, the private school on the corner—*Cliffy C**ts*, the boys at Madeleine's school used to scream at them from the safety of the upper deck of the number fifteen bus. They simply tossed their long, shiny hair and lifted their noses haughtily at the scruffy, disgusting youths from King George, the huge, forbidding state school that Madeleine went to—was *forced* to go to—just down the road.

She wasn't following them, she consoled herself as she turned round and started back in the opposite direction, she just happened to be walking the same way. She liked the look of them—the tall, very striking-looking girl with thick, brown curly hair and blue eyes and the smaller, red-haired girl with long, straight hair and a freckled face . . . she wondered what their names were. She liked their uniforms—burgundy skirts, white blouses and dark green jackets in winter, light green short-sleeved shirts in summer. Madeleine longed to wear a proper uniform, not just the "plain-shirt-and-dark-skirt" rule that no one really followed. It would save her the embarrassment of choosing what to wear each morning from an ever-dwindling supply of clothes. And why was it dwindling? she asked herself furiously each morning. Because she was getting fat. Because she was eating too much. Because she hated her school and the people in it. She hated being the odd one out, the foreigner, the girl with an accent, no matter how hard she tried to conceal it, and the funny clothes and parents who couldn't speak English. She turned round one last time and saw that the two girls had come out of the shop, each bearing a bag. *And* they had money to buy things, Madeleine thought glumly. Another thing she hated about her life. Her parents had no money. None whatsoever. There was enough for the bare essentials—*napi adag* in Hungarian, their language. Enough to house, feed and clothe the three of them—Imre, her father; Maja, her mother; and Madeleine. Madeleine tried to hide from them just how much she hated wearing the hand-me-downs and cast-offs that Maja's clients, the people whose homes she cleaned, periodically gave her. Especially the women who'd seen the cleaning lady's daughter and exclaimed in surprise over the exceptionally pretty girl with long, thick, dark-blonde hair, the dark-brown eyes fringed with thick, black lashes and those wonderfully high, Slavic cheekbones. Madeleine had stopped accompanying her mother to her cleaning jobs whenever she had a free moment from school after one of them commented that the child was getting a little big, wasn't she? How old did Maja say she was? Thirteen? She looked more like eighteen, what with those full breasts and heavy-lidded, almost sleepy eyes. Madeleine had looked the other way, her face burning in anger and embarrassment. It wasn't *her* fault her breasts had suddenly increased in size. She'd had nothing to do with it—the opposite, in fact. She stood with her hands over her chest most of the time, wishing that the men at the bus stop or behind the counter at the grocer's would stop looking at her in that way. She hated them. In fact, there weren't many things about her life and her surroundings that Madeleine did like. Books. She loved books. Books were her escape. She read everything and anything she could get her hands on, in Hungarian or English. She'd read everything her parents had managed to bring with them when they fled to the West, which wasn't very much, and everything she'd found in the houses of their Hungarian friends in London—again, not very many. She'd devoured everything in the school library and in the public library up the road. Her mother was beginning to despair of ever finding enough for her daughter to read when one of her clients, an elderly English lady with an entire house full of books had invited Madeleine to "borrow whatever took her fancy." There was enough in Mrs. Jameson's house to keep Madeleine occupied for the next three years, Maja said excitedly to her husband that evening. They were both relieved. It was a never-ending source of pain and shame to them that they'd failed to find the opportunities that were supposed to exist for them in the West and pass onto their only child the advantages they'd been taught to believe they hadn't had. Maja Szabo, once a writer of children's books, now a cleaner, wasn't so sure. Sometimes, when she had enough energy and the will to think about it . . . the life they'd left behind in Budapest was a whole lot better than the one they had now. But she rarely allowed herself to think that way—she'd go mad if she did.

Ten-year-old Paola Rossi slammed the door behind her so hard that the panes in the stained-glass windows framing the drawing room rattled. She ran straight down the marble-floored corridor to her room, flung open the door and threw herself on her bed, pummeling the silk counterpane with her fists. She was furious. Her half-sister was coming to stay for six weeks—an *eternity*!—and she'd been forbidden to go to Sardinia with her best friend Daniela and her family. It just wasn't true! She pushed her face into the soft white pillows and let out a scream of frustration. There was a tap at the door—her mother.

"Paola, darling . . ." Francesca began.

"Go *away!*" Paola screamed, her voice muffled by the pillow she held against her face. There was silence for a moment. She rolled over onto her stomach, still hugging the pillow and thought about how unfair life was. She *hated* Amber—she simply hated her. It wasn't enough that Amber was four years older than her, that Max was always saying she was cleverer than Paola, or even that Amber was the "real" daughter, the one whose mother was actually *married* to Max—Francesca, as everyone knew, was Max's *mistress*, not his wife—an important, all-consuming distinction, as far as Paola's young mind was concerned. The fundamental truth was that

Paola couldn't bear to share Max with *any*one. She adored her father absolutely and unconditionally. For her, there was no one in the world as handsome, strong, rich, witty, wonderful as Max. She thought the world of him. Her mother sometimes hinted, ever so gently, that Max did have his faults . . . but Paola's adoration was unwavering. The only thing wrong with Max, she declared to her slightly worried mother was the presence of the other family in his life. Angela, Amber and Kieran. Without them, Max would be perfect. Without them, Paola often declared, *her* life would be perfect. She would be the center of his universe, not just a weekend appendage. Francesca said nothing but was secretly rather alarmed.

Paola choked back another sob. Amber was coming. To stay. She let out another stomach-churning scream.

Francesca walked into the sitting room in the elegant, spacious apartment on via San Giacomo right in the heart of Rome, bought for her—and Paola, of course—by Max, and paused. She wasn't sure quite what to do. Max had rung that morning with his request—no, make that his *order*—and there wasn't a damn thing she could do about it. Amber was coming to stay for six long weeks and she and Paola were expected to make her welcome. She crossed the room to one of the pale silk-covered sofas and sat down, biting her lip in exasperation. She'd been looking forward to sending Paola off to Sardinia with her school friends and to having Max to herself for a little while, and now she had to put up with his daughter. It was bad enough putting up with his wife. She reached for her cigarettes.

"Madame?" Bella, her pretty maid, poked her head around the door. "Should I take the fish out? For the dinner?" Francesca frowned. Damn! She'd almost forgotten her dinner party that evening. She looked at her watch. It was almost five. Just enough time to slip out to Marco's, her hairdresser, and have her hair washed and dried . . . she put down her lighter and cigarette reluctantly.

"Yes, the monkfish. Do it the way you did the other weekend . . . you know, steamed, with linguine and salad. Something simple, hmm?" Bella nodded and closed the door. Francesca got up and took a quick, critical look at herself in the mirror. She looked beautiful. As always. The irritation she felt with Max hadn't registered on her perfect features. Long, shoulder-length, thick and glossy dark-brown hair; dark, sultry eyes; heart-shaped face and full, sensual lips. She studied herself. Francesca Rossi's face and body were her fortune—she had them to thank for her present position in life and her lovely apartment in Rome, of course—and she intended to make sure things stayed that way. Max had no idea. He had no idea that Francesca had spotted him long before he'd seen her; that the quick, furious tryst in the empty powder room in the hotel lobby had been her idea and that she'd planned it almost from the moment she'd set eyes on him striding up the gangway to the First Class section of the Alitalia flight to London.

* * *

Francesca was nineteen, from a tiny town outside Pescara on the Adriatic coast. She was beautiful and ambitious and, just like every other pretty girl from the provinces, already dreaming of better things, of a better life. She polished up her French, set about improving her English and started work as an airline stewardess in 1964. When she pulled up the zipper on her smart, green Sorella Fontana-designed tunic with its long, elegant skirt and jaunty cap, she knew she'd found a way to make her dreams come true. Everyone who was anyone in those days flew Alitalia. She'd served the beautiful and fabulous Sophia Loren, the handsome Jean-Paul Belmondo, Alberto Sordi, Mastroianni . . . even the divine Brigitte Bardot. By 1967, the year she saw Max Sall in the departure lounge at the brand-new Leonardo da Vinci Intercontinental Airport, businessmen, sports personalities, the rich and famous . . . everyone, it seemed, was taking to the skies. She knew who he was; his face had been on the cover of *Time* magazine a few months before. He was the young, dynamic deal-maker who had risen from nowhere to the top of London society, marrying the pretty eldest daughter of some English lord or the other. The papers had been full of it. The girl's parents had been dead set against the marriage and Francesca remembered seeing pictures of the mother, Lady Somebody, almost in tears at the wedding chapel. Francesca had seen Max Sall a few times at the airport, always leaving or arriving in a chauffeur-driven car, walking so fast to wherever it was he was going that he left a trail of men and women running after him, trying to keep up. He was handsome as well as rich. A definite bonus. When she saw him coming up the gangway, she made a quick and instant decision. She knew she didn't want to wind up like many of her friends, the mistress of some aging, used-to-be-dashing pilot, barely making enough money to support one family, let alone two. No, she wanted more, much more. All she had to do was make sure, by the end of the short two-hour flight to London, that he knew who *she* was. And that he wouldn't forget her. He didn't.

And it wasn't because of what had happened after—well, during, really—their explosive coupling in the powder room, no matter what her mother said. Paola hadn't been planned; Francesca hadn't wanted to trap Max that way. No, Paola was an accident. Although, Francesca thought to herself, looking around the beautiful flat, she'd turned out to be a *happy* accident—Max wouldn't dream of leaving her, not now. He had honor, an almost old-fashioned sense of duty, especially where his children were concerned. He was downright tribal in his desire to have his offspring around him, no matter what other people said, including his own wife. Francesca knew that the news of his "love-child," as the papers had called Paola, back then, was probably the source of Angela Weymouth's all-too-evident pain. At times, she almost felt sorry for her. Silly woman. Didn't she know? How did she think she would ever manage to hold onto a man like Max? *La Rosa Inglesa*, the Italian press dubbed her. *The English Rose.* With her ice-blonde hair, her impossibly thin, delicate frame . . . didn't she realize Max would seek something else? Max didn't need or want an English Rose. He needed someone like Francesca: sensuous, hot-blooded, passionate, as he himself was. Of that, Francesca was sure. Well, *almost* sure. Sometimes the questions of a ten-year-old unnerved her. *Why doesn't he marry you, Mama? Porché no?*

She shook her head quickly as if to stop thinking about the past, smiled briefly at her reflection in the mirror and picked up her trademark black leather handbag. She glanced at Paola's shut door as she walked down the corridor. She would come round. She always did. Let her have a good cry and a sulk for an hour or so—she would ask Bella to make her favorite dessert, flambéed bananas and vanilla ice cream, for an after-supper treat. Then she could come into the drawing room and greet Francesca's guests. Paola always liked that bit, all the guests fussing over how beautiful and how like her mother she was. That would win her round. She opened the front door and stepped out.

≋5≋

Amber's flight to Fiumicino was mercifully empty. She sat stiffly in her Business Class seat and tried not to think about the six weeks ahead of her. Leaving home had been dreadful. Kieran hadn't even bothered to come and say goodbye. He was furious at being left alone and had been cold and withdrawn for days. She'd pleaded with him—it wasn't her fault, it had been Max's idea. *Please, Kieran, don't be angry with me*, she'd said tearfully, but he had simply ignored her and sloped off to join his friends. Amber could only stare miserably after his disappearing back.

She turned to look out of the window. Rome spread herself out tantalizingly before them as they prepared to land. Buildings tilted dangerously up and towards them and through the convex pane of the window Amber could see streets and cars bulging in and out of view. Within minutes, with a gentle bump, they touched down.

"Welcome to Rome, ladies and gentlemen," the captain's voice sounded over the speakers as the plane taxied to a halt. The doors were flung open by gleaming, smiling stewardesses and Amber glared at them. Hadn't the bitch Francesca been one of them once? She stood at the top of the stairs, her eyes blinking against the Mediterranean light. Outside it was warm and dry. She walked down the steps, gusted on both sides by blasts of hot air as the engines were shut down and the noise abated. She walked across the tarmac, head down, eyes concentrating on her feet, trying not to look around her. Birds were singing; the air was full of the scent of lavender and mimosa, the sound of a thousand horns from the traffic in the distance. She tried not to think about what lay ahead.

In the arrivals hall, a driver was waiting for her, holding aloft a placard with her name scrawled unevenly across it. She raised a tentative hand, relieved it wasn't Francesca. She climbed into the back of the waiting car and quickly pulled a book out of her bag. She didn't want to have to talk to anyone, least of all Francesca's driver. They swung out of the airport parking lot and headed into the city. It was just after 6 p.m. The evening light was slowly dissolving; dusk was falling over the hills surrounding the city. Half an hour later, they pulled up outside an impressive-looking stone façade, somewhere in the center of the city. She gazed up at the ornate, porticoed entrance, her stomach already threatening to tie itself into knots. She had never been to Francesca's home before. Apart from two disastrous summers, once when she was seven and two years previously, when she was twelve, she'd never spent more than an afternoon in Francesca's or Paola's company—and she liked it that way. It was bad enough that everyone knew they existed; she didn't have to like or even acknowledge them.

She opened the car door and stepped out. As her cases were taken from the boot, the heavy, wrought-iron gate in front of her buzzed open and she found herself standing in a chilly, marble hallway, waiting nervously for the Enemy to arrive.

"Amber. *Buona sera.*" Francesca's husky, heavily accented voice rang out in the entrance way. Amber turned to face her. She hadn't changed at all—the same tiny, tanned figure, dressed immaculately in white with gold jewelry flashing every time she moved. Shoulder-length glossy brown hair, perfectly made-up face . . . yes, Francesca looked exactly the same. "Did you have a good flight?" she asked, ineffectually waving away the smoke she had just blown in Amber's face. Amber nodded shortly, following her inside the house. Francesca was being polite—the last time they'd met, she'd screamed at her and Kieran, swearing at them in Italian and telling Max she never wanted to see their damned faces again. Amber followed her impossibly high heels as they clacked down the wide, cool corridor, the driver hurrying behind them carrying her bags. She coughed loudly as Francesca blew another cloud of smoke in her direction and beckoned her upstairs. There was no sign of Paola.

Francesca stopped outside one of the rooms along the corridor. "I thought you would like this room," she said, opening the door. "You can take a little rest before dressing for dinner, no? We will be six at table this evening." In spite of herself, Amber's eyes widened. It was beautiful: warm, terracotta floor tiles, pale yellow walls with white, billowing curtains at the windows. A bowl of fresh peaches had been put out on the pretty dressing table; their warm, soft scent filled the air. She turned around to mutter her thanks but Francesca had already disappeared. She walked over to the windows, pushing aside the curtains and opening the shutters and leaned out as far as she could, letting the warm evening air play over her face and neck. Cars jostled with pedestrians and the little, tinny-sounding Italian scooters she somehow recognized as being quintessentially Italian. Horns sounded, people laughed . . . it was strange, being right inside a city like this. It wasn't the quiet austerity of Holland Park or even the noisy aggression of Ladbroke Grove. Romans seemed to view the street as just another part of their living rooms—down the street, a few yards away, there were cafés and ice-cream shops, tiny little boutiques with people wandering in and out. Everyone was tanned and lightly dressed. In her sensible skirt and jumper Amber felt overdressed and overly . . . *English*. There was something about the way Italian women dressed . . . she caught herself quickly. No, there was nothing about Italian women she liked. Nothing at all. She turned from the window and looked ruefully at her suitcase. What was it Francesca had said? Dress? For dinner? Why on earth would she do that?

It took Paola a second to note that her half-sister had grown even taller—how was that possible?—and actually, rather prettier in the two years since they'd last seen each other. She couldn't actually remember her very well. Tall, skinny, not nearly as pretty as Paola, thankfully; a loudmouth. Always showing off. But the tall, slender, not skinny—even at ten Paola knew the difference—teenager in front of her said nothing, not even hello. The two sisters glared at each other, neither prepared to give way. They couldn't have been more different: Amber in her schoolgirl pleated skirt and plain cotton shirt with her unruly hair scraped back in a ponytail and neat socks and sandals. Paola stared at them. Socks? In summer? Paola was wearing a fitted white cotton dress with pretty buttons and matching ribbons in her long, silky, dark hair. She looked so much more sophisticated and grown up than the imbecile before her. Well, she *was* English. Francesca had warned her.

Across the room, Francesca watched nervously as she chatted to her two friends, Maria Luisa Tonone and Manuela di Gervase, both mistresses of well-known local politicians and therefore comrades in The Cause. The three equally beautiful women came from similar backgrounds and had similar axes to grind. Francesca often thought she would go mad if it weren't for the two of them. At times like these, she thought to herself—looking at Amber's tight little face—one needed all the support one could get. Damn Max! Why did he always have to have things his way?

"Amber, you will have some wine?" Maria Luisa asked, walking over to the couch where the girls sat, stiffly ignoring each other.

"No. I don't drink," Amber said sullenly. Maria

Luisa turned back to Francesca, raising her eyebrows fractionally. Francesca shrugged. She rang the bell for Bella. Might as well start dinner. The sooner the sulky teenager was sent to bed, the better. She ushered everyone to the table.

From her seat next to the impossibly elegant Manuela, Amber watched Paola's angry face and the way she jealously guarded against her mother even *looking* in her direction—and was comforted to see Paola was as upset as she was. She'd been taken aback at the sight of her, dressed in an almost identical outfit to her mother. Her *mother*? Amber would have sooner died than wear anything Angela wore. She looked around her as they waited for the first course to be served. It was so unlike home. The apartment was expensive and ornate; everything in it was exquisite and not-to-be-touched. At home, things were expensive too, but *comfortable* and expensive, not the austere, overdone glamour surrounding her here. Couches at home were meant for lying in and watching TV; there were record players and radios in all the rooms and books, too—here, there were only expensive-looking paintings and stiff, upright chairs covered in pale, shiny material that looked as though no one had sat on them, ever. The dining table was marble and cold-looking, not like the huge oak table in the kitchen at home. And the maid, Bella or-whatever-her-name-was, was *nothing* like Mrs. Dewhurst or Krystyna, back home. She looked more like a model than a maid.

The conversation around her was in Italian—fortunately, Manuela could barely speak English and Maria Luisa's grasp of the language didn't really extend beyond the usual pleasantries—*A glass of wine? 'Ow are you? 'Ow you like Roma?*

She ignored everyone and tried to concentrate on the food. It seemed never-ending. There was salad to begin with, a plate of crisp, palest green lettuce, tiny, sweet and ripe tomatoes and slivers of moist, black olives; then pasta in a sweet, herb sauce with threads of sliced zucchini and char-grilled yellow peppers; fish; followed by a small dish of ice-cold, lemon sorbet and *then* a tiny piece of chocolate cake served with an exquisitely decorated cup of bittersweet coffee. Amber ate everything on her plate. She was a little worried to see none of the others followed suit: everyone else, including Paola, simply ate a mouthful or two of each course, and pushed their half-full plates to one side. Was there something wrong with the food? she wondered. But no one seemed to notice her. The three women talked almost non-stop, leaving her and Paola to avoid each other's glances, or glare at each other when they couldn't. She tried to calculate the exact number of days, hours and minutes she would have to be in Rome . . . but couldn't. It was too depressing. She finished her meal as quickly as she could and slid from the table without even bothering to ask. No one was paying her any attention anyway. She marched to her room holding her head as high as she could. Six weeks? She would *die*.

≈6≈

It was a dull, wet Saturday morning. The first Saturday without Amber. Becky lay in bed, watching the rain splash against the window pane, miserably wondering what to do. Every Saturday for almost as long as she could remember, she and Amber ate breakfast together. Sometimes it was slices of hot buttered toast and marmalade at Becky's; sometimes it was waffles and maple syrup, cooked by Krystyna at Amber's. After breakfast, they'd go to the ice rink on Bayswater, or to the pictures or, if the weather was good, to Holland Park where they could ride their bicycles. Then it was lunchtime, followed by their homework and usually an hour-long session of paper dolls until Amber got bored. Then there was tea, a video or TV to watch, and then dinner . . . and then bed. Amber often slept over at Becky's. Sunday mornings were Becky's favorite because they were a repeat of Saturdays' *and* there was no homework. Now, she thought to herself, she had almost two whole months without a single Saturday or Sunday morning with Amber . . . what would she do? She stared at the grey light outside her window so long and so hard her eyes began to hurt. She swung her legs out of bed and got up. Perhaps her mother would have some idea of what she could do.

"Don't you want to come shopping with me?" her

mother asked, surveying her daughter's miserable face.

"No, not really."

"Not even if we get you a new pair of jeans?" Becky shook her head.

"No. Maybe when Amber gets back."

"Darling," Susan began, as gently as she could. "Amber won't always be around, you know . . . sometimes you have to do things by yourself, without her."

"No, I don't," Becky said, painfully earnest. "Of course she will. I *told* you."

"All right, all right," Susan said hurriedly. She glanced at her watch—it was already 9:30 a.m.; in half an hour, the shops would begin filling up. "Well, what can we get you? You don't want a pair of jeans . . . how about some new pencils?"

"Yes, please. And a new sketchbook." Becky's eyes brightened. Susan was relieved. If there was one thing she could count on, it was that Becky could always be cheered up by the promise of a new sketchbook or a box of paints or a new set of pencils. She didn't know where this talent in her daughter had come from—only that she had an imagination that astounded Susan, and that she was breathtakingly good.

Later that same day, after her mother had come back from the shops bearing a lovely, brand-new sketchbook and a set of beautiful watercolor pencils, Becky put her things in a bag and set off down the road to the library. She'd discovered a set of

American art books, big, beautifully illustrated books with a *How to Draw* section at the back where she copied sketches of horses and animals and learned how to draw an eye in profile and what the best techniques for rendering the texture of hair might be. As she walked up the steps to the large, elegant Victorian library, she noticed someone standing in the foyer, as if unsure where to go. She looked at her as she passed—a tall, plump girl with blonde hair tied into uneven pigtails. She looked familiar. Becky thought she'd seen her somewhere before but couldn't remember where. She walked quickly to the art section, found the books she wanted and settled herself in at one of the desks, excited by the prospect of a whole afternoon spent drawing. It was one thing she could do, she supposed, whilst Amber was away—practice her drawing. Amber couldn't draw at all; it bored her. She opened her sketchbook, enjoying the look and feel of the crisp, white paper; pure, empty space, waiting for her pencil strokes to occupy it and give it life. She selected two pencils, a soft number two and the hard, sharp number three and began copying from the art book propped up in front of her. Hands, fingers, the arm in motion . . . her pencil strokes covered the page. She chewed a strand of hair, concentrating intently on getting it right, copying to perfection.

She almost jumped out of her skin when a voice beside her broke the silence to whisper that her drawings were good, really good. She looked up, annoyed. It was the girl she'd seen in the foyer.

"Really, they are," the girl said, looking over her shoulder at Becky's sketchbook and the book from which she was copying. "You can't tell the difference." Becky glared at her—how rude of her to just march up to her desk like that and interrupt her when she was *working*. But the girl didn't seem to notice Becky's frosty stare. "Are you going to be an artist?" she asked, asking the one question Becky loved to hear. Her irritation melted.

"Oh, *yes*," she said happily, warming immediately to the strange girl. There was a second's silence.

"I'm Madeleine, by the way," the girl said, hitching her bag on her shoulder, as if to leave.

"I'm Becky."

"I know."

Becky stared at her, taken aback. What did she mean?

"I heard your friend calling you the other day," Madeleine continued. "You know, the tall girl with brown hair."

"Amber?"

"I don't know her name. I just heard her call yours. You went into the shop at the top of Westbourne Grove, then into the bookshop around the corner. I saw you."

"What? What were *you* doing? Following us?" Becky looked at her, puzzled.

"Oh no," the girl said, shaking her head. "I have to walk that way back from school, too. I often see you on the way."

"What school d'you go to?" Becky asked her. She certainly wasn't at Radcliffe.

"King George."

Becky's eyes widened. She'd never actually met anyone who went to the enormous, forbidding school just down the road. "The *comprehensive*?" she asked, regretting the words as soon as they'd escaped her mouth.

"Yes, unfortunately," she said, obviously embarrassed. "You go to Radcliffe, don't you?" Becky nodded. There was another short silence. "Well," Madeleine said, turning to go. "I suppose I'd better get home."

"Would you . . . would you like to come round?" Becky asked before she'd had a chance to think about it. There was something about Madeleine she rather liked, and she wanted to make amends.

"What? To your house?"

"Yes, for tea."

"Oh. Well, I'll have to tell my mum," Madeleine said, a little surprised by the suddenness of the invitation. "Can you wait a few minutes? I only live up the road." Becky nodded eagerly. Suddenly the first Saturday without Amber was turning out not quite as dull as she'd feared. She watched as Madeleine hurried off, her satchel swinging awkwardly against her legs.

Susan Aldridge opened the door to a smiling Becky and a new friend, a large, rather mature, very pretty girl with pigtails, wearing the most unusual combination of clothes—a grey woollen skirt, a yellow-and-black striped T-shirt, blue socks that fell in a heap around her ankles and a pair of too-big tennis shoes. She dragged her eyes upwards.

"Mum, this is Madeleine. She goes to King George," was Becky's introduction as she led the way inside.

"Oh. Hello, Madeleine," Susan said, wondering where Becky had found her. In the twelve years they'd lived in Holland Park, Becky had never so much as spoken to anyone from King George, as far as Susan knew. She smiled at the girl, hoping she didn't look too surprised. Madeleine smiled shyly back.

"We're going to go upstairs. Can we have brownies for tea? Like the ones you made last week?" Becky asked, leading Madeleine upstairs.

"Yes . . . yes, of course. I'll bring them upstairs when they're ready," Susan said, pleased that Becky had found a new friend. She rarely voiced it but she sometimes thought Amber and Becky spent too much time together; including others in their little world might not be such a bad idea. She was pleased as well that Becky had found someone outside of Radcliffe, even if she did look older than Becky. Some of the other parents at the exclusive school got on her nerves terribly, never mind their daughters. It had been a hard decision to send Becky to Radcliffe. Neither she nor her husband had relished the idea of sending their daughter to a private school but, faced with the alternative of King George, they'd balked and paid up. Having Amber, who was so refreshingly down-to-earth despite her father's fortune, at the same school was an added and unexpected bonus. Susan didn't want to send

Becky away to boarding school, as she'd been sent away as a child—all in all, it seemed, Radcliffe was the easiest and most practical solution. Becky's door slammed shut at the top of the stairs. Susan smiled to herself: perhaps the enforced six-week absence wouldn't be quite as bad as they'd feared.

Madeleine looked around Becky's room in awe. It was lovely. She fingered the ribbons on Becky's ballet shoes, touched the sharpened points of her colored pencils on the desk and sat down gingerly on the quilted counterpane. It was nothing like her own home. From the minute Becky's mother opened the door downstairs, she'd understood there was no way she could take Becky back to her own home. She watched in silence as Becky brought out things for them to do. To *do*? In Madeleine's house, there was nothing to do: she sat in her room and read, sometimes went through to the sitting room to watch television or on the rare occasions her father was home before she went to bed, they talked. The idea of having *things*—scrapbooks, sketchbooks, pencils and paints, records, teenage magazines . . . they were as foreign to Madeleine as Madeleine's home would have been to Becky with its dusty, Hungarian books, the smell of cooking that somehow never left the wallpaper and the faded pictures of Budapest and Péter on the walls. Everything in Becky's home was beautiful. When Becky's mother came upstairs an hour later with a tray of the most delicious chocolate cakes Madeleine had ever seen, let alone tasted, her anguish was complete. Becky's mother was *so* nice. She was kind and funny, not prickly and awkward like her own mother. She spent the rest of the afternoon in a frenzy of comparisons, each one leaving her feeling more wretched than the last.

At six thirty, her stomach bursting with brownies and milk, she reluctantly got up from the soft sheepskin rug on the floor and said she ought to go home. Becky's invitation for her to come again after school—any time—seemed real. Even her mother said she hoped they'd see her again. As Madeleine shut the front door gently behind her and walked down the road, she felt something warm and friendly open up inside her. For the first time since they'd arrived in England, almost six years ago, Madeleine felt she'd met someone who could— *might*—become a friend. Becky was the sort of friend she'd had at home, back there in Budapest. She thought of Mara Nádas who lived three streets away and Krisztiána Gyllenborg, the girl who'd been her best friend at primary school. She usually tried not to think about them. It hurt, especially when she looked around her at the girls and boys whose company she was now forced to keep; her nickname at school was Shabby Shabo; they couldn't even spell her name. Still, Shabby Shabo was better than Fatty Foreigner, which was what Josh Barnes, the most horrible boy in the school— the most horrible boy in the universe, as far as Madeleine was concerned—had started calling her. She walked up Ladbroke Grove towards home, trying not to think about the big, comfortable house she'd just left where someone could be in the kitchen, three floors down, and not know if anyone else were at home.

≈7≈

The apartment was empty when Max arrived. He glanced at his watch as the driver brought his cases into the hallway. It was almost three o'clock—where the hell were they? Shopping, most likely. Francesca could shop for Italy. He wondered how on earth she'd managed to persuade Amber to go along. He walked towards the kitchen, loosening his tie. He'd actually intended to come to Rome a week earlier to see how Amber was settling in, but so many other things had claimed his attention, not least his bloody wife. At the thought of her, he grimaced. He'd sent Angela to Klaasens, a first-class, extremely discreet clinic just outside of Brussels, to be "taken care of," as they so politely put it. For the first week or so, it seemed to work. Things were going well, they were able to report. But unfortunately she'd somehow managed to persuade someone— the son of another patient, it seemed—to smuggle her in some brandy. She'd fooled them for a few days and then she'd been discovered—her progress disappearing down the drain, along with the brandy the staff had found. Max shook his head in annoyance. What the hell was he supposed to do with her? He looked at his watch again. Whatever the solution was, it would have to wait. He had a few phone calls to make. He opened the fridge, took out a dish of olives and a beer and walked through the empty apartment to his study.

At his large, glass-topped desk he pulled a bank of phones towards him and flicked open his diary, running his index finger down the list of numbers he'd scrawled in the margin . . . Kaplan, Kimchiko, Kramer. There it was. Jeff Kramer. He picked up the phone and dialed. In New York, the man on the other end of the line answered on the second ring. Max spoke for a few minutes, then hung up. He leaned back in his leather chair, his fingers pushed stiffly against each other, resting against his lips. His mind was working quickly. It was the first time he'd dealt with the East Germans—someone on their side had made contact via a mutual acquaintance. They were looking for dollars in exchange for a number of East German marks, a large consignment of East German-manufactured Trabants and the guarantee of a lucrative construction contract in Uzbekistan, one of the Soviet republics to the east of the Baltic sea. Max nodded to himself; the East German marks could be sold off to Polish or Czech contacts—no problems there. He would earn commission on both transactions. He would have to look around for a consignee for the cars—a Middle Eastern or African contact would be best. It would be next to impossible to arrange a European or American deal. South America was probably too far away and the Asian market was already flooded with

Japanese and Korean imports . . . yes, Iran, Iraq, Sudan . . . those would be the most likely markets. He'd have to get on the phone again. The last part of the deal—the construction of a hydro-electric plant in the north of the country—again, he'd have to do some digging around. He would find the partners, build the consortium and take a hefty finder's fee from both parties. He picked up the diary again and began thumbing through his lists. Five minutes later, he had the three names he wanted. He picked up the phone again and began to dial.

≈8≈

Angela's head felt as though it would fall off her neck. Her throat was parched, her eyes hurt from the light and her body . . . she had the feeling if she didn't hold on to something—the sides of the bed, for example—she would simply float away. She turned her head towards the window. Even with the thick, unyielding curtains drawn, the light was too much. She turned the other way. Her eyes fell on the photograph of Max and the children that that witch of a nurse had propped up on the TV. *Something to remind you of home!* she'd said cheerily before giving the bedcovers one last shake and disappearing. Angela tried to shout after her—I don't *want* to be reminded of home, you silly cow—but she was too exhausted. Besides, the woman probably wouldn't understand. She was French or Belgian or some other such godforsaken nationality. She hesitated for a second. But she'd spoken English to her a few minutes ago . . . was she in England? No, Belgium. That was what Max had told Mrs. Dewhurst to tell her. The bastard. He couldn't even be bothered to tell her himself. At the thought of it, her eyes filled with tears. She slid further down in her bed. The sheets were stiff and cold. She began to tremble. She'd been without a drink for . . . she tried to calculate . . . almost three days now. She knew from previous attempts that the first week was the hardest, but it was hard to think in terms of a week when she couldn't even get through the next five minutes. She was sweating with the effort of trying *not* to think about a nice, cold glass of beer or a sharp gin with lime or the soft, hot warmth of a brandy or . . . she began to cry softly. What the hell was she doing here? What had Max done to her? What had she done to herself?

Her mother's words flew at her, as if it was only yesterday she'd stood in front of the long mirror on the landing at Haddon Hall, her mother and Mrs. Bambridge and her sister, Mary Ann, fussing around her, pinning flowers in her hair and trying to get her to stop nibbling her nails. She'd been twenty-one and so in love she'd thought nothing could ever spoil the happiness in which she felt herself bathed. Max . . . she owed *every*thing to him. She didn't care what her parents said or thought—she didn't care that her friends found him terrifying or that her sister was half in love with him, too. She didn't *care* what anyone thought. Max had taught her that. Do it for *you*, he told her, often. Not for anyone else.

"Angela!" her mother cried out sharply. "Will you stop fidgeting! I can't get this pin in."

"Sorry," Angela murmured, looking at herself in the mirror.

"Mary Ann, will you and Mrs. Bambridge please get me some of those white roses . . . you know, the ones the florist delivered . . . I think they're in the conservatory, on the wooden bench. I'll need a row to put in her hair." Angela watched as her sister and the housekeeper disappeared down the stairs and her mother slowly stood up. "Darling," her mother began, looking stern and nervous and hesitant, all at the same time. Angela looked at her, surprised to see tears forming in her mother's eyes.

"What is it?" she asked, wondering if it was simply something all mothers did—cry at their daughters' weddings.

"Darling . . . I . . . I just want to say this one thing to you. Daddy made me promise . . . darling, if there's anything . . . if it doesn't work out, *for whatever reason* . . . you know you're always welcome back here. You do know that, don't you?"

"Mummy, don't be silly. I'm getting *married*. I'm not going off to the moon, you know. We'll only be down the road. In London. You're supposed to be *happy* for me!" Angela tried to laugh it off.

"I know, it's just . . . it's just that Max . . . well, he's different from us, darling. He's . . . we don't know *any*thing about him, you know. Daddy's very worried."

"You shouldn't be." Angela's voice hardened. "He loves me. I love him. That's all that matters."

"Oh, darling." Lady Weymouth dabbed at her eyes with a handkerchief. "That's what you all say, in the beginning. I used to think that too. *Imagine!* But there's something about him . . . I just don't *trust* him. I'm sure he loves you, truly I am . . . but . . ." she broke off suddenly. Mary Ann and Mrs. Bambridge were climbing back up the stairs.

"There aren't any white roses," Mary Ann said crossly, flouncing into the room.

"Oh? I thought there were. Oh well, these'll just have to do," Lady Weymouth said, pointing to the pink roses and turning away from her daughters. Angela swallowed. What was she supposed to say?

She pushed back the covers, trying to get rid of the memory. Fifteen years had passed since that day and the pain was as raw as it had been ever since she realized her mother was right. She swung her legs out of bed. She could hear voices in the corridor—it was obviously visiting time. A man's voice . . . speaking French. She knew there was a film star in the room next to hers. She couldn't remember the woman's name. And the wife of somebody important at the end of the corridor . . . she'd heard the nurses talking about her the day she'd arrived. Women. A whole sanatorium full of women. Drink, drugs, depression . . . were those the only choices for women like herself?

She felt for her mules under the bed and pulled her silk dressing gown off the back of the door. She felt like a walk. She had to get out of the room.

*   *   *

"*Je m'appelle Angela*," she said in her schoolgirl French and smiled at the young man opposite who quite obviously couldn't take his eyes off her. They had somehow wound up alone in the plush visitors' room down the corridor.

"Bruno." The young man blushed. He hesitated, then held out a hand. Angela took it, enjoying the moist, nervous palm in hers and wondering how quickly she could get him to bring her a bottle of whisky, brandy, anything. "*Vous . . . vous êtes malade*?" he enquired tentatively. Angela smiled.

"*Non. Oui.* A drunk." She laughed. He smiled, then laughed with her.

"*C'est quoi . . . un drunk?*" He was young. Eighteen at the most. He was probably visiting his mother.

"*Rien. C'est rien. Avez-vous quelque chose à boire*?" she asked, suddenly feeling quite reckless. He lifted an eyebrow. Ah, not so young after all. He held up a finger. Angela giggled.

"Deux minutes. Two minute. Okay?" He jumped up. Angela's heart lifted. A drink! He was tall and thin, with the lanky, awkward look of a young man just barely out of adolescence. Angela giggled again as he opened the door to the corridor and peeped outside. In the space of five minutes, they'd become accomplices. She loosened the belt on her dressing gown and fluffed out her hair. She didn't know quite what he would want from her in return, but she would gladly have given him anything. Anything at all.

"*Voilà!*" The door opened and he was back carrying not one but *two* precious, precious bottles of Courvoisier. Angela could have wept. She jumped off the couch towards him. He held up a warning hand. *"Pour ma mère,"* he whispered. "But I give to you."

"You angel," Angela whispered back.

"Mais pas ici. Not here." He did want something after all. Angela swallowed. Just looking at the bottles was making her dizzy. She had a craving for a drink that was stronger than any desire she'd ever known.

"Fine. Follow me." She opened the door, quickly checked the corridor and pulled him after her.

She was oblivious. She lifted the bottle to her lips and gulped, slowly at first, then greedily. He watched her, anxious for her to finish her pleasure so he could start his before a nurse came looking for him, or her. She put the bottle down, climbed into bed and lay back, watching him slide quickly out of his jeans and into the cold bed with her. Within seconds he was on top of her, grabbing at her nightgown, pulling it aside, sliding a hand over her breasts, her neck, down her stomach . . . she kept her eyes firmly on the two bottles sitting on top of the TV next to the picture of Max and as he thrust into her once, twice, three times . . . and then collapsed against her, she actually grinned. It was over in seconds. She closed her eyes as he hurriedly shoved himself back into his boxer shorts, ran a hand through his hair and smoothed down his shirt.

"Ça va?" she asked him dreamily, reaching for the bottle again. Her dressing gown fell open, ex-

posing a small, reddened breast. She saw him look away. She shrugged. *"Merci,"* she said, nodding at his "gift." Although it was hardly a gift, she thought to herself wryly, moving as delicately as she could out of the patch of dampness he'd left behind him.

"OK. Bon, il faut . . . je me casse." He seemed anxious to disappear. "I come back. *Mercredi.* You will be 'ere?"

"Oh, yes. I think so. Bring me another," Angela murmured, the bottle already at her lips. He smiled suddenly.

"OK. *A bientôt.*"

"*Sayonara*, sailor." Angela lay back against the sheets as he slipped out into the corridor. Heaven. Pure heaven. The brandy burned its familiar way down her throat, erasing her headache, her exhausted mind, sore eyes . . . sore heart. She felt immediately better.

≈9≈

A month had passed—a whole month without Amber—and to her immense surprise, Becky found she wasn't spending each day counting the minutes until she was due to arrive and, after the first week, she'd stopped writing in her diary every evening just in case she forgot something important to tell her when she got back. She had school to occupy her, in any case and of course, she now had Madeleine. Madeleine had been round to her house almost every day for the past fortnight and although she'd never even suggested Becky come round to hers, Becky found herself growing more and more curious about Madeleine's home. She knew Madeleine's mother had been a writer and that her books had been banned—she had to ask her parents what that meant—and that her father had been an optometrist—again, she'd had to ask her parents what *that* was—and that they now lived a very different life from the one they'd had, back there. Becky couldn't imagine what had happened to them that they now had to work in such menial jobs—her mother was a cleaner, her father a factory hand—but Madeleine was reluctant to discuss them, or to invite Becky back to her house. But Becky was curious, and persistent, and eventually, one Friday afternoon, she got her way. After having been asked three or four times in the course of the afternoon, Madeleine finally gave in.

"But it's not a bit like your house," Madeleine warned, casting her mind back to the dingy, damp hallway at home.

"It doesn't matter," Becky said earnestly. She couldn't understand Madeleine's reluctance. After all, how different could it possibly be? She thrust her feet into her favorite white sneakers and jumped off the bed. "Ready?" she asked, suddenly impatient.

Madeleine nodded glumly. She looked at Becky as if trying to picture her in her room. She looked impossibly clean and fresh—her long, shiny, auburn hair had been brushed and parted into two identical, glossy ponytails, falling on either side of her small, lightly freckled face. Her hazel-green eyes shone, her clothes were bright and neat—she looked like someone who'd never set foot in Riverfleet, Madeleine's horrible, ugly council block. She sighed and got off the bed.

They walked up Ladbroke Grove together, Madeleine falling silent as they neared the top of the road. At the junction with Barlby Road, they turned left. Becky looked around her. In the space of less than ten minutes, they'd left the elegant, white-stuccoed world of Holland Park behind. Here, there were only blocks of flats, forbiddingly uniform. Madeleine turned right into a small street that led to the railway track and walked up to one of them. *Riverfleet.* Becky watched as Madeleine reached into her satchel for a bunch of keys. She opened the front door and beckoned her in. The dark hallway stank of urine and another, sharp, sour smell. Becky's mouth turned downwards in dismay.

"You *live* here?" she said, her eyes widening as she took in the peeling paint and the "Out of Order" sign hanging askew on the lift door.

"'Fraid so," Madeleine said glumly.

"Gosh." Becky couldn't think of anything else to say. They walked up the stairs to the fourth floor in silence, Becky struggling to hold her breath in case she breathed in anything . . . *dangerous*. The stopped outside a white door. Madeleine produced the same bunch of keys and opened the door.

"Mama?" she called out as they entered. Becky looked around her, half-fearfully.

"Igen." She heard a woman answer, a sharp

sound, like a reluctant question. It was dim inside the Szabos' flat—the clear early summer day outside had not made it past the front door. The air was musty, a folded away kind of air, heavy with the scent of damp linen, unfamiliar cooking and something else, something she couldn't quite place. Becky's eyes adjusted to the gloom as they walked in. It was small—so *small!*—a bedroom to the left, a closed door in front of them, a narrow hallway and then, on the right-hand side, the bathroom and on the left, the sitting room. To the side, through a beaded, patterned curtain, was the kitchen. She followed her into the sitting room. Her mother was lying on a dusty pink velvet sofa, her feet up, resting. In her hands was a heavy book, bound in green, with unfamiliar lettering on the cover. Becky's eyes darted around the room, picking up the details her art teacher said were so important—the cover of the book, the color of the sofas, the pattern on the faded net curtains . . . the type and number of plants struggling to survive on the tiny balcony outside. She filed the scene away in her memory—she would retrieve it later, in a drawing. It was unlike anything she'd ever seen before.

Mrs. Szabo looked up, surprised to see someone standing hesitantly behind her daughter. She put the book down and struggled upright, smoothing her fair hair and tucking it behind her ears.

"Oh. *Mi bajvan*, Madeleine?" She got up from the couch. She was thinner than her daughter, pinched-looking where Madeleine was ripe, and unsmiling. She wore a cotton dress over which a woollen cardigan was buttoned, and thick black tights—in the late spring, the effect was curious. Her hands, when she held them out, were rough and puffy. Becky saw that the nails were ragged; they were hands that spent time in water. She smiled timidly at her. Mrs. Szabo appeared not to notice.

"Mama?" Madeleine asked nervously. She said something to her in Hungarian. Becky listened, fascinated by the unfamiliar sound and intonation coming from Madeleine whose English voice she'd only just become accustomed to. They argued quietly for a minute or two then Mrs. Szabo nodded curtly at Becky and disappeared out of the room. Becky hovered next to Madeleine, wondering what the argument was about—had she done something wrong? She'd barely said a word since they entered. "Um, have a seat," Madeleine said awkwardly, plopping herself down into the depression made in the sofa by her mother. Becky sat down gingerly on a chair opposite and looked around the room. It was crammed full of furniture and books—books everywhere, in the language she couldn't quite read. The combination of consonants and accents was difficult: *Péter Esterházy, Imre Kertész György Konrád.* She mouthed the words to herself silently. In the corner of the room was a great, dark sideboard, a pair of crocheted lace cloths hung over its sides, yellowing with age. Becky looked at the collection of photographs. In their oval, convex lenses, sets of grandparents and relatives stared back blankly at her and she searched amongst their faces for some semblance of Madeleine. It was there, just visible in their high, smooth cheekbones and piercing dark-brown eyes. She turned to Madeleine.

"Who's that?" she asked, pointing at the picture that occupied pride of place amongst the collection. In a tall, gilt-framed black-and-white photograph, a beautiful young man looked out from beneath an grey beret. He wore a soldier's uniform and his beret sat at a jaunty angle on his head. There was another, larger, picture of him on the wall opposite.

"My brother," Madeleine said, her face suddenly tight. Becky looked at her, impressed. A grown-up brother, and in uniform?

"He's awfully good-looking. Is he in the army?"

"He's dead." Madeleine's voice was flat, cutting her off sharply. Becky stopped, shocked. "Would you like something to drink?" Madeleine asked after a moment or two. Becky shook her head mutely. Dead? She'd never known anyone who'd died. How did he die? she longed to ask, but there was something in the unhappy, defensive set of Madeleine's mouth that stopped her. She understood now what it was in the flat she hadn't been able to grasp, at first. It was sadness. The air was heavy with the scent, and taste, of sadness.

Across the room, watching Becky from her position on the couch, Madeleine suffered mutely. Of course the visit hadn't been—*wouldn't* be—a success. It wasn't just the awfulness of her home, or her mother, disappearing as soon as Madeleine walked in the door. It was everything. The photographs of Péter, the persistent, lingering smell of cabbage, the plastic covering on the sofa that still hadn't been taken off—everything was so different and alien, she was sure, to a girl whose mother came to the door every afternoon, a glass of milk and a plate of biscuits waiting on the big dining-room table with its cheerful bunch of flowers and pretty teapot in the middle. No doubt Becky wanted to leave as quickly as possible. Why would anyone want to stay in a place like this when a light-filled, sunny bedroom was available, stuffed to bursting with objects of luxurious, rich desire? She got up suddenly, wanting only to get rid of her and for things to go back to the way they'd been before. She'd been perfectly happy in her own, solitary world. In fact, she thought bitterly to herself as she practically pushed Becky out of the room, she'd been stupid to think she could ever have made friends with someone like Becky. Girls like Becky belonged to girls like Amber—that was why they were best friends. Why had she ever thought otherwise? Ignoring the look of hurt incomprehension on Becky's face, she closed the front door and leaned against it, her face hot with embarrassment and disappointment. She listened for a second, then she heard Becky's footsteps slowly walk away down the walkway, heading for the stairs.

"Why don't you go round tomorrow afternoon?" Becky's mother said, looking at Becky's unhappy face at dinner that evening. "Take her mother a bunch of flowers; that'd be nice."

"I don't think Madeleine likes me," Becky said miserably, toying with her food.

"I'm sure she does, darling," Susan said sooth-ingly. She glanced at her husband for support but he was too busy trying to read a report and eat at the same time. "You don't realize it, I know, but you're a very lucky girl . . . your father and I spoil you, you know. We oughtn't to but . . . when you meet someone like Madeleine, you realize just how lucky you are. Now, finish your potatoes. I'll help you pick a bunch of flowers tomorrow afternoon after school. You can take them round at tea-time." Becky looked gratefully at her mother. She always knew what to do.

Madeleine looked up. She'd heard a tap on the front door. She put her book down in exasperation and got out of bed. Probably the neighbors—their cat was always climbing into the Szabos' balcony and getting stuck, unable to climb back. She walked down the short corridor to the front door and un-latched it, pulling it open.

"Oh." Her mouth fell open. Becky was standing in front of her holding an enormous bunch of glorious, yellow sunflowers in one hand and a drawing pad and pencils in the other. She looked nervously at Madeleine.

"Hi," she said cautiously. Madeleine stared at her. What on earth was she doing? "I brought these . . . for your mum," Becky said in a rush. "I thought she might like them, they're really pretty and my mum said . . ."

"It's not her birthday or anything," Madeleine said, frowning at Becky. "What d'you bring those for?"

"I just thought she'd like them." There was a short silence. Becky cleared her throat. "Madeleine, I was just wondering . . . I was going to ask you yesterday but . . . well, d'you think I could draw you?" It came out in a rush.

Madeleine looked at her incredulously. "Draw me? What ever for?"

"I don't know. I'd just like to. I've only ever drawn my parents . . . Amber can't sit still for long enough. Please say yes. *Please*."

Madeleine paused for a moment, as if she didn't know whether or not to trust the eager, almost pleading smile on Becky's face. Then she opened the door and stood aside as Becky walked past. She took the flowers from her and put them in the bathtub—her mother was still at work. She led the way back into the sitting room, trying not to show just how pleased and surprised she was. She'd spent the previous night repeating to herself all the reasons why she was better off without Becky and by morning, she was almost convinced. Now Becky had suddenly turned up on her doorstep, and the pleasure and longing for a friend that Madeleine had been experiencing ever since the day she'd gone up to Becky in the library came flooding back. She smiled to herself and walked into the sitting room where Becky was already setting out her things. That was another thing Madeleine liked about Becky—she rarely wasted time.

Maja looked at the picture Madeleine had propped up on the kitchen counter when she'd left for school that morning and had to grip the sides of the cooker against the wave of grief that ripped straight through her. It was uncanny. The little girl, Madeleine's new friend . . . she'd chosen to draw Madeleine sitting on the sofa in the living room, her head turned slightly, a curtain of thick, wavy dark-blonde hair falling across one eye. She'd captured the texture and feel of her hair perfectly—Maja reached out a hand to touch the drawing surprised by the smooth, unyielding feel of the paper and the tactile, almost photographic quality of the image. But it was the background that caught her eye. Just above Madeleine, exactly in the center of the drawing, was the photograph of Péter. Maja stuffed her hand in her mouth and turned, unable to bear the image. She stumbled blindly into the bathroom, violently sweeping aside the bottles of shampoo and tubes of toothpaste that were kept there, and fell to her knees.

≈10≈

Amber watched in fascinated repulsion as Paola and Francesca prepared themselves to leave the apartment each morning. From behind the curtains in the drawing room, she could see them primp and preen themselves in the enormous hallway mirror before stepping into the hallway and into the elegant wrought iron lift. Paola was only ten—*ten!*—yet she behaved as though she were at least six years older, certainly older than Amber. Getting ready for school was a ritual that could take up to two hours before she pronounced herself ready. She went to a private *lycée* about three blocks away from the house, for which she required the services of the driver each morning and where she took lessons in a combination of Italian, French, English and Spanish. A polyglot. Amber was reluctantly impressed. School ended at two o'clock but there were scores of afternoon activities, including a weekly visit to the hairdresser—Amber couldn't quite believe her ears—and to the manicurist every Saturday morning with her mother. As she watched the two of them, she slowly realized that Francesca was grooming her daughter in the only way she knew how to grow up pleasing and desirable to the opposite sex, as she herself was. To Amber, the shopping expeditions, the conversations about clothes and make-up and fashion at the dinner table were about as alien to her as the idea of actually having a mother in the first place. She couldn't remember a time when Angela hadn't been someone *she* had to take care of, not the other way around. To think of actually going to Angela for advice? She shook her head.

Yet there was something about the closeness between Francesca and her daughter . . . it would have killed her to admit it but she was almost envious. Watching the two of them giggling together as they opened parcels in the drawing room or the way Francesca would brush Paola's long hair at bedtime . . . she realized, for the first time, that those were things she'd missed out on—most of the time Angela barely registered her presence. And even though she had Becky's mum to fuss over her every once in a while, it just wasn't the same. At the thought of Becky, she made a small face to herself. She missed her terribly. She'd written to her almost every day and, to Becky's credit, she'd replied. But lately her replies had been full of someone else, a girl called Madeleine. Amber experienced that old, familiar sense of panic—she wasn't about to lose Becky too, was she?

≈11≈

Becky's heart gave a sudden and completely unexpected lurch. Above her, looking rather puzzled by her sudden inability to speak, was Kieran, Amber's older brother.

"She'll be back on Friday," Kieran repeated irritably, wondering what was wrong with her. He'd known Becky Aldridge since . . . well, forever. She and Amber were inseparable, always had been. He looked at her and frowned. She'd suddenly grown up—long, shiny auburn hair; green eyes; pretty face; small, petite body . . . hell, she must be fourteen? Fifteen? He'd thought of her as an irritating little kid for so long. He looked at his watch.

"I'll . . . I'll come back on Friday," Becky stammered. Her face had gone bright red. Kieran shrugged.

"OK. She should be back in the afternoon. Well, I've got to run . . . see you around," he said, picking up his motorcycle helmet from the table in the vestibule. Becky turned to go down the steps. "Hey," Kieran suddenly spoke. "You can come along if you want," he offered, rather liking the way her whole face lit up as she turned back to face him. "If you haven't got anything else to do."

"Me? Oh, no . . . no . . . there's nothing . . . what? Come with *you*?" The words tumbled out of Becky's mouth. She stared at him.

"Yeah. I'm just going round the corner. I'm picking up some records from a friend. You can sit on the back."

"Of your bike?" Becky nearly fainted in breathless anticipation. She looked down at herself. She was still wearing her uniform.

"Just tuck your skirt up," Kieran said casually, walking towards her. "It's only a minute down the road." Becky nodded, too delighted to speak. She followed him to the bike parked in front of the house.

Sitting on Tim's bed, twenty minutes later, Becky gazed at Kieran. She couldn't understand why or how he'd suddenly transformed himself in her eyes from an aloof, brooding presence at Amber's house to this handsome, funny, witty young man against whose firm, strong body she'd pressed her own as they rode up Holland Park Avenue, her hair whipping about her face. She looked at him from under her lashes. He was standing in the corner of the room, picking records out of a series of stacked plastic boxes. She had never before noticed the way his thick, curly hair sprang away from his forehead, like Amber's, or the way his lashes were dark and full against his blue eyes. Why hadn't she noticed those things?

"Here, d'you want one?" Tim, his friend, casually offered her a cigarette. She took it nervously, hoping her fingers wouldn't shake. She watched Tim carefully, doing exactly as he did but trying not to inhale the smoke. She almost choked. Neither of them seemed to notice. In fact, neither Kieran nor Tim took much notice of her at all. They talked in a kind of private language, full of references and jokes Becky couldn't catch but thrilled to the sound of, regardless. She didn't care if she didn't get the jokes. It was enough to be in the same room as them. She sat on the bed and watched their every move, feeling a little ridiculous in her prim grey uniform. She pushed her socks around her ankles and loosened the straps on her pinafore . . . anything to make her look less childish.

The record selection took another ten minutes. Finally, with a small pile under his arm, Kieran turned to her. "Ready?" he asked. She nodded vigorously. She scrambled off the bed and followed them downstairs.

"Hop on," Kieran said, fixing the strap of his helmet under his chin. She watched Tim glance quickly at her legs as she pushed her skirt up. She blushed. She paused for a second before laying her cheek against Kieran's back and holding tightly onto him, feeling the hard plane of his stomach beneath her fingertips. She felt the vibrations of the motorbike course through her, making her shiver. She wished the afternoon would last for ever.

"Here." Kieran handed her the joint, blowing the smoke out through his nostrils, looking at her with the faintly sardonic expression he favored. She took it, her fingers shaking, and took a cautious drag. It made her feel rather sick. She let her hand fall to her side after passing the joint back to him and waited. She wanted him to touch her again—anywhere—wanted to feel his hands on her, the light but firm pressure signaling a new kind of longing for contact—she who turned from her mother at night and rarely, if ever, kissed her father. She *wanted* him to touch her. She lay absolutely still, waiting. Her whole being felt as though it were concentrated in the fingers of her right hand as it lay on the counterpane next to his. Casually, almost indifferently, Kieran finished smoking, rolled over towards her and propped himself up on one elbow, his body balanced precariously above hers, his curly brown hair falling into his face as he looked into hers. Becky forgot her nervousness, forgot the nausea in the pit of her stomach, forgot everything as he lowered his face to hers—and then the sweet, hot surprise as he kissed her. She held her mouth slightly open, waiting for the sensation in her lips and mouth to leave her. It didn't. Her mouth was on fire, burning to the touch and feel of his tongue as he traced lazy circles around her lips and inside, just inside where the smooth, silky lining of her mouth began. He

raised his lips and she could feel herself moving towards him, her hands moving around his neck to
bring him back, to seal the distance between his
wonderfully heavy mouth and the erotic heat it generated and her own, timid kisses. She was both
afraid and delirious at the same time. She felt his
hand move up her thigh, parting the damp flesh, his
finger stroking the soft skin and then she sat up,
shaking with the fear and excitement of it.

"Hey," Kieran murmured in protest as she pulled
away from him. He caught hold of her waist, pulling
her back down. She struggled and broke away,
breathing heavily. She panicked.

"I'd . . . I'd better go home," she said quickly, hearing her own high, breathless voice. She looked down
at Kieran, who was lying with a hand over his eyes,
his chest rising and falling. Becky was filled with a
sudden thrill—*she* had done that? *She* had made his
breathing ragged and uneven and *she* had caused
the look of pained exhaustion on his face? She was
awestruck. It was her first taste of power and as much
as she was afraid of it, she wanted to feel it again.
She wanted to test it, to push him beyond what she'd
seen and felt that afternoon . . . she wanted to make
sure it would happen again and that she, little Becky
Aldridge, could make someone as cool as Kieran Sall
weak with wanting her. She tugged down her T-shirt
and tucked her hair behind her ears. Kieran lay still,
not saying anything, not moving. She hesitated. "I'll
come round tomorrow?" she said, more of a question
than a statement. Kieran didn't say anything. "When
Amber's back . . ." her voice trailed off. Kieran rolled

over onto his stomach, burying his head in his arms. Becky's hand faltered on the doorknob.

"Yeah. See you later," Kieran said, his voice muffled. Becky opened the door and walked slowly down the stairs. What a day. In the space of a few hours, it seemed her whole life had changed. *Amber. Kieran. Madeleine.* The two months she'd been dreading were finally almost over, bringing with them a new set of friendships—and complications.

≈ **12** ≈

Amber's first reaction to Madeleine was one of surprise. Whatever else she'd pictured from Becky's descriptions, the large, very beautiful girl sitting on the bed in the place she usually sat wasn't it. To begin with, she was wearing the most odd combination of clothes—a pair of tight brown corduroy trousers; a man's shirt buttoned over a polo-necked sleeveless top; striped socks and clogs. *Clogs?* No one Amber knew wore clogs. The effect was startlingly bizarre. She pushed a pile of freshly laundered clothes off the armchair in the corner of the room and sat down. Madeleine looked at her, a shy smile playing around the corners of her mouth. Becky hovered nervously in the background. She desperately wanted Amber to like Madeleine. Madeleine would like Amber of course. Everyone liked Amber.

"What's King George like?" Amber asked curi-

ously. Like Becky, she'd never even spoken to anyone from the school down the road.

"Horrid." Madeleine gave a wry smile.

"Why d'you go there then?" she asked.

"Because. We're poor." Next to her, Becky
blushed. Madeleine didn't. Amber liked the way she
said it, almost challenging her to respond. Her eyes
met Amber's. Dark eyes, fringed with thick, long
lashes . . . intense eyes, almost black. With her
thick, wavy dark-blonde hair; her almost faultless
English with just the faintest hint of an accent and
her odd, haphazard clothes—to Amber, after her six
weeks in Rome, she was exactly what was needed
in their prim little world.

"Well then, you must come round here more often,"
Amber said, grinning. Across the room, Becky
breathed out a cautious sigh of relief. Amber liked her.

"I will."

Later that afternoon, Madeleine reluctantly got up
from her position on the bed, and turned to Amber
and Becky.

"I'd better go," she said, pulling a face. Amber's stories of her summer in Rome, her "other" family, the
clothes she'd been forced to wear . . . it was another
world, to Madeleine. Everything was mentioned casually, in passing: going shopping; having her hair
cut; private school lessons . . . these were scenes
that in Madeleine's world could not and would not—
ever, she sometimes despaired—take place.

"Well?" Amber's voice brought her back to the present. Madeleine started. She hadn't been listening.

"What?" she asked. Amber was looking questioningly at her.

"Tomorrow. We're going to the pictures. D'you want to come?"

"Oh. No, no . . . I can't. I . . . I have to stay at home. To help my mother." Madeleine stammered automatically. She couldn't ask her mother for money to go to the pictures, much as she would have liked to go. "Thanks anyway," she added, walking to the door.

"See you later," Becky called as she closed it behind her.

"Yeah, bye!" Amber's voice floated down the stairwell. Madeleine opened the front door. An idea had suddenly come to her, out of nowhere. Or perhaps it was the little white lie that had slipped out. *I have to help my mother*. Well, she thought to herself, suddenly excited, she *could* help her mother, in a way. She could get a job. She was sixteen. Lots of girls in her class had Saturday jobs. They spent their money on clothes and make-up . . . and money for the pictures. If she wanted to spend time with her new friends and do the things they liked to do, she'd have to have a bit of money. And if her parents couldn't afford to give her pocket money, as theirs did, well, she ought to stop feeling so bloody sorry for herself and earn it! She practically ran all the way home. It was a brilliant idea. Why hadn't she thought of it before?

"A job?" Maja looked at her daughter in alarm. "When?"

"On Saturdays. Just once a week."

"But what about your homework?" Imre asked, lifting his head from his plate.

"Papa, it's only one day a week. I'll have plenty of time for my homework," Madeleine said gently. Imre nodded uncertainly.

"Well, I suppose there's Mr. Dorman," Maja said, hesitating. She looked at her husband. "You could . . . you could do the dusting and the polishing on Saturday mornings. I do the heavy stuff on Wednesdays . . ." she broke off, considering. "All right, I'll ask him this week. It's not very much money, though," she said, spooning boiled potatoes onto Madeleine's plate.

"I know. It's just to have some pocket money. All the girls at school do it." Madeleine didn't mention Becky. Maja's only comment after Becky's last visit was that the flowers must have cost a fortune and it was all very well for the rich to waste their money. She hadn't told her mother about Amber. From Becky, Madeleine gathered that Amber's family were rich—*seriously* rich, not middle-class, middle-rich, like Becky's.

"Okay. I'll speak to Mr. Dorman on Wednesday." Maja sat back down. They finished the meal in silence, each preoccupied in their own way with the worries of the day.

"She's nice," Amber agreed, having taken back her rightful position at the foot of Becky's bed. "But she wears the weirdest things."

"I know. They're really poor," Becky said. "And, her brother died. Can you imagine?"

"Really? When?" Amber stared at her, wondering just how it was that Becky always managed to find out the most intimate secrets of everyone's lives.

"I don't know exactly," Becky admitted, plonking herself down on the bed next to Amber. "He's awfully good-looking, though . . . there's a photo of him in the sitting room. He was in the army. I bet he was a spy." Amber snorted. Becky's imagination was notoriously overactive.

"Oh, come on. He probably fell ill, or something. Honestly, Becky . . . you make up the weirdest stories."

"I didn't make it up! *You* ask her, then."

"Why should I? If she wants to tell us, she will," Amber said, rather primly.

"Oh, you're so bloody *righteous* sometimes, Amber," Becky said, stung by her skepticism—and her implied criticism. She was always harping on about the *truth*. As far as Becky was concerned, the truth was often boring. Imagining things was much more fun. She picked sulkily at the threads in her bedspread. Amber ignored her and picked up a book. There was silence in the room for a few minutes. Becky looked enviously at Amber's tanned arms and face. She looked wonderful, all long, brown curls and long, brown limbs. In that moment, she looked so much like Kieran. At the thought of him, her stomach lurched. She hadn't said a word to Amber about Kieran . . . she didn't know how to. She fiddled with her quilted counterpane—she wanted to go over to Amber's and see him, but when? And how? What would she say to Amber? The question spun around in her head until she felt dizzy. She lay back on her pillows, ignoring Amber's strange look, exhausted. It had been a tiring day. She'd spent it worrying about Amber; worrying about Madeleine; worrying about Kieran . . . and now she could see Amber beginning to worry about *her*. She closed her eyes. There was altogether too much worrying going on. In the short space of six weeks life had gone from being a pleasant, interchangeable routine of school, Amber's house and art to being an seesaw of emotions, each more intense and unpredictable than the last. She'd waited so long for Amber's return; now that she was here, all she could think about was getting rid of her in order to see Kieran. And she'd felt bad about asking Madeleine to come to the pictures with them. She'd seen Madeleine's obvious embarrassment. Sometimes, Becky thought to herself, her eyes closed, she felt things too deeply. She sometimes wished she weren't quite so sensitive to everyone and everything around her. Amber was so thick-skinned— people's slights and petty upsets bounced off her, away from her . . . she was tough. She didn't suffer on behalf of anyone the way Becky often did. Sometimes Becky longed for a little of the same.

≈13≈

Madeleine looked up at the façade of Mr. Dorman's house curiously. It was purple, unlike all the other cream and light pink houses in the road, a deep, loud purple with a gold door and . . . she squinted . . . *mirrored* windows? She'd never seen anything like them. She stared at their reflection—her mother fumbling with the keys, she standing open-mouthed beside her. She shut her mouth and followed her mother into the hallway. An enormous elephant's foot greeted them, standing directly in front of them—a large, black foot, complete with tough, blackened nails and dark, bristly hair. Madeleine looked at it in alarm. She turned to her mother but Maja had gone straight through to the kitchen, obviously immune to Mr. Dorman's strange tastes.

"So." Maja handed her an apron and a pair of gloves. "Kitchen first, then the rest of the downstairs. Bathroom on the first landing, and the two spare rooms and then upstairs, Mr. Dorman's bedroom and his bathroom. In that order. *Igen*?"

Madeleine nodded, taking the gloves and apron. She shuddered as she walked past the foot, and the zebra head hanging just above her own. Maja showed her where everything was—cloths; dusters; vacuum cleaner; mops . . . everything she needed in her new job. She showed her how to wipe the mirrors, where to put away the crockery; how to make his bed. She would be paid the princely sum of £2.50 an hour and Maja estimated it would take her four hours. Ten pounds seemed a fortune to Madeleine. "I'll come back for you at one o'clock," Maja said, picking up her coat. "Don't waste time," she said sternly, one hand on the door handle. Madeleine rolled her eyes.

"I *won't.* I can manage." Maja opened the front door and slipped out. She had another job to go to.

The work was harder than it looked. It took almost an hour to clean the kitchen. She wondered what it must be like to use a plate and leave it wherever you liked, knowing that someone else would take it, scrape it clean and wash it, putting it back alongside all the other dishes in the cupboards that lined the kitchen walls. Mr. Dorman obviously had other things to think about—even the teaspoons used to stir his coffee were left lying in puddles of spilled milk. Madeleine stacked the dishwasher, scoured the pots. It didn't look as though he was much of a cook—everything was burnt. She was curious; from the look of things, he obviously lived alone. No woman could possibly have tolerated the mess. She tidied the contents of the fridge—three bottles of champagne and a paper bag of mushrooms—emptied the rubbish bin and wiped, polished and dusted until every surface gleamed. As she peeled off the gloves and wiped her face with the back of her hand, she wondered how her mother found the strength to do this kind of work, day after day. Cleaning offices was one thing, but clearing up the debris left by a spoiled, middle-aged man who couldn't even boil an egg was another thing altogether. She walked upstairs to the first bathroom.

Two hours later, she reached the master bedroom. She looked around the room with interest. It was large and airy with an enormous double bed, a huge wooden chest of drawers and little else. Whatever Mr. Dorman did, he seemed to have a passion for animals. A large skin lay draped over the bed—Madeleine couldn't quite identify the animal, a leopard or a tiger; she wasn't entirely sure of the difference—whilst another skin lay across the floor. The walls were white and completely without adornment. She made the bed as her mother had shown her, gathering the pile of dirty linen and putting it into the basket. Maja would do the washing on Wednesdays. She dusted the side tables, vacuumed the floor and polished the chest of drawers. She looked at her watch. Fifteen minutes left. She moved quickly into the bathroom. It was much like the bedroom: large, white, and almost empty. Madeleine cleaned the sink, the taps and the cupboard doors and was just about to go downstairs when a small picture in a frame sitting on the shelf above the toilet caught her eye. She lifted it carefully. A young man was smiling into the camera, a good-looking, grinning young man. She wondered who he was. Mr. Dorman's son, perhaps? He was tanned, with wavy dark-brown hair, dark eyes. She liked his smile.

"Madeleine?" Maja's voice floated up the stairs. Madeleine jumped, putting the picture back immediately and closing the door behind her. She ran down the stairs. Maja stood at the bottom in her coat, running a finger along the table Madeleine had dusted. She nodded. Clean. "Finished?" she asked, straightening the vase of flowers on the dining table.

"Yes. Everything's done." Madeleine followed her mother as she quickly inspected each room. Maja seemed satisfied.

"So . . . you think you can manage the house? On Saturdays?" Maja asked her as they walked up the road to the bus stop.

Madeleine nodded eagerly. "Oh, yes, it's not that difficult . . . I mean, it's not that much work," she added hastily, not wanting to sound dismissive.

"*Kiválló*. Okay. So you come back next week. You did a good job today." She reached into her bag, drew out her purse and selected a ten-pound note. Madeleine's first wages. Madeleine took it and slid it into her pocket, smiling widely. Her mother was notoriously hard to please—if Maja thought she'd done a good job, then she had. She walked along beside her, fingering the lovely, crisp banknote, dreaming of what she'd buy and how long it would last.

Amber heard the front doorbell. She glanced at her watch. Almost five thirty. It was probably Becky, or Madeleine, or one of Kieran's friends. She heard Krystyna's voice as she went to open the door— yes, it was Becky. She could hear her voice and the sound of her light footsteps as she walked upstairs. Amber pushed her books aside and waited for her to come through the door. There was a sudden gust of volume from Kieran's room—she heard the door open and shut almost immediately. She frowned. Maybe one of his friends had come in at the same time? She waited. Five minutes passed, then ten. She opened her bedroom door. She could hear the faint boom and the telltale acrid scent of Kieran's "cigarettes" creeping out from under his door, across the landing. But no Becky. She peered over the banisters, wondering if she'd been caught by Angela, lying on the divan in the upstairs drawing room? But there was no sound. Angela was probably asleep. She was about to walk downstairs when she heard Becky's laugh, clear and high, coming from Kieran's room. She stopped, puzzled. What on earth was she doing in there? She walked over and stood with her head pressed against the door. There it was again—Kieran's voice and the sound of Becky's laughter. She tapped on the door. There was no response. She rapped on the door again, louder. She could hear Becky's voice quite distinctly. It sounded funny . . . deeper, slower. She tapped on the door again.

"What d'you want?" Kieran's voice came at her through the door.

"Becky? Is that you?" Amber was still puzzled. Since when had Kieran ever paid any attention to any of her friends? There was a sudden silence, then she could hear Becky giggling. That was enough for her. She pushed open the door. It took her a few minutes to properly register the scene in front of her. Becky was lying on Kieran's bed, her long reddish hair out of its ponytail and falling over her face—she was wearing a skirt, which had slid up her thighs, Amber noticed dimly—and Kieran's hand was on her bare knee. *On her knee?* She was smoking, too . . . one of his funny cigarettes. The air in the room was thick with smoke and . . . something else. Tension. Sweat.

"What on earth . . ." Amber began, her eyes wide with confusion. Becky was blushing furiously. Kieran looked at his sister coolly.

"Will you knock before you come charging in here?" he said, sliding his hand around Becky's knee and stroking the soft skin on the back of her leg. Becky shifted uncomfortably. Amber's eyes narrowed. It suddenly dawned on her. Of course—she understood perfectly. "I did knock," she said shortly and turned, slamming the door behind her so hard it made the statue on the landing jump. She ran down the stairs, her face on fire, yanked open the door to the shoe cupboard and pulled out a pair of trainers. She wanted to get away from the house and the scene before her eyes. Becky? And *Kieran*.

Becky lay back against Kieran's pillows and tried not to look upset. Kieran was concentrating on extracting the maximum pleasure from his last few drags on his joint. She felt awful. The look on Amber's face said it all—how *could* you? Not only had Becky suddenly slipped off, away from her, she'd chosen Kieran . . . Becky's face burned with shame. She ought to have said something, warned Amber, somehow. But how? Nothing had happened—yet. She caught a lock of hair and began twisting it agitatedly. Kieran didn't seem to notice. In fact, he seemed totally unconcerned. He'd barely looked up as Amber came through the door, his only comment a rather frosty one about knocking on the door. Becky sighed. There were so many things about this family she just didn't understand. She felt as though she'd spent her whole life around the Salls but she was no closer to *knowing* them than she had been the first day Amber invited her to her home and her mother stared blankly at them both as if she didn't know her own daughter, never mind her new friend. She'd been fascinated by them—that much hadn't changed . . . by their nonchalance and the separate, barely connected lives they all pursued in that enormous house. Becky's home was so *normal*, so middle-class and boringly predictable . . . walking across the road to Amber's was like stepping into another world, moving to another country. Becky was fascinated by the Salls. Something about the intensity of their lives, the way their emotions were always on display, captivated her. Perhaps it was the artist in her? At times she longed to escape the safe, easy predictability of her own home, and less than two minutes away from her was its antithesis—dangerous, volatile, unstable. She was drawn to them. To be the daughter of a millionaire banker with another, illegitimate family to be shared; to have escaped from Hungary at the age of ten, like Madeleine, leaving a dead brother behind—*those* were the kind of emotional credentials Becky sought. What was special about being the only—albeit precious—child of a professor from Richmond and his suburban wife?

Kieran finished his joint, blew a cloud of smoke out of the corner of his mouth and resumed his steady caressing of her knee. She submitted herself to his touch without protest. She would think about what to say to Amber—but later, much later. For now, it was thrilling to think of herself slipping easily, naturally, into the Salls' household. Kieran Sall's girlfriend . . . it had a delicious, thrilling ring to it.

≈15≈

The weeks, for Madeleine, flew by. She actually rather enjoyed her new job, letting herself in just after 9 a.m. and leaving just after 1 p.m. Mr. Dorman was never at home. She sometimes put on a record on the big stereo in the living room as she stacked the dishwasher and turned on the washing machine, dancing clumsily with the vacuum cleaner up the stairs as she sucked up the dust. On the fourth Saturday after she'd started, she let herself in and was surprised to see the debris of a large, rowdy party, probably from the night before. The house was in a total state of disarray. There were empty champagne bottles in the bathroom, bottles of beer and wine lying under the sofas and stuffed in the overflowing bins; the remains of canapés and light snacks trodden into the carpet and strewn across the beautiful dining-room table. She walked through the rooms, amazed at the mess left behind. Even the bathrooms were full of bottles, wine glasses and soggy triangles of bread, still with their pinkish smear of salmon pâté or dark, lumpy caviar. She wandered into the master bedroom. The party—or a couple of the participants—must have ended the night in there, she thought, bending to retrieve a lacy bra from the foot of the bed. She held it, fingering the pretty scrap of red silk in her hands, wondering enviously who on earth had breasts *that* small.

She decided to start at the top of the house and work her way downstairs. She picked up all the glasses, bottles and empty packets of cigarettes, stripped the bed of its sheets and thrust the still-damp towels into the wicker laundry basket. She dusted, polished and vacuumed up every trace of the night's festivities. She pulled a pair of fresh, new sheets out of the cupboard, throwing them over the bed and gingerly smoothed the leopard-skin cover over the bed. Suddenly, she heard a door slam downstairs. She listened for a second . . . perhaps it was her mother? She heard a cupboard door open, and the chink of glass, then the sound of the radio being switched on. Mr. Dorman, perhaps? She stood still for a moment, unsure of what to do. Should she go downstairs and say hello, or simply continue working and ignore him? What was the protocol? She decided to go downstairs.

She could see a pair of legs flung over a sofa, a man's jacket lying on the floor. A briefcase stood open on the bottom step, its contents spilled over the hallway floor. From the sound of his heavy, regular breathing, it seemed as if the man stretched out on the sofa was resting. She walked across the hall as quietly as she could, not wanting to disturb. She reached the kitchen door, pushed it open gently and promptly knocked over the bucket and mop she'd left standing behind the door. There was a crash and the sound of spilling water. Madeleine cursed as she hurriedly bent to retrieve the bucket.

"Goddamn, Maja," the man grumbled from the sofa. "Keep it down, will you? I'm trying to get some sleep." Madeleine turned. He hadn't moved from his position—all she could see were his legs. He'd kicked off his shoes and looked oddly vulnerable, lying there in his socks, the sharp crease of his trouser legs peaking to expose a strip of tanned skin. Madeleine blushed. She cleared her throat.

"Er, excuse me, sir . . . it's not Maja. I'm Madeleine,

her daughter . . . I'm helping out on Saturdays." She moved forward, away from the kitchen and stood before him in the hallway, a duster still clutched in her hand. The legs moved; a torso and head appeared. Madeleine looked at him with some confusion. It was the young man she'd seen in the photo.

"Oh." He sat up, running a hand through his hair. "Right—yes, she did say. I'd forgotten. What did you say your name was?"

"Madeleine, sir."

"I'm Mark Dorman. And you don't have to call me 'sir.'"

"Yes, sir. I mean . . . yes, Mr. Dorman."

"Mark."

"Mark." He was American—he had the lazy, playful drawl Madeleine associated with film stars and Hollywood leading men. She looked down at her hands, unsure of what to say. He swung his legs off the sofa and stood up. Madeleine raised her eyes. He was tall and broad-shouldered; he had pulled off his tie and the apex of his throat and chest appeared dark against the white of his shirt. His hair was shorter than in the photograph, cut close to the scalp. She looked into his dark, almond-shaped eyes and blushed suddenly, furiously.

"Well, don't let me interrupt you," he said easily, bending down to pick up his tie and jacket. Madeleine stood still. He left his briefcase and its contents lying on the floor and grabbed a banana from the table. He grinned at her briefly and walked up the stairs, two steps at a time. Madeleine stood where she was, the heat in her face slowly beginning to drain away. She finished the rest of her chores quickly, still somewhat dazed. There was no sound from upstairs. Mr. Dorman—Mark—must have fallen asleep.

"What does he do?" she asked her mother that evening, as the three of them sat down to supper.

"Who?"

"Mark. I mean, Mr. Dorman." Maja looked at her, frowning.

"Why are you so interested in what he does? It's none of your business. You clean his house, that's all."

"I know, but . . ."

"No 'buts' . . . pass your father the vegetables." Maja's voice was sharp. Imre looked up, wondering what all the fuss was about. Madeleine sighed and did as she was told. She was quiet for the rest of the meal, listening to her parents talking, pushing the food around on her plate. She was suddenly not hungry. She excused herself just as Maja got up to bring a pot of tea to the table—she wanted to be alone. Maja said nothing as Madeleine cleared away her own plate and disappeared into her room.

Once inside, she took the unusual precaution of locking her door. She stood for a minute with her back pressed against the door, breathing deeply. She crossed the room and lay down on her bed, dreamily watching the late summer rain fall in sheets against the window, oblivious to the wet, slapping sound of water on glass and to the murmur of her parents' voices through the thin partition wall.

Closing her eyes, she waited for Mark Dorman's face to float into view. She could feel her own heartbeat in her throat and a shy warmth stole over her. She smiled to herself and began replaying their three-second conversation over and over in her mind. *And your name?* She felt again his eyes on her, the way he'd smiled at her as he left the room. It was a pity she'd spent half of the encounter staring at the floor. Madeleine turned over and pressed her cheek against her pillow. Her skin felt warm. Mark Dorman. She couldn't wait for Saturday.

But Mark Dorman didn't appear on Saturday, nor on the Saturday after that. Three weeks went by and there was no sign of him. Each time she opened the door, she thought her heart would burst with the anticipation of seeing him lying on the sofa or coming down the stairs. Each time her disappointment hit her like a blow. Maja was concerned; she'd never seen Madeleine so distracted. She sat silently with them at mealtimes, picking at her food, speaking only when spoken to, breaking off her answers in mid-sentence and looking past her mother and father to the empty space in the sky beyond the window. *Eat something*, Maja kept urging her, but for the first time ever, Madeleine couldn't. She didn't feel like eating, she didn't feel like talking, she couldn't sleep properly. At night, alone in her room with only the sound of the occasional car passing outside on the street for company, she ran over his face and his words in her mind's eye, over and over again until the actual event had been replaced with a much more thrilling fictitious one, in which Mark Dorman stayed behind in the sitting room to talk to her. *Talk* to her! She had no idea what they could possibly talk about but it was enough to imagine his eyes on her . . . his hands, too. She stopped, unable to bear the pleasure the thought evoked. She went about her ordinary chores in the house, whispering his name softly to herself under her breath, longing for Saturday, breathless at the thought of seeing him.

She had just about given up all hope when, the following Saturday, a rainy, wet, miserable day, she walked up the steps to his front door and found it ajar. Her heart suddenly gave a lurch—was he at home? She pushed open the door cautiously. Yes! His briefcase was lying in the hallway, together with a small suitcase. He must have come back from a trip. His umbrella was propped up against the wall, leaving a small puddle of water on the wooden floor. She walked into the narrow hallway, shaking the water from her own umbrella and tried to calm her breathing. The house was quiet. She glanced at her watch. It was just past nine o'clock. She took off her coat, hanging it behind the kitchen door and smoothed down her skirt. Where was he? She peeped into the living room but there was no one there. It was as tidy as she'd left it the week before. She crossed the floor and opened the French doors that led to the dining room—again, nothing. Must be upstairs, she thought, chewing the inside of her lip. She climbed the stairs. He wasn't in the study off the first landing, nor in the spare bedroom. She climbed a further flight. The door to his bedroom was open and she cautiously stuck her head round. She froze. Mark was indeed in his room—he lay stretched out on his enormous bed, half-covered by the leopard-skin rug, fast asleep. Madeleine blinked. He was fully clothed—he'd even forgotten to take his tie off. One shoe lay where it had fallen off his foot at the edge of the bed, the other was still half on. He'd obviously fallen asleep in a hurry. She stood in the doorway, gazing at him for what seemed like ages. He looked so . . . handsome, peaceful . . . she struggled a little to find quite the right words. She had learned English so quickly—everyone was amazed at how she picked it up, the accent and everything!—and she was someone who liked things to be described accurately . . . a gift from her writer-mother, perhaps. But at times she found English too simple. Handsome? Yes, Mark Dorman was certainly handsome. But not in the movie-star way she'd first thought of when she heard his voice. He was also boyish: he looked like someone who played tennis every day and swam just for the fun of it. He was tall and graceful at the same time. She liked the way he ran everywhere, as if his energy couldn't quite be contained in the elegant townhouse with its polished floors and velvet curtains. She'd somehow managed to glean from Maja that he was thirty-two and that he came from California, which, as far as Madeleine was concerned, was a bit like coming from the moon. California! Golden sun, golden men and women . . . the golden life. It suited him. She wondered what on earth had made him come to dreary, gloomy London.

The sleeping man made a small sound. Madeleine was just about to turn and run back down the stairs again when he opened his eyes.

"Hey," he said sleepily, trying to focus.

"Oh, I didn't mean to wake you. I'm sorry . . . I was just . . ."

"No problem. I must've just dropped off. What time is it?"

"It's half past nine," Madeleine said, glancing quickly at her watch. She'd probably been standing in the doorway for all of fifteen minutes.

"Shit. I'd better get moving." He levered himself out of the bed and swung his legs around. He sat for a moment, his head in his hands.

"Are . . . are you alright?" Madeleine ventured. He looked tired—and not very well. He lifted his head. His eyes were a little bloodshot, she noticed. He shook his head slowly.

"Yeah . . . got in from New York this morning . . . one hell of a hangover, that's all."

"Oh."

"I need some water." He stood up rather unsteadily.

"No . . . no, stay there. Sit down. I'll fetch you some," Madeleine said immediately, turning to run back down the stairs. She heard him say something—she couldn't quite catch it—then heard him fall back against the bed. She ran into the kitchen, fetched a bottle of water from the fridge and a glass, then rummaged in one of the drawers—she'd seen a packet of aspirin somewhere in there . . . she found it and ran quickly back upstairs. Mark was still stretched out, his eyes shielded from the light by his forearm.

"Here," Madeleine said, walking round to his side of the enormous bed. He opened an eye and squinted at her. "I've brought you some aspirin as well."

"Maja, you are an absolute angel," Mark groaned, lifting himself up on one arm.

"No . . . no, it's Madeleine," Madeleine said quickly, stung by the way he'd forgotten her name.

"Right. Sorry . . . too much alcohol last night." He smiled at her lightly, taking the aspirins and the glass of water from her. His fingers touched hers.

"Were you at a . . . party?" she asked as he tipped his head back and swallowed the tablets and water in one gulp.

"Not quite. First Class—champagne all the way from JFK to Heathrow."

"Oh." Madeleine couldn't imagine what First Class or any other class in the air might be like; she'd never been in an airplane in her entire life.

"You speak English a whole lot better than your mom," Mark Dorman said, shaking his head as if to clear it.

"Well, we've been here for quite a while," Madeleine said, blushing. She liked his eyes on her even if it unnerved her.

"How long?"

"Um, six years."

"Still, that's pretty fast. How old are you?" Mark was looking at her rather strangely.

"Six . . . sixteen." Madeleine's voice faltered.

"Sweet sixteen, huh?" He yawned, stretching. Madeleine couldn't take her eyes off him. "Okay. Well, I'd better get moving. Thanks for the water, and the drugs," he said, tugging at his tie. Madeleine nodded, not wanting to leave. She watched him shrug off his jacket, tossing it carelessly onto the floor. He started unbuttoning his shirt and then paused. "Maybe you could start downstairs?"

"Yes, yes . . . of course. I . . . I'll vacuum the kitchen. I mean, dining room."

"Sure. Whatever." And with that, Mark Dorman disappeared.

≈ 16 ≈

For the umpteenth time in the past five years, Max cursed Angela as he strode through the house, loosening his tie and throwing his jacket over the banisters for Krystyna or someone to pick up. It was 8:30 a.m. on a Wednesday; he'd just come in on the early-morning flight from Paris and he was about to host one of the most important breakfast meetings of his entire bloody career and he was going to have to do it alone. Damn her. She'd been back at home after being asked to leave the Klaasens clinic a couple of months earlier—there had been some fuss, something to do with one of the guests or the son of one of the guests . . . the supervisor had been too embarrassed to explain properly. Max had hung up the phone on her. He wasn't interested in the sordid details.

"Krystyna!" he yelled, running up the stairs two at a time.

"Sir." Krystyna appeared at the foot of the stairs.

"Everything ready?" Max turned to look at her briefly.

"Yes, sir. Everything's set. The caterers are here. I've prepared the guest rooms on the second floor, just in case Lord Henning would like to rest after your meeting. There's fresh—"

"Great." Max cut her off abruptly. "I'll take a quick shower. Lay out something suitable for me, will you?" He disappeared into his suite of rooms. Krystyna nodded, a little uncertainly. Something suitable? What did that mean? She hesitated for a second, then followed him upstairs.

"That'll do. Yes, that's fine," Max said, coming out of the vast bathroom with only a towel wrapped around his waist. She stood up, not knowing quite where to look. The dark-blue and white pinstriped suit she'd selected seemed to meet with his approval. She smoothed out the trousers and picked up the discarded plastic wrappers.

"Will . . . will there be anything else?" she stammered, the blood rising to her face as she tried not to stare at her half-naked employer in front of her. There was a moment's hesitation as Max looked at her, then he shook his head, still wet at the temples from his shower.

"No. Thank you, Krystyna. I'll be down in a few

minutes." She turned and walked out of the room as steadily as she could. She let out a sigh as she walked down the stairs. It wasn't the first time she'd been embarrassed in front of him. There was something so . . . so . . . *powerful* about Max Sall. She'd been working for him—them, really . . . most of her time was spent looking after his poor wife—for almost a year and he was still able to make her blush like a teenager whenever he turned his steel-grey eyes on her. She *was* a teenager, she reminded herself as she walked into the kitchen. She was barely twenty. Working for the Salls was the first proper job she'd had, apart from working on the farm back home in Warsaw. She'd never met people like them before—rich, famous, unhappy. Apart from Max himself, it seemed as though only Amber had somehow managed to hold herself together: unlike her brother and mother, she seemed to take everything in her stride. Her brother. Krystyna rolled her eyes. Kieran was a mess. She was surprised Max hadn't noticed. He was so like his mother— where Angela was drunk most of the time, Kieran was high. You only had to look at him to know. Yes, she thought to herself as she walked through to the breakfast room to make sure everything was perfect, just as Max wanted it, he was a complete mess. She felt sorry for him. Except when he tried it on with her, of course.

Still knotting his tie, Max ran lightly up the stairs to the guest rooms on the second floor to double-check everything was as it should be. He opened the door to the main bedroom and frowned. The curtains were drawn and the room was still in semi-darkness. He walked over to the window and threw them open. There was a sudden noise from behind him. He wheeled around, almost knocking over the vase of fresh flowers Krystyna must have placed on the dressing table. He narrowed his eyes. There was something in the bed. It took him only a second to register what it was. "What the *hell's* going on?" he roared. There was a sudden squeal and a movement from under the bedcovers. He strode over to the bed and yanked back the cover. It took him a few seconds to recognize the girl huddled semi-clothed next to his son. Becky? Becky Aldridge? Amber's best friend? Wasn't she supposed to be in school? He stared at the two of them. There was an awful, shocked silence. "Get dressed and get out," he said finally through gritted teeth. "I'll be back in five minutes. I don't want to see you in here. You," he said, pointing at his son. "In my study. *Now!*" He turned on his heel and strode out.

"Oh my *God*," Becky said, beginning to cry. "You told me he was away," she wailed, dragging the sheet up to her chest and scrambling around for her clothes. Kieran said nothing. He lay on his back with his eyes closed, not even bothering to get up. "Kieran," Becky said, nudging his ribs. "Get *up*. Your dad wants to see you. Oh God, what are you going to say?" Kieran didn't respond. He put out a hand and fished for his joint. "How can you just lie there?" Becky cried, hurriedly pulling on her clothes. She knew it had been a bad idea to stop by the house

on the way to school. Even though they hadn't actually *done* anything . . . Kieran was strangely content to lie next to her semi-naked body, smoking a
joint and occasionally touching her. Becky liked it
like that—she was too scared to go all the way and
yet scared she would lose him if she resisted. This
way, they both got what they wanted, although, listening to other girls in her year, the fact that he
didn't want to sleep with her . . . not yet . . . well, it
was a little odd. But now . . . she began to cry in
earnest. She was terrified of what her mother would
say—what her father would say. And she was terrified of meeting Max on the way down. The way he'd
looked at her . . . that awful mixture of surprise and
anger and . . . disappointment, too. She turned to
Kieran, who had almost drifted off to sleep again.
"What are you going to tell him? You will tell him we
weren't really doing anything, won't you?" she
pleaded as she tried to pull her hair into a ponytail.
Kieran was silent. "*Please*, Kieran . . . you must tell
him—"

"Shut the fuck up, Becky," Kieran interrupted her,
blowing out a long chain of smoke rings and rolling
over. Becky stopped. What had he just said?

"B . . . but . . . aren't you going down?"

"No. Now shut up. I'm trying to get some sleep."

"But Kieran—," she began again.

"I *said*. Shut the fuck *up*. I'm trying to get some
sleep. That's why I came in here. Shut the door on
your way out, will you?" And with that he stubbed
out his joint, pulled the covers back up over his
head and turned to face the wall. Becky finished

dressing in silence. Her fingers were still shaking as she opened the door and crept down the stairs. It was well past nine. School would have already started. What was she going to tell Amber? Ever since Amber had walked in on her and Kieran a few weeks earlier, things between them had been somewhat strained. Amber pretended not to care, but Becky knew differently. Inside, she was sure, she was seething. There was a possessiveness about Amber these days that Becky had never seen in her before. She couldn't work out whether Amber was worried she was losing Becky—or Kieran. She'd always been fiercely protective of Kieran but these days, in Amber's eyes at least, he could do nothing right. She pushed open the front door as quietly as she could. Everything was changing so fast, only this time, she couldn't talk to Amber about it. She couldn't talk to anyone.

Krystyna paused, a basket of freshly baked croissants in her arms. There was a thud, a shout and the sound of something breaking. She turned to look at Mrs. Dewhurst.

"Did you hear that?"

"Nope. And neither did you." Mrs. Dewhurst was uncharacteristically firm. Krystyna looked at the doorway.

"But . . ." she began, hesitating. She could hear someone being dragged, quite literally, down the stairs. She hoped it wasn't Angela.

"But nothing. Leave 'em to it. Come on, you'd best get those croissants in the oven. His lordship'll be

here any minute now." Krystyna followed her reluctantly into the kitchen. Whatever it was, the breakfast meeting in less than an hour was far more
important.

≈17≈

Madeleine looked around her once, twice . . . then
slid her hand inside. She pulled the sheaf of photographs towards her, hesitating before lifting it clear
of the drawer. She paused for a second. She
shouldn't, she *oughtn't to*—she was only supposed
to be cleaning his study, not snooping through his
personal things. She leafed quickly through the photographs. What was she looking for? She didn't
know. She listened again—no sound from downstairs. Mark Dorman had left for work a few minutes
after she'd arrived.

The photos were all of places she didn't recognize: a city full of tall buildings and yellow cars in the
snow, a beach somewhere, and people she'd only
ever seen in magazines . . . beautiful, smiling people—she held her breath. The same girl was in several of the shots. Madeleine studied her intently.
Long, glossy, dark hair, a strong, wide smile . . . in
one of them, Mark had his arms around her. A
girlfriend, it was obvious. Madeleine pulled a
face. Of course. She could hardly bring herself to
say the word. A girlfriend. She pushed the photos
away from her and got up. She wasn't sure she

could bear to look any further. She was being ridiculous. She had a silly, schoolgirl crush on someone who was old enough to be her father—well, not quite, perhaps. But the truth was, Mark Dorman could barely remember who she was. Her mother suspected as much—she'd threatened to send Madeleine to one of her office jobs if she didn't stop mooching around the house with a face as long as a *drzitnaye*. A horse. An old, sad-looking horse. Madeleine closed the drawer shut with a snap and stood up. It was time to get back to her real job, back to the real world. Cleaning. She picked up the duster and polish and walked reluctantly out of the room.

But the following week Mark Dorman surprised her. Madeleine stared at him as if she hadn't quite heard him right. A party? He was inviting her to a party?

"Who? Me?" she repeated, frowning. She stood with a duster in hand on the landing, looking down the length of the narrow staircase at him.

"Yeah. If you could get here around five—the caterers will be gone by then—you can tidy up and get things ready. It'll start around eight. What's the matter?" He squinted up at her. Madeleine had gone bright red.

"Oh . . . no . . . I just thought . . ." she blurted, embarrassed beyond belief. For one mad, brief second, she'd thought he was *inviting* her to a party, not asking her to clean in preparation for one. She recovered herself. "Yes, of course. Yes, I'll be here at five." She turned to go back upstairs, afraid he would see her flaming cheeks.

"No, wait . . . what's wrong?" Mark put down his briefcase.

"Nothing," Madeleine said, practically running up the stairs. She pushed open the bathroom door and leaned against it. What an idiot, she grimaced. What a complete, utter idiot! Why on earth would he invite her to a party? What the hell was she thinking?

"Are you all right, Madeleine?" Mark's voice sounded outside the door. Madeleine jumped.

"Yes, yes . . . I'm fine. I'm . . . I'll be out in a minute," she called nervously.

"Okay. I'll be downstairs. We can go over what needs to be done."

"Yes. I'll be there in a second." She waited a few minutes, dried her face with one of the clean hand-towels she'd laid out earlier and opened the door. She walked cautiously downstairs.

Mark was lying on one of the purple velvet sofas, reading. He put down his magazine as she passed in front of him and waved her over. She sat opposite him, knees pressed together, hands in lap.

"Okay. Let's sort out what we need to do. There'll be twenty, maybe thirty people—not too many. We'll open up the dining table and let people help them-selves to food and drink—here, let me show you . . ." Mark got up. Madeleine watched as he walked quickly over to the table, felt around underneath the gleaming cherry-wood top for a mechanism that al-lowed the table to open up and slid it out to its full length. "It's really easy, look. Come over here . . .

can you feel that?" He caught hold of Madeleine's hand as she stood beside him, guiding her fingers towards a small metal latch. Madeleine froze, holding her breath. "You try it." She found the latch and did as his fingers directed, sliding the latch into place. The top moved back easily. "See?" Madeleine nodded. Her fingers tingled where he'd touched her and she moved back a pace. It was more than she could cope with, standing that close to him.

"Um . . . shall I . . . which plates and things shall I use?" she asked, moving to the other side of the table. Mark didn't seem to notice.

"Oh, the caterers will bring all of that. It'll be a buffet, you know . . . finger food, cocktails . . . that kind of thing."

"Oh." Madeleine had never been to a cocktail party. She had no idea what they were like. She wasn't even sure why he'd asked her to come in—the caterers seemed to be taking care of most things. "Shall I get . . . flowers?" she hazarded a guess.

"Hey, that's a *great* idea. Get some flowers from the guys down the road. Anything you like. Brighten the place up. Fan*tas*tic." He smiled at her.

Madeleine blushed again. She liked the way he was so enthusiastic about everything. Mark Dorman was just about the most positive person she'd ever met. It made such a change from the dour, worn-down pragmatism that ruled her own home. She mumbled something about finishing the washing up and hurried into the kitchen, afraid for the second time that afternoon that he would see her reddening face.

*　　*　　*

On Friday evening, she stood in the doorway to the living room, admiring the effect. The flowers she'd chosen—huge, spiky orange ones with a single bloom on a slender, dark green stem—she couldn't remember what the florist had called them—looked fantastic against the stark, dark interior with its purple and deep burgundy furnishings. She loved Mark Dorman's home, so different from hers. Space, calm, pleasure . . . pleasure in one's surroundings; a sensory delight. The sensation was alien to her. She remained in the doorway for a moment or two, captivated.

By nine o'clock, the cocktail party was in full swing and Madeleine was reluctantly preparing to leave. She'd told her mother she would be home by eight and she was already an hour late. She slipped out of the kitchen, untying her apron and made her way upstairs to the spare room on the first floor where she'd left her bag. It was a warm evening and most of the party-goers had wandered out onto the terrace. She stood at the window in the semi-darkness, looking down at them. She couldn't see Mark. He'd disappeared as soon as the first guests started to arrive. Madeleine had stood by shyly in the kitchen, watching as one beautiful woman after another came through the front door, each pausing to check her reflection in the enormous mirror she polished once a week. None of them had so much as glanced in her direction. She looked down on them now—watching the way one woman tossed her long blonde hair over one shoulder, laughing at something the man beside her said; red-tipped hands holding a glass of champagne; the way she lifted her shoulders, the charming little shrug— never in a million years, Madeleine thought to herself, would she learn how to do that . . . to be full of flirtatious, easy charm. Madeleine's approach to men—insofar as she had one—was to blush and run. She turned from the window and picked up her bag. It was time she headed home.

"Oh, there you are," Mark's voice broke in on her thoughts. He was standing in the doorway. Madeleine started. She hadn't heard him come upstairs.

She blushed furiously. "I was just going. I . . . I told my mother I'd be home by eight," she said, wishing she didn't sound quite so schoolgirlish. "I'm already late," she added, looking at her watch— anything but at him. The sight of him in his black jacket and pale-green shirt was making her feel quite breathless.

"You haven't had a glass, yet," he smiled, coming into the room. "And I haven't thanked you yet," he added, flourishing a bottle and two glasses.

"For what?" Madeleine was genuinely puzzled.

"For helping to make it a great success. I think it's going down *rather* well," Mark said easily. "Isn't that what you English always say?"

"What?"

"Rather."

"I don't know. I'm not English, you know."

"I keep forgetting." Mark laughed. He poured champagne into the two flutes and held one out to her. The room was almost dark but he made no move to switch on the light. He walked over to the window and looked down on the terrace, just as she had done. "Yeah, I think everybody's having a pretty good time."

"Are they all friends of yours?" Madeleine heard herself ask. She held the glass nervously between her fingers. Mark took a sip.

"Some. Acquaintances, most of them."

Madeleine nodded. She didn't really know the difference. "Who's the girl—woman—with the dark hair?" she asked as casually as she could. She recognized her immediately from the photograph.

"Nikki?" Mark peered out of the window. "She's an old friend."

"She's really . . . beautiful," Madeleine said wistfully.

"No more so than you," Mark said quietly, beside her.

Madeleine blushed furiously, not knowing what to say. She took a cautious sip of champagne but the bubbles went straight up her nose and she spluttered.

"Here," Mark leaned across and tilted her glass away from her. "Don't put your nose inside it, just your lips . . ." he laughed at her. "It's not 7UP!"

"I know," Madeleine protested, embarrassed. "It's fizzy."

"It's champagne," Mark said dryly. But he made no move to stand back. Madeleine remained where she was, absolutely still. He was close enough to touch. And then everything happened rather quickly. One minute she was standing holding her champagne glass and looking onto the terrace, the next she felt his arm against hers as he took the glass out of her hand and slowly turned to face her. Then his face blotted out what little light spilled in from outside and she felt the firm, insistent pressure of his lips against hers. But this was no schoolgirl kiss—this was not the gentle, almost chaste kiss she had dreamt of. Mark's lips were hot and prob-ing . . . he seemed to demand something of her, something she had no idea how to give. There was a pause—a questioning?—and then Madeleine's response. He kicked the door shut behind him and walked over to the single, spare bed. Madeleine closed her eyes, aware only of a persistent clamor-ing in her head and the touch of his hands as he peeled first one layer of clothing away from her body, then another—then the last.

≈18≈

Max didn't pretend not to be studying the man sit-ting opposite him in the smart, Knightsbridge restaurant. He took a sip of coffee, enjoying the way it curled, thick and bitter, against his tongue and lis-tened to the man talk. His mind was busy, filing away facts, dates, places . . . digging in his memory banks to place him in the network of contacts and acquaintances within which Max worked. The con-tact was the result of his successful breakfast meet-ing, but at the memory of the chaos he'd had to sort out beforehand, he winced. Kieran . . . he had no idea what was wrong with the boy, or what to do about it. He'd taken after his mother, no doubt about it. Such a disappointment. Weak-willed, vain and ineffectual. Kieran wasn't the son he'd planned. It was funny, he mused for a second, allowing his mind to wander, Amber was much more like him—she was tough, determined, independent. All the things he'd hoped Kieran would be. It was a great pity. Such qualities were ultimately wasted in a girl. He forced his mind back to the present. Talal Baroudi, the man Lord Henning had sent his way, was looking enquiringly at him.

"Sorry . . . you were saying?" He took another sip of coffee.

"We were wondering if you had any contacts. Anyone on the inside." Max nodded slowly. He had to make a quick and instinctive decision. Could he trust Mr. Baroudi? He nodded again. The man in front of him was Lebanese. From a middle-class, Christian banking family. His suit was expensive and beautifully cut; on his little finger a diamond twinkled discreetly. His shoes were Italian and carefully polished. Details, details . . . God, as Max knew, was in the details.

"OK. Let me make a quick call. There is someone . . . a man I used to know. He's in Tehran at the moment. If anyone can set you up with the Russians, he can. I'll be back in a moment." Max pushed back his chair and walked quickly to the front desk.

*　　*　　*

Talal Baroudi watched him go, impressed. In ten minutes, Max Sall could set up a meeting that would have taken him a year to arrange. The man's list of personal contacts was vast and seemingly unique. It was what he'd been told in Beirut. There were lots of middlemen in the Middle East—it was something of a regional joke. Talal himself had a private telephone directory that was the envy of many. But no one could command the ear of a dozen presidents and heads of state, *thc* most important and influential business tycoons and most of the world's financial leaders like Max Sall. It was why he was good and it was why he was so damned expensive. But if this meeting was anything to go by, he was worth every last cent of his two percent commission fee. An unusual man, too, Talal mused, picking up his coffee and one of the hotel's delicious biscuits. He knew a little of Max Sall's unorthodox domestic arrangements—the alcoholic wife in London, the beautiful mistress in Rome . . . homes all over the world. Lucky bastard, he thought to himself, grinning. His rise from personal chauffeur to business mogul was well known and endlessly discussed. But very little was known about where Max Sall had actually *come* from. There were rumors. Some said he was Jewish, born in Germany and had escaped the infamous camps; others said he was Russian, or even Armenian, that he'd arrived in England as a penniless teenager. It was true there was something in the man's voice . . . not an accent, just the *faintest* trace of something . . . an inflection, an awkward grammatical construction every once in a while. Max himself was silent on the subject. He never gave personal interviews, had turned down dozens of requests by biographers eager to sensationalize a life that was actually already pretty damned sensational. Talal shrugged. Who cared where Max Sall was from? What was important was whom he knew. And whom he could persuade that Talal Baroudi was someone worth doing business with.

"He'll see you in Copenhagen in a week's time." Max came back to the table. Talal nodded, smiling. "I've let him know you'll cover all expenses," Max added as he sat down. He scribbled a number on a card and handed it over. "Call that number when you get into town." Talal nodded again. Their meeting was concluded. "How's Laila?" Max asked, gathering his things. Talal looked up in surprise.

"She's fine . . . I didn't know . . . you know my wife?" he asked incredulously.

"We met once, a long time ago. She worked for Alitalia, I believe?" Talal nodded, impressed for the second time that morning. Not many people would ever have guessed that the matronly Laila Baroudi's real name was Lucia Marciano and that she'd met and married Talal Baroudi on a weekend stopover in Beirut against everyone's advice . . . but that was typical of Max Sall. He never forgot anyone. Ever. "Send my regards, will you? She ought to remember me." Max picked up his umbrella and raincoat, nodded at Talal and quickly left the hotel.

Talal lingered for a moment by the table, slightly

unnerved. Had there been something . . . was there something in the way Max had said "she ought to remember me"? He stood up, alarmed to find his heart beating unusually fast.

≈19≈

Madeleine pulled down her underwear and closed her eyes. She counted to ten. When she opened them, she told herself, the familiar, monthly stain would be there . . . and the whole thing would be forgotten and life would go back to normal and . . . she opened her eyes. Nothing. White, clean fabric, not a drop of blood, not a spot. She swallowed. She sat down on the toilet seat and buried her face in her hands. It was almost two months since that terrible, beautiful evening at Mark Dorman's. Almost two months since the morning a few days later when he rang Maja and said he wouldn't be needing a cleaner any more; something about moving to New York. Madeleine didn't look at Maja when she stuck her head round the corner to tell her.

Now, sitting on the toilet seat, she lifted her head, tears spilling down her smooth, plump cheeks. She wasn't stupid or *that* naïve—she knew what had happened to her and what she ought to do next. The question was how? She looked at her hands. Even if she managed to persuade her mother to give her another cleaning job, it would take her . . . she began the calculations . . . thirty weeks to raise £300.

When she'd first realized her period was late, she'd rung one of the abortion helpline numbers she'd seen on the number fifteen bus. *Pregnant? Afraid? Call 01-679-9999 for confidential advice and support*, the advert ran. Madeleine rang the next morning. £299, including VAT. She said thank you and hung up, confident—at that time—that her period would come and that she'd never need the advice and support they offered—at £299 a pop, mind. At her present rate of employment, helping Maja at some office back near the house, it would take her six and a half months to raise the money she needed, at which point the baby would practically be born. She wiped her cheeks. She was a practical girl, she reminded herself, calm and capable. There were few options in her present circumstances. She needed to find the money for an abortion, she had to tell someone what had happened to her and she couldn't tell her parents. There were only two people in the whole world who might be able to lend her the money—Becky and Amber. They were also the only two other people in the whole world she could tell.

She flushed the toilet, blew her nose and opened the door. It was a Thursday and the flat was empty. It was the first time she'd missed school, ever. She'd told Maja she wasn't feeling well, and it was true. She felt sick, an all-over, unspecified kind of sickness that made her feel nauseous and ravenous at the same time. She felt her stomach under the waistband of her pajamas . . . bloated, soft, tender to the touch. She felt huge, as though she'd burst out of her skin at any minute. She crawled back into bed, hugging her hot water bottle against her stomach, trying not to think about what was going on inside her and what she was about to—would have to—do.

Amber took one look at Madeleine's face and did not hesitate. "I'll lend you the money. Don't worry about it." Becky looked at her gratefully. As much as she would have *liked* to help Madeleine, there was no way she could lay her hands on £300 without her mother knowing, and then there would have been an awful lot of explaining to do. Mindful of her own secrets, the less she had to talk about such issues, the better.

"Are you sure you don't mind?" Madeleine said, tears threatening to spill down her face.

"Mind? Madeleine . . . don't be silly. I'll get it for you now, if you like." Amber half-rose from the bed.

"No, no . . . you don't have to do it now . . . I have to phone the . . . *place* . . . first." Madeleine said, wiping her eyes with the back of her hand. She hadn't expected such instant generosity. She'd barely known Amber three months. A wave of nausea suddenly hit her and she got up and ran towards the bathroom.

"Poor Madeleine," Amber said, looking at Becky. A sudden, awkward silence sprang up between them, the first such silence in the ten years they'd been friends. Becky looked at the floor. Amber looked at her, dismayed. Overnight, it seemed to her, everything had changed. She couldn't bring herself to ask Becky whether she . . . somehow, as soon as Madeleine broke her news, she'd heard Becky's faint gasp, her quick intake of breath . . . and she'd known. Yes, Becky had done it and no, she couldn't bring herself to even *think* about it. There were other things to think about. Becky had brought Madeleine into their lives and turned the cozy, familiar friendship between them into a different kind of friendship between three. Fortunately for all of them, Amber and Madeleine liked each other, immediately. The bond that had held Becky and Amber together since forever stretched, easily and naturally, to accommodate Madeleine, almost without them noticing. And now Becky and Madeleine had moved on, slipped free of their childhood bearings, without her. She was aware of having been left behind somewhere, not that she was in any hurry to catch up. She wasn't afraid of what they'd done—although the consequences, for Madeleine, were pretty terrifying. No, she certainly wasn't afraid and she wasn't in a hurry . . . she'd just never met anyone she'd even consider doing it with. Somehow all men, when measured against the yardstick of masculinity that Max had provided for her, faded, blotted out by the intensity of mood and passion he generated. She got up from the bed and walked out of the room.

Angela turned her head as Amber knocked on the door to the drawing room and entered. She put down her glass carefully, and prepared her face with a smile. She listened to her daughter for a minute then got up from her chair by the window. She walked over to the elegant sideboard and picked up her handbag. She pulled out a soft, leather purse, opened it and took out a thick wad of notes.

"Here you are, darling . . . I think there's enough in there. What color are you thinking of?"

"Yellow," Amber said without batting an eyelid. "I thought something yellow would be nice."

"Yes, something bright and cheerful," Angela agreed, walking back to her chair. "Do send them my congratulations, won't you? I have met her before, haven't I?" she asked, suddenly anxious.

"Yes, Mother. Sophie comes round all the time." Amber held the notes in her fist. She moved back towards the door. "Thanks," she said, as she opened the door. "It'll be a really wonderful wedding. I'll take some pictures and show you." Angela nodded dreamily as Amber closed the door gently behind her. By morning, she'd have forgotten Amber had even come into the room, asking for £300 to buy a wedding outfit for her best friend from school.

≈20≈

The three of them met at the entrance to the station at Ladbroke Grove at nine o'clock on a Saturday morning, two weeks later. As if by prior arrangement the weather had changed—a light drizzle shrouded everything in a sad, dour greyness to match their mood. They bought their tickets to Richmond and walked upstairs to wait for the train. No one said a word. Amber wanted to say something, *do* something that would make Madeleine feel better but a tight, brittle air had come over Madeleine, forestalling anything even approaching affection. Becky trailed behind the two of them, looking lost and unsure of herself. Like Amber, she too wanted to touch or hug Madeleine but couldn't or didn't know how. The train approached, swaying and clattering its way into the station. The doors opened and the three of them were quickly swallowed up.

Madeleine sat alone, her head turned away from the other two, concentrating on the back gardens and vegetable allotments that slid past the window. She didn't know which was worse—thinking about what was going to happen or thinking about what *had* happened. Both were painful, although the first was pure conjecture. The latter . . . well, she found it hard to think about it without panicking that it might never happen again—that after this brief, fleeting incident, she would never find anyone with whom she might experience the same, completely unexpected surge of emotion that ran through her when Mark Dorman touched her, or the answering shock of desire in her, electrifying in its intensity. She thought back to the moment he'd collapsed on top of her, his head buried in her neck, gasping . . . in pain? She'd touched him, half-fearful, but his hand sliding slowly over her breasts and stroking the soft skin of her stomach had sent the most wonderful, hot glow coursing through her. No, not in pain . . . she could feel his smile against her skin . . . just . . .

a great feeling. It was good—better than good. *She* was good. He told her. His words sent another rush through her, spreading from somewhere between her thighs, across her body and into her face. She pressed her head against the pillow, feeling the heat of her tears in the corners of her eyes. But before she could bask in the afterglow or even turn her head to rest against his, there was a shout from below. Mark Dorman disentangled himself from her with a speed that made her head spin. In a matter of seconds, he was dressed again, running a hand through his hair and then . . . he was gone. She'd waited for what seemed like ages but he didn't come back. And after that, when she'd dressed herself and the heat in her body had subsided and she'd walked downstairs, she'd seen him locked in an embrace with someone, a slim, young woman with a black dress slit all the way down her back and long, golden hair under which his arms were buried. She'd opened the door without a sound and walked out into the cool night.

She turned away from the window and looked at her hands. At that moment, Amber reached across the gap between the rows of seating and touched her once, ever so gently, on the knee. She looked up. Becky smiled timidly at her. Whatever happens, the two of them seemed to be saying, you're not alone. She looked at their faces, and was grateful. The train pulled into Richmond Station and the three of them stood up. Time to get moving, to move on.

PART TWO

～21～
Menorca, Spain
1983

Paola tossed back her hair, adjusted the thin straps on her sundress and walked out of the bathroom. Out of the corner of her eye, she could see the bar owner, Didier—Didi to his friends—looking at her as he polished first one glass, then another, slowly, holding each goblet up to the light, watching her reflection in the fat, convex surface in his hands. It was a game between them: she pretended not to notice, he pretended not to care. Inside, however, her heart was thumping. Didier Juneau owned Didi's, the hip, trendy bar that Paola and her friends went to every afternoon right in the center of Tamarinda, opposite the old baroque church on Plaza España. It was four o'clock on a Friday afternoon, the last week of the summer holidays. On the Sunday, she and Francesca would fly back to Rome.

"Are you looking for someone?" Didier called out, catching Paola off-guard.

"Me? No, no . . . I . . . I was just . . . going to make a phone call," Paola said, flustered. She sounded silly and if there was one thing Paola hated—apart from her sister, of course—it was sounding silly.

"Phones are over there," Didier said, indicating the bank on the wall behind her. Paola was forced to turn around. He gave the bar counter a half-moon swipe, watching the way her ass swung in her thin, cotton dress as she walked towards the phones. She half-turned, caught him at it and they both smiled. The game was on.

"What were you *doing* in there?" Bernadette hissed, as Paola sat down next to her. They were sitting with Enrico and Pablo, the teenage sons of family friends ordered by their mothers to chaperone the two girls on their last visit to town.

"I'll tell you later," Paola whispered. She took a sip of her Campari and orange juice, the ice having completely melted in the fifteen minutes she'd been gone. But it had been worth it. She had won a date. She would have to sneak out of the villa at ten that evening but Max was away and her mother wouldn't notice—or if she did, she knew she wouldn't tell. She looked at Enrico—a boy. A pleasant-enough, handsome-enough daytime companion but still, a mere boy compared with the man whom she had arranged to meet. Didier was in his thirties, not his teens. Paola was bored with Enrico and his friends.

She wanted to have fun—real, grown-*up* fun. She lit a cigarette.

Félipe, the head barman at Didi's, watched Paola walk away from the bar and turned to Didier, grinning.

"*Mierda*," he said. "You've hit the jackpot."

"I know." Didier grinned back. "Classy, isn't she?"

"*Hombre*. You know who she is?" Didier shook his head. "Max Sall's daughter. From the *Italianna*."

Didier looked at him, his eyes widening. Of course! He hadn't recognized her. He picked up another glass, his grin widening. "How old is she?"

"Old enough. They all are." Félipe shrugged. The little teenage girls who hung around the bar at night weren't as little as they looked. They grew up fast in Menorca. It was one of the reasons he'd moved here from Madrid. Didier grinned again. In fact, he thought to himself, he had a whole lot to grin about. Paola Rossi . . . one of the richest "little" girls on the island. She'd agreed to meet him later on at Tabac, on the waterfront. He'd seen the look in her eyes: half-afraid, half-flirting. He'd seen it in many of the sixteen-year-old heiresses who leaned against the counter at Didi's, their breasts pressed against the thick, mahogany ledge, a sensual hunger in their faces. He knew exactly what it meant. There were many beautiful men—men in their twenties and thirties—wandering about the island, some legitimately, some not. Many of the teenage girls discovered they were suddenly bored with their high-school boyfriends with their crew-cut hairstyles and their preppy, studiously casual clothes. To them, the beautiful men represented danger and freedom and something mysterious to which they were slowly and steadily pulled. Didier was one of them. Paola had spotted him; or he her. Either way, Didier knew exactly what was going to happen. He'd seen it—*done* it—a hundred times before.

At exactly quarter past nine, Paola slipped out of bed, fully dressed and tiptoed into the bathroom for one last look at herself. She shut the door behind her and switched on the light. She'd chosen a long, pink silk skirt that clung to her thighs and flared around her ankles; a tiny, white ruched top with tie-up straps and flat white sandals with a pretty coral-pink shell detail. She brushed her gleaming dark curtain of hair one last time, touched up her lipstick and switched off the light, satisfied she looked at *least* three years older than her fifteen years of age. She lifted up her bedroom window, tucked up her skirt and carefully clambered out, crossed the lawn and hopped onto her little scooter. She freewheeled down the hill for a few minutes until she was out of earshot, then kicked it into life and roared off into the night. Her pulse was racing—she had timed things to be exactly fifteen minutes late. Long enough to make him wonder if she were coming, and not too long that his ardor cooled. Another one of Francesca's extremely useful tips.

"Hi," she said, winding her way as seductively as she could through the crowded tables. There weren't many men in the bar who could take their eyes off her, she noticed with satisfaction as she walked towards him. Didier's own eyes widened appreciatively as she sank down gracefully next to him. No apologies for keeping him waiting, either. He'll admire your nerve, Francesca had often told her.

"Hi. I thought you'd forgotten," Didier said, smiling lazily at her.

Paola shrugged and smiled. "Oh, I'm always late," she said airily. She fished in her purse for a cigarette. She had to do something with her hands. He was *so* good-looking and *so* grown up, sitting opposite her in a worn leather jacket, his long brown hair curling around his neck and the unmistakable shadow of an evening beard on his face. Her heart began to race.

"What are you drinking?" he asked.

"A Campari . . . no, a whisky," she said quickly. Didier nodded approvingly and snapped his fingers for a waiter. Seconds later, her drink appeared. She took a gulp. Didier watched her, still smiling. He leaned forward.

"How old are you, Paola?" he asked, his eyes on the opening in her top through which the gentle swell of her breasts could be seen.

"Eighteen," Paola lied boldly, taking another sip.

He leaned back. "You want to go to a party?" he asked, lighting a cigarette himself.

Paola nodded enthusiastically. "Whose party?" she asked, her eyes lighting up.

"Oh, just some people I know. It's on the other side of town. One of the villas in the hills."

"Ooh, fantastic. That sounds *really* neat." Didier

raised an eyebrow. She blushed—too childish perhaps?

"Yeah." He got up, stubbing out his cigarette. "Okay. Let's go. My car's over there by the curb." He pulled out a crumpled note and left it on the table. Paola hastily swallowed the last of her whisky and followed him.

"D'you . . . is it okay? What I'm wearing?" she asked as they hurried towards the car. Didier looked down at her and casually draped an arm around her shoulders.

"I wouldn't worry, *chérie*—I plan on seeing you . . . *without* any of this," he said with a laugh, lightly touching the straps of her top. A shiver of excitement ran straight through her. She had two days left on the island and she'd promised herself before they'd come that *this* time she wasn't returning to Rome the only virgin at the *lycée*. Daniela, Roberta, Pascale . . . her best friends had all done "it" and Paola was determined not to be left out. Only she wasn't about to lose "it" to some pimply-faced, sweaty-palmed teenager in their class. Someone like the nice, dependable Enrico or the boring Pablo. She was going to do "it" with someone older, *much* older—someone much more experienced who would teach her a thing or two, not the other way round, as Daniela and Pascale reported. They reached his car. He opened the door for her—she dimly noticed it was a bit of a rustbucket, not the kind of car she was used to travelling in—but then he slid into the driver's seat, turned to her and cupped her face in his hands and then . . . well, she didn't notice anything except the feel of his hands as he unbuttoned the first few buttons of her top and started his gentle exploration of her body.

"Didier," she murmured after some time had passed. She'd somehow wound up half-lying on him, wedged between his hard-on and the steering wheel, equally hard. "Shouldn't we . . . what about the party? Won't we be late?"

"Fuck the party. I've got something much better in mind." He let his hand slide down her thigh. "Come on. We'd better go, or I'll wind up getting arrested for public indecency." Paola giggled, shivering as his hands left her and started the engine. She disengaged herself and sat back in her seat, noticing that the windows were all fogged up.

It was a ten-minute drive back to Didi's where he lived above the bar. He parked the car, grabbed her hand and hustled her through the side entrance and up the back stairs before anyone really had a chance to spot him. Félipe was covering for him that evening—he'd known, even if Paola hadn't, that they would be back at his place within an hour.

In a smooth, well-rehearsed move, he shrugged off his jacket, grabbed two glasses from the sideboard and collected a bottle of whisky as he pulled Paola down onto the daybed beside him. Five minutes later, he had successfully divested her of her top, sandals and his hands were working their way steadily up her beautifully smooth and firm legs. Paola Rossi was rich. She was also hot. He was the first—he could tell it by the way her legs trembled and the sharp intake of breath every time his hands hit a spot—perfect timing, as far as Didier was concerned. A hot, rich virgin. Who better to initiate her into the ways of the world than himself? He was good at it. He ought to be. He'd had enough practice. Perhaps this one would hang around long enough for him to reap the benefits. The *real* benefits. His hands began their work.

≈22≈
London, England

"Oh, for *fuck's* sake, Sall. *This* is what you do." Jake Higham-Burton leaned across the bed and snatched the checkbook out of Kieran's hands. He flipped to the back of the book and tore out a single leaf. "Here. How much d'you want?"

"Shit, I don't know. How much . . . how much d'you think we need?"

"Depends. How high d'you want to get?"

"I don't know. Pretty high. *Very* high." Kieran giggled suddenly.

"Right. Make it five hundred pounds."

"Five hundred pounds? Are you *nuts*?" Kieran's eyes opened wide. He tried to grab the checkbook back but Jake lifted it above his head, laughing.

"Come on. He won't even miss it."

"How do you know? Give it here . . . he's *my* father, you know."

"All the more reason. Don't be such a scaredy-cat. He won't even know it's gone. See . . . that's why you take the check from the *back* of the book, not the front." Jake tossed the checkbook across the floor. He fished around for a pen and laid the clean, empty Coutts' check on his knee. "There," he said, writing Kieran's name with a flourish. "Now you sign it. I don't know what his signature looks like." Kieran looked at him doubtfully. "Come *on*, Sall. D'you wanna get high or not?" Kieran took the check from him, drew in a deep breath and scrawled an approximation of Max's signature on the appropriate line. "Fantastic! Easy as pie. Now, come on. Let's get to the bank before they close," Jake said, leaping off the bed. "And *then* we can drop by the Prince."

"Shit, Jake . . . what if . . ." Kieran began, still sounding doubtful.

"There *are* no 'what ifs,'" Jake said, sounding exasperated. "Get a move on! Where's your coat?"

"Okay. I'm coming. I'm just—"

"Shit out of dope." Jake finished the sentence for him. "And coke. And anything else that takes our fancy. Ready?" He held open Kieran's bedroom door. Kieran pulled on his coat and stuck his head cautiously around the corner. "He's not here, you chicken shit. He's in bloody Japan. By the time he gets back, you'll have your dosh, we'll have the stuff and you, my boy, will be so fuckin' high . . ." Jake began to laugh again. Kieran frowned and shoved him down the stairs in front of him. He wanted to get out of the house, fast. Stealing money from Angela's purse was one thing—stealing a check from Max's study was another. The two of them ran down the front stairs, giggling nervously.

*   *   *

It was easy. An hour later, he and Jake were in the back of a black cab speeding towards an address in Bethnal Green, £500 in crisp twenty-pound notes in the back of his jeans, laughing so hard the driver kept turning round to make sure they were all right.

"Thanks, mate," Kieran said as they were deposited outside a block of flats. He shoved a twenty-pound note through the window. "Keep the change."

"Come on, HRH is home." Jake was clearly excited.

"How d'you know?"

"That's his car over there." Jake pointed to a silver BMW with darkened windows parked on the other side of the driveway. Amongst the battered Morris Minors and Minis, his car looked a *little* out of place, Kieran thought to himself as they walked into the building's entrance and waited for the lift.

"Prince. My man." Jake led the way in, suddenly sounding very different from the public-school-turned-university-drop-out Kieran knew. Prince was an alarmingly tall, well-built man of indeterminate age whose biceps were bigger than Kieran's thighs. He swallowed nervously as Prince stood aside silently to let them pass. The sitting room, if it could be called such, was almost empty save for a single La-Z-Boy rocker in one corner and the biggest television Kieran had ever seen. He watched in nervous awe as Jake outlined their needs, indicated the cash they'd brought and were willing to spend—and rolled a spliff which the two of them shared as Prince neatly weighed and bagged their order. It was over in less than ten minutes. Prince barely looked at Kieran. Stammering his thanks, he followed Jake out into the hallway, scarcely able to believe their luck. The two of them ignored the elevator and ran down the twelve flights of stairs, whooping like schoolkids. It was a little harder to get a taxi back into the West End, and Jake grumbled that they really ought to have asked the driver who brought them there to wait. But half an hour's walk down Roman Road was a small price to pay for the five hundred pounds' worth of Class A drugs sitting in plastic bags and stuffed into their coat pockets. Kieran couldn't wait to get home—and get high.

≈23≈

Amber put her bags down and stood awkwardly in the middle of the tiny room. There. It was done. At university. At last. She closed the door behind her and promptly burst into tears. She couldn't believe she'd finally arrived. After all the arguments, the shouting, the sulking—and the last-minute help from the most unexpected quarter—she was finally, irrevocably at university. She blew her nose and sat down on the edge of the unmade bed, looking around her. A narrow, empty room with just the bare essentials for a first-year student: bed, desk, built-in wardrobe and a small sink. The whole thing was no bigger than her walk-in closet at home. She touched the pile of linen that had been left at the foot of the bed. Cold, hard, bleached. She swallowed. Well, whatever she was feeling, Madeleine and Becky were feeling too, she told herself sternly as she pulled her suitcase towards her. Madeleine was a first-year medical student at Edinburgh and Becky had found a last-minute place at art school in Kingston. Becky hadn't managed to get the requisite—or any—A-levels and only a telephone call from her father to a colleague in the art history department had saved her from a fate she had decided would be worse than death—Lucie Clayton's, which had been her mother's bright suggestion. Amber smiled faintly at the memory. It had been easy for Madeleine with straight A's in all the right subjects. She'd known she wanted to be a doctor since they'd done their O-levels. But it was Amber's choice that had been the real surprise—and Max's reaction.

"Eh?" Max had lifted his head from the morning paper and looked at Amber as if she'd gone mad.

"English. I want to do English." Amber repeated herself. She was puzzled. Why was he looking at her so strangely?

"Whatever for?" Max asked, shaking his head before going back to his story.

"What d'you mean?" It was just the two of them at breakfast. Kieran hadn't yet come downstairs.

"It's a waste of time," Max said, already irritated. "Do something useful. Learn to type."

Amber almost dropped her mug of tea. "Type? Why the hell would I want to learn how to type?" she asked, her voice rising immediately.

Max lowered his paper again and glowered at her. "Why not? It's a useful skill for a woman. I can set you up with a job somewhere—"

"I don't *want* to learn how to type!" Amber broke in furiously. "I want to go to university! I can't believe you're saying this!" She pushed her plate away from her. Max's face had darkened but Amber didn't care. Her eyes filled with angry tears.

"Will you stop squawking?" Max growled, shaking out his paper in annoyance. "I just don't see the point, that's all. You'll spend three years of your life doing God-knows-what, stuffing your head with all kinds of useless information—and then before you know it, you'll be married. Why waste the time?"

"Says who?" Amber retorted angrily. "Is that what you think all women want? To get married to the first asshole who comes along—"

"Amber! Watch your mouth! I'm only trying to be practical," Max shouted at her. There was a sudden noise in the kitchen. Mrs. Dewhurst popped her head round the door.

"Everything all right, sir?" she asked, looking worriedly at Amber's reddened face.

"Fine. Will you leave us alone?" Max barked at her. Mrs. Dewhurst disappeared. Amber got up from the table and threw her napkin down. She didn't care if it earned her a month's worth of angry looks and cold silences. How *dare* Max trample over her ambitions with such disdainful ease.

"I don't care what you think," she said to an astonished Max. "I'm going to university and that's all there is to it. I don't need your help. I'm the one doing A-levels, not you. And if I get the right grades, I'm going." With that she turned and walked out of the room as calmly as she could.

It took Max almost three weeks to calm down and a further month to slowly be persuaded that it wasn't a complete waste of time and that just because Kieran hadn't lasted more than a term at Nottingham didn't mean that Amber would do what he had done—get himself thrown out. Max had stomped around the house for days after the outburst at the dining table but in the end, it was Francesca who had brought him round, much to Amber's astonishment. She spent hours with Becky and Madeleine afterwards trying to figure out what on earth her motive might have been. None of them could work it out.

She sighed, blew out her cheeks and stood up. Well, all that had happened last year and here she was, the night before her first classes were due to begin—and she was already homesick and confused. Was it what she really wanted? She longed for her huge, soft, comfortable double bed, her own bathroom and shower, the familiar sounds of Mrs. Dewhurst and Krystyna preparing breakfast or lunch or dinner . . . even the muted sound of music coming from Kieran's room and the telltale acrid whiff every time he opened his door. Hell, she even missed Angela's ghostly presence on the third floor. So far, no one had said a single word to her. She began to make her bed. It was almost ten o'clock. She'd seen from the guided tour around the residence halls that there were showers at the end of every corridor and that there was a shared kitchen halfway down. She would finish making her bed, take a bath and make herself a cup of camomile tea before climbing into bed. She had a long day ahead of her. The butter-flies in her stomach were already starting to flutter.

The following morning she was up early, woken by the sound of buses and taxis jostling for space and pun-ters on Oxford Street, some five floors below. She lay in bed in the overheated room, listening to the sounds of the city starting its rush-hour chaos and thought about the day ahead. She was to report to the English Department on Gower Street at 10 a.m. for an orien-tation session that would last until lunchtime. She swung her legs out of bed, picked up her dressing gown and opened her door. Everyone else on her cor-ridor was still fast asleep. She glanced at her watch. It was almost eight thirty. She shrugged. Maybe they were already gone . . . ? She headed to the showers.

Half an hour later as she headed back in the op-posite direction, there were still no signs of life. She closed her door and began to dress, wondering where everyone was and why she seemed to be the only person awake in Evans Hall. She spent a few minutes making sure she had everything she needed for the first day, picked up her bag—a pres-ent from Mrs. Dewhurst—and grabbed her coat, closing her door gently behind her. At the end of the corridor, a door opened and a girl in a white terry-cloth robe stumbled out of her room, yawning widely as Amber drew near.

"Hi," Amber said. A fellow student!

"Mmrhhmm." The girl muttered something indistinct and continued stumbling towards the bathrooms. Another door opened, and then another. Amber looked at her watch. It was nine thirty. Perhaps that was the preferred wake-up slot. She caught the lift to the ground floor and was disgorged onto Oxford Street.

Three hours later, her head spinning from all the things she thought she *ought* to remember, she closed her notebook with a snap. The introduction to the department was over. There were perhaps sixty or seventy new students crammed into the little lecture hall. She looked around her shyly—groups of long-haired girls chatted together as they filed out of the hall; clusters of serious-looking young men in Pringle sweaters and corduroys; a few obviously foreign students; a couple speaking French . . . she felt utterly lost. Everyone seemed to know everyone else. Was she the only person in the entire university without someone to talk to? With a sharp pang, she suddenly understood what poor Madeleine meant about being the outsider. Her facial muscles were exhausted with the strain of trying to look unconcerned, indifferent . . . anything to hide the growing sense of panic. *This* was what she'd fought Max for?

"Hi." She looked up, startled. A very tall young man was standing directly in front of her, blocking her path. Did she know him? "Hi," he said again, extending a hand. Amber paused. "Go on, I won't bite."

His voice was extraordinarily deep, full of laughter. She smiled faintly.

"I'm sorry . . . have we met before?"

"No. But I know who you are."

"Oh?"

"Yeah. You're Amber Sall, aren't you?" He was smiling down at her. Amber found herself in the unusual position of having to tilt her head backwards just to see him properly. He was grinning down at her with easy confidence. Brown eyes, ruddy cheeks, short, sandy-brown hair . . . she liked the way his eyes crinkled at the corners and the fact that he seemed to be looking at her, *really* looking at her—then she frowned.

"How do you know?"

"Saw your picture outside. We had our pictures taken this morning, remember?" Amber nodded, relieved. She'd thought for a minute . . .

"Max Sall's your dad, isn't he?" he went on, saying the very thing she didn't want to hear. She stopped, disappointed.

"Look, why are you so interested in who I am?"

"I'm not. Well, I *am* but not like that. No, it's just . . . in Halls this morning, one of the girls was reading a magazine and there was a picture of your sister . . ."

"My *half*-sister," Amber corrected him, gritting her teeth. Bloody *hell!* Any hopes she'd had about the mini-scandal that had erupted earlier in the summer being forgotten by the time she enrolled had just evaporated. She looked up at the young man. "D'you mind? It's got *nothing* to do with me, all right?

I don't know who you are . . . I don't even know your name . . ."

"It's Henry. Henry Fletcher," he broke in. He held the door to the lecture hall open for her. Amber glared at him and started to march off. "Hey, I'm sorry . . . I didn't mean to, you know, pry or anything. I've just been sitting behind you for three hours trying to work out what to say. Honestly, I didn't mean to piss you off." He sounded genuinely apologetic.

Amber paused, then turned back to him. "It's okay. You haven't. Now, will you leave me alone?"

"Only if you promise to have a drink with me. Tonight. After the seminar." He was laughing at her again. She glared at him—then relented, and smiled. After all, he was the only person who'd spoken to her all day. And there was something friendly and warm about him. She nodded.

"Okay. But where d'you want to go? I don't know anywhere around here."

"Me neither," he said cheerfully. "But it's a university. There's bound to be somewhere. I'll wait for you here after class." He grinned at her again and walked towards the lifts. Amber watched his impossibly tall frame disappear into the lift and then looked at her watch. It was lunchtime. No wonder she was absolutely starving. Allowing herself the tiniest of smiles, she wandered off in search of something to eat. Someone had spoken to her, perhaps it wasn't going to be so bad after all.

At York, the woman sitting opposite Madeleine finally got up, leaving behind the magazine she'd been eyeing since Leeds. She snatched it up and turned to page fourteen. She raised her eyebrows. It was a double-page spread. *The Sall Sisters: Exclusive Pictures!* She looked at the photos of Amber and her half-sister Paola, on whose account a thirty-four-year-old man had been arrested on suspicion of having underage sex, and shook her head disbelievingly. The two sisters couldn't have been more different, as the article seemed to imply. It wasn't the most flattering picture of Amber—coming out of Marks and Spencer, head down, hand already warding off the photographer, but Paola on the other hand looked only too happy to have her photograph taken and had adopted what she obviously thought was a winning smile and pose in every shot. Madeleine remembered the fuss that had been made at the time. Paola had gone missing on the last day of the family holiday; distraught, her mother had called the police. Amber had told them the barest details but the newspapers had been full of the pictures—the police raiding the apartment above the bar; the man—Madeleine couldn't remember his name—being led away in handcuffs, protesting his innocence . . . he hadn't known she was fifteen; she'd lied, told him she was eighteen; a remarkably uncontrite Paola coming out of the station with her mother, the two of them looking more like twins. It had gone on for weeks. Max's wrath had erupted on an almost daily basis. God, the whole thing had been terrible.

She put the magazine down and turned to look at the landscape rushing by. The yellow-green hills

and thickly carpeted valleys blurred as the train hur-
tled north. To Edinburgh. She was on her way to
start the next phase of her life, the definitive one.
She'd been preparing for it ever since the morning
she'd walked into the Careers Office at King
George, put down her completed application form
and fulfilled the hopes and expectations of everyone around her. *Dr. Madeleine Szabo.* She said it
out loud, in English and Hungarian, liking the way it
rolled off her tongue, easily and comfortably. She'd
been practicing saying it since she was sixteen.
She'd watched Amber and Becky agonize for
months over their respective career choices, but
that didn't apply to her. Madeleine's decision was
hardly a choice. Wealthy people had choices, that
much she already knew. That was what money gave
you—the freedom to choose. *I will be this. I will be
that.* Like trying on a dress, and setting it aside or
handing back a pair of shoes to the sales assistant—*no, I'll take the other pair, please.* Or even . . .
she let her mind wander dangerously for a second . . . to keep something, a child, perhaps . . .
she swallowed. She'd sworn never to think about it.
That was all in the past. Now she had the future to
look forward to. She was going to *do* something with
her life, *be* somebody. She imagined her father talking to their neighbors or to his Hungarian friends at
the community center: *of course you remember
Madeleine . . . she's now a doctor, yes, we're very
proud of her . . .* or her mother, casually letting it slip
while cleaning Dr. Evans' house, just around the

corner from Amber's. Everything would be solved, all wounds healed, with her success. Nothing could compare with that. There had been just the one, tiny, fleeting moment of doubt when Amber announced her choice—English. Madeleine's head had gone up, quickly—oh, to be in a position to choose something you *really* loved . . . English . . . but she swiftly squashed the thought. Amber and Becky had choices, she reminded herself sternly. She didn't. And that was that. She put down the magazine, wondered how Amber and Becky were getting on on their first day away and turned to look out of the window once again.

≈24≈

What did he expect? Francesca asked herself, puffing furiously on a cigarette. She had practically seen it coming—although, she reminded herself quickly, that was exactly what Max had accused her of—seeing it coming and failing to do anything about it. But what? Her daughter was running wild and there didn't seem to be anything she *could* do. The girl needed her father. Maria Luisa and Manuela had confirmed her worries; she was *acting out*, whatever that meant. Francesca had long ago given up trying to discipline her little girl. Not so little now, she reminded herself. She grimaced. She stood up and crossed to the windows, pulling aside the heavy damask curtain and looking out across the rooftops to the gardens of the Villa Borghese at the end of the boulevard. It was wet and windy; autumn had arrived early. She had made the decision to take Paola out of the *lycée* and send her to a small but exclusive finishing school in Lausanne, just for a year. Paola could—hopefully—finish her baccalaureate, be free from all the distractions of Rome and her friends . . . and then they'd see. She stubbed out her cigarette and turned from the window. Max had been predictably furious at her but what was she supposed to do? He was rarely around these days, always flying off to the Far East or the U.S., far too preoccupied with new business ventures and deals to pay Paola much attention. Why, even *she* was beginning to feel a little neglected. The last weekend he'd been there, she'd found to her surprise that she was acting a little . . . well, clingy. She, who never, *ever* asked the kinds of questions a wife would ask—*When will you be back? What time will you be home? When are we going to spend more time together?*—she was horrified as well as surprised. So was Max. He narrowed his eyes at her at the breakfast table and ignored her.

She heard Paola's door open suddenly and turned, putting as cheerful a smile on her face as she could.

"*Cara,*" she said, holding out her arms. "Why don't we go shopping, just the two of us? I have the list of things you'll need for the new school—look, it's exciting . . . furs, and a new coat . . . evening dresses, a suit . . . come. We'll have lunch at Veneto's together, then we'll spend the afternoon in town." Paola nodded, a trifle ungraciously. She wasn't looking forward to her new school *at all*. In fact, she was dreading it. Even the promise of a new winter wardrobe couldn't raise a smile. She walked dejectedly back to her room under Francesca's worried eye.

On her first morning at art school, Becky looked around her at her fellow first-year students and immediately cursed Madeleine. She'd rung the evening before after she'd arrived at her halls in Edinburgh and the two of them had swapped arrivals stories, hoping to cheer each other up. Madeleine's last words to Becky had been "don't worry about it. Everyone's probably as nervous as you are." Well, they weren't. No one looked even *remotely* nervous. There were twenty-odd first-year students sitting in a loose circle, smoking—*smoking?*—listening with half an ear to the lecturer, whispering to one another and, when they were silent, looking distinctly bored. She stared at them. Why did they all seem to know each other? When had they met? Why hadn't she met anyone? She looked down at her pleated tartan skirt with her pale lemon yellow sweater that picked out the yellow threads in the tartan weave and flat, sensible shoes, and was mortified. Neat, pretty, tasteful—*completely* out of place. Opposite her was a tall, slim girl with blonde hair twisted in a thousand exquisite braids, denim overalls already splashed artistically with paint and a striped sweater fraying at the elbows: a proper art student. Next to her were two dark, intense-looking young men who smoked cigarette after cigarette, nodding wearily as the lecturer spoke. Becky was the only one carrying a notepad—everyone else seemed to retain every word, effortlessly: *no need to write anything down, it's all up here, man* . . . she swallowed, and turned her attention to the lecturer. Small, thin and wiry, he seemed more like a first-year student than a professor of art. What the hell was he saying? Something about pain, loss, death? She looked around her again, puzzled. She was here to learn how to *draw*, not talk about the death of her cat, or her mother, neither of whom were deceased. But everyone else was talking . . . talking, talking, talking. She looked down at her skirt again. Had she stumbled into the wrong course by accident? She leaned forward, listening intently and caught the eye of the braided goddess opposite. *Wrong, wrong, wrong,* the girl's expression seemed to say. Wrong clothes, wrong attitude, wrong place. Next to her studied, gorgeous insouciance, Becky felt awkward, naïve . . . and unbearably plain. What was that rubbish Madeleine had said? No one here was nervous. If anything, it was the opposite. Everyone present—except her, of course—looked as though they'd been at art school all their lives.

Six hundred miles to the north, Madeleine wasn't actually faring much better, despite her confident words. "Look at the person standing next to you," the elderly professor who was in charge of their orientation said, "take a good, long look at the person on your right and on your left." People began to shuffle nervously. "Because," he went on dramatically, "in six months' time, one of you will be gone. A third of you will make it through. Welcome to the Royal Infirmary, ladies and gentlemen. Not for the faint-hearted." With that, he turned on his heel and walked out of the lecture hall. Sixty-odd eager young men and women stood still in silence, avoiding each other's eyes. After a few minutes someone giggled and people began to stir. Madeleine looked around her. There were very few women in the group—six, eight . . . thirteen, she counted quickly. The rest were rather uniformly dull, young men. One of the girls was rather pretty with a relaxed, secure air about her. Within minutes, a group had formed around her. People began talking, suddenly, all at once. Up and down the room, young men turned to the person on their right, then on their left . . . it quickly became something of a joke. *Hullo, I expect you'll be gone next term* . . . Madeleine stood alone at the back of the hall, watching as the men on either side of her moved forwards, away from her. So, university wouldn't be any different, she thought to herself as she shouldered her bag and made her way to the exit. That was how it had always been. At nearly six feet tall, still forty pounds heavier than she ought to be, she was practically a giant, even in a group that was mostly male. Women looked at her pityingly; men backed away. Madeleine didn't need to be told how people responded to her. She wasn't blind. *You've a lovely face, Madeleine, you should do something about your weight.* Everyone said it— teachers, friends, parents—*parents* of friends. Becky's mother had tucked an arm into hers about a month before they were due to start at university and tried to have what she thought was a friendly, motherly conversation. She'd even offered to take Madeleine along to her WeightWatchers class . . . Madeleine shook her head. She didn't know how to explain to her that she couldn't afford it. And no amount of persuasion on Becky and Amber's part could change what she could see with her own eyes. Becky had some daft notion that people were intimidated by her, her height and imposing stature; Becky even thought she was lucky—everyone im- mediately respected her, even people who didn't know her. She wasn't someone to be trifled with; even at nineteen she was a *serious* woman. Madeleine saw it differently. She wasn't imposing, she was *fat*. Overweight. End of story. She opened the swing doors and paused, turning to take a look at the hall full of people with whom she was now stuck. The group around the pretty girl had grown. She was now the center of laughing, admiring at- tention. Madeleine just had time to notice she was wearing jeans, a pink V-necked sweater turned the other way around and a chain of glowing, white pearls around her slender neck before the doors swung shut.

≈25≈

Jake was right. It did get easier. The second time he did it, the pang, as he scrawled "Max R. Sall" along the dotted line, was really more of twinge. By the time he deposited the fourth check—for £1,000—into his account, he merely blinked as the cashier counted out the notes. One of the advantages of banking at Coutts, he acknowledged. Cash, on demand. None of this waiting around for days for a check to clear. He slipped the envelope of crisp fifty-pound notes into his jacket and stepped out onto the Strand. Besides, he reasoned to himself as he flagged down a cab, Max had left him with little choice. He'd been given the most paltry of allowances—barely enough to keep him in cigarettes, let alone drugs. All over that stupid fuss about university. He hadn't wanted to go in the first place. As usual, it had been Max's idea. Kieran wanted to stay at home, with Angela. It was a good thing he'd been kicked out to be honest. God knows what might have happened to him if he'd stayed at university. No, he was much happier at home. Especially now that Amber was gone. At the thought of her, he frowned. She'd made the most awful fuss about going herself and made him look like a right idiot.

"Where to, guv?" A black cab had pulled up in front of him.

"Bethnal Green," Kieran said automatically,

climbing in. "And I'd like you to wait for me when we get there . . . shouldn't be long."

"Right you are." The cab swung around and headed east.

"Here," Prince said casually, "you should try it. It's beautiful, man." Kieran swallowed nervously. Prince handed him a syringe filled with a dark-yellow liquid, a strip of rubber and indicated to him to roll up his sleeve. Kieran swallowed again. Heroin. He knew what it was. There was a young girl passed out on the chair at the end of the room, her arm hanging limply to one side, a dreamy, vacant expression on her face. Up and down her arm Kieran could see the telltale track marks—and bruises, too. "Let me help you." Prince's hands were already on him, rolling up his sleeve and preparing the tourniquet. Kieran felt powerless to resist. His body was weak with nerves and longing. He watched in fascinated horror as Prince deftly wrapped the rubber strip around his arm just above the elbow and tapped professionally at the blue vein passing down the center of his forearm. In seconds, the vein began to bulge. Just as he'd seen it on television or in films, Prince held the thin, long needle up to the light, flicked against it once, twice and with a grin, sank it straight into Kieran's arm before he could protest. The hit was almost instantaneous. He slumped forward, clutching Prince's arm as his mind exploded with the sweetest, most powerful rush of emotion he'd ever felt . . . he thought he would pass out. "Easy, man," Prince was saying as he swayed back and forth. His voice seemed to be coming from miles away.

"I . . . sh . . . shit, I . . . whoa," he slurred, as wave after wave of pleasure coursed through him. It was incredible—his eyes snapped open. Everything was so bright, so clean, so unbelievably . . . *beautiful.*

"Take it easy, bro . . . lie down on the carpet. Here, close your eyes . . . that's it, cool." Prince's voice guided him gently. He curled up on the dirty brown carpet, closed his eyes and began to drift. Images crowded his brain—the milky-white skin of Becky's stomach, the pink, almost shy nipples; her red hair, falling over his face; the view from his bedroom window at home; Angela . . . her smile . . . the sound of his motorbike engine, the feel of it between his legs; he began to whimper softly . . . and then to drift. His last coherent thought was of Max—his furious face on so many occasions . . . too many to count. And then there was silence. Blissful silence.

"Yo, man. Hey, dude . . . wake up. Wake *up!*" Someone was pushing at him, shaking him awake. He struggled to sit upright, his head spinning.

"Wh . . . wh . . . what's happening . . . what . . . where am I?" he mumbled, wetting his lips and trying to get rid of the bits of . . . what? Hair? . . . that had somehow found their way into his mouth. He wiped it with the back of his hand.

"Easy, dude. You've had a bit of a trip. You're coming down. Take it slow . . . that's it." He narrowed his eyes, trying to focus. Prince was crouched in front of him, kneeling on the carpet. He slowly eased himself upright, holding onto his enormous forearm for support. "Okay?" Prince asked him, bending down to pick up his jacket. Kieran nodded a little uncertainly.

"Wh . . . what time is it?"

"Three. You've been out for half an hour. You okay?"

"Yeah. I'd better . . . get going," Kieran said with difficulty, casting a worried look at the still sleeping girl in the corner of the room.

"No worries. Here, this is what you came for." Prince handed him several small bags of dope, coke and assorted pills. "And would you care for any of this?" He held up a tiny bag of greyish white lumps. Kieran hesitated for a second, then nodded slowly. Prince grinned. "Four hundred and fifty pounds a bag, sir. Best there is." Kieran reached into his jacket and peeled off a stack of notes. He handed them over without a word. "Here, I'll throw these in," Prince said, taking the bundle without even bothering to count. "You'll need 'em." Kieran took the teaspoon, syringe and packet of needles and slipped them into his pocket. Jake would know what to do with them. He fled downstairs. Unbelievably, his taxi was still waiting.

≈26≈

Henry smiled down at Amber as he passed her a pint of beer. It was their third date in two weeks—hardly a record—but he was in love. Hopelessly. "Cheers!" he shouted above the din of music and chatter. He couldn't see her eyes in the dim light but he could sense her wide, generous smile. Of all the things he liked about Amber, her smile was his favorite. Warm, quick and sunny. When she smiled her whole face lit up, like dawn over the water at Kariba. The thought startled him.

"You're not listening to me," Amber prodded him in the ribs.

"I can't *hear* you," he protested. "What?"

"Can I borrow your notes from this morning? I was half-asleep in the lecture."

"Of course. You can borrow them any time." He gazed down at her. Should he say something? Something a bit more meaningful than the usual subject-related chitchat and asking for each other's notes? She had to know by now . . . he'd asked her out three times in a row, but that was the thing with Amber: she was friendly and funny and open and all of that, but he'd seen it once or twice, the shutters coming down firmly on subjects she didn't want to talk about—her family, for one thing, *especially* not her father. He didn't want to risk it. He didn't think he could bear her coldness. She'd cut someone off mid-sentence the other week, some Sloane Ranger babbling on about her sister . . . no, he definitely didn't want to risk losing the warmth in her that had attracted him from the minute he saw her.

As if on cue, they both turned back towards the band—some amateur student effort. Henry couldn't stand the wailing but the posters had been lying around all over the ground floor in the department and he'd grabbed one as an excuse to ask her out again, so there they were, suffering together in silence. Well, not quite. It was unbearably loud.

"Shall we go somewhere else?" Amber shouted to him after the fourth—or fifth, or sixth—set. Her eardrums were aching. Henry nodded enthusiastically. He took her empty glass and began forcing a path for them through the crowd.

"God, that was dreadful," he said as they burst through the swing doors onto Gower Place.

"Well, it was your idea," Amber laughed, wrapping her scarf around her neck.

"I was desperate," Henry grinned at her.

She looked at him, puzzled. "To hear *them*?"

"No, to find another reason to ask you out."

"Oh." There was a moment's hesitation. Henry tried to see her expression. His heart was suddenly racing. "You don't need a *reason*," she began slowly. He let out a breath. There was the sound of a smile in her voice. "I—"

"Amber," Henry suddenly broke in. "I really like you. I mean, really. *Really*." He could have kicked himself. He sounded like a complete and utter idiot. They were standing on the street corner underneath the horrible yellow glare of a street light. He looked down at her, at her eyes sparkling mischievously over the rim of her red and yellow striped scarf. It seemed the most appropriate thing to do under the circumstances—he bent his head towards her and kissed her.

It was definitely the sunshine in her face. Later that night, lying in his too-short bed, Henry went over the entire evening, minute by precious minute. Sun-shine and warmth. Other people in the program complained that Amber Sall was stuck up, aloof, cold . . . he didn't see her like that at all. To him, she was a strange, perfect contradiction. There was something exotic about her that was hard to put his finger on. She wasn't like any of the cheery, red-faced English girls he'd known—and been out with—in his teens; yet she was thoroughly, thor-oughly English. They shared the same sense of hu-mor; liked the same bands; enjoyed the same books. She'd lived in London all her life yet she didn't seem to have any particular attachment to it. When they spoke about what they wanted to do, where they wanted to go when they'd finished, Am-ber took it for granted that the whole world was open to her, for her. And it wasn't just because she was rich. Somehow, without knowing it, she'd touched the nerve in him that was still as raw as it had been the day he'd arrived in England, five years ago. Five long, cold and damp years, years without the sun. Henry couldn't live without the sun. He sometimes felt as though he were drowning in England, in the gloom and the watery grey light. The fact was, Henry wasn't the ruddy-faced, rugby-playing En-glish public schoolboy he appeared to be—he wasn't English at all. He was Rhodesian, or Zim-babwean, as it was now called. His father was second-generation, the son of a settler, whose roots in the African soil, in the end, proved surprisingly easy to uplift. Henry grew up thinking of himself as African; apart from a single visit at the age of eight to a distant relative on his father's side in Yorkshire, he had never been to England, to the country his parents, bafflingly, insisted on calling "home." At fifteen, when he was already nearly six feet tall and one of the most popular students at Hillhurst, the exclusive boys' school just outside Salisbury, his parents began talking of returning "home." In 1979, a few months after the fall of Ian Smith's regime, they packed up their belongings and fled. *The country*, George Fletcher declared, *was going to the dogs.* It was his favorite phrase. Henry's two older brothers, Joshua and Martin, both finished university in Britain and escaped from the rain and damp as soon as they could, Joshua to Sydney and Martin back to Africa, to Johannesburg. Now there was only Henry to return at weekends to the pleasant cottage in Cambridgeshire to which his parents had fled—although quite from what, Henry wasn't sure. They rarely talked about their old life. Henry's father had found work as a branch manager in one of the banks in the small village of Trincham and his mother settled remarkably quickly into a seemingly endless round of fêtes and fairs for which she spent all week baking.

Henry was sent to Clark Hall, one of the many minor public schools not far from home. Within a month, he'd perfected his new English accent and was indistinguishable from all the other ruddy-faced boys with whom he shared a dormitory. With his natural curiosity for new phenomena and his outsider's desire to prove himself, to fit in, success came easily to Henry. By the time he reached sixth form, the handsome, likeable school prefect was as English as the best of them. He couldn't have said why he preferred it that way.

Their family, according to George, had been one of the lucky ones. In later years, as the economy began to flounder, many of the white settlers who had stayed on, returned—only poorer, more desperate and more bitter than the Fletchers. *In the nick of time.* It was another of George's favorite sayings. Henry didn't see it that way. For him, it was as though a part of him had been severed and the only way to staunch the blood was to forget about it. Which he had done, until Amber Sall came along.

≈27≈

Madeleine closed her eyes as she grasped the scalpel and gingerly prodded the body lying on the slab in front of her. Gritting her teeth, she made an incision as the professor had instructed them, intending to cut in a sweeping arc across the stomach, ending just below the navel. Nothing happened. She pressed the blade again, harder. Still nothing. She opened her eyes. The smooth, alabaster skin under the harsh neon lights looked rubbery to her, shiny and utterly resistant to her touch. She tried a third time. The blade slid in cleanly, there was a faint sound of air escaping, like a gasp of breath and the body beneath her hand suddenly moved as the gases inside the stomach were released. Madeleine gave a short, horrified squeal. Next to her, a female student fainted.

Twenty minutes later, as the class was walking out of the mortuary, everyone talking excitedly about what had happened, Madeleine felt someone fall into step beside her. She turned her head in surprise. It was Tim, the third-year teaching assistant who sometimes helped out at lectures.

"Happens every year," he said, smiling at her. "Don't think you've been singled out for punishment." Madeleine blushed.

"I shouldn't have squealed like that," she said, looking down at him. He was a good head shorter than her, thin and nervously intense—in lectures, he was always fiddling with something; his glasses, pens and papers, a cup of water. "Dr. Morland probably thinks I'm an idiot."

"Oh, I wouldn't worry about it." He waved her anxiety aside. "It's just gas. You get a build-up of gastric gases in the corpse . . . quite powerful, too, some of them. I've seen corpses practically lift themselves off the table and flop back down again. Then you get a number of students fainting . . ." he laughed. Madeleine smiled faintly. "Well, I'd better be off," he said, looking at his watch. "Got a lecture of my own in about five minutes. See you later. We're having drinks at the Three Crosses this evening on Union Street. Bring a friend, if you like." With that, he disappeared, leaving Madeleine standing staring after him as he hurried down the corridor, his white coat flapping behind him as he walked. *We're having drinks this evening.* Who was the "we?" And why had he invited her? She reached up a hand, touching her hair self-consciously. She suddenly realized she was the only student left in the corridor. She looked at the clock on the wall, then pulled her dog-eared timetable out of her pocket. 11 a.m . . . Pathology. Room 321. She hurried to the elevators.

The pub, when she entered, was crowded and smoky. She recognized a couple of her fellow students standing in one corner of the room and was just making her way cautiously towards them, unsure of her welcome, when she heard someone shout her name from across the room. "Madeleine . . . over here!" She turned. It was Tim and two other students whom she'd never seen before—they must be third years, she thought as she walked over to their corner. "Great you could make it," Tim said, pulling up a chair for her. "It's good to see you." Madeleine sat down, shyly flattered by his enthusiastic welcome. "What'll you have?" he asked, getting up from his own seat.

"Um, just a half pint, please," Madeleine said. She put a hand nervously to her throat and smiled at the other two, wondering what to say.

"Paul and Mitchell," Tim said as he came back with the drinks. "Chaps, this is Madeleine. First year. A *real* fresher—almost conked out in pathology this morning," he laughed. Madeleine smiled a little self-consciously. She couldn't quite work out why she'd been singled out to have drinks with them but Paul and Mitchell seemed nice and genuinely interested in what she had to say. Within minutes, she was do-

ing what she'd always done when faced with someone's unexpected interest in her—she began to re-
pay the debt. She was amusing, interesting,
funny . . . she felt herself slide into what Amber
called her Miss Congeniality role. *Thank you for
showing an interest in me, thank you for taking the
time.* It drove Amber crazy. But Madeleine couldn't
help it. The tracks along *that* particular personality
trait were very well worn. She slipped right in.

Becky stared at the painting on the wall. Polly, an
impossibly tall, long-legged girl was standing in
front of her work, defending it. Becky stared in silent
admiration at the swirls and whorls of lurid color—
pink, cerise, lilac and deep, almost incandescent
purple—at the thick, tactile quality of the paint and
the wonderfully abstract, confident abandon with
which Polly had interpreted the assignment. The invited critics leaned forward in their chairs to discuss
the work. Becky felt faint with nerves. It was her first
public review and she had no idea what to expect.
Each student was allocated twenty minutes in which
to outline the concept and thinking behind their
work, and then it seemed to be the job of the critics
to tear the student apart, limb by limb, feeble idea by
feeble execution. Around her, everyone else was
nervous, waiting reluctantly for their turn. Polly's
cheeks were flaming as she spoke, but she de-
fended her project bravely, even articulately. Listening to her, Becky felt the butterflies in her stomach
take off, circulating around until she thought she'd
faint with nerves and exhaustion. She hadn't slept

all night, staying in the studio with two other students, struggling to finish her own—ridiculously weak, she feared—set of drawings.

"Next!" Beverly, their tutor, called out. "Samantha. Are you ready to go? Becky? Pin up your work next to Samantha's. You'll be on after her." Becky got up from her position at the rear of the review space and picked up her work. She watched the critics tear into Samantha for their allocated twenty minutes as if in a dream. When her own turn came and the first critic, a horrible-looking man in a green shirt and a bright yellow bow-tie, took one look at her work and asked her, in a voice dripping with sarcasm, if there was anything, *any*thing at all, that could possibly distinguish her work from a pile of shit, despite the gasp from the rest of the room, it took Becky a moment or two to understand exactly, precisely what he had asked . . . then she burst into tears and fled.

Listening to their horror stories on the phone, Amber was too embarrassed to report how well everything seemed to be going with *her* classes. She hadn't even wanted to mention Henry, but Becky wormed it out of her. Everything seem to have fallen into place. She loved the program, she liked living in halls, she'd made one or two friends . . . compared to the torture the other two were facing, she had nothing to complain about. Nothing at all. Except . . . there *was* something. She didn't bring it up with Becky, of course, but perhaps Madeleine would have an idea? It was Kieran. She'd gone home at the weekend, hoping Max would be there so she could report how well it was all going but of course, he was away. She'd dropped off a load of washing for Krystyna then gone upstairs to see if Kieran was in. They had barely spoken since she'd left at the beginning of term. He was angry at her for going in the first place, especially since he'd screwed things up so spectacularly on the university front, but Amber wanted to make amends. Krystyna said he was in, had been in *all day.* Amber was a little puzzled by the strange look she'd given her but shrugged it off and walked upstairs.

She was shocked. And worried. Kieran looked absolutely dreadful. His hair was lank and greasy, his skin lifeless and dull. He looked as though he hadn't eaten a decent meal in weeks. She sat down on the edge of his bed, wondering what the hell was going on. Kieran brushed aside her concerns with a feeble wave.

"I'm brilliant. *Bri*lliant."

"You look awful." Amber glanced around the room. It was a pigsty. "Has . . . has Max seen you?" she asked tentatively.

"Oh, fuck Max." Kieran yawned, rolled over and shut his eyes. Amber got up from the bed and went to the window. She pulled open the curtain, ignoring Kieran's protests. The room was flooded with light. In it, Kieran looked worse than ever. She bit her lip. She ought to talk to someone about him, but who? Talking to Max would be pointless and besides, Kieran would think she was telling tales. Angela? No point there, either. She absolutely doted on

Kieran. She wouldn't be able to do a thing, anyway. She looked at her dozing brother. She'd always looked after him, protected him from the worst of Max's rages, even though she was his younger sister. He ought to have been the one to look after her. But it hadn't worked out that way. Kieran wasn't as tough as she was—he'd been an awful cry-baby as a child. Whenever Amber had fallen off her bike or out of a tree she had simply picked herself up, dusting down her scraped knees, but Kieran had bawled for hours, demanding the maximum sympathy from anyone in hearing range. It hadn't exactly endeared him to Max, who wanted tough, feisty children, not cry-babies. And when Angela started to slide, Kieran simply couldn't stand it. Amber had been too little to remember her when she *wasn't* perpetually drunk and crying, so it hadn't been quite the same loss for her.

"Hey, sleepy-head," she called, walking over to the bed. She wrinkled her nose. He stank, too. "I'm going to send Krystyna up, okay?" But Kieran didn't answer. He appeared dead to the world. She sighed. At least she could organize for his room to be cleaned. It was filthy. He could sleep in her old room for the time being. Krystyna could sort it out. She closed the door gently behind her.

"It's obviously drugs," Madeleine said to her. Amber was silent. "Did you see anything . . . needles, packets, things like that?"

"Oh, I don't think it's *that* serious," Amber said

quickly. "It's just the dope. He must be smoking huge amounts of it. Anyhow, I got Krystyna to clean him up. He was quite cheerful by the time I left."

"Well, if you say so. There were a couple of junkies at my school, you know. It sounds awfully like them."

"No, no . . . not Kieran. Anyway, where would he get the money? He's always complaining that Max hardly gives him any money. Heroin's terribly expensive, isn't it?" Madeleine didn't reply. If kids at King George could find a way to feed their habit, she was sure Kieran could. She listened to Amber's descriptions of her course and Henry with a wry smile. It was almost the end of term and Madeleine had barely spoken to anyone in her program. Apart from Tim, of course. He was a lecturer's assistant and he was supposed to talk to the junior years, so it hardly counted. They rang off, promising to ring each other the minute they got home for the Christmas holidays.

≈28≈

He was shown into a small, private sitting room, asked if he would care for anything to drink and was brought the morning's papers to read while he waited. It wouldn't be more than ten, fifteen minutes. Mr. Beaton was *most* apologetic . . . he was running late. Max nodded, handed over his overcoat and sat down in the plush leather armchair. He looked around as the assistant left the room. Not bad, he mused . . . on the twentieth floor of the Euston Tower, dark oak paneling, antique furniture, a few tastefully chosen paintings hanging on the walls. He shook open the paper. *Lord Sainsbury, 96, Dies.* He stared at the headline. *Andrew B. Sainsbury, Baron Sainsbury of Drury Lane, dies at the age of 96, of complications following a stroke.* He put the paper down, momentarily stunned. It had been almost thirty years since the day he'd met Lord Sainsbury for the first time and probably three, four years since they'd last crossed paths. And indirectly, it was through him that he was waiting to see Geoff Beaton, the managing director of British Railways. He pulled a face. No, in fact, it was directly through him.

He was seventeen when he began working as a driver for Sainsbury's. He'd lied about his age, and the fact that he had a driver's license. He'd had enough of the butcher's counter by then. The manager at the Kentish Town branch had kept an eye on him—the young lad was a good worker, quick off the mark and popular with the housewives, too. Sainsbury's was expanding in the years following the war. In 1954, they opened the biggest food supermarket in Europe, in Lewisham High Street. He put in a word for young Max. The firm was trying out something new, an idea imported directly from the U.S.: the Lewisham High Street store was completely self-service. Max's first promotion was from swilling out the butcher's counter where the housewives placed their orders and waited for the butcher and his team to hand over their goods, to working in the meat preparation room, behind the shop, hacking, slicing and packaging the meat to be displayed in the newly designed refrigeration units. He hated it. There wasn't even the opportunity to flirt. He spent two miserable weeks learning a bewildering array of cuts of meat before imploring the store manager to give him something else.

"Can ye drive, lad?" the Scots manager asked him.

Max nodded. "'Course I can."

"And have ye a license?"

"Yes."

"Right ye are, then. Mr. Andrew's lookin' for a replacement driver. His lad's down with the 'flu. S'only for a couple of weeks, mind." Max didn't stop to listen. He peeled off his blue and white striped butcher's apron, flung it in the bin at the rear of the store and scrubbed his hands till they bled. He spent the weekend learning how to drive the neighbor's ancient 1933 MG until he was confident he'd at least got the hang of it. But when he presented himself at the rear of the store on Monday morning and took one look at the gleaming maroon and black Bentley R-Type with its elongated, elegant prow and plush leather interior, he nearly balked. Fortunately, at least in the long run, the manager assumed the look on his face was distress at not having the right uniform or white gloves or something and not sheer fear at having to drive the damn thing.

They got off to a rocky start. Lord Sainsbury was demanding and impatient and often wound up shouting directions through the glass partition that separated them. More often than not it was on the tip of Max's tongue to tell Lord Sainsbury to shut up—but he couldn't, and didn't. And then one day, everything changed.

He was waiting for Lord Sainsbury outside his Kensington home one morning. The schedule was to drive him to the head office at Blackfriars, then onto the Chief Accountant's office in Streatham before going out to Essex to inspect a couple of possible new store sites. It was a blustery spring day. He started the engine as soon as he saw Lord Sainsbury emerge from the front door and jumped out, as was the custom, to open the door for him. As he drew near, he noticed his employer was in a truly foul mood. They were not to go to Stamford House, it transpired, but to Dover, over a hundred miles to the east, to pick up a Professor Solomon Blumenthal, a refrigeration engineer whom Terence, Lord Sainsbury's eldest son, in his *infinite* wisdom, had invited to work for them in their new research and development department but who, it turned out, *couldn't speak a word of bloody English*. Lord Sainsbury's voice rose with indignation.

"What I'm supposed to do with a bloody refugee who can't speak English, God only knows. Where'm I going to find a German speaker at . . ." he consulted his fob watch, "eight o'clock on a Wednesday morning? I *ask* you!"

"I can, sir," Max said quietly.

"Eh?"

"German, sir. I speak it. Fluently." It was the first time he'd admitted to it since arriving in England. He met his employer's incredulous gaze in the rear-view mirror.

"And how did that come about?" Lord Sainsbury, despite his annoyance, was intrigued.

"Jewish, sir. German-Jewish."

"I'll be damned."

He spent the next three years acting in the capacity of personal assistant to Lord Sainsbury, as well as driving him around. Lord Sainsbury wouldn't have anyone else beside him. In those three years, he built the beginnings of his most valuable asset: his list of contacts. When he married Angela Weymouth in 1963, few people could have known that the handsome bridegroom whose family was represented by Lord Sainsbury and his four sons had arrived in England twenty years earlier with nothing other than a dog-eared teddy bear and a small packet of three diamonds—all of which he still had.

And now Lord Sainsbury was dead. Max's eyes were uncharacteristically bright when Mr. Beaton's assistant popped his head round the door to usher the visitor in.

≈29≈

Paola was too excited to do anything other than stare in awe at the fabulous opulence surrounding her. La Boum was the hottest nightclub in Geneva and it was evident from the admiring glances she received from both men and women that she was one of its hottest guests. Within minutes she'd managed to distance herself from the three girls she'd come with—all the way from Lausanne huddled in the back of a waiting taxi after escaping from school. On her left was a row of the biggest, meanest-looking and most menacing bouncers she'd ever seen and on her right, a queue of the young, beautiful and desperate whose names unfortunately weren't on the guest list. It was the job of the men on the left to keep out those on the right. Paola's name was on the coveted list thanks to Sophie de Cordonnier, the sadly rather plain-looking daughter of a French film actress who knew all the right people and had managed to get herself and her friends on the right list.

She deposited her fur cape, smoothed down her skin-tight dress and followed the crowd into the club. She made her way to the bar, ordered a White Russian and stood, sipping it and leaning elegantly against the steel and glass bar as a group of young men next to her fought over who would speak to her first. This was *much* more her scene, she thought to herself as first one young man introduced himself, then another. By the time she'd finished her drink, three more had been lined up on the bar's shiny surface and she found herself listening with half an ear to a nasal-sounding American drone on and on, and watching the movements of an older, *much* better-looking man next to him, obviously one of the group, yet holding himself somewhat apart.

"So where are you from?" the American asked, unable to take his eyes off her. He was the son of a Texas oil magnate, as he'd told her within the first five minutes.

"Rome. Paris. Menorca. Take your pick." Paola was bored by him. She looked over his shoulder but the man next to him had disappeared. "Who was that?" she asked, wishing he would shut up and disappear himself.

"That's Prince Georg," the American said proudly. "He's a good friend of mine."

"Really?" Paola's voice carried with it all the insinuation that word could produce. The man reddened.

"Yeah, we're staying together at the Leconte in town. There's a group of us. You should come visit. What are you doing tomorrow?"

"Who knows?" Paola said, giving him the benefit of a faint smile. Her mind was racing. A prince? Her mother couldn't fail to be impressed. There was one snag—they had to be back in school before dawn. She would just have to find a way around it. Prince Georg. How divine.

*   *   *

She spent the rest of the evening on the dance floor, happily having shaken off Dave, the rich-but-boring American, but sadly failing to find herself in the arms of her prince, as she now thought of him. The club was packed to the rafters with beautiful men and women dancing wildly, shouting at one another and at the barmen, rubbing tanned, naked shoulders together and throwing back their heads to reveal perfect teeth, hair and smiles. Sophie, Martlne and Véroniquc had managed to find her and were watching in open-mouthed admiration as Paola *actually stood up on* one of the glass tables, kicked off her shoes and gyrated her hips to the cheers of the crowd at her feet. It was almost dawn before the four of them, only semi-conscious, crawled into the back of the taxi that had been waiting since midnight and sped back along *Lac Genève* towards the school where, thank God, their absence hadn't been noticed.

News of her exploits whipped around the school at breakfast the following morning and by lunchtime, she was a bona fide celebrity in the school of 200-odd girls, most of whom could only dream of being as daring as Paola Rossi. From then on, it was easy to find girls to cover for her and the following Saturday, she was able to leave Brilliantmont in the legitimate company of Jenna de Rosnay, a senior at the school, for a weekend exeat to stay with Jenna's aunt, the Comtesse d'Harcourt at the family château just outside Geneva. By lucky coincidence, Jenna was distantly related on some third cousin's side to Prince Georg's family. Her aunt claimed they had spent summers in France together as children although Jenna confessed she could hardly remember him. Their weekend stay in Geneva included a trip to the penthouse suite at the elegantly old-fashioned Hotel Leconte where, true to his word, Dave the American, his equally boring teenage sister Catriona, Prince Georg of Hollhein and Thüringen, a quiet Frenchman named Philippe, two Danish models and two rather surly Germans, Günther and Fabian, were staying. Paola and Jenna spent a very pleasant afternoon with the group, drinking champagne and peach juice and picking delicately at trays of canapés that arrived every ten minutes throughout their visit. Paola was in seventh heaven.

"A prince?" Francesca was, as Paola had predicated, suitably impressed. "What sort of prince?" Italy was famed for its plethora of principalities whose heirs had titles and sometimes precious little else.

    "I don't know . . . he's German . . . I can't remember the name of his castle. He's ever so old-fashioned but he's lovely, Mama . . . he lives in a hotel in Geneva, the one we went to—I told you about it—and he's invited us, me and Jenna, to stay with him at Christmas, in Austria. Jenna's aunt already said she can go. Please say I can go . . . *please*?"

    "Well, I . . . I'll have to think about it, *carissima*, I'll talk to Max . . ."

"*Promise* me you'll persuade him, Mama. I'll die if I don't go!"

"Yes, yes . . . of course I'll talk to him. Don't be so dramatic. I'll call you back on Monday, all right?" Francesca put down the phone and sighed. Paola was most definitely not in Max's good books. A fortnight spent in the company of a minor German prince might not be *quite* the right thing to restore her to her father's good wishes. And she was still only sixteen.

Paola planned each and every outfit of each and every day with single-minded, military precision. By the time the Christmas holidays arrived, she was ready. She had spent a small fortune ensuring there would be no conceivable occasion at which her wardrobe might let her down. On the morning she was due to leave for Vienna airport from where they would be picked up by Prince Georg's private plane, she stood in the hallway adjusting the angle of her suede, fur-trimmed hat, and making sure there were no imperfections in the outfit she'd chosen to travel in. A black suede jacket, belted at the waist, a black cashmere polo-necked sweater, just visible under the wide, fashionably stitch-edged lapels, dark-grey woollen trousers and smart, patent leather knee-high boots. With her hat and matching dark brown suede bag, she looked every inch the beautiful, chic heiress. She was particularly comforted by the thought that Jenna, while perfectly presentable—even pleasant-looking—was no match whatsoever for her doe-eyed, sensual beauty. She applied lipstick, a few dabs of powder and then turned to Francesca for the final stamp of approval.

"*Belissima!*" Francesca cried, overcome with pride at the sight of her beautiful little girl looking so smart and sophisticated. She hugged her one last time before allowing her driver to pick up the three suitcases, two hat boxes and two make-up cases—all Vuitton—into which Paola had crammed a fortnight's worth of clothes.

Ten minutes later, sitting comfortably in the back of the silver Jaguar, Paola quickly ran through the inventory of her bags in her head. Skiwear—four different jackets, six pairs of ski pants, two different pairs of boots; an assortment of cashmere sweaters and matching scarves; eight long evening dresses in silk, satin and fine knitwear; four pairs of jeans in fashionably dark denim; a selection of crisp, white shirts and beautifully detailed belts; jewelry, hats, boots, shoes . . . silk and cotton pajamas and her fluffy angora-trim dressing gown . . . more make-up than she could possibly use in twelve days and enough skin cream to last a month. Everything was lying between layers of tissue paper and scented petals. It did look rather a lot to be taking on a two-week holiday but . . . she would be in the company of royalty—and two models—and she ought to dress accordingly.

She and Jenna met at Vienna airport. "*Merde,*" Jenna exclaimed when she saw Paola's cases. "We're only going for two weeks!"

"I know," Paola said defensively, "but I didn't know what to take. So I took everything."

A sleek black Range Rover was waiting for them at the little airport in Innsbruck. Within minutes, they were winding their way through the spectacular Alpine landscape towards the Arlberg where Prince Georg's family home of Hochüli lay. They read the signs pointing to Untergürgl, Obergürgl and Hochgürgl, laughing over the tongue-twisting Austrian dialect. The drive took about an hour and then they were pulling up at the gates of what looked to them both like a fairytale castle, complete with turrets, fluttering flags and enormous, iron-studded oak doors. Paola, for once, was lost for words. Three footmen walked out to meet the car and silently and quickly disposed of their bags. A plump, smiling, matronly woman welcomed them on behalf of his Royal Highness and ushered them through the castle walls and into an inner courtyard. Surrounded by snow-covered pine trees, with the princely flag fluttering from one of the castle's four main turrets, the place was magical.

Paola and Jenna had been given adjoining rooms in the eastern wing, next to the two Danish young ladies and Catriona, the young American, the woman told them as they trotted after her. She led them down one long, portrait-adorned corridor after another until at last she stopped outside a set of doors. She opened them to reveal a suite of two bedrooms, a shared living room and a bathroom that was the size of a modest Roman apartment in itself. Each bedroom was lavishly and tastefully decorated and included a four-poster bed, an entire wall of dark, gleaming wardrobes and an elegant little writing table situated in front of a window with the most magnificent view over the Alps. Paola lay against the plump, down pillows on the big, four-poster bed and watched as two young maids entered, carrying their cases and requesting permission to unpack. She nodded silently, stifling a giggle as she and Jenna looked at each other. The maids opened the cases reverently, gently laying out their gowns and outfits and hung everything neatly on silk-covered hangers, carefully smoothing out the tissue paper for reuse at the end of their stay. When they had finished, they respectfully informed the two young ladies that dinner would be served at eight, in the dining hall at the end of the southern wing. The Prince and his companions had left to go skiing that morning in Lech and would be back shortly.

"Ohmigod, it's *magnificent*!" Paola shouted to Jenna as the maids left the room, lying back on the pillows and tossing her cashmere cape across the room. Jenna had gone into her own room. Paola looked around her. The castle, despite its vast size, still managed to be warm and intimate. Her room was big, but not overwhelmingly so—the ornate cream-colored plasterwork of the ceiling and deep red walls combined to make the room cozy and rich, not cold. The furniture was exceedingly elegant—dark mahogany dressers with polished brass handles, the plump four-poster bed with its Irish linen sheets and wonderfully delicate, paisley-patterned silk counterpane; burgundy drapes around the bed which matched the deep red of the walls. Portraits of what she assumed were royal relations adorned the walls, tastefully framed in dark, almost black wood. In one of the window reveals, a set of cushions had been fixed to form a comfortable, padded seat. She got up and walked over, sat down in the little bay window and looked outside. Everything was white, a delicate, frozen landscape of pine trees, undulating white lawns and frozen streams leading down the valley in which the castle nestled. On the far side of the valley, the mountains rose again, craggy, snow-covered sheets of rock, silhouetted elegantly against the brilliant blue, winter sky. She shivered with pleasure. It was six o'clock. She crossed the room and opened Jenna's door. Two hours to go until dinnertime. It would take them almost that long to decide what to wear. Time to get down to business.

Paola was besotted. Not just with Prince Georg, but with the whole, wonderfully decadent, indolent crowd. She loved all of them—the models Kina and Holly, Jenna . . . Philippe, Günther and Jürgen . . . even Dave and his sister Catriona weren't so bad. Most of all, she loved Prince Georg. He was a quiet, rather formal young man—she'd found out he was twenty-six, ten years her senior. This time there wasn't any point in lying about her age—since her exploits at the beginning of the summer, everyone knew she had only just turned sixteen but, as she pointed out, a century ago, she'd have been married off at fourteen and produced two children by her sixteenth birthday "so please stop teasing me about it!" Everyone grinned. Technically she was the youngest member of the group but . . . as the men said to each other, she looked like she'd teach *them* a thing or two. Those legs . . .

She spent her days flying down the slopes, listening to the cold wind rush past her ears, her heart thudding with the excitement and fear of hurtling down the mountainside with only the slim, black-clad figure of Prince Georg in front of her. She would slice to a halt minutes after him, her hair falling around her face and watch his eyes light up in appreciation, both of her sporting abilities and her looks. Jenna and Catriona couldn't keep up with her—they cried after watching Paola and the Prince swoop past them on the first day. The two models, Holly and Kina, were too terrified of falling to even risk putting on skis. But whatever they lacked in terms of courage off the slopes, they more than made up for in their willingness to do and try *anything* off the slopes. Paola, who had seen her fair share of drugs growing up in Rome and summering on Menorca, was astounded. Joints, lines, pills, poppers, pipes . . . they'd arrived with a veritable apothecary in their cases. Every evening, after half a dozen bottles of the finest wines, the real party would begin. Holly—not, Paola suspected, her real name—an impossibly thin, icily beautiful blonde from some small town near Copenhagen, would line up the evening's selection. There would be a short discussion as to the order of inhalation, which to try first and so on, and then silence for fifteen minutes as the party made short work of the selection in front of them. On the first evening, Paola was dumbstruck. Of course she'd tried a little pot, downed her fair share of alcohol and even once swallowed something that one of the girls at school had smuggled into a party—nothing much happened; her head felt woozy for a while and she'd woken up the following morning with the most spectacular hangover . . . but other than that, she'd pretty much stuck to cigarettes and the occasional joint. Looking around her at the group sprawled out on the oriental rugs in one of the half-dozen drawing rooms on the ground floor, it was clear that she was now in *very* different company. Getting high—seriously high—was a must. She held out her hand for the little white tablet that someone offered her and, taking a sip of champagne, swallowed.

Half an hour later, she was laughing harder than she'd ever laughed before. Everything everyone said set her off. She sparkled, throwing back her head, tossing her hair wildly from side to side . . . she slid off her seat and somehow wound up half-sprawled across the floor, one hand on Holly's thigh as she listened to Dave recount the *funniest* story . . . something about a bear, a dog and a model . . . it was so funny, she couldn't stop giggling. She was vaguely aware of Jenna frowning at her, but that in itself was so funny . . . she began to giggle again.

The days flew past. Best of all were the evenings, when she and Jenna spent hours in front of the mirror getting ready for dinner; trying on different outfits, putting their hair in rollers then pinning it up or letting it cascade down their backs—they were very different from the blonde, sleek beauty of Holly and Kina but they were so much more *fun*. Dave turned to Prince Georg and Philippe as if in confirmation. They nodded enthusiastically.

On their second to last evening, Paola wore her long black silk dress with the wide, flared sleeves and open back. Her hair was up, piled loosely on top of her head and fastened with a black velvet rose. She borrowed Jenna's black suede high-heeled boots and sheer stockings.

"Bravo!" shouted Dave, clapping from one end of the long table as she and Jenna were shown in. A cigarette hung from his lips as he appraised them. Prince Georg handed her a glass of champagne, his fingers touching Paola's, immediately sending a little charge of electricity running through her.

"Where are Holly and Kina?" Jenna asked, looking around. Neither they nor Catriona had come down yet.

"Oh, they decided to skip dinner," Prince Georg said quickly. "They're tired." There was an odd atmosphere at the table—Dave was already quite drunk; Günther and Jürgen seemed edgy, tense.

Only Prince Georg and Philippe seemed normal: aloof and slightly stoned, as always. Prince Georg clapped his hands, once. The door opened immediately and the maids began serving dinner—paper-thin slices of veal, cooked in a rich, wine sauce; tiny, buttery potatoes; freshly picked snow-peas and lightly sautéed mange-tout . . . the food, as always, was superb. Neither Paola nor Jenna ate much. They picked daintily at the veal, a spoonful of peas here, a mouthful of potato there . . . Prince Georg kept filling and refilling their glasses, smiling widely.

About an hour later, Paola realized she was a lot more drunk than she'd thought. She was having trouble concentrating on what Dave, sitting to her left, was saying. Philippe, sitting on Jenna's right, was leaning over her, saying something. Suddenly, the lights in the room dimmed, then went back on. She looked up in surprise, but no one else seemed to notice. She felt Dave's hand on her thigh, sliding slowly up her leg, but she couldn't focus properly . . . she wanted to tell him to stop, to take his hand away but she found she couldn't open her eyes, or move her hand. Somewhere in the distance, she heard someone shouting. There was the sound of a chair being scraped back, hard . . . then a door slamming. Someone began to laugh. She felt someone's hand steal round her shoulders . . . and then Prince Georg's voice, saying something to her, softly, in her ear. She relaxed. It must be *his* hand, she thought to herself as the lights plunged and dimmed again—it must be him running his hand up and down my arm, across my neck, pulling at the dress. There was the sensation of air hitting her bare flesh . . . where were the others? she thought to herself as she began to slide into a thick, befuddled sleep. Were they still in the dining room? What had happened to everyone else? To Jenna and Philippe and Dave . . . and Gün . . . Günth . . . ? There were hands all over her, too many hands . . . her last conscious thought was of someone covering her mouth with his hand while her dress was peeled roughly from her body. Then she remembered nothing. Nothing at all.

She woke slowly, in waves, opening her eyes, struggling to focus then sinking again. She was in bed, buried under the eiderdown, her head lolling against the feather pillows. She tried to sit up. Her head felt heavy, wobbly . . . she felt sick. She lay against the pillows for a few minutes, opening and closing her eyes, still drifting in and out of sleep. A few minutes passed. The swaying, woozy feeling in her head slowly began to subside. She was able to open her eyes and look around. The curtains had been pulled back; someone had put fresh flowers in the room; her clothes were folded neatly on the chair by the window. She looked down at herself. She was wearing a silk nightdress—not her own. She frowned. She must have passed out at dinner . . . too much wine? She didn't remember drinking that much. She slowly swung her legs out of bed, walked unsteadily to the dressing table and sat down heavily. She stared at her face in the mirror. She *looked* the same . . . her make-up was smudged and there were circles under her eyes but she looked all right. So what was the niggling, dark sense of foreboding? She shivered suddenly. Something wasn't right . . . she couldn't put her finger on it, but there was something wrong. Something had happened. She frowned with the concentration of trying to remember. Had something happened to her? Whose nightgown was she wearing and why couldn't she remember coming to bed? She pulled the nightdress off over her head. And then she saw it. Just above her left nipple, clearly visible against the pale, mushroom-colored skin. A bite mark. The teeth marks were startlingly visible. Someone had bitten her . . . hard. She stared at herself, too afraid to even touch it. She swallowed. She had no idea who it could have been, or when it could have happened. It couldn't have been anyone at dinner . . . of course not, that was ridiculous. So how had it happened? She sat in the still, grey light, her mind racing, struggling to remember something, *any*thing. She couldn't. Everything was horribly blank.

PART THREE

≋30≋
New York, USA
1986

The three men shook hands. Outside, the rain beat relentlessly against the window. From the eighty-eighth floor, the streets below them were completely shrouded by the cloud and fog. Max picked up his coat and briefcase and smiled briefly at the two men before walking ahead to the lift. He still had a few calls to make. Negotiations on this latest deal were almost at closing stage and as usual, Max was the figure who had brought the two parties together. An unlikely alliance: Walter Sprague, the Brooklyn realtor, and Morgan Covic, the City Planning Commissioner. Sprague had been working on the acquisition of a semi-derelict building on 55th and 5th Avenue in midtown Manhattan for over two years. It was a complicated sale with obstacles at almost every corner—planning permission wouldn't be easy; the underlying land wasn't for sale; the land lease would run out in thirty years' time—the list was endless. Sprague wasn't a man to give up easily, however, and had doggedly pushed his way through until the final set of negotiations between the owners of the building and the owners of the land on which the current building sat—and the deal stalled. It looked in danger of falling apart. Sprague had invested almost everything he had in putting together the financing for the project: if it succeeded, it would make everything he had done to date pale beside this, which he knew would be the finest residential skyscraper in the world. Everything was in place and the pressure to pull it off was beginning to mount. Sprague was a desperate man by the time he contacted Max Sall. Everything centered around the sale of the land—and the owner, an elderly New York billionaire by the name of Frank Carradine, wasn't playing ball.

Max had taken the call in his study in Menorca, looking out across the lavender hills towards the shimmering skin of the sea. He told Sprague he would see what he could do and agreed to call him back in a few days. He put the phone down, frowning. Frank Carradine. Something was stirring at the back of his mind. He knew the name—he could put a face to it, but there was something more . . . he turned back to the view of the sea, deep in thought. Fifteen minutes later, he had it. He picked up the phone again and began to dial.

*　　*　　*

The doorman at Max's Manhattan apartment was smiling broadly as Max stepped out of the car.

"Afternoon, Mr. Sall," he said, holding the umbrella over his head. Max nodded his thanks. "Uh, this just came for you, sir," he continued, holding out a white envelope. Max took it and walked inside. He opened it on the way up in the lift. Two front-row tickets to see the New York Knicks play at Madison Square Garden that evening. The compliments slip was signed simply "with thanks, Walter," Max smiled. The tickets were a nice gesture. Of course, Sprague couldn't know he hated basketball. Then it occurred to him—Amber and her boyfriend Henry were staying with him for a few days . . . perhaps they might like to go? He slid the tickets into his breast pocket and opened the front door.

The spacious apartment was empty. Amber and her ridiculously tall and confident boyfriend, Henry, had arrived a few days previously after both graduating from university with first-class honors. Despite his initial reluctance, Max was proud of her—the only one of his three children to hold a degree. Max wasn't a man given to introspection but he did sometimes wonder if his ambivalence towards higher education was a result of his having been deprived of one. He walked into the sitting room, loosening his tie and poured himself a drink. He sat down in one of the leather seats and turned on the stereo. It was unusual for him to have an afternoon at home like this—he had intended to come home, pick up the phone and spend the afternoon catching up on business but the deal he had just struck, for some reason, had put him in a pensive mood. He leaned back and let the strains of Schubert's *Piano Quintet in A* wash over him. He was pleased with the morning's meeting. Amber had asked him, not so long ago, what the secret to his success was . . . he'd smiled vaguely and shrugged. Contacts, friend, acquaintances . . . he'd murmured something along those lines. He took a sip of his whisky. It was true. Take the deal he'd just helped make happen. On the face of it, an impasse. Walter Sprague, a self-made man from Ohio trying to strike a deal with Frank Carradine, the reclusive New York billionaire. Carradine didn't need the money, he didn't need the sale and he certainly didn't need some aggressive little *putsch* from Toledo, Ohio threatening him with lawsuits and the like. But Max had remembered something. Frank Carradine wasn't the name he'd always gone by—Max knew him as Fausi Carrady, an Iraqi Jew from Baghdad who had arrived, near-penniless, in London in the 1950s, trying to get to New York. Back then, Carrady was a hustler, a man specializing in barter, the oldest form of trade. In the years immediately following the war, there were many countries who either had no hard currencies of their own, or faced politically motivated trade embargoes. Either way, bartering was the only means of procuring essential or important foreign goods. Wood might be exchanged for a shipment of sardines which might be exchanged for metal, or a consignment of books. Carrady was a natural barterer but he lacked the contacts to ensure the circle of sale did not collapse. He met Max Sall, briefly, through a mutual friend in 1956. Max helped put together the connections that made Carrady his first real money—money that he used to set himself up in Brooklyn. A shipment of pistachio nuts from Iraq was successfully bartered for a shipment of egg yolks that had arrived from Shanghai and several hundred bolts of raw silk. Max helped get the egg yolks to a cake manufacturer in the Midlands and the silk to Debenhams. Carrady was a little put out at the terms Max proposed—but his hands were tied. He was grateful. And, as Max found out almost forty years later, he had never forgotten it. *That*, he found himself wanting to say to his daughter, was how it was done.

≈31≈

Walking along 5th Avenue with a sullen Henry at her side, Amber was silent, anxiously wondering if she'd done the right thing. They'd been in New York a total of four days—long enough for Amber to decide she wanted to stay, and that she wanted to stay without him. She'd tried to bring the subject up at breakfast in the corner deli that morning . . . but it was clear Henry didn't approve.

"What?" he'd spluttered, staring at her in disbelief. "Here? Stay in New York?"

"Yes. Why not?" Amber said, her heart sinking.

"But . . . you've never . . . why didn't you say? I

mean, what'm I going to do? Why can't you get a job
in London? You never said you wanted to stay . . ."
his voice trailed off miserably. Several customers
around them looked up.

"I only just thought about it," she said, sounding
unconvincing even to her own ears. Henry looked
away. "And anyway, it'll only be for a while. For the
summer, maybe."

"Oh, yeah? And who's going to arrange that?
Daddy?"

"It's not like that," Amber shot back immediately.
She could feel her cheeks burning. Henry knew how
to hit a nerve. Until she'd left home at eighteen, Amber hadn't realized just how long Max's shadow really was—nor how trapped she was within it. She'd
spent the first few months at university trying to convince those around her that she wasn't the stuck-up
heiress everyone assumed she would be. She'd
failed. No matter how hard she tried, the specter of
Max's millions, as Henry called them, haunted her.
No one could—or would—believe she was just like
any other student, worrying about money, finding a
flat to live in, agonizing over this man or that . . . the
fact that her sister was always in *Hello!* magazine
on the arm of one unsuitable rich young man after
another; the fact that her father had bought her a
trendy Clerkenwell flat in her second year and the
fact that she'd snagged Henry Fletcher, whom most
girls at school would have given their back teeth to
speak to . . . it all seemed to add up to an image of
her that was so far from the truth, she wanted to
scream at them—*I'm not stuck up; I wasn't born*

*with a silver spoon in my mouth and I'm just as in-
secure and lonely sometimes as the rest of you!*—
but her pride somehow held her back. The famous
Sall reserve. Max hated weakness—and Amber, of
course, had always been strong.

After those first rather painful few months, she
leaned to ignore the catty remarks when Max or
Paola appeared in the media and managed to put
on a brave face when those who had become firm
friends in her classes sat outside the Union bar at
the end of the year planning summer trips to far-
flung places to which she certainly wasn't invited. It
hurt at first—she would have loved to go backpacking around Thailand or South America or wherever
it was Sophie Ellerton and Mandy Bosworth were
planning to go. But she had Henry. Several times
during the three years she was at UCL she wondered to herself if she *hadn't* had Henry . . . would it
have been different? Would she have made more of
an effort? Madeleine was always telling her how formidable her exterior was—the way she carried her
chin just a fraction higher than everyone else; the
slight frown that always seemed to be hovering between her eyes; and that icy, piercing blue—but
Amber always shook her head. Madeleine said it
had taken her ages to pluck up the courage to
speak to her, and even then it was Becky she'd first
approached. *"Soften up, Sall"* was her favorite expression. But Amber just didn't know how.

"So tell me . . . what's *Daddy* going to do for you
this time?" Henry demanded again, dragging her
back to the present.

"Max has nothing to do with this!" Amber was suddenly close to tears. "I'm perfectly capable of getting a job myself, you know. I'm going to apply for an internship. It'll just be for the summer and then I'll be back in London and we can . . . carry on."

"Yeah, right. Of course. Carry on. And what the hell am I supposed to do in the meantime?" Henry's tone was bitter. His face was turned away from hers. She recognized the obstinate set to his mouth. She sighed. It was hard trying to please everyone. She wanted desperately to show Max the three horrible years at UCL had amounted to something, that it hadn't been a waste of time. Sure, she'd come back with a first-class degree but, as Max pointed out, that was to be expected. He hadn't said it in so many words but the implication was there—the Sall brains were responsible for that, not Amber. He'd never once asked her what university was like, whether she'd enjoyed it, or what she planned to do next. Somehow her achievement had wound up being his. She'd left the dining room in tears.

"Look, it's only for the summer." She tried to smile placatingly at Henry. She was torn. A couple of evenings earlier, she and Henry had been lying sprawled out on the plush carpet in the sitting room watching television when Max came home unexpectedly. He'd joined them, even poured them both a glass of brandy and settled himself in the couch opposite. He was going to be on television, he told them, loosening his tie. Some interview with a journalist—he didn't know why he bothered to do things like that any more. Amber caught Henry's admiring glance. She knew, despite his sarcastic comments, that Henry positively worshipped Max—Max was the kind of father Henry desperately wished for. When the three of them turned to face the television, she saw the pride and longing in Henry's face. It ought to have pleased her. It didn't. It was Henry who whistled approvingly at Max's face and commented on his tie, his suit, the way he handled the journalist—a pretty but earnest-faced young woman. Amber lay beside him in silence. After Henry's adulation, anything *she* said would have sounded false, or worse, silly. Max said nothing, just sipped his brandy slowly, concentrating on the screen. When it was over—half an hour of such intense dialogue it made Amber squirm in embarrassment, not for Max, of course, but for the poor young woman—she waited, half-fearful of what he would say when his face faded from the screen. He had completely dominated the interview, turning the questions he didn't like back on her, making the journalist stumble over her words and lose the thread of the conversation.

"She was crap," Henry pronounced confidently, propping himself up on one elbow to look at Max. Amber nodded. But Max surprised her.

"No . . . I liked her," Max said mildly. Amber and Henry stared at him. "She was good. She knew her stuff. Pretty, too." Henry nodded uncertainly. He wanted to agree with Max, of course, but he'd given her such a grilling . . . she'd looked close to tears at one point. "Don't often get that in a woman," Max said, getting up from the couch.

"What?" Henry couldn't keep the disappointment

out of his voice. He'd obviously been relishing the thought of Max's company all evening.

"Looks *and* brains. It's usually one or the other." And with that, Max left the room.

"He is just . . . so . . . cool," Henry whispered, reaching out for Amber's hand and pulling her closer to him. She was silent. She couldn't tell him what had suddenly been revealed to her; what Max's comment had brought about in her. Release. It was nothing—a throwaway, tossed-out little phrase—but everything suddenly became clear. She knew at that moment exactly what she wanted to do, what she wanted to be. Diana Morton or whatever-her-name-was had suddenly shown her the way. She *could* do it all— worry about her looks and her figure and clothes like every other girl on the planet, especially with some-one like Paola in the picture—*and* use her brain with-out fear of turning men like Max and Henry off, away from her. It was something to be admired: to be pretty *and* clever . . . Max had said so. *He* admired it. He liked Diana Morton. She wanted him to like her, too.

"Promise me it'll only be for the summer," Henry's sulky voice broke in on her thoughts again. She nodded quickly, relieved he'd begun to come round. She wasn't sure she could handle another long, drawn-out argument.

"I promise."

"And you'll phone me every day?"

She nodded again. "Every day." The thought sud-denly filled her with dread.

≈32≈

While everyone else was celebrating the end of their degrees, the third-year students at Edinburgh had only just started their clinical rotations. At the precise moment Henry and Amber were arguing in a Manhattan deli, Madeleine was coming to the end of an eighteen-hour shift.

"Here," Dr. Semple, the consultant pediatrician, took the needle from Madeleine's shaking hand. "Allow me. Do pay attention," he said in a voice that indicated impatience and a bored acceptance of the incompetence of the medical students who were sent his way. He held the infant's tiny wrist, deftly felt for the cushion of flesh just below the elbow and before Madeleine could blink, had inserted the tiny needle, taped the drip mechanism and soothed the squealing child. He turned to her. "That's how it's done, Ms. Szabo, quickly, quietly and with the minimum of fuss. Saves your own nerves, and those of the child, no doubt." His voice rang out around the ward. Several of the nurses looked away, stifling their giggles. Madeleine looked at him, her cheeks reddening. She'd been trying to insert the needle into the infant's arm for almost fifteen minutes, without success. The truth was she was so tired she could barely see what she was doing. She'd been on ER duty for almost twenty-four hours straight, with only a brief, thirty-minute nap in the junior doctor's common room at three that morning. It was now nearly five the following afternoon and she simply couldn't keep her eyes open. Dr. Semple looked at her. "Take a short nap, Ms. Szabo. Fifteen minutes should do the trick. Call me if anything *else* goes wrong." He nodded curtly at her and disappeared. Madeleine held the infant in her arms and smiled sheepishly at the ward nurses.

"Here, I'll take him," one of the nurses said, holding out her arms for the baby. "You go on . . . there's a foldout bed in the staffroom at the end of the corridor. Go on. I'll wake you in thirty minutes." Madeleine looked at her gratefully. Her whole body felt heavy and stiff, her movements leaden. The desire for sleep was so strong . . . she stumbled off down the corridor, her brain already beginning to shut down before she'd opened the door.

A second later, she woke with a start. The nurse was standing in front of her. She scrambled to her feet.

"A new case has just come in," the nurse said apologetically. "I let you sleep for as long as I could. Gastroenteritis—he's nine years old. I've sent for the junior houseman."

"How . . . how long have I been asleep?" Madeleine asked, as she smoothed down her coat.

"Nearly an hour," the nurse said, following her out of the door. "The baby's doing fine. Matron's on ward rounds at the moment, otherwise I'd have let you sleep longer."

"An hour?" Madeleine stared at her.

"Feels like seconds, doesn't it?" the nurse agreed, smiling in sympathy. "You'll get used to it, don't worry." Madeleine said nothing as the two of them swept down the corridor. Used to it? She didn't think so.

Six hours later, almost dead on her feet, she pulled her handbag from her locker and walked in a daze towards the elevators. She had twelve hours off. She knew exactly how she would spend them. Asleep. She pressed the button for the ground floor impatiently.

"Bye, Madeleine," one of the nurses called out to her as the lift finally arrived. "Straight to bed. Get some sleep!" Madeleine smiled faintly. She didn't even have the energy to raise her hand. She walked into the lift and was almost asleep by the time they hit the ground floor.

≈33≈

Becky scoured through the newspapers for the third time that morning. She lay on the sitting-room floor in her parents' house looking increasingly glum.

"Cup of tea, dear?" her mother called from the dining room. "Are you hungry?" Becky shook her head.

"No, I'm okay, thanks. Just looking through the paper."

"You'll find something soon, darling." Susan

Aldridge came through the doorway. "And there's no rush, you know."

"I *know*, Mum. But I don't want to spend the next six months back in my old room as though nothing's changed." Becky's voice was sharp. She'd been back at home for almost a month and convenient as it was, after three years away, it was a *little* hard to adjust.

"Of course not, darling," her mother said automatically. "I'm only saying . . . you stay here as long as you like. We love having you back home." Becky said nothing. "What would you like for supper?" her mother went on, undaunted by Becky's silence.

"I don't know . . . I can't think about supper now. It's only eleven o'clock!"

"Well, I'm just popping out to the shops and if there's anything you'd fancy—"

"Mum! Please! I'm trying to find a job. I don't *care* what we have for supper," Becky said through gritted teeth.

"All right, all right. Well, I'll be off, then, darling. I'll see you in a little while." Becky nodded, turning back to the paper. Phew. An hour or two on her own. Bliss. She picked up her pen.

Half an hour later, the house quiet and empty, she admitted defeat. She shoved the paper aside and got up. There just weren't many jobs being advertised for a recent fine art graduate—with a Third Class degree, to boot. The latter was a sore point. After three years at one of the country's most radical art colleges, she'd realized she was neither talented nor "clever" enough to take part in the emerging conceptual art scene. She was a competent illustrative artist, someone who would probably wind up doing greetings cards, she'd overheard someone say once, cruelly. At the time, she thought she would never recover from the slight, but now, she no longer cared. If art was all about shocking people into staring, repulsed, at images of dead bodies and the mangled remains of birds—as the third-year student who'd won the coveted Gordon Manning Prize last year had done well, good luck to them. Being an artist, she'd quickly discovered, wasn't about being able to *draw*, as she'd assumed. It was about being able to think—nothing to do with talent or technique. If she'd wanted to learn how to think, she'd once explained to Amber in exasperation, she'd have joined the philosophy department. She wanted to *draw* and *paint*, to be an *artist* . . . but no one else seemed to share her view. Who cared? She stopped, embarrassed at her own thoughts. Who was she kidding? She *always* cared what other people thought.

She looked at her watch. It was almost noon. She was bored. There wasn't even the distraction of Amber just across the road. She'd hardly seen Amber all year—she was always off with Henry, doing something exciting and fun. Like now. The two of them were in New York. She rolled over onto her back, staring at the ceiling. It was funny. In the beginning, when Madeleine joined them, it had been fine. Madeleine was clever in the way Amber was clever . . . quick, witty, hard-working. Becky wasn't, but it didn't seem to matter back then. She had art.

She'd been born with a talent with which no amount of hard work could compete, and that had been enough. She was the one they both envied. But then, just before their A-levels, things had started to go downhill. She wasn't studious, like the two of them, and exams terrified her. She'd very nearly blown her chances of going to university because she was so afraid of taking them. And she, who was always teasing Amber about getting Max to pull strings for her—not that she ever did—*she'd* had to ask Daddy to pull them for *her*. Without him, she wouldn't have got into art school in the first place. Fat lot of good it had done her. Here she was, barely a graduate, unemployed and with no signs of imminent success. Jesus. She sat up. She might as well go over to Dan's. It was a bit of an effort, getting from Holland Park to Finsbury Park where he shared a squalid squat with three other students . . . no longer, she reminded herself. They were all graduates now. But her mother had been so alarmed at the sight of the tattooed and much-pierced Dan the first time Becky had brought him home that she really didn't feel like going through it again. But why his *tongue*, darling? Whatever for? She could hardly tell her mother it made sex that bit more exciting. Her mother probably thought she was still . . . untouched.

Later that evening, sitting astride Dan and watching his face contort itself into the familiar mask of pleasure and pain, she was surprised to find herself thinking about Amber again. She supposed it must be to do with being at home again. In the three years since they'd left school, she and Amber had slowly but inexorably drifted apart. If she were honest— and, sliding off Dan's sweaty body and into the tangle of sheets beside him, she told herself sternly she really ought to be—in their first year, she'd been rather jealous of Amber and Madeleine. They both seemed to find their places easily. Amber had started going out with Henry almost immediately and Madeleine was so absorbed in her classes she'd practically ceased to exist. That first Christmas when they'd all returned home for the first time, it had been just the teeniest bit strained. Henry, whom Becky privately found rather intimidating and Madeleine confessed she found boring, absolutely dominated everything—Amber, the Christmas party, the conversations . . . he wouldn't leave Amber alone, not even for a second. He even insisted on coming shopping with them, *to the sales!* Becky had thought it wise not to invite Clifford, the man she'd mistaken for a tutor and slept with in the first week of term only to find out he was an unemployed graduate from about three years' previously who hung around the first-year students pretending to be one of the faculty. He quite liked Becky, he told her several times during the course of the first term. He "quite liked" lots of the new first-year students, she later found out, but by that stage, she was really quite low on confidence and at least he paid her *some* attention. But the holidays, despite everyone's best intentions, hadn't been the unbridled success they'd all hoped for.

And that had been the beginning of the slide. She still thought of them as her best friends—her art school friends complained about it all the time—but deep down, she knew the situation was actually rather different. This summer, when she and Amber could have rekindled their earlier closeness, especially with Madeleine still in Edinburgh, Amber immediately announced she was off to the States, with Henry. So that was that. Becky was left to contemplate the next moves in her life on her own. She slid out of the bed and picked her way across the clothes, records, books and debris that Dan seemed to think were necessary to establish ownership in the squat of six friends, and walked into the bathroom. Outside, the traffic rumbled by on the Seven Sisters Road. The grey, muggy and dirty interior of the house matched the grey, muggy and dirty environment outside. Ugh. She sniffed cautiously at a used washcloth and immediately put it down; no telling *what* it had recently been used to wipe.

≈34≈

Henry walked down Madison Avenue without really noticing the luxury goods on provocative display in the windows of almost every shop he passed. He wasn't really looking. He wasn't even really thinking. Bits of his conversations with Amber over the past few days drifted in and out of focus. *It'll only be for a few weeks . . . you'll find lots of things to do in London . . . it'll be good for you, me, us . . .* the phrases kept on tumbling out. He didn't know what to do, think or feel. As much as he tried not to show it, a real sense of panic had swept over him as soon as she announced she wanted to stay without him. *You can't*, he'd wanted to shout at her. You can't leave me. But they were in a restaurant, which she'd probably planned, and short of making the most monumental scene, there was little he could do. They'd walked along 5th Avenue afterwards but to his distress, he hadn't been able to say much. That was the thing with Amber—once she set her mind on doing something, nothing could stand in her way. She was the most determined person he'd ever met. It was why he loved her. She was strong and she made him strong.

He paused outside a jeweler's. He was overreacting, he knew it but couldn't help it . . . something flashed and caught his eye. Right in front of him, sitting in splendid isolation on its cushion of black velvet was the most spectacular solitaire diamond—a single, fiery stone on a platinum band. He gazed at it, his mind racing. She would laugh at him, at it . . . it was such a ridiculous statement to make . . . he pushed open the door and walked in. Within seconds, an exceedingly pretty and well-dressed young woman had materialized at his side. Oh, yes . . . the engagement ring in the window. A beauty. A De Kooningen diamond. She casually mentioned the price. Henry almost fainted: $22,000.00. He thanked her and hurried out. But the thought kept whirling around in his head. It would show Amber just how serious he was. That he wasn't to be trifled with. That after three years, he *knew*. He quickly consulted his guidebook. He needed to find something more appropriately priced. He headed downtown, towards the Village.

Almost two hours later, he'd found exactly what he was looking for. A small, elegant ring of white gold with a single, smallish square-cut diamond. He handed over his card and tried not to think about the overdraft he would incur as the sales assistant rang up $875.99 and began the gift-wrapping of his purchase. Ten minutes later, the box firmly inside his pocket, he made his way back to the Upper East Side to Max's apartment where he hoped Amber would be waiting. He was due to fly back to England a couple of days later. He would take Amber out to dinner that evening and surprise her. And then he would fly back to England alone, safe in the knowledge that she really and truly did belong to him, whatever plans she'd made for the summer.

Amber saw it coming. She knew as soon as Henry cleared his throat in the restaurant—which he'd insisted on choosing—and said he had something important to say to her. Her heart sank. He pushed the little box across the table towards her, smiling warily. She looked at it for a second, then opened it, carefully smoothing out the paper, the ribbons, the tape, as if she knew it would be repackaged. She opened the lid.

"Oh. Oh, Henry . . . you shouldn't have."

"Don't you like it?"

Amber swallowed. "It's beautiful, Henry. It's . . . lovely. But you shouldn't have—"

"I wanted to. I thought . . . I thought you'd like it." Henry's voice was almost pleading.

"I do like it. Honestly. It's beautiful. But I don't need—"

"It's got nothing to do with whether you need it or not," he broke in angrily. "I love you. I want to marry you."

"I . . . oh, shit, Henry." Amber looked around her. She suddenly felt utterly trapped. Sitting opposite her was Henry . . . the Henry she'd known since her very first day at UCL. Henry who'd been so much a part of her life for the past three years that it seemed impossible to contemplate another three years without him. "It's lovely, Henry," she said, her voice wavering slightly as she spoke. "But I can't. *We* can't. We're too young. We've got our whole lives in front of us . . ."

"And I want to spend mine with you," Henry said stubbornly. His face was flushed. He was pleading now.

"You can't say that. It's a huge decision . . . we need more time."

"Maybe *you* need more time. I don't." She looked at his face. It had closed and retreated into its familiar, stubborn shell. Amber let out a sigh. It wasn't going to end well.

"I do need more time. I'm sorry, Henry. I can't. I just can't." There was a horrible silence. Neither of them had finished eating. Then Henry pushed back his chair, opened his mouth as if to say something to her, then turned on his heel and left. He didn't take the ring. Several people around them looked at Amber as discreetly as possible, wondering what the argument had been about, looking knowingly at the little black box that lay next to her side plate.

"Is everything okay, ma'am?" a waiter hovered near by. Amber nodded. Then she signaled for the bill. There wasn't any point in sitting there alone. She paid and left, trying not to notice the sympathetic glances as she walked out into the warm evening air.

Henry didn't come back to the apartment that night. Amber lay awake almost until dawn, going over their conversation, wondering if she'd done the right thing . . . wondering if she hadn't just made the biggest mistake of her life. No, she whispered into her pillow. It had taken her a long time to realize it but Henry was definitely not the man for her. She was tired of being leaned on—she wanted to lean on someone else for a change. She didn't want to be the strong, practical, capable one; she wanted him to take the lead. But he couldn't and wouldn't. Their relationship had started off being about her family—*you're Max Sall's daughter, aren't you?*— and it had pretty much ended that way—*so what's Daddy going to do for you now?* Three years in be-

tween of Henry falling in love with her father; her
home; her glamorous—at least as *he* saw it—holidays . . . she'd been so grateful to him for his friendship and companionship at university that she
hadn't really seen their relationship for what it really
was. Henry wanted to *be* somebody . . . and he
thought that being with her would make him so.
Well, he was wrong. Being Max Sall's daughter
wasn't as easy as it looked. For Amber, being Max's
daughter was mostly about never being good
enough. She wasn't as pretty as Paola, she wasn't
a boy, like Kieran and she certainly wasn't as clever
as Max himself. Whatever she did, Max wasn't satisfied. The irony was, she'd been going out with
someone for the past three years who was his polar
opposite—far too easily satisfied. Everything Amber
did was okay with Henry, as long as it kept him in the
picture and in her life.

She turned over in bed, unable to sleep. She
wanted more out of everything. More of a challenge,
not less. Settling down now with Henry would be
like . . . she struggled for the image . . . a slow, suf-
focating sleep. Not death, nothing so dramatic. A
long, gentle snooze, punctuated only by summer
visits to *Casa Bella*, which Henry absolutely adored.
She looked out of the windows at the Manhattan
skyline, the skyscrapers lit from the inside so that
the buildings remained visible even in the inky
blackness of night. Mile after mile of steady yellow
and white lights, the whole city powered up, it
seemed, by some internal, invisible heartbeat . . .

the city that never slept. She dimly wondered where Henry was. The thought produced almost no reaction—no jealousy, no worry . . . nothing. She had said to him the separation would last the summer. As the first strands of watery light began to swim across the sky, she knew she'd lied. She wanted the separation to be longer, much longer. Forever, in fact.

Two days later, she was left standing outside the International Terminal at JFK wondering at the speed with which everything had unraveled as she watched Henry thread his way through the crowd and disappear up the escalators. She'd insisted on coming with him to the airport, although now she wondered why she'd bothered. He'd barely spoken to her in two days. It was strange how little there was to talk about after three years, she thought to herself as she waited for Max's driver to pick her up. She'd left the ring out on the kitchen counter the night she'd come back alone, not knowing what to do with it. She couldn't keep it. The following morning it was gone. Apart from the briefest exchange, Henry hadn't said a word to her. He'd left without looking back.

   The driver pulled up beside her. She took one last look behind—Henry was gone—and turned round. She stared at her hands in her lap. And then lifted her head. She was twenty-one. She was in Manhattan. Alone. This was what she'd wanted, wasn't it?

≈35≈

A week later on the Monday morning at nine thirty on the dot, she presented herself to the receptionist in the lobby of the *New York Chronicle*. Max had gone to meet someone in Moscow or Warsaw, she couldn't remember. Before he'd left, he'd done as he'd promised and secured her an interview—not a job, he'd warned her—with an old friend of his at the *New York Chronicle*. Donovan McCorquodale had agreed to see her—the rest was up to her.

She smoothed down her skirt before stepping into the lift and ascending silently towards the thirty-fifth floor. She was ushered, equally silently, into his office.

"It's not glamorous," he said after the introductions, smiling and nodding at her at the same time. Amber shook her head.

"Oh, I know," she said eagerly. "I don't care what I do . . . anything at all. I really didn't want to ask Max, but he offered to call you and . . ."

"Good, good . . ." Mr. McCorquodale broke in hurriedly. "Well, we'll start you off as an assistant to the junior copy editor. Sandi Jackson's her name. You'll be a kind of gofer . . . you know, check dates, place names, get her coffee, that kind of thing. How long're you here for?"

"Just the summer."

"Fine. Maybe later on we can give you something with a little more oomph! I'll talk to Max, see what we can do." Donovan laughed heartily at his own description. He turned back to his papers, waving her out and promising to look in sometime and see how she was getting on. She was ushered out of the office and back into the lift. Within seconds, she was back down on the ground floor and was told to report to Personnel the very next day.

Sandi Jackson's "office" was simply a single desk in a room absolutely full of desks—there must have been close to fifty people working in the open-plan space. Amber looked around her, bewildered, as Joe Tucci, the desk editor, sped down one aisle of desks, then the next.

"Sandi? *Sandi*!" he yelled. A young woman stuck her head above a partition and squinted in their direction.

"Over here! I moved desk!" she shouted. Joe gave a wave and led Amber over. "Hi," Sandi said, thrusting out a hand as Joe introduced them. "Welcome."

"Amber's father is a *personal* friend of Mc-Corquodale's," Joe began immediately, to Amber's horror.

"No, no . . . not really . . ." she interrupted hurriedly, horrified.

"Oh, don't worry about it. If you've got contacts, use 'em!" Sandi laughed, revealing a row of startlingly white, perfect teeth. "So what're you doing here?"

"She's gonna be your assistant," Joe said, raising his eyebrows significantly.

"Neat." Sandi's smile was still wide.

"Yeah, she's gonna be working here for the summer. Then she goes back to England," Joe said, pleased to be the fount of such important information.

"Neat." It seemed to be all she could say. Amber glanced from one to the other. She hoped the job, whatever it turned out to be, would be a *little* more stimulating than her colleagues.

It wasn't. By the end of her first week, she discovered that there were so many nuances within the corporation—assistants to assistants; assistants to juniors; juniors and deputies to managers; assistant managers, their juniors and *their* assistants—she had to laugh. Her job seemed to consist mainly of running out into the Manhattan streets at 8:18 a.m. precisely to fetch coffee, not only for Sandi but for the six or seven other junior copy editors and sub-editors who worked in a five-desk radius around them; answering the constantly ringing phones and fielding Sandi from unwanted callers; photocopying reams of documents and only occasionally proof-reading Sandi's already-corrected copy for any mistakes she might have missed . . . boring in the extreme. But while the job itself wasn't anything to write home about, living in New York was. She loved the city from the moment she'd set eyes on it. Taking the subway every morning along with four million other New Yorkers, rushing around with a coffee and muffin in hand, listening to the symphony of car horns at 9 a.m. . . . she felt thrillingly, nerve-tinglingly alive.

She put up a hand to touch the back of her neck. And another thing: she'd cut her hair. The day before, on her way back home from the *Chronicle* offices on 7th and West 23rd, she'd passed the chic little hairdressers on Madison. She hesitated for a moment, putting up a hand to finger her tumbling mass of curls . . . and then she'd pushed open the door and entered.

"All of it?" the stylist asked her, her eyes widening.

"All of it." Amber said firmly. She looked at her reflection in the mirror in front of her—a swathe of dark-brown curls that reached halfway down her back, falling over her face, almost hiding her eyes. She'd had long, curly hair forever, for as long as she could remember. In fact, her hair had been her defining feature. *Amber, you know . . . the girl with the curly hair.* She closed her eyes as the stylist started work.

An hour later, she stared at herself, not quite believing the face in front of her. Her brown hair was now almost black, cropped very close to the skull. Her face, shorn of its cloudy frame, was a stranger's—dark, thick eyebrows, sharp blue eyes . . . cheekbones, the curve of her jaw . . . she turned her head slowly under the admiring glance of the stylist.

"It's . . . nice," she said at last, shyly pleased.

"Nice?" the stylist repeated scornfully. "Honey, it's

gorgeous! To *die* for!" She laughed, whipping the salon cape off Amber's shoulders. Amber smiled. Americans were so much more expressive than the English. Everything was expressed in extremes, in superlatives. To die for! She glanced again at her reflection. She looked exactly as she felt: young, tremulous, fresh. A fresh start.

A month later, she walked into the elevator, six cups of coffee balanced precariously on a paper tray in one hand, a bag of bagels clutched tightly in the other. Bagels and coffee. Part of the daily routine, part of her job. She pressed the button with her elbow and turned to face the doors. It was the end of August and the city was still sweltering. She could feel beads of sweat trickling down her back. Thank God she'd cut her hair off, she thought as the doors opened. Running around in the heat with a cloud of curls would have been unbearable. She stepped gratefully into the cool, air-conditioned space. She handed out the coffee, organized the fair distribution of bagels and sat behind her computer, waiting for Sandi to toss the latest drafts for correction over the partition between them and start work.

"Hey, Amber," Sandi called to her over the partition. Her head appeared suddenly, her expression frantic. "Can you do me the *hugest* favor?" Amber nodded, wondering what was wrong. "I've been doing a little freelance work on the side," she said, her voice lowered, "and I've really fucked up. I was supposed to do a piece on some housing projects in Harlem for the *Village Voice* and I *totally* forgot. Like, *totally*. Would you be an angel and get some back-ground notes for me? Like, *today*?" Amber's heart leapt. A chance to get out of the office!

"Of course," she said, hoping she didn't sound too enthusiastic. "What sort of piece?"

"Oh, I don't know . . . some editor up there wants more human-interest stories, you know . . . how people in the city live, that type of thing. There was a piece on some Haitians in Flatbush last week and they want something on another group. I should've gone over the weekend but I totally, *totally* forgot." Sandi smiled her most winning smile. Amber couldn't quite understand why she was trying so hard—she would have given her back teeth to get out into the city and see a little more of New York. So far, she'd just about covered Lower Manhattan and even she knew there was more to the city than the elegant high-rises and skyscrapers that ran as far as the eye could see.

"Of course," Amber said again. "When d'you need it?"

"Like, *tonight*?" Sandi said, rolling her eyes in mock desperation.

"In that case, I'll leave straight away," Amber said, grinning. "Do I need to ask permission from anyone?"

"No, just go. I'll say you're on some errand or something. It's sorta true." Amber wasted no time. In five minutes flat she had her bag, a notepad and a small camera and a vague idea of what she was supposed to do. Sandi had hurriedly explained what she needed: notes and observations from which she could spin a short story—1,500–2,000 words—and a couple of pictures. She would be back in the office some time in the afternoon and Sandi could write the article that evening.

She left the offices and caught the subway up to 125th Street, emerging out into a world that was so far away from the one she'd just left as to be in another country altogether. She walked out of the station and stood on the sidewalk, gaping. Gone were the immaculate sidewalks and canopied entrances; gone were the designer stores and the well-heeled crowds; gone, too, was the cosmopolitan, diverse population of downtown. Here everyone, with one single, painful exception, was black. She felt her color take possession of her, quite literally. People turned to stare at her as they walked past, singling her out. She began to walk away from the station, down the wide, once-graceful boulevard, towards a cluster of high-rise apartment blocks. She had no idea where she was going. Manhattan, she knew, wasn't that wide . . . sooner or later, she'd run into the river. The segregation around her was total, complete. It was 1986, she kept reminding herself. Not 1834. She was in New York, not Johannesburg. So what was going on? There were almost no signs of commercial life on either side of the street, except for liquor stores. Groups of men milled around the entrances aimlessly, smoking and surreptitiously drinking out of brown paper bags. Once or twice she saw a police car flash by as it drove through an intersection at top speed. She continued walking. The housing stock had obviously seen better days—the elegant brownstone buildings were semi-derelict, weeds growing out of the windows on the second and third floors. Several buildings were boarded up entirely, ironically by the Muhammad Ali Co., she saw, making a note in her pad. And where were the women? In the hour or so she'd been walking, apart from one or two women clambering down the steps of a bus and immediately disappearing down a side street, there were almost no women on the streets.

She stopped outside a Woolworth's department store. A Burger King sign hung above the door. She was hungry and thirsty and there were no smart delis anywhere in the vicinity, no restaurants or diners lining the sides of the streets. Burger King it would have to be, she thought, walking up to the counter. She looked around. It was a little odd—the restaurant, if it could be called such, was little more than a counter and a few tables within the department store. She shrugged, taking her place in the line. She ordered a burger and a Coke and took her tray to a free table, ignoring the questioning glances around her. Next to her, a young man sat down, his hostile glare washing over her with unmasked suspicion. Opposite him, an elderly woman fumbled with her tray, collapsing unsteadily into the seat. Amber watched out of the corner of her eye as the young man, a bandana tied around his dreadlocked head, dripping with gold chains and attitude, slowly and meticulously began cutting his burger into tiny, bite-sized pieces. Amber watched in amazement as he leaned over and began feeding the elderly woman, piece by piece, with infinite care and tenderness. She felt a prick of tears behind her eyes as she heard him address the woman as "grandma," making sure she ate everything and gently wiping her toothless gums when she was finished. She pushed her own plate aside, afraid she would suddenly burst into tears. The sight was incongruous and terrifyingly touching. The young man suddenly caught her eye. Amber dropped her own. His aggressive contempt towards her was clear and equally terrifying. She was more than just an outsider in the community into which she'd unknowingly stumbled. She was the enemy. She got up and left.

Later that evening, after having handed Sandi a full five pages of her handwritten notes, she lay on the couch at home, the TV on mute, and slowly went over in her mind what she'd seen that morning. She jumped up and grabbed a notepad. She had never before felt such an urge to *write* something, to express what she'd seen, putting her observations into words. She did now. She wrote for almost three hours without stopping. When she had finished, she put down her pen, walked over to the plate-glass windows and stared down at the city. London held no such extremes, she thought to herself. Of course there were divisions—living where she did, in Clerkenwell, the tensions between the working class who had lived there for decades and the new, suddenly affluent yuppies who were moving into the area at an alarming rate, were obvious. But *this* . . . she had never seen such differences so crudely expressed. Her image of New York had been over-turned, violently, in the space of a morning. She *had* to write about it.

In the morning, she shyly handed Sandi a three-page typed essay. "It's nothing," she said, trying to be as offhand as possible. "I just thought . . . if you've ever got the time . . . you might just look through it and, you know, let me know what you think."

"Sure," Sandi said, smiling widely. "By the way, those were really great notes you made yesterday. I *loved* the whole grandma scene. Thanks." She took the sheets from Amber without even looking at them. "I'm *real* busy this week and next, honey," she said smoothly, "but I promise, as soon as I get a chance, I'll have a look through your stuff. Now, we've got a whole bunch of proofs to get through for tomorrow's Scene & Heard section. Can you start with these?" She handed Amber a pile of uncor-rected proofs. And that, thought Amber wryly, was that.

Except, of course, it wasn't. Three days later, she picked up the *Village Voice* and turned to the CityScape section, eager to see what Sandi had done with her notes. It took her a second to realize that the editorial piece in front of her hadn't been adapted from her notes—it was her *piece*, the es-say she'd given Sandi . . . in its entirety, word for bloody word. Sandi had simply handed in what Am-ber had written. She scanned the column anxiously. *A World Apart. By Sandi Jackson*. There was no mention of Amber Sall or of the background work she'd done. Not a single word. She stared at the piece in utter disbelief. How could Sandi have done it? She'd stolen her work. She'd obviously read the piece the night Amber had given it to her and sent it onto the *Voice* first thing in the morning. It was theft! She crumpled the paper angrily in her fist. It was her first professional lesson. Never, ever, give anything away, not even your notes. She threw the paper angrily into the nearest bin.

≈36≈

The private jet taking Max and two other businessmen to Schönefeld airport in East Berlin was standing on the runway at Heathrow, engines ready for take-off, waiting. Five minutes passed, then another ten. Max looked out of the window at the darkened runway—there was nothing to be seen. From his seat he could see the two pilots talking over the radio to someone. Another five minutes passed. He began to get impatient. The single stewardess came through from the cockpit and smiled at the three businessmen.

"Sorry to keep you waiting, gentlemen. We've just received word of an additional passenger. He'll be on board in a moment. Sorry about the delay." Max grunted. The price he'd paid to be flown into East Berlin ought to have secured him against any delays, no matter who was joining them on board. He made a small sound of impatience and turned back to his paper. A few minutes later, the door at the rear of the plane opened and the passenger for whom they'd all been waiting emerged. He heard the stewardess usher the man in, showing him to the only spare seat—in front of him, of course. He sighed, moved his legs out of the way and glanced upwards. He paused, surprised. Standing in front of him was a young, black man in a long, dark overcoat, carrying a briefcase. Max looked back down at his paper, aware he'd been staring. Private flights to Eastern Europe did not normally include young men—particularly young, black men. He wondered who he was. Everyone on board was staring at him. He seemed unperturbed—probably used to being stared at, thought Max. He was exceptionally good-looking. He nodded to Max, but said nothing.

The plane began to taxi out to the runway. Opposite Max, the young man settled himself into his seat, folded away his coat, and withdrew a sheaf of papers from his briefcase. Max glanced at them—Cyrillic script. He was reading Russian. Now he was really intrigued. As the plane readied for take-off, he found himself wondering who on earth he could be. He tapped his pen against his teeth thoughtfully. The flight was two and a half hours long. Perhaps he'd strike up conversation once they were airborne and find out. Max loved an enigma.

"Russian, eh?" Max leaned forward after the smiling stewardess had placed a bottle of champagne before them. Tendé declined the glass she proffered.

"Coffee, black . . . thank you," he asked her. He turned his attention to Max. "Yes. You speak Russian?"

"A few words," Max said, waiting for the attendant to bring Tendé's coffee before lifting his own glass. Tendé shrugged. "Max Sall." Max held out a hand.

"Tendé Ndiaye."

"Hell of a name. Where's it from?"

"Me? Or the name?" His English was flawless. Better than Max's. He was definitely intrigued.

"Both. Either." Max leaned back in his seat, amused by the young man's confident tone.

"Mali."

"West Africa? Former French colony?" Max knew a little about the vast but underpopulated country.

"Spot on."

"And—if you don't mind my asking—what are you doing on this flight?"

"What are *you* doing on it?"

"Business."

"Same here." He wasn't giving anything away. Max grinned. The two businessmen beside them tried to look as though they weren't listening—not very successfully. Max saw that the young man had them all in the palm of his hand. As he chatted, it occurred to him that Tendé Ndiaye was enjoying their curiosity. But he could see too that he was quietly amused by their patronizingly liberal attempts to explain his presence among them to themselves—*who are you, where are you from, where are you going and what are you doing here*—he looked as though he'd heard a thousand variations of the same from a thousand different sources. He watched in quiet admiration as the young man returned to his papers.

Max too had his own reading to do. The two and a half hours passed quickly. As they fastened seatbelts and began their descent into East Berlin, Max suddenly put a hand into his breast pocket and drew out a card.

"Look, if you're ever in London or New York, give me a ring. It was interesting talking to you."

"Thank you. Well, if you're ever in Bamako," Tendé said, smiling at the remoteness of that possibility. He handed over his own card. Max looked at it briefly. *Dr. Tendé Toumani Ndiaye. Deputy Minister for the Environment. Government of the Republic of Mali.* He pulled a face—impressive. He was aware the young man was watching him. At the door to the plane, they shook hands. A car was waiting for Max across the tarmac, as arranged.

"Can I give you a lift anywhere?" he asked as they ducked heads and walked out onto the steps.

"Thanks, but no. I have people coming for me." He indicated a car making its way towards the plane, its lights dimmed. Max nodded. He'd probably never see him again. A shame; there was something about him that Max had enjoyed. Enormously.

Angela frowned, swaying on her feet. She clutched the phone to her, struggling to understand what was being said. Kieran—arrested? The whole thing just wasn't making sense. She looked at herself in the mirror in the hallway as the disembodied voice on the other end of the line described a string of procedures, none of which she understood. She had dressed carefully that morning, although she couldn't really remember why. She looked rather well—very well, in fact. A long white linen skirt, a pink, silky top; her hair had been washed and set by Corinne, the new maid . . . she was barefoot but there were plenty of shoes in the cupboard. She turned back to the phone.

"What?" she asked again.

"Mrs. Sall. I think you'd better come to the station. It might be best before . . . the press get here, you understand? Your son's not in a very good way."

Angela swallowed. "Yes, yes . . . um, can you . . . could I speak to him?"

"I'm afraid that's not possible, Mrs. Sall. Do you have a lawyer?"

"A lawyer? Whatever for?" Angela was suddenly alarmed.

"Mrs. Sall. Your son has been arrested. Look, is your husband available, perhaps?"

"Oh, God. No . . . no, he's . . . away. Oh. Well, I suppose I'd better come, then. Where did you say you were?"

An hour later, accompanied by Corrine and Mrs. Dewhurst, Angela hurried into the police station at Wandsworth, looking wildly around her. Despite everyone's efforts, she'd swallowed almost half a bottle of brandy before coming downstairs.

"Kieran?" she called, rushing up to the front desk. The young policewoman on desk duty managed to catch hold of her before she went rushing through the set of double doors. A desk sergeant was called and it was explained to her that she could go in to see her son, but on condition she promised to behave. Corrine and Mrs. Dewhurst watched as the duty officers exchanged glances, then led her in.

"Kieran? Oh my God . . . Kieran? What have they done to you?" Angela shrieked as soon as she entered the room. Kieran looked up.

"Mrs. Sall." The inspector in charge of proceedings got up to stop Angela from flinging herself at Kieran. "Mrs. Sall . . . please. Do sit down. Please." Angela began to cry. Kieran looked back down at the floor.

"What have you done to him?" she asked tearfully as she was led to a seat opposite him.

"Well, we were rather hoping you might be able to help us establish what he's done to himself," Inspector Fraser said, eyeing the sniffling Angela with ill-concealed alarm. She looked almost as incoherent as her son.

"What do you mean?" Angela whispered. She glanced across the table at Kieran. She could barely recognize him. Why wasn't he talking or looking at her? His face was closed in that petulant, little-boy-lost look she knew so well. He was disheveled and very badly dressed. His trousers were torn, his shirt had several buttons missing, his hair looked as though it hadn't been washed in a week—no, a month . . . she started crying again. Who had done this to her darling boy?

"We found a fairly substantial amount of mari-juana on your son, Mrs. Sall, together with a large amount of cash and—this is why we've called you in—an assortment of jewelry, checks drawn on your husband's account and made out to your son, as well as these . . . er, art pieces, as it were . . ." he coughed and indicated two large vases she recognized dimly as having been in the dining room at home for almost as long as she could remember. She turned around to face Kieran.

"I'm not sure I understand," she said, her voice shaking. "I . . . gave those to Kieran. I asked him to . . . er, to *sell* them for me. Isn't that right, dar-ling?" she turned to Kieran. He still didn't look up.

"Mrs. Sall," the inspector said gently. "I understand what you must be going through. We're not here to make this any more difficult than it needs to be. We wanted to ascertain ownership of the goods found in your son's possession, that's all. It's fairly clear what he intended to do with them. I'm afraid there's really nothing you can do for him at this moment, except arrange for a lawyer, of course. Will you be appointing someone yourselves?" Angela could only stare dumbly at him. All of a sudden, she was excruciatingly sober. Max. She would have to tell Max. And Max would kill him. All she could think about was what Max would say. She allowed the policewoman who had shown her in to lead her out. Kieran didn't look up, not once, not even as she turned to him with a look of such desperate fear that Inspector Fraser himself had to look away.

≈38≈

Paola lay on her back, closed her eyes against the blinding glare of the sun and tried to fall asleep. Red and pink splotches danced across her eyelids as the heat rose. It was nearly midday and she could almost hear her mother admonishing her for lying out in the sun at that time. Francesca was indoors in the villa somewhere, supervising the frantic last-minute preparations for the party they were throwing that evening for Max's fifty-sixth birthday. It had been planned for almost a year and was to be *the* social event in the Menorca summer calendar. She and Francesca had decamped to the island at the beginning of the summer so that Francesca could organize things exactly the way she wanted. Paola wasn't so wrapped up in her own world that she couldn't see just what the party meant to Francesca—it would be one of the few occasions where Francesca got to reign, and in public, too. It was to be *her* party, a social gift to him from her. Everyone who was anyone on the island had been invited, as well as over a hundred guests who were arriving from various places around the world. The caterers had been in residence for nearly three days and a small army of staff had been drafted in to clean and polish the entire villa until it gleamed everywhere. Paola herself was sick of the noise and constant buzz; she couldn't wait for the party to start. And for it to be over. She had a reason to look forward to it being over—Amber and Kieran would be coming later that afternoon, of course. Although she'd heard the most *monumental* rumours about Kieran . . . something to do with drugs, the police . . . perhaps he wouldn't be coming after all. She heard Francesca making soothing noises to Max: *he's young, it's a mistake, he'll settle down . . .* but Max didn't seem to be listening. At least Angela wasn't coming. She'd been checked into yet another clinic. From the sounds of it, Kieran really ought to join her.

Anyhow, she thought to herself as she rolled over onto her stomach, even if Kieran wasn't coming, there was still Amber to contend with. Ugh. How perfectly awful. To make matters worse, these days Max was just full of Amber's accomplishments. She'd got her degree, she'd got a job with some newspaper in New York and she was about to start working for some stuck-up financial magazine in London . . . bully for her. It was probably Max who had got her the jobs in the first place. She'd apparently broken up with her boyfriend, Francesca told her. Not quite the Miss Perfect she'd always been. Paola just hoped she wasn't going to come to Menorca to look for another one. Well, Paola had her own weapons in place, including the dress she had just bought for the party. Just thinking about it made her feel all warm inside. It was black, a stunning black lace and skin-tight leather affair. It had cost a small fortune but from the moment she'd seen it in the windows of Ferragamo, she knew she had to have it. She and Francesca had treated themselves to a weekend shopping in Paris on their way down to Menorca. Paola had to admit that the stunning black and white dress her mother had bought at Dior was equally gorgeous. The two of them would look *so* good together . . . a real birthday treat for Max. He would be the envy of every man in the villa.

She opened her eyes. The villa was a blinding flash of white. It was time to go in. She had to be careful—she wanted to deepen her tan, not burn. There was nothing less attractive than a face shedding skin every time one smiled. She was perfectly golden. A few minutes in the pool and she would have the beautifully heightened glow she'd been hoping for when the party finally began.

Inside, Francesca was supervising the flower displays. Enormous arrangements of tropical flowers had been brought up to the villa by van. They lay around in the baths and available sinks in the house, waiting to be taken out and displayed. Several rather good-looking young men wandered in and out, holding the arrangements aloft, smiling appreciatively at Francesca and her beautiful daughter as they tried out location after location. The enormous living room had been completely cleared of furniture and the patio doors had been opened onto the terrace with a gleaming barbeque pit and bamboo bar at one end, next to the shimmering blue plane of the pool. Citronella braziers had been planted all along the garden wall, framing the pool; by 7 p.m. they would look spectacular against the turquoise water and the billowing muslin curtains.

"Darling," Francesca called, seeing Paola wander in. "What do you think? Here or over there?" A young man stood by patiently as Francesca considered the best possible position for a huge bouquet of lilies, thick, fiery orange azaleas and palm fronds.

"*Mama*," Paola rolled her eyes. "I don't know." Paola wasn't about to be drawn into the circus. She ignored Francesca's cross glance and disappeared down the hallway into her bedroom.

By five o'clock, a sense of calm had begun to descend on the villa. Amber had indeed arrived alone at three o'clock; Paola had heard her being shown down the corridor to her room. She hadn't bothered to come and knock on Paola's door and Paola hadn't bothered to knock on hers. She was alone, Paola could hear, which meant the despicable Kieran wasn't coming after all. Max arrived shortly afterwards. She could hear him booming around the place, yelling for things to be brought to him . . . his suit, his tie, his shoes . . . but Paola didn't want to risk bumping into Amber so she stayed in her room. Of course, the five o'clock calm was simply the lull before the storm. None of the guests were staying at the house, Francesca told her, except, of course, for Amber and some African Max had met on a flight somewhere. The party was due to begin at seven and at five thirty, Paola began her preparations.

First there was the long, hot, scented bath, followed by a quick cold shower. Her hair had been washed and set in enormous rollers that morning by Francesca's hairdresser, who would also be on hand throughout the evening for any unforeseen emergencies. She wrapped herself in a huge terry-cloth robe and padded through to her dressing room. She sat in front of the mirror and inspected her face for any flaws. The rosy, golden glow she'd been cultivating all morning was indeed evident— she would need the minimum of make-up to enhance it. She started, as always, with her eyes. She knew exactly what suited her: dark-brown shimmering powder on the lids, a soft, smoky pencil line below. Two or three coats of mascara, thickening and lengthening her already long lashes, then a careful grooming around the eyebrow area and a dash of gel to keep her brows in place. She studied the effect in the mirror. Her cheeks received a dusting of golden powder; her lips were carefully drawn with the plum lip pencil she liked . . . two coats of lipstick and a careful blot. Perfect. She stepped out of her robe, sprayed herself with perfume and a shimmering body mist to give her a golden, sparkling glow and walked to the closet to retrieve her dress. *The dress.*

It took her almost ten minutes to slide into it and fasten every button, delicate lace ribbon and zip. When she was done, she turned around to face the mirror. She had never looked better. For a brief, fleeting moment, she wished Prince Georg and the crowd she'd been forced to abandon could have seen her. She was lost for a moment, remembering the horrible ending to what ought to have been the romance of the decade. It was all that awful Dave's fault.

It had taken a few days for the niggling sense of unease she felt to disappear. It wasn't anything she could really put her finger on, just a horrible feeling that something rather unpleasant had happened to her and she couldn't remember what. The bite marks had slowly disappeared, leaving her with even less to hold on to. And everyone was being exceptionally nice to her, even the usually withdrawn prince. She sometimes caught Jenna looking at her a little too intently, but then she'd quickly look away again and somehow, Paola didn't quite have the nerve to ask her what was wrong. By the end of her stay, the memory had faded, not quite disappeared . . . a tender, slightly uncomfortable area inside her head which hurt if she dwelt on it too long. She pushed it to the back of her mind, determined to forget about it. The holiday had gone splendidly; the prince seemed to like her very much indeed . . . Holly and Kina had promised to introduce her to their agent in Paris when they all got back . . . it all seemed to be going so well.

They all returned home with promises of meeting up in the Bahamas in the spring. Prince Georg kissed Paola's hand rather formally as they parted company in Innsbruck. She and Jenna boarded the plane for Vienna. They still had the Christmas holidays in front of them—they would meet at the beginning of term in Lausanne. And that, Paola thought, was that. Except, of course, it wasn't.

When she got back to school in January, she detected a distinct lack of warmth on Jenna's part. All attempts to talk about the little holiday in Hochüli were met with a rather frosty silence. She had stopped inviting Paola to accompany her to town or to her aunt's or to bunking off classes and taking the train into Geneva. By the end of the second week of term, it was quite clear that Jenna de Rosnay's circle of friends at the exclusive finishing school no longer included Paola Rossi—and Paola couldn't understand why. It was a bit of a blow. Not only was Jenna a year above Paola, in the beginning, the cachet had functioned the other way round—Jenna was nowhere near as pretty or popular or daring as Paola Rossi and it had been considered something of a catch for them to hang out with the beautiful and popular junior. Not any more. To make matters worse, Paola couldn't seem to get in touch with any of the Hochüli crowd. Prince Georg simply didn't return her calls; the telephone numbers she'd been given for Holly and Kina didn't work and Dave, the horrible American, was never at home. She couldn't work out what had happened.

In the end, it was Véronique who told her. Rumors had been flying round the school ever since Paola and Jenna had returned—that Paola Rossi had slept with four men—*four!*—and had allowed them to take photographs of her which the men put in their famous *cahier noir*—a photographic diary, if you like, of the famous girls they'd slept with and which, it was whispered, Dave Hahn, the American, would sell to the papers should cashflow ever demand it. Paola listened to Véronique's story in horrified silence.

"But . . . why me? Why didn't they choose Jenna?" Paola stammered. There was a moment's hesitation.

"Well, they choose someone . . . you know, of not quite the same . . . *level*," Véronique explained as delicately as she could.

Paola stared at her, uncomprehendingly. "What on earth are you talking about. I'm rich. My father's loaded."

"Yes, but you're not . . . well, your mother's not *married*, is she? I mean, she's only his girlfriend." Paola listened to Véronique's snobby little voice outlining the reasons why Paola Rossi and not Jenna de Rosnay had been hand-picked for their ritual *tableau*. Her cheeks were flaming by the time Véronique von Riedesal, the daughter of a German count, had finished.

Then she rang Francesca and demanded to be taken out of the school. Immediately. It was Paola's first introduction to the tiny, possessive and closed world of European minor royalty. She might have oodles of cash at her disposal and an enviable lifestyle but, as she had been so rudely reminded, she had no status. And that, in their eyes, made her easy game.

Well, all that was in the past, she reminded herself sternly as she pirouetted one last time in front of the mirror. She would never, ever be humiliated in that way again. Ever. She'd had to tell Francesca, of course—minus a number of important details—and Francesca was gratifyingly outraged on her behalf. But one truth remained: no matter what Francesca said or how much she sympathized with Paola's "dreadful ordeal," it was clear that fundamentally, Véronique was right. Paola *was* Jenna de Rosnay's social inferior and until and unless Max did something about it, she always would be. Unfortunately for Paola, Max didn't look as though he was in any hurry to set about improving Paola's position on the social ladder. Not that he'd been told about it. Wild horses wouldn't have dragged the humiliating story out of Francesca, and certainly not out of Paola. And although she and her mother did their best to put the story behind them, there was that one, niggling little question . . . what had happened to the photographs?

As the months passed and nothing further seemed to happen, Francesca allowed herself to relax a little. After all, she reasoned, her daughter seemed to have survived the earlier scandal with that horrible man, Didier Juneau. If there were a few amateur photographs floating around of Paola having sex with Prince Georg . . . so what? From what she'd heard, the haughty aristocrat had done it with just about every available heiress on the continent. What was so spectacular about Paola Rossi? Listening to Francesca's reasoning, Paola said nothing. It was true she could hardly remember the details of that night, but there was certainly more than one man involved and she wasn't sure that "sex" quite covered what appeared to have gone on.

"Paola!" Francesca was coming down the corridor. Paola gave a little start. She'd been daydreaming again. She quickly fastened the last zip on her leather and lace ensemble and began carefully pulling the rollers out of her hair. Her Manolo Blahnik shoes—beautiful, strappy high heels with thin leather ties—stood in the corner of the room, waiting to be worn. Francesca tapped on the door. She opened it and gazed fondly at her daughter. "*Bellissima*," she mouthed, nodding in approval. Paola smiled. She knew she looked absolutely stunning.

The bathroom was full of steam. Amber took down her dress and padded barefoot across the cool marble floor. After the humidity of New York, the dry hot days and cooler nights in Menorca were a welcome relief. As was the fact that no one had paid her arrival very much attention. She hadn't wanted to come, especially not after Angela's frantic telephone call, but she'd promised Max she would and anyway, Kieran was out on bail and could wait. She sighed. Sometimes, she thought to herself, she longed to belong to a normal family like Becky's, the sort of family where *nothing ever happened*. At the thought of Becky she winced. She'd promised to stop by as soon as she'd arrived back in London but then there'd been the fuss with Kieran and now Max's party . . . she made a mental note to go over as soon as she got back. Becky had said something to her about bumping into Henry—another reason Amber was strangely reluctant to go over. She didn't want to know what Henry was doing.

She slipped the dress she'd found in Angela's wardrobe over her head, smoothed down the skirt and turned to look at herself in the mirror. She looked fine . . . a little plain, perhaps? It was a flowery, slightly girlish long-waisted dress with puffed sleeves and a rather fussy neckline. She bit her lip— it somehow looked a little childish on her. She'd never quite managed to find her own style, always teetering between being over- or woefully under- dressed and she simply didn't have the kind of lithe, tanned figure her sister did that could make any- thing she wore look delectable—and unnecessary, of course. It had been one of Henry's favorite com- ments: *Your sister always looks as though she's just got out of bed. Which is where I and every other man on the planet would like to see her.* She tried not to let the comment sting. She picked up a brush and tried to do something with her hair. It was in that horribly awkward stage between being too short and too long. She'd realized, walking into the office just after she'd cut her hair, that not everyone was as enthusiastic about it as the stylist had been. Kieran had laughed at her as soon as she'd walked in the door the previous morning—which, considering the trouble *he* was in, was rich, Amber thought to herself angrily. He told her she looked like a bedraggled lamb ten minutes after shearing. She told him to fuck off. She looked at her watch. It was six thirty. She ought to stop worrying about her bloody dress and go off in search of Max to give him his present. She'd found the boxing gloves, worn and signed by one of Max's heroes, Muhammad Ali, by chance in a shop in Lower Manhattan. They were expensive but she knew he'd love them. She'd had them cleaned and boxed in a beautiful cherry maple and glass case. Bloody heavy to lug around but worth the smile on his face, she thought. She carefully applied a bit of lipstick, switched off the lights and closed the door. She could hear the band warming up outside on the patio and the caterers moving back and forth as she wandered down the corridor. Despite being in the same house as Francesca and Paola, she felt a small stab of excitement. She'd been asked to do a small piece on the party for a London style magazine. It would be her first real story and she was nervous. *Lots of glamour*, the editor had said. *What people are wearing, who came with whom . . . that sort of thing*. It wasn't quite the gritty debut she'd been hoping for, but a good writer ought to be able to write anything, she told herself sternly.

Lost in thought, she turned the corner and ran straight into Paola. Her heart plummeted. If she'd been worried about her dress before, now she was positively frantic. She looked about ten years old next to Paola's sophisticated, stunning little number. There was a short, tense moment as the two sisters eyed each other warily, then Max's voice broke the silence as he walked towards them smiling. He was obviously in an exceptionally good mood.

≈39≈

Tendé Ndiaye nosed the little sports car around the hairpin bends, enjoying the feel of the engine's power under his hands and the breeze around his face. It was an unexpected break for him—two days in Menorca at the invitation of Max Sall, whom he'd met by chance on one of his trips to East Berlin—but he was glad of it. It wasn't the sort of thing he usually did. These days, his life was all work and no play, but the invitation had been followed by a phone call and the suggestion that there was something Max would like to talk about. He'd phoned his father at home in Bamako and delayed his return.

He took his eyes off the road for a second. It was seven o'clock in the evening and the sun was casting elongated black shadows across the road. It was breathtakingly beautiful. The air was thick with the scent of lavender, pine and something else, unidentifiable to him. The sea appeared and disappeared as he navigated the bends; tall ruler-straight lines of stiff, black cypress trees framed each glimpse towards the glittering, blue surface. The Mediterranean sun was so different from the sun at home. In Mali, the sun was fierce, a constant, throbbing sheen that sent everyone scurrying indoors between the hours of noon and two o'clock in the afternoon, blinding everything in its glare. The sky at home was rarely blue—it was white, the color and texture having been seared out of it by the time the late-morning prayers were over. Houses rose and fell; white apartment blocks towards the harbor; elegant, red-tiled villas as he started to climb the hills. There was wealth here, and taste. Through wrought-iron gates he glimpsed luxury cars and yachts tethered to small trailers. As he rose, through the rear-view mirror he saw dreamy, still swimming pools, only occasionally punctured by a lone human head or a group of splashing children and the splendidly crisp lines of one white, modernist home after another.

Max's villa, *Casa Bella*, was at the top of the ridge, he'd been told. He quickly pulled over and checked his map. A steep alleyway rose up the hillside to his left. An ornate, wonderfully thick wooden door was recessed into the wall; above him, a yellow and white striped awning bellied in the breeze. A house, growing organically out of the wall that encased the slope wore the sleepy-eyed demeanor of an aging yet handsome woman behind sunglasses; the white wooden shutters were closed. Small, decorated balconies jutted out like shelves; enormous pots of geraniums—blood-red; pink; velvety-purple—adorned the façades. He half-smiled to himself. Life here must be good. He pulled out into the road again and continued on his way.

Casa Bella. He pulled into the driveway and switched off the engine. He was early; the drive had been quicker than expected. He smiled as he released his body from the awkward confines of the small car. Perhaps the Alpha Romeo Spider had made it shorter than it seemed. He picked up his bag from the back seat and walked up the drive. A pretty, smiling maid greeted him and led him through the house. She showed him his room for the night and explained in halting English that the party would begin at seven, on the patio. Was there anything he needed? Tendé shook his head. He looked around the room appreciatively as she closed the door behind her. Large, spacious, light-filled . . . his own private shower and terrace overlooking the hills to the left of the villa. He looked at his watch. It was 6:15 p.m. Just enough time to have a shave and a long, hot shower. He unpacked quickly, laying his snow-white *boubou*, the long, delicately embroidered tunic and narrow matching trousers that men in his country wore, still in their plastic wrapping, on the bed. He stripped, wrapped one of the white towels the maid had left for him around his waist and walked into the bathroom. Nothing had been spared to make guests feel comfortable, he noticed, as he turned on the shower. Toiletries, towels, hairdryers, toothbrushes, shaving sticks . . . everything had been thought of. He knew little of Max Sall's domestic arrangements. Like everyone else, he knew

Max "operated" two families but he was unclear as to whose domain he was currently in—the wife or the mistress. Well, he'd soon find out. He stepped under the scalding jet of water, pleased he'd found the time to attend what promised to be one hell of a party.

The hallway and enormous lounge were already filling up by 7 p.m. Tendé stood at the end of the corridor, surprised by the number of people who'd arrived in the forty-odd minutes he'd spent getting ready. It was obvious from the couples walking up the driveway and gliding through the house that this was one of the biggest events in the Menorca social calendar. Enormous-waisted men in crumpled linen suits were accompanied by stick-thin blondes, each one dripping with more gold and diamond jewelry than the next. He raised an eyebrow. It was hard to tell the trophy wives apart. He recognized a few of the men: Lord Montagu, the English tobacco king; Wolfgang Gmeiner, the German industrialist; one or two politicians; a film star . . . it was quite a gathering. He moved out of the doorway.

"Tendé!" Max's voice rang out across the patio. Amber turned. She saw a tall, slender figure coming towards them. Her eyes widened in surprise—who on earth was he? "Fantastic! I'm so glad you could make it!" Max had stepped forward and was enthusiastically pumping the hand of a man wearing the most unusual, beautiful outfit: a long, billowing white shirt, almost a dress, reaching to his ankles and, peeping out from beneath the embroidered hem, a pair of trousers in the same snow-white cotton. On his head, he wore a small skullcap, of the same cloth, but edged with lace. He was black—a rich, dark, velvety blackness; against the white cotton of his outfit, his skin shone. She barely had enough time to take in any further details—dark eyes beneath thick, straight eyebrows; high, taut cheekbones and full, dark lips. She was dimly aware she was staring but couldn't help herself. She turned to Max. "Amber, meet Tendé, Dr. Ndiaye . . . the man I told you about. We met a couple of months ago in Berlin." Amber shook her head slightly. She hadn't a clue who he was talking about. She held out her hand. His grasp was firm.

"Very pleased to meet you," she mumbled, hoping her surprise hadn't been too obvious.

"Likewise." He gave a quick smile. A private, guarded smile.

"Come, Tendé, I want to introduce you. There's someone I want you to meet." Max was already pulling him away. He turned before she could say anything else and was immediately swallowed up in the small crowd. Amber remained where she was standing. A great breath of tension suddenly pulled up, taut, inside her as her eyes followed Max and the tall stranger around the room until they disappeared through the French doors and into the candle- and laughter-filled night.

Snatches of conversation floated past. *You must come when it's cooler, we'd love to have you . . . Well, that's exactly what I said. I told him, point blank, you mustn't expect . . . Did she really?* Amber drifted past. She caught sight of him once or twice. She smiled tentatively, thinking perhaps he had seen her; but no . . . no sign of recognition in the inscrutable face. They weren't brought together in the crowd. She was surprised at herself. She'd met him for a second, a brief second . . . ridiculous for her to wait about all evening in this peculiar state of tension, hoping to bump into him again. She busied herself with taking mental notes for her piece, chatting to one or two of Max's friends whom she recognized from various parties over the years. She looked down at her dress from time to time, wishing she could slip away down the corridor and find something else to wear, but what? In her puffy sleeves and loud, floral print she looked like a child! No wonder Tendé whatever-his-name-was steered clear. He hadn't yet seen Paola. Amber was watching anxiously for her arrival. Paola loved to make an entrance.

She looked again for Tendé and saw him standing by the pool, deep in conversation with someone. She watched in fascination for a moment as his face and dress were lit up by the watery reflection bouncing off the rippling surface. Even from where she was standing she could see the frown of concentration on his face. His gestures were animated, intense. Whoever he was talking to—one of Max's friends, a short, grey-haired man in a ridiculous pastel suit—looked up at him in something close to awe. Amber skirted the dancers as unobtrusively as she could, wanting only to draw near to him; to hear the sound of his voice and to find out just what it was he was saying that seemed to render the man looking up at him speechless. *Yes, of course, the French have their interests . . . we wouldn't expect them not to, non? But it's more a question of how we share the spoils, not when.* Amber edged closer. Snatches of their conversation floated past her. *But we'll go to the Russians, too—we're not fussy. We'll see how long we can play the two of them off one another.* She stood silently a few feet behind them, her back turned, sipping her drink and listening to the low, mellifluous voice that sent a faint tremor running through her.

She saw Max approaching, a bottle of champagne in hand and an enormous grin on his face. She'd rarely seen him so animated, happy. He draped an arm around Tendé's shoulders and, spotting her, turned him round to face her, coming towards her. She felt her heart lift. She saw, as his face moved slowly towards her, how beautiful he was. Not the sleek, unblemished perfection of male beauty as she knew it from films and magazines; Tendé's face was too intense, too drawn to be classically beautiful. No, his attraction stemmed from something else. There was the faint presence of tension underneath the smooth, black surface; thin lines ran around the corners of his mouth, etched by some internal struggle that only he was privy to; at his eyes, too, an extra fold across the lid when they narrowed in silent, rapid appraisal of everything around him. He was watchful, alert. As Max brought the two of them together, again, Amber felt the sharp pull of desire—more than anything, she wanted to *talk* to this man who had appeared out of nowhere and whose presence had disturbed her in a way no man had ever done before. She watched, mesmerized, as the two of them approached her again. Max smiled at her and waved her over. She drew closer.

"Having a nice time?" Max asked. Amber nodded, almost too happy to speak. The two men smiled at her. Her heart was in her mouth.

"Are you . . . did you meet . . . how d'you know . . . ?" she asked Tendé, stumbling awkwardly over the words.

"Your father? How did we meet?" he finished the question for her, smiling faintly down at her. Amber nodded and took a swallow of champagne to hide her confusion. "We met on a plane to East Berlin, a few months ago. He invited me to the party. I'm on my way back home . . ."

"And where's that?" Amber asked, aware that her heart had started to beat a little faster. She suddenly wanted to know everything she could about him.

"Ah, Bamako. Mali."

"West Africa?"

"Oui."

"What do you do? I mean, East Berlin's a long way from Bamako." She realized as soon as she'd spoken how silly the words sounded. "I didn't mean it like that. I just wondered . . . Max said you were a doctor . . . ?"

"I work for the government. I'm not a medical doctor." Tendé's voice stopped her. She looked up at him quickly. His expression was blank. "And you?" he asked, out of politeness, it seemed to her.

"Oh, me? I'm studying English. I want to do . . . to be a journalist." She was on edge—she who was *never* intimidated, by anyone, ever. He said nothing. "Would you like another drink?" she asked after a moment or two. She needed one; there was something so unsettling about him, and about her desire to please him, to win his approval, to make him notice her. He shook his head. He blinked slowly, his gaze taking in everything around him, spoken or unsaid. She drained her glass, a little too quickly. It wasn't only the champagne going to her head. She looked round for a waiter, desperately needing a refill, something to do with her hands whilst she wondered what to say and how to keep him talking to her. She cast a quick glance towards the pool—blast! There wasn't one in sight. "I'm just going to get . . . to fill this up," she said quickly, lifting her glass and wondering how on earth she could indicate to him that she'd be back, that she didn't want to leave his side or end their conversation, stilted as it was. He nodded, seemingly indifferent.

Amber hurried across the garden to the bar. Her heart was pounding. She wondered how old he was—obviously closer to her age than Max's. She'd never met anyone so . . . poised, so intellectually alert and composed. There was a calm, intelligent confidence about him; she'd never met anyone like him. His voice and manner hinted at a depth of experience of the world that she longed for. His reserve had the opposite effect—she wanted only to be close.

The barman handed her a fresh glass. She pushed her way back through the garden, hoping to reach Tendé before Max or another of his friends claimed his attention. She could see him, standing alone where she'd left him, quietly enjoying the sights and sounds around him. And then suddenly, everything went disastrously wrong. Paola appeared, dressed to kill. She was almost unrecognizable in a skin-tight dress with slits and straps all over the place and the most ridiculously high-heeled shoes. She looked absolutely stunning. Tendé simply wouldn't be able to resist. Amber looked on dumbly, watching in an agony of jealousy as heads turned across the garden to watch her sister make a beeline for the most interesting person in the room. Amber drained her glass of champagne and turned away, unable to bear the sight. The rest of the evening passed in a blur of disappointment. She caught sight of him and Paola once or twice, his head bent low, her arm on his . . . and was shocked by the rush of hatred that swept through her. Paola could have her pick of anyone in the room; why did she have to pick *him*?

It was almost two o'clock in the morning when she decided she'd had enough. Three hours of catching sight of them, dancing, laughing and then, even worse . . . they'd both disappeared. She'd had far too much to drink—the garden and the shimmering surface of the pool were beginning to merge. She set down her half-empty glass on one of the tables in the living room and walked unsteadily across the patio into the living room. She wanted to strip off her clothes, stand under the blast of her shower for five minutes and then crawl into bed. The party around her showed no signs of slowing down. She looked around her once, twice—no, he was nowhere to be seen—and then headed down the corridor to her room.

Just as she passed the door to Paola's room, it opened suddenly and Paola stepped into the corridor, closing her door quickly behind her. In the semi-darkness, the two sisters stared at each other. Amber felt the rage she'd experienced earlier rise in her.

"Going to bed already?" Paola asked, an arrogant smile playing around the corner of her lips. Even in the dim light, Amber could see that she'd been kissed—her lipstick was prettily smudged. As if to emphasize the point, Paola put up a hand, touching her lips appreciatively. Amber longed to slap her. She nodded curtly. "*I'm* not. I've been . . . dancing with Max's new friend. Oh, I saw you talking to him earlier. He's gorgeous, isn't he?" She looked up at Amber. Amber's finger itched. "*Much* more my type, though, I think. He's a bit too . . . I don't know . . . experienced for you, don't you think? I mean, compared to Henry . . ." her voice trailed off meaningfully.

"Didn't know you had a type, Paola," Amber said quietly, choosing her words carefully. "I rather thought you'd go with anyone, no?" She watched in satisfaction as Paola's cheeks reddened. And before Paola could say anything further, she walked off. She slammed her bedroom door behind her, tears of anger and disappointment brimming, threatening to spill. So Paola had got her claws into him . . . well, if there was one thing she *wouldn't* do it was fight with Paola over a man. And not only because Paola was sure to win. The thought of having something that Paola had touched made her feel sick. Just as Paola made her feel sick. She yanked her necklace off and threw it onto the floor. Dr. Tendé-*whatever-his-name-was* was obviously not as clever as he looked. He ought to have seen straight through Paola, to the cheap little slut Amber knew her to be. Oh, well . . . his mistake. Paola would soon tire of him. She turned on the shower and stepped in. But, she thought to herself as the water hit her face, she couldn't imagine ever tiring of Tendé . . . and the truth was really quite simple. When she thought about Tendé and Paola, it hurt. Why did Paola always have to ruin everything? She had the feeling she'd be competing with her half-sister for the rest of her damned life.

PART FOUR

≈40≈
London, England
1990

Madeleine cursed as she battled her way up Tottenham Court Road. It was windy, cold *and* raining—a horrid, depressing combination—and of course she'd forgotten her umbrella. She was struggling to get back to the hospital with an armful of books, two plastic bags containing case notes she ought to have finished reading ages ago, and a paper bag, already falling to pieces, in which she'd carefully placed a dozen eggs, a carton of milk and four packs of cigarettes—basic supplies for a week. She had her first surgical case in little over an hour and she didn't want to be late. She turned down Middleborough Street and into the driving rain. A second later, a gust of wind nearly blew her off her feet; she stumbled, there was the quick, awful sensation of something slipping through her fingers . . .

and then, of course, her bags crashed to the ground and the carton of milk burst—all over a pair of black, well-polished brogues and a pair of dark tweed trousers. Swearing and apologizing at the same time, she bent down in the rain and tried to retrieve her broken eggs, empty milk carton and sodden cigarettes.

"I'm awfully sorry," she stammered, straightening up. Fortunately, the eggs had broken in their plastic container and not on the gentleman's legs.

"Not to worry," she heard him say dryly, shaking his trouser leg and sending little droplets of milk scattering onto the pavement. "No damage done."

"I'm really sorry," she repeated, looking up at him. He was a little taller than she, she noticed—middle-aged, with short grey hair and grey, rather cold eyes behind his glasses. He shook his trouser leg again, nodded curtly at her and then walked off, leaving her to pick up her soiled goods from the puddles on the ground.

An hour later, she was just donning her gown and mask in preparation for surgery when the doors to the ante-theatre swung open and the consultant strode in. She looked up. It wasn't the familiar figure of Dr. Harrigan, the surgeon whom she'd been ex-pecting. She peered at him over the rim of her sur-gical mask. Oh no, it couldn't be . . . yes, it was . . . it was the man she'd bumped into in the street, barely an hour earlier. She blinked in confusion. He was a doctor? She'd never seen him before. Was he new to the department? She just hoped he wouldn't recognize her. An inept, clumsy resident was the last person he needed to assist on the operation before them. She tied her gown with slightly shaking fingers and followed him into the operating theatre.

The case was a long and complicated one: a twenty-two-year-old man, with stage C-3 colon cancer, rare in someone so young. For almost six hours straight, Madeleine worked with the consultant surgeon and a senior resident to carefully cut the tumor away from both the colon and the stomach wall to which the tumor had attached itself, ensuring they had taken as wide an arc around the affected site as possible, together with samples of the lymph nodes around the groin. From her notes, Madeleine knew that the tumor in this case was a surprise—the young man on the table before them looked healthy enough, despite the cancer, she'd heard the two senior doctors say as they opened him up. He'd apparently been suffering stomach pains and cramps for some time and although he'd twice seen a GP, the fact that he was so young had almost ruled out the possibility of cancer and no one had thought to look for it. His girlfriend had brought him in the night before; the pain in his stomach had worsened over the past few days and they were both worried. A CAT scan of the colon had immediately shown the radiologist what was wrong.

She watched in respectful silence as the surgeon closed the stomach flap and neatly and precisely stapled the two sides together. If the young man were lucky, all he would be left with was a scar running almost the entire length of his stomach. The two senior doctors seemed to think he had an outside chance—with chemotherapy and the right attitude, he might just make it. She helped the theatre nurses clean up after the operation and prepare the table for the next case. It was dark by the time she peeled off her mask and gloves and threw them into the bin for incineration. She glanced at her watch— she'd been in theatre for almost seven hours straight.

"Dr. Szabo?" A voice broke in on her thoughts. She was sitting in the hospital canteen with a cup of tea, going over in her mind the procedure they had just performed, when someone interrupted her. She looked up. It was the surgeon, the man on whom she'd spilled her milk. She swallowed a mouthful of burning tea. If he recognized her from the morning's earlier encounter, he made no sign. He looked down at her, unsmiling. "I believe the person sitting over there by the window is the girlfriend of the young man on whom we've just operated," he said in his dry, Scots voice. "Would you be so kind as to let her know the surgery was successful?"

Madeleine nodded quickly. "Of course," she said, getting up hurriedly from the table. "Shall I . . . what shall I tell her . . . about the prognosis?" she stammered.

"*Dr.* Szabo," he said in a tone that indicated he thought her anything but. "You assisted at the procedure, did you not?" Madeleine looked at him warily, wondering what he was about to say. "And you read the case notes, did you not?" She nodded again. "Then extrapolate from what you saw and read and give the poor woman some information. She looks in desperate need of it." And with that, he turned on his heel and walked off, leaving a red-faced and rather angry Madeleine behind.

It was almost a week before she saw him again. She was heading back towards ICU to check on the young man as part of her morning ward rounds when she caught sight of him striding towards her, his white coat flying out behind him, his face full of a thunderous rage. She turned and gaped as he strode past, a clutch of nervous housemen and registrars following him, each wearing a more worried expression than the last.

"What's going on?" she asked the staff nurse ten minutes later, as she walked past the nurses' station.

"It's the Brown girl. The one he operated on last week. She went into a coma this morning and the lab results aren't back yet on the tissue samples he sent for biopsy. He's on the warpath for the pathologist. Poor bloke. I don't fancy being in *his* shoes this morning." Pat Miller, the usually cheerful staff nurse, looked glum. "He's been in here all morning, upsetting my staff."

"Who is he?" Madeleine asked, picking up the case notes on her own patient. "How come I've never seen him before?"

"Alasdair Laing, the head surgeon. He's brilliant, don't get me wrong . . . but a pain in the arse to work with. He's been in the States, on some exchange scheme with a medical school in Boston. Pity they didn't keep him . . ." Pat's voice trailed off suddenly.

Madeleine looked up, and blinked. She closed her eyes briefly, wishing the ground would open up and swallow them both. In front of them on the other side of the counter stood Alasdair Laing, a look of withering disdain on his face.

"Dr. Szabo . . . when you've *quite* finished," he said, sending a shiver of despair down Madeleine's spine, "would you see to it that Charles Mortimer's new regime is implemented? You'll find the necessary instructions in his notes." He turned around and marched out of ICU.

"Oh, well," Pat Miller said, pulling down the sides of her mouth and shrugging. "He never liked me much anyway." Madeleine smiled faintly. Could it get any worse?

It did. At eight that same evening, her bleeper went off, rudely jolting her out of the ten-minute nap she'd been luxuriating in. She glanced at the message. *Report immediately to ICU.* She leapt up, smoothing back her hair and shoving her feet into her shoes. What could have happened? She raced down the corridor, her heart thumping. As soon as she pushed open the doors to the ward, she realized what she'd done. Or rather, what she hadn't done. Dr. Laing was standing at Charles Mortimer's bedside, a look of exasperated rage on his face. Madeleine almost died. How *could* she have forgotten? she asked herself over and over again as the case notes were revised and the new drugs ordered immediately from Pharmacy. Why on earth hadn't she done it as soon as she'd been told that morning? With flaming cheeks, she handed the clipboard back to Dr. Laing, avoiding the matron's eye and trying her hardest to keep a calm, professional look on her face. She felt like bursting into tears. Her chances of getting onto a good surgical rotation team were slipping further and further away. The word would soon go round the senior consultants that Madeleine Szabo was forgetful, clumsy and inept and no one would want to work with her. The teams were highly competitive—getting on the right one was notoriously difficult. What the hell was wrong with her? She watched in embarrassed silence as Dr. Laing discussed the patient's new regime with the ICU staff. Not once did he look her way.

≈41≈

She saw them as soon as she walked in the door. Propped up carelessly against the landing wall. She stopped on her way up the stairs, pulled the top canvas towards her and looked at it properly.

"Charlie, wait . . ." she called up the stairs. "Hang on a minute." She stood back, considering them. Six works in all—oversize canvases, resting against one another. She wondered who the artist was.

She looked at the painting. It was several layers

deep. A sunset, almost photographic in its quality and intensity . . . the purples and reds of the poem were painted in thick, rich horizontal stripes across the broad canvas. From blood-red to the palest, most delicate pink, almost translucent. Overlaid on the layer on top of the sunset were the most unusual markings—cartographic marks . . . wind direction, wind strength, isobars, barometric readings . . . she vaguely recognized them from the weather reports on the television. Contour lines of storms, areas of high and low pressure and electricity build-up. She peered intently at the painting, trying to "read" it . . . was it a map of some sort? There were charts . . . tiny, scribbled names . . . Rotterdam, Le Havre, Calais, Long Beach, Monrovia, Cape of Good Hope, a mixture of harbors and ports around the world. And finally, the last layer of work . . . mark-making . . . what looked to be thousands of tiny, white stenciled marks . . . small, irregularly shaped ovals and oblongs, covering the entire surface of the sunset and the "map," thicker in places, thinned out and solitary in others. Incredible, Becky thought to herself, standing up. It must have taken the artist forever to cover the canvas. She looked at the other paintings and saw similar themes: a large-scale, lusciously colorful image as a background, some sort of calligraphic layer of information on the middle layer and the "marks," colonizing the space of the canvas in the foreground. The paintings were so unusual, hovering somewhere between cartography, poetry and art.

"Becky!" Charlie called her from the top of the

stairs. "What on earth are you doing down there?" he shouted down to her.

"Coming," Becky shouted up automatically. She made a quick note of the artist's name—Saba Mehretú. Unusual. She hurried upstairs.

On Monday morning, she walked into work with a bounce in her step. Morag, the gallery owner, looked up as she came through the door.

"Had a good weekend?" she asked, smiling.

"Wonderful. Morag, listen. I've just seen something . . . d'you have a minute?"

Rushing for the bus that evening, she hugged herself with glee. She'd done it! She'd managed to convince Morag not only to take a look at the paintings, but . . . if she liked them, to stage a show. It was the break Becky had been waiting for. She'd been working as an assistant curator at EC1, a small, East End gallery, for almost a year. It was a fantastic job—she adored it. She sometimes couldn't believe she'd waited so long to actually *do* something with her degree in art and stop pretending she was one day going to become An Artist. It was seeing Amber and Madeleine back in London again almost two years ago that had done it. Amber was now a bona fide journalist at the prestigious London-based *Financial Digest* and Madeleine was Dr. Madeleine Szabo, on her way to becoming a first-class, world-class surgeon. Becky . . . well, Becky was a temp when they met for dinner. It had been a strange evening—the three of them back together again after almost two years. After the last time Becky had seen her, Amber had suddenly decided to go back to New York. She'd spent two years working for some local newspaper, getting the kind of experience she needed, she told them. She wanted to make absolutely sure no one could ever accuse her of trading on her name, or on Max's contacts. It had been pretty low-key stuff—neighborhood affairs; petty crime; the birth of the local girls' soccer team—but she'd earned her stripes and was proud to say she'd done it. Becky remembered looking at her across the dinner table, speechless with admiration. Madeleine had graduated near the top of her class, of course, and had won a place to do the next part of her training at UCH in London. When the time came for Becky to relate her activities—well, there wasn't much to say, really. She drank to their success and, blinking back tears, swore that the next time they met, there would be an achievement of hers to toast as well.

What was peculiar was the speed with which things fell into place, once she'd decided to do something. She'd seen the advertisement in the paper the Monday after their meal. *Assistant curator sought. Young, alternative gallery. Fine Art, incl. photography, sculpture and installations. Experience preferred but not necessary.* Becky wasn't even sure what "alternative" meant. She put together a CV, penned a quick covering letter and shoved it in the letterbox, praying that something would come of it. The following week she had an interview and the day after, a job. Morag, the gallery owner, was a cheerful woman in her late thirties from Glasgow who had done exactly what Becky had—taken a degree in Fine Art from the illustrious Macintosh School of Art . . . and then sat back for four years wondering why there were no jobs on offer. She'd lived with a group of fellow Scottish artists/waiters/secretaries in an old loft space on Charlotte Street in the East End and got to thinking, along with a few others, that the abandoned industrial buildings in that part of the city would be perfect spaces for showing art—in particular, the kind of art that didn't make it to the established galleries in the West End. There were a few of them at first: EC1, which she'd started on her own; the Showrooms just down the road from them on Shoreditch High Street; Cavalier on Bingham Street and the just-opened in VA, the Institute of Visual Arts, on Rivington Street. There wasn't much else going on in the run-down and semi-abandoned streets east of Liverpool Street but there were lots of broke artists living in the loft spaces above the empty shops—and Morag knew most of them. Slowly, her reputation for spotting a good, up-and-coming artist or recognizing a trend, grew. She'd had two major successes in the three years she'd been open which meant that there was a little extra money in the bank for the first time and that they could afford to take a risk or two, should one come along.

So when Becky burst in on a Monday morning announcing she'd just spotted the most *amazing* paintings—*you just have to see them, Morag . . . the woman's a genius, I promise!*—she agreed quite readily. She and Becky put on their coats and walked over to the house where Becky had seen them. It had been a birthday party—some friend of Becky's fiancé, Charlie. Becky had immediately tried to find the artist and it turned out that she'd left that party to go to another. So Becky had spent the rest of the evening traipsing around Shoreditch, going from one party to another, looking for a woman named Saba Mehretú. When she finally found her, she realized not only was the young woman an extremely talented artist, she was a potential media star. She was in her late twenties, half-Swedish, half-Ethiopian; brought up in Detroit, Michigan, and just arrived in London. She was also absolutely gorgeous. By that time Becky didn't care whether she was nice or not—she was young, exotic and talented. Nothing more was needed. She handed Saba a business card, extracted a number from her and promised to be in touch.

"Well, what d'you think?" Becky asked, unable to keep the nervousness out of her voice. Morag stood for a moment, considering.

"I think . . . I think they're beautiful. Does she have a gallery? Has she shown anywhere?"

"I don't think so. I . . . actually, I forgot to ask."

"Well, find out. I think we can definitely build something interesting around her. They're beautiful." Becky almost hugged her. They walked back to the gallery, talking animatedly. By the time they pushed open the gallery doors, they'd decided on a title for the show—*Mark Up*—which both of them loved, and a range of dates. The next step, which Becky would handle alone, would be to bring Saba into the gallery for the first round of serious talks and negotiations.

She'd never been shown in London before but Saba turned out to be a shrewd operator. She walked into the gallery wearing paint-splattered jeans, dusty sneakers and a Chanel pink and white checked jacket, complete with pearl buttons and matching necklace. She was petite with tawny, caramel-colored skin and enormous grey-green eyes; her hair was a cloud of dark-brown curls and the silver bracelets on her left arm jangled every time she spoke. Becky could only gape at her. In her mind, the advertising and marketing of the show was already taking shape. Huge, black and white billboard-sized photographs of the artist; small, exquisite prints of sections of her paintings . . . extracts from her poetry, small samples of new work-in-progress. With luck, EC1 could become as famous as Saba Mehretú was—or would be. Becky could feel it. And she had discovered her.

Morag listened to Becky's plans for the publicity surrounding the show. It was clear from the look on her face that she was impressed with what she'd come up with. For the first time since she'd started at EC1 she had something she could really call her own and she understood the thrill of watching something she'd created slowly begin to take shape.

After the contracts between EC1 and Saba had

been signed and all the legal issues resolved to both Morag and Saba's satisfaction, the work of putting the show in place began. Becky had the six enormous paintings removed from the hallway and brought into the gallery storeroom. There were eight other pieces in Saba's studio of a smaller size and dozens of loose-leaf sketches and drawings in her portfolio. The two of them spent a very pleasant morning going through the portfolio, selecting pieces for the show. They decided on twenty pencil and ink drawings, Basquiat-like in their collage quality with bits of photographs, scribbled notes and small patches of color woven into the blend. Becky thought plain light beech frames and an off-white passe-partout background would be best for showing the pictures off, and Saba agreed. They set a date for a photograpreher friend of Saba's to come round and take the black and white photos Becky wanted; it all seemed to come together very nicely. They had almost three months until the opening; Saba promised to finish the eight smaller works in that time and left Becky to get on with the task of marketing and organizing the show.

It was almost eight by the time Becky got home that evening. Morag had practically thrown her out of the office, laughing. *Go home! Go on with you!* She'd collected her coat and reluctantly left.

She pushed open the front door, wondering if Charlie was back. The house was empty and quiet. She walked through to the kitchen. Everything was calm and clean, a sure sign that he hadn't yet arrived. She smiled to herself and walked upstairs. In the big bedroom that was theirs on the first landing, she peeled off her work clothes and rummaged around for something more comfortable. Five minutes later in a pair of sweatpants and a warm wool sweater, she walked downstairs and opened the fridge. Charlie was probably at one of his business dinners—she found it difficult to keep track of where he was and who he might be out with on any given night. Charlie was one of those businessmen who found it difficult to explain exactly what he did. Other than going to lots of dinners. He was very handsome, *extremely* popular, from a very nice, well-connected family; he'd been to all the right schools and although he'd been kicked out of university after only a term, the experience didn't seem to have had any lasting effect—or caused any damage. Becky almost laughed out loud, remembering Charlie's description of how he'd got the job in which he'd been for the past ten years and which seemed to suit his charming, rather lazy attitude.

He'd done the "backpacking" thing for a bit after his summary dismissal from Durham. He'd gone to Nepal, inhaled enough opium to last him a lifetime, spent a year on a farm in the outback and then returned to London, suitably matured. Or so he said. A friend had suggested "something in the City" and so Charlie had dug out a list of firms that hired graduates, forgetting for the moment that he wasn't actually part of that select group and had chosen two with the nicest-sounding names. The following week he'd had two interviews on successive dates and one with an invitation to lunch. He arrived late to the first interview having lost his way in the maze of narrow streets around Bank but found his interviewer apparently "out of the office" and was shown to a very comfortable sofa and given a stack of magazines to read until Mr. Sherburne-Burridge arrived. He spent an enjoyable hour reading *Tatler* and *Vogue*, ignoring the more financially minded magazines on offer and finally, just after 3 p.m., a short, rotund man ambled in, clearly having enjoyed a very good lunch. Charlie was shown into his spacious office, asked a few questions about school (Harrow); university (Durham, but sadly cut rather short); contacts in the City (none) and sports played (lots). He was a little wary—surely it couldn't be that easy. But it was.

A week later, he started work as a trainee investment analyst (he confessed he had no idea what that actually was) but over the next ten years, managed to work his way up and past Mr. Sherburne-Burridge to his current position as an arbitrager, which Becky could never seem to pronounce, much less remember. Whatever it was he did, it seemed to pay very well. In addition, of course, there was his inheritance. Charlie was an only child. His mother had died when he was a teenager and his father passed away when he was twenty-three. He therefore found himself at the age of twenty-four with two homes—his trendy bachelor pad in Islington and a large, suburban family home in leafy Dulwich. When he met Becky, through a mutual friend, he suddenly realized he was completely alone in the world. He told her she reminded him of his mother, a red-haired woman of considerable beauty and charm, or so he said. Becky, too naïve to understand the full implications of the statement, was flattered. It took him three months to persuade her to move into the Dulwich home with him—and that had been a year ago.

She kicked the refrigerator door shut and walked to the oak dining table she and Charlie had found on holiday in Spain. They'd had it shipped back to London at almost four times the cost of the table itself. It was beautifully solid and aged and softened the rather austere stainless steel kitchen that Charlie had insisted on installing. She looked around her at the calm, understated luxury; the little touches that made the place so desirable to her and to the people she showed it to—look, she felt herself saying silently . . . I lack for nothing. An Aga stove; Zanussi dishwasher; Brabantia bread bin and Duralit toaster. Charlie had even allowed her a few "artistic" touches—blinds, instead of curtains and that eye-catching Persian rug in the hallway—rust, olive-green and burgundy—not the sort of crisp, clean, blues and whites that Charlie liked. She loved having friends over, even the art crowd whom Charlie, surprisingly perhaps, liked. After all, it was at the party of a publishing director whom Charlie knew that she'd seen Saba's paintings. David Mallam had inherited a small but prestigious publishing firm from his parents who specialized in modern art and Saba had apparently met his glamorous wife, improbably named Dot, at a gallery. She'd complained about lack of space, having only just arrived in London, and Dot had generously told her she could store the paintings at the enormous loft she and David shared just off Fournier Street. An odd place for a publishing director to live, Becky had remarked to Charlie, but Charlie just tapped the side of his nose and said it wasn't only artists who knew a good thing when they saw one. He'd been thinking of investing in a bit of property around there himself. Becky smiled and shook her head. Charlie. He was completely incorrigible.

She pulled out one of the chairs and sat down with her plate of sliced apple, coleslaw and Wiltshire ham. She poured herself a large glass of red wine and pulled the newspaper he'd left there that morning towards her. She flicked through the headlines until she found the TV section and scanned it quickly. Nothing much. She concentrated on her coleslaw and ham, her mind already drifting back to the upcoming exhibition.

She was almost asleep by the time Charlie came home. She could hear him stumbling around downstairs, probably rather the worse for wear. Sure enough—a thud and a stifled swear word. She rolled over, amused. A few seconds later, the door opened softly and Charlie's head appeared.

"Are you asleep?" he whispered.

"Not any more," she whispered back.

"Oh. Sorry. Had a bit too much to drink, I'm afraid." He walked over rather unsteadily to the bed.

"I can tell," she said, wrinkling her nose. Cigar

smoke and port. Charlie was thirty-four with the tastes and mannerisms of a fifty-year-old.

"Can you really? How awful of me." He sat down next to her, smiling. He slid his hand underneath the silk counterpane and fumbled his way to the bare skin of her stomach. "You're wearing a nightdress," he said, sighing heavily.

Becky laughed. "So?"

"So? You promised you wouldn't."

"When?" she asked, genuinely surprised.

"This morning. Remember? I told you I was off to have dinner with Gleesman tonight and you asked if I'd be late and I said yes and would you please wait up for me wearing nothing but this." He fingered the chain around her neck with his other hand.

"I don't remember a word of *that* conversation," she said, wriggling away from his cold hand.

"Oh yes you do." He bent his head. His lips were almost as cold as his hand. His tongue was warm, though, and quickly found its way into her mouth bringing with it the sweetness of port and a faint taste of chocolate. "Take it off," he murmured, tugging at her nightdress. She obliged and sat up, pulling it swiftly over her head. Charlie paused for a moment and switched on the little bedside light. He liked looking at her, he told her. At the pale, small breasts, milky-white skin and the little whorl of her navel that he told her was like an orange. He shrugged his way out of his own clothes and slid into the bed beside her. He was already hard. Becky wouldn't have minded a little more of the foreplay and teasing—the parts she liked best—but, she thought to herself as he pulled her on top of him, the best bit of all was having a fiancé like Charlie come home to a house like theirs and to a life like hers. She was twenty-five. If she thought about it, which she tried not to, she hadn't thought it would be so easy. She had everything and everyone she wanted. From where she'd been a year ago, everything had suddenly and dramatically gone right. Their wedding was planned for the following spring, with Amber and Madeleine as bridesmaids. Neither of *them* had boyfriends. Back then, when it seemed as though they had everything and she nothing, she had to admit to feeling just the tiniest bit superior in that department. Becky Aldridge hadn't spent a day of her life as a single girl, not since she'd hopped semi-naked into Kieran Sall's bed and discovered just what the combination of small, rose-tipped breasts, smooth alabaster skin and pretty legs could do to most men.

≈42≈

Amber had heard about a small trick: focus on something else and the minutes will pass. She tried to focus on something else—anything else—but couldn't. She felt the muscles in her legs contract in pain and glanced down at the pedometer. Four miles—*was that all?*—which meant she had two more to go. Six miles a day. That was the target she'd set herself and that was what she'd reach, even if her legs gave out before she got there. She continued running. On either side of her, men and women were doing the same thing. They sounded like a stampede of angry beasts—twenty pairs of legs hitting the rubber at the same time. She ran on.

Fifteen minutes later, it was all over. She did the obligatory stretches, wiped the sweat from her brow and headed to the showers—the best part of any workout. She'd made it part of her going-home routine, three times a week. Sitting on her bum in front of a computer all day long, she complained to Becky, was sending it southward. She showered and changed in record time, left the gym *and* caught a bus on which there were actually free seats. A luxury. She got home just before the eight o'clock news was due to start.

As she came through the front door, she heard the blips on the answering machine. Someone had just rung. She switched on the lights, threw her coat over the chair and walked over to the machine. Six messages—the little red light flashed angrily. She switched it on and walked over to the fridge. All from Max, thankfully. Although it was nearly a year since the last of the silent, menacing phone calls, she still felt a sense of unease every time she picked up the phone. Henry—she was sure of it. She listened to Max's deep voice filling the flat. She was to call him in Menorca the minute she got in. There goes the news, she thought as she pulled the phone towards her. She would have to catch it at ten. She dialed his private number.

"Hi," she said, settling herself down in the sofa

with a glass of wine. "I just got your messages. What's up?"

"Where have you been?" Max's voice was petulant. "I've been calling you all day."

"I was out of the office today, interviewing someone. I've only just got back. I was at the gym."

"Oh. Well. Listen, I need a favor." Amber raised her eyebrows. A favour? Max asking her for a favor?

"What sort of favor?" she asked cautiously.

"I need to get something written. A piece . . . a journalist's piece. It's to do with this project we're setting up. I need you to go out to Bamako—"

"Where?" Amber sat upright.

"To Bamako. Mali. I need you to go there some time in the next month. It's got to be before the—"

"Max. I *work* for a living! I can't just get up and go at a moment's notice. And besides, what project are you talking about?"

"It's not at a moment's notice—you've got holiday, surely? This is important, Amber. I need to have something written about this deal . . . look, why don't we meet this weekend. I'll come to London, if you like. We'll go out to dinner and I'll explain the whole thing."

"But why can't you . . . I mean, you must have hundreds of other journalists you can ask. Why me? And it'll look odd, anyway . . . me writing an article about one of your projects."

"That's the whole point. I don't want it known that I'm involved. Look, I'll give you a ring on Saturday, all right? We'll have lunch at my club." And with that, Max rang off, leaving a rather annoyed and mystified Amber sitting on the couch staring blankly at the television screen. She took a sip of wine. There was something else. Tendé Ndiaye. It had to be something to do with him. Amber had seen him once since the party some four years previously. He and Max had become unlikely firm friends, despite the nearly thirty-year age gap. She was annoyed to find her reaction to him hadn't changed at all since the party. A slight intake of breath, a faint but discernible quickening of the pulse. He piqued her interest, that was all—or at least so she told herself. She couldn't bring herself to inquire or think any further on what might have happened between him and Paola. The last time she'd seen him, he and Max had stopped over in London for a day en route to somewhere in the Far East. She'd been at home, they'd exchanged a total of oh, fifty words and it hardly seemed the place or the time to bring up the subject: by the way, did you sleep with my sister? Or she with you? He seemed wary of her, as he had been the first time but before she could think of a way to progress the conversation, Max had come into the kitchen and the two of them left shortly afterwards for dinner. Of course, the encounter had brought him right back into the frame of her mind and it took her a few weeks to shift him out again. A diffident and beautiful man. For a while she amused herself making up adjectives to describe him: compelling; controlled; complex. She stopped. There was no use letting her imagination run away with her.

Now Max had brought him firmly back. Blast. She wondered what the project was about. Max had become increasingly distracted in the past few months. He was always away in the Far East; Australia; New Mexico . . . he'd been strangely hesitant to say where exactly and what he was doing. The last time she'd been home, there had been an enormous delivery of books for him. Amber had tried to take a quick look at what he was reading but the boxes were firmly taped shut. And since the whole messy affair with Kieran, his study and bedroom were securely locked when he wasn't in London, so no chance of finding out there. She took another sip of wine. Well, whatever it was, she'd find out soon enough. She picked up the phone again. Madeleine had left a message the night before.

Max came into the dining room at his club, all smiles and looking exceptionally well. Tanned, fit, beaming. Amber's heart sank. Whatever it was he wanted, it wouldn't be small, or easy. Max had never asked her for a favor in his life. She wasn't sure he'd ever asked *any*one for a favor.

"Darling," Max came over to the table. Amber's heart sank even further. When had Max ever called *any*one "darling"?

He waited until they'd both finished eating and the little cups of espresso coffee had been brought to the table. He dabbed delicately at his mouth with the napkin and leaned back in his chair.

"I want you to write something for me," he said, getting straight to the point. "An opinion piece. I'll explain to you what I need and you can decide how to do it." Amber nodded cautiously. Max had already assumed, of course, that she would do it. She put down her cup and listened. The story, when it came, was fascinating.

For a few years now, Max told her, he'd been feeling somewhat restless. Nothing major, just a feeling that some of the old joy had gone out of his game; and by that he meant his business dealings. He was at his peak—enough money to ensure that even his grandchildren would never have to work, should they so choose. He was respected, feared and disliked, in almost equal measure. There were very few deals of a certain nature that didn't involve Max in some way and his influence extended well beyond those affairs in which he got personally involved. Professionally, he was at the top and there really wasn't anywhere else to go, except down, perhaps, and that, of course, was out of the question.

When he met Tendé Ndiaye on a plane to East Germany in 1986, his interest was piqued. A young, multilingual junior government minister with an enviable grasp of languages, cultures, socio-political nuance and world events . . . who could fail to be charmed by the man? Max had gone back to London after his dealings in East Berlin were complete and on the spur of the moment, had decided to look up Mali in the handsome encyclopedias that lined his study walls. There wasn't much to read. He'd ordered a few French books on the country—there seemed to be more information available in French—and then, purely by coincidence, he'd been waiting to see an old friend in his offices in the

City one day and had been given a *National Geographic* to thumb through as he waited. The cover story was *Mali: the Salt Kingdom* and it had taken Max all of five minutes to devour the article, excuse himself from the meeting and run down the stairs, much to the surprise of the receptionist. Never one to lose any time, he'd jumped in a taxi and gone straight to the British Library where he'd made a note of every book, magazine and article available on two issues: salt and Mali. Within a week, his secretary had delivered the books he'd ordered and he sat down to read. It took another fortnight but at the end of it, he had an idea. A mad, crazy, almost laughable idea . . . but it gripped him like nothing in the past few years had.

Mali, he explained to a wide-eyed Amber, had been an immensely wealthy empire at one time, built largely off the back of the trans-Sahara trade. Cities like Timbuktu and Djenné were almost mythical centers of power, learning and culture to generations of Europeans. Salt was so valuable to the peoples south of the Sahara that in places like Timbuktu, it was traded weight for weight with gold. But by the middle of the eighteenth century, other trade routes had opened up, other dynasties had risen and the power and influence of the Mali Empire were vastly diminished. The French colonized almost the entire middle strip of West Africa, naming it Western French-Soudan and for decades, its decline was almost complete. *Why couldn't you have shown this much interest in my history lessons?*

Amber wanted to say to him. She'd never seen Max so animated.

The article Max read in the *National Geographic* was mostly historical—dozens of beautifully shot photographs of the arid landscape, the splendid ruins at Djenné and Timbuktu, the mosques made entirely from mud and so on. But what really caught Max's imagination were the pictures and short descriptions of the salt mines at Taoudenni and Téghaza in the far north of the country. One description—he couldn't remember it word for word—involved an old, blind man who'd spent his life guiding the camel strains carrying salt across the desert to Timbuktu. As he got older, he began to lose his eyesight but refused to give up his job. Some of the younger men used to test him and ask him where they were. The blind old man would stop, pick up a handful of sand and sniff it. He always knew exactly where they were from the smell of the sand.

"Is that really true?" Amber asked him, smiling. Max's enthusiasm was catching.

He shrugged. "Who knows? Does it matter?" He signaled for another coffee and continued.

The article had made reference to the fact that there was enough salt lying beneath the surface of the Sahara to fulfill the growing demand for industrial salt in the developed world. The problem wasn't the quantity of available salt: it was getting it out. He spent a month poring over technical and scientific journals, familiarizing himself with almost everything there was to know about the damn substance—and made a call. He invited Tendé Ndiaye to his party in Menorca. And then he outlined his plan. He wanted to build the world's largest salt mine on the site of the world's oldest mine.

Fortunately for him, Tendé was also immediately gripped by the idea. As the Deputy Minister for the Environment, putting together the feasibility study for the project would have fallen under his jurisdiction. Very quietly, with the help of a scientist he'd known back in high school, he began a series of investigations. They studied the techniques the miners used—laboriously digging by hand to get to the first layer of salt, approximately a foot and a half below the surface of the ground. This first layer of salt was of poor quality, containing stones and sand. Medium-quality salt could be found in the second layer, about six feet down. But the best quality salt was deposited in layers extending for up to thirty feet below the surface of the ground—pure, white, flaky salt. The best available. The miners would cut in methodical layers then employ people to split the first, second and third layer and to cut the slabs to the right size for camel transportation. The tablets of salt were loaded onto the camels but not before each miner had stamped his tablets with his family symbol. The social structures of the peoples around the salt-producing areas were intimately bound up in the trade.

"But won't bringing in a modern plant ruin a traditional way of life?" Amber asked.

Max frowned. "Well, that's exactly what I want you

to write about. I want a piece that'll point out the *benefits* of bringing the whole thing up to date. Good God, these people live in the Middle Ages. Think of the opportunities something like this will bring!" It was on the tip of Amber's tongue to remind Max of his position when she had first brought up the idea of going to university but she remained silent.

"What does Tendé Ndiaye think of this?" she asked quietly.

"He's in a dilemma," Max shrugged. "He's stuck. If he gives the project his blessing—and did I tell you, he's about to be made Minister—then he'll have the traditionalists on his case. If he opposes it, he'll have the Prime Minister to answer to. The bottom line is that the country has to modernize. He knows it, I know it . . . but it's tricky. Getting public opinion behind the project's our best chance of success."

"And you think one little article in the FD's going to do that?"

"No, but it's a start. We need backers, of course . . . and an article like that'll be read by thousands of people. The right people. When they start taking an interest, other journalists will and the whole thing'll start snowballing. I've seen these things happen before."

"And when does this . . . article . . . have to be written?"

"Sooner the better. Now, this is what I've arranged." Amber sat back and listened in amazement as Max outlined her travel plans, dates and her rendezvous with Tendé Ndiaye at his home in Bamako.

"You've worked it all out," was all she could say when he finally stopped talking. Max looked terribly pleased with himself.

"Well, it was both of us, really. The thing is, we have to act on this fast. One of the things Tendé was doing in East Berlin was talking to the East Germans about rural industries and development. They didn't focus on the salt industry, but give them time—they will. It's a winner, Amber. We can't go wrong." Amber looked at him. It was probably the first time she'd ever heard anything close to passion in her father's voice. Max wanted this project to work. "I know what you're thinking," Max said suddenly. "I don't do this kind of thing. I put people together; I'm not a projects man. But I'm tired of it. I'm tired of always being the middleman. I want to be the frontrunner for once in my life. I want to *make* something. I want to produce something tangible, something I can hold in my hands."

"But you do make things . . . you make money."

"Money. Yes, I make money. That's the Jew in me." Amber looked up, startled. "No, I don't mean it like *that*. I mean . . . we . . . Jews . . . we're always the go-betweens, the fixers, the middlemen. We put our money in our heads, education, business . . . things that can't be taken away from us. That's what I remember my father saying."

"You . . . you've never talked about them before. I don't know anything about them," Amber said hesitantly.

"No, I don't suppose you do," Max said quietly, looking at his hands. Amber held her breath. "Anyway, that's all in the past." He looked up, a determined look on his face. So . . . where shall I send the tickets? To your home?"

"*Where* are you going?" Becky had obviously never heard of Mali.

"Mali. It's in Africa."

"Whatever for?"

"I've got a job to do, an article on the desert. Boring stuff. How's Charlie?"

"Oh, fine. He's away this week. Can't remember where. Paris, Milan . . . somewhere like that."

"Great! I mean, let's have dinner then, you, me, Madeleine. I'll find out when she's off duty." Amber corrected herself just in time. It wasn't that she didn't like Charlie, she just found him irritating. He was not a man who wore his privileges lightly.

They rang off and Amber turned back to the pile of magazines Max had so thoughtfully provided for her. Salt. It wasn't exactly what she'd planned to spend the weekend reading but . . . Max had asked her and he so rarely asked for anything. She felt duty bound to comply. If she were honest, she was also flattered.

≈43≈

"Dr. Szabo." He inclined his head. Madeleine went scarlet as she picked up her coffee cup and sat down in the only free seat in the little café—opposite him. She'd managed to escape from the hospital for a quick, fifteen-minute coffee break and she was sick of the muddy water they served in the hospital canteen. Just her luck to run into him in here! There was a short silence. She had forgotten to bring a book or a newspaper with her and she didn't even have a folder of case notes to study. There was nowhere to look but down, at her cup. She took one scalding mouthful after another, hoping she didn't seem too desperate to get away yet not relishing the idea of another fifteen minutes spent in silence sitting directly in front of the one person in the world to whom she had absolutely nothing to say. The minutes ticked by. Dr. Laing drank his own coffee— black, filter, she noticed absently—at an unhurried pace, reading the *Lancet*. "Mortimer's pulled through," he said suddenly, looking up. Madeleine swallowed hurriedly, burning her tongue.

"What? Oh, yes . . . yes, he's doing much better. He'll be leaving ICU tomorrow, I think."

"Yes. Tricky one. Still, surgery went well. Got it all out." He nodded to himself.

Madeleine hesitated. "Dr. Parker thinks he ought to . . . go through with the chemotherapy they've recommended," she said, wondering if she'd overstepped the mark. There had been a bitter row between the oncology consultants and the surgical team.

Dr. Laing shrugged. "Well, I suppose it can't hurt," he said dismissively. The clinical trials in colon cancer were inconclusive, Madeleine had read in a previous issue of the *Lancet*. It had made the decision whether or not to offer chemotherapy as a treatment that much more difficult. Madeleine had been with Dr. Parker and the senior resident when they'd told a bewildered Charles Mortimer that *he* would have to make the choice whether to go through with the treatment—it was too early to say whether it would help his survival chances or not. Parker had been furious at Laing's recommendation of surgery only. *Typical bloody surgeon*, she'd overheard him say to a colleague as they walked out of ICU. *Cut it out. End of story.* From his tone, Madeleine had gathered that it probably wasn't the end of the story.

"He's very young," she ventured after a moment. "It's hard to believe it can happen to someone of his age."

"Yes, that's the interesting thing about this particular cancer. You'll see from his medical history that his grandfather and father both suffered from the disease, although neither of them actually died from it. We know this sometimes happens in families . . . the disease will strike each successive person a generation earlier. Grandfather in his sixties, father in his forties and the young man in his twenties. Nature's way, we imagine, of getting rid of the defective gene. Eventually it surfaces in one too young to have reproduced and the gene dies off." Madeleine stared at him. It was the longest speech she'd ever heard him make, and by far the most interesting. She nodded. It made sense.

"So does that make his chances of survival any weaker?" she asked.

"Not necessarily. We took out a fair bit—the lab results indicated there was no metastasis anywhere else in the colon and it hasn't yet spread to the liver. He's lucky. Came in just in the nick of time." He put down his cup. "Similar case. In the *New England Journal of Medicine*. July 1988, I believe. A young man in California. Look it up when you've a moment." He stood up and pushed back his chair. He inclined his head again, picked up his raincoat and walked out before she could even say thank you.

≈44≈

In a brief ceremony at the Palais de Justice in Bamako lasting not more than twenty minutes, Tendé Tourmani Ndiaye was sworn in as Minister for Mines, Energy and the Environment. He shook the hand of the President, surprised as always by his firm, emotional grip; then it was the Prime Minister, the Speaker of the House and finally, his father, the Minister of Justice. Mohammed Ibrahim Ndiaye made no obvious sign of recognition—the young man in front of him was simply another civil servant, undergoing the same ritual he had undergone some thirty-five years earlier. If, as he held the young man's hand in his own, he exerted a little more pressure than was strictly necessary, or normal . . . well, that in itself too, was normal. At thirty-two, his son had done exceptionally well.

There was a smattering of applause, a few wide smiles for both father and son; then it was over. The protocol officers hovered around, making sure photographs of the new minister were kept to a minimum, that the invited journalists kept their questions brief and short and that the working day held as little interruption as possible. The President, flanked as always by his deputies and one or two security officers, left the hall first. As he left, the remaining ministers visibly relaxed, one or two coming up to Tendé and congratulating him in a heartier, friendlier manner. They then left the compound and drove to the Mandé, one of the newest hotels in Niaréla, the exclusive neighborhood in the center of the city where Tendé's mother and a number of businessmen and politicians were waiting for them.

Waiters hovered discreetly as the group was seated. There were few people in Bamako who did not recognize the greying head of the Minister of Justice, or his wife, the singer. Mandia Diabaté was already famous when she married Mohammed Ndiaye. Tendé had grown up with the framed photographs in which statesmen like Nkrumah, Nyerere and Mugabe, their arms draped around his mother and father, were captured, smiling. In the hallway at the family's home in Paris where Tendé had spent most of his school holidays, there was a picture of a very young Mohammed, the first socialist President Moussa Traoré and Yuri Andropov, the former leader of the Soviet Union, standing together outside the Kremlin, a clutch of bodyguards just visible in the background. It was a sign of how complex the relations between public and private, East and West, Europe and Africa, could be. It was also a sign of how successfully the Ndiaye family managed the divisions.

As the group around him ate and drank, showering congratulations on him and his parents, laughing uproariously at everything that was said, Tendé's mind wandered. The portfolio of Mines, Energy and the Environment was one he'd coveted, almost from the moment he'd stepped into government. It was one of the most important new ministries in the country. He was an economist, faithful to that discipline's principal tenet: the way forward, for developing nations, was through the economy. Only through successful and careful, careful economic development could the country make progress. The manner in which this country or that achieved the desired development was open to debate—socialist, capitalist, communist . . . even as a teenager, Tendé had understood that. His subsequent studies at the exclusive lycée in Bamako, followed by his bachelor's degree from Lyons confirmed his opinion, and much more. At home, in Mali, he was familiar with the capitalist *laissez-faire* doctrine France had left behind, despite the country's earlier flirtation with Marxism and its colonial legacy. Studying in Lyons had taught him something about the wider European context of that doctrine— going into the heart of the beast, his father had said to him, smiling a little. *Understand them and you will understand us.* He understood.

Later, when his father decided to send him to Moscow to study, he knew why. At the time, it had been a hard decision to bear. The weather, the language, the people . . . it was as unfamiliar to him as anything he'd ever experienced. He spent a year studying Russian at a private language institute, just outside the city, then two years at the prestigious state university in Moscow. By the time he was ready to leave Moscow he felt he was just beginning to get under the skin of the country, cracking the ice. The Soviet Union itself was undergoing a series of wrenching crises. It was an interesting time and Tendé emerged from it a more interesting man.

From the USSR, he went in the opposite direction. Columbia University in the early eighties was a radical and heady place to be. Tendé enjoyed every single, precious moment. He took classes by his hero and mentor, Edward Said; he listened to lectures by the brilliant philosopher Jacques Derrida; he traveled to Princeton to hear the elite African American academics; he read Marx and Fanon and Senghor; he joined the student societies, debated vigorously in public and in private; he explored every inch of New York, including the parts no one, not even Americans, cared to see—he knew the Bronx as well as he knew the Village and the myriad districts and communities in between.

And then, five years later, his doctorate under his arm, he went home. He spent a year working in the Ministry of Finance; a year working in the private sector with six months' secondment in Paris and then he formally entered government. In just three short years, he had risen from Assistant to the Junior Minister to Special Advisor to Deputy Minister. By anyone's accounts, it was a remarkable achievement in one so young. But for those who knew Tendé, it was simply part of the Plan. And not once

in thirty-two years had he deviated from it. Sometimes, looking at his handsome, closed face, his
mother wondered a little. He was so determined, so
quietly confident. No one, she knew, was *that* confident, or assured—it was impossible. But whatever
her private worries, Tendé seemed to take everything in his stride. Unlike his sisters, she and her
husband had never had to worry about their youngest son. She looked across the long table at him.
He was leaning back in his chair, watching the
group around him celebrate his success. She raised
her glass of chilled white wine. Tendé caught her
eye and raised his own. *I ka kènè.* Congratulations.
They both smiled.

≈45≈

They both came out of the elevator together. Dr.
Laing nodded curtly at Madeleine and pushed open
the hospital main doors. She followed, tightening
her scarf around her neck. There was a cold wind
blowing in between the tall buildings. They were
both walking towards the café. It was obvious. There
was a moment's hesitation as he slowed his pace
fractionally and she hurried up.

"A bit chilly this morning," he said as she drew
level.

"Yes. I thought spring was supposed to be on its
way," Madeleine said, grimacing.

"Well, this would be considered summer where I'm from," he said after a second.

Madeleine glanced at him. "You're Scottish, aren't you?"

"Indeed. From Aberdeen."

"Oh. I've never been that far north. I did my degree in Edinburgh . . ."

"I know."

"Oh." Madeleine didn't know what to say. Luckily they'd reached the café. He held the door open for her. They'd walked there more or less together and it would have seemed rude to leave and find a chair on her own.

"What will you have?" He solved the dilemma for her.

"A coffee, please. White. Thank you."

"Not at all." He smiled briefly and walked off towards the counter. Madeleine watched him go. It was true he made her nervous as hell but there was something unexpectedly warm about him. She realized it was the first time she'd seen him smile.

"Here we go." He brought the mugs to the table and sat down opposite her. The café was almost empty. She wrapped her hands around the steaming mug, grateful for its warmth. They began talking about upcoming cases—Madeleine was scheduled to assist at an appendectomy at four that afternoon; at midday the following day, a stomach obstruction that had been in the process of referral when she'd left the previous evening . . . and finally, a thoracic surgery on the Friday. She was currently a "floater," assisting surgery wherever and whenever she could. In a week or so, she would apply for—and be given—a place on a surgical team, hopefully the team of her choice. Despite his abrupt bedside manner and the fear he inspired in the junior staff, Dr. Laing's team was the most sought-after amongst the junior doctors. Compared to the genial, avuncular Harrigan, for example, surgery with Laing was a fierce, almost religious experience. His hands were steady, his instructions clear and precise. In his presence, Madeleine thought, nothing could go wrong. She wondered if it would be presumptuous . . . if she dared . . . could she?

"I was wondering," she began, her heart thumping. "About the surgical teams next week . . . I was wondering if there was any room left on yours?"

"Make an application like the rest of the world, Dr. Szabo. The personnel manager will have the necessary forms."

Madeleine blushed to the roots of her hair. It had come out all wrong; she hadn't intended to sound as though she were fishing for favors. She wished the ground would open and swallow her up. "Of course . . . I didn't mean . . . I just . . ." she stammered, kicking herself.

"Szabo. Are you Hungarian?" The question was a surprise.

"Yes. Yes, my parents are. I am."

"A lovely country."

"Have you been there?" Madeleine's voice was almost disbelieving.

"Once. To a conference in Budapest, quite a few

years ago now. A nation of very talented doctors, I must say." Madeleine half-waited for the adjoiner—*and you, quite obviously, are not one*. But it didn't come. Instead, they spent a very pleasant twenty minutes talking about Budapest—the boulevards, squares and churches of Madeleine's childhood. She even dared to tease him a little about his pronunciation. *Szent István körút* . . . not St. Stephen's Avenue. He gave up, almost laughing. As they put on their coats and headed back to the hospital, she found it hard to believe this was the same man she'd come in with. His smile, when it came, was a pleasure. She found herself wanting to make him smile again and again.

They met by accident a few more times in the canteen and at the café. It seemed as if the ice had been broken. He gave her a copy of a paper on pediatric surgery, written in Hungarian—a colleague of his, he said, handing Madeleine a thick sheaf of typed notes. Her heart sank. Her own language had remained a child's language, frozen in the mind and vocabulary of a ten-year-old . . . but he seemed rather pleased to have found it for her and she took it, smiling her thanks. The next time they met, they were on their way home. He asked how she'd found the paper, she explained a little about her lack of medical vocabulary and they laughed together. And then he invited her to eat with him at lunchtime one day, a small Hungarian restaurant on Marylebone High Street, not far away. She accepted without even thinking about it, touched by his kindness. It seemed completely natural, she told Amber over the phone. He had a taste for some goulash, he told her: *gulyás leves*, she corrected him. Soup, not stew. She asked if he'd ever had *töltött csirke* . . . stuffed chicken . . . or *képosztá* . . . spring vegetables. He shook his head. The hotel at which he'd been staying hadn't run to such exotic tastes. She laughed.

Over the stuffed chicken and *halászlé* that she'd ordered, she learned that he was fifty-one, from a small town outside Aberdeen, that his father had been a farmer and his grandfather before him. Alasdair was the first in the family to leave behind the land and livestock and take up the pen and book, never mind the scalpel. He'd done most of his training in Scotland, at the royal infirmaries at Dundee and Edinburgh, then moved to London and into a teaching hospital. He'd risen quickly through the ranks of academia; a visiting fellowship to an American university soon confirmed his position at the forefront of experimental surgery; from there, it had been several years on the visiting professorship and lecture circuit until he'd decided to come back to London to take up his present post as the head of the surgical department.

"And your family?" Madeleine asked, glancing quickly at his wedding band. There was the faintest hesitation.

"My wife lives in Edinburgh," he said slowly. "She's . . . not well. We have a ten-year-old son."

"Oh. I'm sorry."

"No need," he said briskly. "Now, what'll you have

for afters?" Madeleine looked back down at the menu. She really couldn't eat another thing, but . . . *somlói galuska* or *diós és mákos kalács*? Sponge cake or her mother's favorite, walnut and poppy seed cake? She couldn't resist. She watched, smiling, as he ordered both dishes—*we'll just share, shall we?*—and laughed out loud as he closed his eyes in bliss at the first mouthful of the deliciously light, moist sponge cake.

"She's got MS," she told Amber a week later. She'd found out from one of the nurses.

"That doesn't make her any less his wife," Amber said dryly.

"I know."

"Madeleine, he's fifty-one. He's your professor. And old enough to be your father. I don't know him but I just don't think it's a good idea."

"Well, nothing's happened. I mean, two lunches and a few coffees . . . it's hardly . . . anything, is it?"

"That's how these things always start," was Amber's dire prediction.

At first, she'd tried to shrug it off. Amber was absolutely right. He was far too old—and far too married. Besides, there was nothing going on, she told herself sternly. Exactly as she'd told Amber: two lunches and a few coffees. Although the last lunch had lasted almost three hours. She found him surprisingly easy to talk to. It was impossible to connect the interesting and interested man sitting in front of her listening intently to her talk about herself, with the dour, aloof consultant who'd been so rude to her the first few times they met. It was as if she'd suddenly opened a door in him, one that led to a completely different person . . . someone with a dry, sharp sense of humor, a great, deep laugh and a generosity she would never have guessed at beneath the somber exterior. He was very attractive— silvery grey hair; light, grey-green eyes beneath dark lashes; a nice, square jaw with a cleft that became more pronounced when he smiled. She liked the shape of him—tall, solidly built, the kind of man you could really lean into, especially if you were Madeleine's size. Alone in her tiny studio flat above Warren Street tube station where, every ten minutes, she could feel the tubes pass one hundred feet below her, she plugged in the kettle and tried to stop thinking about him. She couldn't. Madeleine's relations with the opposite sex had been . . . well, pretty disastrous, really. Apart from the whole, horrid episode with Mark Dorman about which she never spoke to anyone, *ever*, there had been a few rather awkward encounters in the ten years since, and that was it. If she thought about it, which she tried not to, the longest relationship she'd ever had had been with Mark Dorman and that hadn't been a relationship at all. There had been that week-long thing with Barnaby Johnson in her second year but she'd been a good head and a half taller than him and she always felt the two of them looked ridiculous. She'd broken the news to him as gently as she could and he actually looked rather relieved. She suspected his pass at her one evening in the union

bar had more to do with homesickness and the upcoming exams . . . and she'd been right. A fortnight
later, she saw him holding hands with Philippa
Somebody-or-other who was petite and waif-like
and suited him infinitely more.

And that was it, really. The two other one-night
stands . . . she   half-smiled   at   that—one-hour
stands, more literally—didn't count. A drunk, rather
sweaty encounter the night of their third-year finals
and once, at someone's party. She'd been rather
surprised to find herself the object of some resident's attentions, and that was all it took. Becky was
always saying it was because Madeleine was insecure about herself and lacked confidence, but it
wasn't strictly true. Madeleine had plenty of confidence. She wasn't afraid to ask questions in class;
she wasn't shy about putting herself forward, or arguing her point. She was good at what she did and
she knew it. It was just . . . with men. There was
something about having had the kind of teenage
years she'd had . . . always worrying about money,
an only child, having to take care of her parents in
the way she had . . . the early responsibilities had
left a mark on her. She somehow thought the romance and the silliness, the falling in love and the
parties and drinking champagne . . . she somehow
believed that wasn't for her. She was Madeleine
Szabo, six feet tall, one hundred and fifty pounds
(on a good day); daughter of immigrants whose
place could never be quite assured. As Amber said
to her, she felt as though she had to earn every
bloody thing that came her way. Around men espe-

cially, it made her slightly withdrawn and defensive and *that*, Amber said, was the reason Madeleine had never been in love. It was just rotten luck she'd fallen for a dog like Dorman but *please* don't let it ruin everything else, will you? Madeleine nodded doubtfully. It was easy for Amber to say.

Oh, stop it, she said to herself, getting up and going to the kitchen. She began the washing up from the night before. As she turned on the tap, she looked at her reflection in the window above the sink. She didn't look that bad. Her hair was a bit messy but it was long and thick . . . perhaps she should start wearing it down? *Stop it*, she said again, more firmly this time. *He's twice your age. He's married and he's not the least bit interested in you. So stop it*. She finished the washing up still thinking about him.

≈46≈

"Angela?" Amber called out, walking up the stairs to the drawing room on the first floor. There was no sound. She pushed open the door. Angela lay asleep on the divan by the window. Amber paused. She looked at her. With her long blonde hair falling over one arm, her face half-hidden by the curve of the other, she looked peaceful, almost child-like. Her blouse was buttoned up wrongly—she must have missed the first button. It gave her a lopsided air. Her legs were hidden by a thick, cream-colored

blanket but her feet were bare, sticking out from underneath it. Her soles were dirty, Amber noticed immediately. She'd obviously been walking around the
house barefoot. Amber felt a contraction in her
chest. A half-empty glass stood alone on the white
carpet beside her. There was nothing else in the
room. No books, no television, no magazines. Whatever else her mother did all day elsewhere in the
house, in this room she did nothing. Just lay at the
window, her dirty feet covered by a clean, thick blanket . . . staring at the street below. Amber turned
abruptly from the image in front of her and gently
closed the door before walking back down the
stairs.

She wandered into the kitchen. There were new
housekeepers and cleaners about, she noticed.
One of them, a slim, pretty young woman who had
introduced herself earlier as Siobhân, gave her a
friendly smile. No, she didn't know where Kieran
was—she hadn't seen him for a few days. Amber
turned down the offer of a cup of tea and continued
wandering through the rooms on the ground floor.
Max must have had the decorators in, she noticed.
There were subtle changes in the furniture and the
color of the walls . . . a new set of curtains in the
dining room . . . a large, beautifully polished cherry-
wood dresser now stood in the hallway. Where did
he get the time and energy to notice things like that,
she wondered, in between his proposals to boost
the economies of a dozen Third World countries
and building salt mines in places she'd never heard
of? She ran her fingers along its glossy surface—

not a speck of dust. Whatever was going on upstairs on the first floor of the house, standards above and below Angela hadn't slipped, not a bit. She looked at her watch. It was almost two. She had arranged to meet Becky to go shopping.

"Will you tell Kieran I said goodbye?" she asked Siobhân. "And Mrs. Sall as well. I'll be back in a couple of weeks."

"Of course." Although Siobhân was all smiles, there was something about her Amber didn't quite trust; she smiled too much. Amber missed Krystyna. She'd married an Englishman and moved to the home counties. Amber couldn't quite imagine what Krystyna made of them but she certainly hadn't wanted to go back to Poland. She picked up her coat and scarf and left.

"Come shopping with you? Of course . . . but why?" Becky's voice had sounded puzzled over the telephone. It was one of their long-standing arguments. Amber's fashion sense was practically non-existent, especially according to Becky's rather stringent standards. Yet Amber had always steadfastly refused to allow Becky to do anything other than comment. Two years in New York had done little to improve it, Becky wailed, as soon as Amber got back. But Amber was adamant. She liked what she wore. She didn't care if she sometimes got her colors wrong or styles a little out of season. Wrong? Out of season? Out of this world, more like, was Becky's sarcastic rejoinder, but Amber didn't really care. This time, however . . . it was different.

"Well, I might have to go out," Amber said, trying to sound nonchalant.

"Where? In the desert? I thought you were going to the Sahara."

"Yes, well . . . there might be this . . . I might have to go to dinner in Bamako, the capital. Before the desert. And there's this man," she added hesitantly.

"A *man*?" Becky sounded even more surprised. "What man?"

"He's one of Max's colleagues . . ." Amber began, regretting she'd opened her mouth.

"Oh, *no* . . . not you as well! Don't tell me *you* fancy some geriatric businessman." Becky laughed. She'd just spent an hour counseling Madeleine as to why Dr. Laing was *completely* wrong for her.

"What d'you mean 'me as well'? Of course not. He's not old. He's only thirtyish."

"And he's Max's colleague?" Becky sounded dubious.

"Well, sort of. I don't really know what they do but there's a small project they'd like me to take a look at and so I'm going for two weeks and there's nothing more to tell you."

"Of course there is. Don't you dare fob me off. What's going on?"

"*Nothing's* going on. Nothing at all. I've only met him twice," Amber said, feeling herself blush as she said it.

"Where's he from? English? French?"

"No, he's from there. He's from Mali."

"*What*? He's *African*? *Black*?"

"So?" Amber was immediately defensive.

"So . . . ? *Every*thing. Does Max know?" Becky squealed.

"There's nothing *to* know!" Amber said sharply, her cheeks burning. She'd known Becky would re-act that way; God, she could be so Little England at times. He's *African*? She heard the words again, and the alarm behind them. But her question had unnerved her. Did Max know? *Oh, for God's sake*, she muttered to herself, by now quite annoyed. *There's nothing to know. This has nothing to do with seeing Tendé Ndiaye again. I'm going to do a job. For Max. Period.*

"Don't tell me you're planning to wear that?" Becky looked shocked. Amber flushed. They were in Self-ridges.

"What's wrong with it?" Amber asked, her cheeks flaming. She was under the impression her dress sense had improved since her stint in New York.

"It's ridiculous. You're twenty-five, not forty-five. *Honestly*, Amber." Becky plucked the offending dress out of her arms and propeled her towards an-other rail. "D'you want this man to notice you or not?"

"I never said anything about . . ." Amber hissed, alarmed.

"You don't have to. Now, what about a couple of bikinis?"

"I'm going to *work*, Becky. It's not a holiday."

"I know. But you've got about as much chance of grabbing his attention in those," she waved disparagingly at the clothes Amber had picked out, "as you would in a sack. Come on, show off your figure. It's still worth showing, you know." Amber went even redder.

≈47≈

Tendé was one of the first passengers off the plane. He walked quickly down the steps towards the waiting car, shrugging off his jacket as he walked. Even at eight thirty in the evening, the temperature was in the eighties.

"*Bonsoir, m'sieur*," Majeed, his driver, greeted him. He nodded. It was good to be home. This time he'd been away almost a month. The car glided across the tarmac and was soon lost in the early-evening traffic heading towards the center of the city. As they crossed Pont du Roi Fahd over the sluggish, dirty-brown Niger, he looked out of the window at the city, slowly coming alive. It was the middle of Ramadan—the fast had been broken a couple of hours earlier and the city was beginning to pick up. Restaurants were full and the cheaper, curbside vendors selling small plastic cartons of *riz au gras*, *tô* and *saga-saga* were already busy. They turned onto Avenue al-Quds and headed for Tendé's house in Hippodrome, close to the old part of the city. As the car swept past the two familiar hotels, Le Djenné and Le Relax, Tendé felt himself begin to unwind. They drove through Missira, past the stadium and turned onto his street. Outside his walled compound, two armed sentries stood guard. One of them, a new recruit to the job, walked over to the car. He peered inside.

"*Vous cherchez*?" he demanded in French, his AK-47 dangling casually from one shoulder, like a handbag.

"*I ni sògòma, ni òwo?*" Don't you recognise him, idiot? The driver hissed the words at him. The guard jumped back, caught off guard. He leapt to attention, made a great show of ushering the car in, shouting at the second guard to "Open the gates! Close the gates! Open the door!" Tendé smiled to himself as he got out of the car. Home indeed. The air was dry but not yet dusty. The rains were finally over. He paused for a second on the verandah, inhaling the sweet scent of the jasmine that his mother had planted and instructed the garden boy to water every day. The verandah, which ran along the length of the three-bedroomed bungalow, was dotted with her enormous, burnished clay pots—fragrant jasmine in some, flamboyant purple and white hibiscus and tiny, pink tight-petaled roses in others. Mandia was forever smuggling seeds and cuttings in from her visits to Europe, determined to make them bloom. He smiled to himself. In fact, if it weren't for his mother, he thought, the whole place would have looked exactly the way it did when he'd moved in, almost a year ago. Thanks to her efforts, at least it looked lived-in. He pushed open the heavy wooden front door, feeling it creak stiffly under his hands.

It probably hadn't been opened in a few weeks. Lameen, his house boy—a misnomer; Lameen was older than he was—lived in the quarters at the back of the house and came in every day through the kitchen door. He dropped his bag on the polished wood floor and reached for the lights. In a second, the room was flooded with light. He looked around. It was a pleasant, simply furnished room. Mandia had thrown out all the standard, government-issued furniture that came with the house. She had hung long, indigo tie-dyed patterned curtains from Cote d'Ivoire at the windows and scoured the local marché for elegant pieces of mahogany colonial furniture; two long grey-covered sofas sat opposite one another in the center of the room, an ornate, wooden coffee table between them; bookshelves at one end of the room and the long, pale wood dining table Mandia had cajoled—and tortured—the local carpenters into making at the other.

He walked through the living room to the kitchen and opened the fridge. Lameen knew of his arrival; there were several ice-cold bottles of Castle beer in the shelves, as well as a covered plate of food. He took out a beer, pulled off his tie and walked back into the living room. The guards had carefully placed his suitcases next to the door. Lameen would open them in the morning and efficiently sort through his clothes. By the following evening, everything would hang, cleaned and neatly pressed, in his wardrobe. It was indeed a bachelor's existence. And that was how he liked it. Despite his mother's by now not-so-gentle nagging.

*   *   *

He woke early the next morning and for a second lay in bed, confused by his surroundings. The early-morning call to prayer had woken him. He glanced at the little bedside clock—it was 5 a.m. Outside he could hear the cockerel crowing and the sound of someone opening cupboards in the kitchen; Lameen was busy preparing breakfast. Of course. Ramadan. He was back at home. He pushed back the thin cotton sheet and walked towards the shower. He'd been traveling since the start of the fast and as such, had been exempted. He gave a half-groan. Two weeks until Eid. He stepped under the lukewarm water. That was another thing he'd have to remember to bring back from his next trip overseas: a water pump. The limp trickle splashing its way across his chest simply didn't cut it. He needed something far more vigorous to prepare him for the day ahead.

At exactly seven fifteen, Majeed pulled the car around to the front of the house and opened the door for Tendé. He grabbed his briefcase and, still reading his notes, got into the back seat. From there it was a short twenty-minute ride to the ministry. He had a full, long day ahead, without even so much as a sip of water. He passed a hand over his face. It was the first step in getting their project off the ground. Max's daughter, the journalist—he'd met her very briefly—was due to come out to Bamako in the next couple of weeks, just after the end of Ramadan. A good thing it wasn't the other daughter, he half-smiled to himself. He'd practically had to tear himself away from her at that party Max had given a couple of years back. He snorted. If anything would bring the project crashing to a halt even before it had begun, that would—fooling around with Sall's daughters. That was the thing about rich, European men, especially men like Max. Nothing was off limits: business deals, bribes here and there, the greasing of a palm . . . they took everything in their stride. But not their daughters. *That* was sacrosanct. In ten years of dealing with them, it was a rule Tendé had always obeyed. Besides, it wasn't the sexy little one coming out to the desert, it was the serious, rather forbidding one. He couldn't really remember what she looked like—tall, slim, very short hair. Almost boyish, he seemed to recall.

The car swept into the parliament complex. A uniformed sentry jumped forward as soon as it stopped. Tendé got out, adjusting his tie. He'd decided to wear a suit today; he would be doing a lot of talking and convincing and he needed to emphasize his familiarity with the West and their way of doing business. Wearing a suit at home also made him slightly uncomfortable—too damn hot, for one thing—but he knew he was at his sharpest when he was uncomfortable and if there ever was a day he needed to be at his best, this was it. He couldn't afford to make a single mistake. There were many at the table, he knew, who wouldn't be averse to seeing the cocky youngster trip up or over himself. And this time his father wouldn't be around to smooth the way. This time he was on his own. He picked up his briefcase and walked into the hall.

Francesca, unusually, was alone. She sat forward on the edge of her silk sofa and reached for a cigarette. Paola was out with her friends and wouldn't be back until late, if at all. She lit up, exhaling slowly. She inspected her nails. Something was bothering her. No, not *some*thing—Max. Max was bothering her. Paola was bothering her. She took another long, slow drag. She was forty-five years old; unmarried; no career other than bringing up a daughter who was rapidly turning out to be more of a headache than Francesca had ever bargained for; she had a very generous allowance from Max and a reasonably full social life as one of Rome's most charming hostesses—and that was it. She was well aware the "it" in question was more than many women had, but lately she hadn't felt quite as satisfied with herself and the course her life was taking as she used to be. There were several reasons. The one which weighed upon her most heavily was to do with a little scene at a spring engagement party she and Paola had attended at the weekend. At first, it had seemed great fun, the two of them dressing up and getting ready together. Francesca had had her hair cut the day before; a short, chic bob which António, her cherished stylist, had told her was right at the cutting edge. The bob was just a little asymmetrical, the ends flying outwards rather than in.

Francesca herself had been a little doubtful. She thought it made her look older, but António had been so persuasive and she'd given it a try. Paola agreed with her—it was a nice cut, granted, but too radical a departure from the long, glossy look Francesca had always favored.

So . . . the day hadn't started well. Francesca was nervous about her hair and to make matters worse, her skin had broken out that morning—tiny, reddened spots just beneath the surface. It was stress, of course. But knowing what it was didn't help to make it feel any better. By the time they both got into the car, Francesca was beginning to wish she'd stayed at home, or spent a day at the spa. She certainly didn't feel like having her new look raked over by two dozen critical eyes. The garden party they were going to was her best friend Maria Luisa's engagement party. Her wealthy industrialist lover, Giancarlo di Gervase-Toscini had, to everyone's astonishment, finally done the right thing—he'd divorced his wife of thirty-odd years and proposed to Maria Luisa. She was forty-five, two years older than Francesca and suddenly in a different league. Francesca had pretended to be as pleased as everyone else—admiring the enormous solitaire diamond ring, discussing wedding dresses and dates and venues and cakes until she thought her ears would burn. And then there had been the comment . . . *but you'll be my bridesmaid, of course . . . I mean, maid of honor . . . no, bridesmaid, no? . . .* and Francesca had colored under Maria Luisa's apologetic glance.

She wasn't sure why it should upset her now, at this point. As she kept reminding herself, she had the best of both worlds. She always had. She was the mistress, not the wife: she got to see him at his best, not his worst. Max saw her when he wanted to see her, not when he had to. And she had his child, which brought her security. But at the same party, she'd been chatting—no, flirting—with one of the many handsome young Italians that Maria Luisa always seemed to have on tap at her functions. They'd been talking in the quiet, intimate tones that usually indicated the opportunity for something a little more intimate when Francesca noticed the young man's eyes wandering. She frowned. She hated that. She brought her glass up to her lips, pretending to sip the martini he'd just brought over for her and looking discreetly around her to see who or what he was staring at. She nearly dropped her glass. He was staring at Paola. Francesca followed his gaze. She was standing a little to their left, chatting—no, flirting—with an almost identical handsome young man. Francesca was stung. She and her daughter were in competition for the same men? She swallowed the rest of her drink in one go and marched off, much to the surprise of Luigi-or-whatever-his-name-was.

Inside Maria Luisa's huge and elegant palazzo apartment, she escaped to the bathroom. She felt like bursting into tears. There was a pretty little sofa in one corner of the ornately decorated room. She remembered sitting on it almost twenty years ago—not the same one, obviously; Maria Luisa had the decorators in every two years—but in that same position, with her legs tucked under her waiting for Maria Luisa to finish in the toilet behind the glass screen. She remembered their conversation as if it had been a few weeks ago. Giancarlo had just bought the elegant but crumbling apartment for Maria Luisa and the two of them were giggling over how quick and easy their escapes had been from provincial poverty to jobs in the city and then to this. Francesca had just announced she was pregnant and it was clear Max was going to provide for her. At twenty-four, just two years older, Maria Luisa was now an official mistress; whatever happened to Giancarlo or to their relationship, she now had assets—and, of course, a beautiful place to live.

"D'you think he'll ever leave his wife?" Francesca had called to her through the door.

"Who cares?" Maria Luisa laughed, getting up and flushing the toilet. She walked out, her eyes shining. "*This* is much, much better. Look at it!" She flung her arms wide, indicating the beautiful apartment with its views out towards the hills and its huge, high-ceilinged rooms. "Can you believe it? I come from *Bari*, for crying out loud. Did you ever think this would be ours?"

"You're right. We have so much more fun!" Francesca laughed, getting up. And at that time—and for many years afterwards—it was more or less true. Max was great fun to be with. He *appreciated* her; her beauty; her ability to run a house; give parties; bring up their daughter to be beautiful and pleasing and hanging onto Max's every word. He was a good, thoughtful lover; he wasn't possessive or pathologically jealous, the way Giancarlo was, for example. Max never asked Francesca what she did when he wasn't around. He never questioned her spending habits, her taste for clothes, exquisite furniture, even cars. On those occasions when he'd been away from her for months, rather than weeks, he never asked her if anyone else occasionally took his place in the wide four-poster bed with the view directly onto the Villa Borghese. It wasn't that he didn't *care*, Francesca thought to herself, it was more that he considered it her business, just as Angela and all the other dalliances she knew him to have were his. A perfect *liaison*. Not a marriage, not a contract . . . a *liaison*. He was the French-speaker—she never asked him where he'd learned it—and the term seemed to satisfy him.

The light was fading, turning that special color of gold for which Rome was so famed. The Eternal City. The sun's rays spilled in through the heavy damask curtains and cut swathes across the parquet floor. But at that moment Francesca didn't feel like thinking about eternity and age and life. She was worried about herself and Paola and a sudden chill that had come over the circumstances of a life that up until now at least, she'd found satisfactory in almost every way. She stubbed out her cigarette. Should she start thinking about how to make her situation a little more secure? But how would she go about it? She'd never thought to question Max's arrangements for herself and Paola. Should anything happen to him—God forbid—where would they stand? Watching Maria Luisa's all-too-evident happiness she understood for the first time the real precariousness of her position. While she was young, beautiful and desirable, there was nothing to worry about. She was sure enough of her charms to make sure Max would come back and would keep coming back. But once those were gone, what then? She understood now that the act of marriage was also a contract, and it was one Max hadn't offered. A contract that outlived beauty and lust and passion—all the wiles Francesca had cultivated to assure her own security. The irony of the situation was that Angela, that drunk ice-queen, had secured for herself the things Francesca couldn't. And she hadn't even had to try. As far as Francesca knew, Angela hadn't slept with Max in almost a decade. But Angela came with something Francesca didn't—she came with a pedigree and a host of connections that Max wanted and needed. Her dowry, if you like. And that, when you really thought about it, was what it boiled down to. Paola's little *affaire* with the prince that had ended so badly proved it. Francesca Rossi, no matter how beautiful or desirable she made herself, was still Francesca Rossi from Corvara, a tiny hillside village about thirty miles from Pescara, population 790 of whom at least one hundred were relatives. She saw now that it could not be and would never be any different for Paola. Granted, Paola had grown up in vastly different circumstances—comfortable homes, the best schools, not that those had done her much good— all the toys, clothes, shoes she could possibly want.

Paola had had everything except the same security Francesca herself now craved. She saw how her daughter had learned from her: how to please Max; how to be pretty and charming and a man's delight. Paola had spent her whole life looking for and never quite achieving Max's attention.

For the first time in her life, Francesca prayed her daughter wouldn't do as she had done—settle for second-best. Even if what they had was a damn sight more than most women got. She stood up, her hands going automatically to smooth down her skirt. She wondered where Max was. He hadn't been to Rome in almost a month. That was another thing: she didn't know quite what he was up to at the moment. Whatever it was, it seemed to involve constant travel to Africa. Francesca shuddered. Why anyone, least of all Max, would want to go to Africa was beyond her. Nothing but famine, brutal wars and the most terrifyingly poisonous snakes. She'd seen them on TV.

≈49≈

Madeleine sat opposite Alasdair Laing and thought her heart would burst . . . or break. It was their second dinner and this time there was absolutely no mistaking what it was. A date. He had asked her out on a date. Technically speaking it wasn't illegal, other than the fact that he was the head of the team on which she worked. She was no longer a student.

The decision to accept was hers and hers alone. Of course she accepted. She'd blushed bright red when he asked her and nodded, suddenly too shy to speak. And now here she was, sitting across a small table from him in a small French restaurant around the corner from where he kept a flat. There was an invitation lying unspoken between them all evening. Would she? Should she? She bent her head to her plate, unable to think about what might happen.

He was a good listener. For the first time since she'd come to Britain she found herself willing to answer his quiet questions—to talk about herself; her childhood; her parents. She nearly talked about Péter, but stopped herself just in time. She hadn't talked to anyone about him, ever. No one in her new life knew anything about the manner of his death. Madeleine simply cut that part of her life out of her new, English personality and no one ever knew. She didn't know whether she could bring herself to say his name out loud. It didn't seem right, somehow, to bring him back to life in front of a stranger. And yet, the odd thing was, Alasdair didn't seem like a stranger to her. Not any more. She'd learned in the past month or so to separate the austere surgeon from the quiet, serious man who listened to her talk with his forefinger pushed up into the folds of his cheek and who never, not once, took his eyes off her as she spoke.

"What do they do, your parents?"

"My mother's a cleaner. Offices, peoples' homes . . . and my father works in a factory."

"And before?"

"Well, my mother's a writer. She used to write children's books." Madeleine gave a short laugh. "And my father used to work in a factory as well. But in Hungary he was a specialist, a manager in a glass factory. They made lenses for microscopes. Kovacs. You've probably heard of them." Alasdair nodded.

"Do they like it here? In Britain?" He took a sip of wine.

Madeleine shrugged. "I don't think they really think about that, you know. It was my father's decision to leave. He had an opportunity . . . so we left. They didn't think about what it would be like. My mother never says, or at least never in front of me. I think she hates it. Wouldn't you?"

"I imagine so."

"But why are we always talking about me?" Madeleine asked suddenly. It was true. Alasdair seldom spoke about himself.

"Because you're much more interesting," he said with a quiet, wry smile. She could feel the heat rising in her face.

"Don't say that," she said, looking at her empty plate again.

"Why not?"

"Because it's not true. I don't feel interesting. I feel strange and sometimes awkward and . . ."

"Why?"

"You know why." She lifted her eyes. She didn't know if she could bring herself to say it. She suddenly felt her eyes fill with tears. "Is this going to be

one of those stories . . . you know, the one everyone knows? Successful older man looking for a little excitement on the side . . . young, silly girl . . .
you know how it goes. You know how it ends,
too . . ."

"Don't." She looked up. There was pain in his
voice and in his face. He shook his head slowly from
side to side. "Please." He reached across the table
for her hand. It was the first time they'd touched.
Madeleine felt the heat slowly drain from her face
and gather itself in her fingers held within the circle
of his own. "I will never leave my wife, Madeleine.
Never. I don't know what I'm doing here with you and
I don't know what I'm asking. I've never met anyone
like you . . . I think you're the most extraordinary,
brave woman I've ever met and . . ." he let out a
breath slowly. "If you want me to leave you alone, of
course I will. It won't affect anything, not professionally, not in any way. I promise you that and Christ, I
don't know what else to say." He looked away from
her as if he couldn't bear to hear her response.

The next few minutes were hard for her to remember or to reconstruct exactly what happened,
and when. She remembered making some sort of
sound . . . a denial? An acceptance? She couldn't
remember. They both started to talk at once; the
waiter appeared; there was a short discussion
about the bill and then somehow, she could never
work out how, she was standing next to him, her
face pressed into his neck and his arms going
around her. There was a blast of chilly air as they
stepped outside the restaurant and then he kissed

her. She felt herself pulled into his coat, felt his arms press into the small of her back and the scent and taste of his aftershave as she moved her face against his. Whatever it was she'd been meaning to say in the restaurant, after this . . . there was no going back. Madeleine would have happily died on the spot. The feel of his arms around her, his weight against hers, his body something she could hold onto . . . and the smell, the smell of him . . . she drew in great gulps as if she couldn't possibly get enough. That strangely specific male scent—aftershave, soap, sweat . . . she pressed against it as she had done against the touchline of her father's chest when he taught her to swim at the municipal pool at Lukács Fürdö. It was the same scent that Péter had on his way out to meet Rózsa, his girlfriend. Memories flooded through her, releasing a wave of emotion and longing. She held on. Tightly.

She had nothing to compare him with. The first touch, the drawing up into the warmth of the mouth; the tongue . . . so insistent and sure of itself, finding its own way inside and around her mouth; the sweet wetness and the corresponding rush of feeling, down there . . . she gasped, as if bitten, or stung. He seemed to understand and anticipate her reaction—there was a gentle hug where she was expecting something else; a kiss, a whisper. To her astonishment, she found within her a secret reservoir of emotion. Her climax, occurring long before his, took both of them by surprise. The pleasure and tremendous sweetness he aroused in her lasted long after his weight had slid from her body and the sound of his breathing had died down. With his hand cradling her head, her long blonde hair spread across them both, she slept a dreamless, sound-less sleep next to a man for the first time in her life.

≈50≈

Amber knew straight away. Before Madeleine even had a chance to explain or describe the circum-stances leading to the most magical moment in her entire life, Amber knew.

"You've done it, haven't you?" she asked, taking one look at Madeleine's unusually glowing face.

"What?"

"Don't 'what' me! You've slept with him, haven't you?"

Becky's head shot upwards. "Slept with who?"

"Oh . . . please . . . do we have to talk about it?" Madeleine's face was bright red.

"Are you kidding us? Post-mortem. *Now.*" Amber and Becky propped their chins in their hands and stared across the kitchen table at a squirming Madeleine. She looked away, a dreamy expression drifting across her face. Becky and Amber looked at each other and grinned. "Come on, Szabo. Out with the details. All of 'em." Amber was quite firm.

Much later, when Becky had reluctantly left them to meet Charlie at Waterloo, Amber turned to Madeleine and asked the question she'd been dreading all evening.

"And his wife? What does he say about her?"

"Oh, Amber . . . I don't know. We . . . he doesn't talk about her. He'll never leave her, he told me that right at the beginning. They have a ten-year-old son. I don't know her name, I don't know anything about her except that she's ill and that she lives in Edinburgh . . . weird, isn't it?"

"What is?"

"Well, I might have seen her, when I was there . . . you know, in the street, or in a café. You never know."

"No, you don't know and sometimes it's better that way." Amber paused. What was she doing? What could she say to Madeleine? Don't fool around with a married man? Because you'll get hurt? It didn't always follow. Look at Max and Francesca, for example . . . perfectly happy, perfectly content. Now that she was older, Amber had to admit to a certain grudging admiration for Francesca and the way she'd organized her life. She couldn't imagine Angela being quite so willing to play second fiddle—and with a child of her own. It had never occurred to her to wonder how Francesca and Paola felt about being Max's weekend family. Not that being the weekday family was anything to celebrate, she thought quickly. But . . . looking at Madeleine now and seeing for the first time the real, *glowing* and sensual Madeleine behind the frown and the baggy, frumpy clothes . . .

what harm could it do? "You like him, don't you?" she asked.

"Yes," Madeleine replied simply. "Yes, I do."

Later that evening, after Madeleine had gone, Amber looked at the suitcase lying open-jawed on the living-room floor and experienced a faint shiver running through her. She looked at the case—silver, sturdy, with her initials on the snap-and-lock levers. It was madness, really, flying off to the middle of Africa to write an article on a subject she knew nothing about. Not true, she corrected herself quickly. She now knew more about salt than she'd thought it was possible to know. Still, flying six thousand miles away to stay with a man she'd only met twice before . . . honestly, this was one of Max's most outlandish ideas. Actually, she corrected herself again, she wasn't going to be staying with Tendé Ndiaye. She would be staying at a guest house on the grounds of his parents' home. If she were honest about it, too, she ought to admit to being just the tiniest bit disappointed. In fact, if she were being honest about the whole thing, she would also have to admit to the reason she'd decided to go to Mali in the first place. Of course she was doing it for Max. It was the first time Max had ever asked a favor of her and of course she wouldn't let him down. But she'd experienced the same, faint flutter she always felt on hearing Tendé's name. She wanted to see him again. Suddenly Max's suggestion seemed the right one.

She stood up and walked over to the window. From her top-floor flat she could see over Canonbury Square all the way up to Upper Street. She loved the little flat although the five flights of stairs to get to her front door sometimes caused her to wince. Max had bought it for her as soon as she came back from New York. A graduation present, he'd called it. She often felt guilty, looking around her at her friends and colleagues and seeing just how far removed her own life was from the pressures that everyone else had to face: rent, mortgage, bills . . . the day-to-day finances that always seemed to culminate in a build-up of tension just before the end of the month—and then the release of payday. She watched Becky go through the cycle month after month, although quite why she worried so much was a mystery to Amber. She had Charlie to take care of all those unpleasant things, as she so often said.

It was the perfect size for her—two bedrooms, a nice sunny living room and a recently remodeled kitchen and bathroom. It had the added distinction of being next door to the flat in which George Orwell had written *1984* and several other classics—there was a shiny blue plaque on the wall outside announcing his tenure in the building. The previous owner hadn't done anything to the flat since the sixties, Max told her, and he'd brought in his interior designer to do something about the place before Amber moved in. Fortunately she and Amber had managed to collaborate on colors and fabrics and carpets before Max completely overwhelmed it with his austere, somber tastes and the result was a warm, quirky flat filled with Amber's personality and collection of odd, sometimes very beautiful things. The haberdasher's cupboard in which she kept her crockery, for one thing. She turned to look at it. She and Henry had found it at a jumble sale near his parents' home in Trincham. She paused for a moment. Henry. She hadn't thought about Henry in ages. Funny how someone who had once been at the center of your life could suddenly be outside of it, completely. She and Henry had been so close. Of course, that had been part of the problem, but still . . . they'd shared what seemed now to be unbelievable intimacies; at times she thought no one knew her better, not even Becky. But that closeness had just disappeared, overnight, almost. When she'd said the words "I don't think I'm ready for this" he'd shut the door on her and walked away. At the time she was grateful—the coziness of their relationship was stifling to her. But at times, like now, she did wonder what had become of him. Becky had bumped into him once, a few years ago. He was working in a bank or something, she said. Amber raised an eyebrow. It didn't sound like Henry. Then again, she didn't know him. Not any more.

She'd had a few boyfriends since then; nice, safe young men, not unlike Henry, all cut from pretty much the same mold. Although that was the odd thing about Henry—perhaps it was the thing that had attracted her in the first place. Henry wasn't actually who he seemed. It had taken him a while to "confess" to her. She'd been a little surprised by it—

why did he think of it as a confession? So he wasn't English . . . so what? Why was it such an issue? But the more she got to know him, the more she realized there were things leftover from his childhood in Zimbabwe that he could never fully resolve. When he'd first told her he wasn't from Trincham and that he'd grown up somewhere so different as to be another planet, it wasn't fully clear to her what he expected her to say. He seemed to be saying he'd lost something and that he could never go back but to Amber, it just didn't make sense. So what if his parents had left the country? So what if they hadn't supported the changes taking place?

"No, you don't understand," Henry said to her, his dark eyes clouding over. "It's not about *them*. It's about me."

"Er, yes . . . but I still don't get it. *What's* about you? What's the issue?" But somehow Henry couldn't say. Amber suspected he didn't know himself either. She knew he'd grown up in a very small town called Makuti, somewhere near the border with Zambia, and that he'd been sent to boarding school in Salisbury— a very posh, pseudo-English school called Prince Edward Academy which at that time was reserved only for white boys, and that something had happened at that school that had caused him to question everything he'd ever understood about the world and his place within it . . . and that before he'd had a chance to fully understand his new situation, his parents had announced they were moving "home."

"Don't you see? That *was* home. It still is." Sometimes he nearly drove her crazy with his inexplicable longing to belong somewhere. For Amber, the idea of home was such a contested notion—Holland Park with Angela whom she couldn't quite bring herself to call "Mum"? A Monday to Friday location with Max? Menorca with its servants and the ever-present threat of Francesca's arrival? Amber actually thought you were better off *not* having a home, or at least a rather more flexible interpretation of one. Henry didn't agree. It was all right for someone like Max, he declared. Max was strong enough to make his own rules. Henry hero-worshipped Max. Amber knew Max was so much closer to Henry's idea of a father than his embittered bank manager father who had never recovered from the shock of leaving Africa. Henry mysteriously called it his *bwana*-complex. His father had grown up on the same farm Henry was born on, Avonlea—*Can you imagine, Amber? They're in the middle of Africa. Avonlea?*—and had grown up thinking he was the master of all he surveyed. He'd been a *bwana*—master—since before he could walk. It was the right and privilege of every white child in Cecil Rhodes' country.

"So why is it a complex?"

"Because no one in Trincham calls him 'master.' He's just like everyone else. No one runs around after him or does things just because he says they should. No, he's got to earn his place and his position the hard way."

"Well, you ought to be pleased for him. Surely that's a better way to live than this . . . other way?"

"It would be, if he could only do it. But he can't. He hates getting up every morning and driving himself to the bank. He *hates* having to report to men half his age and he especially hates the fact that there's no one at home to kick around or yell at, just because he can." Amber was silent. "I hate him." Henry rolled over onto his back and stared at the ceiling. "I hate them both."

What had happened to them? she wondered. What had happened to Henry? She suddenly wished she could call him and say "Guess what? Guess where I'm going?" He would be so jealous, she thought, smiling wryly. It was the one thing he'd talked about endlessly. "I want to take you there, to show you where I come from." She'd shrugged it off at the time. Henry began for her there, in England . . . in London. She didn't care where he'd been before that, or why it should matter so much. She'd never succeeded in thinking of him as African—it seemed silly. She wondered idly what Tendé would make of him. Or what Henry would make of Tendé. At the thought of him, her stomach gave another funny lurch. Three days to go. Stop it, she told herself sternly again. Stop. *Stop. Stop.*

≋51≋

"What do you mean you don't know where he is?" Max looked at his wife in exasperation.

"Well, I don't. I'm sorry, I don't know. I saw . . . I saw him last week, I think . . ." Angela stammered, her voice already becoming shrill.

"Last week? You live in the same house, woman!"

"He doesn't have to report to me every time he comes in or leaves the house," she said angrily.

"Perhaps he ought to," Max snapped. "A *week*? Anything could have happened in a week."

"Like what? He's not a child, Max," she tried reasoning with him.

"Said who? He's acts like one, he lives like one . . . and you bloody well treat him like one!"

"I do *not*," Angela protested, her lip quivering. It was old, familiar territory. Max had always blamed her for Kieran's weaknesses. *You spoil him rotten*, he shouted at her over and over again.

"Don't start that crap with me, Angela. I haven't got the time or interest. I want you to find out where he is, what he's doing and why he's not at home. If I'm subsidizing that lazy fool and his pathetic lifestyle, I want to know where he is, at all times. Is that clear?" Max glared at her. Angela dropped her eyes. The contempt in his glance was too much to bear.

The door slammed and Max was gone. She sank down on the divan and put her face in her hands. She didn't think she could go on like this. At first it had been wonderful having Kieran at home all the time—Amber was so busy with her new life at university and her job and besides, she and Amber had never really got along, even when she was little. Kieran was her baby, and Amber had always made it painfully clear she thought very little of her mother, just like Max. It was true Kieran had been involved in more than his fair share of scrapes, but that was the way Angela looked on them: scrapes . . . the kind of silly stuff teenagers did all the time. Although the last "scrape," stealing close to £15,000 from Max's account and spending it on God knew what kind of drugs . . . well, even she had to admit that was pushing the definition of the word just a little far . . . but all children went through their growing-up phase. Kieran's had just lasted a little longer than most, that was all. God knew he didn't need another blazing row with Max or to see the contempt in his father's voice as he told him to get a life or get out. No child deserved that, Angela thought, tears coming easily now.

There was a tap at the door. She straightened up, wiped her face hurriedly and turned.

"Who is it?" she called.

"It's me, ma'am. Siobhân. Shall . . . shall I come back later?"

"No, it's all right, Siobhân. Come in." She sighed. It was ridiculous, really. Siobhân had seen her at her absolute worst, crawling around on the floor like a child, unable or unwilling to get up, brush her teeth, her hair, put on her clothes . . . so many times in the past couple of months she'd held her hand, brought her a drink, slid tablets down her throat and promised her she'd get through the day, sober or not . . . and yet the silly protocol between servants and their employers that Max insisted upon made her address Angela as "ma'am." It was ridiculous, really. Siobhân was probably closer to Angela than anyone at present, her children included. *And whose fault is that?* Max had roared at her the last time she'd tried to bring it up. She wiped her face again and tried to smile.

"Are you . . . all right, ma'am?" Siobhân asked solicitously. Angela nodded.

"I'm fine. Is there . . . could I perhaps have . . ."

"I've brought you something, ma'am." Siobhân moved forward with a tray. Tea, a buttered scone and a large glass of wine. Angela sighed and nodded gratefully.

"Thank you, Siobhân. You're an absolute darling." She picked up the wine glass and took a gulp. "Oh, and Siobhân," she paused, a single drop of wine running down her chin. She quickly wiped it away. "I've got to go out this evening . . . some charity dinner that I can't get out of. Would you be a darling and help me get dressed?"

"Of course, ma'am. Shall I run you a bath?"

"Please. That would be lovely." Angela drained the last of the wine. The scone and tea lay untouched. "And would you get out my silver Dior dress? It's on the second rail in the dressing room. The sparkly, long one. I'll wear it with those silver sandals . . . you know, the ones with the diamond in the front." There was a second's hesitation.

"Of course. I'll bring it in while you're having a bath." Siobhân picked up the tray and empty glass. "I'll see if it needs ironing and lay it on the bed for you."

"Thank you, Siobhân."

Half an hour later, Angela looked at the dress on

the bed and frowned. It was the wrong dress. Siobhân had brought up a long, white dress by . . . she
peered at the label . . . Valentino. She couldn't even
remember buying it. She tied her dressing gown
around her and opened the door. Her dressing room
was a whole room next to her private living room.
She'd originally had a walk-in closet just off her bedroom but as the size of her wardrobe grew, it became impossible to house the hundreds of dresses,
shoes, coats, furs, hats and *things* that Angela spent
huge amounts of money on. She opened the door
and walked in. There were three long rails running
the entire length of the room. She moved between
them, going to the second rail where she thought
she'd hung the silver Dior. Her fingers pulled through
the hangers . . . no, there was no silver dress. She
frowned. She was sure she'd put it there, next to the
green and gold Dior . . . she shook her head. The
room was full of clothes in their plastic sheaths,
some with the price tags still dangling. It would take
her hours to find it. Oh, the white dress was fine. She
switched off the light and walked back to her room.

Siobhân was waiting with a hairdryer and a bottle
of her favorite perfume. Angela sat down in front of
the mirror and allowed Siobhân's gentle hands to
tease her hair into shape and bring her face to life.

"Oh, and one last thing, Siobhân . . . I think I just
heard Kieran come in. Would you let him know his
father is looking for him? Tell him not to go out tonight, please." Siobhân nodded.

"Of course, ma'am."

"Not that Max'll be home himself," Angela muttered under her breath. She turned and walked a little unsteadily down the stairs. Clive was waiting for her at the door. She checked her reflection in the mirror downstairs—everything looked fine, in place—and walked out, leaving the front door wide open.

Siobhân walked down the stairs and closed it. She'd done a fairly good job with Mrs. Sall's hair, she thought to herself as she watched Angela slide gracefully into the back seat of the Jaguar. She looked at the clock on the wall—a quarter past eight. Mr. Sall wouldn't be home that evening, Mrs. Dewhurst had already told her. The kitchen and dining room were spotless; there was nothing further for her to do downstairs. She listened for a moment—no, Mrs. Dewhurst had already gone home. She popped into the kitchen, quickly unlocked the larder cupboard and switched on the light. She walked to the back of the larder to where the wines were kept. There were hundreds of bottles in there, stacked to the ceiling, some in unopened crates on the floor. She bent down and lifted the lid off one of them. She pulled out a bottle. 1990 Châteauneuf-du-Pape. Siobhân knew very little about wine. She was from a tiny village outside Dublin—whiskies were more her domain. This one looked nice and old; there was dust on the crate and dust on the bottle . . . it ought to be good. She pulled a bit of straw up and around the empty hollow where the bottle had been. If anyone saw, they'd assume it was Angela. She stuffed the bottle inside her cardigan and hurried out to her bedroom.

Smiling to herself in anticipation of a Friday evening spent watching TV with a good bottle of wine, she slid her key in the lock. It wasn't locked. Had she forgotten to lock her door? She was getting as bad as Angela. She gave a short laugh and pushed open the door. "What the . . . !" She almost leapt out of her skin. She slammed her door shut behind her. "How . . . how did you get in here? What are you doing here?" She looked at Kieran sitting calmly on her bed, smoking a cigarette. Her eyes widened in fear as she took in exactly what he was sitting on. Dresses. Angela's dresses, to be more exact.

"I might ask you the same thing," Kieran said, his eyes narrowing. "Did my mother give you that, too?" he pointed a burning cigarette at the wine bottle. Siobhân stood rooted to the spot. "Cat got your tongue?" he asked, smiling nastily.

"I . . . I was only . . . I was just taking them to get them cleaned," Siobhân stammered, her heart racing. Had he . . . ?

"These as well?" he asked, unfolding his hand. Angela's diamond and sapphire earrings lay nestled in his palm. "And those?" He pointed to a matching diamond and white gold necklace and earrings set, still in their Garrard's black velvet box. Siobhân looked at the floor. She'd been caught. Red-handed. There was an awful silence.

"I'm . . . I'm sorry. I . . . I just wanted to . . ." she began, her mind swirling. How the hell was she going to get out of this one? If Kieran called the police, which he looked as though he might do, it would all come tumbling out. This would be the third time she'd been caught stealing from her employers—she'd managed to fake a set of references for Mrs. Dewhurst but there would be no fooling the police. "Jesus, Kieran . . . please don't tell your mam . . . I'm really, really sorry . . . I don't know what came over me . . . please don't tell Mrs. Sall . . ."

"Shut the fuck up." Kieran's voice was cold and hard. He swung his legs around and stood up. He walked towards her. She thought for one mad second that he was going to hit her. She flinched, dropping the bottle of wine. It hit the carpet with a dull thud. He grabbed her by the shoulder and pushed her downwards, hard. She knelt on the carpet and looked up at him, recognition of what he wanted dawning slowly in her eyes. There was a moment's hesitation, then she reached up and began to un-buckle his trousers. He laughed. "Over there. I wanna sit down while you do this." He walked to-wards the chair in the corner of the room. "I won't tell if you won't," he said, running a hand through his hair. "And I'll show you where to sell them."

She was good at it. It was over in a few seconds. Kieran closed his eyes briefly as he came, grabbing the sides of her head. She had long, curly black hair which she usually wore tied up, away from her face. He rather liked the sight of his hands buried in it. He eased himself out of her mouth and sat back, watching as she wiped her mouth with the back of her hand. She'd swallowed, too. He rather liked that as well. He still held the earrings in his hand.

"I'll come by tomorrow. If you're nice to me, I'll tell you where to get the best price." She said nothing. "Or I could return these, you know . . . just let Max know where I found them . . ."

"I'll be here," she said flatly. "Please don't tell Mrs. Sall. I'll return the dresses tomorrow."

"No, keep them. Like I said, it'll be our secret." Kieran pulled up his zip. "And if you're going to steal her clothes, at least take the ones she hasn't worn yet. You can take them back to the shop." He stood up and walked out of the room. Like Angela, he didn't bother to close it behind him.

He walked downstairs, humming under his breath. It had been ages since he'd had sex—or a blowjob . . . same difference. He'd enjoyed it. Funny girl, though. Pretty enough, but too quiet for his liking. You couldn't tell what she was thinking and that smile . . . bloody relentless. He wondered who'd hired her. Stupid, as well. Kept on asking him not to tell Angela. It she'd had any sense it was Max she ought to have been afraid of. It was Max who would call the police and fire her, not Angela. Angela probably wouldn't remember what jewelry she had, or how many dresses she'd bought. Strange.

Alone in her room, Siobhân got up from where she'd been kneeling and sat on her bed. Kieran had hauled the last six dresses she'd taken and tossed them on the floor. She sat with her hands on her knees, biting the inside of her lip. He'd forgotten his cigarettes. She reached across the bed and took one, her fingers trembling slightly. She lit up and

leaned back against the pillows. She needed something to drink—wine, water . . . anything. Anything to
get rid of the taste he'd left in her mouth. She exhaled
slowly, watching the smoke rings rise and distort.

≈52≈

The sky in Bamako was the color of plum, an angry,
darkened mass of clouds lying low on the horizon,
occasionally sending gusts of cool, arid air across
the city. It was the rainy season and the river was
swollen to a dirty grey-orange. A man was waiting
for her just inside the modest terminal building,
holding up a handwritten sign. *Madame Amber Sall*.
She waved in friendly recognition.

"Hello." She smiled her thanks as she pulled her
suitcase behind her. "Thanks for coming to pick me
up. It's a bit chaotic in here!" The tall, thin man
stared impassively down at her.

"*Par ici, madame*." He indicated the way, snapping his fingers impressively and garnering the immediate attention of half a dozen young boys
swarming around the arriving passengers. Of
course. French. Amber could have kicked herself. He
shouted something and a small, bright-eyed boy in a
Playboy Bunny T-shirt jumped forward, grinning. He
took hold of Amber's suitcase, obviously jeering at
his friends who stood watching in envious silence as
he followed the tall man and *la blanche* outside. The
humidity was intense—a thick, sweaty second skin,

despite the imminent arrival of rain. Dieudonné, as he was improbably named, informed her that they would be going to *le Ministre's* house then the following day, she would go to Timbuktu by plane and from there, by four-wheeled drive to Téghaza.

"And how long will it take? To get to Téghaza, I mean?"

"Sometime two, four days." Dieudonné shrugged. Obviously time, for him, was not of the essence. Amber frowned. Max had said she was to be away for ten days. If it took her four days to get to the damned place and four days to get back . . . bloody hell.

"And Tendé? M'sieur Ndiaye? Is he . . . here, in Bamako?"

"*Non*. M'sieur Tendé is at Téghaza. *Il est déjà parti.*"

"Oh."

From the back seat of the air-conditioned Mercedes, Bamako flew by. They crossed the grey, sluggish river, drove down one wide boulevard after another and then turned off into what was obviously one of the wealthier, older suburbs. It was surprisingly green after the arid semi-finished construction landscape around the airport. Here there were thick, dark green trees; thin, needle-sharp palms; wild, overgrown explosions of color in the clambering bougainvillea and flat, cantilevering flame-orange trees. Colorful, hand-painted signs at every junction pointed the way to the *Résidence de l'Ambassade de France* or to *Salon de Beauté Aminata*. They pulled up in front of a high white wall topped with curls of barbed wire. A uniformed sentry stood to attention as the gates swung silently open. The wheels crunched noisily over the gravel and they came to a stop under the carport of a large house with brilliant white walls, deep arched verandahs and dark, moss-green shutters.

A uniformed maid and a young boy dressed in khaki shorts and shirt stood stiffly to attention as Dieudonné opened the door for her. A sharp word from him and the boy took her case from the boot of the car. They walked through the darkened, cool rooms of the labyrinthine house, passing through a courtyard and turning down corridors until finally, the maid stopped before a tall, beautifully carved wooden door and pushed it open. The room inside was enormous, sparsely furnished and to Amber's tired eyes, an absolute oasis. The boy carefully laid her suitcase down on a small ornamental bench at the foot of the bed and he and the maid silently withdrew.

Amber looked around her. The room was beautiful—light, delicate green walls; dark polished wood floor and two or three pieces of what looked to be colonial-era furniture; a low, wide bed covered in a striking abstract-patterned cloth of greens, rust-browns and blacks; a small writing desk in a corner and two large white wicker chairs covered in the same material as the bedspread, looking through the almost floor-to-ceiling windows out onto the wide verandah with a vast assortment of plants in terracotta pots. Whoever was responsible for the décor in Madame Ndiaye's house obviously had very good taste. She walked across the room to the door on the opposite side. A large shower-room with a toilet and bidet behind an ornate, wooden screen. She looked at herself in the mirror above the sink, thinking she looked rather the worse for her ten-hour journey. She looked at her watch. It was six o'clock in the evening. Almost on cue, the sound of the prayer call wafted through the air outside, a soft, melodic moan. She could hear people moving about in the courtyard below. It was time to take a shower and a rest—she had no idea who was at home or what the evening schedule of the house might be. In fact, she had no idea about anything, other than the disappointing fact that Tendé Ndiaye was some two or four days' journey away. She was hungry, too, but there was nothing to eat in the room and she wasn't sure she could find her way back through the rambling house to find anyone to ask about food. She headed straight to the shower. The water pressure was low but it was hot. Half an hour later, she rinsed the shampoo from her hair and walked over to the bed. She was exhausted. Despite it being a daytime flight, she'd hardly slept a wink the night before.

She lay down, naked, on the sheets, listening to the faint sounds of people moving around outside and to the crickets beginning their nocturnal buzz. Nightfall was swift—through the shutters she could see the light dying all at once. She lay on her back, savoring the tropical heat that enveloped her—no distinction between her skin and the air surrounding her; all was once. She thought sleepily, dreamily, of an alarm clock before lassitude claimed her and she tumbled headlong into a thick, dreamless sleep.

She woke the next morning, dragged out of sleep by the early call to prayers. She opened one bleary eye, looked at the little alarm clock on the bedside table and lay back, surprised. She'd slept for almost twelve hours straight. It was 5:30 a.m. Outside the dawn was breaking and faint strips of white light appeared through the shutters. They would leave for the domestic airport at 8 a.m., Dieudonné had told her. She would fly to the small airstrip outside Timbuktu and from there a four-wheel-drive vehicle would take her to Téghaza. She lay in the dissolving darkness, wondering what on earth she'd let herself in for. Suddenly, the planned trip which in London had seemed like a rather mad but essentially *exciting* thing to do, now began to take on the air of an unplanned nightmare. She wanted to crawl back into the safety and anonymity of her London flat, get on the Tube at 8:15 a.m. as she did every morning and go straight back to the world that she knew and felt safe in— not the shadowy world of Max and his contacts and the deals that he made across it. She closed her eyes. Timbuktu? Was she mad?

Yes, she decided, looking outside the window as the tiny plane juddered to a halt. She was mad. Quite mad. The pilot, a young Frenchwoman—half Amber's height, she actually had to sit on a cushion in order to see above the bank of instruments!—killed the engines and turned to smile at her.

"Voilà. On est là." Her arm circled a graceful arc, indicating nothing. Amber peered out of the window again. There was nothing. Literally nothing. A small, low building, almost covered in sand, a couple of mules wandering around . . . a broken-down Land Rover standing lopsidedly nearby, its back wheels missing. After the intense hum of the small six-seater plane over the past two hours, the silence was overwhelming.

"This is it?" she asked, unclipping her seatbelt.

"I'm afraid so. There's the old town, about three miles to the south. What did you say you were doing here?"

"I'm not staying in Timbuktu. I'm going north—to Téghaza." The pilot raised her eyebrows.

"Alone?"

"No. I'm meeting . . . well, a driver's supposed to meet me here. Although I can't see him yet. Then someone's meeting us up in Téghaza."

"Bonne chance!" the young woman laughed. Amber's heart sank even further.

"What d'you mean?"

"Oh, don't worry. Don't listen to me. Probably your driver is waiting for you. Here," she finally managed to push open the door and release the drop-down stairs. A single airport official was waiting for her on the ground. "'Ave a good trip!" she called as Amber gingerly descended to the ground. "I will be here on

Saturday to bring you back. I hope!" she added, laughing again. Amber rolled her eyes. That was all she needed in her present state of disquiet. She handed over her bag to the man at the foot of the stairs and followed him across the hot, sandy tarmac to the single airport building.

Ten minutes later she was sitting in the back of a government-registered Toyota Land Cruiser, enjoying the cool air-conditioning and looking around her dubiously at the three bodyguards plus driver sitting in the front two rows and behind her at the second Land Cruiser with four men and their submachine guns sprawled casually across their laps. It was all remarkably well organized, if a little over the top, she thought to herself as they pulled away in convoy from the airport and headed out towards the vast, open expanse in front of them—the Sahara desert. The driver, who had introduced himself as Abdoulaye, spoke English well and was certainly friendlier than his companions. He had looked at Amber's alarmed face as she took in the bodyguards, the guns, the ammunition . . . and laughed.

"Unfortunately, it's *necessaire*," he said, smiling widely. "There are many bandits on the road to Téghaza."

"B . . . bandits? What sort of bandits?" she stammered.

"Thieves, murderers . . . Tuareg peoples," Abdoulaye grinned cheerfully. "Don't worry—we are well protected!" Amber smiled weakly.

* * *

The road out of Timbuktu could hardly be called one. It was little more than two dusty tracks in the shifting sand. Amber felt the wheels of the vehicle shudder as they tried to bite into the soft, sandy surface below the wheels. The landscape around them was creamy white, undulating hills interspersed with dark green shrubs and small bushes struggling to survive in the arid sand. Through the feathery leaves of the shrubs, Amber caught glimpses of the far-off dunes—they rose, seemingly solid and majestic, like giant crescents left casually behind by some celestial artist in perfect, half-moon shapes. It was almost 11 a.m. and the sun was rising to its highest peak. Slowly the colors of the land began to shift from grey-white to pure white, all color bleached out by the merging overhead of the sand and sky. Inside the car, thankful for the air-conditioning, Amber let her head rest against the window as the talk around her rose in the musical language she had been hearing for almost a day now and in which words, sentences and meaning blurred hopelessly. Abdoulaye had said it would take them all day to reach Téghaza. With any luck, they would be there by nightfall. She looked outside the window. It was hard to believe they would ever be *anywhere* in this vast, empty stretch of nothingness.

By four o'clock that afternoon, after two or three stops and a handful of dates, she was tired, thirsty and hot, despite the cooler interior of the car. Outside, the brilliant oranges, dusty reds and egg-yolk yellows of the sands somehow intensified the heat so that she lay back against the soft seats, sweating uncomfortably. Apart from a few camels and the odd robed Tuareg, they hadn't seen a living being for miles. Two of the men were asleep in front of her, their heads lolling as the vehicle shuddered and juddered its way across the sand-gravel track that was the only road heading north. The sky was beginning to throw up its evening display: the shadows on the ground were lengthening; overhead, delicate white traceries of clouds were slowly turning orange, then delicate pink, then flaming saffron-gold.

An hour later at evening prayers, they came upon a row of kneeling men, their plastic sandals lined up neatly in the sand. Under a row of makeshift tents made from spindly wooden poles and sheets of sacking, thirty or forty figures knelt in supplication, the soles of their feet raised towards the Land Cruisers as they bowed facing Mecca. Abdoulaye pulled the vehicles to a stop and the men got out. Leaving their guns in the car, they pulled out two jerry cans of water and their prayer mats. Amber watched in half-embarrassed silence as they washed their feet, hands and faces, and, like the group they had just passed, bent down and prostrated themselves in the sand. Their heels flashed and disappeared as their prayers rose around her, the sound sweet and human in the vast expanse of nothingness stretching out before them.

"Madame?" Abdoulaye's face appeared at the window. "You like to eat?" He indicated a plate of rice and what looked like small Cornish pasties. Amber smiled her thanks, opened the door and stepped down into the soft, still hot sand. There were a few straggling trees and bushes nearby. She took a quick look around her, extracted a wad of tissues from her handbag and with as much dignity as she could muster walked to the nearest one and quickly squatted. She walked back to the cars. The men, out of a touching delicacy, had turned their backs. She accepted a plate from Abdoulaye and sat on the door ledge and ate with them.

"About one hour, two hours . . ." Abdoulaye said, squinting into the dying light. "We will reach." Amber nodded thankfully. An entire day spent cooped up in the back of a jolting vehicle was exhausting, despite the fact that she'd barely moved an inch since she got in that morning. They finished eating in companionable silence, each taking it in turn to pour lukewarm water from the enormous cans into the plastic cups Abdoulaye had so thoughtfully provided. They brushed the crumbs from their clothing and jumped back into the cars.

She was almost asleep by the time the vehicles finally pulled into a clearing beside a row of half-lit bungalows. Under an inky, pitch-black sky illuminated by a slowly rising perfectly symmetrical moon and bright, steady stars, the men unloaded the vehicles. Amber stood by as they carried their guns, provisions, water canisters and boxes into one of the small houses. Abdoulaye called out something to one of the men; seconds later, there was an answering shout and the door to one of the bungalows was flung open. Amber turned slowly. In the doorway, framed by the light spilling out around the contours of his body, was Tendé Ndiaye. She swallowed, picked up her bag and moved out of the darkness.

≈53≈

Becky scanned the list for the third time, making sure that everyone who was on it had received an invitation. She was as nervous as all hell. Morag was on her way back from New York, coming to the opening straight from the airport, but Becky had assured her that she had absolutely everything under control; there was absolutely no need to worry. She was good at this sort of thing. Satisfied, Morag had boarded her plane for JFK—she was off hunting down new artists and Becky was left to organize and run it on her own. But she was still nervous. Amber was still in bloody Mali and Madeleine knew absolutely nothing about the art business. She just prayed she'd got everything right and that nothing would go wrong. There were 240 people on EC1's list. Morag updated it on a monthly basis, adding and occasionally dropping a name here and there. She guarded her list the way some people guarded a piece of jewelry or a family secret; she knew the success or failure of the gallery depended almost entirely on who was on the list, and how many pieces they were prepared to buy in any given season. Becky had almost missed the whole rival gallery owners' section in Morag's Rolodex. There'd been a mad scramble to find enough invites for the fifty or sixty additional names but luckily, she'd managed it just in time and they'd all gone off the week before. The wine and canapés had been ordered: sixty bottles of good red wine, sixty bottles of white and thirty bottles of champagne. She'd had no idea how much to order, so she'd rung the National Portrait Gallery and pretended to be a student writing a piece on the organization of private viewings—a stroke of genius on her part, she thought. It seemed like an awful lot of wine but . . . with three-hundred-odd people turning up it would probably go quite quickly. She'd invited absolutely everyone from her old art school—this was Becky Aldridge's night and she wanted to make sure *every*one saw it. Well, it was actually Saba Mehretú's night, she reminded herself. Saba was the artist, not her.

She got up from her desk and walked upstairs to the gallery space. She made sure all the lights were working properly, that the pictures were hung and positioned perfectly and that the place was spotless. She stood in the doorway admiring it. They had painted one end wall a deep, rich red. Against it, Saba's three large canvases looked better than ever. The color lent a certain warmth to the room—with the exposed brickwork at the opposite end, it looked every inch the modern, cutting-edge space both she and Morag wanted. She stacked a pile of the small catalogues on one of the display cases, adjusted a couple of blooms in the huge display at the entrance and stepped back. It was all done. She looked at her watch. It was nearly four o'clock. She would pour herself a quick gin and tonic and then go downstairs to change.

At six on the dot, the buzzer sounded. She swallowed a last mouthful of gin and tonic, dabbed some perfume on her wrists and hurried upstairs. It was the caterers. Six young men and women in black outfits just as she'd requested—and the wine and food. There was a tense moment when the manager said it was the first time she'd ever seen food served at an art gallery—Becky stared at her—but then Saba arrived and they had to get all the stuff in . . . there wasn't any time to wonder if she'd done the right thing. No food? She took a quick look around—no one else seemed to think it strange. She squashed the thought.

"Where's your kitchen?" It was the catering manager.

"Kitchen?" Becky repeated. "We don't have one."

"Oh." The woman looked confused. "Well, it's just that you ordered hot canapés. The breaded shrimp and the satay sticks . . . we'll need somewhere to warm them up."

"Oh, shit. I didn't think of that."

"Ah."

"Becky." Saba came through the doorway. She looked gorgeous in a long white dress with a leather jacket and diamante long-drop earrings. Becky turned. "Are you sure about this?" she asked, gesturing at the plates of food being unloaded from the van. "I mean, I don't want anything to get on the paintings."

"Oh, it . . . it won't. Um, don't worry . . . we'll make sure nothing happens. There's . . . it's all insured, anyway," she added quickly. Was it? She had no idea. A familiar sense of panic began to rise in her—things were starting to go wrong.

"Well, if you're sure . . ." Saba said dubiously. She turned to look at the gallery. The framed prints were safe behind their Perspex screens but the large works . . . she bit her lip.

"Don't worry," Becky said, watching her nervously. "It'll be fine." She turned to help the staff stack the boxes of wines.

"Have you got a table ready?" One of the men came through the door.

"What for?"

"To put the wine glasses on."

"Oh . . . um, you could bring up my desk . . . here, I'll show you . . ." Becky was beginning to really panic. She hadn't thought of all the tiny details; she'd assumed the caterers would take care of everything. It was a company Morag had used before, and she'd just assumed they would know what to do. The young man looked a little put out. "Come on, help me bring it up." She ran down the stairs. Shit, she didn't even have a tablecloth to cover it. Oh God, this was all going horribly wrong. She was sweating.

Ten minutes later, a quarter of an hour before the doors were due to open, they finally had a makeshift table and had covered it in sheets of white paper that one of the girls had found. It actually looked okay. For the first time since the doorbell went, Becky allowed herself to relax. It had been a bit of a bumpy start, but things were beginning to fall into place. She and Juliet, the catering manager, had decided against serving the shrimp and chicken satay—they'd have to charge EC1 for them, of course, but at least they wouldn't be serving up cold, soggy food. Becky nodded gratefully. Whatever you say. It was unfortunate that there wasn't a large refrigerator or a bathtub full of ice—the white wine was lukewarm, as was the champagne. "Don't worry, after a few glasses, no one'll notice," Juliet said. Becky nodded distractedly. A taxi had just pulled up outside. With relief, she saw it was Morag. She rushed to the door.

"Hi," she said, stepping outside and helping Morag with her cases. She'd come straight from Heathrow and looked absolutely shattered. She also looked incredulous.

"Hi, Becky . . . what's going on? What's all this?" Morag let her case drop. She pointed to the wine table standing in the middle of the gallery. "What's that table doing there?"

"It's the wine . . . we . . . I forgot to organize a table from the caterers so we took my desk from downstairs and . . ."

"No . . . what's it doing in *there*? Next to the paintings?" Morag sounded alarmed.

"Oh, well . . . there wasn't really any space to do it downstairs and—"

"Get it to the corner of the room. *Now!*" Morag left her bags and a surprised taxi driver at the side of the road and practically ran into the gallery. "Quick! You . . ." She pointed to the chap who had dragged the desk up from Becky's office. "Pick up that end. Here . . . let's put it over here." She turned to Becky. "Keep it away from the work. I don't want anyone splashing—" she broke off as one of the girls came through balancing a tray of tiny, plump cherry tomatoes and feta cheese sticks. "What the . . . ?"

"Er, canapé, madam?" The girl seemed confused. Becky froze.

"Canapé?" Morag turned to Becky. "Are you mad?" At that moment, Saba walked in. Becky looked at the ground. "Er, just a second," Morag said, grabbing Becky by the arm. She fished a twenty-pound note out of her wallet. "Would you pay the taxi driver and bring my bags in," she asked the waiter who was standing staring open-mouthed at the scene unfolding in front of him. "We'll be back in a second." She and Becky disappeared downstairs.

"Oh, God . . . I'm sorry, Morag," Becky began as soon as they got into the office. She was pale.

"Becky, have you lost your mind? Food at an opening? I thought you knew how to organize these things. We're not insured. If anything happens to the work . . . what on earth were you thinking?" Morag looked at her. Becky swallowed. She was afraid to speak, on the verge of tears. "Look, guests are going to start arriving in a second. Pull yourself together. We need to get rid of the food—tell them to stick the trays here in the office. What've we got upstairs? White wine and water?"

"And red wine . . . and champagne." Becky sniffed.

"Champagne? Who . . . have we *paid* for this?" Morag was beginning to sound angry. Very angry.

"I'm really sorry, Morag," Becky said again.

"So you keep saying. Jesus, Becky . . . this is going to cost a fortune. This has to come out of Saba's share, you know." Becky stared at her.

"I thought . . . I thought . . ." Becky began miserably.

"God knows what you thought. Look, one of us has to be upstairs. I'm going back up. You sort yourself out and get up there as quick as you can. We'll talk about this later." Morag shook her head. She turned and walked out the door, leaving Becky shaking in the middle of the room. A few minutes passed. Upstairs, Becky could hear Morag greeting people as the gallery began to fill up. She looked at her watch. It was 7:15 p.m. She had to pull herself together. And fast. She took a deep breath, wiped her face and opened the door.

"Becks!" She turned. Charlie was weaving his way towards her, clutching two bottles of champagne. Becky's heart sank. He was absolutely plastered. Behind him were two of his "city boys," as he called them. She knew he liked the fact that she ran a gallery—not that she'd be running it for much longer . . . she'd never seen Morag look so furious. Charlie liked the fact that Becky's crowd was so different from his. Art-gals, he called them. So much more fun than the women he came across on a daily basis. Becky was secretly rather embarrassed by his descriptions of the secretaries and personal assistants who fluttered around him all day long and she would sooner have *died* than told Morag he sometimes referred to her as an "art-chick"—as opposed to Becky, who was firmly an "art-chick*lette*"—but it was all meant in fun and Charlie could be devastatingly funny at times. "Becks!" He came up to her, throwing an arm round her shoulders and gave her a quick, rather slobbering kiss on the ear. She moved away. A drunk and boisterous Charlie was the last thing she needed tonight.

"Darling," she said, grabbing him by the arm. "I'll be back in a minute. Just got to see to something." Charlie was too drunk to notice her agitated state. She'd just seen Morag staring open-mouthed in horror as Penelope Gottlieb and Domenic Barclay walked in—they owned a gallery further down the road. Wasn't she supposed to have invited them? Had she fucked *that* up as well? She hurried towards her. This was rapidly turning out to be the worst evening of her entire life. Surely it couldn't get any worse.

It did. There was another hasty, furiously whispered conversation in the toilet with Morag—of *course* she wasn't supposed to invite rival gallery owners. What the hell was wrong with her? Even if she hadn't organized a viewing before, didn't she at least have a modicum of common sense? There was Saba, their precious artist, happily flirting with Dominic Barclay . . . *well, you can kiss your little find goodbye*. Morag was livid. And then, just when she thought it couldn't possibly get any worse, Charlie started dancing in the middle of the gallery and one of his friends lit a cigarette. Morag got one of the waiters to throw the three of them off the premises and Becky had to run down to the toilets to avoid hearing Charlie swearing and shouting for her to come and help him. She waited for a full fifteen minutes, sitting on the toilet seat, too shocked to cry . . . until the girl who'd been waiting outside threatened to relieve herself on the floor.

"Sorry," she mumbled as she exited the toilet. The girl looked at her suspiciously. What the hell had she been doing in there alone for fifteen minutes? Becky hurried upstairs again. She looked around the room cautiously. It was now 10:15 p.m. The little crowd was beginning to disperse. Morag was chatting in the corner to a couple Becky recognized; they were artists who often came into the gallery. There were several of her erstwhile arrogant fellow students standing huddled in another corner—she was sure they were laughing at her. She wanted the evening to be over as soon as possible. She wanted to get into the back of a cab and not have to look up at the world until she was safely at home. Her career was over before it had even properly begun.

"Hi, excuse me . . . Becky? Becky Aldridge?" She turned. The voice was deep and strangely familiar.

"Henry!" She blinked in surprise. It was Amber's ex-boyfriend. Henry of the silent, tortured calls at midnight. "Oh, my God . . . what . . . ?"

"Hi, I wasn't sure . . ."

"How . . . what are you doing here?"

"I'm a friend of Saba's. She mentioned your name a couple of times and I thought it must be you. Red hair and all that . . ." he smiled. "I just got here."

"Oh, lucky you. You missed it, then," Becky said, feeling a sudden and alarming rush of tears.

"Hey . . . what's wrong? Becky?" Henry was looking down at her, concerned.

"Oh, don't mind me," Becky turned away. "I'm just . . ." She moved away from the doorway.

"Here . . . come over here. What's the matter?" Tears were streaming down Becky's face. He led her quickly away from the room.

"I'm sorry," she said indistinctly through her tears. "I've just made the worst possible fuck-up of my life. I've completely ruined the show. Morag's going to give me the sack first thing tomorrow morning and . . ." she stopped, unable to go on.

"Tomorrow's Saturday," Henry said gently. "Look, obviously I don't know what happened earlier but it doesn't look like a complete disaster to me. Everyone looks pretty happy, in fact. I met Saba on the way in and she seemed fine. Here, use this." He pulled a handkerchief out of his pocket. Becky took it gratefully.

"I'm really sorry," she sniffed.

"Nothing to be sorry about. Let me get you a glass of water." Becky nodded gratefully. They were standing at the back of the hallway. One or two people coming up the stairs from the toilet looked her way but everyone by now was either too tired or too drunk to really notice. She blew her nose as Henry reappeared with two glasses of water. "D'you want to sit down somewhere?" he asked, looking around. Becky shook her head.

"I just want to go home," she said.

"Come on. I'll take you."

"Oh, no . . . don't be silly. I'll get a cab. Honestly. I live miles away."

"It's no problem at all. Come on. I think the party's pretty nearly over anyway. Have you got a bag or a coat?"

Becky nodded. "My stuff's in the office. But really, Henry . . . I can just take a taxi."

"Nonsense. Get your bag. I'll wait for you up here." She blew her nose one last time, tucked her hair behind her ears and walked downstairs to her office. Henry was being dreadfully sweet—funny, she didn't remember him being sweet at all. Actually, the thought of sitting alone in a taxi suddenly seemed rather sad. Some company on the way home would be good. And when she got home, Charlie would be there. Hopefully. She had no idea where he and his friends might have gone. She picked up her bag and coat and ran upstairs.

"Ready?" he asked lightly.

"Yes. I'd better tell Morag . . . I won't be a minute." She was trembling as she walked into the gallery to find her. But Morag was unexpectedly calm. She took one look at Becky's tear-stained face and told her to go home and get a good night's sleep. The unexpected kindness threatened to trigger another rush of tears but luckily Henry suddenly appeared beside her and led her away before she made an even bigger fool of herself. As if that were possible, she told him, getting into the passenger seat of his car.

"These things happen, Becky," he said as he started the engine. "From what you've said . . . it was your first show, right?"

"And my last."

"No, it won't be. You'll see. By Monday morning it'll all seem different. You wait and see." Becky said nothing. "Look, have you had anything to eat all evening?" Henry asked as he pulled out into the traffic.

"No, I . . . well, I just forgot. There was so much to do . . ."

"There's a really good Thai restaurant on the corner of Old Street. Let's grab something to eat . . . spring rolls or some soup or something and then I'll take you home. It's only 11 p.m. and I bet you're starving. What d'you say?"

Becky looked at him and smiled. "Gosh, it's really nice of you, Henry. I . . . I'd love some Thai soup."

"Great. Let's go there then."

The soup was wonderfully hot and the atmosphere inside the little restaurant was loud and cheerful and exactly what she needed. Within half an hour, she'd almost forgotten her earlier despair. Henry was an amusing dinner companion and by the time he settled the bill and they were walking back to his car, she'd forgotten that the last time they'd met, he'd called her an idiot. He was fun to be with. He'd asked her lots of questions about her job; about herself . . . she'd shown him her diamond ring and they'd talked about Charlie. He'd told her he worked for the Eritrean Refugee Council and hadn't been in the least bit patronizing when she confessed she had no idea where Eritrea was. She'd always been rather in awe of Henry with his easy confidence and his tall, boyish good looks. She always had the impression he thought her rather frivolous with her art-school vocabulary and her faux-Bohemian ways.

"You called me an idiot, once," she said as they got into his car again. Henry had the grace to look embarrassed.

"Mmm. I remember. Sorry about that."

"No, I probably deserved it."

"I doubt it," he said dryly. "I used to be . . . actually, I can *still* be a bit of a pompous ass. Or so my friends tell me."

"Well, not tonight. Thanks. Really. I was feeling so low."

"It happens, doesn't it?" He started the engine. "I remember when Amber and I split up . . . I thought the world was going to end." Becky looked at him. It was the first time he'd mentioned Amber all evening. He pulled a face. "You get over it, though."

"Yeah. She was supposed to be here," she said, after a minute. Henry was quiet. "She's in Africa, actually. She's back next week."

"In Africa? What . . . what's she doing there?" There was a forced note to Henry's voice. Becky wondered if she'd said the wrong thing.

"She's got an assignment. Some article on the desert."

"I see. Well, lucky her. So . . . where am I going?" Henry turned to look at her. There was pain on his face, Becky noticed. Still. It had been four years since they'd broken up and whatever Amber said, it was clear Henry was still hurting.

"East Dulwich, I'm afraid," Becky said, suddenly feeling very sorry for him. "It's a bit of a trek."

"Not for this little gal," he said, gently patting the dashboard. Becky had to laugh. His car was positively ancient.

"Darling," Charlie mumbled as Becky opened the bedroom door and switched on the light. She was surprised to find him at home. She and Henry had sat in the car for a few more minutes outside her house—there were no lights on; she'd assumed Charlie wasn't yet home. They'd made a vague promise to stay in touch but Becky could see he didn't mean it. He'd been very kind to her that evening but she could see the news of Amber had thrown him and she wouldn't blame him for keeping his distance. She'd watched his lights disappear down the road and was surprised to find she'd almost forgotten about the disaster at the gallery earlier that evening. "Come here, darling," Charlie slurred again, stirring. She quickly switched the light off.

"Go back to sleep," she whispered, taking off her clothes. She walked into the bathroom. She closed the door and switched on the light. She looked dreadful. There were tearstains on her face and her mascara was halfway down her cheeks. She gave a rueful smile. She'd sat like that opposite Henry Fletcher the whole evening? No wonder he felt sorry for her. She quickly washed her face and brushed her teeth. What an evening. She switched off the light and slid, naked, into bed. She knew from long experience that Charlie would roll over, attempt to touch or even kiss her and promptly fall asleep. She was right. She felt a hot, rather sweaty hand grope around for a breast, a nipple, anything . . . he nuzzled against her cheek, his hand fell slack and he began to snore again. Her last thought before she too slid into dark nothingness was of Henry. Of his face looking across the table at her—and of his smile. She liked his smile.

≈54≈

On the other side of the city, just before dawn broke, Madeleine lay awake, thinking. Next to her, shrouded in the duvet cover, was Alasdair's large form, barely stirring. She was thinking about the weekend just past; she'd been home to see her parents as she did whenever she had a day off, and of course, her mother had noticed there was something different about her. She was wearing her hair down . . . and a pair of new boots? Very nice. And the scarf? Madeleine wasn't sure how to respond.

"This? Oh, it's just . . . something I found the other day," she mumbled, blushing. She'd never been able to hide anything from her mother. Maja's eyes followed her as she got up and went through to the kitchen.

"So? How's work?" Maja asked her as soon as she came back.

"Fine, nothing new. I've been on call for ages. Listen, I was thinking . . . would you and Papi like to take a holiday this year? To Budapest?"

Maja looked at her in alarm. "A holiday? To Budapest? No . . . don't be silly. It'll cost the earth . . ."

"Ma . . . I told you. I can pay for it . . . it's fine. I'd like to, honestly."

"Madeleine, that's enough. If we want to go to Budapest, your father and I will find the money. Besides, who wants to go there?"

"Ma, how long have you been away? Maybe it's changed."

"Madeleine, that's *enough*!" Maja's tone was sharp. Madeleine sighed. It was always that way. They were proud of her success, of course, but they were also afraid of it. Madeleine knew Maja was afraid of the changes she seemed to think Madeleine's success would bring—a slow moving away from them; forgetting her language and culture; a reversal of the roles of parent and child? Madeleine longed to tell her that the reversal of roles had occurred the minute they arrived in Britain and, perhaps more importantly, didn't they realize that she had a right to a life of her own? That if she didn't come to Kensal Rise every Saturday and Sunday it might be because she was on call, or out with a friend or, God forbid, had a social life? But it was no use saying any of that to Maja. She was so quick to take offense, especially now, and Madeleine couldn't bear to see the hurt look on her father's face if Maja so much as hinted that Madeleine didn't want to come home. With Alasdair away every weekend to his home in Scotland, it had worked, up until now. But he'd asked her if she wanted to go away with him in June to Paris—he had been invited to a conference and they could spend a few days together exploring the city . . . would she like to come? Madeleine had looked at him, her blue eyes shining. *Like* to come? Was he mad? She would have given anything to go. All she had to do was put in an application for leave and find some way of telling her parents she'd be gone for a week. She tried again.

"Mama . . . things have changed at home. It's not like it used to be. You could visit Péter's . . . you know . . . it'll be good for you."

"And since when do you know what will be good for us?" Maja retorted, her face reddening. Madeleine sighed. There was an awkward silence.

"Well, I'm going on holiday," she said a few minutes later, as casually as she could. "Some friends of mine from the hospital are going to Paris. It's only for a week."

"Paris? You're going to Paris?" Maja was surprised. "Well, of course . . . now that you're all fancy and a doctor and everything . . ."

"Oh, for God's sake, Mama. There's nothing fancy about it. It costs nothing to go to Paris. We're taking the ferry."

"Who's going to Paris?" Imre had come in the room.

"Your daughter. Imagine."

"That's wonderful, Madeleine. A beautiful city. You must see *la Tour Eiffel* and the Louvre." Imre's reaction couldn't have been more different. Madeleine looked at him gratefully.

"I will, Papi. Listen, I was just saying to Mama . . . why don't you two take a holiday this year? Go back to Budapest. I can arrange it."

"Oh, I don't think so. We're fine where we are. It'll be so expensive . . . so many other things we could spend the money on."

"Like what? *I'll* pay, Papi. It'll be a Christmas gift or something." Madeleine was almost pleading with him. What else was there to spend the money on? They refused to move out of the tiny flat they'd been given when they arrived. Madeleine had done her best to make the small improvements that she'd thought necessary: a washing machine, a new TV, even a new sofa—bought after much arguing and endless comments from Maja. What else did they need so desperately that two weeks in Budapest had to be foregone? She was earning a junior doctor's salary now; it wasn't much but it could certainly pay for a holiday every once in a while.

"No one's paying and no one's going to Budapest. That's final." Maja got up from the new sofa and marched into the kitchen. Imre looked at his daughter and gave a resigned shrug. Madeleine felt like screaming.

Now, in the safety of Alasdair's room, watching dawn break over London through the blinds, she thought about it again. She would simply buy the tickets. She would buy the tickets, book a hotel room and that would be the end of it. Once they were bought, Maja wouldn't waste them. There'd be a bit of an argument, perhaps a couple of days of sulking and then she'd start looking forward to it. And it would certainly help Madeleine feel better about going to Paris with Alasdair. Although nothing was ever said, Madeleine couldn't help but feel guilty about the material and social improvements in her own life when measured against the stagnation of theirs. And the last thing she wanted was to spend ten days away feeling guilty and miserable.

Alasdair stirred. Madeleine stretched her body against the length of his, luxuriating in the mixture of pleasure and trepidation she felt whenever they were together. She could feel the heat of his body through the tartan pajamas he wore . . . she smiled to herself suddenly. *Tartan* pajamas! Sometimes when she caught sight of him in the hospital striding purposefully from one operation to the next or from a lecture hall to a team meeting, she had to stop and think—was this the same Alasdair who held her at night, whose body she held and caressed and in whose grey eyes she saw a reflection of her own pleasure? She had to stop, trembling, in the cold corridors of the emergency room or rush to the bathroom to blot the tears that came upon her from time to time, without warning.

He rolled towards her, still asleep. A shaft of light suddenly slid into the room through a crack in the curtains. Alasdair had pushed back the duvet cover and lay on his back, breathing softly. She propped herself up on an elbow and looked at him, at the dark, silky hair that covered his chest, tapering to a point below his navel, now covered by his pajamas; the skin at the base of his neck, pulsating gently; the pale white underside of his arms . . . she pushed her face into the side of his warm neck and waited for him to wake up and for his hands to slowly move from comforting caress to erotic touch. They now spent all their weekday nights together whenever Madeleine's schedule would allow. He'd asked her to resign from his surgical team because, as he told her, watching her face light up with delight, she distracted him during surgery and his mind wandered when it shouldn't. Mistakes might be made. It was a small disappointment to her to be back on Harrigan's team but she knew he was right. Besides, it made seeing him unexpectedly during the day that much more special. She went about her job in the operating theatre and on the wards in a calm, fluid state of suspense, her senses charged by an inexplicable sexual tension; no one had ever drawn such a response from her. There were days when she thought she couldn't bear it. Once or twice when they were making love, watching his face shudder as his own pleasure was wrung from him, she caught herself thinking—fleetingly—of Péter . . . was this what he felt? Was that curious mask of intensity followed by an exhaustion so complete she sometimes thought Alasdair dead to the world . . . was that how it was for him, too? She quashed the thoughts immediately. It was weird and wrong to think about Péter at such times, but she couldn't help herself. It was as if, in Alasdair, fragments of her life and self that had been blown apart suddenly came together, comfortably finding their place in spaces inside herself that she'd thought empty and cold. Alasdair brought warmth. He brought warmth to her and he made things whole. His presence occupied and healed her mind, her body and her heart.

She felt his hand slide over her stomach and the brush of his lashes against her cheek.

≈55≈

Henry's hand hesitated over the phone. He frowned. It wasn't like him to be so indecisive. He picked it up, and seconds later replaced it again. What would he say? "*Oh hi, Becky . . . how're you feeling? I was just calling to . . .*" To what? He stared at the phone. The unexpected news of Amber in Africa had disturbed him. He picked up the phone again.

Five minutes later, he put it down, wondering if he'd done the right thing. Becky had sounded a little surprised to hear from him but she'd agreed to meet him on Friday night for a drink. She'd sounded . . . he wasn't sure . . . flattered? Was that the right word? Yes, flattered. He pursed his lips. He hadn't meant to flatter her. He just wanted to find a way to hear more about Amber. Or did he? He wasn't even sure why he suddenly wanted to find out more about her. They'd been apart for four years, long enough for both of them to get on with their lives. Henry had been out with countless girls since Amber; he wasn't the type to stay single for long. But by the sounds of it Amber had got on with her life in a *proper* way, doing something that counted. He had no idea what she was doing in Africa but whatever it was, it was better than sitting in a dingy office in Clapham, sifting through a thousand application papers a day for Eritrean refugees seeking asylum. It wasn't the politically charged, *necessary* job he'd dreamed of doing when he left university, but it paid the rent and for a while, at least, it kept him sane. He watched the few friends he'd kept in touch with from university one by one succumb to the pressure of jobs, girlfriends, annual holidays and eventually a mortgage and prayed that his life would turn out differently.

It was perhaps that which he missed most about being with Amber. Amber wasn't like other girls—women, he reminded himself quickly. She was different. It wasn't just the fact that she was wealthy; Amber lived life on an entirely different scale from most people he knew. She did what she wanted, when she wanted, how she wanted. She could be and do literally anything. And there was Max. Henry longed for a father, mentor . . . *friend* like Max. To be able to influence the course of history, to jet around the globe as if it were one's own private playground; to call on world leaders at one's whim—those were the qualities Henry most admired in Max. Henry wondered what it must be like to open a newspaper and see your father's face, read his words . . . *that* was what he admired. Not a petty little bank clerk of a father whose maudlin loyalties lay with a country that didn't even exist any more. *Rhodesia.* What a joke.

Someone thumped a pile of files on his desk, rudely bringing him back to the present. He stared at them. How long would it take to wade through them and what effect would it have? None. He looked up at the poem he'd seen on the Underground a few days before and had hurriedly copied into his notebook. He'd stuck it on the wall above his desk. It seemed to sum up his present situation in the most exemplary way. His lips moved over the first line . . .

I have known the inexorable sadness of pencils

and continued soundlessly to the last. . . .

*Dropping a fine film on nails and delicate
    eyebrows,
Glazing the pale hair, the duplicate grey standard
    faces.*

Henry didn't want to be one of the pale grey faces. He wanted to be back there in the sunlight surrounded by people with wide, shining smiles and a bright future and at times like these, more than anything in the world, he wanted to be with Amber.

*   *   *

The following Friday, at quarter past six, he looked at his watch and pushed a stack of papers away from him. It was time to meet Becky. He was un-characteristically nervous. He wasn't sure what it was that had thrown him off-balance the whole week. Was it seeing Becky Aldridge again? He'd never much liked her when he and Amber had been together—he'd seen her as a little silly, somewhat pretentious . . . rather inconsequential, in his eyes. But last week, at the gallery . . . she'd looked so damned vulnerable and miserable and he'd been able to cheer her up. She was so grateful and it made him feel good. And once she'd calmed down, she was surprisingly good company herself. Pretty and funny and very feminine. He liked that about her. But there was the surprising bit of news about Amber. She'd gone to Africa. He wasn't prepared for the jolt of envy, jealousy that had gone through him. He'd always wanted to take Amber there. She might have known about the rest of the world and been to places he'd never even heard of but Africa was *his*. It was his home. He ought to have been the one to take her there. He hadn't even dared to ask Becky if she'd gone with anyone. But he hadn't been able to stop thinking about it all week, either. The week had been a bit of a nightmare, actually . . . torn between thinking about the way Becky's face had lit up when he suggested going to Thai Gardens and imagining Amber somewhere in the middle of the Sahara. It was driving him crazy. The only thing he could think of doing was to call Becky again. And now he was on his way to meet her. He hoped he wasn't making a huge mistake. Opening up old wounds. Becky was engaged, so why had he asked her out? And why had she accepted?

Standing nervously by the door of the Lamb and Flag in Covent Garden, Becky was asking herself exactly the same question.

≈56≈

Amber was sitting outside the bungalow on the front steps, watching a luminous, silvery moon rise almost vertically in the silky black sky overhead. A lattice of stars hung immobile, their lights burning steadily, not twinkling. The silence was profound. In the still, dry air, a rustle from half a mile away sounded close to her ear. There was a strange sound like air hitting a sail—with a start she realized it was a bird, its wings flapping as it soared into the night sky. She wrapped her arms around her knees, marveling at how quickly the temperature had dropped. It was hard to believe it had been close to 105°F that afternoon. Now it was closer to 60°F. She looked out over the perfectly level, white expanse of the salt flats, admiring the way the moon threw a watery silver shadow over the land, turning everything bathed in its light to a ghostly sameness. From the bungalow next door, she could hear the sounds of the men preparing to sleep, rolling out mats and taking buckets of water outside to wash. Everything had to be brought here—there was no electricity, no water, no telephone. There was nothing except the sea of salt spread out before them and, on the far horizon, the beginnings of the Air Mountain range and the Tibesti foothills.

"Beautiful, isn't it?" She turned. Tendé had come out silently and was standing behind her. She swallowed and nodded. It was their second day in the desert. In two days' time, they would set off for Timbuktu. They would spend a night in the old city and then fly back to Bamako on Saturday. And then it would be back to London and to work. Amber doubted the reality of the world outside this place. In just over a day, she had found herself almost totally submerged into the binaries that the desert provided—dust and wind, sunlight and shade, the tan, yellowing sand and the relentlessly blue-white sky. And the silence. A deep, blood-rushing-to-the-temples, awe-inspiring silence. She had never experienced anything like it—and now, after just two days surrounded by it, she couldn't quite believe in the world she knew existed outside this time and space. "Makes you think," Tendé continued softly, his voice coming to her just above her ear. "Jesus spent forty days and nights in it. So did the Prophet. I feel like I know why."

Amber turned her head to look at him. "It's the most powerful place I've ever been in," she half-whispered. It seemed rude to break the silence by speaking.

"It's almost inhuman . . . you're afraid of it and

drawn to it at the same time." Tendé remained standing behind her.

Amber shivered. "D'you think it will work?" she asked. "You and Max . . . your idea?"

"It depends," he said after a moment, coming to sit beside her on the step. "It depends on what you mean by 'work.' Will it be built? Of course. The idea in itself is too . . . *romantic*, almost, for it not to work. Everybody will want it to succeed. The bigger question of what it will trigger . . . that's more difficult."

"You mean development? And progress? Surely those are . . . *good* things for the country. Max says—"

"Max says many things," Tendé said quietly. "He's a businessman. He sees things in business terms, black and white, profit or loss, that's all." He was quiet for a moment. "And that's how it should be. If there's anyone who could get a project like this off the ground without the complications and compromises that come when you go to people like the World Bank, for example . . . well, it's him. And in the end, I'd rather do business with Max Sall than the IMF. It's cleaner."

"But are you saying that there might be problems with this scheme? Things that aren't quite so good for you . . . for the country?" Amber asked, her mind accelerating, as it always did, when she spoke to him. In two days she had realized Tendé Ndiaye was by far the most interesting person she had ever encountered. The speed with which he moved— physically and intellectually—was daunting.

"Of course. Look around you. Why do you think we

need armed guards? We've been fighting a quiet war of secession in our country for decades. The Arab North—the Tuareg—don't want to be part of the black South. That's what the guns and the kidnappings and the killings are about. If this mine goes ahead—and it will—it'll make this part of the country one of the richest provinces. D'you think they're simply going to sit back and allow the South to distribute the fruits as we see fit?"

"But what can you do? I mean, you say yourself that it's going to go ahead . . . ?"

"It has to. You've seen the countryside around here. People here die of diseases that the rest of the world has forgotten about: polio, malaria, TB, malnutrition. The desert way of life is finishing; there's nothing for the younger generations here. They want TVs and cars and access to schools. Well, those things have to be paid for, somehow. A scheme like this can lift a whole region out of despair. Max has to get the financing right, I have to work on the politics. But that's the way it should be. That's our problem, in Africa. Money and politics—they're too close. The economy ought to run on its own steam, with its own internal culture and logic. What we don't need are politicians poking their noses in every other week and grabbing what they can before things have a chance to mature."

Amber was silent. She knew next to nothing about the country or its problems. She knew even less about the relationships he spoke of—money, politics, the economy. But she was fascinated. Sitting there in the silvery darkness, in the middle of the Sahara next to a man whom she'd met a total of three times in her life and whom, she knew with an absolute certainty, she would follow anywhere he asked her to go . . . everything else—Max, London, her friends, her career, those aspects of herself that she had not even been aware of—suddenly fell into place. It was as if she had been looking at herself in an out-of-focus frame. Now, for the first time in her life, everything was painted in detail-sharp relief.

"A calculated risk," she said suddenly. "You have to take it. You won't know how it'll turn out but you can't afford not to."

"Yes." She could feel him appraising her silently.

"I suppose that's what draws Max to this place. He once told me he was sick of putting things together for other people to act on. He wants to be part of the action, not behind the scenes."

"He's an interesting man," Tendé said after a moment. "When I first met him I thought he was like lots of other businessmen you meet . . . charming, sharp, powerful . . . you know, the usual." Amber nodded. "But when he called me again, to come to the party in Menorca, there was something more . . . unusual about him. I don't know. I was curious. I read a bit about him in that biography, the one that was published a few years ago. Not very good . . ."

"He was furious about it," Amber smiled. "He said they'd got it all wrong."

"Yes, he doesn't strike me as the biography type. I can't imagine him telling anyone anything about himself. Never mind a stranger."

"No, he's very . . . he's silent about his past. I . . . we . . . don't know anything."

"But he's committed to this project. Really committed, I mean. Lots of people express interest in doing something like this but he . . . look at you. He sent his daughter. Why are you here?"

"Because he asked me to," Amber said simply. She could feel him looking at her.

"And will you do as he asks?"

"He hasn't really asked for anything. He wants a story on this place—he hasn't told me what to write or what to say. I suppose he knows it wouldn't work that way."

"Do you know what you will write about?"

"Yes. Yes, I do."

"Then I look forward to reading it." He smiled suddenly. "Good night, Amber Sall." She turned in surprise. He stood up and disappeared back into the night. Behind her, she heard the front door of his bungalow close. She felt immediately bereft.

The following morning, she was just about to turn on the rather rusty tap in the makeshift shower when she saw something move out of the corner of her eye. She froze. She was standing naked in the cracked white porcelain tub. It moved again. She turned her head ever so slowly, her stomach contracting in fear. It was a spider. The biggest, ugliest, strangest-looking spider she had ever seen in her life. Flat as a pancake, a dull brown color, almost indistinguishable from the ochre-colored walls, long, tentacle-like legs . . . she screamed as it ran across the bowl towards her foot. She leapt back and screamed again, all thoughts of modesty vanishing as she backed into the room where her clothes lay strewn around the floor, entangled within her bed sheets. She looked wildly around for a towel, a T-shirt, anything . . . and then the door was flung open and Tendé burst into the room, Abdoulaye close on his heels. There was a second's stunned silence before Amber dived into the pile of clothing and bed sheets, frantically trying to cover herself up, blurting out the words, "It's just . . . a spider . . . in the bathroom." And then Tendé turned on his heel, bumped into a shocked-looking Abdoulaye, whose eyes were almost popping out of his head, and slammed the door shut behind him.

"Are you all right?" he barked through the closed door. Amber's face burned.

"Yes . . . yes," she called out, "I'm sorry . . . it was just . . . I wasn't expecting it. It caught me by surprise."

"This is Africa, Miss Sall. You should expect to find such things." She heard his footsteps across the concrete before they disappeared into the soft sand. She could have kicked herself. How silly . . . and embarrassing beyond belief. It would take her a while to forget the look of stunned surprise on Abdoulaye's face as he took in her naked body scrambling frantically for cover—or the look of scornful disdain on Tendé's. *This is Africa, Miss Sall.* Oh, the shame of it! She ought to be made of sterner stuff. How was she going to face him after this?

*   *   *

But nothing further was said. When she'd sufficiently gathered her wits and emerged sheepishly
from her bungalow, Tendé was already out in the
salt fields with the men. There was only Abdoulaye
for company, and he delicately avoided her eye all
morning. Apart from a curt nod and a brief exchange when he returned at lunchtime, Tendé
hardly spoke to her all day.

Amber couldn't believe that she'd come all this
way and with such a sense of expectation, only to
blow it all by squealing over a silly spider and appearing even more gauche and childish than she
had when they'd first met. She lay awake on their final night in the desert, unable to sleep, desperately
trying to hang on to things—sights, conversations,
images—anything to delay the inevitable moment
when she would step out of the Mercedes at Bamako Airport and disappear out of his life. But apart
from the one all-too-brief conversation they'd had on
the bungalow steps, they were rarely alone together.

All too soon their brief three-day sojourn in the
desert was over. They woke before dawn on the last
day to begin the long drive back to Timbuktu. She
folded the few things she'd brought with her, cleared
away her notes and tidied the bed. She stood in the
watery half-light, listening to the sounds of the men
outside clearing up their temporary camp. There
was the smell of coffee. Not for the first time she
marveled at the ability of the men to make shelter in
the most unlikely of places. She had no idea if they
were married, had children, or more than one wife,

but from the first day she'd arrived, she'd been impressed by their silent efficiency in moving from task to task . . . cleaning a gun one minute, firing up a little coal stove and slicing onions in preparation for dinner the next. She looked around the room. There was nothing to indicate she'd ever been in it. In a few hours she would be gone from here, probably forever. She would never come back. Of that, she was absolutely sure. A tap at the door startled her. She picked up her bag and opened it. It was Tendé.

"Ready?"

"Yes. Just making sure I haven't left anything behind. I don't suppose I'll be back here again," she said with a half-smile, glancing around. He looked at her, but said nothing. She shut the door behind her and followed him to where the men were already loading up the vehicles. Abdoulaye appeared out of the semi-darkness, took her bag and handed her a tin mug of dark, thick coffee. She drank it gratefully. It would be hours before they would stop to eat and drink.

"Amber," Tendé called to her from behind one of the Land Cruisers. She turned to him. "I'm going to put you in the front vehicle, with Abdoulaye and myself. The guards will drive behind us." Her heart lifted in the most ridiculous manner. She nodded as casually as she could. She ate a piece of the flat, sour bread the men had cooked, drained her coffee and walked up to the car, happy beyond belief.

Fifteen minutes later, the vehicles loaded up and their possessions secured, the convoy began winding its way slowly across the sand towards Timbuktu. Amber sat alone in the back seat, staring at the back of Tendé's head as they climbed and swayed over the sand dunes to reach the flatter ground where they could pick up speed. The sun had risen rapidly and now the desert spread out before them in a sea of yellow and ochre corrugations, nothing in front or behind but the same. There was no road—just a track. The young man at the wheel drove as if by instinct, the car shuddering over the shifting, flurry surface. Tendé and Abdoulaye were speaking quietly in their own language and the soft, low murmur made her drowsy . . . she began to doze.

It was the change in engine pitch that woke her, and then everything happened at once. She opened her eyes to see the wheel being wrenched from under the driver's hands, saw Tendé's arm shoot forward to steady him, then the world turned upside down. The enclosed space of the car tilted dangerously, swaying this way first . . . then a sudden thud, and again, to the right . . . it gave way, completely. They were flung against the seats, upside-down, and something struck at her head; Tendé and Abdoulaye were flung against one another. It happened so quickly there was no time to react, to shout . . . to do anything. Everything flashed before her—the yellow sand, the black shapes of the men's heads . . . their arms, a bag sailing through from the rear. Suddenly the world righted itself again. A second thud and then the car was careening uselessly away through the sand, hitting nothing and finally coming to a stop. There was a shocked silence. Then a yell from Abdoulaye . . . they were all right! The car wasn't damaged. They'd been turned upside-down, that was it . . . that was all. The driver turned an amazed face towards them, his eyes wide with glittering tears. *Everything okay? Everyone okay?* Amber heard a door open and then Tendé was beside her, his hands on her as he pulled her slowly upright.

"Are you hurt?"

"No, no . . . I was just . . . thrown a bit," she struggled to sit up. Her skin tingled where he held her.

"You sure?"

"Yes . . . I'm fine. What happened?"

"We were lucky." Tendé's hands left her as he closed the door and got back in the front. "But you," he spoke to the driver in their language. The driver smiled sheepishly, nodding . . . Tendé appeared to be praising him for his skill in bringing them out of the skid, unhurt. Abdoulaye nodded enthusiastically. Boubacar—he was introduced to Amber and she reached across and shook his hand. There was an air of hilarity in the car. Look what they had just survived! Boubacar started the engine cautiously and it kicked into life immediately. They looked at one another in relief. The car rolled back to join the track from which they'd been flung. Slowly, the empty, silent vastness around them closed over the incident, as if it had never happened. Their relieved chatter gave way to silence, each lost in thought as they contemplated what might have happened.

At Timbuktu they were met by the same blonde pilot. She and Tendé obviously knew one another. Amber sat in silent and unaccustomed anxiety as they kissed and exchanged small talk. He slipped in and out of Bambara, French and English without even blinking. It was horrible—and impossible—to believe that in less than forty-eight hours, she would be on her way home and might not see him again. If he noticed her agitation, he gave absolutely no sign. He was as impassively polite to her as he had been at the party, three years ago. Tendé Ndiaye, she suspected, was not a man who let down his guard or allowed anyone behind the professionally polite screen he projected to keep everyone at a distance. Even a joke shared with Abdoulaye and Boubacar, she noticed, was a joke shared on his terms, on his cue. Everyone around him treated him with the same cautiousness she was used to seeing people treat Max with—like a beautiful, healthy predator, something to be admired and feared, equally.

And then, all at once, it was Monday. She was staying at his parents' house, in the lovely room she had occupied only five days previously. Five days? She could scarcely believe it. It seemed a month ago that she'd awoken at dawn, listening to the sounds of prayer. The house was empty; his parents were away, Salah told her. She ate dinner alone the night they got back—Tendé had some official function to attend, he told her. If it didn't go on too late, he would drop by to say goodbye. If not, he wished her a safe and pleasant trip home. Amber, listening to his disembodied voice over the phone, wanted to cry.

The evening was spent in a roller-coaster ride of emotions, every time she heard a noise in the house. Finally, at almost half-past midnight, she resigned herself to the fact that he probably wasn't going to come and slowly made her way back through the house to her room. She left a note for him lying on the side-table downstairs thanking him for his hospitality and leaving her London number in case she could ever return the favor.

She left the next morning feeling lower than she'd ever thought possible, and boarded her flight. Eight hours later, she was sitting in the back of Max's car, looking at London through the splattered droplets of rain on the windows, wondering just how she was going to put Tendé Ndiaye at the back of her mind, or better still, out of it. She was nothing to him—that much was obvious. His business partner's daughter; a journalist . . . not even a friend. She swallowed. Hot, bitter tears of disappointment had been burning at the back of her throat for almost a day. She wanted nothing more than to be in the quiet of her flat where she could give vent to them and—please, God—emerge on the other side of this crushing experience. For the first time in her life, she had a glimpse of what life might be like for Angela—to fall in love with someone who didn't want or need, or even notice—you. She slid down in the seat, angry at Tendé, angry at Max and most of all, angry with herself. How could she have let herself even *think* that there might be something more?

Kieran's mind was racing, working faster and harder than it had done in almost a decade. He wasn't really listening to the conversation going on around him—he had An Idea. Across the sitting-room floor, his old friend and partner-in-crime Jake Higham-Burton was in earnest discussion with the two men he'd invited to the flat. Kieran couldn't remember their names. But the Idea was growing in the back of his mind as he watched them talk. He and Jake had bumped into one another after an almost two-year gap in their friendship. Kieran hardly recognized him. He'd cleaned himself up. He'd been given an ultimatum by his father—either he got his act together and did something with himself or he'd cut off his allowance, throw him out of the house and recommend the army. Jake had sobered up on the spot. He hadn't given up the dope, of course, but he'd somehow weaned himself off the harder stuff and the result was that for the first time in almost ten years, he could actually remember what he'd done the night before and the distance between waking and sleeping wasn't the blurred, unarticulated mess it had been for so long. And he'd done it without rehab or the loving support of his by now *not*-so-loving parents. What the hell would he do without his monthly allowance? Nothing, was the answer, and he set about putting his life back on track.

Kieran's life was still a spectacular mess but there was something about seeing Jake's renewed purpose and his determination to *do* something that was infectious. Somewhere in the muddled recesses of his brain he dimly remembered what it was like to do something that Max approved of. It had been so long ago that he could barely remember the glow of satisfaction when he came back with a good school report or made a comment that made him smile. It had been Amber for so long. *She* was the golden girl in the family. He and Paola—not that he ever spent time thinking about Paola—but all of a sudden and in connection with The Idea, she'd popped up in his mind. He took another drag on his joint and watched the three men talk.

"Listen," he said suddenly, breaking into the conversation. They looked up. "Listen to this. This is fucking *brilliant*." He saw Jake frown. "No, no . . . really, man . . . listen. You know my sister, right?" Jake nodded slowly, still frowning. "What we *really* need to do is get *her* involved. Get her to get her friends to come . . ."

"What, that fat doctor friend of hers and the other one . . . what's her name . . . ?" Jake scoffed.

"No, not *Amber*, you idiot. Paola. If we could get Paola on board, that's all we'd need. She's *so* fucking cool."

"Paola who?" one of the other men asked.

"Paola Rossi. She's my sister. Well, half-sister."

"Paola Rossi . . . you mean the . . . what is she? An actress? The one who hangs out with all the models? She's your *sister*?"

"Who *is* this guy?" the other man asked.

"Kieran Sall." Kieran stifled a burp and stretched out his hand.

"Should I know you?"

"You might know my father."

"And he is . . . ?"

"Max Sall."

"*Max Sall*? No fucking *way*! You're Max Sall's son? Really?"

"Yes, really," Kieran said sarcastically. Jake was watching him closely. Kieran turned to him. "It's a brilliant idea, mate. Admit it. If she came, we'd get all her friends to come. Paola knows everybody: actresses, singers, models . . . the lot. And once they come, everyone else will."

"He's right, you know," one of the men said. "Digger." He held out his hand. "And Will." Kieran shook both their hands. He inhaled and coughed.

"It's just an idea," he said, trying to sound modest. "But she's really cool—knows all the right people."

"Okay. We need to talk about this. Between *us*," Jake said quickly, indicating himself and Kieran. "I'll give you a ring later on, Will. Keep this to yourselves for the moment, will you?"

"No problem. Nice meeting you, Sall." Digger and Will got up. Kieran could barely contain himself. It was so long—so fucking long—since he'd had anything in mind other than how to find money for his next hit or whether he could summon up the energy to pay Siobhân a visit. Jake showed the two men out and came back into the room.

"What the fuck was that all about?" he asked, rounding on Kieran.

"Nothing, honestly. You were talking . . . I was thinking . . . it's a great idea, Jake. Really."

"This is *my* venture, Kieran . . ." Jake began, looking angry. "This was *my* idea." Then he stopped. "But you're right. Paola would be awesome."

"And I know she'd do it. She'd be *so* up for it."

"Kieran, when was the last time you spoke to Paola?" Jake was watching him closely.

"Oh, not so long ago," Kieran said vaguely. Jake frowned. "Okay. Well, a while ago. When we were teenagers, actually. But it doesn't matter. I'll talk to her this . . . this weekend. Oh, man . . . this could be so fucking *great!*" Jake said nothing. He'd never seen Kieran Sall so animated. In spite of himself—the nightclub was his idea, remember?—he was excited. Paola Rossi was always in the gossip columns; she was always photographed hanging out with the right crowd—the models, aspiring actresses and starlets who made up the European party circuit. Getting her to come to the club on a regular basis and bring all her glamorous friends would be a massive boost. The fact that they were all European—*proper* European . . . French, Italian, Spanish—would add another layer of glamour to the place. Lots of young, tanned flesh on display . . . yes, Kieran had had a brainwave. He was amazed he still had the capacity.

"Look . . . go home, think about it, talk to Paola, Max, whoever. Let's meet again in a week's time. I need to put some stuff together. I've only got about half the money I need. I still need to do some digging."

"Maybe Max could help," Kieran said, his eyes shining.

"Don't push it, Sall," Jake replied, laughing in spite of himself. He'd seen Kieran high, stoned, unconscious, half-dead . . . you name it. He'd never seen him excited. It was quite a sight.

Max looked at his son through narrowed eyes. It was a fortnight since Kieran had asked to see him— he'd been so busy with the whole Téghaza project— but Kieran had insisted they meet. It was important. Now, finally, sitting across the desk from him in the study which had been off bounds to Kieran for the better part of four years, he was surprised at what he saw. Kieran in a state of animation? He leaned forward.

"Are you asking for money?"

"Absolutely not. Jake's handling the money. It's his idea, anyway. All I'm asking is for you to help me get in touch with Paola. And to ask if it's all right with you, of course." There was a sudden silence. Max got up from behind his desk and walked to the window. He would never have admitted it to Kieran, but he was touched. The boy wasn't asking for money—for once!—he was asking for support. He turned round.

"Okay. I'll be in Rome next week and I'll talk to her about it. I'll speak to you in a fortnight or so. Good enough?"

Kieran nodded. "Thanks." He got up. They looked at each other for a moment.

"I was just going to get Siobhân to bring some coffee. Want some?" Max was as surprised at the invitation as Kieran was. He'd spoken without thinking. Kieran jumped as though he'd been shot.

"No, no . . . that's okay. I'd better . . . run. Thanks, thanks . . ." And with that he bolted from the room. Max stared after him and shrugged. Well, well, well . . . perhaps this was the beginning of a new chapter in Kieran's life. He sincerely hoped so. He'd been surprised at his own reaction—almost hopeful. He thought he'd given up hope where Kieran was concerned. It just went to show. Blood. Thicker than water. Thicker than anything.

He picked up the little brass bell and rang for Siobhân.

≈58≈

Paola listened to her father with widening eyes. At first she didn't quite understand—Kieran wanted her to open a nightclub for him? She looked at her mother. Francesca was frowning.

"No, not exactly. They—he and a few friends of his—they've come up with an idea for a club. Now, I don't know anything about nightclubs but they want it to be something like Annabel's, you know, the London club in Berkeley Square." Max continued eating. The two women regarded him warily.

Francesca's eyes also widened. Annabel's—now *that* was different. Annabel's was exclusive and frightfully successful. She and Max had been there a few times in the past. But she still couldn't quite see where Kieran fit into the picture. For the past few years it had been nothing but one horror story after another. God only knew how Max had kept the boy out of jail—and now he was backing him in opening a nightclub? "No, I'm not backing him," Max replied testily. "This is *their* venture. They're not even asking me for money. What they *are* asking for is support. For some reason," he broke off and pointed his fork at Paola, "they seem to think this young lady will help bring in the right crowd." He stabbed a piece of veal. "Although why they think the riffraff you hang around with is the right crowd is beyond me." Paola said nothing. She was too stunned to speak.

"But what do they want her to do?" Francesca asked.

"Nothing. Show up from time to time. Be there on the opening night . . . bring her friends . . . I don't know. You know more about these sorts of things than I do. But I told Kieran I'd support him and that I'd ask you to do the same. And that's what I'm do-ing. If you want to come to London to talk to him . . ."

"Oh, yes . . . yes! When?" Paola broke in excit-edly. Max looked at her.

"Whenever you want. I'll be going back on Sun-day morning. I won't be there during the week but Kieran'll be there. Angela's there." He ignored Francesca's glare.

"Oh! This will be so much *fun!*" Paola was thrilled. "Will they call it Paola's? After me?"

"Don't be silly," Francesca broke in sharply. She wasn't pleased about the suggestion at all, especially the bit about Paola staying at Angela's. "It might all come to nothing. Weren't you saying you were suspicious about anything Kieran turned his hand to?"

"That's in the past," Max said, visibly annoyed. "He's straightened himself out. Turned over a new leaf. This could really be the making of him." He took a sip of wine. "About bloody time." He signaled to the waiter for the bill.

Back in her room later that evening, Paola lay on her bed and thought about the clothes she would take to London. She was *so* bored of Rome and every time she suggested moving somewhere—Paris, New York, Madrid—Francesca just looked hurt and tried to change the subject. And now Max had announced this little plan out of the blue and she realized just how badly she needed something new in her life. Hanging around the city with her friends was fine but they never seemed to *do* anything. It was always the same old stuff—shopping during the day, going to the beauty salon, clubbing at night, always making sure they were seen in the right places with the right people but, if the truth were known, Paola was getting pretty fed up of the "right people." Francesca didn't seem to realize but the "right people" in Rome were the same little clique of about fifteen families and Paola had slept with almost all of the eligible young men—as had most of her friends—and they were getting pretty bored with one another. That was the thing about not having a job or a career or anything. Nothing ever happened. Not that she particularly wanted to work. She just knew life was becoming rather predictable and if there was one thing Paola hated—as everyone around her knew—it was being predictable.

She rolled over onto her stomach, hugging her silk pillows. Yes—Kieran's surprise little invitation couldn't have come at a better time. She tried to re-member what Kieran looked like. She hadn't seen him since he was thirteen . . . and she was eight, nine? If he was anything like Amber . . . she pulled a face. Actually, he couldn't be anything like Amber. He'd been in trouble too often. Little Miss Goody Two-Shoes would never have done the things Francesca said Kieran had done—stolen money from Max; sold drugs; sold his mother's jewelry to *buy* drugs . . . he sounded like a real rebel. A bit more like her than Amber.

So . . . she went back to the subject at hand. Her new suede mini-skirt and perhaps a white blouse and a matching jacket? Yes, very cool. Oh, and those thigh-high boots she'd seen in the window at Bottega. Those would look fabulous with her short skirt. And some new jeans . . . the new, faded ones . . . the ones they ripped up to look old and worn. A pair of those with a leather jacket, perhaps. She made a mental shopping list. She and Francesca could go the following day. Although Francesca hadn't seemed as pleased as Paola or Max; she was probably worried Paola would sud-denly decide to move to London. Of course she wouldn't. But it would be fun to have a place there, especially now that she was going to have a nightclub named after her. London was *the* place to be—everyone said it. She hugged the pillow to her again. Fabulous. Just when life was looking boring, something brilliant had turned up.

≈59≈

Kieran did a double take. *That* was Paola? *His sister?* He swallowed. He had never, ever seen anything quite so exquisite. Next to him Jake gave a long, low whistle. Paola stepped out of Max's Jaguar, shook her mane of glossy dark-brown hair over her shoulder and turned to look rather disparagingly at the house. She was wearing a skirt—a minuscule scrap of black leather, actually; thigh-high black leather boots—the high-heeled kind, the ones you saw in . . . *those* videos, thought Kieran suddenly—a white long-sleeved T-shirt that clung to her curves and showed her nipples quite clearly and a fur wrap around her neck. She looked stunning.

"That's your fucking *sister*?" Jake growled. Kieran nodded, unable to take his eyes off her. When was the last time he'd seen Paola? Ten years ago? He and Jake watched her as she walked up the path beside Max, her pert little breasts jiggling and dancing around inside her T-shirt. Kieran looked away, confused.

"Kieran?" Max called out as they walked through

the front door. Jake almost trampled him in the rush to get to the hallway.

"Hi."

"Ciao." Paola was every bit as cool as she looked.

"Well, I'll leave you three to get on with it," Max said, walking towards the stairs. "Kieran, show Paola her room, will you? I've got a few phone calls to make. I'll join you for a drink at six o'clock." Kieran nodded, unable to take his eyes off Paola.

"It's great you could make it," he heard Jake say as he went off to find Siobhân.

"Mmm." Paola was playing it cool—real cool. He liked that.

"Did you . . . was your . . . how was your flight?" Jake was stammering.

"Not bad. S'only a couple of hours. Have you ever been to *Roma*?" Kieran strained to hear her. Her voice was husky and pretty. She spoke English well but with that delicious slurring together of words that Italians did so well. Christ, even listening to her was enough to bring on a . . . he stopped himself. Fuck. She was his sister, for Christ's sake. He yelled out for Siobhân.

"Just hang those up over there, will you?" Paola barely looked up as Siobhân and the driver entered with her bags. She was busy inspecting the little suite of rooms she'd been given. Little was the word. She couldn't get over how small the house was— well, the house itself was reasonably large but apart from the rooms on the ground floor as you came in, everything else was positively tiny. The three rooms that were hers for the week on the top floor of the house were no bigger than her bathroom at home—nicely decorated but still . . . just where was she supposed to hang all her clothes? And as for her shoes . . . there was barely enough room in that tiny built-in cupboard for her suitcases, never mind the twelve pairs of shoes she'd brought with her. Plus she intended to do some shopping. She *loved* English clothes.

She pushed open the bathroom door—minute! But pretty. She opened the antique cupboard next to the sink. Just enough room for all her cosmetics. She closed the door.

"And where would you like me to put *these*?" the maid said as she came back into the room. Paola frowned. If she didn't know better she'd say the girl was being sarcastic.

"*I* don't know. You find somewhere. It's not my house." Paola tossed her hair over he shoulder and walked into the little adjacent sitting room. There was a TV in one corner of the room. She picked up the remote and switched it on. News. Boring. She flopped down on the sofa. So . . . London. She was here at last. She'd never been to Max's London home. She knew from Francesca that Angela lived on the second floor and that Max had his study below her on the first floor and that Kieran and Angela's rooms were on the third, just below hers. Five floors in this tiny house? She'd never understood the narrow, squashed homes of the English—even the hotels she and Francesca usually stayed in when they came shopping were impossibly tall and narrow compared to the sweeping generosity of their apartment in Rome . . . it made Angela and her kids look like the poor relations. Paola giggled at the thought.

She heard the maid close the door behind her. At last. She moved back into the bedroom and promptly began pulling out all the clothes the maid had stowed away. She wanted to inspect the outfits she'd planned for the week. The instant flash of appreciation she'd seen in Kieran and his friend's eyes had put her in an exceptionally good mood. If there was one thing Paola loved, it was being appreciated. Now . . . skin-tight leather trousers and a lacy top? Or the jeans with the carefully positioned tear just below her bum? She sighed happily.

One hell of a strange family, Siobhân thought to herself as she closed the door and walked down the stairs. Angela had called her in on her way up—was that Max's daughter who'd just arrived? Siobhân didn't quite know what to say.

"What does she look like these days?" Angela asked, looking out of the window.

"Oh, well . . . you know, quite pretty," Siobhân answered as vaguely as she could.

"She's like her mother, you know." Siobhân stood in the doorway, her arms full of Paola's luggage.

"Yes, ma'am." What else was she expected to say? "Er, will you be needing anything else, ma'am? It's only . . . I'd better take these up." She indicated the bags. Angela nodded and turned away. Siobhân carried on up the stairs and was told to hang the little missy's clothes up.

And then there was Kieran. She'd seen the look of . . . well, what would you call it? Lust? She was shocked. Paola had walked in the door with Max and the two of them—Kieran and his friend . . . they'd just stood there, mouths open. It was disgusting. She was his sister, for crying out loud. And she, Paola . . . she knew exactly what they were thinking. She'd sauntered up the stairs with that bloody mini-skirt so short they could all see her knickers as she walked up, even poor Clive, the driver. Enough to give the poor man a heart attack. Christ, what a family. Well, maybe now that Kieran had something else to occupy his mind he'd leave her alone. She was getting sick of it. She was getting sick of the whole lot of them. Except Max, of course.

Angela could hear them moving about upstairs, the damned click-clack of the girl's heels. Siobhân had shut her door but she could still hear them . . . and Max, shouting down the phone line to someone as usual. She shivered. It was the one thing he'd promised her—twenty-two years ago, to be exact. She wouldn't have to put up with them in her house, ever. Ever. She'd somehow managed to extract that promise from Max and now, twenty-two years later, he'd broken it, just as he'd broken all the other promises he made. Or she thought he'd made. He always said she simply heard what she wanted to hear—he'd never promised a thing.

She stood by the window, thinking about the day she'd found out. She'd been hysterical at the time. The pain . . . she hadn't thought it possible to hurt so much. She'd been sitting down to breakfast by herself—Max was in Paris at a meeting; he was due back at lunchtime. She'd opened the papers and there he was. Max. Coming out of a restaurant somewhere in some city . . . with a woman, her hair flying out behind her, holding onto his arm. She'd snapped the paper shut, stunned. It had to be a mistake. She'd sat in the living room at their old house in Chelsea all morning, waiting for him to come home, praying she wouldn't fall apart. She'd sent the children to Kensington Park with the nanny. She remembered it because it was a cold afternoon and the nanny had protested . . . but she didn't care. She didn't care about anything except seeing Max and hearing how the whole thing was a silly mistake. A misunderstanding. But it hadn't turned out like that. He'd breezed in at lunchtime and then her whole world had collapsed, just like that. She'd confronted him as soon as he walked in the door. He'd ignored her for a moment and then walked into the drawing room. Angela followed him.

"No," Max said slowly, pouring himself a drink. "It's not a mistake." Angela stood in the doorway, staring wild-eyed at him. What did he mean "no?"

"But . . . wh . . . who is she?"

"Her name's Francesca. She's an air hostess. I met her on a flight." Max's voice was calm. Angela was afraid her heart would stop. She was having difficulty breathing.

"B . . . but . . . why? I don't . . . understand," she said. "We're married . . . we . . ."

"Look, I don't want to go into this. It's got nothing to do with you. I . . ."

"Nothing to do with me? Are you *crazy*?" The words burst out of her throat. She turned to stare at him. In retrospect, that had been her first mistake. Max closed up. Immediately.

"I'm not going to discuss this with you. Francesca will stay in Rome. You'll be here. You don't have to like one another . . ."

"Like? *Like*? You . . . *bastard*!" Angela's hands were clenched. She didn't remember how or when she crossed the room or who hit who first. She remembered lashing out at him hysterically and when he slapped her—*whack!*—she remembered just being relieved that it was possible to hurt somewhere else other than the inside of her head. He'd turned away from her. He'd actually slapped her and left her curled up on the drawing-room floor. When she thought about it, her skin crawled. And she . . . what had she done? She'd lain there until the children came running through the door. Kieran was six at the time, Amber was barely two. It was the nanny who'd bundled them out of the room and picked her up, washed down her face and put her to bed. Twenty-two years later, nothing much had changed. Siobhân still picked her up, washed her face and put her to bed. The only thing that had changed in twenty-two years was that Max no longer shared it. Her bed. Back then, she'd been the one to eventually crawl to him, begging him to make love to her again. She was twenty-five years old when Francesca arrived on the scene. She was married to one of Britain's rising young financiers. They had two children, a home in Chelsea, an island villa in Menorca. Max had just made his first million and was on his way to making more. Everyone knew who he was, who they were. Their wedding had made the front pages of all the society papers. Max's affair—if that was what you could call it—was now splashed across the pages of the same papers. How would she explain it to her parents? To her friends?

She wrestled with herself for days: should she leave? Where would she go? Back to her parents? She couldn't bear the thought. And the children? But far worse than that, worse than any of the practical arrangements that ran incessantly through her mind was the thought of leaving Max. She *loved* him. She was still absolutely besotted with Max. He'd walked out the day she'd confronted him—ten days ago—and all she wanted was to see him again. As the days passed without a word from him, her rage slowly turned to fear. He wasn't going to leave her, was he? He wouldn't . . . would he? She'd stopped thinking about leaving him, and now she was terrified he would leave *her*. She couldn't bear it. She began to panic. She could put up with Francesca. She could put up with anything—just come back, please. She phoned his secretary, she phoned his bankers . . . she phoned everyone she could think of.

Well, she thought bitterly, listening to Paola order Siobhân around, that was her second mistake. The relief she'd felt when he came back after three weeks spent God-knows-where . . . the *gratitude* that flowed through her the first time he made love to her again . . . it disgusted her now. She gazed down at the street below. Max's car was parked outside. The sun bounced off the roof—it was a beautiful day. She sighed. Mistakes. She'd spent her whole life making one mistake after another. The biggest mistake, of course, was loving Max. And although few people knew it, the strangest thing of all was that she loved him still. After all this . . . this *shit*, she thought angrily. That was the shameful bit. She still loved Max. She always would.

≈60≈

The wallpaper was peeling and clouds of dust accompanied their footsteps. Paola, following Kieran and his three friends in her brand-new leather jacket and white denim skirt, was furious. She stomped after the four of them, a mixture of disgust and irritation on her face. If there was one thing she hated, it was dirt . . . *and* dust, of course. Every step she took sent up a puff of debris. She followed them into the bowels of the building, squealing every time she touched something.

"Well, what do you think?" Kieran turned to her after half an hour of poking about in the semidarkness. Paola looked up from her handkerchief with a scowl.

"It's disgusting," she said indistinctly through the white linen. "It's dirty and it smells as if *tramps* have been living here."

"They probably have." Jake laughed at her expression. "But it's absolutely brilliant. I can see it already . . . this is going to be bloody fantastic, mate. Can't you see it?"

"No. I can't. I want to go home." Paola was on the verge of stamping her feet. She looked down at her black high-heeled boots. They were covered. Ruined. It was the last straw. They were only a week old. She made a sound of impatience, tossed her hair over one shoulder and started back the way they had come. But it was hard to find her way— every corridor looked the same. She couldn't remember whether they'd come up the left-hand side of the old elevator shaft or the right. Where the hell was the exit?

"Paola!" she could hear Kieran calling to her. "Wait . . . where are you going?"

"Home," she called over her shoulder. She'd had enough. She looked at her boots again—absolutely ruined. Damn Kieran and his friends and their stupid business plans. She'd thought the whole thing was nearly *finished*. Not this great dirty building site. Sure, it would be a different story once it was opened; she liked nothing better than dressing up for the opening of a club or a bar and she was never short of invitations to appear with other beautiful people whose appearance could make or break a venue. *That* part of it she liked. *This* part, she cursed, looking down at her skirt, was disgusting. She ignored Kieran's shouts and eventually managed to find the exit door. She pushed it open impatiently and emerged onto the street. Tottenham Court Road—she didn't even know what part of the damned city she was in. She immediately hailed a passing cab and climbed in. She had some difficulty remembering Max's address but an hour later, after driving around in circles for a while, they found it. She couldn't wait to jump in the shower and wash the dirt from her skirt. She looked down at her boots and skirt. They would have to be thrown away.

Kieran, Jake and Will reached Holland Park almost at the same time Paola did. Kieran was worried about her but Jake and Will were so excited by what they'd seen in the basement of the Centrepoint building at the junction of Tottenham Court Road and Oxford Street—all they wanted to do was get back and discuss their next steps as soon as possible. Digger and Blake, the fifth member of the investment team, were coming over and the five of them were going to sit down together and draw up a preliminary agreement. Max had agreed to lend them his lawyer to look it over—and he'd agreed to chip in £1 million to help them get it off the ground. Kieran had been worried that Jake and Will would think he was trying to muscle in on their idea but ever since they'd set eyes on Paola, they'd been surprisingly agreeable. They'd had a very good meeting with Max and his lawyer and the result was that they'd split ownership of the club six ways, each of the five investors to take a 16.6 percent stake with the single remaining stake split between four investors, including Max, whose return was agreed at two percentage points above the current base rate. Paola would be paid an annual 5 percent of the profits in the first two years with an option to renew the agreement after eighteen months. It all sounded rather complicated but Max had assured them it was better to get things straightened out from the beginning. In truth, Jake had confided to Kieran that he was actually relieved Max had got involved—when he, Digger and Will had first thought about it, they'd realized pretty quickly they had no idea how to actually make it work. Max had been to see the proposed location and agreed it was fantastic.

The old Centrepoint building was a twenty-story sixties office block right in the heart of London's clubland, a five-minute walk up the Charing Cross Road from Leicester Square. The building had been empty for almost ten years—there were rumors of flying panes of glass after a structural miscalculation . . . some even said a passerby had been hit and decapitated. Whatever the rumors, it had been unoccupied almost since it was built.

They were interested in the ground floors—a huge glass-fronted area off the street with a large mezzanine and two floors of basement space. The basement even had direct access to Tottenham

Court Road underground station—from a club or-
ganizer's point of view, an enormous advantage. On
the ground floors at least, the work that needed to
be done was purely cosmetic. Digger and Jake had
visions of a room filled with light, a space with sub-
tly changing colors . . . just enough of an eye-
catcher to attract the attention of people on
street-level but with an absolutely strict door policy.
There would be only one entrance into the ground
floor. Once inside, of course, people could move
freely between the floors, but they had to make it difficult to get in. Exclusive but expansive . . . a brilliant
idea. Digger's father was an architect and would
recommend someone from his own office to do the
job. They'd given themselves six months to get it up
and running. Ambitious, perhaps, but they were all
tired of sitting around all day long, smoking dope
and subsequently their ambitions, away. The five of
them looked at each other and grinned. Everything
was going better than they'd dared hope. Jake gave
Kieran a light punch on the shoulder—he'd turned
up trumps. Who would have thought it?

Upstairs in her bathroom, Paola wrapped herself in
a towel and walked, dripping, into the bedroom. She
could hear the guys downstairs. There had been
one awful moment, coming up the stairs, when Angela opened her door and the two of them had just
stood there on the stairs, eyeing each other. Then
Angela had turned away and slammed the door
shut. She hadn't said "hello" or anything, so Paola
hadn't either. But there had been something in the

woman's eyes . . . she looked half-mad. For a second, Paola almost felt sorry for her. But the slam of the door in her face . . . that was rude. Paola tossed her hair back and continued on her way up the stairs. Angela looked a lot like Kieran. Same light brown hair, large blue eyes . . . not like Amber. Thank God *she* wasn't around. Kieran was much, *much* nicer.

She pulled out a long, black jersey dress with an exposed midriff section. No, a bit showy for dinner. A short denim skirt with black fishnet tights and a plunging V-neck sweater? Yes . . . with the pointy-toed stilettos she'd bought at Christian Louboutin. She dropped the towel and began to dress.

≈61≈

Max and Francesca were enjoying a weekend in Menorca. He'd been in such a good mood for the past few weeks. Francesca was beginning to think her earlier doubts had been totally unfounded. Paola had come back from London with three times as much luggage as she'd gone with and a whole host of stories about how fantastic it was and how much fun she'd had and how Kieran had been so nice to her . . . and on and on. She hadn't said a thing about Angela and Amber had been away, apparently . . . all in all, it seemed as though the trip had been worth it. In fact, it had been more than worth it. It had put Max in a terrific mood—he'd called up on the Friday afternoon and told her to meet him at the villa. Like two teenagers, almost. Francesca was loving the unexpected attention. Day *and* night. She was positively glowing. It was obvious that Kieran's unexpected sobering up and the new-found relationship between him and Paola was a source of great delight to Max. She'd underestimated how much Kieran had troubled him.

She caught sight of one of the maids and asked her to bring them both some coffee on the terrace. A courier had just delivered a newspaper for Max and he'd hurried outside to read it. She clipped her way across the marble floor, smiling to herself.

"*Goddamn!*" she suddenly heard Max yell from the patio. She stopped. What now? She hurried outside. Max was holding out a newspaper at arm's length, scowling.

"What's the matter?"

"Goddamn!" He repeated angrily. "What the *hell* has she written?"

"Who? What?"

"Amber. I expressly *told* her I wanted a favorable report. What the hell has she gone and done? Get me a phone, will you?" Francesca ran into the sitting room. *Christ!* That bloody family! He'd been in such a good mood . . . what on earth had the girl gone and done? She picked up one of the cordless phones and hurried back outside. Max grabbed it, stood up and strode out to the pool, stabbing the numbers with his forefinger. Francesca rolled her eyes. She could feel an argument followed by an evening-long sulk coming on. She could cheerfully

have killed Amber. What had she written about?
She picked up the discarded paper. There it was:
*"White Gold: Bringing the Sands to Life?" By Amber
Sall, Financial Digest Correspondent.* She frowned.
What was all the fuss about?

"No," Amber interrupted Max angrily. "You asked me
to go there, take a look at the place, talk to Tendé
about the project . . . and that's exactly what I did."

"I asked you to write a report *in our favor,*" Max
hissed. "I didn't ask for this liberal crap about a dying culture and the end of a way of life. What the
fuck is this?"

"I'm a *journalist!*" Amber yelled down the phone.
"Not a bloody circus animal! If you'd wanted something so favorable why didn't you write it yourself?
You could have saved me the bother of two weeks
in that *dump* of a place with that *arrogant* man . . .
you could have just brought me the bloody report to
sign! You *knew* I would write about what I saw. You
knew it!" Amber's patience had just snapped. She
was at her desk in the office. Tim, her editor, looked
at her through the glass doors of his office. Keep it
down, he motioned with his hand. Amber colored.
"Look, I'm at work," she said, trying to calm down. "If
you want to talk to me about this, call me when I get
home. I can't talk about it right now. Besides, if you'd
bothered to read the whole thing through, it *is* a favorable report. It just talks about both sides of the issue. Like I've been *taught* to do." She slammed the
phone down.

*   *   *

"Give me that damned paper!" Max barked at Francesca.

"Don't shout at me!" Francesca shot back. She thrust out the offending article. "*I* didn't write it." She got up and stalked off. Max shook his head, shook out the paper and started reading again.

Half an hour later, he grudgingly admitted Amber was right. Okay, so it wasn't quite the congratulatory piece he'd been hoping for but actually . . . it was pretty damned good. A smile began to play around the corners of his mouth. His girl. She'd written a long, honest and rather enjoyable story about salt, about the desert, about the future of a complex culture within a country that was itself only a few decades old. He shouldn't have yelled at her. Hell, he was *proud* of her. He picked up the phone again.

After Max's call, Amber was so angry and upset that she'd asked Tim for the afternoon off. He'd taken one look at her face and agreed. She walked down City Road from her offices at Angel and decided to walk on down to the river. Standing beside the Thames would be a good way to cool her burning cheeks.

It was almost nine o'clock by the time she got back to her flat. She'd walked down to the Embankment then phoned Becky and they'd met for a drink. Becky had actually made her laugh with her story of the opening night of her new artist's show; it sounded as if everything that could have gone wrong, had. Somehow, she'd managed to talk the gallery owner into giving her another chance and now, almost a month after it had happened, it was more or less forgotten. Apparently Charlie had been brilliant that night—he'd taken her out for a Thai meal, driven home by the river . . . honestly, Becky said, without him she didn't know what she'd do. Amber listened, happy for Becky that she'd found someone so special, but feeling more than a little sorry for herself that she hadn't.

She was in a strange mood when she got home. She kicked off her boots, opened the fridge and poured herself the last of a bottle of white wine. Unusual for her to drink alone but tonight she felt in need of something a little more uplifting than the nine o'clock news and a ham sandwich. She took her glass and an apple into the living room and switched on the TV. Her answering machine was blinking—four blips—probably Max. She didn't feel like talking or listening to him at that moment. She would ring him in the morning. She put her feet up, took a sip of wine and tried to relax. The phone rang once, just after 10 p.m. She ignored it. The machine would pick it up and it was on silent. The world outside could wait. Just for tonight.

Tendé listened to Amber's clear, precise voice on her answering machine and left a short message. The newspaper in which her article had appeared lay on the table beside the phone. He looked at it again. It was very well written; balanced, objective and yet strangely poetic, as well. He wasn't surprised. She'd impressed him on her trip to Téghaza. He hadn't really remembered her from the party in Spain—it was her sister who'd stayed in his mind. He'd found Amber rather aloof and a little cold. He was much quicker to respond to the open sensuality of her younger sister although he could tell, just by looking at her, that Paola was dangerous. But in the desert, speaking to Amber, she'd surprised him with her quiet perceptions. He'd overheard the men talking about her after the spider incident. Abdoulaye murmured he could see how a woman like that might stir a man's mind but not his body. He'd stifled a smile when he heard them, silently agreeing—but now he wasn't so sure. She wasn't beautiful in the way he remembered her sister or like the women he was usually attracted to but there was something about her . . . once you'd talked to her you found yourself thinking about her and wanting more. She had one of those faces that was transformed completely by her smile—after two days in the desert he'd found himself wanting to see it whenever he spoke to her. He shook his head. He knew better than to go down that path. Max Sall wasn't the kind of man to sit back and allow someone like Tendé to court his daughter. Either daughter. If he knew what was good for him he'd steer clear of Amber and Paola Sall. And at this point what was good for him was the project—getting it started, getting it off the ground. It was probably just as well Amber hadn't been home. He wasn't sure why he'd called—the article had moved him. Just as she'd moved him. Greatly.

Becky looked at Amber out of the corner of her eye. Why had she lied? It had been on the tip of her tongue to tell her about Henry. Nothing would have happened . . . nothing *had* happened. It was totally, completely innocent. So why did she lie? And now that she had . . . well, how was she supposed to bring it up now? She could have kicked herself. What if Henry ran into Amber unexpectedly? Aargh. She pulled a face at herself.

"You take the first cab," she said to Amber as they stood outside the bar. "You've had a pig of a day. I'll take the next one."

"Are you sure?" Amber looked at her gratefully.

"Absolutely sure. Get that one . . . look. I'll call you tomorrow, okay?" she shouted as Amber got in. She blew her a kiss and watched as its tail lights disappeared up the road. She sighed. She'd gone and made a mess of things, completely unnecessarily. Henry hadn't called her since the Friday they'd met for a drink—why would he? He'd probably just wanted to make sure she was okay. They'd spent the whole evening talking about Amber, anyway. She'd realized when they parted ways that she'd made a mountain out of a molehill over the whole thing. Henry wasn't interested in her—not that she was in him, of course. One drink, a Thai meal and that was it. So why, why, *why* hadn't she told Amber? Or Charlie, for that matter? She hailed the next cab and climbed in.

Thank God it's Friday, Amber thought to herself as her alarm went off the following morning. She lay in bed for a few minutes, listening to the familiar gurgling song of the hot water pipes as the heating came on. She looked at the window pane—it was raining. Of course. Typical. They'd had a week of glorious sunshine and now this. She pushed aside the covers and got up. On the way to the shower she hit "play" on the answering machine. The first two messages were from Max. She was brushing her teeth when Tendé's voice suddenly cut across the sound of running water. She stopped, mid-flow. *". . . so . . . perhaps see you in London one of these days. This is Tendé Ndiaye, by the way."* She almost broke her neck leaping over the bed to get to the hallway in time. Her machine automatically erased messages once they'd been heard . . . she pounced on it. Phew! She pressed rewind, her heart hammering. *"Hello, Amber Sall. Just read your article. I thought it was very good, very impressive. I enjoyed it. So . . . perhaps see you in London one of these days. This is Tendé Ndiaye, by the way."* She rewound it again. *"Hello, Amber Sall . . . "* She stood in the hallway for ten minutes, staring at the machine, quite overcome. He had called. Now what?

PART FIVE

≈62≈
Cairo, Egypt
1991

It was Alasdair's idea to go to Egypt. A winter break—
a few days in the sun. He surprised her with it one
evening after a particularly long day in surgery. He'd
even consulted the personnel department to find out
when she was due time off. He'd arranged everything . . . two days in Cairo, a three-day cruise down
the Nile, ending at Luxor and a weekend in the beach
resort at Sharm-el-Sheikh. They'd pored over the
travel guide together. Madeleine was so excited.
She'd managed to shut out her parents, her course-
work, her waiting operations . . . everything. She
didn't tell anyone, not even Amber or Becky. She was
often on call for six days in a row, so no one would
think it strange she wasn't around. And if she came
back with a noticeable tan . . . well, she'd cross that
bridge when they came back.

They flew out of Gatwick on a typically overcast November day. The skies were leaden and dull and a fine drizzle was settling over the airport as their plane lifted into the skies and broke through the clouds. She slipped her hand into his, noticing not for the first time the faint liver spots and blotches on the back of his hand. He was fifty-two. Twenty-nine years her senior. His eyes were closed; he was snoring gently. She leaned across and pulled the blanket over him. A wifely gesture. She smiled at herself. She felt below her seat for her bag and pulled out a textbook. Alasdair Lang was at the top of his career; hers was only just beginning. She still had plenty to do.

Their arrival in Cairo was chaotic. From the moment they walked out of the plane into the dry, winter heat, Madeleine was captivated. It was so different from anywhere she'd ever been. Hot, dusty, noisy . . . the sheer number of people was daunting. A taxi was found for them—there were literally hundreds of young men surrounding the newly arrived, eager and ready to act as guide, driver, negotiator, all-purpose friend, fiancé . . . smiling as pleasantly as she could, she shook her head—no, no . . . I'm with my husband—and followed Alasdair into the back of the tiny, cramped car. The driver, an amiable young man named Mohammed, talked non-stop all the way to their hotel in a mixture of English, French and Arabic—Madeleine couldn't understand a word. She turned to look out of the window at the city speeding by. Cairo. It was just like the airport, only much vaster. Buses competed with cars, which in turn intimidated the scooters; they showed little mercy towards the cyclists who clung precariously to the edges of the streets . . . and somehow, amidst it all, crowds of pedestrians managed to make their way. She sat with her nose pressed against the window, delighted by the sights and sounds of the city. Alasdair was struggling to hold up his end of the conversation with Mohammed. He'd been to Cairo once before, he told him, as a student. *Ah, now you bring your daughter?* Mohammed asked innocently. Alasdair nodded shortly. Madeleine felt for his hand, and squeezed it.

Their hotel was cool in a dry, air-conditioned, neutral kind of way. A large, comfortable room . . . rose-patterned bedspread, flowered curtains.

"It doesn't look very Egyptian," Madeleine shouted to him as she walked into the bathroom. She was hot and sticky after their dusty journey. His reply was lost as she stepped into the shower. The tepid water felt wonderful. She washed her hair, luxuriating in the feel of the water streaming over her, restoring her body to something approaching its normal temperature. She spent a good half an hour under the spray. When she came out toweling her hair vigorously he had fallen asleep. She bounced beside him on the bed and prodded him—you sleep too much!—and watched in delight as she let the towel drop and he struggled awake, one hand going out automatically for her breasts. He pulled her onto the bed, ignoring her protests at her wet hair, and covered her face with kisses. She lay back and closed her eyes as he parted her knees and slid a hand knowingly up the inside of her thighs. Eight glorious, wonderful days. It almost made up for the snatched weekdays when they were together at home.

The next few days were wonderful. She had long grown accustomed to not being able to share her experiences with her parents—she seldom told Maja when or where she was going—but this time, it was hard. She walked around the *souk* with Alasdair and thought about her father. How he would have loved to see this! And the gifts she could have brought back . . . everything was ridiculously cheap. She fingered a silver filigree necklace and matching bracelet that Maja would have loved. How would or could she explain it? Exploring Cairo together—the wide, chaotic streets; half-hidden tiny back alleys; the food market with its pyramids of brightly colored, unidentifiable spices and the towering stacks of exotic fruits and vegetables; the noisy *souk* with its carpets and handicrafts; the crumbling monuments and semi-preserved colonial buildings and the modern housing blocks designed by Nasser and already turning to ruin . . . it was special seeing it all with Alasdair, listening to his explanations as they moved across the city.

They left Cairo and set sail for Luxor at dusk, the countryside around them bathed in dying shades of sand, pink and red . . . across fields of wavering date palms and sugar cane, the sun made its evening descent. She stood on the deck of their boat with Alasdair's arm around her waist, her head rest-

ing against his cheek. All along the deck, coal braziers were being lit, their scent mingling with a host
of others—lemon, couscous, meat—somewhere on
the decks below dinner was being prepared. She
leaned against him and watched the shore slowly
disappear as night fell and they moved out into the
middle of the Nile.

It was on their third and final night of the cruise
that Alasdair began to feel unwell. The boat had
docked in the afternoon and they were led ashore to
a small hotel at the foot of the wind-sculpted White
Mountain. It was a small, simple bungalow built from
palm beams, salt rock and clay—six rooms that
were almost invisible in the pale, sand-colored landscape. They'd had dinner—a wonderful combination of lamb, rice and apricots—but Alasdair hadn't
eaten much. He'd ordered a brandy, something to
sip as they sat by the coal-filled fire. There were
three other couples with them; and a family of four.
Madeleine remembered hearing the children complaining as their mother shepherded them to bed.
Alasdair looked pale and tired, but he kept insisting
he was fine; it was nothing, he was tired, it had been
a long day. She walked with him to their room, looking on in concern as he undressed and lay down,
faint beads of sweat beginning to appear on his
forehead and upper lip, despite the chilly night air.

"A good night's rest . . . I'll be right as rain in the
morning," he smiled at her, removing his glasses
and pulling the sheets up to his chin. He was alternately hot and cold, he told her. A touch of fever,
maybe . . . nothing to worry about. She sat with him

until he felt into a fitful sleep, tossing away the sheets and then pulling them back again. Around midnight, she rose and walked to the French doors at one end of their room. She opened the doors and stepped outside. The sounds of the natural world came to her—the wind moving almost silently across the dunes, the rustle of leaves and the creaking sound of the enormous palms as they moved to and fro. She shivered in the cool night air. She hoped he would be better by morning.

But he wasn't. He was awake before she was. She opened her eyes to see him sitting upright, holding his stomach, as though in pain. He was pale and tired-looking, as though he'd slept badly.

"What's the matter?" she asked, sitting up in alarm.

"Nothing . . . just a little pain . . . right here." He pointed to his breastbone, wincing. Madeleine looked on, worried. She felt his abdomen. It was a little tight. A pulled muscle, perhaps?

"Shall I ask for something?" she said, wondering if a hotel as small as theirs would have anything. What could she give him? Aspirin?

"No, no . . . it's nothing to worry about. I'll be fine by lunchtime."

But lunchtime rolled around and Alasdair still lay in bed, grimacing in pain every few minutes, refusing anything to eat or drink. The boat was due to leave in an hour. Madeleine walked to reception and asked if it were possible to see a doctor. The young man at the desk was concerned—the hotel doctor had been called away to an emergency at another hotel, some five or six hours' drive away . . . perhaps he could help? What did she need? Some aspirin? She took a bottle from him and returned to the room. Alasdair didn't look well enough to get on the boat; they agreed to stay at the hotel for an extra two days and pick up the boat on its way back. Luxor could wait, Madeleine insisted. It was far more important that he get well. Alasdair was too ill to protest. He slipped back into sleep as she turned on the ceiling fan and refreshed the jug of water.

That night, neither of them slept. He had a fever—the soaking sheets and violent outbreaks of shivering attested to that. In the morning, he was clammy and cold to the touch and could barely sip water. It was at that point that Madeleine started to panic. She ran to the reception desk again. Where was the nearest hospital? The receptionist pulled a dog-eared map from under the counter: in Siwa, about a five-hour drive from where they were. Madeleine immediately handed over Alasdair's credit card—please, get us a car and a driver. The man nodded; he could see the fear in her eyes. She returned to the room, trying not to show how worried she was. Apart from the occasional sip of water, Alasdair had had nothing to eat or drink for two days. He lay back against the damp sheets, allowing her to make the arrangements as quickly as she could. She packed their clothes and bags in a matter of minutes. A driver had been found and she wanted to get to the hospital as quickly as possible.

On the journey, Alasdair said very little, just kept slipping in and out of sleep, shivering despite the fierce mid-morning heat. They arrived in the small town just after three o'clock. A peasant farmer directed them to the hospital—more of a clinic, Madeleine noted, as they pulled up outside the mud-walled building. It was tiny—clean, she was relieved to see—but tiny. The nurse who helped Alasdair into the waiting area wasn't able to speak English but with the help of the driver they managed to determine that yes, there was an X-ray machine. The daughter was a doctor? She would know how to read the X-rays? Madeleine was nodding furiously. The nurse looked a little uncertain but she and the driver wheeled Alasdair down the corridor. They would be back with the films in a little while. Madeleine spent the longest hour she'd known pacing up and down the little, hot waiting room under the curious gaze of half a dozen local patients and their families.

A doctor came running down the corridor, clutching a batch of X-rays.

"You're a doctor?" he asked, holding the blue films up to the light. Madeleine nodded, looking at the film with a sinking heart. It was his appendix. Ruptured.

"He needs to be operated on right away," Madeleine said, turning to the doctor.

"Madame . . . unfortunately, we have no facilities to do such an operation here. You must go to Cairo."

"Can we . . . can we drive there?" she asked, not knowing how far away they were.

"No, you must take airplane. You can reach Cairo . . . one hour, maybe two hours. Not more.

Come, I will explain you the way." She followed the doctor to the clinic door. There was a small, private airstrip, he explained, for the plantation owners. She could find a pilot there. It would cost a lot of money—Madeleine nodded impatiently, yes, of course—but it was the only way. Driving, the doctor explained, would take almost eight hours. As she knew, the patient didn't have eight hours to spare. Septicemia was probably already setting in. Madeleine thanked him, tears of fear beginning to mist her eyes. She ran to where Alasdair was sitting in the wheelchair, looking frail and weak and exhausted.

"He says we need to get you to hospital in Cairo," she said, her heart contracting in her chest. Alasdair simply nodded. She could tell from the way he held his head that his energy was rapidly dwindling. His eyes were closed and he seemed to have difficulty breathing. She bent down, putting a hand on his knee. "I'll get us a pilot, don't worry . . . we'll be in Cairo before you know it." He nodded, heavily, but didn't say a word. She fished his wallet out of his jacket pocket and left him with the nurse. She and the driver roared off in the direction of the airfield. Thirty minutes later, it was done. With the help of the doctor and his nurse, they managed to get Alasdair on board the tiny plane. The doctor stuffed the X-rays in her hand just before the doors closed.

"Get him to the Al-Faisal General Hospital," he instructed. "I will ask for an ambulance to take you there when you get to Cairo." Madeleine nodded, too terrified to speak.

On the plane, his breathing changed—it became

laboured and shallow. She held his hand, talking as soothingly to him as she could, avoiding the worried looks the pilot kept giving them. The flight was short and, true to the doctor's word, there was an ambulance waiting for them when they touched down. The two male nurses took charge immediately, bringing out a stretcher to meet them as the small aircraft taxied to a halt. She got into the ambulance alongside Alasdair gratefully and, for the first time, allowed herself to think it might be all right, after all. The ambulance was new and the team was very efficient. The nurse beside her told her they were taking him to one of Egypt's finest hospitals. Her father would be in good hands, he said. Not safe, not better—but in good hands. She remembered thinking about his words later.

He was rushed through the hospital entrance on a trolley, Madeleine running behind him, still holding the X-rays in her hand. She'd left their bags in the ambulance but no one seemed to care. The urgency of getting this man with breathing difficulties into the hospital as quickly as possible overcame everything. Two doctors in white coats were waiting for them as soon as the crew wheeled him in. One of them grabbed Madeleine by the forearm, asking her a few questions as she stared wildly after Alasdair's disappearing figure. A set of double doors opened at the end of the corridor and suddenly, he was gone. She turned to the doctor, the words barely able to come out of her mouth. She handed the films over and watched as he opened them, too afraid to ask what was going to happen. He took them from her and raised them to the light, scanning them with professional rapidity.

"Yes, we'll need to operate immediately. It's his appendix. Please wait here." And then he, too, was gone. Madeleine walked unsteadily over to the chairs that were lined up along one side of the wall. She swallowed. In the corner of the room was a pay phone. She walked over to it, inserted as many coins as she could find and dialed Amber's number. She desperately needed to talk to someone. The phone rang a few times. She glanced at her watch— it was five o'clock in Cairo, four o'clock in London. Amber was probably still at work. She let the receiver fall and stumbled over to one of the chairs.

He died later that evening, on the operating table. A nurse came to tell her, shaking her gently by the shoulder, forcing her abruptly out of sleep. She stared at her. She wanted to say something, but couldn't. The nurse looked at her kindly, then disappeared. Madeleine was left standing in the lobby, her fists clenched at her sides, breathing deeply and rapidly as if she couldn't swallow enough air or digest what she'd just been told.

It was the First Secretary at the British Embassy who explained to her later that in Alasdair's case, it seemed his appendix had defied the logic of such occurrences and instead of swelling up to bursting point, causing precise abdominal pain, had developed a leak almost immediately upon infection. He had been dying slowly for the past few days. His blood was poisoned, almost right from the start. There was nothing anyone could have done, or so the hospital said. The man obviously didn't know Madeleine was herself a doctor.

"Do you have children, Mrs. Laing?"

Madeleine looked at him, fresh tears forming in her eyes. She drew a deep breath. "I'm not his wife."

"Ah." There didn't seem to be much else to say.

Amber put her head round the door. Madeleine was lying on the bed in exactly the same position she'd left her in that morning. She was awake.

"Hey," Amber whispered, coming into the darkened room. Madeleine blinked and gave a weak smile. "How're you feeling?" she asked, coming over and sitting on the edge of the bed.

Madeleine nodded slowly. "I'm . . . okay."

Amber took her hand. "Have you had anything to eat?"

"No . . . I wasn't hungry. I'm okay." Amber bit her lip. Madeleine clearly wasn't okay.

"Shall I make you something? Some soup?"

"No . . . honestly. I'm fine."

"Mads . . . you haven't eaten anything all day. Come on, have something with me. I'm making some for myself." Madeleine shook her head weakly. Her eyes filled with easy tears. Amber held her hand. She didn't know what to say. Madeleine had been staying with her ever since it had happened—almost three months ago—and rather than getting easier, it seemed to be getting worse. She patted her hand and got up. "I'm bringing you some whether you like it or not," she said lightly. "You're wasting away, Madeleine. Soon there'll be nothing . . ." Her voice trailed off. It was probably not the right thing to say. She watched Madeleine close her eyes and send a trail of fat, hot tears down her cheek. She got up and walked into the kitchen.

She took out the carton of soup she'd bought and began slicing some bread. Madeleine needed help—proper help. Not the kind of help she or Becky or even Madeleine's parents could provide. She just didn't know who to turn to. Where did you get that kind of help?

Alone in the room again, Madeleine struggled with herself. She couldn't help it. She didn't want to cry, she didn't want to lie in bed all day long and she certainly didn't want to make it hard for people around her. But she couldn't help it. There were days when she woke up in the morning and simply had no idea how she'd get through the twelve or thirteen hours before it was time to go to sleep again. Some days she had no recollection of the daylight hours passing. Some days it felt as though she'd been asleep all day. Three months. It had been *three* months and everyone said it would get better. They had no idea. She turned her face to the wall. It was grey. His eyes were grey. Had been grey. She began to cry again.

"Mads?" Amber was shaking her gently awake. There was a bowl of soup and a buttered roll on a tray. "Come on. Have something. Please, Madeleine. *Please.*"

Becky waited until she heard the front door slam shut behind Charlie, waited until she couldn't hear his footsteps any more then slid out of bed. She was amazed at herself—she'd never thought of herself as a particularly good liar, but these days . . . just look at her. She'd called Morag the night before saying she wasn't feeling well, she'd probably stay at home for a day or two . . . nothing serious, just a flu coming on. The gallery was quiet anyway; they were in between shows.

She pulled on her dressing gown and walked into the bathroom. She had an hour to get ready before Henry arrived. A nice long soak in the bath, fifteen minutes to do her hair and make-up and then they'd be on their way. A whole day in a hotel in the Berkshire countryside. Henry had found it, God only knew how. She could hardly stand the excitement that was building up inside her. She turned on the taps and sat on the side of the bath, watching the foam rise. She was having an affair. She whispered the words to herself, still half incredulous. She, Becky Aldridge, soon-to-be Becky Mason, *was having an affair!* And there was no one she could tell. Amber, of course, was out of the question. Especially now, after what had happened to poor Madeleine. Her mother? Absolutely not. Her parents *adored* Charlie; besides, they wouldn't think

Becky could ever be that devious. She thought about Madeleine and the horrible ending to her relationship. It just went to show, she mused, you had to grab what happiness you could, when you could. You never knew what might happen next.

On that startlingly profound note, she slipped into the bath.

An hour later, almost to the dot, Henry rang the doorbell. Becky took a last look at herself in the bedroom mirror and ran downstairs. Minutes later, they were speeding towards the South Circular, heading for the M25. Henry took his hand off the gear stick and squeezed Becky's thigh. She leaned back in the seat, trying to quell the butterflies and tension in her stomach. She always felt this way about Henry, even after six months of clandestine meetings and illicit sex. She couldn't explain it to anyone, not even to herself. Having an affair was just so *not* a part of who she was, or who she'd thought herself to be. The first time it happened she was astounded at herself. She'd calmly buttoned her dress, pulled on her coat and walked off down the road to the Tube station and walked in her front door an hour later, all smiles. She hadn't had to explain anything to Charlie—he was so wrapped up in his job, and she often came home late from the gallery; she had lots of friends he knew nothing about and really didn't care to—it was all astoundingly easy. She would no sooner have thought about leaving Charlie than she would have lopped off her right arm. Everything continued to run as normal: get up in the morning, have breakfast, kiss Charlie goodbye, Tube into work, a day at the gallery, sometimes drinks after work or meetings with potential artists . . . and once or twice a week she slipped off to Henry's where she had the kind of sex she only ever read about in books or saw occasionally on TV—fierce, wild, sometimes rough . . . and then she pulled on her clothes and left him lying face down in the tangle of sheets and clothes that the two of them had made, minutes earlier. She couldn't explain it and she didn't even try. She continued to sleep with Charlie; she even enjoyed it. It was as if she'd been suddenly cleaved in half—the one half functioned as she'd always done . . . sensible, likeable Becky Aldridge; the other was this strange, sensual creature who could be made to do anything. The heights—or was it depths?—of intimacy she reached with Henry, she wasn't sure she would ever want to with Charlie. Henry opened her up, quite literally . . . she went to places in her own imagination she didn't know existed. There was a quiet, dangerous edge to Henry that she had never even guessed at. A kind of desperation to him that frightened her at times but thrilled her just the same. He was different from everything—the person she'd thought he was, the person he appeared to be . . . she wondered over and over again if that was what Amber had seen and walked away from. But it was a question she could never ask. Amber had no idea. And Becky wanted to keep it that way. Henry was *her* business, a private matter, for her and no one else. It helped to think that way whenever she thought of Charlie.

Whatever was going on between her and Henry was no one else's business. She was so confident of her ability to separate the two halves of her life, she never even bothered to take her ring off. Henry would finger it sometimes, absentmindedly, in the lull after sex. He never commented on it and so neither did she.

≈64≈

She walked down the long, white corridor, looking at the names on the doors to her left and right. Borowski, Hammond, Professor Greaves . . . Harrigan. There. She stopped and knocked once, twice. She hoped she was doing the right thing.

"Come in." A voice sounded from within. She pushed the door open.

"Dr. Harrigan? I'm Amber Sall. We spoke on the phone." She was relieved to see him smile in recognition.

"Ah, yes . . . Miss Sall . . . do come in. Excuse the mess . . . in the middle of marking. Please. Do sit down. I'll just move these . . ." He swept a pile of papers off the chair in front of his desk. Amber sat down. "So," he said, going round to his side of the desk. "How can I be of help?"

"It's Madeleine Szabo," Amber said without preamble. "She's one of your junior doctors . . . on your surgical team." Dr. Harrigan nodded slowly. "I'm . . . I'm not sure how much you know about what happened or even if I should be here talking about it but—"

"We *are* aware, Miss Sall," Harrigan said quietly. "A dreadful tragedy. Alasdair had many friends in this department, not just colleagues. I believe I was one of the few who knew . . . what was going on. How is Madeleine?"

"Not good. I . . . I don't know what to do about it or even how to help her. That's why I thought of coming here, rather than trying to find her GP, if she even has one. It's not just a case of her getting better or getting over it. She seems much worse than that to me. She keeps saying it's all her fault, that she should have diagnosed it earlier. Talking to me isn't doing her any good. I wondered . . ."

"If I might have a word? Of course. Is she alone?"

Amber shook her head. "No, she's staying at my flat—she's been there ever since. But . . . not being able to go to the funeral and not really being able to talk about it with anyone . . . I think that's made it harder."

"I understand. When would be a good time to drop by?"

"Any time. Whenever you're free. I know you must be unbelievably busy."

"Alasdair Laing was a friend of mine. If there's anything I can do to help his . . ." He stopped suddenly. "He loved Madeleine. Anyone could see that. I'm so sorry this has happened. I'll drop by this evening. Around 7 p.m.?" Amber nodded gratefully. There were tears in her eyes as she thanked him.

"Nothing to thank. Alasdair was a friend. I miss him. We all do."

Madeleine heard the buzzer. She'd been dozing, on and off, for the past couple of hours. She found it hard to sleep at night and usually lay awake until the early hours of the morning, listening to the night sounds the house made and to the whisper and sweep of the tree outside the bedroom. Last night had been a particularly bad one. Every time she dropped off she saw Alasdair and she would wake with a start. The whole thing had been a dream, a horrible, silly nightmare . . . and then she would wake up properly, realize where she was and the tears would start again.

The buzzer sounded again. Amber wasn't yet home. She slipped out of bed, found a dressing gown and walked barefoot down the corridor. There was a dark shape behind the frosted glass . . . a short, rather large man. She cleared her throat. "Who is it?" She tightened the belt on the gown.

"Dr. Harrigan. Madeleine?" Madeleine stood frozen in front of the door. Harrigan? From the hospital? "Madeleine?" he called again softly. "I was just passing . . . can I come in?" Madeleine looked at her bare feet. Then she unlocked the door.

He led her gently into the living room, took off his coat and without saying anything, disappeared into the kitchen to make her some tea. There was no awkwardness—professionally, as well as personally, Harrigan knew exactly what to do. He brought her the tea, pulled up a chair so that they were close but not touching, and waited for her to speak. When she had finished and he saw there were no more tears left, he pulled a sheaf of papers from his coat pocket and unfolded them, spreading them across the small coffee table.

"Go away, Madeleine. Leave the country for a while." She looked up. "I'd like you to take a look at these. Right now you feel you can never practice medicine again. I understand. It will pass. There are many ways to be a doctor."

"I can't. I'm finished," Madeleine said, not looking up from her tea. "I should have known what it was . . . I should have seen it . . . *done* something." He nodded. She had lost her nerve.

"It's happened to many more of us than you would care to think," he said quietly. "But you are a *good* doctor, Madeleine. This will pass. In the meantime, I want you to think about this, about doing something different for a while. You don't have to make a decision now. Just promise me you'll think about it." Madeleine nodded slowly. He said nothing further. He didn't talk about Alasdair, he didn't say how they all missed him, how sorry they all were . . . none of the usual soothing noises. He left her with something far more useful—a question. About herself.

As soon as Amber opened the door she knew something had changed. There was the faint sound of music coming from the sitting room—Madredeus, the Portuguese group whose music Alasdair had introduced Madeleine to . . . and she in turn to everyone else. She poked her head round the door. Madeleine was sitting on the couch surrounded by papers, notes, the phone book—she'd been busy. She looked up as Amber pushed the door open.

"Hi," she said softly.

Amber gave a wave. "Looks like you've been busy."

"Yes." Madeleine let out a sigh. "Dr. Harrigan came round this morning. I expect you sent him." Amber nodded cautiously. "He gave me these." She held out a couple of sheets. Amber read the first page quickly. *"The International Committee for Migration manages health issues associated with the processing of migrants in sending, transit and receiving countries. ICM's migration health services work with government and other agencies to meet the individual and collective health needs of migrants."* She looked questioningly at Madeleine. "Read the next page," Madeleine said. Amber looked down. *"Psychological and Trauma Response (PTR) in Serbia. Category: Migration Health Services. Summary: This project aims to enable the provision of a timely response to the population's emerging psycho-social needs related to the recent conflict."* She stopped.

"You're going away." It was a statement.

"I have to, Amber. I'll go mad if I stay here. Everything reminds me of him. I can't even walk in the doors at the hospital. I . . . I've lost my nerve. I'm not sure I'll ever practice again."

"Was this Dr. Harrigan's suggestion?" Amber asked, sitting beside her on the couch.

Madeleine nodded. "He said it would help me to get outside of myself for a while—help myself by helping others." She looked down at her hands. "I don't know if it will, but I can't stay here. I've been on the phone all day. I've got an interview in Vienna next Tuesday." Amber blinked. That soon? "Apparently, they're looking for someone in one of their Special Purpose Missions, in Belgrade. They need someone with medical training who speaks English, French and Russian. I suppose there aren't many of us around." Madeleine gave a short laugh. It was the first time Amber had even seen her smile. "It's mostly administrative—helping to train the staff to deal with what they call Internally Displaced Persons . . . you learn the lingo pretty quickly . . . it's a twelve-month contract. It pays well. I hope I get it." Amber said nothing. It somehow didn't seem fair. Life had already dealt Madeleine some pretty harsh blows—and now this? A twelve-month contract in one of the most dangerous spots in the world didn't seem like something to wish for. But it had changed something in Madeleine, switched on a light . . . and for that she was grateful.

≈65≈

"You said you weren't going to cry," Becky said, wiping away her own tears. Amber blew her nose.

"I said I was going to *try* not to cry," she said through her handkerchief. They looked at each other. It was 2:20 p.m. on a Sunday afternoon. Madeleine had just disappeared through the departure gates at Heathrow's Terminal Two, waving until she couldn't see them any more, and now it was just the two of them looking embarrassedly at each other, wondering what to do.

"I'm glad her parents didn't come," Becky said after a moment.

Amber nodded. "It would've been hell. She said goodbye this morning. Her mother had hysterics."

Becky raised an eyebrow. "I can't imagine her mum shedding a tear, let alone having hysterics," she said. "I've never met anyone quite so . . . *pinched*, d'you know what I mean? She's *so* wound up."

"Well, so would you be if you'd been through what she has."

"I suppose so. You know, I'm really going to miss Mads," Becky said as they walked towards the car park. Amber tucked her arm in Becky's.

"Me too. Well, what'll we do now that it's just you and me? Fancy seeing a film? I need something to cheer me up."

"I can't, I'm afraid. I'm meeting Henry at five," Becky said.

"Henry?" Amber frowned. Becky blinked. "Henry who?"

"Oh. Did I say Henry? I meant Charlie." Becky's face was aflame. She tried to laugh it off. "How weird. Why did I say that?" Amber looked at her for a second but said nothing. It wasn't the first time Becky had made a similar slip. They reached Amber's car in silence.

"Becks, are you seeing someone . . . apart from Charlie?" Amber asked as they got in. Becky breathed a silent prayer of thanks. Whatever else Amber suspected it was clear she hadn't made the connection.

"No, don't be silly. It was just a slip of the tongue. I don't know why I said it. I'm meeting Charlie at home at five."

"You would tell me, wouldn't you?" Amber asked, starting the car.

"Of course I would," Becky said, looking down and fastening her seat belt so that she wouldn't have to meet Amber's eyes. She caught sight of her own face in the side mirror. Liar. Bitch. She looked away.

Three hours later, her face resting on Henry's bare stomach, her fingers stroking the fine dark-brown hair that ran from his navel to his cock, she closed her eyes in shame.

"What's wrong?" His stomach shuddered gently beneath her cheek.

"Nothing," she whispered. "I'm just . . . sad, I guess. Madeleine left this afternoon. She's gone to work in Belgrade."

"Doing what?" Henry put a hand over hers and moved it firmly downwards.

"I don't know . . . some kind of medical program. Amber didn't really say. Ohhh. D'you like that?"

"Yes." And that was all it took. She forgot her shame as she watched Henry's face—the most precise register of pleasure she'd ever seen. "Yes. I like that."

* * *

Amber drove back to Islington after dropping Becky off at Hammersmith Tube station. She was emphatic—she didn't want Amber to drive all the way to East Dulwich . . . it was too far, too out of her way. Amber protested that she didn't have anything else to do but Becky was adamant. Amber watched her cross the street, her red hair swinging around her face as she crossed the road. Something had changed in Becky over the last few months, she thought. Nothing she could really define. She was a little more guarded than usual . . . a little more preoccupied. She supposed it was work—the gallery was expanding. Morag had bought someone out a few blocks away and they were planning to divide their artists into two categories—something called "installations and sculptures" in one and "fine art and photography" in the other. Amber said it sounded like a good idea without really understanding what the difference was—other than the obvious ones, of course—but curiously, Becky hadn't really wanted to talk about it. It was very unlike her; she usually bored everyone to tears with her descriptions of the minutiae of the art world and the differences, real or otherwise, between their stable of six or seven artists. But lately it wasn't the art world that was on her mind. Amber just wished she knew what was. She wasn't herself—of that she was quite sure.

She pulled up in front of her flat. It was 4:30 p.m. on a Sunday afternoon and she had nothing to do. She looked at her hands. The ring she always wore on her right index finger was twisted around. She straightened it. *Hope.* Madeleine and Becky had given her a set of three silver rings on her birthday, inscribed with the words *Hope*, *Trust* and *Faith*. She'd lost *Faith* the very first day she wore it and *Trust* had fallen off a month later as she was washing her hands. She presumed it was now lying somewhere along an "S" bend in the bathroom plumbing. She now wore *Hope* on her index finger. It had been a bit of a squeeze to get it on but there was no way she was losing *this* one as well. Particularly as in the other, most important area of her life, she'd given up on it. Hope. After that one phone call from Tendé six months ago, she'd heard nothing more. She hadn't known how to contact him—she had no number for him, no address. She'd toyed with the idea of asking Max but after a single attempt when he'd fixed her with a strange, almost angry glare, she'd given up. She'd waited for him to call her back again . . . but nothing. The worst of it was that not hearing from him didn't result in him disappearing from her mind. It was almost the opposite. It only took a day like today—seeing Madeleine off, worrying about Becky—and he was back, in full force. She had no idea why. In fact, she was getting rather impatient with herself. Why couldn't she just forget him, close the chapter on the whole non-event and get on with things?

Halfway through the meeting at the Presidential Palace, Tendé looked up and caught the eye of his direct superior, the Minister of the Interior. The minister raised an eyebrow. The proposal on the table in front of the ministers and their deputies assembled in the conference room was causing something of a stir.

"What's *his* interest?" the Finance Minister asked, looking skeptically at the report in front of him. Tendé paused for a few seconds before answering.

"Profit, of course . . . it's a huge project and it requires an enormous amount of capital. You don't go into something like this if you're not looking for substantial returns. But there is something more. Max Sall is a wealthy man. A very wealthy man. At this point in his life, I don't believe it's only profit. I think he's genuinely interested—"

". . . in what?" someone interrupted testily.

"In our development. In progress. In giving something back, so to speak." There was silence around the table.

"Why us?" the Deputy Minister for Development asked. "He's not French. There's no colonial interest . . . or guilt?" Several people around the table laughed quietly.

"Who knows? Timbuktu. . . . it's always been a

dream for Europeans, since the Middle Ages. And especially for someone like him. Like I said, he's already made his money. This project . . . this is about *proving* something like this can be done; it's not about the money. Of course it has to show a profit, but I believe he's genuinely interested in a new role, both for himself and for us. I think it's a unique opportunity and we can't afford to waste it. This could be big . . . *very* big."

"It's sustainable," the President's economic advisor spoke. "Ecologically and culturally, too. It would bring massive employment to the northeast." There was a short silence around the table. They were all only too aware of the problems in that part of the country. Unemployment, in the vast arid region bordering the Sahara, was endemic. With it came unrest. The pressure exerted by the rebel Tuareg population to secede from Mali was costly to suppress and dangerous, too. For everyone around the table there could be no question of relinquishing Timbuktu. It was one of the most famous places in the world, a place that men devoted their whole lives to discovering—it was a source of national pride and an important touchstone of national identity. It was unthinkable it should "belong" elsewhere. But for all that, the problems facing the town—and the entire region—were legion. The town, as Max had seen for himself, was slowly slipping into decline and his proposal to develop and construct the world's largest salt mines at Téghaza and Taoudenni *and* build a world-class processing and distribution center at Timbuktu itself was little short of a godsend—it would make the election promises of the previous year seem within reach, for one thing. And make those who invested in the scheme from the beginning rich, for another.

Tendé looked down at the opening paragraph of Max's report. *"Making the Desert Bloom: Investment and Infrastructure Opportunities in the Tombouctoo Region. Tombouctoo, city of fable, once the nerve center of trade and learning in the western Sahara, has fallen slowly into decline. We at Sall Investments, Inc., believe we have a unique solution to the region's dwindling importance and to restoring Tombouctoo to its proper place at the forefront of national and international awareness. Tombouctoo is a name steeped in history and synonymous with the past—we believe it should resonate with the future, with opportunities and possibilities.* He stole a quick look around the table. They had all read the report and despite their grave, impressively impassive faces, he could feel the excitement and interest Max's words had provoked. He himself had been gripped by Max's description of a multi-billion-dollar investment package and the technical assistance he could pull in to make it work. He glanced at the glossy brochure Max had asked his people to produce for the occasion. It hit exactly the right tone—slick, glossy, professional-looking; technical enough to convince the skeptics in the cabinet that he'd done his homework yet poetic and optimistic at the same time. He wondered if Amber had done any of the writing. It somehow didn't seem quite her style. She popped into his head suddenly, unexpected and unannounced. He remembered with precise clarity the fall and shape of her curly hair as she turned to consider a question, or the startling blue of her eyes. He realized with a start that he missed her. It had been almost six months since he'd last . . . he looked up. Amadou Traoré, the Minister of the Interior, had asked him a question. He turned to him, racing to bring his mind back to the scene and issues at hand.

"Who will Sall partner with? You?" Traoré asked again. He was smiling but the question was a serious one. Everyone turned to look at him.

"No," Tendé shook his head. "We—the Ministry—will put out a tender. We'll be looking for a consortium to come together with varying areas of expertise. It'll be public, transparent . . . we'll preselect and then go to full tender. Just like any other project." Around the table, heads nodded. Tendé breathed a cautious sigh of relief. The petty jealousies and nepotism that bedeviled the government—*all* governments, he corrected himself swiftly—had so far been quashed. He only hoped it would stay that way.

The meeting was rapidly pulled to a close. The minister officiating thanked them all for coming, hoped they would take the documentation away with them and study it well . . . if they had any questions . . . the usual closing remarks. Tendé watched as each man—and the sole female minister, Maryse Konaté, the Minister for Transportation—picked up the paperwork he'd provided and slowly walked out of the room. He pushed his fingers against his lips for a second. Max had thrown the challenge their way. It was up to him to make sure his government picked it up. He followed them out of the room, pleased at the way the meeting had run but somewhat less pleased by the way Amber Sall's face kept on appearing in his mind's eye. Above all, Tendé was a man who liked discipline; he liked things to run in an orderly and logical fashion. He didn't like surprises—and Amber surprised him. He was also surprised at himself. Why couldn't he stop thinking about her?

≈67≈

Kieran looked around him. The four of them—he, Jake, Digger and Will—were standing on the mezzanine walkway looking down the glass staircase at the workers installing the last of the light fittings in the floors running parallel to the windows. The architects had come up with the idea of using sound and light as the main design tools in the club. Kieran had immediately liked the idea but Jake and Digger were initially unconvinced. Digger had spent time in New York in the late eighties and for him, Studio 54 and the upmarket Xenon were the clubs to emulate with their elaborate décor and lavish furnishings. But Kieran and Will had different ideas. They both saw Paradise at Paola's in a completely different way—not a disco or a nightclub but a "laboratory for sound and light," as the architect put it to them. Paul Oakenfield, the up-and-coming DJ Will had met in Ibiza the previous summer had agreed to "residence" at their new club, if—and *only* if—he were given free rein with the music policy. Paul was a bona fide star in his own right. Will described seeing thousands of people crowd the beach in Ibiza just to hear him spin and play, so it paid to listen to him; his finger was well and truly on the clubber's pulse.

They'd gradually been won round to his vision of a huge, empty space on the ground floor, pulsating with light and sound, changing color and mood in time to the music, a wild, frenetic space that would fire up the crowd waiting in the inevitable queues around the block and set the pace for the after-midnight party. The five no-alcohol bars dotted around the enormous space were all back-lit, floor-to-ceiling sheets of stainless steel with glass shelving and industrial-sized refrigerators concealed under polished slabs of black Corian. As the outer ring of light-walls changed color, the stainless steel walls picked up on the reflected light casting a warm, soft glow over the bodies and faces pressed up—hopefully—against the bar.

The mezzanine with its glass floor and suspended steel and glass staircase was the DJ's arena. They'd spent almost two-thirds of their initial £2 million on the sound system; as Paul explained, it had to be able to run for extended periods of time and it had to look and sound great. DJs were becoming stars—the same level of presentation and visibility had to be given to them as to any pop star.

Up there with the gleaming desks and rows of synthesizers and turntables were elevated glass floors on which the beautiful people such as the ones Paola would bring in could hang out and survey the scene below.

Equally important to the club's success were the two floors below ground. The VIP White Room, the chillout zone on the floor immediately below was a soothing, minimalist space of white leather sofas, smoked glass walls, its own, fully stocked, fully alcoholic bar and low-level lighting. The room had its own separate sound system with a number of smaller, more intimate spaces for the slightly older crowd to escape to after the madness of the floor above. It had been Will's idea to introduce a VIP membership for the White Room—it would keep the numbers to a comfortable minimum, they could serve alcohol without worrying about drunken guests ruining the place and keeping it small and exclusive would ensure the management could keep an eye on exactly who went in there and what they did. Finally, the lower basement was given over to toilets and spacious restrooms where clubbers could touch up their make-up, sit outside the toilets and chat to one another and freshen up before heading back upstairs.

He turned to look admiringly at Paola as she walked upstairs to where they were standing. After the tantrum she'd thrown the last time she'd been in the place, she was being positively charming. The four of them trailed behind her, the red-faced architect making frantic notes as she pointed out one defect after another. She was very good—a missed toilet-roll holder here, an unvarnished surface there . . . he and Digger exchanged a glance. They had all been less than impressed the last time she'd stomped off moaning about her boots. Paola pronounced herself really pleased with the place, the architect gave a cautious smile and Kieran and Digger breathed a sigh of relief. The opening night of Paradise at Paola's was less than a week away and everyone was exhausted and irritable. Kieran had never worked so hard in his damned life: up every morning at 7 a.m. to be picked up by Will at 8 a.m. Then it was a full day at the club, overseeing the renovations, meetings with suppliers, DJs, security staff, the local council . . . it seemed endless. He was enjoying it, though. He never thought he'd be the one to say it but actually, having something to do each day wasn't as bad as he'd always feared. He actually looked forward to getting up. He'd stopped doing coke as well, which was an added bonus. He couldn't do it *and* get up on time *and* go into work. The four of them still smoked the odd joint during the day, of course, and he needed one to get to sleep at night but compared to where he'd been in the past couple of years, he felt positively glowing with vitality. He stole a look at Paola. She always looked so damned healthy: golden and glowing and *clean*. He loved standing near her just to catch a whiff of her gloriously expensive perfume or the scent of her hair as she tossed it over her shoulder. She gave off an air of perfection that he found hard to resist. She was actually pretty damned hard to resist, period. He watched the four men in the room gape in silent admiration of her. She was wearing some sort of loose, slinky top and skin-tight jeans. He suspected they were all having as hard a time concentrating on her words as he was. The thought made him uncomfortable.

In fact, Paola made him downright uncomfortable. He had no idea how or what to think of her, apart from the obvious reactions, of course. But he knew—in his head, that was—that he oughtn't to think of her as anything other than his sister. The way he thought of Amber. But it was impossible to draw any kind of comparison between the two of them. Amber always made him feel stupid and weak and pathetic. The dynamic of their relationship had been in place for so long that it was impossible to think of it ever changing. Although, he mused, lately he'd detected something different in Amber whenever she spoke to him, not that they spoke often. But once or twice in the past couple of months she'd actually hinted that she thought he was doing rather a good job, and he was surprised by how much he cared. And Max, too—their relationship had suddenly, after all these years, started to improve. He enjoyed watching Max take seriously what he had to say. He enjoyed bringing him down to the club every once in a while, showing him what progress had been made. The last time Max had been down, he'd even clapped him on the back. The gesture had startled him, but filled him with a kind of pride he'd never before experienced.

"Okay. I'm off." Paola turned to him. "Ciao, Kieran.

I'll see you next week." Saying goodbye with Paola, was a ten-minute affair. Three kisses for everyone present, a little hug for him . . . he watched her pick her way across the floor with a growing irritation at the way the workmen around simply stopped what they were doing to stare at her. A mixture of anger and jealousy. He shook his head abruptly. She confused him. He was confusing himself. He stalked off to the toilets.

"Don't tell me you want another favor?" Amber said half-teasingly to Max. They were sitting on the terrace at the newly opened River Café in Hammersmith—not normally the kind of locale Max favored but Amber had drawn the line at meeting him at Garrick's.

"Of course I do." Max smiled briefly. They were interrupted by the waiter. Amber could see Max looking approvingly at his plate of pan-seared salmon and endives. "You're paying for this, by the way," he said as he broke off a piece of bread.

Amber rolled her eyes. "Okay. What's the favor? What's the article? Who's it for?"

"No, this time I don't need you to write anything. It would be a bit transparent. No, just bring your friends along."

"To what?"

"Kieran's club. The opening night's a week tomorrow."

"That's easy; half the city's talking about it." Amber tasted a piece of asparagus. Divine.

"Are they really?" Max looked up, surprised—and pleased.

"And I suppose Paola'll be there?"

"Of course. It's her club, after all."

"Of course."

"Now, now . . . they've worked very hard on this, you know. I don't mind admitting that I'm pleasantly surprised." Amber nodded grimly. "Paola's been really helpful."

"I'm sure. Okay. Well, I'll put the word out but I don't think there'll be any need. My friends are asking if I can get them on the VIP list."

"Of course you can. Just give Kieran the list of names." Max took another mouthful. "Tendé'll be there." Amber almost choked on her wine.

"Really? Bit far for him to come for a party," she said, in what she hoped was a disinterested voice. Her heart was hammering.

"No, he'll be here for other stuff. We're really moving ahead," Max said happily. "He's managed to secure pretty much most of the approvals we need. He says we'll be ready to move in about six months' time. I think we aim for six weeks—but things seem to take longer out there." Max rambled on. Amber had stopped listening. Suddenly a week seemed like an awfully long time.

It was. The days dragged by. Amber found it difficult to concentrate on her work and even Becky complained she seemed distracted. Not that Becky herself was particularly focused. She'd become ever so secretive about where she was going and what she was doing. Amber was convinced something was up, but with the sudden news of Tendé Ndiaye's arrival, her concerns had been eclipsed by a much larger and infinitely more troubling issue—Paola. The stab of pleasure that ran through her every time she thought about seeing Tendé again was matched only in its intensity by the anxiety at the thought of Paola seeing him again. Whatever else would happen at the opening party, it would be impossible to compete with Paola for Tendé's attention—for *any*one's attention. Ugh. Amber lay on the sofa at home in the evenings, a strange fever of anticipation and fear stealing over her. The choice of what to wear was shadowed by the worry that whatever she put on would fade into instant insignificance by whatever Paola would—or wouldn't—be wearing. Amber wasn't normally given to anxious moments spent staring at her naked body in front of the bathroom mirror—that was much more Becky's style—but she found herself scrutinizing herself each evening: too thin, too pale, too boyish . . . and her hair? It was in that terrible halfway stage between short and long. What to do about it? Becky was of no help at all. She was busy, she said . . . work, temperamental artists, Morag demanding too much . . . but on the Wednesday before the all-important Friday-night opening, Amber impulsively jumped into a cab at lunchtime and headed straight for the gallery seeking advice on a haircut and Morag said she hadn't been in all week. She was ill, apparently. Amber looked confused—which Morag noticed, she saw—and made her excuses and quickly left.

There was tension in the air at home. Amber arrived at 6 p.m. intending only to drop her bags and walk round to Greene's Salon and Day Spa on Elgin Avenue. Her appointment was for 6:15 p.m. She caught sight of a red-faced Siobhân scurrying upstairs followed by the sound of breaking glass and her mother's high-pitched yelling. She wondered what was going on. She hadn't actually thought about it—was Angela intending to come as well? Surely not. Francesca would be there, for one thing, and she was sure Kieran wouldn't want that kind of scene on his opening night. She put her bags down and closed the door behind her. Her own nerves were bad enough—she didn't want or need one of Angela's tantrums to upset her any further. She walked quickly down the street.

Inside, at a quarter past nine, Max was standing in the doorway of Angela's rooms, staring at his wife with ill-concealed irritation. Siobhân had just finished laying out the clothes she'd requested on the bed and silently disappeared. Where the hell did she think she was going? he demanded.

"If you think," she said, twisting herself round from her dressing-table mirror and speaking through the Kirby grips in her mouth, "that I am going to miss the most important moment of my son—*our* son's—life, you'd better think again." She turned back to the mirror. Max was silent. "And I don't give a shit that

Francesca's going to be there. Kieran's *my* son, not hers." Paola didn't seem worth mentioning. She pinned up her hair. Her hands were shaking but she was determined not to let it show. There was a movement behind her, where Max had come to stand. She looked at him in the mirror. He brought his hands up, suddenly, placing them on her bare shoulders. She swallowed. They stared at each other for a minute.

"You look . . . good," he said finally.

"Thanks," she whispered. She couldn't remember the last time Max had spoken to her in anything but anger. She looked at herself. Blonde hair piled in large curls on top of her head, eyes made up in smoky black eyeliner; thick, luscious mascara; a hint of blusher; deep red, beautifully drawn lips. Siobhân was as good, if not better, at it than the girl at the salon. Max's hand slid from her shoulder. She caught her breath. He pulled aside the silk collar of her dressing gown and cupped her breast. They remained frozen in front of the mirror, watching each other. She closed her eyes as his fingers slowly found a nipple and touched her, lightly, a whisper of a touch . . . the way he used to. He slowly pulled the swivel chair around to face him. Without taking his hand away, he bent his head and kissed her, hard. The taste of his tongue was exactly as she remembered it—she couldn't bear to think of the last time she'd felt its familiar, hot probing. She clung to him, her hands going automatically towards his belt. She felt the familiar, sweet convulsions begin before he was even inside her. "Max," she groaned, not caring that they were lying on top of the very dress Siobhân had spent an hour ironing or that he hadn't even taken his trousers off.

"Shh." Max's face was a strange mixture of lust and disgust. She saw it just before he exploded and closed his eyes, as if he couldn't bear to see what he'd just done. There was silence for a few seconds then he gently moved her off him. She couldn't look at him. She drew her knees up to her chest and wrapped her arms protectively around her nakedness. She needn't have bothered. He got up without a word and left.

Amber looked up as Angela came down the stairs. She looked beautiful. She was wearing a white trouser suit with black stiletto-heeled boots and a lacy black camisole just visible beneath the jacket lapels. Her hair was loose and curled flatteringly around her face—perfect make-up, nails polished . . . she looked better than she had done in years. She suddenly felt ashamed of herself for doubting why Angela should come—Kieran was her favorite, he always had been. It was only right that she should share his success.

"You look lovely," Amber said as Angela reached the bottom step. Angela looked at her and smiled, a tremulous, nervous smile that made Amber's heart contract. Angela's hands were trembling; the only outward sign of the effort she knew it must have taken her to get that far.

"So do you, darling," Angela said, fishing in her black clutch bag for a cigarette. "Very grown up."

"Thanks," Amber smiled dryly. "Where's Max?"

"Er . . . I think he's coming. He . . . had to . . . went to change." She blushed as she spoke. Amber looked at her quickly. But before she could comment, she heard Max's footsteps coming down the stairs.

"Ready?" he asked with a smile.

"Is . . . Kieran already there?" Amber asked. She didn't feel up to asking about Tendé.

Max nodded. "Last-minute panic, no doubt. Shall we?" He didn't look at or address Angela. The three of them walked out and got into the waiting Jaguar.

≈68≈

Inside the club, excitement and pandemonium were at fever pitch. The press had been sniffing around all day, wheedling to get on the guest list; trying to bribe the doormen to give up the names of the invited so they could phone back to their editors and be the first to announce that yes, Princess Stephanie was arriving and no, that wasn't Sting in the back of the BMW that swept round the back. The story of the club made good copy—four sons of wealthy businessmen, including Kieran Sall and Jake Higham-Burton; named after Paola Rossi, Kieran Sall's half-sister and Max Sall's infamous love-child; an all-star guest list including several of Paola Rossi's European friends . . . it was a younger, hipper version of Annabel's—a new generation of entertainment entrepreneurs was about to be born.

The official opening was at 10 p.m., although Kieran explained to Max as he showed him, Angela and Amber around, that the club would normally not open its doors until midnight.

"We want people to come here and dance, not drink," he said. Max raised an eyebrow. "You can buy anything at the bar, juice, virgin cocktails, water . . . whatever. If we open at midnight, it means people go out and do their drinking before they get here. It's less hassle for us." At twenty-five pounds a head with the capacity to hold 3,500 people on a night . . . pretty soon they ought to be laughing all the way to the bank. Sorted. As Digger would say. Just then, Digger ran up the stairs towards them.

"Your sister's here," he said, panting. "With her mum. Phwoar. Oh, sorry, Mr. Sall . . . didn't see you back there." He had the grace to look embarrassed. Max smiled. Angela stared off in the distance. Kieran dashed off after him. Amber and Angela walked gingerly down the glass staircase, leaving Max to deal with Francesca's arrival. The music had steadily been increasing in volume and the whole place was now pulsating with the beat from the £1 million sound system. Halfway down the stairs Angela was stopped by a very good-looking young man—one of Kieran's friends? Amber smiled and continued on her way. Through the changing light-walls she could just make out the silhouettes of the crowd outside. Flashbulbs were going off every other second and the enormous men in suits and walkie-talkies glued to their mouths were patroling the entrance. A velvet rope was periodically lifted to allow the VIPs into the White Room.

She followed a group of tanned, skeletal girls on stilettos into the room. She really liked the chillout zone—it was comfortable with great music and a very cool, laid-back atmosphere, despite it rapidly filling-up with the kinds of people she would normally never speak to—courtesy, no doubt, of Paola. Italian and French seemed to dominate the airwaves. She went up to the bar and ordered a Flirtini cocktail from the über-cool female bartender. She leaned against the bar and took a sip. It was as delicious as it sounded. She looked around the room. She'd never seen as much tanned, perfect flesh on display in her life. Kieran and his friends had really pulled it off. A shriek suddenly went up in the corner of the room. The doors opened and Paola and two or three young women swept in dramatically, followed closely by a photographer who was immediately muscled out of the room. No photographers in the VIP zone, obviously. Amber watched from across the room as her sister squealed and giggled with the rest of the model crowd—luckily the lighting was low and Paola didn't look her way. They were too busy inspecting each other's outfits to notice anyone else, anyway.

She moved away from the bar, choosing a spot less crowded at the back of the room. She sank down into the spongy white softness of the sofa and stretched her legs in front of her, admiring the swirl of fabric her new flared trousers made at the ankle.

She heard Paola's noisy group leave the room, shrill comments and cries in half a dozen languages. *Bella* this, *bellissima* that. She sipped her cocktail and watched discreetly as a couple whom she ought to have recognized and didn't argued quietly over who should go to the bar for a refill. The music was good. She watched the DJ in the corner booth organize and prepare his vinyls with the precision of a surgeon, sliding the shiny black disks out of their covers, stacking them up in careful order on the empty desk beside the turntable, headphones on, a face of concentrated bliss . . . she wriggled her toes in her new boots. The cocktail was strong—she hadn't eaten since lunchtime and the mixture of vodka, Cointreau and fruit juice was potent as well as pleasant. She sat back and closed her eyes, letting the sound of the music wash over her.

"Asleep already?" There was laughter in the voice. Her eyes flew open. For a second, she didn't register. Then she sat upright, a cold flash of excitement running through her.

"Tendé! You're here!"

"Patently. And you? You look like you're dozing off." He smiled and sat down opposite her. He was alone.

"Me . . . no, no . . . I was just enjoying the music." He looked at her dubiously. "Really." She put a hand to her hair. He was different tonight, she noticed immediately. Much more relaxed than the last time she'd seen him. He was dressed in black—a plain black shirt under a suit jacket and trousers, no tie. She could feel her smile spreading across her face.

"So . . . I just got here. Kieran told me you were in here. Is Max around?" he asked, looking around the room.

"He was upstairs. With my mother . . . and Francesca," Amber said carefully. Tendé was smiling.

"I see. Should be an interesting night. What're you drinking?"

"Um . . . a Flirtini," Amber said, giggling.

"Sounds good. Does it work?"

"Too early to tell."

"That can be changed." He got up and walked towards the bar. Amber sat back, amazed at herself. She'd done nothing but agonize over this man for the past year and a half; spent most of her free time thinking about him or thinking about how to *stop* thinking about him; she'd spent the past week in an agony of indecision over what to wear, how to look, what to do with her hair . . . things she normally never paid attention to. And now here he was, standing in front of her, larger than life—and she'd somehow managed to slip into a tango of easy, flirtatious banter. She was amazed at herself. *Proud* of herself.

She watched him walk back carrying a Flirtini for her and what looked like an ordinary martini for himself.

"Am I the only one flirting tonight?" she asked as he set her drink down on the table between them.

He shrugged. "Do I need to flirt with you, Amber Sall?" Amber almost choked.

"Tendé!" They both turned. Amber groaned inwardly. He'd done it again! Max! Amber could have murdered him. She sat back against the cushions and watched the two men hug like long lost bloody brothers. She couldn't *believe* it! "Let's find Kieran and Paola . . . show you around the place. You've met Paola, haven't you?" Max's voice trailed off as he started walking towards the doors. Amber closed her eyes. She wasn't sure she could bear the sight of Tendé being dragged off to meet Paola. His voice, close to her ear, startled her.

"Don't go." And then he disappeared.

As had happened at the last party, she kept catching sight of him—across the packed dance floor or at the end of the bar or once, being led up the glass staircase by a beaming Paola. But their eyes never seemed to meet; she was left with a glimpse of his back or the flash of his profile illuminated by the slow surge of light as the walls changed color. The crowd had a register all of its own: a sea of hands waving dreamily in the air, people dancing wildly, pushed up against each other, cheek to cheek, hip to hip—at times it seemed as though the swaying, chanting bodies moved as one.

Amber kept to the fringes, tipsy, enjoying the vicarious thrill of being next to them, knowing that somewhere in the crowded mass Tendé was also seeing it, hearing the music thumping from the massive speakers and watching the beauty on display. Paola was clearly too busy posing for photographers, laughing wildly in the arms of one young, handsome bachelor after another, clutching other models and paparazzi princesses to spend any time with him. In the hour or two she circled around the edge of the dance floor, Paola kept stumbling across her field of vision, but never with him.

At midnight, she saw Max preparing to leave with Angela and Francesca in tow. She blinked. The photographers would have a field day! Tendé was nowhere to be seen. She was on the point of pushing her way forwards to say goodbye when a hand caught hold of her own, tugging her gently backwards.

"Leaving? Already?" It was him. She turned to him, eyes sparkling.

"No . . . not asleep, not leaving, just enjoying the scene," she laughed.

"Dance with me." Without waiting for an answer, he pulled her through the pulsating crowd.

They were so close there wasn't a part of them that wasn't touching. This was nothing like the discos and bars she'd been to with Henry or the parties she'd been dragged to by Becky or like anything else she'd done. The beat was palpable; she felt it in his heartbeat, in the feel of his arms, his thighs brushing against hers . . . he was a good dancer and she took her cues from him. Around them, hypnotized by the sleek, sliding synths of the DJ whom everyone seemed to know, half-clad girls twirled their long hair round and round; men, torn between watching the girls and guzzling down quarts of free Evian, tried to keep up. They were laughing together, delighted by the energy and lithe vitality of the dancers. She buried her face in his shoulder, giggling. His hand slid around her, coming to rest in the small of her back and she arched closer, instinctively.

"Let's get out of here."

They burst through the exit doors, still laughing. A photographer's bulb went off as they ran, holding hands, into the light, fine drizzle that had just begun to fall. It was warm, despite the rain—after the heat and sweat inside, the fresh air was a relief. The queue to get in was still forming, winding its way around the block. Amber followed Tendé under the curving staircase at the rear of the building. All at once, it was dark and quiet in the shadows; the faint thumping beat of the club's music could be felt through the ground. Tendé stopped and leaned against the wall, pulling Amber towards him. Her last thought, as his head blotted out what little light there was spilling into the hidden corner, was that she hoped she wasn't dreaming. It was the most sensual, erotic kiss she'd experienced. Slow, teasing, hungry. She could hear her own heartbeat in her ears as she returned his kiss, arms sliding of their own accord under his jacket and across the hard, flat plane of his chest. They said nothing. She opened her eyes to find his watching her. In the darkness, his hand moved up the front of her shirt, a practiced, pleasure-giving gesture . . . she wanted more. But it was he who stopped. The mood of laughing spontaneity that had gripped them both in there, on the dance floor, suddenly evaporated. Outside, in the air that had begun to cool, a different mood took hold.

"Amber Sall." He said it slowly, testing the sound against her mouth. She didn't know how to respond. The pleasant, dreamy effect of several Flirtinis on an empty stomach was quickly dissolving.

"Tendé Ndiaye," she said, after a moment. He laughed.

"Not bad, not bad . . . I've heard worse." His hand tightened around her back. She breathed in the smell of him, close to his neck. His skin was deliciously warm and soft.

"How do you say it?" she murmured.

"It doesn't matter. You say it well."

"No, really. How d'you say it? What's the difference?"

"Amber Sall. Are we going to stand here all night arguing over my name?" His chuckle reverberated through his chest.

"No."

"So what are we going to do?"

"We could . . ." Amber took a deep breath. They both hesitated. And then turned together and hailed a cab.

"This is so strange," Amber said, propping herself up on one elbow to look at him.

"Why?"

"Well, because it's all happened so quickly. This." He smiled. "What's funny?" she asked, sliding a hand underneath the duvet, seeking out his chest.

"You think this is fast?"

"Well, I mean . . . we only . . . really met this evening, at the club. And now you're here. In bed with me."

"You spent almost a week with me in the desert, or have you forgotten?" He turned to face her.

"Of course not. But you barely talked to me!"

"We talked for a long time," he said, shaking his head at her.

"No . . . just the one night. We talked about the project, about Max, that was all." He was quiet for a few minutes.

"I thought about you . . . often, after that," he said finally. He rolled over onto his back. "There were many times I wanted to . . . I don't know, call you . . . get in touch . . ."

"Why didn't you?"

"Because." He passed a hand over his face. "Because I didn't think it was the right thing to do." Amber looked at him uncertainly. A chill suddenly ran through her.

"And now . . . ?" she asked in a low voice.

"I don't know. I like you—very much. But this will be . . . complicated."

"Why? Why should it be any more complicated than . . . than anyone else?"

"I come from Mali, Amber." He turned to face her. "I'm Moslem. I'm African. I'm also a government minister trying to put a project together where your father is the major stakeholder. And then there's Max."

"Max has nothing to do with this," Amber said, frowning.

"You don't think so?" Tendé's voice had suddenly acquired an edge to it.

"No. It's none of his business. Besides, he likes you. He likes you more than he likes any of us, I can tell you!" She tried to make a joke of it. Tendé was quiet.

"Amber Sall. D'you know what it means in Arabic? Amber?"

"No."

"Jewel. Something precious."

"I didn't know you spoke Arabic," she said, a sudden feeling of vulnerability washing over her.

"Enough to read the Koran and order a beer."

"You're not supposed to drink," she said dryly.

He laughed, pulling her closer. "Ah, you're too quick for me. I like that about you, you know."

"You're not so slow yourself," she mumbled against his skin. But the feeling of fear hadn't left her. What was he saying? She pulled her head free. "So . . . so what are we . . . you . . . going to do?"

"I don't know."

"But there is a way, isn't there? I mean, of course it's just . . . you know, the beginning . . . but if it . . . if we like each other, surely all the other things . . . we'll find a way around them? Won't we?"

"N'sha'allah."

It wasn't quite what she wanted to hear.

Becky watched Morag's mouth move up and down but after the first couple of sentences, she was no longer listening. *Very good references, I'm sure you'll find something else. Just hasn't been the same.* The phrases drifted right over her head. She couldn't quite grasp that they were being addressed to her, that Morag was speaking *to her.* That she had been fired.

"I'm sorry, Becky," Morag was saying. Becky looked up, surprised. There was real discomfort on Morag's face.

"Oh. No . . . don't worry about it. It's . . . it's fine." She stood up. "Well. I suppose . . . I suppose I'd better . . . you know, sort things out . . . tidy up." She genuinely wanted to spare Morag the embarrassment of their predicament. She'd been fired. For the first time in her life.

Charlie was away in the States. She pushed open the front door, bent down to retrieve a couple of letters addressed to Charlie and a thick wad addressed to her that she recognized as being from her bank. She was probably overdrawn. Again. Lately, her spending had begun to spiral out of control. She had never been very good at keeping track of her expenses—she was the type to shove bills and bank statements into drawers and hope that Charlie would find them and pay up, or if it was really, *really* bad . . . why, they'd phone her, surely? In that way, she drifted from month to month, never knowing exactly where she stood. But with Charlie taking care of all the living expenses it didn't really matter. If, towards the end of each month, she had her credit card refused for one purchase or another, well . . . it was only over a new pair of shoes or, lately, some fancy new underwear . . . nothing to really worry about. Once payday had come and gone she could always go back.

She shoved the letters—there were about twelve of them—into a drawer in the kitchen and took off her jacket. She poured herself a glass of wine and walked upstairs to the living room. It was chilly and empty in the large room. She kicked off her shoes and sat, feet curled under her, on the pale new leather sofa that she'd persuaded Charlie to buy and stared at the empty TV screen. She couldn't even be bothered to turn it on. She sat there for a while, sipping at her wine and thinking about what had happened that day. Morag had asked her to leave. Straight away. She'd been let go. Sacked. Fired. For some odd reason, Morag seemed to think she'd given Becky enough warning—but Becky couldn't remember a single incident.

She picked up the phone lying on the marble coffee table and quickly dialed Henry's number. As soon as she heard his voice, she burst into tears. He promised he'd get there as soon as he could.

An hour later, she heard his tap on the front door. She ran down the stairs, fresh tears streaking her face and opened the door. The sight of him—tall, strong, solid—made it worse. She flung herself into his arms. He staggered with her into the hallway and quickly closed the front door. She who had been so calm all day could barely speak for crying. He stroked her silky red hair, smoothed the tears that slid down her cheeks and eventually managed to get her into the kitchen and put a large brandy in her hand. He knew he oughtn't to give her any more to drink—he could see an empty bottle on the expensive oak table but he couldn't think of anything else to do. He wasn't surprised she'd been fired. Of late Becky seemed to put her own pleasure before everything else, and that, he'd recently discovered, seemed more or less centered around himself. He wasn't quite sure what to make of it. They were having an affair. Or, rather, Becky was having an affair since Henry, technically speaking, wasn't involved with anyone. He was terribly involved with Becky, he realized, but he didn't know how to stop it or indeed if he wanted to. She seemed to think he was someone else—he had no idea who or what—but the resulting erotic tension between them was something he'd never experienced and half-feared he was addicted to. He and Becky never spoke—they fucked. All the time. They played elaborate games, they invented fantasies for each other, they acted them out. Becky had once told him she needed him the way some people needed cigarettes, or a drink. It had been a crude, rather shocking thing to say and he saw that she herself was a little afraid of it, but, Jesus . . . it made the few hours they spent together each week so highly charged he often found himself alone at his desk thinking about it the following day and experiencing the helpless, instant kind of hard-on he'd had at thirteen.

Sure enough, twenty minutes later as they sat upstairs on the sofa and he stroked her head and her sobs lessened, both their thoughts turned elsewhere. She carefully put down the glass of brandy she'd been nursing. Five minutes later, he was enjoying the guilty thrill of undressing her in the bedroom she shared with Charlie. Her fiancé. He tugged her skirt downwards, running his hand over the perfectly smooth pale skin of her stomach, burying his head in the soft flesh of her stomach and reaching around to cup her buttocks, bringing her closer. She ran her fingernails lightly down his back. He shivered at her touch. She was so small and so fragile. Everything about her was pretty and feminine and delicate. He liked watching her undress, watching the way she took off her pretty underwear and folded it neatly, the triangle of lacy panties, wispy, silky bras, cups always turned inwards. He slid a hand beneath the fold of her ass, caressing the fine, soft skin on the inside of her thighs. Becky's breathing changed. He shrugged off his trousers and slid into her bed. Charlie's bed.

The phone rang suddenly, shattering the quiet. Becky paused for a second, then picked it up.

He got out of bed, quietly, and walked into the bathroom. He splashed some water on his face and stood in the doorway for a second. It wasn't Charlie. It was a woman—he could tell from the squeals. Amber? His heart gave a sudden, unexpected lurch. Christ, he thought to himself, catching a glimpse of his anxious face in the bathroom mirror. What are we doing? I'm still in love with Amber; I'm screwing her best friend who's getting married in less than six months' time. I'm in his house, his bed . . . what the fuck are we doing? He listened to

Becky's exclamations for a few more minutes. He heard her say goodbye, promise to meet whoever she was talking to the following day. And then the click of the receiver. He stepped back into the bedroom. Becky was looking at him a little strangely, he noticed. Her eyes were shining.

"You'll never guess what," she said, almost triumphantly, it seemed to him.

"What?"

"That was Amber. You'll never guess who she's going out with." He was aware of a pressure in his head as she spoke.

"Who?"

"Tendé something-or-other. I can never pronounce his last name. The guy from Mali. Remember I told you her dad was doing a project there? Well, it's his business partner. Imagine. She's crazy." Henry was completely and utterly unprepared for the lightning flash of rage and jealousy that tore through him. In less than a second, his past raced to catch up with him. An African. Black. With Amber. He stumbled into the bathroom.

≈69≈

Madeleine's first impression of Belgrade was that it appeared astoundingly normal for a city at war. People on the wide, tree-lined streets, cafés open for business, trams running . . . it looked much like any other European city. No, the young Serbian inter-preter sitting in the front seat corrected her. Bel-grade itself isn't at war.

"For the moment, it's happening elsewhere—almost everywhere else, to be precise. We're very lucky, in some senses, to be stationed here." Madeleine said nothing. She looked at the city flash-ing past the windows. Square, imposing concrete bunkers; mass housing; ornate, classical buildings like the ones she remembered from Budapest; the odd minaret poking up here and there; churches . . . a strange sandwiching of East and West. She'd read a little about the city and the country, such as it was, before coming. The intricacies and complexities of this corner of Europe had taken her mind off other things, thankfully. It meant she arrived in better shape than she'd been in for the past few months.

She was taken straight to the apartment where she would live for the next twelve months. A small, top-floor flat in an old building in the center of town; the handsome, five-story pinkish-grey building was peeling on the outside and the lift didn't work but there was parquet flooring and tall, elegant win-dows that looked out onto a jumbled maze of red-tiled rooftops, satellite dishes and telephone lines strung from street corner to balcony. She thanked Marko, the interpreter and Pascale, the ICM official who had come to the airport to meet her, and de-clined their offer of coffee and dinner later that eve-ning. So much had happened in the past three weeks, she needed some time on her own to digest everything and time to reflect on what she was doing . . . or about to do. They would come by in the morning to pick her up; it would take her a few days to find her way around the city. If there was anything they could do . . . she shook her head, smiling. No, no . . . she was fine.

She closed the door behind them, hearing their footsteps die away as they walked down the stairs. The door on the ground floor clanged shut, the noise echoing all the way up the building. Then there was silence. She was alone. She crossed over to the window in the living room and looked out onto the street. It was grey, a typically overcast, south-eastern European day. The quality of the light was familiar to her. Budapest lay to the north of Belgrade but there was something of the same atmosphere—both cities lay on the same river, after all: the Danube. She'd seen the signs along the ride into the city although she'd noticed most of the street names and signs were written in Cyrillic script, not in Latin. Madeleine's grasp of the Cyrillic alphabet had all but disappeared since their flight to the West—she could barely remember the letters. As they drove through the streets, she was able to read one re-curring sign. *Ove je Srbija*. This is Serbia, Marko translated glumly for her. She'd wondered what it meant.

The flat was modestly furnished: a large double bed, clean sheets and towels and a fairly large cup-board in one corner of the bedroom; a sofa and two chairs in the living room; a sideboard stacked with odd plates and an assortment of cutlery; kitchen with appliances in reasonable working order . . . it was small and compact and no more than she needed. She spent an hour unpacking her suitcase, hanging up her clothes and familiarizing herself with the contents of the cupboards—pots, pans, the ubiquitous Italian coffeepot. Yes, there was everything she needed. There was even a small black-and-white television in the living room. She walked over and plugged it in. Three channels, RTV Belgrade and two others whose names she couldn't pronounce. It was all in Serbo-Croat. Milosevic's face appeared almost every five minutes. She watched for a few seconds and then switched it off.

She sat, hands on knees, for a few minutes on the sofa, looking cautiously around her new home. For the first time in a long while, she felt at peace. The break with England and Amber's flat which she'd come to associate with the sound and taste of her own tears had been clean—and necessary, she saw that now. In a new place with new sounds and smells and air around her, it seemed possible to breathe again. Begin again. It was 9 p.m. Outside the spring evening was rapidly falling. The sounds of traffic, of street vendors shouting at the passersby floated up to her open windows. She got up, closed the shutters and walked through to the bedroom. She took off her shoes, lay down on the bed, fully clothed and closed her eyes. In a moment, she thought to herself, she would get up, take a shower or a bath, whichever was available, and pull her nightdress out from its new place in the cupboard across the room.

She woke up the following morning. It was bright daylight outside.

Her new job was everything Harrigan had said it would be—and more, and worse. From the minute she walked into the organization's headquarters in the Skadarlije quarter of the city, she knew he had, quite literally, saved her life. The staff at the ICM mission were the usual mixture of international aid workers, NGO bureaucrats, technical advisors and translators but they were a new breed of worker to Madeleine and it was *all* so new, so chaotic, so intense. Six or seven languages were in constant and noisy ebb and flow, people were always rushing in and out of rooms, there were meetings, more meetings . . . by the end of her first day she couldn't actually remember why she'd been sent there in the first place. There just wasn't enough time or space to absorb it all. At the end of the day, Gordana Marjanovic, a cheerful, seemingly tireless medical student from Belgrade University who had given up her studies to join the ICM, told her the local journalists had dubbed Serbia the "Land of Mordor." Madeleine looked at her blankly.

"You know, from Tolkien. *Lord of the Rings.* Haven't you read it?" Madeleine shook her head. "Oh, well . . . you'll soon find out what they mean. Look, d'you want to have a coffee?" she asked, picking up her bag. It was on the tip of Madeleine's tongue to decline, but then she nodded. Yes, why not?

They walked down Zeleni Venac, the central

boulevard, towards the city center. There were groups of long-haired, bearded young men gathered in clusters at the street corners, selling a bewildering array of goods from little metal stands. T-shirts with the words "Freedom or Death"; music tapes featuring Serbian folk music; even key chains with a skull-and-crossbones motif—Madeleine shuddered. Gordana seemed not to notice. She led her down a series of narrow alleyways, turning right and left until she stopped outside a small café where, she said, the best Turkish coffee in Belgrade could still be found. Gordana was obviously known to the patrons—several people stopped by their table to say hello, ask how things were . . . hell, she answered cheerfully, lighting a Lucky Strike. Everyone in Belgrade smoked, Madeleine observed. The air inside the little café was thick with the pungent tobacco smell of the local cigarettes.

"I'm lucky," Gordana said, sipping her coffee and fingering the full packet that lay on the table. "I can buy foreign cigarettes."

"Lucky?" Madeleine smiled faintly.

"You don't smoke?" Madeleine shook her head. "That will change. Three months. You'll see."

By the end of her first week, she knew she wouldn't make it past three weeks, never mind the three months Gordana had spoken of. She had never picked up a cigarette in her life but after a week of fifteen-hour days, reading the kind of reports that landed across her desk and realizing for the first time exactly what the job entailed, she reached for a Lucky Strike. She lit up, coughing as she inhaled but thankful for the distraction—she wasn't sure if she could continue reading the report that had just been tossed her way. Rape as a weapon of war. She smoked three in a row as she read the testimony of a nineteen-year-old Moslem girl from Posavina, in the north of Bosnia. Gordana was right. This was a country descending into madness; for the first time in months, anger surged through her. Islington and Amber and Becky; her job at UCH; even Alasdair and Egypt fell away from her as she picked up sheet after sheet. She had no idea what she was doing or even what she was expected to do. Her job, insofar as she understood its parameters, was to train aid and humanitarian relief workers in the field in how to deal with victims of exactly the kind of abuse contained in such reports. As part of a team of Italian psychologists and doctors recently arrived in Belgrade, their mission was part of a joint UNHCR-University of Florence initiative to improve services in the areas of mental health and psycho-social trauma. The loss of confidence which had haunted her for the past three months simply vanished. She spent a fortnight calmly rationalizing her own training with what had to be done, smoking her way through a packet of Marlboro Lights that Gordana had thoughtfully provided and slowly coming to terms with what she was expected to do in her new role—and how to do it.

A month into her new position, a very different

Madeleine had emerged. Thin, with short, cropped hair—in the circumstances, her long, thick blonde hair was nothing but a nuisance—a cigarette burning between her fingers and perpetually in jeans, no one at home would have recognized her. Yes, Harrigan was right. In saving others, she would save herself.

≈70≈

It was almost six weeks since Tendé had slid out of her bed and gone off to an early-morning meeting with Max. She'd woken up that morning and watched him dress with her heart in her mouth. Where would they go from there? His answer the night before had said little. She hadn't known whether to be hopeful or full of despair. They were in the first few delicate stages of any relationship— push too hard and she would lose him; she knew the rules. But at the same time it wasn't as if he lived in Camden or just across the river. There were some 6,000 miles and two continents between them. If she didn't push now, when would she?

"Is this . . . a permanent goodbye?" she asked from the bed as he put on his tie. He stopped and turned around.

"Goodbye?"

"Yes. You know . . . an *au revoir* or an *à bientôt.*" She tried to sound flippant. She didn't look at him.

She couldn't. He walked over to the bed and sat down on the edge, reaching for her hand.

"Of course we work this out. I told you last night, no?"

"No, what you said was—"

"N'sha'allah."

"Yes. Which means . . . ?"

"If God wills it. He will."

"How can you be so sure?" He traced the edge of her ring. *Hope.* He turned it over and pointed to it.

"This." He bent his head and kissed her. "And this." He straightened up. "I'll call you later."

And he did. He'd asked her not to tell Max, seeming convinced that Max wouldn't take the news well. She thought he was overreacting—Max liked him, a lot, she pointed out—but he was adamant. The other part, the political sensitivity of the news while their project was only just getting off the ground . . . that bit she understood perfectly. Particularly now, with Kieran's joint venture having got off to such a blistering start, anything that involved Max Sall or his offspring was bound to find its way into the news. So she told Becky, on pain of death, and was rewarded by Becky's immediate and obvious joy. In fact, she was rather touched by it. Becky's happiness almost outdid her own. They spent a wonderfully girly day shopping, drinking coffee and gossiping—only Becky hadn't been quite so ready to share the details of how her life was going. She was increasingly vague about the wedding; there was the awful news of her losing her job at the gallery but strangely, she didn't seem to care. She was more interested in the details of Tendé . . . when was he coming back; would Amber go to Mali again; what did Max think.

"Whoa, you're running ahead of me," Amber laughed. "I don't know. I haven't told Max. Tendé seems to think he'll have some kind of fit . . . I don't know why. Anyway, he's coming back to London next month. I guess we'll see what happens."

"A whole *month*? I couldn't wait that long." Becky was emphatic.

"I can," Amber said mildly. "Right now, I feel like . . . like I could wait forever."

"That won't last," Becky said knowingly. They both laughed.

The best bit, Amber thought to herself as she sat down at her desk at work, was that Tendé was as good as his word. He did call. Not every day, sometimes not for a week . . . but he spared her the nail-biting, agonizing wait-by-the-phone that she'd so dreaded. If he said he would call on Thursday, he did. She learned very quickly that this wasn't to be like anything she'd experienced before. Tendé was thirty-three—five years older than her, yet he seemed to belong to another age and time. He was precise, with no capacity for small talk and, it seemed, with very little time to waste. He was as busy as Max—no two weeks were the same; no two days alike. She hadn't thought very much about his position in government but she quickly understood that over there, the boundaries of a government minister's job were not as clearly or neatly drawn as those she was accustomed to seeing. His job was not over at 5 p.m, or at 8 p.m, as hers was. His seemed to drift over twenty-four hours, each day bringing with it a fresh set of issues, problems, sometimes opportunities. He talked quite frankly about the challenges and difficulties he faced. A small anecdote during a quick phone call on Sunday morning could contain a whole world of subtle and hidden meaning—just as it had done in the desert, her mind raced to keep up.

In his study at home in Bamako, Tendé put down the phone and realized suddenly how lonely his life had become. It hadn't always been that way. As a student in France, then Moscow and finally in New York, he'd been no different from anyone else. He'd partied hard, played hard, had his fair share of women and missed lectures but somehow, since he'd come back home, he'd thrown himself into the business of politics and his country's development with such a passion he'd had little time left over for the things he enjoyed. Used to enjoy, he corrected himself. Apart from the night in London with Amber, the last time he'd been to a nightclub had been almost a year ago with his sister Lassana and her rather stiff Swiss husband. He smiled to himself. The Rail Band had been playing and on impulse the three of them had gone to the infamous Hôtel Buffet de la Gare in downtown Bamako—a wild night. Werner, Lassana's husband, had surprised them both by insisting on staying until the band packed up at dawn. But that was a year ago. The thought

brought him up short. Was it possible? Had he become so lost in his world of meetings, deals, dashing around from one country to the next . . . had he
simply lost track of all the other things he used to
enjoy? Perhaps that was why the night in London
had turned out so unexpectedly. He'd realized ever
since their few days in the desert that Amber Sall
was somebody special. The realization had come to
him slowly, yes, but perhaps in the best way. That
night it was hard not to be affected by the atmosphere in the club. He'd known, even as Max extended the invitation to him some weeks earlier, that
he would come. He'd even arranged his schedule
to be in Paris the week before. A thin line, of
course . . . a ticket to Europe paid for out of government coffers and the decision to stay over the weekend was his, but he'd wanted to see Amber again.

When he saw her sitting alone in the lounge sipping a cocktail—appropriately named, he remembered with a smile—a tremendous feeling of
pleasure swept through him; he'd found it hard to
banter with her as they always seemed to. He'd
wanted her, right there and then. The rest of it . . .
dancing, slipping outside, jumping in a cab and going back to her place . . . it had seemed to him to be
nothing more than a natural extension of the on-off
conversation they'd been having for six months—
ever since she'd come to Téghaza.

It was six weeks since he'd seen her. He would
be flying to London again within a month. Max had
finished putting together the preliminary documents
to form the basis of a feasibility study and together

they would review the lists of engineering consultants who had expressed interest. It was moving faster than either he or Max had anticipated. There was something about the allure of the desert, the ancient salt industry, the dream of bringing the desert to life . . . the few people Max had spoken to had already been sold on his idea. But they were treading carefully. Although it was the first time Tendé had ever been involved in anything quite so large, he knew from the experience of watching others that it was vital to keep his finger on the details, not to let things slip away from his attention and to make everyone and everything around him accountable, at all times. Until the project was on more stable ground, he wasn't going to risk a thing by making public his involvement with Amber Sall, and he certainly wasn't going to tell Max.

Besides, he had no idea how things with Amber would turn out. It was still early days. It was another thing he'd learned to be cautious about—women. There were one or two encounters in his past he could quite easily have done without. Proceed with care: it was a lesson that seemed to have served him well. Until he met Amber, of course. Oh, well, he thought to himself as he put away the reports and notes he'd been reading all day, there was still plenty of time to figure out what to do. He would see her again in a few weeks' time. Under the unusual circumstances, keeping their relationship to themselves would give them a bit of time to work it out, between them. No one else. Max hadn't asked him what he'd done that evening or even where he'd stayed. It wasn't his business, even if it was his daughter. He switched off the light and walked slowly through the house.

It wasn't quite true. Someone had seen them leave the club together. Paola. But by that time she was under the benign and heady influence of a new drug Kieran had persuaded her to swallow—something called Ecstasy. Paola had never had anything like it. He and Will were busy transferring the little white tablets from a large bag to tiny squares of folded paper and slipping them into every available pocket when Paola walked in the offices behind the White Room and stopped, a smile of half-recognition spreading over her face.

"What are you doing?" she asked, coming to sit on the edge of the desk. Kieran was blushing furiously but Will had already swallowed his first pill and was feeling exceptionally loving towards everyone around him.

"Try it. It's the best thing ever."

Paola hesitated. The last time she'd swallowed a little white pill her world had all but collapsed.

"Go on. It's Ecstasy. Have you ever tried it?"

"No. What's it like?" She leaned forward. Kieran found himself staring down her cleavage.

"Brilliant. It just makes everything . . . so, so cool. And happy. You just feel so happy." Will was strangely inarticulate.

Kieran looked up. "Here, let's both take one." He held out his hand. "It's totally safe—no hangover, no headache, nothing. Go on, let's do it together." He popped one in his mouth. Paola reached out and took the other pill. She examined it for a second and then put it on her tongue. Kieran handed her a bottle of water. She swallowed and waited for something to happen. There was nothing—not even a fizz as the tablet dissolved and slid down her throat. They sat there for a few moments, looking at each other. Then she shrugged and got off the table.

"Big deal. Nothing's happening."

"It will, baby," Will promised her, leaning back in his large leather chair. He and Kieran grinned at each other. Paola walked off, swaying slightly. She'd also had too much to drink. She pushed open the double doors and made her way back towards the White Room. She needed another drink. She saw two of her friends standing at the bar and sauntered over. It happened slowly at first. She felt a rush of warmth steal over her as she looked at Helena and Patrizia, two minor models whom she barely knew but had invited anyway.

"*Hi!*" she said, joining them at the bar. They both turned. Within seconds, Paola was chatting away as though they were her closest friends. She really, really *liked* them, she realized, as they sipped cocktails together, laughing. Helena was *so* beautiful and Patrizia was just lovely. She giggled and whispered and laughed with them. All of a sudden, it was the best evening of her life. She wanted to share her remarkable discovery. She whispered to them that she had something that could turn the night into an absolute blast . . . did they want any? Of course. She left them and hurried back to the office, hoping Kieran and Will would still be there. It was empty. She rushed up the back stairs and hurried down the corridor that led to the dance floor. The doors at the end opened suddenly and she saw Amber and Tendé sweep past, holding hands. She stopped for a second, momentarily stunned. She'd seen Tendé as soon as he walked onto the dance floor. She'd even whispered to Daniela who really was her best friend that she was determined to get him—*look how gorgeous he is!*—but she'd lost sight of him as Kieran and Will and Digger kept dragging her off to be photographed or to meet someone. She stood in the middle of the corridor expecting to feel annoyed . . . why was he holding hands with Amber? But nothing happened. She still felt all warm and glowing inside. She shook her head and continued down the corridor in search of Kieran.

Half an hour later, she was back in the office after having been swept onto the dance floor, watching Kieran unlock a drawer and pull out a little plastic bag of pills.

"They go fast," he said, shaking out a dozen. "But don't tell anyone where you got them. If you need more, come and find me." She nodded. She held out her hand. Kieran stood up and held her fingers as he dropped six pills slowly into her palm. Her fingers felt hot and tingly where he held them. She was sitting on the edge of his desk, as before, one leg dangling in front of her. She brought her head up. There was a sudden jolt of electricity between them. She pulled her palm back. His hand came to rest on her thigh. She caught her breath. His head moved closer . . . the warmth inside her suddenly boiled over . . . and they kissed. The knowledge of who they were disappeared slowly as his tongue entered her mouth and his hand slid her dress up her thigh. This is wrong, she heard her own voice inside her head but she couldn't stop. He pulled her towards him, one hand finding its way inside her dress and under the tiny string of her underwear. She tried to pull back . . .

"Yo, Kieran!" Digger was running down the corridor towards them. They sprang apart, Kieran swearing under his breath. Paola quickly slid off the desk and walked, shaking, towards the door.

"Paola," Kieran called softly as she pushed the door open. She ignored him—and Digger—and disappeared.

The rest of the night passed in a haze of dancing, laughing wildly with her friends, tossing back one cocktail after another. She didn't see Kieran again. Just before dawn, she pulled on her coat and walked outside. Clive, Max's driver, was parked by the curb. She climbed in and asked him please not to wait for Kieran but to take her straight home. Clive was surprised. In almost three months of driving Paola Rossi around he'd never once heard her say "please."

Max threw down his pen in frustration. He didn't know what was wrong with this warring family. The day after the opening Paola had surprised everybody and suddenly announced she was leaving for Rome and she wasn't sure if she wanted to come back. Kieran hadn't come home that day; no one knew where he was; Amber was behaving most peculiarly and didn't want to come to Menorca for his birthday the following month . . . she had other plans; she was vague. Francesca hadn't spoken to him since she and Angela had met at the door to Paradise and Angela seemed to think the momentary lapse in their frosty relations on the night of the damned opening signaled a thaw. What the hell was going on? He fished for his glasses. He'd been having headaches for a month and had finally given in and gone to see an optician. Amber said they suited him. He wasn't so sure. They made him feel suddenly middle-aged.

"You're not middle-aged," she'd said, grinning at him. He felt ridiculously, momentarily pleased. "You're old." He'd stared at her, annoyed.

But she was right. He would be sixty-two on his next birthday in less than a month. It had been a good year. Business-wise things were going well. Very well, in fact. Some of the criticisms that had been leveled against him in the past few years were about to be turned on their head with the announcement that Sall Investments, Inc. was to be the major shareholder in a new company, Salzman Holdings, an untypically sentimental throwback to his own beginnings. For years, despite his obvious financial successes, he'd been unable to shake off the rumors that persisted in the City about him: an outsider, a Johnny-cum-lately, a shark . . . Max had never lost the sense of not quite belonging to the Establishment. The feelings of abandonment and loneliness that he felt—must have felt, since he rarely admitted to them, even to himself—standing on the quay at Harwich, not knowing where to turn had never quite left him. He looked at his children. If there was one thing he could be proud of, regardless of their other shortcomings, it was that they never had to feel what he had. They were secure financially, socially, culturally. He hadn't said anything to anyone, not even Francesca who was most likely to be the recipient of confidences whispered late at night, but Kieran's turnaround and the grudging acceptance of Paola into the London family fold had meant a lot to him, even more than the deals that he'd made in the past twelve months. Seeing Kieran with his friends at the opening night, watching his beautiful daughters, so different from each other yet so special in their own ways . . . there was no one he could share it with. No one would have understood exactly, precisely what it meant to see the photographers straining to catch one last shot of Paola Rossi as she escorted her friends in through the VIP door or to watch Kieran give last-second instructions to the security guards through his walkie-talkie. These were his kids. In thirty years he'd gone from polishing the windscreen of Lord Sainsbury's car to standing on a glass platform, his wife and mistress by his side, watching the whole of London pay homage to his children's success.

And now here they were, fighting. Giving him a headache.

He sighed and turned back to his papers. His reading lists were divided into two piles. On the one hand, he read technical papers with headings like "Cut and Blast Mining" and "Brine Evaporation." He was learning about the different techniques employed to extract salt from the earth. Like many self-taught men, Max was a voracious reader. He plowed through the manuals, reference papers and technical journals with ease. Vacuum plants, cylindrical vessels, steam chambers . . . he quickly grasped the principles involved and was able to apply them directly to the Téghaza conditions. When the feasibility reports came in, he wanted to be able to understand exactly what they meant.

Next to his technical stack, however, were other articles and information about salt. He read that the expression "not worth his salt" came from ancient Greece where slaves were traded for salt; he read that special rations of salt given to Roman soldiers were called *solarium argentium*, from where the English word "salary" is derived; and that in 1259, Charles of Anjou levied the *gabelle*, a salt tax, to finance his conquest of the Kingdom of Naples. As much as he enjoyed brushing up on his technical expertise, he enjoyed the other stuff—the human stuff. He knew that when it came down to it, at a meeting with engineers and miners, for example, being able to say to one of them that the Erie Canal in the U.S. had been called the "ditch that salt built," referring to the salt tax revenues that paid for its construction . . . little anecdotes like that would win him friends amongst the managers and board of directors. Or amongst Tendé's men. Did they know that in 1930, Mahatma Gandhi led a 200-mile march to the Arabian Ocean to collect untaxed salt as a protest against British rule? He chuckled to himself. Amber would have called him a cynical bastard. He preferred to think of it as good business practice.

He picked up his pen again, his good humor restored.

Back in Rome, Paola lay on her bed for the second afternoon since she'd got back, unable to think straight. The memory, hazy as it was, of what had happened in the office that night just wouldn't leave her. Every time she turned her head or paused in conversation or closed her eyes, it was there. She was frightened by it—of course she was. But worse than that, she was frightened of herself. She couldn't talk to anyone—not Daniela, not Francesca and certainly not Kieran. She'd bolted from the office as soon as she heard Digger's voice, too stunned by the awful, *sickening* realization in her that she liked it . . . she *liked* what his mouth was doing to her and his hands and that *she wanted more*.

She gave a groan and turned over in bed, pressing her knees tightly together as if that would dispel the urge that had come over her to part them and let his hand go . . . she blocked the thought. It was wrong. It was sick. Evil. There wasn't any other way to describe it. But she was confused. She'd seen Kieran for a total of perhaps six days in her whole life. She didn't *know* him—that was the whole point. Max said—this is your brother; this is your sister—but they weren't. Paola couldn't think of herself as someone who had siblings. Growing up, she'd barely spared them a minute's thought. Hating Amber . . . well, that was easy. Amber was easy to hate. She was rude and prickly and competitive, nothing like the sister she'd hoped for when she'd been old enough to understand that she had one who didn't live with her. She could still remember the disappointment she'd felt on seeing Amber for the first time. She must have been . . . what . . . four? Five? She dimly remembered her and Kieran coming to *Casa Bella* but she hated the gangling, bossy girl who barely spoke to her and made fun of her attempts to speak English—not that she could speak Italian or Spanish or French, all of which Paola could speak fluently by the time she was four. They hated each other. She didn't really remember Kieran on that visit. An older, elusive presence. He'd disappeared to the beach every day for the week that they were there. No, she had no memories of him. Nothing.

She'd met them again the summer Kieran turned thirteen. She remembered it because he'd wanted to go to town with the school friend he'd brought along with him but Francesca had said they were too young to go out alone at night. Max wasn't there. There was a screaming match between Francesca and the headstrong Kieran that had left her mother exhausted and tearful and resulted in Kieran, his friend and Amber being sent back to England in disgrace as soon as Max arrived back. And that was it. She'd never set eyes on him again until . . . she squeezed her eyes shut, unable to think about it any more.

"Paola?" Francesca was coming down the corridor. Paola groaned. She didn't sound pleased. There was a short rap on the door.

"Yes," Paola called out after a second. Francesca swept in. She didn't *look* pleased.

"I've just been on the phone with Max. What's all this? He says you're not going back. What about the nightclub?"

"I don't feel like doing it any more," Paola said, shrugging.

"Now, just you listen to me a minute, young lady—" Francesca kicked the door shut. Paola looked up, startled. Her mother was angry. "I cannot believe how selfish you are." Paola's mouth opened in shock. "Did you see how *happy* Max was that evening? Did you see how proud he was of all of you? Did you?" Paola couldn't answer. She'd never seen her mother so furious. "He has done nothing but provide for you all your spoiled life. The one time you could do something for him . . . you *can't be bothered*? Well, let *me* tell *you* something about being bothered. You *will* be bothered. You will get up, you will pack a bag of suitable clothes and you will go back to London every Friday *for the next three months*. Is that clear? Your brother's success depends on you putting in an effort, just as you agreed to . . . or have you forgotten? Jesus *Christ*, Paola. What did I ever do to bring up such a spoiled brat?" And with that, Francesca turned around, walked out of the door and slammed it hard. Just as Paola used to.

She sat in total silence for a few minutes after Francesca had gone, too shocked to move. She'd never heard Francesca defend Kieran. In fact, she'd barely heard her *talk* about him, or Amber. Nothing positive had ever dropped from Francesca's lips about them, ever. And she certainly hadn't realized the whole event had made Max proud. Why hadn't he said something? And why had she called her a spoiled brat? She wasn't spoiled . . . she was confused and hurting and there was no one to share it with. She laid her head on one of her pillows and felt something hot and wet slide down her cheek.

In London, Kieran wasn't faring much better. He'd spent the last few hours of the night on Will's floor, unable to face going home and seeing Paola, or Amber, or Max. When the deal about the club had been done Max had made a huge fuss about converting one of the guest suites on the top floor into Paola's set of rooms. Now that she was going to come to London on a regular basis, he said, she needed somewhere to stay until she decided if she liked it enough to buy a place of her own—or, rather, for Max to buy it. Kieran didn't think he could stand seeing her come downstairs in her see-through white nightdress and calmly slide into place at the breakfast table. He'd almost choked the first time he saw her.

He stayed at Will's for two days, much to Will's irritation. He couldn't figure out why Kieran just didn't go home. On the Sunday morning, unable to stand the thought of getting into the same tired and dirty clothes, he'd finally walked outside, hailed a cab and jumped in, his stomach already in knots. But when he got home, he discovered from Siobhân that Paola had left the day before; Max was sequestered in his study reading something for a meeting on Monday morning and Amber, of course, was at her own place. There was only Angela in the house. He made his way cautiously up the stairs. He couldn't face Angela at that very moment and disappeared into his rooms. He stood under the shower for almost thirty minutes, hoping for some relief from the persistent image in his head—of Paola's mouth and the long, glossy curtain of her hair. He switched off the taps violently.

It was Siobhân who told him some time during the following week that Paola would be coming back every weekend for the next couple of months. He was so surprised and relieved he forgot to ask her how *she* knew. He shrugged and walked off, a sweet relief flowing through him. He would apologize to her, explain . . . it was the drugs, the excitement of the evening . . . it would never happen again. He ran up the stairs two at a time, whistling.

Paola said nothing, just sat in the expensive new leather chair that Max had ordered for her living room and looked at her nails. When he'd finished mumbling his apologies, she just nodded and said it was okay. No problem. She didn't smile; she barely even looked at him. He backed out of the room, cursing himself, feeling more miserable than he had done in a long time. She left to go to the club before him—she was meeting some friends in town, he heard her say to Max. They would go out to dinner and then she'd bring them round later on. Well, Kieran thought to himself, brushing the lint off his jacket, at least she'd agreed to keep coming. Digger, Jake and Will had been besides themselves on the opening night at the gorgeous young things she'd brought in tow. May it long continue, had been Jake's last words. He squirted some gel in his hand, ran it through his hair and took a quick look at himself in the mirror. He'd never really paid too much attention to the way he looked—he was tall and broad-shouldered. It had always been enough of a winning combination to ensure an above-average success rate when compared with his peers. Now he scrutinized himself anxiously—light brown hair cut short around the sides and falling forward into his eyes; startlingly blue eyes, like Amber's; a straight, narrow nose with the same sculpted tip as Angela's; square jaw . . . no, he looked nothing like Paola. Absolutely nothing. There was no resemblance . . . not a drop. Maybe they *weren't* really brother and sister after all. Maybe . . . maybe Francesca had lied. She would know. And from the little he knew of her, he wouldn't put it past her. Francesca was capable of anything. On that much more optimistic note, he left the room.

Something had to give. Something was about to fall. The delicate, precarious balance in which all of her life was suspended was about to topple, she could feel it. Charlie; Henry; her mounting debts; no job; lying to her parents about having been fired . . . any second now, something would give. Charlie had given her one of his credit cards "just to tide you over" he'd said, characteristically generous, before leaving for a week-long trip to Singapore. She'd checked the balance, found there was £15,000 available to her to spend—and promptly gone mad. Even now, three days after the shopping binge, there were unopened bags under the bed and sacks full of cosmetics and shampoos and creams that she would never use. Something about walking into the store with all that spending power at her fingertips . . . she found herself saying "yes" to everything that was offered. And of course, in Harvey Nichols, everything was on offer, always. Beautifully wrapped parcels containing the prettiest things: caramel and peach-colored bras; a silk kimono; a pair of high-heeled mules; pure white cotton panties with delicate *broderie anglaise* edges; fishnet tights and a black lace garter . . . things she would never wear in front of Charlie but that Henry liked to see her in. In the week he was away Henry slept over in the huge, soft double bed and slept well, every night.

A month after she'd been given the card, she realized with a shock that she really oughtn't to let him see the bills. She'd woken up early one morning and by chance, really, had been downstairs when the post came flying through the letterbox. She quickly pulled her bills and his statement out of the pile and made a mental note to do the same the next month. She had no idea how much she'd already spent. Somehow, the figure of £15,000 was still in the forefront of her mind but of course that was impossible . . . she'd spent *loads* since then.

Plus, Charlie had begun to notice there was something different about her. He didn't say much but once or twice she'd caught him looking at her rather strangely. She'd developed the habit of putting on a listening face when he came home in the evenings and started on about his job and the people and the little deals and on and on . . . Becky would simply drift off, nodding every once in a while, making the appropriate noises. It was easy, really. Charlie didn't want to *talk*—he just wanted someone to listen. She would sit opposite him, feet tucked up under her, a large glass of red wine on the immaculate coffee table between them and simply drift off. Sometimes she thought about Henry, sometimes she thought about the things she'd bought during the day, about getting a new job . . . different things. Once she'd sat there in front of him going through the last few minutes of the last time she and Henry had sex. It was quite thrilling, really, listening to Charlie drone on and on and picturing Henry's face contracting in such intense pleasure as he'd come inside her for about the third time that particular night.

"Sorry?" She'd snapped back to the present with a jolt. Charlie was looking at her, frowning.

"What's the matter?" he repeated.

"With me? Nothing . . . nothing. Why?"

"You've gone all red. All over your face." She got up immediately and hurried out of the room. Inside the bathroom she switched on the light. He was right. Her face had broken out in an angry, red blush. She realized with a stifled giggle that she turned herself on just sitting there thinking about Henry. She splashed some water on her face and opened the bathroom window to cool herself down.

"Probably just a bit of a flu coming on," she said lightly as she walked back into the living room. "I get really hot sometimes."

Charlie nodded slowly.

No, something was about to break. She wasn't sleeping as well as she usually did. Charlie had been back from Singapore for over two months and it didn't look like he was going anywhere else soon. It had upset her rhythm. She'd become used to him dashing off to the States or Europe or the Far East every other week or so. It had given them—she and Henry—a rather pleasant routine . . . not every day, not every weekend, but often. Unpredictable enough to be a thrill and yet often enough to stop them becoming desperate. But now, with Charlie having been at home for almost sixty days straight, she was beginning to get restless. If Henry had also been unemployed . . . well, it would have been perfect, from Becky's point of view at least. But he wasn't. He went to work every bloody day which meant that seeing him in the daytime when Charlie was himself at work was impossible. She was trying to work out how to engineer a weekend away, saying she was going somewhere with Amber, for example, when Charlie surprised her. Completely.

"Are you looking for something, Becky?" His voice was quiet. Becky whirled round. It was 7:15 a.m. and she'd crept downstairs to pick up the post before he got to it. It was the sixth of May. Statements usually came in on the second or third.

"No . . . I was just getting the post. Coffee?" she said brightly, hoping she hadn't gone red.

"What's going on, Becky?" He held a sheet of paper towards her. She glanced at it, her heart sinking. It was indeed a credit card statement. Someone— Charlie—had gone through every single line, underscoring purchases, question marks against balances; red lines across every item. Hotel bills; telephone bills . . . all of it. She looked up. To her horror, there were tears in his eyes. She broke down. Right there and then. He forced it out of her— every single, sordid little detail. How long it had been going on, when they'd first done it, where, how; she thought the questions would never end. Did Amber know she was screwing her ex-boyfriend? Did her parents know? What was he like? Charlie was crying, standing in the hallway in his dressing gown. Becky covered her ears. The sound was horrible. She'd never seen Charlie cry before. She'd never seen a man cry before.

In the morning, he left for work and said they'd sort it out when he got back. She spent the longest day of her entire life sitting immobile in the living room, watching the television with the sound turned off, going downstairs to make nothing more than a cup of tea, agonizing over what was going to happen until his key turned in the lock at 6 p.m.—he was home early, she thought with a sudden flash of hope.

She didn't even give him a chance. She begged him, on her knees . . . it was over, she would never see him again, she didn't know why she'd done it . . . she was sorry, sorry, sorry. She wept and couldn't stand up, she grabbed his legs as he tried to walk out of the room—she was almost hysterical by the time he picked her up and carried her to bed. He gave her a glass of hot milk and some aspirin for her head and stroked her hair until she fell asleep, shattered and exhausted by the outpouring of tears and fear. She woke several times in the night to find him sitting in almost the same position, right next to her, his hand still resting on her matted hair. It was a Wednesday night—wasn't he going to get some sleep? He had to go to work in the morning, didn't

he? Charlie just shook his head. He didn't say anything more. Becky was very afraid of what would
happen next.

Amber picked up the phone. It was almost 6 p.m.
and she was working late. She had a deadline for
the following morning and the story wasn't coming
together as she'd planned.

"Hello?" She was brusque. There was silence on
the other end for a few seconds. "Hello?"

"Amber?" It was Becky.

"Oh, hi. Listen, Becky, can I call you tomo . . .
what's the matter?" Becky had started crying.
"Becky?"

"C . . . can . . . can I come round?" She was
heaving great, deep breaths. Amber was alarmed.

"Of course. What's the matter? What's happened? Where are you?"

"Downstairs."

"Downstairs where?" Amber was confused.

"In the lobby."

"Hang on. I'll be right there." Amber replaced the
receiver and ran to the elevators.

Becky was sitting on a chair near the wall of public
telephones. She looked terrible. Her hair was pulled
back into a rough ponytail, her clothes were disheveled and she'd obviously been crying for hours.
Her eyes were thin, puffy slits in a red and blotchy
face. Amber could only gape at her. Becky would
never leave the house looking like that unless something really terrible had happened. She took hold of

her arm and gently led her into one of the private meeting rooms behind the reception desk. She pulled out a chair, helped her into it and turned to close the door.

"Becks . . . what's going on?"

"Oh, Amber . . ." Becky had started crying again. "It's Charlie."

"Has something happened to him?" Madeleine's face flashed suddenly before her.

Becky shook her head. "It's me . . . he's . . . he's thrown me out."

"Oh." Despite Becky's distraught state, Amber was relieved. Whatever it was, it could be sorted out. "Oh, thank God," she said with a short laugh. "I thought it was something . . . you know, more serious." Becky looked up.

"It *is* serious. I can't go back. He won't let me," she said through her tears. Amber patted her arm.

"Look, I'm going to put you in a taxi and send you round to mine. You can stay there as long as you like until the two of you sort it out. I'm sure you will. You're getting *married*, Becky. This is nothing . . . a little argument. It'll blow over."

"No, it won't. You don't understand what I've done," Becky said indistinctly.

"Well, whatever it is, can it wait? I've got to get something finished for tomorrow morning. You go home to my place in a cab and I'll be home later. Probably before ten. All right?"

"I haven't got any cash," Becky said miserably. Amber stuck a hand in her pocket and pulled out some notes.

"Don't worry about a thing. Go home. I'll go up-stairs and get the keys. There's wine in the fridge and I think there's some leftover food as well. You look like you haven't eaten anything all day." Becky numbly shook her head. Amber gave her a quick hug and dashed back upstairs.

Five minutes later she saw Becky off in a taxi and went back to her desk. Whatever the crisis was, she was sure they'd sort it out. Although Becky had seemed pretty hysterical. She tried to concentrate on the job at hand. She would hear all about it later.

The flat was dark when she finally got in. She switched on the hallway lights, wondering if Becky had already gone to bed. She walked into the living room and stopped. Becky was sitting in darkness on the sofa, her head in her hands.

"Becky?" She put her bags down. Becky lifted her head. "Shall I put on the light?" Becky nodded, wip-ing her face. "Did you . . . have you had something to eat?" Becky shook her head. Amber sighed. "Look, whatever the argument was about—"

"I've been seeing someone else." Becky's words fell into the darkness. Amber switched on the light and walked over to the sofa.

"Oh, Becky." She sat down next to her and put an arm round her shoulders. It was more serious than she'd thought.

"Amber." Becky's voice was tight. "I wanted to tell you this before . . . I just never . . . it just didn't seem like the right time. I'm sorry."

"Don't be silly. You don't have to tell me anything. It's Charlie you should be thinking about."

"No, I do . . ." she took a deep breath. "It's . . . Amber, the guy I've been seeing . . . it's Henry."

"Henry? Henry who?" Amber was confused.

"Your Henry."

"Henry *Fletcher*?" Amber's voice was incredulous. She pulled away from Becky.

"I'm sorry. I should have told you. It just didn't seem . . ." her voice trailed off.

"How long has this been going on?" It was the same question Charlie had asked. Becky's face crumpled.

"A while. A few months."

"A few months? But . . . how . . . where did you . . . why didn't you just *say*?" Amber stood up, agitated. She wasn't sure which had upset her more—the news that it was Henry or the fact that Becky had been hiding it from her.

"I was going to, honestly. But I just couldn't find the right time. You're always so busy—"

"Don't." Amber stopped her. "Don't make excuses, Becky. Please." She didn't know what to say. There was silence in the room, broken only by Becky's sniffling. "I'm going to bed," she said finally. "I can't think about this right now. You can sleep in the spare bedroom—there's sheets and towels on the bed. I need to get some sleep. I've got to be at work early tomorrow morning." She turned to leave the room.

"Amber," Becky sobbed. "I'm sorry."

"I know. Me too. I'll see you in the morning." Amber walked out and shut her bedroom door. She didn't know what to think, much less what to say.

It was the drugs, of course. Paola accepted Kieran's explanation and no more was said. She continued to come to London every Friday afternoon and returned to Rome on Sundays. Max was happy, Francesca was happy, the boys—as she called the four of them—were happy. Everyone was happy. Except her. She managed to hide it; she dressed up with extravagant care; she waltzed into the club with her friends at midnight; they danced on the bar with the beautiful people—to everyone around her she seemed to be having the time of her life. She and Kieran were seldom alone. She steered clear of the little white pills and got wasted on Bellinis instead. She came back at dawn each night, left her Blahniks downstairs on the marble floor and walked up to her room, barefoot. Most nights she left Kieran behind at the club—Clive spent all night waiting for one or the other to come stumbling out of the side entrance and flop into the car.

Once inside her rooms upstairs, she would shower, wash the smoke and sweat from her hair and tumble into the cool, wide bed. She would lie awake for an hour or so, tossing and turning until at last she fell into a deep, heavy sleep. She would wake up in the early afternoon on Saturdays, wander down to the salon on the corner or meet friends who lived in London or those who'd come over for the weekend with her, and in the evening, they'd start to party again—some nights starting at the club, other nights going to dinner or somewhere else before making their way there after midnight. Fairly soon the pattern had settled into a routine. Max had started to travel a lot again, often somewhere in Africa, Francesca said. Paola assumed he was with Tendé. She'd said nothing about seeing him and Amber together that night. As far as Paola was concerned, the less she thought about that night, the better. And anyway, she hadn't seen Amber since then. She never came to the house at Holland Park and no one seemed to talk about her when Max wasn't around.

One night she and Kieran just happened to be leaving Paradise at the same time. It was early for both of them. She was tired and was standing in the vestibule of the side entrance, trying to light a cigarette when he pushed open the doors and saw her there.

"Hi."

"Ciao." She lit her cigarette. "Going home?" she asked, blowing the smoke in his direction. She was nervous.

"Yeah. Had enough for tonight. Digger and Jake are handling things. Is Clive outside?" He opened the door. "Yeah, he's here. You coming?" He tried not to look at her.

"*Si*." She ground out her cigarette with her heel and followed him into the car.

Inside, they sat as far away from each other as possible. Kieran looked tired, she noticed. He looked out the window as Clive started the car and pulled away from the curb. Luckily there were few photographers around.

"Are you coming to *Casa Bella?*" she asked suddenly, breaking the silence. Kieran looked at her. It was Max's birthday the following week.

"Dunno. Are you?"

"Maybe." They were both quiet. Paola's heart was beating fast. She didn't like sitting so close to him, looking at his hands and remembering . . . she looked out of the window.

It was almost three when Clive pulled up in front of the house. The lights were all off. Max was in Mali and even Siobhân had gone away for a week to Dublin. They walked in together, careful not to make any noise. Angela was the only person at home and she was probably asleep.

"D'you want something to drink?" Kieran asked as they put their bags and things down on the dresser. Paola hesitated.

"Sure. I'll have a brandy."

"You go upstairs, if you want. I'll bring them up." Paola nodded. She kicked off her shoes and walked upstairs. She looked at herself in the bedroom mirror—she might as well have a shower. It would take Kieran a few minutes to find the brandy and bring it upstairs. She walked into the shower and quickly stripped. The water was wonderfully warm and relaxing after a night spent almost non-stop on the dance floor. She dried herself and pulled a pair of pajamas out of the cupboard.

Kieran was already sitting on one of the floor cushions when she came through to the living room. He'd brought up a bottle of one of Max's finest brandies and put two goblets on the table. He poured one for her as she walked towards him, toweling her hair.

"Bet that feels good," he said, glancing down at his own smoke-filled suit.

"Yes." She picked up her glass. "Cheers."

"Cheers." Kieran smiled. "Good night, wasn't it?" She nodded and sat down on the floor opposite him. They began talking about the night—who'd come, who'd been seen leaving with whom, what this one or that was wearing. Suddenly the awkwardness of the past month began to melt. They talked in low whispers, stopping to giggle with a hand over the mouth; Kieran doing a mean imitation of Jake ogling the models as they filed in under his eye. He refilled their brandy at least twice before stretching himself out on the floor beside her with a cushion under his head. It was dark outside—in a corner of the living room a paper light glowed. He turned his head to say something and caught the smell of her freshly washed hair. It was still damp at the ends. Slowly, they slid down until they were lying facing each other, eye to eye. She was so close he could feel her breath on his face. As it had the last time, the knowledge of who they were came up between them—he could see it in her eyes as his hand moved towards the front of her pajamas and slowly began to unbutton them. It disappeared. She slid a hand down the front of his trousers. He was aching for her. He began to kiss her, softly, slowly at first. She unbuckled him. He ran his lips across her face, into the hollow of her neck . . . The taste of perfume just at the collarbone . . . further down. His tongue circled first one taut, hard nipple, then the other. Paola moaned softly as he continued his exploration, her own hands pulling his clothing away from him until they both lay naked beside each other on the floor. This can't be wrong, he thought to himself as he entered her. It cannot be. Nothing that feels this good can be wrong.

Later, when it was almost light, he pulled on his clothes and crept out of the room. Paola was fast asleep, her hair spread out like a silk covering over her back. He slipped down the stairs to his own room, his heart beating fast. He drew the curtains, throwing his clothes over the mirror in the corner of the room and slid into bed. He did not want to see his face in the morning when he awoke.

≈72≈

Max was over the moon. He'd always wanted to learn how to fly. He and Tendé had been discussing it for hours. It was the most practical thing to do. They would keep a small aircraft at the domestic runway in Bamako—it would make getting to Téghaza much easier. After a particularly hard drive there on the last trip, Max told him he'd lost the will to live by the time they actually got there. So—a small Cessna, a twelve-seater . . . Max would take lessons in the U.K.; in the meantime, they'd hire a standby pilot—Tendé had no wish to learn how to fly, he said, laughing—and within a couple of months, Max would be able to fly himself and anyone else they had to take along. It was the perfect solution. He asked his assistant to find the nearest flying school, organize a course of lessons and get him a list of places where he could buy a plane. Now. It was vintage Max.

Within three months, as promised, he got his pilot's license and made the most exhilarating trip of his life with a co-pilot from Gibraltar, where the plane was registered, across the Straits to Morocco and then down over the Sahara to Tamanrasset in Algeria where they refueled, and onto Téghaza. Tendé's men had built—or cleared—a crude landing strip not far from the bungalows that were the project's temporary headquarters.

They were waiting for the first wave of consulting engineers to come and view the site. A vast, white-hot area of some 2,500 square miles, the consultants had recommended a mixture of solar evaporation and vacuum evaporation. Max, exactly as planned, was able to discuss the relative advantages of different extraction techniques with some authority. Tendé looked on as he talked to the government advisors who had been brought to the site ahead of the engineers. He smiled. Jumping out of a plane that he'd flown himself, striding across the desert raising great storms of white dust, Max was in his element.

The engineers were driving up from Timbuktu. A French-Canadian firm had won the tender to do the feasibility study; everyone was looking forward to their arrival. Max and Tendé discussed the upgrading of the bungalows—a couple more, if necessary—for their accommodation. The site survey would take up to three months.

"I'm glad I'm not staying here for three months," Tendé murmured as they drew near the bungalows. "Rather them than me."

"They're getting paid enough for it, believe me," Max said as they pushed open one of the doors. A scorpion ran across the floor. He lifted an eyebrow. "Maybe not."

The next few days were spent driving across the concession, the engineers familiarizing themselves with the terrain, poring over the enormous maps they had brought; setting up survey posts in the chalky sand. They brought drawings with them— large, beautiful blue-tinted sheets covered in their delicate spidery calligraphy, areas dotted in, criss-crossing lines, whole sections of the landscape shaded in blue, yellow, pink. Max looked on, listening to Tendé talk of sector development and product diversification. It was hard to believe the emptiness in which they stood would one day be transformed into anything resembling the glossy CAD drawings spread out over the hood of the Jeep. They still had a long, long way to go, Tendé reminded him as they set off back to base that afternoon. The temperature was almost 110°F . . . a dry, furnace-like heat that swallowed you up as soon as you stepped out of the car. The generators were on full blast as they drove up to the bungalows—they'd had to bring in two enormous 75kvA Ingersolls to power the air-conditioners in the four renovated bungalows and provide the engineers who were staying with all the comforts—radio; satellite telephone link; electric kettles . . . even a toaster. The men who'd come up from Timbuktu with Tendé—the drivers, guards and laborers—looked on in silence as the equipment was carried out from the cars into the temporary homes.

"What are they thinking?" Max asked Tendé as they walked from one bungalow to the other. Tendé shrugged.

"They're used to it . . . white men and the amount of stuff they bring. Look at the tourists. They can hardly move for their cameras, tripods, backpacks, sleeping bags. These people have seen it all before."

"It's obscene," Max murmured as two men carried a portable refrigerator in followed by at least thirty crates of beer.

"If it's the *touboub*—the white men—doing it, it's not so bad. The problems come when some of my men—the government guys—arrive. Like I said, the local people are used to the whites living with all their paraphernalia. They've been coming to Timbuktu for centuries. The Tuareg can stomach that. What they can't stand seeing is how we—black Malians, from the South—now come with the same. Especially when it's their land," he waved his hand around, "that's making it all possible." Max was silent for a moment.

"But surely it's for the good of the country?" he asked, sounding exactly like Amber.

"What country? Mali was the brainchild of the French. Who also tried to create an independent state for the Tuareg, by the way—Azaouad. You've never heard of it?" Max shook his head. "Look, it's the same for them as it was for us, with the French. More autonomy, if not full independence, better prospects, a share of the development pie. The same. In the end, it all boils down to money. The other stuff—different cultures, different races, different ways of life . . . if everybody comes to the table with a full belly the differences magically disappear."

"And that's why you're behind this project?" Max paused. As much as he knew about Tendé and the country he was about to invest most of his wealth in, there were acres of its history about which he was almost completely ignorant. He enjoyed their discussion. Working with Tendé was a million miles away from the early-morning breakfast meetings in New York, the cozy lunches in London, the after-dinner drinks in Paris . . . the grease that made his deals in the West bear fruit. Working here was different. The ideas that floated around over and above the lunches and dinners were big, huge issues about "progress" and "development" and "freedom." Tendé was nearly thirty years his junior. Sometimes he looked at the man and wondered what *he'd* been doing at thirty. Making money. Max had been making money since he was fifteen. There had been a brief, momentary flirtation with the idea of Palestine-Israel. One of the boys from the orphanage—Max struggled to remember his name—had gone there almost as soon as the war ended.

He'd joined some local fighting unit against the British and had come back to London to recruit members. He and Max—Dov! That was his name ... it came back to Max suddenly, in the desert—they'd met up and gone to a café in Willesden. Max could still remember it. Black-and-white checked tablecloths and bottles of watered-down ketchup. He'd listened to what Dov had to say but the ideas he spoke of—independence, freedom, the Jewish State—meant little to him. Max was concerned with making money; *that* was freedom to him; money meant independence. He listened to Dov but he didn't see. That had been at the beginning of his career, he mused. Funny how the same words were coming back to him now.

"What can we do, Max?" Tendé gave a half-smile. "*I* believe economic development is the only condition and basis for peace. There are many people who don't share my view, in my own government. But if we don't attempt to put schemes like this into practice the people here will always be poor. Sure, they have their culture, their way of life, but the world has changed. *Is* changing. Soon these people will have television and radio—many of them already do. They see a different world, a world with Ingersoll generators and refrigerators and cars. It's like I said to Am ... to a friend," he went on quickly, "they want to have the choice, like everyone else. Camel or car. I know which *I'd* choose." Max nodded. He looked around. It had taken him forty years to get to the point where he could afford to talk about issues like these. He wondered what Dov was doing at that very moment. He believed he'd been right to turn his offer down. The thing was, not only was he in a position to talk about the issues, he could *do* something as well. *That* was what forty years of making money had done. Without his wealth he wouldn't be where he was. Standing in the middle of Africa, quite literally, in the clear, dry desert air looking up at the vast volume of white sky tinged with just a hint of blue; in the distance the hazy outline of scorched rocks; and further back still, the beginnings of the canyon walls and the petrified landscape surrounding the Empty Quarter.

He saw the head engineer, Guy Leblanc, coming towards them. An ironically appropriate name, he chuckled to himself as the man drew near.

"Guy," he said, grasping the man's hand. "All settled in?"

≈73≈

There were five of them in the car. Madeleine; her immediate senior, Sven; two Italian psychiatrists and Goran, the young ICM interpreter, stopped at the corner of Cara Dusana and Tadeusa Koscuska, adjacent to the lush green Kalemegdan Park. They were waiting for two British journalists who were seeking cover for a trip to Sarajevo. Heavy fighting had broken out around the city a month before and the team were on their way to bring supplies and relief to the ICM refuge in the town of Ilidza, about two miles from Sarajevo. Everyone was nervous—the reports of fighting and the accompanying brutalities had touched everyone in the office. True or not, there was no way to ascertain the stories except to visit the areas in person. In exchange for driving under the white-flag protection of the ICM, the journalists had agreed to do what they could to publicize the plight of the women they were about to see.

Everyone wore flak jackets over their T-shirts—it was a hot spring day but no one was looking at the weather. The bureau chief at the Associated Press had told them to watch for snipers around Ilidza and to avoid going anywhere near the UN HQ in Sarajevo itself. Madeleine sat in the back with Dr. Carinelli and his assistant, a pleasant, round-faced young woman named Antonia. They passed round chocolates and cigarettes in an attempt to keep their nerves from fraying.

At last the journalists drove up in an extremely battered Volkswagen Golf with a spider's web fracture in the top left-hand corner of the windscreen and bullet holes along one side. Madeleine's eyes widened as she saw the car but she said nothing. The little convoy drove east out of the city.

They stopped in Tuzla for lunch, chatting to the Swedish and Argentinian UN peacekeepers who were sitting at the next table in the small café in the center of the town. They were optimistic. Tuzla was a haven of peaceful co-existence, they said, between the three warring factions—the Serbs, the Croats and the Moslems. Madeleine noticed a sad-faced older man listening to their conversation in the corner of the café. He got up and passed their table as he left, muttering to himself. She couldn't understand the words but the sentiment was clear—you don't know what you're talking about. She looked doubtfully after his back as he shuffled out.

"You English?" One of the journalists sat down in the empty seat beside her. She looked up.

"Yes." She didn't feel like explaining anything further. In England she was Hungarian. In Serbia she was English. It made things a lot simpler.

"London, right?" He rolled a cigarette carefully between nicotine-stained fingers.

Madeleine nodded.

"Yeah, me too. Can always tell a Londoner." He smiled wanly. "I'm Doug, by the way. That's Martin." He pointed with his cigarette to Martin across the room. He got up and ambled over.

"I'm Madeleine." They shook hands.

"So . . . how long've you been here, Madeleine?" Doug asked, inhaling gratefully.

"Two months."

"Long enough."

"Yes. It feels like much longer," she said. "I'm beginning to forget what the outside looks like."

"Wait till you've been here half a year," Martin said with a faint laugh. Madeleine looked at him. He was scruffy in the way all foreign journalists she'd seen were scruffy—a permanent stubble, hair falling into their eyes; clothes thrown on in the middle of the night or day; jeans that looked as though they hadn't been taken off in months . . . they were both wearing dark-green camouflage jackets over flak vests and T-shirts, despite the loveliness of the day outside.

"How long have you been here?" she asked.

"Two years, off and on. We do get out every once in a while. Not like them. Poor fuckers." He waved a hand around the café. "Tuzla's all right, for now. We left Sarajevo last week. That's where we've been living up till now. But we've been ordered to pull back to Belgrade."

"Is it that bad?"

"It's worse."

"Shall we press on?" Sven interrupted them, getting up. They nodded reluctantly. The group broke up. Madeleine made a quick detour to the toilet. She looked at herself in the cracked mirror above the sink. She was virtually unrecognizable. Even to herself.

When she came out a few minutes later, the café was almost empty. She pushed the door open and walked outside. The dark-blue ICM van was already reversing out of the parking lot.

"Here," Doug shouted to her from the VW. "Jump in with us. We're rendez-vousing at Ilidza in an hour, anyway."

She signaled to Sven who was rolling down the window. It is okay? No problem. "See you there," he shouted. She climbed into the back seat.

"Sorry about the mess," Doug said sheepishly. The back seat was covered in cigarette wrappings, empty bottles of beer, newspapers and—a gun. She swallowed.

"Just push it all to one side."

"Are you both armed?"

"Er, yes. We're not supposed to be, but . . . Christ, in this place, you can't afford not to be," Martin said grimly.

"We're not." Madeleine looked at the vehicle ahead of them, its white flag of neutrality fluttering bravely in the wind.

"You should be. Bet they don't tell you that back in London."

Madeleine said nothing. In truth, it was a relief to be sitting in the back seat with the two men— strangers, she thought to herself. But in this time and place, the fact that they were all three from London made them seem safer and more solid, somehow, than the multinational, multilingual crew in the back of the blue van. Plus, they were armed.

She settled down amidst the rubbish and clutter in the back seat, listening with half an ear to their non-stop, slightly manic chatter. It was strangely reassuring.

They passed through the first two checkpoints on the road to Sarajevo without any problems. Doug even chatted briefly to one of the policemen at the second checkpoint in pidgin Serbian. Madeleine dozed on and off in the back, exhausted. The loud drone of the engine made it difficult to join in the conversation.

They were about a mile outside Ilidza when the first signs of trouble appeared. Madeleine woke up as soon as Doug killed the engine. She struggled upright.

"What's happening?"

"Dunno. They're checking papers, I think." Doug lit a cigarette. Their little Golf was about 400 yards from the van. For a moment it looked as though the soldiers would wave them through. Doug started the engine. And then it suddenly went horribly wrong.

"Fuck," Martin said, picking up his camera. "What's he doing?" The three of them strained to see. One of the soldiers had opened the door to the van and was gesticulating with his gun—get out. Madeleine could see Sven getting down from the driver's seat and Goran jumping out on the other side, walking round the van to try and talk to the soldiers. Two more armed soldiers appeared, both shouting and gesturing to the passengers inside the van to get out.

"What's happening?" Madeleine said, fear beginning to rise in her. Doug's hand was twitching on the gear stick. Martin was busy filming.

"Oh, fuck." There was a sharp intake of breath from Doug. Madeleine's hand went out automatically to the window—one of the soldiers had reversed the butt end of his rifle and hit Sven across the face. The two doctors were screaming. She could see their open mouths through the windows of the van. Now more soldiers had appeared, out of nowhere. The blue van was surrounded by militia in their black uniforms and terrifying-looking hoods.

"We'd better get out of here," Doug said, putting the car into reverse.

"No . . . no!" Madeleine shouted as he began moving backwards. One of the soldiers looked up and started pointing at their car. Another took aim.

Doug started reversing the car at breakneck speed, Martin still hanging out of the window filming the whole, sickening scene. Madeleine watched in horror as the soldiers began hauling the ICM workers out of the car. Doug manoeuvred a violent, tire-screeching swing and threw the car forwards. There were shots ringing overhead and the sound of bullets hitting the road. Madeleine's last glimpse was of Sven kneeling in the dust as a soldier casually, almost lazily, put a bullet through his head.

There was no time to think. Doug pushed the Golf to its limit, the engine screaming in protest as they tore back towards Tuzla. Just before the town, he swerved wildly left and the car plowed through a cattle grid and onto a bumpy rural track. The three of them were silent as they flew over ruts and stones. He seemed to know where he was going, zigzagging back towards Sarajevo, avoiding the main route on which they'd been before the shooting started. At last they emerged onto a tarred road. Doug slowed down for a moment.

"Anything behind us?" he asked Martin in a low voice. Martin shook his head. The road ahead was open and clear. In the distance, above the hills, white plumes of smoke kept exploding into the sky. In the back seat, Madeleine was calm. As soon as he reached the city limits, Doug put his foot down again and they tore through the city at ninety miles an hour, dodging the burnt-out buses and concrete barricades that the Serbian Territorial Army had erected on the way. There was no one on the streets. The sun was clear and bright above them and there wasn't a soul in sight. Again Doug seemed to know exactly where to go. They pulled up half an hour later in front of a pock-marked building. The Hotel Sarajevo. It was full of foreign journalists and aid workers. Doug burst into the lobby, his hair standing wildly on end, demanding a radio-linked phone. Martin and Madeleine trailed after him. She had nothing on her, not even a toothbrush. It was supposed to have been a day-trip to the front line to establish a network of support. Martin followed a group of BBC reporters to show them his footage. Madeleine was left standing at the front desk.

"Stay with me." Doug suddenly appeared at her side. His hand pressed down on hers, hard. She nodded wordlessly.

She lay beside him in the dark, hearing but not really listening to the low rumble of artillery fire on the horizon and the occasional thud as something—a rocket, a grenade?—exploded closer to home. There was no question of sex. They lay together in shocked, suspended disbelief, turning every so often and touching, as if to reassure the other that they were still there. Warmth, another living, breathing body; even the clearing of a throat or the rumble of her stomach—she hadn't been able to eat that evening—were comforting. They couldn't sleep so they began to talk. Hesitantly, at first, then with ease. She found herself saying things—surprising, secret things—that she'd never said to anyone else. Alasdair, Péter, even. She could barely bring herself to think about it, much less say it . . . the baby. The child she'd . . . lost. Once she started, she couldn't stop. Words just kept tumbling out. They talked about Budapest and *somlói galuska* and *töltött csirke* . . . things she'd talked to Alasdair about. He got up at one point and rummaged in his bag for something—a bottle of *Hercegovacka loza*, the local spirits. They took turns drinking straight from the bottle. The fierce, rough liquid blazed a trail down her throat. On an empty stomach, she thought to herself as he passed the bottle back. But she didn't get drunk. She lay beside him, surprised and slightly alarmed at the unexpected urge in her to share something of herself with a stranger.

"Who's Péter?" he asked her, his voice coming from just above her ear.

"My brother. He died a long time ago."

"How?"

"He . . . was shot." She turned into the warm flesh of his arms and chest, her mouth moving against his skin as she spoke. "We were running away, from Hungary."

"Bloody hell. So . . . this . . . this *madness* . . . it's not the first time . . . you know something about it, then?"

"A little. I was quite young. I didn't really understand what was going on." She closed her eyes, remembering.

It was Imre who wanted them to go. Endless discussions with Maja, with Péter. He was nineteen then, a university student and youth member of the underground resistance movement, the Hungarian

Democratic Forum. He didn't want to leave. Running away, he told his parents angrily, solved nothing. Better to stay and fight than run and hide. But Imre and Maja worked on him, slowly, all through the cold, bitter winter of 1972. By the spring, he'd reluctantly agreed to come. They decided on the Austrian border—once they got across, it would be relatively easy to apply for asylum. The Austrians had taken in a number of prominent Hungarians; Maja was a banned writer . . . they knew they at least stood a chance.

For weeks Madeleine sat in class with the rest of her friends and kept the secret bound up inside her tightly to herself—no one knew that the pretty, lively ten-year-old with twin blonde pigtails was about to leave, disappear. One minute she was sitting on the edge of someone's desk, the next she'd be gone. They left on 12 February 1973. Madeleine remembered sitting in the back seat of the borrowed car, squashed beside Péter and their two suitcases, listening to her father's terse, worried voice as they drove east on the pretext of visiting relatives in his father's village, close to the Austrian border. Madeleine had never been outside Budapest before. She remembered looking out of the car at the rosy winter sun casting inky, elongated shadows on the pristine white surface of the snow-covered fields around them. They left the car on the outskirts of the forest, covering it with branches while Madeleine held onto her bag, chewing the end of a pigtail and trying not to be sick. She was afraid. It sometimes seemed as though the fear she'd experienced that night had never quite left her. She remembered odd things about the hour that followed—the crunch of the forest floor underfoot; the grip of Maja's hand; the steady, broad backs of Péter and Imre as they led them through the trees to the Austrian border post where they were headed. It was Madeleine who heard the rustle behind them, who stopped suddenly and turned before Péter and Imre could; she pulled her hand out of Maja's and dropped her bag. There was the sound of metal scraping against metal, a shout . . . men's voices . . . she remembered the way Maja screamed to Péter to run . . . the shot . . . the cold, wet snow on her face as Maja and Imre grabbed her and dragged her forwards and, just before they reached the fence, that last glimpse of someone lying face down in the snow, one arm flung away from him and that awful, awful red stain spreading from beneath his stomach and staining the gleaming whiteness around him. Not him. Not someone. Péter.

"Are you asleep yet?" Doug's voice suddenly brought her back to the present. She shook her head, her eyes full of tears. It wasn't often she thought about that night. "Come, let's try and get some rest," he whispered, pulling her close. "It'll be a tough day tomorrow." She nodded, allowing herself to be enfolded in his arms, not trusting herself to speak. She finally dozed off just as a watery dawn broke across the city's skies.

The following morning, there was pandemonium in the hotel lobby. The back of the hotel had just been hit; a mortar had exploded in the TV editing suite and two local technicians had been killed. The BBC had ordered all of its foreign journalists out of Sarajevo. The UN hotel had also been hit, and people were wondering aloud if the TO was targeting foreigners. Above the noise, senior journalists could be heard shouting for calm. Madeleine stood with Doug in the dining room, looking around.

"Do we . . . know what happened yesterday?" she said in a low voice.

Doug looked at her, then nodded. "They were shot. All of them. We're hearing reports that it was Arkanovici." Madeleine looked at him questioningly. "Arkan. Serb nationalist militia leader. He makes the TO look like children." He was quiet for a moment. "I liked Sven," he said finally, heavily. "What a fucking waste." Madeleine was quite. Somehow it didn't seem quite real. Martin came up to them.

"What are you planning to do?" he asked them, somehow addressing them both. Madeleine looked at Doug and lifted her shoulders.

"I don't know. I suppose I'll have to try and get back to Belgrade. Can . . . is it possible to get word through to my offices?"

Doug nodded. "We'll relay the info to London and they can send it on. There are no phone lines left in Sarajevo."

"I'm going back, mate," Martin said, not looking at Doug. "I've got . . . well, you know what I've got. I'm going to hitch a ride out of town with the UN. There's a convoy leaving at 11 a.m. You?"

"I'm staying, mate." Doug looked at Madeleine.

She nodded slowly. Yes, she thought suddenly. Why not? The UN were airlifting all foreign journalists out. She didn't want to be airlifted back to London. There was a sudden thunderous crash from the front of the building. People around them started to run for their rooms, gather their things . . . everyone was anxious to get the hell out of town. Martin shook hands with both of them, then leaned forward and hugged Madeleine suddenly.

"Look after yourself, love," he said thickly, turning away from them. He was crying. Madeleine hadn't shed a single tear since the ambush the day before. He disappeared up the stairs.

"Are you sure about this?" Doug asked her, fingering his unshaven chin nervously. There was another explosion outside.

"I'm sure." Madeleine was calm. "I'm a doctor. There are people dying outside. I can't leave."

"Okay. You ready?"

"I don't have anything with me," she said simply. "My wallet—that's all. I don't even have my passport. It was in the van."

"Let's go, then." He grabbed her by the arm and they ran outside. The Golf was still standing where he'd parked it; there was some fallen debris from one of the explosions on the roof, bits of glass, papers . . . dirt. The car was unlocked. He jumped in, pushing the door open for her. There was a second's hesitation as she turned her head to look at a plane circling overhead, then ducked into the car as she realized it was dropping its payload of bombs somewhere on the city. The ground shook for a few minutes. Doug started the engine. They tore out of the parking lot behind the hotel—what was left of it—and began a mad dash through the central streets of Sarajevo. It was nine o'clock in the morning.

"Where are we going?" Madeleine shouted to him above the noise of rocket explosions and sniper fire.

"Towards Bjelave. It's in the east of the town. A friend of mine, Murad, lives there. It's close to the university hospital. I think we'll be safer there." The car swerved violently to avoid the body of an elderly man, lying face down in a pool of coagulating blood. They fell silent, concentrating only on getting to wherever it was they were going—alive.

≈74≈

Undetected. Unseen. Like anything that goes unnoticed, Kieran and Paola sought out opportunities to meet when and wherever they could. No one saw a thing. Paola spent the summer flying back and forth to London; a few weeks here and there in Menorca; a fortnight in New York; a shopping trip to Paris with Francesca. Autumn was almost upon them when she and Kieran decided on the spur of the moment to go to Menorca for the week. It was late September. The club was doing so well—better than any of them had dared to hope. It had been Jake's decision to open on Fridays and Saturdays only, with just the White Room open to members during the week. It was a smart move; it seemed to make the public

more desperate to be seen there. The window of opportunity, as Digger put it, was small and exclusive,
exactly as they wanted. Max was pleased Kieran
and Paola would be going off for a week in the sun.
They looked like they needed it, he said on his way
out of the house. Kieran was looking rather under
the weather—circles under his eyes, tired all the
time. It would do him good. Strangely, Francesca reported the same; Paola hadn't been very well of
late. She'd lost weight. Yes, it was a very good idea,
she said to Max. What a relief the two of them
seemed to get along so well.

They flew into Menorca on a Monday morning.
Paola had cheered up immensely. The strain of
what was going on was getting to her. She was torn
between confusion and guilt, her moods swinging
like a pendulum from despair to exhilaration. She
had no idea what to think; who to talk to; what to do.
To say there was no future in it was the understate-
ment of the month, the year . . . the century. Eternity. It was wrong. Sick and wrong and nothing
would ever change it. Yet she couldn't get away.
Kieran needed her. He said so a thousand times a
day. She was hypnotized by him—the sound of his
voice, his arm, sliding down hers; the taste of his
mouth . . . she was hooked. She looked around her
quickly at the other passengers, then relaxed. No
one here knew who they were.

   The villa was quiet and peaceful. There was only
Andréa, the maid, around and she left every evening to go back down the hill to her apartment in

town. They were completely alone. On their second morning, they woke up at midday and made plans to spend the day at the beach. They carried towels and books and loaves of ciabatta bread and walked down the rocky incline to the sea. They swam in the turquoise, waveless sea, floating on their backs until their cheeks burned, then turning over to let the cool water rush past their ears. The beach was a ribbon-strip of white sand and steep red and orange-striated gold rock towering above it. The villa stood perched at the top of the hill—from the water's edge it bobbed over and under of her line vision as she treaded water, watching Kieran's brown head as he dived and swam beneath her. They swam round the small headland into a patch of darker blue water. It was cold there and Paola wanted to turn back but Kieran swam on. They reached the shore but it was a rocky beach and Paola wanted to lie in the sand. Kieran laughed at her and tossed pebbles across the still surface of the water. Paola sat on the edge of a rock and watched him.

They swam back just as the sun was beginning to lose its late-summer heat. The air was cooling by the time they reached the villa. Paola wandered off to shower while Kieran rummaged in the kitchen for food.

The bathroom was full of steam when he entered. Through the glass door he could see the rosy pink outline of Paola's body as she stood under the hot stream. He pulled off his shorts and T-shirt and opened the door. A gust of warm spray hit him in the face. Paola squealed as he squeezed in beside her. He took the sponge from her and held it above her face, drenching her already-flattened hair and sending rivulets of water down her neck and breasts. He pulled her to him, burying his face in her shoulder. They turned the taps off together and wandered, arms around each other, still dripping, into the bedroom. Their footsteps dissolved into pools of glistening water on the tiled floor.

Francesca walked through Customs with a smile on her face. She hadn't bothered to phone the villa to let them know she was coming. She wanted to surprise them. She had to admit to feeling rather more kindly disposed towards Kieran, now that he and Paola seemed to have found a friendship. She hailed a taxi as soon as she was outside. She glanced at her watch. It was nearly eleven. She'd caught the last flight from Rome and had had to wait for over two hours in Barcelona—some technical delay. She'd brought tons of food with her; far more than the three of them could eat in three days. She settled herself happily into the back seat of the Mercedes limo and watched the lights of the island speed by as they climbed into the hills.

The villa was completely quiet and dark when she arrived but the silver Mercedes was in the driveway—they'd forgotten to put the car away. She looked at her watch again. It was only half past eleven. She paid the driver and waited as he hauled her bags into the hallway. They must be asleep, she thought, as she switched on the lights. She frowned. There were clothes lying all over the floor and half a sandwich lay uneaten on the dining-room table. She bent down and picked up Paola's bikini bottoms. Silly girl. What was she doing shedding her clothing in the living room? She pushed open the sliding doors that led to the bedrooms and tapped on Paola's door. There was no answer. She opened it quietly and poked her head round the door—the bed was empty. It was still made up. There were a few of Paola's clothes and shoes lying around but she obviously hadn't been sleeping there. She frowned. Where were they? Perhaps they'd been watching TV in one of the spare bedrooms and had fallen asleep? She walked down the corridor. There was light flickering from under the door in one of the rooms. She smiled and pushed open the door.

It was days before she could recall what she'd seen as soon as the door opened without wanting to be sick, physically sick. There had been a stunned silence, followed by a trembling so hard she thought she would fall over. They hadn't noticed her at first. Paola's back was to her. She was . . . she couldn't even bring herself to describe it . . . she was *sitting* on him, his hands moving slowly up and down her back. Francesca stood in the doorway, the light spilling out around her, frozen. He'd seen her first. He hadn't even tried to move. She walked over to the bed and pushed her daughter as hard as she could—and slapped him. Twice. Across the face. And then she'd run from the room, shaking with re-vulsion and fear. Paola had run after her, holding a sheet to herself, crying silently. She'd told her to get back inside her room and to stay there until the morning. Francesca had locked herself in her bedroom, sitting on her hands on the edge of the bed, rocking back and forth, looking at the telephone and knowing she had to call Max. She couldn't sit there all night the only person who knew what was going on—what had been going on. She had to call and tell him, tell someone. But she was afraid. She walked into the bathroom, her face crumpling, and swept away the cosmetics that had been placed there so carefully by Andréa, shoving them aside, hearing the bottles crash and break against the marble floor. She fell to her knees, retching.

Kieran left on the first flight in the morning. He left before anyone got up. He called a taxi and climbed in without taking so much as a bag with him. He flew back to London, alone, and waited for the storm to break over his head.

≈75≈

"I need something cheerful," Amber said to Tendé as she came into the room.

"Like what?" He straightened up from putting a CD into the stereo. A woman's melodic, soulful voice filled the air.

"Anything. I just need to do something light and entertaining and . . . and cheerful. You have no idea what we've been through in the past couple of months." She walked over to stand behind him and wrapped her arms around his waist. "This is good," she said, listening to the music with her cheek against his back. "What is it?"

"My mother."

"Really?" She smiled. "You know, from where I'm standing your family seems just about perfect."

"Oh, no . . . no." Tendé shook his head, smiling. "We have our moments, too, believe me."

"No, but mine . . . I still can't quite believe what's happened. I don't think any of us can."

"Try not to judge him, Amber. He probably doesn't understand it himself."

Amber sighed. "I know. You're right. But whenever I look at him I just can't get it out of my head—"

"What d'you think it's like for him?" Tendé interrupted her gently.

"Why are you so bloody magnanimous? You never even liked him," Amber protested, stepping away from him. He turned round and caught her arm.

"Because. He's your brother . . ."

"And she's my sister!" she said hotly.

"Exactly. You ought to show more compassion." Amber stared at him, her temper beginning to rise. He shook his head at her. "Don't. Don't get angry. We've got other things to worry about right now. They'll get over it. You said it yourself. They've both been sent to . . . what d'you call it? . . . counseling? They'll find a way. Now, you wanted something light and cheerful?" She nodded reluctantly. "Let's go to dinner. You want to eat *à l'Africaine*?" he smiled at her. "And then we'll go dancing. There's a new club that's just opened in the center of town. Some of my friends will probably be there." Amber's eyes lit up. It was her second trip to Mali. The first one, almost a year earlier, had been on very different terms. She came willingly into his arms.

"I'm sorry. I didn't mean to get angry with *you*. I'm just . . . tired, I guess."

"I know. But we'll go out tonight and have a good time. Max arrives on Saturday so let's make the most of this. I have a feeling things are going to get a lot more complicated." Amber shook her head against his neck.

"No, he'll be fine. I promise."

"We'll see." Tendé kissed the tip of her nose. "You want to take a shower before we go?"

"Yes. It's so dusty. It wasn't like this the last time I came."

"It's the Harmattan. The winds that blow down from the desert. It'll be like this for a couple of months, I'm afraid. Today's not so bad, actually. Sometimes you can hardly see more than a few feet in front of you."

"Yuck. It's horrid."

"You'll get used to it."

She pulled away from him and searched his face. "Will I? And the other things?"

"You'll get used to those too. Now, come on. You said you wanted a cheerful night. Take your shower and get ready. I'll make a few phone calls and then we'll go. *D'accord*?" She nodded. "Now go." He steered her in the direction of the bathroom.

*   *   *

He heard the sound of running water and walked slowly through the living room into his study. He paused at the doorway, running a hand round the back of his neck. He was also tired. It had been a punishing few weeks of traveling, meetings, facing the press—the feasibility study had suddenly shown everyone just what wealth the country was sitting on and the media scrutiny of the proposed deal had been intense. Max was arriving in two days' time— and on top of it all, Amber had decided that now was the time to tell him. He still wasn't sure the timing was right, especially after the upheavals in their family in the past few months. In fact, he wasn't sure it would ever be right. Amber seemed to think he'd take it in his stride. He liked Tendé so much, and he would want her to be happy . . . she had a dozen reasons why it wouldn't be the shock Tendé predicted. He had one large, looming reason why it would be—he was black. He and Amber had argued incessantly over it.

"Your sister's married to a Swiss guy," she kept pointing out.

"It's not my parents we're dealing with, Amber. They don't care. It's not about color with them, you know that. They couldn't care less."

"Well, it's the same with Max. He won't care. I promise."

"So why haven't you told him already?" Tendé asked.

Amber was silent. "Because . . . because you're frightening me," she said eventually.

"That's bullshit and you know it."

She turned away. "Okay. Well, we're going to tell him soon, aren't we?"

"Whenever you're ready."

And now she was. He picked up the glass of water she'd left on the sideboard. It was unusually dusty. The winds were particularly strong this year, he thought to himself as he swallowed. He was flying up to Téghaza ahead of Max the following morning. Amber would meet Max at Tendé's parents' home, where he always stayed when in Bamako. She wanted to tell him alone, she said, and let him get used to the idea before he flew himself up to meet Tendé in Téghaza on Sunday morning. He turned. Amber was ready and waiting by the door. She looked beautiful. Her hair was longer now and fell around her face in thick, dark curls. He liked it when it was long. He liked holding the wayward curls in his hands. The short, spiky cut of a few months ago he found too boyish, severe.

At the restaurant, the newly opened l'Akwaba near the Hippodrome, he watched her order *riz gras* and *nkontomire*, a Ghanaian dish. *Akwa'aba*, the waiter told her, meant "welcome" in Twi, one of the many Ghanaian languages. Her French was good and she chatted unselfconsciously to the waiter and the proprietor who came over to greet them. It was one of the things he liked about her. She wasn't like so many of the Europeans in town who either fawned over the locals, proclaiming everything "wonderful" and "amazing" or like those who treated everyone and everything with a weary, seen-it-all-before contempt. Amber treated Mali the way she treated everything else—it was life. Sure, there were differences but she met those intellectually, not emotionally. Beggars were beggars. Flies were flies. And the Harmattan was horrid. The *nkontomire*, when it arrived, was delicious but the *riz gras* was disgusting. Rice cooked in tomato soup. He laughed delightedly.

They left the restaurant at midnight—in Bamako, like in Paris, he explained, the nightlife of the city didn't really start until after midnight. The weekend began on Thursday night—tonight—and would continue until Sunday afternoon. The Sunday early-evening prayers signaled its end. Amber nodded. She liked the call to prayer that resonated throughout the city although Tendé pointed out that in his neighborhood, and his parents', the mosques weren't allowed to carry loudspeakers which was probably why. She disagreed. For her it gave the day a different set of rhythms; people moved according to a slightly different beat. In London, she argued, the day was divided by the two rush-hours; her daily movements were engineered to occur either before or after the onslaught.

"D'you know how I can tell it's a Sunday morning?" she asked as they walked towards his car. He shook his head. "It's the absence of noise," she said. "There aren't any cars on the street. I get woken up by the silence."

"You ready for some silence now?" Tendé shouted to her over the extraordinary din of music and laughter in the club. She nodded, sucking desperately on an ice cube to cool her down. It was almost four. They'd been dancing for hours. They said goodbye to Tendé's friends and fought their way through the crowd to the car. He was incredibly well-known. All sorts of people had come up to him in the four hours they'd been inside the *boîte*. Older men, obviously friends of his parents' generation; his own friends, the young men in suits and jeans who looked and acted pretty much like men in their thirties any-where—leaning against the bar with a beer in one hand, idly nudging each other when a good-looking girl walked past; the owner of the club and the DJ—and the girls. Amber was amazed at how beautiful the women were—stunning creatures, so beautiful and elegant it hurt your eyes to look at them. She felt like a thin, ghostly shadow standing next to them with their brilliantly made-up faces and clothes from another world. There were one or two who looked at her in frank disapproval—or disappointment, she couldn't tell. They laid their arms on Tendé's forearm and made clucking noises of . . . dismay? Sympa-thy? She couldn't tell. Curiously, she wasn't jealous. She'd never felt worried or insecure with Tendé, not as she had been with Henry. He used to engineer things to *make* her worried. She stopped. She really didn't want to think about Henry because that would mean thinking about Becky—and she wasn't ready to think about *that*.

"Tired?" Tendé's voice broke in on her thoughts. She turned to him in the darkness of the car and put a hand on his knee.

"No . . . yes . . . hot. And thirsty."
"I know. It's the wind."

She wanted to switch the light off when they were lying in bed, in the tangle of damp limbs and touches that would turn any second now to caresses but he put out a hand to stop her. He liked seeing her face when he made love to her—it was usually hard to know what women feel in that moment of inarticulate sweetness—because Amber's face was unusually expressive and he loved watching it. She mumbled a protest but sank back into the sheets, squealing as he pulled her on top of him so that she lay along the length of his body and her blue-grey eyes were directly above his. Her face was lightly freckled. He drew her mouth into his, wanting to be swallowed by her, whole and complete. They lay there like that for a while, their heartbeats fused until she—not he; he laughed—couldn't stand it a second longer and moved, sliding onto him, swallowing him now, properly. He was the one who closed his eyes then. His inarticulate pleasure was complete.

They woke just a few hours later to the sound of Tendé's watch. He groaned and sat up. It was 6:30 a.m. He glanced at Amber, who was already drifting off back to sleep. He shook his head to clear it and slid carefully out of the bed. There was a car coming to fetch him at seven and take him to the airport. He had to hurry. He walked, naked, into the bathroom. His skin felt dry and itchy as it always did at that time of year. It wasn't hot—not enough for the air-conditioning, at least—but it was uncomfortably dry. He took a quick, cool shower, brushed his teeth and stowed away a few things in his overnight bag. He and Max would be returning to Bamako on the Tuesday. He paused for a second. By then, he'd know. He knew he appeared to Amber as though he didn't really care what Max thought, but of course he did. He would never say it to her but he was more than a little nervous of his reaction. He couldn't say exactly what it was he feared. Tendé was a man who liked to keep things in neat, separate-if-possible categories. Work was work; politics was politics; love was love. In Amber, however, the boundaries were blurred and the contexts were murky; it wasn't a situation he relished.

Amber woke up a few hours later. She lay in the semi-shuttered darkness listening to the sounds of the outside world and reveling in its unfamiliarity. Somewhere outside, beyond the high wall they'd driven through when they arrived the night before, dogs were barking. A cockerel still crowed. Someone was riding a bicycle up and down the street, ringing the bell and calling out something—for sale, perhaps? She turned her head. There was a glass of water beside the bed. She drank thirstily. It was ten o'clock. Max would have arrived already. He enjoyed staying at Tendé's parents house—he couldn't stand the hotels in Bamako, he said. It was like being in London or New York, except the telephones rarely worked and there was seldom any hot water. She sat up and examined her legs; her skin was so dry. She got up, stretching her arms above her head, yawning. There was a knot of excitement and apprehension in the pit of her stomach. Max had no idea she was there. She would appear at their home that morning, surprising him. Tendé had thought it a bad idea—*what if he has a heart attack?*—but how else would she do it? They would have lunch and then everything would be out in the open; Max would have had time to get over his surprise . . . a glass or two of wine to celebrate and she would go out to the airport with him. Over and done with by 3 p.m. and then everyone could get on with their lives. Tendé had already told his mother. As soon as Max was informed, they would make it public.

An hour later, her skin still oily from the lashings of body lotion she'd poured over herself, she walked into the sitting room and looked around her with interest. It was strange; they'd been together for nearly a year and yet this was the first time she'd seen his home, where he lived. She liked the feel of the bungalow—masculine and quite dark . . . it suited him. There wasn't much furniture: a leather sofa, cane chairs covered in a rather nice blue and black pattern; low coffee table. In one corner of the room was a stack of CDs and records. She wandered over. She'd never heard of most of the bands . . . mostly African, by the look of them. She picked up his mother's CD. *Mandia Diabaté—Live in Concert at the Palais des Nations*. There were several of her albums amongst the stack. She was a handsome-looking woman but she and Tendé were not alike. He'd told her he took after his father, not his mother. She seemed rather formidable. She put the CDs down and picked up one of the framed photographs on the sideboard. Yes, he looked like his father. He was standing with Yasser Arafat and . . . she squinted . . . Gaddafi of Libya? Yes. She put it down. There was another one of a light-skinned young woman, her head turned towards the camera, slightly out of focus. She was very beautiful— thick, curly black hair; dark, sleek eyebrows; coffee-colored skin and a wide, red-lipped smile. She stared at it for a few seconds before putting it down. An old girlfriend, no doubt. She turned away from the display. The door to the study was open and she stood in the doorway, looking in. There were many books, a desk with a laptop computer and printer, two telephones, an open briefcase stuffed with papers; newspapers in English, French . . . Russian. *Russian?* She walked in and picked it up. Another of the many things she didn't know about him. She turned away and walked off to find the cook. Perhaps she could help with preparations for lunch. Anything to take her mind off Max's imminent arrival.

"D'you know . . . it'll be Christmas soon," Doug said softly. Madeleine looked up.

"Christmas?" The thought seemed preposterous.

"Yeah. It's the fifteenth today, right?" She looked at her watch.

"Yes, I suppose you're right." They looked at each other. That meant they'd been in the flat on Provare Street for seven months. Seven months of slowly deteriorating living conditions . . . so slow that you got used to it. The stranglehold that the Serbian army had placed on the city was choking it to death, hour by hour. All but the most basic supplies—bread, petrol, matches—had dried up and the winter was beginning to set in. A flourishing black market had sprung up and was now firmly in the hands of the criminal mafia. The price of goods began to rocket: an egg could cost £1.50 on the black market and that winter, the average monthly wage was roughly the same. The real danger as November slipped into December, was the cold. Almost all the trees in Sarajevo and the suburbs had been cut down, so people were now turning to books. Murad, in whose flat they were living, commented one night that people were making inventories of what they were burning—whole personal libraries were turned to fuel. In a rare display of black humor, he told them that Lenin and Marx were the first to go, followed by cheap, romantic novels. Shakespeare and Chekhov were saved till last. Madeleine laughed that night until her sides ached. She'd almost forgotten how.

But in the Croat-controlled areas west of the city, prices were still relatively low. A huge smuggling operation sprang into action between the Croat inhabitants of the city and the outlying regions. But the territory the smugglers had to cross at night was largely controlled by Serb forces—hundreds were wounded or killed by snipers. Many of them were brought to the University Hospital where Madeleine worked, sometimes for twenty-four hours straight. Yet neither of them could think about leaving. Doug was obsessed with recording and bearing witness to the slow murder of the city and Madeleine could scarcely remember what life had been like before. Murad had been a journalist, before—now he was a "fixer," bringing in precious supplies of food and medicine from places neither Madeleine nor Doug could bring themselves to ask about. She and Doug were friends and occasional lovers, sharing what had once been Murad's parents' bedroom. They had both gone to visit relatives in Goradzde about a week before the fighting broke out and had never returned. Sometimes when the strain of operating without anesthetic or turning patients away from the hospital doors got too much to bear, Madeleine would turn to Doug at night and sex was a welcome, if temporary relief. London seemed like another life.

And yet . . . there were other things, too. Other

reasons to stay. She had never experienced such calm within herself, such surety about what she was doing and where it might take her. She had found a source of strength in herself that had nothing to do with the old touchstones of personal fulfillment and "happiness" such as she'd struggled with for so long, back there. In Sarajevo, under the most desperate conditions imaginable, she had somehow found herself. In the midst of the terror and the sickening squalor, she felt herself strangely released. She wrote sporadically to her parents and to Amber. The UNHCR personnel who brought medical supplies to the hospital, whenever they could, would always take letters back for her and once or twice, someone had actually delivered one through.

"Mads." Doug looked up from the newspaper he was reading. Somehow, despite it all, the two daily newspapers, *Oslobodjenje* and *Vecernje Novine*, were still being produced. Doug was able to follow a little of what was written.

"Mmm?"

"I don't believe it! There's a production of *Hair* on at the National Theatre on the twenty-fifth. On Christmas Day. Shall we go?" His tone was incredulous. Madeleine looked up, smiling.

"Yes," she said slowly. "I'd like that. I'd like that very much." He squeezed her shoulder as he walked to the kitchen to make some tea. She looked at her hands. They were rough and calloused now, the knuckles reddened and raw-looking. No hand creams, no after-surgery lotions, no long hot soaks in the bath. She smiled suddenly, thinking of Becky.

She'd always been so darned fussy about her hands. She wondered what she was doing. She hadn't written to Becky since . . . well, almost since Alasdair died. Sadness and grief and hardship weren't really Becky's department, or so she said. Good-time girl, that was her. She pulled a face. Becky too seemed like another life.

At that moment, lying on his shabby sofa in London, Henry began to realize that actually, maybe Becky was right. He'd been dead set against it when she'd first brought it up but now . . . well, maybe it wasn't such a bad idea after all. In less than a month he'd be leaving England behind for a new job—and a new life, he hoped—where he'd always longed to be. Back home. In Africa. He'd seen the advertisement in the back pages of the *Daily Telegraph* and applied on the spot. He'd been hired after a telephone call and a quick check of the records at Prince Edward Academy. He was going out to help an elderly English couple run a guest house at their farm halfway between Chinhoyi and the small town of Zave, about 125 miles to the northwest of Harare. Ironically, the farm lay at the foothills of Mount Fletcher. That, the delighted Mrs. Fairfield said, had clinched him the job. The salary was deplorable by British standards but he would have his own cottage on the estate, a small share of the profits and the chance to live where he'd always wanted to— back home. He quit his job at the Refugee Council the minute he'd had their confirming letter. He left the same day. He'd never really given a damn about the refugees anyway. He couldn't understand why they were clamoring to get out of Africa—he was clamoring to get *in.*

And then there was the question of Becky. She'd been staying with him since Charlie had thrown her out. They'd drifted into a strange kind of limbo—without Charlie's shadow hovering over their shoulders, things between them had fizzled out, almost to a halt. She'd been so miserable those first couple of months. Amber, it seemed, hadn't taken the news well. She kept saying she wasn't upset about him, she just couldn't believe Becky hadn't told her, or lied. He had to offer Becky a place at his; she'd sooner have died than gone back to her parents and without a job, and very little money . . . well, what else was she going to do? She moved in and now, after nearly eight months, she seemed like a pretty permanent feature. Thinking about Amber with . . . *that* man . . . had nearly killed him. It still did every time he thought about it. Maybe leaving the country would help him get away from it all. He'd told Becky, of course. She'd gone very quiet and then gone into the bedroom and shut the door and, the truth be told, he actually couldn't be bothered to get up and go after her.

She'd come to him, finally, a few days later, with An Idea. Why didn't she come with him? They could both help to run the place. She was good at . . . at cooking and decorating and making guests feel comfortable . . . she'd be brilliant at it. She could come for a few months—she'd borrow the air fare from her parents; he wouldn't have to pay—and then they'd see. If it didn't work out, she would come back. Simple as that. It would be a whole new life for him out there. It might be lonely, too, with only Mr. and Mrs. Fairfield for company . . . and they sounded old and settled. With her there, they'd do things together; he could show her the countryside he was always talking about; they could go camping together . . . go to the beach. He refrained from telling her that Zimbabwe was landlocked and didn't *have* a beach.

At first the idea filled him with dread. He wanted to get away from the mess he'd made in England, not bring it back with him. But Becky wasn't pushy; she just told him to think about it and actually, the more he thought about it, the better it began to sound. She was good at putting a home together— in the few months she'd been at his place, it was almost completely transformed. Her things were all over the place: little baskets filled with interesting magazines; books in the toilet that he actually found himself reading; her cosmetics on the shelf. She'd found a pair of bed sheets in one of the cupboards and turned them into curtains in his bedroom; she nicked flowers from the park down the road and put them in a jug on the table in the kitchen . . . yes, she was good at that sort of thing. Plus his clothes were always washed and it was rare for him to come home and not find something to eat.

He heard her key in the lock. She'd been round to her parents'.

"Becks?" he called out. She came up the stairs, her face pink and rosy from the cold. She was wearing a white woollen hat with matching gloves—she looked pretty and fresh, just as she had done when they first met. He didn't like thinking of her in the weeks after leaving Charlie, her face permanently squeezed in pain, tears sliding down her cheeks. He liked her smiling and sunny with clean, sweet-smelling hair and nice knickers. "Becks," he said, getting up from the couch. She looked at him expectantly. "I've decided. Yeah. Let's do it. Let's go together." She looked at him with such gratitude he thought his heart would burst.

"Oh, Henry. You won't . . . it'll be great, I promise. It'll be wonderful. You'll see." She came and sat beside him on the couch with her hat and gloves still on. He pulled one off, turning her hand round in his. He looked at her fingers. He'd never asked her what she'd done with Charlie's engagement ring, that huge, almost vulgar diamond. He'd probably asked for it back.

"Yeah, it'll work out. I'll tell the Fairfields tomorrow. They did ask if I had a wife." She turned to him and kissed him. Her lips were cold but her tongue was hot. He opened the front of her coat.

It took longer than they thought to get everything organized. Ironically, it was Henry's visa and work permit that held them up. All through January and February he waited in line at the Zimbabwe High Commission in Trafalgar Square. Becky began to think they might never leave. She had money for her air ticket and she held £2,000 in traveler's checks, courtesy of a small jeweler's shop in Camden where she'd sold her ring. *The* ring. Henry didn't ask where she'd got the money and she didn't say. She had another reason for wanting to leave England. Her overdraft currently stood at at least double that amount and she didn't see why she should sell her ring to pay *that* off. It wouldn't—so what was the point? Charlie had never said a thing about paying back the expenses she'd racked up on his behalf and she wanted to leave it all behind.

Finally, in the last week of February, Henry had his British passport stamped with the necessary permits and they were able to leave.

They landed at Harare International Airport on a beautiful, hot autumn day. They were in the southern hemisphere, now, he told her, although strictly speaking, Zimbabwe was actually in the tropics. But most of the country was at relatively high altitude and as such, was cooler than most of the surrounding tropical countries. They took a bus into town and stayed a night at the Courteney Hotel in the center of the city, a pretty hotel with a pool. Becky turned to him as he came in the room, her eyes shining. It was exactly as she'd pictured it—lush, green, pretty flowers. She was going to *love* Zimbabwe, she declared. He looked at her blankly. Harare had thrown him—it was nothing like the rather sleepy, quiet city he'd known as a teenager. He wasn't sure quite what he'd expected but the tremendous surge of anticipation that had gripped him as soon as they landed had all but disappeared. No one recognized him, no one seemed in the least bit interested that his British passport gave his place of birth as

Gweru, which was where his father had once had a farm. Black Zimbabweans, far from recognizing him as some sort of long-lost brother regarded him the way they regarded all white tourists—a quick chance to make a few dollars and a necessary evil to be smiled at and discarded as soon as he walked past.

He phoned the Fairfields from the lobby and told them they would be with them the following afternoon. They were to take a bus from Harare to Chinhoyi and phone from there. It was only a half-hour drive to Chinhoyi, Mrs. Fairfield said—they'd come to the central bus station to meet them. Becky wondered how they were going to lug their five suitcases onto a bus but . . . she shrugged. They'd managed. In the meantime, didn't he want a swim? Henry shook his head. He couldn't explain it to her—he didn't want to sit by the pool with the other translucently pale guests, being waited upon by servants in their bleached white uniforms like tourists on a cheap holiday.

"But we *are* tourists," Becky said, puzzled. "Aren't we?"

"*You* might be. I'm not." Henry was sullen. Becky sighed. She didn't know what had come over him since they'd arrived. He'd suddenly become so moody.

"Well, I'm going for a swim," she said, tying the straps on her bikini. Henry didn't look up. She picked up her towel and walked out. He was being silly. A swim would do him good after their ten-hour flight. She had hardly slept a wink. Falling asleep in the late afternoon sun was *exactly* what she needed.

When she came back there was a note from Henry on the bed. He'd gone for a quick walk and would meet her downstairs in the bar in an hour. She shrugged. He probably needed some time to get used to being back. She'd forgotten how long it was since he'd been here . . . had he come to England as a baby? She couldn't remember. She peeled off her swimsuit, noticing she'd already gone a nice, healthy pink and disappeared into the bathroom.

She was wearing one of those pretty dresses, Henry noticed as he walked into the hotel bar. A few young white men were hovering near her and he felt a tiny flicker of pride. He walked over, put his hand on her shoulder and kissed her, on the lips . . . she was pleased. He pulled up a stool next to her and watched as the other men sloped off to nurse their drinks in silence. She's mine. Hands off. It was a language universally understood. He ordered a beer and some *boerewors*—South African spicy sausages. She tasted it when it came and pulled a face.

"Yuck. It's like haggis." He laughed at her expression and finished it off. Three beers and two *boerewors* later, his good humor was restored. He enjoyed watching Becky get tipsy on her South African white wine and order a plate of chips—laughing at her when the barman asked with a straight face, "Cheese and onion, madame, or salt and vinegar?"

"Fried potatoes," Henry translated for her. "French fries." The barman nodded. Ten minutes later she had a plate of pale, rather soggy chips.

"What do people here eat?" she asked innocently. There was a small sound from the barman— laughter? Henry colored.

"Sadza, mostly. It's a kind of porridge," he said in a low voice. "That's the staple food."

"Is that what you eat? It sounds horrid."

"Er, no. I mean . . . well, you'll see. There's all sorts of things. Anything you want."

Becky nodded. "I think I'm really going to like it here," she said happily. "I really do." Henry lifted his beer. He hoped so. He hoped *he* would. To him, it was still unsettlingly strange.

"Henry? Henry Fletcher?" Someone shouted his name. Henry looked up. A large, very red-faced man was standing beside a white pick-up truck waving at them.

"That must be them," he said to Becky. He waved back.

"Blimey." Becky stared at them. Mrs. Fairfield looked like a walking tent. A walking flowered tent. She wasn't at all what she'd expected. They started dragging their cases over.

"Hullo! I'm right, aren't I?" Mr. Fairfield shouted as they approached the truck. It was a double-cab, rather battered pick-up. A small, lithe black man was crouched in the back of the truck.

"Henry Fletcher." Henry stuck out his hand. Mr. Fairfield took it, pumping it enthusiastically. "And this is my girlfriend, Becky." Mr. Fairfield almost took Becky's hand off its socket. Wincing, she turned to Mrs. Fairfield. She smelled of rose-water and talcum powder and beamed at them both. Mr. Fairfield shouted something to the man in the back who immediately sprang down and began stacking their cases. Becky rushed forward to help but was shyly brushed aside. She turned—they couldn't just stand there and let him do all the work?—but Henry was talking to the Fairfields. They clambered into the truck, the Fairfields in front; she and Henry in the back seat and the poor man out in the back crouched beside the suitcases with no protection from the burning sun.

"Is he . . . will he be all right there?" she asked Mrs. Fairfield as they set off. "I mean, there's plenty of room here in the back. We could squeeze up, if you like." Henry nudged her, annoyed. She turned to look at him, puzzled.

"Oh, don't worry about Mishak, dear. He's fine. They don't feel the heat," she said blithely. Becky opened her mouth to say something but Henry nudged her again. Don't. She sat back, astounded. What on earth did she mean?

The ride was short and the landscape breathtaking. It was almost English in its rolling, lush greenery and neatly bordered farms, nothing like what she imagined Africa to be. No wonder Henry missed it. It was beautiful. They turned off the main road by a cluster of majestic-looking, grey-green trees and rode down a track that could have been somewhere in rural France. A row of evenly spaced trees on either side of the track had grown to intertwine their branches overhead; they sped down the dusty track, filtered green light dappling the road, casting long dancing shadows in the late afternoon sun. They pulled up in a yard full of old trucks and the disemboweled remains of pick-ups and the kinds of old cars you didn't see in England any more, she noticed—a Morris Minor, a Ford Capri. Becky looked about her in surprise as they got out of the pick-up. A row of men had appeared as soon as Mr. Fairfield drove through the open gate; they now proceeded to take the suitcases from Mishak and walked in single file towards the main house. It was a long, curving thatched-roof house, in mock Tudor style with thick, blackened beams and painted a bright white. A cerise bougainvillea covered almost the entire west-facing side of the house; in the garden beyond were plants the color and texture of which Becky had never seen. It was English; and yet it was not. Creepers, hibiscus flowers, golden shower creepers, the dazzling glimpse of a turquoise pool . . . she turned to stare, open-mouthed at Henry.

"You'll have the cottage at the foot of the gardens," Mrs. Fairfield was saying to them as she led them through the house. "It's got pretty much everything you need, I think you'll find."

"You've got a lovely home, Mrs. Fairfield," Becky said, following her.

"Call me Daisy, dear." Becky had to stifle a giggle. "The guest cottages are on this side of the property. There's six of them altogether. We had them built last year. In the same style as the rest of the estate. Pretty, don't you think?" She pointed at them through the French windows. Henry and Becky nodded dutifully. "Well. I'll leave you two to get settled in,"

Mrs. Fairfield said, lumbering away from the windows. "We do laundry on Tuesdays—Charlene will come in and collect it and bring it back, the boys will tend to the garden and there's someone comes in to do the pool once a week. I never swim but you're welcome to use it when we don't have guests."

"And getting into town . . . shopping and stuff like that?" Henry asked.

"You can use the old Morris. It used to be mine but I can't fit behind the steering wheel these days!" Mrs. Fairfield burst into peals of laughter. "And if there's anything heavy, you know, anything big, you can ask Horace for the pick-up. He usually goes into town every other day. There's a small supermarket just past the junction on the main road and there's a Woolworth's in Chinhoyi." Henry nodded. It all seemed straightforward and exactly as they'd said. He turned to Becky.

"Well, thanks very much, Mrs. Fairfield. I'm sure we'll find our way around pretty soon. We'll . . . er, leave you to it," he said, a little uncertainly.

"Oh, call me Daisy. Do. There's a bit of food in the refrigerator, and milk and cereal and so on for tomorrow. And if you need anything, just shout for Charlene. Now, I must find what Horace is up to. If I don't keep an eye on him . . ." she let out another guffaw and disappeared into the kitchen. Henry and Becky looked at each other and grinned.

"Come on, then . . . might as well go home," Henry said, pushing the French doors open. A small bush dog was lying in a corner of the patio, growling menacingly as they passed. They walked down the green lawn to the cottage at the foot of the slope. It was thatched, like the main house, and almost entirely covered in white bougainvillea and a reddish, ivy-like plant. Henry pushed the door open cautiously.

"Oh." Becky stood in the entrance, gaping. Plain whitewashed walls, a terracotta-tiled floor, simple furniture and long, almost floor-to-ceiling windows. The ceiling was low with simple hanging paper lanterns; there was a console with a rather old TV and a video machine. She walked into the center of the room and slowly turned around. "It's lovely," she breathed. Henry looked relieved. He walked into the bedroom. Becky followed him. A low, wide double bed lay in the center of the room surrounded by a white, billowing mosquito net. The windows in the bedroom were shuttered. Becky walked across and opened one. It looked out directly onto the pool at the top of the incline. Becky couldn't wait to take photographs to send to her parents, Madeleine . . . Amber. She wanted to show them that despite the stupid mistakes of the past year, she'd landed on her feet and that she was going to be okay. Really okay. She felt a slight twinge as she pictured them looking at her new home, her new life. After what had happened, she wasn't sure if Amber cared.

The first few days passed quickly. There was a lot to see and learn. Becky wondered out loud how Henry had ever thought he would manage alone. There were the guest cottages to be cleaned and swept each day; the gardens had to be overseen; in the office at the "manor," as she and Henry quickly dubbed it, there were phone calls, bookings to be confirmed, a calendar of activities to be planned. It would be Henry's job to lead expeditions from the farm to Lake Kariba; they had a man, Jock, whom they paid to take their clients on the five- and seven-day trips they organized down the Zambezi River but it was Henry's job to collect them from the game lodge at Mana Pools at the end of each trip and bring them back down. It was a lot of driving, he said to Becky as they traced the route on a map. For a Mom-and-Pop outfit such as the Fairfields ran, everything was surprisingly well-organized. They put on one or two expeditions a month, of groups of anywhere between four to sixteen people, charging an astronomical amount for the privilege, which the British, American, German and Swedish tourists seemed only too happy to cough up. Where did the money go? Henry wondered. It certainly wasn't being spent on the farm—as far as he could make out, the farm pretty much ran itself. The workers weren't getting any of it, that was certain. He saw them in the early mornings or late afternoons coming back from the fields; a ragtag crew of barefoot men in tattered overalls, sharing a laugh or a cigarette, falling silent whenever he approached. These were not the smiling, happy faces of the farm workers of his childhood—these men were sullen, their faces etched with worry the way some in other parts of Africa drew elaborate tribal markings to identify this one or that. The men on the Fairfields' farm were tired and resentful with an anger lying just below the surface of their burnished skins made dusty and grey from hoeing and digging the ungiving earth. He wondered what the Fairfields actually grew. Tobacco, he was told a few days later. They owned a piece of land that stretched almost to the horizon. But tobacco prices were falling and it was hard to get the labor they needed at the prices they wanted. Tourism seemed a fail-safe option and one to which many of the white farmers around them had turned. Problem was, Horace Fairfield confided to Henry, he wasn't getting any younger and running around after rich Americans all day could wear one out, even if some of the women . . . he winked heavily and passed a handkerchief round his red, sweating face. Henry grunted. Horace Fairfield made him feel rather ill. But it was a job, he reminded himself half a dozen times a day. A job in the sun, back home, where he thought he belonged.

Amber knew Max had arrived. She could tell by the way the house suddenly changed pitch. The dogs next door started barking, there was the squeal of tires on the gravel and the sound of feet running to meet the car. She smoothed down her dress, quickly adjusted the straps of her camisole top and got up from the chair she'd been sitting in, waiting for the moment to arrive. She walked to the door. Sure enough, Max's greying head emerged from the back of the Mercedes. He looked up as she opened the door. If he was surprised or shocked to see her in Bamako, he made no sign. He shut the door behind him carefully and walked towards her, his expression almost completely blank.

"Max," she said, coming out of the shadows and moving into the blinding afternoon light.

"Amber." Max walked forward and kissed her, once on either side. His grasp on her upper arm was firm. "Tendé's father told me you were here." Amber nodded cautiously.

"Were you . . . shocked?" she asked nervously. Max was still for a second. Then he shook his head.

"No. Not shocked. Surprised, maybe." Amber frowned. Max's tone was so unlike him. Calm, detached . . . it wasn't him. She led him inside, into Tendé's sitting room.

"We . . . I . . . we didn't know how to . . . you know, tell you," she began awkwardly. "I wanted to say something in London. But with everything that's happened, we just thought it would be . . . better . . . nicer . . . to tell you out here."

Max nodded slowly. "Well, that was considerate of you," he said mildly. Amber looked at him. Was he joking? Was he angry? She couldn't tell. The Max sitting on one of Tendé's low, comfortable chairs was not the Max she knew.

"Would you like something? Some tea? Coffee?" she asked, aware of how stilted her own voice must sound. She wished he would just get angry, if that was what he wanted to do. She wasn't sure how long she could continue sitting there, politely asking if he wanted this or that. She was worried—polite acquiescence was not Max's way of doing things. She glanced at her watch—it was nearly two o'clock. He was due to fly out to Téghaza at three and she couldn't wait for Majid to come back and get him. All this calmness was making her nervous.

"He didn't say anything else?" Tendé's voice crackled over the line from Téghaza. Amber shook her head. It was nearly five o'clock. Max would be with Tendé shortly.

"No . . . nothing. It's as if I never said anything." Amber bit her lip. She didn't like it when Max acted out of character. If there was one thing you could be sure of with Max it was his personality. "He just seemed to take it in his stride."

All Tendé said was: "That can't be."

PART SIX

≈77≈
Rome, Italy
1993

Francesca was silently appraising the middle-aged man seated opposite her. He seemed kind, somewhat avuncular, a little on the short side and tending towards the rotund but not unpleasant—and staggeringly rich, of course. Otto von Kiepenhauer was a friend of Maria Luisa's husband, Giancarlo, and Francesca knew that *she* had been invited to the intimate dinner party to size him up as it were . . . Maria Luisa's not-so-delicate way of telling her it was time for her to start looking elsewhere, if only as a way of forcing Max's hand. Maria Luisa knew it would be a difficult task—she'd told Francesca as much—but still, they weren't getting any younger, she pointed out, and Giancarlo had a list of men as long as his arm who would give anything to sit next to Francesca Rossi. Francesca had given in, reluctantly, and now found herself sitting opposite the German industrialist-turned-hotelier listening with half an ear to his conversation and mentally running over a number of different scenarios in her head. She didn't much care for Germans—too straight-laced and fussy, as a general rule—but when she heard Otto talk about his latest venture, a luxury hotel somewhere in the middle of Africa, her ears pricked up.

"Where did you say your hotel was?" she asked, leaning forward slightly and watching his face flush as he stared down her deep and tanned cleavage.

"My lodge? Yes . . . it's very beautiful. Very luxury. Tip-top. Only the best." Von Kiepenhauer was only too happy to expand on his theme.

"I'm sure it's stunning," Francesca said smoothly. "But *where* is it?"

"Ah. Namibia," Von Kiepenhauer said, spearing an asparagus happily. Francesca frowned. Where? "Do you know it?" he asked her.

"No . . . never heard of it. Where is it?"

"Aha. Well, you see . . . I'm not surprised." Francesca raised an eyebrow. What was the man trying to say? "No, no . . ." he continued, chuckling. "I don't mean it like *zat*. What I mean is—it's a completely new country. A new name. A *silly* name, if you ask me. No, you would have known it by its *real* name, *Südwest Afrika*. Southwest Africa, *hein*?" He said the last with a flourish. Francesca continued to look puzzled. "Next to South Africa, just south of Angola. You don't know it?"

Francesca shook her head. "I've never been to

Africa," she said apologetically. "It must be beautiful. Tell me about it." Von Kiepenhauer was only too pleased to oblige. Francesca caught Maria Luisa's approving eye as she leaned forward and fixed Otto with her eyes. She smiled to herself.

Two hours later, almost bored stiff with his talk of giraffes, lions, water buffalo and animals she'd never heard of, Francesca allowed Otto to help her into her coat.

"Ach, but you must come and see it for yourself," he said as he struggled with the sleeves. "I have a wonderful lodge at Usakos, on the way to the coast. You would love it, I'm sure of it. Nothing but peace and quiet and the animals . . ."

"My dear," Francesca turned to smile sweetly at him. "How kind. But I'm more of a . . . *Hilton* . . . kind of woman, I'm afraid. But my daughter, Paola, would *love* to come. She absolutely adores animals and camping and all that sort of stuff. Doesn't she?" she turned to Maria Luisa who was standing open-mouthed, next to them. She nodded quickly.

"*Si, si* . . . Paola is very . . . *natural*, no?" She shot Francesca an alarmed look. So *that* was what she was playing at. But Paola . . . natural? She didn't think so.

"Of course she must come. But I tell you, my place is luxury hotel. No camping. Tip-top." It seemed to be Otto's favourite expression. Francesca smiled vaguely.

"I'm sure it is, *cara*. But listen . . . why don't you come round for dinner before you go back to . . .

Na . . . Nam—how do you call that place? Yes, Nam*ibia*. When are you leaving?" She was all smiles and pouts. Maria Luisa was impressed. And Francesca was doing the right thing, after all—taking care of her daughter. After Paola's last escapade—which they'd managed to keep out of the papers, thank God—the poor girl was doing nothing and going nowhere fast. She kissed Francesca on both cheeks, murmuring to her that she was doing the right thing. Francesca turned to Otto. "So . . . we'll see you tomorrow evening? About 7 p.m.? Lovely." She walked through the enormous palazzo doors leaving a cloud of expensive perfume and a slightly bewildered Otto von Kiepenhauer behind.

"Are you crazy?" Francesca sat back, surprised by the vehemence in Paola's tone.

"*Me?* Am *I* crazy?" she repeated, annoyed. "Paola . . . you don't have so many options, you know. You've been back in Rome for what . . . almost two years now, and what have you done? Nothing. Absolutely *nothing*! If you think I'm going to let you sit around here for the next two years, wasting your time . . ."

"Go on, rub it in!" Paola yelled at her, tears springing to her eyes. Francesca sighed. Christ—what had she done to deserve this? Paola had been in and out of therapy for almost eighteen months until the last therapist had reluctantly said there wasn't much he could do for her. Francesca just didn't know what to do. *Missing a father figure; identity projection; low self-esteem* . . . the phrases the psychologists threw at her simply made no sense. Paola seemed even unhappier going twice a week to the various and expensive "experts" who had been recommended to her by various people, including Maria Luisa and Manuela who seemed to spend all their time in the elegant offices of half a dozen of Rome's top therapists—people Francesca hadn't even realized *existed* until the whole thing had started. And now they'd been through them all.

"*Cara*, I'm not rubbing anything in. It will be wonderful for you—a change of scene, nice hot weather . . . and Otto is a *very* nice man. Really. You'll see. Now, dry your eyes, darling, please. And let's go shopping for something nice for you to wear. What do you say? Hmm?" Paola looked at her sulkily.

"Okay," she said finally, relenting. Francesca breathed a sigh of relief. Thank *God* she still liked to shop. She wasn't sure what she would have done if that had disappeared as well.

"*Buono*. So . . . let's get ready, darling. I'll have the car brought round in an hour, okay? We'll go to Maria Bolga's new shop, the one on the corner, near YSL. She had some lovely new things in when I stopped by on Monday." Francesca got up from the bed, relieved. It hadn't gone quite as badly as she'd feared.

By the end of the evening, Paola had to grudgingly admit that Francesca was right. Although Otto looked old enough to be her father—not that he was anything like Max—he was charming and extremely attentive and . . . safe. There was something in his rather old-fashioned manner that Paola liked. He pulled out the chair for her, fussed over her wine, her food, made sure she ate enough—when was the last time a man had actually encouraged her to eat *more*? She couldn't remember. She looked across the table at her mother, now deep in conversation with the one German friend she had in Rome, the impossible-to-pronounce Suzette von Riedesal zu Thürlinger-Grachvogt . . . Suzi to her friends . . . an older, so-ugly-she-was-handsome expatriate German who had married an Italian and was now fashion editor of Italian *Vogue*. She caught Francesca's eye as she looked across anxiously to Paola . . . was she having a nice time? Was Otto good company? She saw Francesca settle back into her chair in relief. Yes, Paola *was* having a nice time. Otto was very nice. And much as she hated the thought of wildlife, his descriptions of a luxury game lodge in the middle of Africa with a huge swimming pool and sundowners on the terrace overlooking the animals' watering hole did sound . . . well, intriguing. By the time dessert was served, she'd accepted his invitation to fly out to Namibia. He offered her the use of his private jet— whenever she wanted to come, it would simply take her from Ciampino to Windhoek, the capital city, and then onto the private airstrip he'd built beside the lodge. She would love it. She would never want to come back to Europe. It was on the tip of her tongue to ask what the shops were like but Francesca broke in delightedly. She'd obviously been listening.

"Ah, Otto . . . what did I tell you? She'll *love* it. Absolutely love it." She raised her glass. Suzi followed suit—the goings-on at the table hadn't escaped her eagle eye. Paola blushed prettily. She'd only agreed to go out and *visit* him—it wasn't as if she'd accepted his hand in marriage . . . although the thought only made her blush even harder. Besides, she thought to herself, lifting a glass of water quickly to her lips, it would show that bloody Amber a thing or two. She wasn't the *only* one in the family to do something adventurous and head off to Africa. At the thought of Amber, her lip curled. It was always the same with her. Everyone had been shocked at the news that she and Max's best friend, darling Tendé Ndiaye, had been carrying on behind his back for almost a year before they told him. The news had stunned everyone. Everyone except Paola, it seemed. But by then no one wanted to hear what Paola had to say—about anything. She'd just been on the verge of finally getting Max's attention after the whole horrible, silly fuss about her and Kieran, and then Amber, of course, had to spoil it all by announcing *her* little secret. Typical.

A month later, Paola climbed into the back of the waiting BMW and, after a tearful farewell to Francesca, was soon speeding towards Ciampino where Otto's private plane was waiting to take her on the nine-hour journey to Windhoek International Airport, where she would spend approximately an hour going through the immigration formalities before setting off again for his airstrip at Outjo. The lodge was in the hills between Okahandja and Us-akos, close to a tiny village called Tsaobis. Paola stumbled over the unfamiliar pronunciation. For the first time in almost two years, she was looking for-ward to something. The thought of leaving every-thing behind suddenly appealed to her: Francesca's anxious face; Max's stern unforgiving one; the bor-ing escapades of her friends . . . although most of them could no longer be called escapades, in truth—settling down, this one getting married, that one engaged—it was enough to make her turn and run screaming towards Otto and his offer of two weeks spent in the sun. She'd been a bit worried about it being Africa, of course, but Otto had as-sured her it was nothing like the Africa she saw on the news—if she ever watched it. There were no snakes, no creepy-crawlies, no famines. Namibia was almost Europe, he said proudly. Beautiful weather, gorgeous sunsets, excellent food and wine and the biggest skies she would ever see. It was a paradise, he said—his own, private paradise.

And if his private plane was anything to go by—the rest would be fantastic. Even Paola, who'd never sat in an economy class seat on an aircraft in her life, was impressed. The plane was exquisitely fitted out—cream, plush carpeting, seats that folded out completely and soft, cashmere rugs. The single flight attendant was equally exquisite and as for the pilot . . . Paola settled herself into her chair and ac-cepted a glass of champagne with a gracious smile. Why didn't Max have his own plane? she wondered.

This was the only way to travel. Her spirits lifted with the plane as they soared into the sky above Rome. It was eight thirty in the morning. With luck, she would be having dinner that evening in Africa. The thought thrilled her. She thought briefly, fleetingly of Kieran—and then pushed his face firmly to the back of her mind as she'd been taught. She plugged in her headphones and leaned back, listening to the tape her friends had made for her, a selection of songs from her favorite radio station, Radio Ketchup.

Surprisingly, she found she'd slept most of the way. It was still broad daylight as the captain prepared to land at Windhoek airport—peering out of the window all she could see were the blue-brown outlines of hills and the perfect, unending blue sky. The plane touched down with hardly a bump and within minutes, Paola was descending the stairs onto an almost empty runway with the vast sky yawning above her. It was surprisingly cold, despite the sunshine. It was June but in the southern hemisphere they were in the middle of winter. Winter in Africa? She'd never heard of such a thing but she had to admit, pulling her cape around her, in the shadows it was absolutely freezing. A black man in uniform came up to her and told her in strangely accented English that she had to clear Customs first before getting back on the plane. It would only take a few moments, he said. He escorted her into a small and very neat little airport building. The signs were in German, English and a third, rather odd-looking language, a little like Dutch, she thought. The formalities were quick and painless and within minutes, as he'd promised, she was being walked back across the tarmac to her plane. She hadn't even had time to look around. The light was blinding, even at five in the afternoon.

They took off again, heading northwest, as the pilot told her. She watched the land stretching out beneath the plane. The colors were sharp—yellows, rusts, the mauve-green profiles of hills. Ahead of them, a range of blue mountains suddenly burst out of the flat plain—Paola had never experienced anything quite so empty and vast. There was nothing below them—no cities, no towns, not even a village. It was quite deserted. Every so often a shape appeared; as she squinted into the vastness below her, she saw that it was a herd of animals, their huge, elongated shadows racing along ahead of them. Antelope, the pilot announced, racing across the grassy plane. The sky was beginning to turn pink on the horizon and it spread like a blush, tinting the deep blue and making it appear even more luminous and delicately beautiful.

The airstrip lay like a thick black tongue in the green-yellow grass. Paola watched it rise up to meet them as the plane descended. The lodge was still under construction—she could see half-finished chalets and the signs of a road being built. There was a flash of blue in one corner—a pool, perhaps?—and the dark-brown angles of the rooftops . . . and then a bump and the ground rushing past them. The plane shuddered over the slightly rougher terrain. Paola's

Louis Vuitton bag went flying as the plane braked sharply, and then they were there. The door was opened, the steps were lowered. The exceedingly good-looking pilot stood in the doorway and thanked Paola for joining them. It ought to have been the other way around, Paola thought to herself as she walked out into the sunset. It was hard to believe she was in Africa, or that she'd just spent the better part of a day in the air. She'd never felt so refreshed and excited after a ten-hour journey in her life. She would definitely have to tell Max to get one of his own. It was a must.

Otto wasn't at the plane to meet her. A uniformed servant approached with a string of men behind him, ready to unload. Paola watched in surprise as all sorts of things were lifted carefully out of the hold: crates of wine; hundreds of brown cardboard boxes; bolts and rolls of fabric . . . when her two cases finally appeared, they looked absolutely lost amongst all the stuff they'd flown down with. The pilot saw her looking and smiled.

"Herr Kiepenhauer usually has me make a couple of trips a week," he said, indicating the supplies. "They're nearly finished up at the lodge so we bring down the essentials."

"What's in the boxes?" Paola asked as they waited for the servants to finish loading.

"Oh, all sorts of things," the pilot said, laughing. "Frau Meisler, the interior decorator, puts in a new order every day. You'll meet her in a minute." Her tone was neutral. They got into the van and were soon speeding up the hill towards the main building.

*   *   *

"Paola!" Otto was standing on the steps as the van pulled up. He seemed delighted to see her. She was given a hand down by the pilot and handed over to Otto like a gift, she thought, as she was passed from one man to the other. It was a rather pleasant thought. "You've arrived! Welcome . . . welcome to Outjo . . . to paradise!" Otto was excited. The sun was a fiery sliver on the horizon—braziers were being lit around them. He barked out a few commands to the pilot and the stewardess in German and they immediately took their leave. He welcomed her inside the enormous building. It was perched on top of a hillside with sweeping views down to a silvery lake and to the mountains beyond. It was the restaurant and entertainment center of the lodge, he explained, tucking her arm firmly in his and walking towards the bar. The room they were in—if it could be called a room; more a series of different spaces—was curiously German in its décor. Brass candelabras hung from the ceiling, the walls were a mixture of the Tudor-like beam construction she vaguely associated with skiing holidays in Bavaria . . . a stone-flagged floor; plush leather couches and wrought-iron tables next to the patio. It was like a hotel in Gstaad or Kitzbühl, transplanted to the middle of Africa. The only incongruity were the staff—black men and women in traditional black uniforms, the women with frilly starched aprons and the men with white caps perched awkwardly on top of their heads. She wondered why there were so many of them, and why they were in uniform—the lodge was patently not finished and there certainly weren't any guests around . . . she shrugged. A door opened at the end of the room and a tall, thin woman bore down upon them. Otto looked up, smiling.

"Ah . . . Frau Meisler. Gretha . . . do meet Paola Rossi. A most charming young lady. Paola will be with us for a fortnight. Such a short visit, my dear," he turned to her, spreading his hands ruefully. Paola tossed her hair over her shoulder.

"Well, I might come back again, you never know," she said flirtatiously, enjoying the look of panic in Frau Meisler's hooded eyes. Mmm. A little competition? She looked forward to winning.

A week later, however, she had no idea whether she'd won or not. Strangely, Otto made absolutely no demands on her whatsoever, other than being a beautiful and charming dinner companion. He spent most of his days striding around his vast empire, shouting at workers, conferring with the German overseers and fretting about whether it would all be completed in time. Paola gleaned that the opening of the luxury lodge was scheduled to coincide with political talks in the region—von Kiepenhauer had very generously provided the use of his lodge for the upcoming peace talks with the neighboring country, Angola. Quite what the talks were about, she had no idea. All that concerned her at the moment, she confided to Francesca over the phone, was that she didn't think he liked her. Not really.

Francesca listened to Paola with a frown. Well, the little German was more devious than she'd given him credit for. What a clever man! He was making

Paola come to him, not the other way around. He must have known that making himself unavailable would pique her interest—and her pride. He'd already figured her daughter out. Paola simply wouldn't be able to *stand* losing. She listened to Paola's long list of complaints: he never said how pretty she looked, or how well she was fitting into the strange surroundings, or what good ideas she had . . . except at dinner, of course, and then it was in front of that skinny dragon, Frau Meisler. In fact, Paola said tearfully, she wondered if she'd been brought there just to annoy Frau Meisler. Maybe *she* was about to become Frau von Kiepenhauer and this was his way of . . . well, she didn't know quite what he was doing but it just wasn't *nice*, being ignored like that. It wasn't nice *at all*. Francesca listened rather worriedly . . . never mind Otto, Paola was racing dangerously ahead. She made the appropriate soothing noises and told her not to worry. She was sure Otto liked her very much indeed. She put the phone down, amazed at the speed with which things had moved along. It was less than six weeks ago *she'd* been the one invited to dinner with an ulterior motive . . . now she was consoling her daughter? She lit a cigarette, hoping her little plan wouldn't turn out to have anything other than the best possible consequences for Paola—and for everyone concerned.

Madeleine raised her glass. Across the table, Doug, Murad, Alija . . . the people she'd come to know as closely as her own family over the past two years, blurred. She was leaving. She was being transferred to New York where she was about to start a new job after two years of living, working, fighting and sometimes nearly dying in a place that, as someone in the media had recently remarked, "was like being in a thirty-year war where you are never sure where your enemy is. And where your worst enemy can become overnight your closest friend, provided he is an enemy of your most immediate enemy." It was like being in a game of endless mirrors where nothing was as it seemed. Just as she'd received her papers and the terms of her new contract had been hammered out, the fighting in Bosnia-Herzegovina had entered a new phase of its strange and twisted logic. Moslems and Croats who had hitherto been fighting on the same side against the Serbs, had just turned on each other. Everyone was predicting the worst. At night, when the rumble of artillery had died down, Madeleine lay next to Doug and wondered aloud if she were doing the right thing.

"'Course you are. It's important, what you're doing. I mean, the stuff you do every day . . . most doctors can do that. But this new stuff . . . putting together the case for rape . . . that's going to have a huge effect, Madeleine, not just on one life, but on thousands. You've got to go." Madeleine was silent.

"What about the hospital?" she asked finally. Everyone knew the doctors working there often relied entirely on Madeleine's efforts to get drugs and essential supplies through the UN forces.

"They'll manage." Doug lit a cigarette. "There's no question of staying, Madeleine. You're almost all in. Look at you." She turned away from him. He was right. Twenty-seven months of working in conditions that most people simply couldn't imagine had taken their toll. She wasn't sure anyone would recognize her. Sometimes she no longer recognized herself. Amber was going to meet her in London in a week's time. For the first time in a *very* long time, she found herself worrying about how she looked. She took the cigarette from him and inhaled deeply. She was nervous, too, about returning to London. It would mean seeing her family again—she'd grown farther away from them than she'd ever thought possible. It had come as something of a relief not to have to worry about what Maja thought or whether anything she said or did would hurt her father's feelings . . . she'd been free of them and of everything else. She couldn't even remember the last time she'd thought about Alasdair. All that seemed to belong to another life, another her. She passed the cigarette back to Doug. And what of him? What now for them?

"We'll be fine, Mads," he said, reading her thoughts and pulling her head across the pillow closer to his. "You and me. I know it's been . . .

weird. There's so much else going on . . . but it'll be fine." She was quiet. At times he seemed to know her better than herself, and at others, he was a complete stranger to her. She sometimes wondered how it had ever happened. But that was the thing about being where they were. You wasted very little time thinking about things like that. She pushed her face into his neck and closed her eyes. The smell of chloride and disinfectant never quite left them, no matter how often or hard they scrubbed. Just to be able to smell something else. Something fresh and clean, untainted by the death and suffering around them. She tried to recall Amber's face. In the two years since she'd seen her all sorts of things had happened to them both. Amber was now dividing her time between Bamako and London; she was making a name for herself in journalism, as everyone had known she would. She and Tendé were talking about getting married. He was rising fast in his government. As she read Amber's news in the sporadic letters that got to her, she marveled at how effortless it all seemed to be. She wondered what had happened to Becky. Amber said she'd moved to Zimbabwe with Henry. Madeleine still remembered the day she got that letter. Amazing to think that with everything else going on around her she'd still been able to express surprise at that little piece of news. She'd gone round the corner of the hospital, ignoring warnings from the nurses about snipers along Marsála Titu Avenue and stood with a leg pinned up behind her on the wall and read Amber's letter from start to finish. And now on Thursday, almost two years and three months since she'd said goodbye to her and Becky at Heathrow, she was going back.

Amber paced up and down the waiting area in Terminal Two. Madeleine was coming in on a flight from Geneva. Amber herself had only just come back from Bamako—these days, the flight from London to Bamako via Paris had become just about as familiar to her as the daily ride down Upper Street on the seventy-three bus had been. Once. Now, whenever she was in London, it was easier and quicker to jump in a cab or allow herself to be driven around by Clive. It made her feel even more like a visitor in her own city but Tendé was right . . . there were only so many hours in the day and she always had so much to do. She began to fiddle with her hair. It was long again, and the constant shifting from damp to dry climate wasn't helping. She wondered what Madeleine would look like—in all the time she'd been gone, she'd never once sent a photograph. She'd made a joke once about having lost so much weight that she'd had to punch extra holes in the single belt she had. Amber scanned the passengers coming through—no, no one who even looked remotely like Madeleine. She looked up at the information board. Baggage in hall. She ought to be . . . she stopped suddenly. There she was. Her mouth fell open as Madeleine walked past the Customs official and stopped to light a cigarette.

"Madeleine?" Amber walked over to her. Madeleine looked at her and smiled—the same, wide, beautiful smile. Amber realized there were tears in her eyes as they hugged.

"Amber . . . God, it's so good to see you." Madeleine tried to wave away smoke with her hands. Amber bent down and picked up her bag.

"Is this all you have?" she asked gently. Madeleine nodded.

"Didn't have time to go shopping," she said, smiling ruefully.

"Probably not a great deal to buy," Amber said lightly. "Come on. Clive's outside."

She studied Madeleine as discreetly as she could— the same blonde hair, cut short now . . . lopped off, she corrected herself. It resembled nothing so much as a cut. The same smile, bright blue eyes, and there the resemblances ended. Madeleine as she had been was a voluptuous, sensual person; the gaunt, painfully thin person next to her had nothing to do with those adjectives. This Madeleine was taut and edgy. Amber put a hand on her arm.

"What d'you fancy doing? We could go straight to mine . . . or maybe you'd rather see your parents first?"

Madeleine sighed. "A film. I'd love to see a film. I can see my parents tomorrow. I've been dreaming about going to the pictures ever since the job came through."

Amber smiled. "There's loads on. Let's pick up a *Time Out* on the way home and choose." She settled back in the seat. Some things, she was relieved to see, hadn't changed at all. Madeleine had always loved going to the movies.

*   *   *

She stayed in London for a fortnight, slowly adjusting to life on the outside of the madness in which she'd been living for so long. It took her a while to get used to things . . . little, normal things. The way Amber ran down the flight of stairs each morning to the Italian delicatessen on the corner and came back with huge, flaky croissants and freshly ground coffee; the absence of the dull thud of mortar shells and the fact that the telephone worked, *all the time*. She walked outside at midday and was shocked to find so many people on the street—but slowly, a day at a time, she slipped back into the pattern of life in an affluent city at peace and learned not to duck every time a car horn sounded. She hadn't heard from Doug since she'd arrived. Somehow, deep down, she knew it was unlikely their relationship, such as it was, would survive. He had been good to her and good *for* her at a time when she desperately needed it and she was in no doubt that she'd done the same for him. But Doug had his own demons. She'd never been entirely sure of his reasons for coming to Yugoslavia—Bosnia-Croatia-Serbia, she kept reminding herself; Yugoslavia barely existed any more—and he hardly ever spoke of his life before arriving there, or after, for that matter. He seemed to believe he was destined to stay. Madeleine had thought that way for a while. But the unexpected offer of a job in New York working with the UN, the International Court of Human Rights and the ICM had proved too tempting to resist. She still found it hard to believe she had left the war.

Even now, sitting on the café on Upper Street reading a newspaper amongst a tribe of young women in slingback shoes and sunglasses, it still seemed unreal.

It had come about very quickly. A new, tripartite committee had been set up hastily in New York, charged with changing the legal definition of rape from being a crime against humanity to being a war crime. When she'd first been contacted through her own offices in Belgrade, she'd wondered why on earth she'd been touted for the position. Why me? she wanted to say. What can I offer? But, as Doug pointed out, she'd been tending to the victims of such organized rapes for over two years . . . who better to advise the committee on the lasting physical and psychological effects that the women— Croat, Serb and Moslem alike—had suffered? She remembered leaving the hospital early one morning, not long after the news had been sent to her, walking back through the narrow streets, suddenly wishing for a coffee that didn't taste of formaldehyde or for a morning spent sitting by a window, reading a book. The force of her longing startled her. She realized she'd all but forgotten what life—real life, her own life—was like away from this place. She'd stopped for a second, savoring the memory, then a shout from above brought her back to the present. Someone was gesticulating at her from an open window: *Get out! Get out of here! Quick! There are snipers in the street behind!* She turned and ran.

Now, with her coffee in front of her and a pair of Amber's sunglasses pushed up on her forehead, she was slowly learning to believe in it and to look forward to the future. She would spend a month in Geneva, familiarizing herself with those aspects of the law that were deemed important and necessary in her new role and then she would fly to New York where, she was told, she could expect to be based for a minimum of twelve months. A whole year. She'd never been to America. Amber was sure she would love it. She wasn't sure. The few Americans she'd met in Belgrade seemed touchingly naïve and optimistic about the world—and they'd been among the first to run home when it turned out to be not quite as pleasant a place as they seemed to think. Well, she was about to spend a year in their world and find out for herself.

She looked up and saw Amber making her way across the road towards her. It was a beautiful early summer morning. Sunlight bounced off car windows and the group on the pavement was bathed in light.

"Hi," Amber said, flopping down into the chair beside her and letting a pile of expensive-looking bags crash to the floor. "I'm exhausted!"

"What've you been doing? Shopping?" Madeleine looked at her purchases. "What've you been buying?"

"Two years' worth of birthday and Christmas presents—and you're not to argue," Amber said firmly. Madeleine stared at her.

"Presents? For who?"

"For you, you silly bird. And I'm not taking no for an answer." She signaled to the waiter for a coffee. Madeleine was quiet for a moment.

"You didn't have to," she said eventually. "I'm . . . it's not like before . . . I'm pretty well-paid, you know. I've had two years' worth of salary going into my account and I've not spent a penny, really."

"It's not about the money, darling," Amber said, shaking her head. "Of course you can buy your own stuff. You just won't, that's all. And the new ICM Special Representative needs more than one pair of jeans and two T-shirts. Now, you can try them on when we get home and if anything doesn't fit you can take it back this afternoon." Madeleine shook her head, smiling. Amber. Still so bloody bossy. "What are you smiling at?" Amber asked, frowning at her.

"You. You haven't changed a bit."

"I should hope not. I always thought I was pretty perfect," Amber laughed. "Oh, Madeleine . . . I'm so glad you're back. Even if you are dashing off again. But at least in New York I feel you're safe. I can visit you there."

"I hope so. Doug said I was probably safer in Sarajevo," Madeleine said, smiling at the thought. "Anyhow . . . let's go home. I can't wait to see what's in those bags!"

A week later, Amber hugged Madeleine again and watched her disappear through the departure gate at the newly opened Terminal Four. It was sad, but she had a lot on her own mind. She thought back to her meeting the previous morning. It had started out as a routine catch-up; she knew Tim liked to see her at least once a month to go over her reports and articles and she'd initially thought this meeting would be no different. Tim was in a rather serious mood, but that often happened and she'd thought nothing of it. But about ten minutes into their chat, she'd sensed something else was on his mind. It took him about a minute to tell her.

"It's your father, Amber. We've had some unsubstantiated reports . . . nothing's been confirmed yet, I hasten to add, that he's held several meetings in Paris with Galli, the Tuareg leader. Now, there could be nothing to it but we're also hearing rumors of a failed coup attempt—and the man behind it, Boubacar Sidibé, was coincidentally at several of the same meetings. I'm putting someone on the story—"

"No. Let me do it." Amber broke in, breathing fast.

"I can't. Out of the question. Now, what I'd like you to do is—"

"Tim. *Please.* I know more about Mali than probably anyone in the current affairs department. You know that's true. I can do this, I know I can."

"Amber, I'd like nothing more than to hand over the dossier and say 'get on with it'—I know you'll do a fantastic job. But—and it's a serious 'but'—it's your father. It's too close to the bone. It goes against everything we stand for. Objectivity, dispassion . . . you know the score as well as I do."

"You can't do this to me, Tim. You can't bring me in here and tell me this . . . and then tell me you're putting someone else on the job. At least let me work with whoever's covering the story. I don't care if I don't get credited. But I can't walk out of here knowing that this is going on and that I'm not part of it. *Whatever* the truth is. Plus, it'll be almost impossible for any of the other reporters to get the access they need in Bamako. I can. I can get us in anywhere. *Please*, Tim." There was silence in his office for a few minutes. Tim looked at her, his mind turning over and over. Finally he threw down his pencil and stood up.

"All right. I'm putting Gale Scroggins on it. You can work with him. I'm not running your name alongside the story and if it gets too hard or I think you're compromising yourself—or us—in any way, I'm pulling you off it. Is that clear?"

Amber stood up. "Perfectly clear." She picked up her bag and turned to go. At the door, she paused for a second. "And thanks, Tim. I appreciate your . . . trust." She gave a quick smile and walked out, her legs shaking. What the hell had she just agreed to do?

Now, as she slid into the back seat and watched the airport flash by, she thought about the conversation and about the job she was about to do . . . and how she was going to tell Tendé. Or not. She was due to fly back in a couple of days' time—she'd reluctantly agreed to have dinner with Angela and Kieran that evening. It was the last thing she wanted to do. Walking into the house at Holland Park was like walking onto the set of some strange, alternate reality TV show. Angela waltzed around in caftans and leather moccasins—she'd suddenly sobered up, taken up Buddhism and frequently got her fashion sources wrong—and Kieran spent most of his time glowering in his room. The staff had all been replaced for about the third time in the past two years. Siobhân was long gone; another girl had taken her place: Maíre . . . something like that. She'd lasted about six months then she too had handed in her notice. Amber couldn't remember who was now looking after Angela but the thought of spending three hours that evening in the company of her mother and brother was enough to make her want to crawl home and lie down. They were exhausting, both of them. Kieran especially. He played the role of tragic victim only too well. He was learning from Angela. She sighed.

On her last evening at the lodge, Paola dressed with even more care than usual. She was quietly determined to make sure Otto von Kiepenhauer wouldn't forget her. There was something about the man she found strangely compelling. He wasn't like any of the men she'd been attracted to in the past—quite the opposite, in fact. He was short, balding and old. *Not* the kind of man she'd always seen herself with. But there was something lovely and solid about Otto. She liked the way he smelled, for example, a subtle mixture of expensive aftershave and cigar smoke; she liked his smile and his mannerisms—always attentive, always polite . . . nothing seemed to ruffle his smooth, polished exterior. He looked and acted like someone who'd seen everything at least once before and could therefore take everything in his stride. He gave off the same unmistakable air of power that Max did—nothing too obvious, just the way he issued commands without ever contemplating his needs would not be met; the way he talked about his businesses and plans. The world was truly Otto's oyster, as it was for Max. He'd made his money in manufacturing, or so he said—Paola knew that the name "von Kiepenhauer" must have come from money somewhere down the line—but in the late seventies, he'd looked at the rapidly expanding German tourist industry and jumped in. His tour company, Zeus, took Germans where they'd never been before. China, Russia, Chile and now, Namibia. Working on the maxim that it was better to cater to one tourist willing to spend $1,000 than a thousand tourists spending $1, he had carved out a niche in the marketplace—luxury travel and tours to destinations so far off the tourist radar that he often had to provide everything: landing strips, roads and the finest *sauerkraut* included. He never took "no" for an answer and was so powerful in the field of high-end tourism that entire governments prostrated themselves before him, hoping for their country to become the next addition to the Zeus stable of exotic locations.

All this Paola learned not from Otto himself, but from Frau Meisler. She still hadn't quite got to the bottom of the story between the tall, rake-thin woman and her jovial host but whatever there might have been between them, Paola was determined to end it. The only problem in her plan was Otto himself. He was as charming as ever, but not a hint of romantic interest. Not a *hint*. She was driving herself crazy trying to work out why. She fastened the diamond studs in her ears and checked her reflection. She stared at herself for a minute. Her face had changed; it was thinner now, her cheekbones were more prominent and a set of fine, delicate lines around her eyes were suddenly visible. She was growing older, of course. She now looked more than ever like Francesca, right down to the tiny lines around her mouth and the determined set of her chin. She sprinkled a few drops of perfume between her breasts and stood up. Her lime-green silk skirt flared gently over her hips and the white silk top showed off her tan—how could Otto resist her? she wondered, frowning. She was perfect. Even her toes matched her outfit—a pretty pale pink picked up in her coral necklace and matching bracelet. She slipped her feet into her green slingbacks and brushed her hair one last time. She had one last night to make an unforgettable impression. Although the invitation to come back to Outjo had stayed open, there were no immediate plans, and despite herself, Paola began to panic a little. What if he didn't want to see her again? What if—God forbid—he didn't really like her? What if she'd been a disappointment? On that rather depressing note, she closed the door to her room and walked outside.

She needn't have worried. Dinner, for once, was without the formidable Frau Meisler. She'd gone into Windhoek at lunchtime, Otto told her, and would be back the following day.

"She sends her regards," he said, smiling at her across the table and expertly decorking a bottle of wine. "And hopes to see you here again very soon." Paola nodded doubtfully. "And you? Are you sad to leave?" Paola nodded again.

"Yes, very," she said in what she hoped was a voice of lingering regret.

"You had a nice time here, *hein*?"

"Oh, yes. Lovely. It's such a shame it's come to an end." She looked at him from underneath her lashes.

"Perhaps not an end . . ." Otto mused, his fingers playing with the stem of his wine glass. "I will be in Rome again in a fortnight's time. Perhaps I can call on you there?"

"That would be lovely," Paola said quietly, following Francesca's advice. *Enthusiastic but not desperate. Willing but not pushy.* Otto's face lit up. He raised his glass.

"To Rome, then." Paola did the same. Was it, she wondered, a declaration? And if so, of what? She swallowed her wine, not quite sure what to feel.

Francesca was much clearer. In the weeks following Paola's return, she talked endlessly, giving tips, advice, sermons . . . anything she thought would help the situation on its way. She was quite clear about the goal: Paola was to be Mrs. von Kiepenhauer and nothing, *nothing* would deflect her from her task. Paola was quite shocked at the single-mindedness with which Francesca pursued her objective.

"You don't want to end up like me, darling,"

Francesca told her as they sat side by side in the hairdresser's. Paola looked at her from underneath the scarf covering her hair and frowned.

"What do you mean? Everything's okay with you and Max, isn't it?"

"Oh, yes . . . things are fine. But you know, if anything should ever happen to Max . . . it's not automatic, you know."

"What isn't?"

"That I'd be taken care of. That we would be okay. It would all go to Angela, you know. That drunken bitch."

Paola was stunned. "But of course it won't. Max must have . . . you know, put something in his will or something. He wouldn't leave us with nothing, would he?"

"No, no . . . but that's assuming he's made a will and that his affairs are up-to-date. Maria Luisa was telling me only the other day . . ." Francesca immediately launched into a horror story of a man and three mistresses. Paola could only stare at her mother. She'd never quite thought of it like *that*. She *liked* Otto. The fact that he had tons of money was as far as she was concerned simply a part of his personality, like his penchant for nice cologne or the way he ended his sentences with "*hein*." She couldn't separate his money from him. But Francesca was putting an entirely different spin on things. She wanted Paola to be safe. I *am*, Paola insisted crossly. Francesca had other ideas. She would only be properly safe when she had a ring on her finger and the unassailable right to half of her husband's wealth. In some ways, Paola was thankful Francesca now had something other than the affair with Kieran to focus on. It made a change from her painful attempts to *understand*, as she put it. No amount of telling her that there *was* nothing to understand—it had just happened—seemed to satisfy her. But now there was something else to obsess about.

By the time Otto finally called on her, his fate was sealed. Faced with Francesca's steely charm and the sight of Paola descending the stairs each evening in a succession of stunning evening dresses, the poor man had no choice. Over dinner in Tizú, the fashionable new Sicilian restaurant on via Spinoza, he proposed. He wasn't sure who was more pleased—Paola or her mother.

The first Amber heard of the engagement was when a thick, cream envelope sailed through the letterbox. Three envelopes, to be exact. One addressed to Max and Angela; one for Kieran and one for herself. She was in the drawing room downstairs with Angela, watching in surprise as Angela reached across the coffee table not for a glass of wine or a beer but for a cup of tea—*and* with a steady hand. Amber raised her eyebrows. She'd never seen Angela sober. She heard a tap at the front door and the sound of something hitting the floor. She got up, confused—was it possible? Had Angela finally kicked the bottle?—and walked to the door. She came back, bearing the envelopes and handed Angela the one addressed to her and Max. She slit the envelope and slid the heavy card out. *Francesca Marina Rossi requests the pleasure of your company . . .* she looked up. Angela was studying her. Her own envelope lay untouched beside her.

"Paola's getting married," Amber said, surprised.

"Oh, good. Francesca'll be pleased," Angela replied tartly. She reached for a biscuit. Amber's eyes widened. She couldn't remember Angela ever reaching for something to eat. There was silence as Angela bit into the crisp shortbread. "These are rather nice, darling," Angela continued, pushing the plate across the table. Do have one. Daphne made them this morning, I think."

"Daphne?"

"The new cook. She started last week. I had a hell of a time choosing, I can tell you. I went for ugly this time."

"Ugly?" Amber was having difficulty following her.

"Mmm. Couldn't stand having those pretty girls around me any more. Did nothing but steal my things."

"Things?"

"Darling, why are you repeating everything I say?"

"Am I?"

"Yes. Now, I'm going upstairs to meditate, darling. I'll tell Max you came round, shall I?"

"Oh, er . . . yes. Although I'll probably see him next week. I think he's coming out to Bamako."

"Oh? And where's that, darling?" Angela got up and brushed a few crumbs from her turquoise blue caftan. Amber looked at her, puzzled.

"Bamako? That's where I live." Was it possible Angela had no idea where she was? "It's in Africa."

"How nice. Well, I expect I'll see you when you get back. Bye, darling." And she was gone. Amber remained where she was for a minute, studying the invitation card, her mind racing. Who the hell was Otto von Kiepenhauer? And why were they having two ceremonies, one in Rome and the other in Namibia? She looked at the card again. The wedding itself would be held in Rome and the reception three days later, at a place called Outjo Lodge, some one hundred miles north of the capital, Windhoek. Paola in Africa? She couldn't quite picture it. She wondered what Max thought.

At that moment, Max was staring at a note that Theo, his lawyer of many years, had written, advising him for the second time that year to update his will and consolidate some of his interests. Perhaps surprisingly for someone in his position, he hated doing anything that hinted, however remotely, at his own mortality. He hadn't revised his will since he'd cut Kieran out of it some six years earlier—the fit of rage that had precipitated the decision had been dimmed momentarily by Kieran's success in the nightclub stakes but his standing had plummeted again following that dreadful business with Paola. Max couldn't quite remember what the last revision to his will had been. He vaguely recalled giving Amber the largest control in his fortune but that was before she'd sprung the news of Tendé on him. He sighed and put down the note. Across the desk stood a vase of summer roses—one of the maids must have put it there. Reds, yellows, rich pinks. He looked at the veined, curling petals; a few of them were almost in full bloom. He pulled one out, admiring the tightly knit folds and its perfect, delicate symmetry; over the next few days, a leaf would open up here, allowing a second to unfurl over there . . . he sniffed at it. Mutti loved roses. The thought came to him suddenly, startling him with its swiftness and intensity. Mutti. He hadn't thought about her in . . . decades. He swiveled around in his leather chair and pulled open one of the drawers in the cabinet behind him. There was nothing in the little drawer save a small black suede pouch. He took it out and fingered the tasseled cord, then reached inside. He unfolded the piece of paper and shook the three diamonds out, watching as they tumbled into his palm, each catching the light in a different way. Still there. Always.

He closed his hand on the jewels, wondering just what Mutti would have made of it all—one of her grandchildren going off to live in Africa with a Moslem; the other marrying a German whose father would surely . . . he stopped. He couldn't bring himself to think any further on that issue. Her grandson; an emotionally stunted, doped-up addict, still living at home and, apart from one foray into the business world that had ended in disaster—although nothing to do with the business, *per se*—totally devoid of ambition or drive. An alcoholic wife and a distracted mistress . . . what would Mutti have said? She would have been proud of his success, of course—

or would she? Max had been too young and many of the values his parents would have instilled in him . . . there just hadn't been the time. He'd done his growing up alone, finding his own moral rudder and figuring out what was right and wrong by himself. At times like these, he felt their absence most keenly. What would his father have said? Of the two of them, he found his father much harder to recall. Mutti was easier—little things, like the smell of roses or the way a cake sometimes sat in the shop window . . . the color of a particular dress . . . those details brought her back to him. But recalling his father was much harder.

He rolled the gems between his fingertips. Had *he* been a good father? The question now plagued him. Francesca clearly thought what had happened between Paola and Kieran was his fault. His alone. He'd been astounded. She'd marched Paola off to a series of quack therapists—at least in Max's eyes— and the girl had emerged from it none the wiser. He hadn't known what to do with Kieran. Forget it. That was the easiest route. He'd spoken to him just once. *We're prepared to forget it ever happened.* That was what he'd said. Kieran had just looked at him and closed his bedroom door. Max didn't know what to do, or say. Francesca had plenty to say and in the end, Max had grown bored listening. It was over. Finished. A big, ugly, horrible mistake. Let the two of them put it behind them and get on with their lives. *Get on with their lives?* Francesca had screamed at him. *How? They need help!* She'd silently presented him with the bills for the "help" she'd sought for

Paola but to be honest, he couldn't see that it had done much good. Paola simply continued to flit about as she'd always done; hanging out with the same crowd she'd brought to Paradise, spending vast amounts of money on things she absolutely didn't need or want: a new car; new clothes; holidays . . . the list was endless. Fortunately for everyone, the scandalous truth hadn't made it into the press. And for that, Max was grateful. In fact, outside of the family, no one knew what had happened. He'd had to sell their shares in Paradise pretty quickly. It was clear that the boy was in no fit state to continue. Kieran had limped along half-heartedly for a couple of months before Max took matters into his own hands. But he'd actually made a profit, and from the little he heard about such things, Paradise had only gone on from strength to strength. It sometimes irked him that he'd been forced to sell when he had. If he'd kept his stake in it would be worth a whole lot more.

He sighed. It was back to the question of wealth again. *His* wealth—his will. He crumpled up Theo's note. He would deal with it later. He was leaving for Téghaza in the next couple of days and there was still a lot to do. The first mine was almost completed and the processing plant was well under way. There had been a few tensions in the area and Tendé was worried. Max smiled. For all his thoroughness and his grasp of what was going on, Tendé wasn't as quick as Max. Max had foreseen trouble, long before they'd broken ground. He'd arranged a meeting with the Tuareg leaders from the main political parties almost immediately. He wanted to show them he was committed to working with them in the region, not against them. Max knew only too well what it was like to be an outsider. He knew the history of the Tuaregs was a difficult and marginal one and the meetings were an attempt to broker a deal *before* trouble broke out, not afterwards. He had no way of knowing it but somehow, somewhere inside him, he knew Mutti would have approved.

The telephone rang, shattering the peace. He tossed Theo's note into the wastepaper basket. He would get round to sorting out his will later. Right now, there were many other far more pressing issues to attend to. He picked up the phone.

≈79≈

It was the first thing she saw when she walked in the room. Hanging above the fireplace was a large oil painting, almost Rothko-esque in its use of color and abstract form—it was stunning. She paused in front of it, a glass of wine in her hand.

"Who's the artist?" she asked the hostess, the impossibly beautiful Nadège O'Connor.

"Oh, that? That's a Marimba. Godson Marimba." Nadège waved an elegant hand.

"Who is he?" Becky was intrigued. She'd hardly expected to find a painting of interest anywhere in Zimbabwe and certainly not at the house of any of the people she and Henry called friends.

"I don't know, really. He's one of Gid's finds,"
Nadège said vaguely, turning back to her conversation. Becky walked over and studied it. Marimba had
captured the beautiful, lazy slide of colors she'd
come to associate with Zimbabwe—blues turning to
green; slipping into brown; browns lightening until
they too slid into grey, then white. It was definitely
Rothko, although there was something more or-
ganic about the shapes he used—not quite square,
not quite circular . . . his shapes were undefined,
reminiscent of the ruins at Great Zimbabwe that
Henry had taken her to see when they'd first arrived.
Huge, powerful, almost maternal shapes. She stood
back from the painting, admiring it from a distance.

"Does he have any more?" she asked. But
Nadège wasn't listening. Becky turned and wandered out onto the patio. She looked for Henry but
couldn't see him. She watched the knot of men
gathered around the barbeque look up as she
passed, silently appraising her—young, pretty, not
yet married and, the all-important distinction as far
as they were concerned—white. She hated it. She
hated them. In fact, she pretty much hated everything about this place. She was longing to go home.
Henry, she was sure, would never leave. Although
he'd admitted to finding it difficult when they'd first
arrived, he loved it now—he'd found his place. No,
he would never leave. Becky, on the other hand, had
never felt quite so . . . useless . . . in her life. *Use-*
less. Zimbabwe had no use for her, and the feeling
was mutual. At first, playing husband and wife in the
little cottage tucked away in the countryside that re-

minded her of England . . . it had been fun. She'd enjoyed making a home and helping Mrs. Fairfield with the other cottages. She'd even had ideas about how to expand the business; but after a while it became clear to her that she was the hired help, employed to run around after Mrs. Fairfield and take over the messy task of supervising her servants. And in fact, she was lucky to be employed at all— the original job advertisement had been for Henry, not Henry-and-a-girlfriend. She was paid a tiny sum, cash in hand, at the end of every month. It barely covered her cigarettes and the petrol for her increasingly frequent trips to Harare. If it wasn't for Harare and the new circle of friends she'd found, she would have been on the plane back to London ages ago. Even if she'd had to borrow the money.

She'd met Nadège O'Connor, a beautiful Anglo-Irish girl married to Gideon Bayne who, coincidentally, had been at the same school as Henry—not such a coincidence, as she later came to find out. The tiny white community in Harare all knew one another; they'd been to the same schools; shared the same friends and were in and out of each others' beds . . . a perpetual merry-go-round of partners and shared grievances. Henry couldn't stand them. Wild horses wouldn't drag him down to their endless parties and polo matches but Becky, bored to tears on the farm, found them a welcome, urban distraction. And they adored her. Nadège had "found" her wandering through the marketplace in Chinhoyi, searching for fabric to make curtains, and had immediately adopted her. She and Gid were on their way to the luxury safari camp at Doma, just to the north of Chinhoyi, and had stopped for petrol and something to eat. Nadège caught sight of a pale redhead in the most charming pink flowered sundress and floppy straw hat and had immediately jumped out of the Land Rover.

"Hey! You . . . you in the hat!" she shouted across the women selling piles of silver and shimmering green fish. Becky turned. "Yes! You . . . can you hang on a moment?" Becky watched as a pair of long, tanned legs in minuscule khaki shorts descended from the car. "Hi, I'm Nadège," she said, walking towards her and extending a hand. "Your hat . . . it's beautiful. I couldn't help noticing it. And your dress. So pretty." Becky stood there amidst the curious onlookers and immediately fell in love. Nadège was gorgeous—tall, willowy, ash-blonde . . . an immaculate person, she felt. Everything about her was perfect, from the matching shorts and scoop-necked T-shirt to the fashionable black and white bandana and blue, John Lennon-style sunglasses. Starved of fashionable female company for nearly twenty-four months, she drank in the sight of Nadège and her husband, the handsome Gideon, and stood there, gasping for more. And Nadège was certainly fashionable. She'd done a bit of modeling, she told Becky—there were a couple of photographs of her in their lovely home in Borrowdale—and worked for a few months in PR but she'd met Gideon in Chelsea in the spring of 1992—love at first sight and all that and had immediately packed everything up to come out to Zim, as she called it.

She and Gid had two beautiful children although they seemed curiously absent from their parents' lives. They spent most of their time with the two live-in nannies, Nadège explained—*a really fantastic arrangement; the cost of labor here is so cheap, you wouldn't believe it and the girls just adore Lisbeth and Maryam; they couldn't live without them* . . . it left her free to concentrate on the things she liked doing. Such as? Becky asked tentatively. Nadège certainly didn't have a job. She shrugged. Riding, mostly. And entertaining Gid's business associates. It seemed to take up inordinate amounts of her time.

Nadège introduced her to the smart, fashionable set of white Zimbabweans and expats who lived in the northern Harare suburbs and who, as Henry helpfully pointed out, would much rather be living in Chelsea or Sloane Square except that these days, their Zim dollars wouldn't even cover the cost of a plane ticket and they wouldn't get the servants they needed. He was scathing about her new friends. Becky sometimes wondered if there was more to the story than Henry was telling her—one or two of the men gave her strange looks when she said she was Henry Fletcher's girlfriend.

"Fletcher . . . wasn't he the one . . . he was at PE, wasn't he?"

Becky nodded cautiously. Almost all the men at any one gathering seemed to have gone to Prince Edward Academy.

"Becky, do have some punch," Gideon broke in smoothly on that occasion and led her away. She longed to ask Nadège why Henry seemed to be such an uncomfortable subject but lacked the necessary courage.

She began to spend almost every weekend in Harare, either catching a lift with departing guests or, as had begun to happen lately, simply walking out the front door to where the Baynes' Land Rover was waiting. Nadège sent the driver to get her—there was absolutely no question of her taking the bus into town. Was she mad? *No, no . . . I'll send the driver out to get you. No, don't be silly. That's what he's paid to do, darling.* Becky learned to acquiesce. It generally wasn't much use arguing with Nadège. She usually got what she wanted.

At first she'd loved it—the feeling of anticipation as the driver turned off Lomagundi Road and then drove past the university, then through Alexandra Park with its lovely, English-style houses, past the racecourse and up Gun Hill and then into Borrowdale Road. The houses along the way were almost buried by their trees and flowers of such strange, exotic beauty. There were swimming pools in almost every garden; the high, wire fences of tennis courts and the strips of beautifully manicured, perfect lawns. The names were resolutely English—The Gables; Avonlea; The High House; The Dales. They were as familiar to her now as the trees lining the Chinhoyi Road just before the turn-off to the farm.

The people gathering every evening at the Baynes' or the Baxters' or the Rowes'—the names were almost interchangeable—were an odd assortment of disparate ages, professions and temperaments bound together by the fact that they were wealthy, indulgent and white. The only blacks present at any of their gatherings were the servants. Becky remarked on it to Henry. He shook his head impatiently. When would she ever get it? That was just the way it was. It wasn't any different at the farm, was it? Becky nodded slowly. They would gather beside the pool in the late afternoon, first the women, stretching out languorously on the sun lounges, their faces and the slopes of their breasts tanned and gleaming with coconut-scented oil. Within seconds, a martini or gin and tonic would appear as if by magic on the little carved wooden tables beside each seat, a plate of plump, succulent olives or salted nuts as an accompaniment. The servants padded silently in and out bringing a towel or a forgotten pair of sunglasses; a fresh drink or the telephone out to the six or seven ladies lying prostrate before the sun. Becky found it uncomfortable at first—lying there with practically nothing on, murmuring a thank you every so often as a "boy" carefully placed a drink beside her. Some of the "boys"—well, they were men, really.

"Don't you feel . . . you know, embarrassed?" Becky asked Nadège one afternoon. Nadège was lying on her stomach. She had taken off her bikini top and her two, perfectly tanned and rounded buttocks were parted only by a thin white string—someone had brought her two thong bikinis back from Rio. She just loved them.

"Embarrassed? Whatever for?" she mumbled from beneath her arms.

"You know . . . us lying here half-naked and the servants coming by. I don't know . . . I feel a bit weird."

"Oh, for goodness' sake. They don't pay us the slightest bit of attention. We're not attractive to them, you know."

"D'you really believe that?" Becky propped herself up on an elbow. She gazed at Nadège's perfect form lying next to her.

"It's true. They like . . . different things. Have you seen some of their women?"

"Oh, come on, Nadège. You're from London. I mean, it might be different if you'd grown up here, but you must have had black or Asian friends. Surely."

"Well, of course I did. But that was *there*. It's different back home. You'll see. You'll get used to it. I found it a bit weird when I first came out but it's true—we're invisible to them, except on payday. Then it's one sob-story after another; this one wanting to borrow money, that one having to go home . . . grandmother's died and I don't know what else. It's exhausting."

Becky said nothing. It embarrassed her, to tell the truth. Whatever Nadège or the other women said, she could sense the strained artifice of their situation simmering just below the surface. It was in the glances that the "boys" gave to one another as one of the women turned over, exposing reddened nipples and pale white breasts as they reached for a sarong or a towel; it was in the faintly contemptuous way Josiah said "yes, madam," every time she asked for something . . . it was everywhere. But no one else seemed to see it. Or if they did, they pretended not to. She found that she'd started talking to Amber again, in her head. If there was one person she could have shared it with, Amber would have been the one. She would have understood. But she'd ruined the friendship with her stupidity and her cowardice and she couldn't see how to repair it.

"Striking, isn't it?" Gid's voice broke in on her thoughts. She was still standing in front of the painting.

"It's beautiful."

"You won't believe how much I paid for it," Gid said, lighting a cigarette. "Got it for next to nothing. Honestly, these guys . . . they haven't a clue. If he were a *real* artist . . . can you imagine?" Becky looked at him, her lip curling of its own accord. Christ, was there nothing human about any of them?

"Where does he paint?" she asked eventually.

Gid shrugged. "Dunno. He's the brother of a man who works for me. He brought it into the office one morning to show someone. I saw it and bought it on the spot. Love the colors. I knew it would look nice above the fireplace."

"Gideon, could you find out where he works? The brother, I mean. I'd like to visit him. See if he has any more," Becky said suddenly. An idea had suddenly come to her.

Gid nodded absently. "Yeah, sure . . . though I'd be surprised if you found anything else. That's the

trouble, see. They do it well once, but they can't repeat it. It's something—"

"That'd be great," Becky interrupted him. She
couldn't bear to hear any more. "I could come down
during the week. Shall I give you a ring on, say,
Wednesday?" He nodded and she quickly walked
off. She found Henry chatting to Kate, a tall, pretty
brunette. She watched Henry playing his favorite
role—experienced bush-hand—and the answering
lighting up of Kate's face. She shook her head. What
was wrong with these people? What the hell was so
special about taking a bunch of overweight, over-
paid tourists up and down a country that wasn't
even theirs to look at animals who, in all likelihood,
would eat them alive? Henry seemed to think he
was some kind of modern-day hero, an African In-
diana Jones, complete with bush hat and chinos. It
was rubbish. The truth of the matter was that Henry
was little more than a glorified gardener. It was Jock
who took the tourists into the bush; Jock who
stalked lions and elephants with little more than a
knife in his belt. And it was Jock who paddled down
the Zambezi with hordes of crocodiles and hippos
circling his canoe—not Henry. She saw him frown
as she approached. She knew he hated being
caught in a lie—and that she was the only one to
catch him. Most of the people at these parties would
sooner have cut off their hands than hopped into a
canoe in a croc-infested river, or slept in a tent. On
that score alone, she thought, they displayed some
sense. Becky hated the bush and everything in it.
She delighted the town crowd by declaring herself

in paradise every time the Land Rover turned into Borrowdale Drive. She still remembered the peal of laughter at the first party she'd attended when she remarked that it was such a relief to open a cupboard or a drawer with confidence, knowing that nothing untoward would slither out.

"Oh, hi . . ." Henry's face was flushed. A combination of beer and Kate's adoring gaze.

"Shall we go?" Becky asked, a little more sharply than she'd intended. She caught the look that passed between Henry and Kate. Oh, fuck it, she thought to herself angrily. They're probably screwing already. She was surprised at how little the thought actually hurt.

≈80≈

Within a month Madeleine had found a small apartment on Lefferts Place, just off Classon Avenue in Brooklyn. Large—for Brooklyn, the gum-chewing realtor assured her. She was on the ground floor; there was a supermarket and a corner deli nearby and on Atlantic Avenue, just a few blocks away, there were the requisite restaurants and trendy bars . . . *everything a young woman like yourself could possibly want*, Cindi said, snapping her gum ferociously. *It's poi-fect*. Madeleine smiled faintly. She signed the lease the following week, handed over the astronomical six-month deposit and received an alarmingly heavy bunch of keys. Was it really necessary to triple-lock each of the four locks on the front door? Cindi looked at her with a long-suffering expression. Foreigners.

"Honey, this is New York. You lock every one of 'em damned locks. You got it?" Madeleine nodded quickly.

She caught the subway back to Brooklyn and walked the three blocks back to her new home. It was July. New York was bathed in sweat. She closed the door behind her, locking just two of the four, and surveyed her new home. A long, rather dark hallway leading into a sitting room, separate kitchen and dining room and a nice, sunny bedroom. The bathroom looked as though it had been carved out of a closet but it was clean and freshly painted. She sat down on the floor. Apart from a mattress that Cindi had been kind enough to lend her until she bought a few things, there was nothing else in the apartment. Nothing. She'd been given a generous enough housing allowance; she really ought to get up and get moving. She needed furniture, pots and pans, plates . . . she looked around her, dazed by the heat. Her suitcases stood in the middle of the living room floor. Home. She was nearly thirty years old and this was her first home. She smiled at the thought.

Six weeks later, she pushed open the door after a particularly long and hard day at work and looked around in surprise. It was actually beginning to look like a home after all. She'd somehow managed to find the time to order a bed; a sofa; a chest of drawers. She'd picked up a couple of potted plants on the way home one evening; there were pictures of her mother and father and Péter, of course, in nice frames on the makeshift bookcase. It was slowly beginning to look real. Being Madeleine, she'd immediately divided her housing allowance into three. One third she sent straight away to her parents; a third she put in the bank and a third she spent thriftily, looking around and using her budget as a means of exploring her neighborhood. It had paid off. She'd managed to furnish a small apartment on what most people would have spent on a single item. On the bedside table—an old wine crate she'd begged off the owner of the Puerto Rican grocery store on the corner—stood a framed picture of Alasdair. She looked at it each night before going to sleep. Of Doug there was nothing. Somehow she knew there would never be anything, either. He knew it. They both did. After the last embrace at the airport in Belgrade it was over, finished with, expended. She felt no regret. She often wondered how it was possible to be with someone in such close, intimate ways, and yet not be there at all at the same time. That was the way it had been with them. She didn't want to go over it or endlessly look for answers. It had been good—and, yes, useful—while it lasted but now it was over and she was alone. Somehow, it felt right.

In any case, as she found out over the next few months, there just wasn't the time to think about Doug or her parents or anything else. Her new job took up most of her time. She found that while she

missed the immediacy of medicine there was something deeply satisfying about the painstaking way in
which they—she; Dari, the brilliant lawyer from
UNIFEM; and Jamilla, the Red Cross representative—worked. The three of them made a good team,
Madeleine with her in-depth knowledge of the physical and mental trauma inflicted upon the women
they sought to represent, Dari with her quick, prob-
ing mind and Jamilla with forty years' experience
working within the international crises management
framework. Charlie's Angels, the department chiefs
at the UN called them, not entirely tongue-in-cheek.
Jamilla was a silver-haired, slim woman from
Bangladesh who had grown up in the U.S. Madeleine sometimes thought her forthright manner
and brusqueness was the result of having refused
an arranged marriage outright in her teens, effectively casting herself outside the circle of her own
family. Dari had filled her in on a few of the details.
Dari herself was an interesting person—Canadian
by birth, her parents had emigrated to Israel when
she was eleven. She'd spent the next ten years in
Ramat Hasharon, a wealthy suburb of Tel-Aviv, then
surprised everyone in her family by falling in love
with a Danish tourist and following him back to
Copenhagen. She'd lived in a small suburb outside
Copenhagen for the next ten years, raising two children and doing her best to become a Danish house-
wife. At the age of thirty, she'd started taking law
classes. It had taken her seven years to gain admit-
tance to the Danish bar by which time her marriage
was effectively over. She'd applied for a job at ICM

headquarters in Geneva, spent two years climbing swiftly up the ladder of gender-related legal issues and had just recently been posted to New York alone. Three single, dedicated and highly articulate women—Madeleine felt honored to be in their company.

The heat of summer slowly gave way to bright clear days of autumn—fall, as New Yorkers called it. October slipped gently into November. The leaves were falling at the rate of ten a second when she got a call from Amber. Paola, her half-sister, was getting married and Tendé had refused to go to the wedding. Would Madeleine come instead? Amber didn't think she could bear to spend a week alone with the rest of her madcap family. It was to be a Christmas wedding in Namibia, on the top of a mountain or something equally ridiculous.

"*Please*. I don't think I'll be able to bear it. Can you imagine? He's fifty years old and owns half of the country."

"Well . . . I don't know . . . we're so busy here . . ." Madeleine bit her lip. As pleasant as it sounded, she couldn't just take off for a week.

"But you must get holidays? Surely a couple of weeks a year, at least?"

"Yes, but . . . well, I'll talk to Jamilla and Dari. See what they say. When is it?"

"December twenty-fifth. You'll be closed that day anyway." Madeleine nodded. She could fly back via London and see her parents. She opened her diary.

"Okay. I'll put in a request for leave." On the other

end of the phone, she could hear Amber sigh with relief.

"Lucky for you," Amber said to Tendé as she put down the phone. "Madeleine's agreed to come."

"Lucky Madeleine," was his dry response as he walked towards the kitchen. Amber sighed and turned to face him.

"I just don't understand why you don't want to come," she said, bringing the subject up for about the tenth time that week.

"I just don't." She could hear him opening the fridge.

"But why not?"

"Because."

"You can't just say 'because,' Tendé. You have to give me a reason. A *proper* reason. What'm I supposed to say to Max?"

"Okay. How's this? I don't want to go because no one in your family acknowledges our relationship; the fact that we've been together for nearly three years; no one even acknowledges *me*. I'm tired of pretending to Max that you're not here, that we're not living together and that we, as a couple, don't exist. And as far as the damned wedding goes, I don't want to spend time as the only African guest at a wedding on top of some hill somewhere in southern Africa where the only other Africans'll be the ones lugging chilled champagne up the hill—and which none of them will ever taste. I don't want to be a part of that." He glared at her. "Is that a good enough reason for you?" Amber was silent. He was right. Of course he was right.

"Okay. I'm sorry. I didn't think it through. *I* won't go either. I'll phone Madeleine and . . ."

"No. No. Paola's your sister. They're your family. You should be there." Tendé stood in the doorway drinking water out of a bottle. Amber frowned at him. She'd almost given up trying to break him of the habit.

"But I don't want to be there if you can't," she said, getting up from the couch and going over to him. "I do understand, honestly I do . . . but it would be fun, though, wouldn't it?"

Tendé shook his head slowly. "No, I'd be grumpy all day and you'd get cross."

Amber smiled, slipping her arms around his waist. "Cross? Me? Never." She leaned against him. She could feel him smile against her hair. "I need to talk to Max, I know."

"When you talk to him, you should have something significant to say," Tendé said quietly. Amber pulled back a little, looking at him.

"What d'you mean?"

"Well . . . it's one thing saying we're together, in a relationship, whatever you want to call it. It's another thing to say . . . that we want to get married, for example." His tone was light. Amber searched his face.

"Don't joke about things like that," she said, her heart suddenly racing.

"Who said I'm joking?" Tendé's voice was quiet.

"Are you . . . what are you saying?" she said carefully.

"What d'you think?"

"Tendé Ndiaye . . . are you asking me to marry you?" Amber laughed suddenly. He grinned at her.

"Well, what does it sound like?" He put the bottle he'd been drinking out of down on the counter and turned to her.

"But . . . how come you've never asked me before?"

"Is it the kind of question one has to ask again and again? No . . . I've been waiting."

"For what?" Amber was amazed.

"For the right moment."

"And this is it?" She glanced down at herself. She was wearing a pair of his boxer shorts and a T-shirt. He followed her gaze.

"Yes. At least, I think it is. Is there ever one?"

"Well, you're the one who's been waiting for it," Amber said, allowing herself to be folded within his arms. "I can't believe you've just asked me to marry you."

"I would've asked sooner. But I think there were things you needed to think about first. You know, see if you could live here, if you could fit into the culture, living with a new religion . . . it's a lot to take on."

"I've been thinking," Amber said hesitantly. "About converting, becoming Moslem."

"I know. I've been watching."

"I want to. I've made up my mind."

"You know that you don't have to. Even the Prophet married a Christian and a Jew. And you're both, no?"

Amber laughed. "Well, technically not really. Max is Jewish, not my mother. It's passed through her, you see." Tendé nodded.

"I know. But . . . I mean it. You don't have to."

"I know," she repeated slowly. "But I don't know how I'm going to live here if I don't."

"What do you mean?"

"Well, you're born Moslem. And here in Mali, it's as much a part of the culture as it is a religion—even *I* can see that. But being born into it . . . well, you have the freedom to opt out of the things that you don't like or don't want to do . . . you drink alcohol and I've certainly never seen you pray . . . but me, if I convert . . . I won't have that choice. And yet if I don't, how will I ever fit in?"

"Of course you will. You'll find your own way. You're already picking up some of the language. You like living here, anyone can see that. You don't have to change your religion to live here, Amber. Islam's not a dogma. Neither is Mali. I know the two seem interchangeable, especially to foreigners, but we've always had people of other faiths in our midst—just look around you. No, you don't have to convert, not unless you want to. And then it should be for different reasons—not because you want to fit in. You already fit in." Amber nodded slowly. "But I won't go to your sister's wedding," he added quietly, smiling. Amber pushed her face into his neck.

"I wouldn't expect you to. You're very stubborn, *husband.*"

"Likewise, *wife.*" They both laughed. He kissed her, hard.

A month later, however, she wasn't smiling. She had just come back from London, from a meeting with

Tim. She wasn't working hard enough or fast enough on the story he'd given her, he complained. And she was the one who'd begged for it. He'd warned her, but she'd insisted and now . . . it was almost three months later and he still had nothing. Amber couldn't say a thing in her defense. He was right. She promised him she'd get onto it immediately. "A fortnight," he said as she left his office. "I'm giving you a fortnight. Gale's been waiting for a month for you to come up with something. I've had to put him on something else. Get your act together, Amber, or you're off the story." Amber nodded and fled.

And now she was sitting at her desk in Bamako and the evidence was spread out in front of her. Max had indeed met with Galli and Sidibé. There were even photographs of the three of them coming out of the Métropole in Paris together. They'd apparently been holding secret meetings at an undisclosed European location—reporters trying to ascertain the meeting place had drawn a blank. She chewed the end of the pen, frowning, and picked up the phone. Five minutes later, she had her answer. *Casa Bella*. Of course. Andréa and Luciana had confirmed it.

She got up from the desk and walked to the window, hugging herself. What next? She knew what she ought to do—send a fax through to Gale immediately, confirming dates and times of meetings. She ought to call Tendé at his office—he had a right to know, of course. She'd kept her part in the whole investigation quiet—she'd had to—but now . . . Tendé would be furious. She knew just how fine the line separating them was: he, a junior government minister; she the daughter of one of the country's largest private foreign investors. When it came out, the link between Max's recent activities and Tendé Ndiaye's choice of foreign—white—bride could be damaging to Tendé. It was like walking a tightrope, he'd often said to her. Two or three steps in the wrong direction could—and would—finish him off.

The prayer call was starting. It was almost six. She stood at the window staring out at a patch of milky-pink sky. It was the beginning of December. The Harmattan winds had started again; a light ochre dusting over everything. In a week or two, the sky would be clouded out completely by the fine powder. She hated it. She stared at her open laptop. Her words were already etched into the luminous screen. What to do . . . what to do. She couldn't think straight. Of course she had to send in what she knew. No question. But . . . it was Max. She had to talk to him first, and find out from him. She reached for the phone again. She had to get to Max before anyone else did.

≈81≈

Whatever else she'd expected when she finally walked into the small house in the crowded township of Mbare, the dreadlocked, chain-smoking man in front of her was not it. Godson Marimba looked up from where he was lying on the floor and nodded curtly at her. He was busy trying to fix a pipe—there were puddles of water on the floor and a large bucket in one corner. Becky stood in the doorway, wondering what to do. Godson Marimba was nothing like any of the other Zimbabweans she'd met—she'd been picturing a quiet, soft-spoken man, shyly grateful for her interest in his work. She'd imagined going to sit in a café where they might discuss his work and art. The man who worked on the pipe and totally ignored her was a whole culture away from the gentle, obsequious servants back on the farm.

"Er . . . Mr. Marimba?" Becky asked as his head disappeared beneath the sink.

"Yeah."

"Um . . . I was wondering . . . my name's Becky Aldridge. Your brother, Sampson, told me I could find you here. I'm—"

"I know who you are. What do you want?" he interrupted her. Becky blinked, taken aback by the directness and hostility in his voice.

"Oh. Well. I'm . . . I saw one of your pieces the other day. I was wondering."

"The answer's no, lady. You're wasting your time. I don't paint any more and I don't have anything left for sale. Okay?" Becky jumped. "So . . . I hope that's answered your questions, lady. Sorry about the wasted journey." He busied himself wrenching apart a bolt.

"Look, Mr. Marimba . . . I saw one of your pieces and—"

"Fucking vultures."

Becky stopped. "What did you just call me?" She was too astounded to continue.

"You heard me." He stuck his head out from beneath the sink and regarded her coolly.

"Wha . . . what're you talking about?" she stammered.

Godson slowly sat up, rubbing his oil-stained hands on his dirty blue overalls. He shot her a dark look. "Tourists. You're all the same. You fly in here, snap up the local art at ridiculous prices and then whisk it out of the country before anyone can say a thing. Then we find out you're selling our stuff in New York and London for fifty times the price. Vultures. That's what we call you and that's why you're not getting anything from me. Now why don't you just fuck off back to your hotel in Avonlea. There are nice baskets for sale in the lobby, you know." There was a tense silence as the two of them stared at each other. Becky's heart was racing—how *dare* he?

"You . . . arrogant *prick*," she ground out finally. Godson gave a short laugh. "How dare you talk to me like that? I came here out of interest. It took me two fucking weeks to find you. I'm not a tourist, I *live* here."

"Oh yeah? Me too. So what?" He was mocking her.

"So . . . so *nothing*. I'm not a dealer or a tourist. I'm not looking to take anything out of the country. I'm just interested in your work, that's all. I'm thinking about starting up a small gallery here and—"

"What did you say?" Godson stopped cleaning his palms and looked at her. "A gallery? You want to start a gallery?"

"Yes, I've been looking around. There's so little here . . . I used to run one in London. I was thinking—"

Godson stood up suddenly, a spanner falling out of his pocket and clattering onto the cement floor. He stared at her for a second, then held out a hand. "Look," he said a little awkwardly. "I'm sorry. I got the wrong impression."

Becky hesitated, then took his hand. "I suppose it's an easy mistake," she said after a moment. "Is there somewhere we could talk for a moment?"

"Not around here," Godson laughed. "Tell you what. I'm meeting some friends of mine at Jazz 105 tonight. You staying in town?"

Becky nodded. "Not in Avonlea, though." He had the grace to look abashed.

"It's on Second Street, downtown. We'll be there around 10 p.m. Why don't you join us? We can talk then. Right now . . ." he gestured towards the tools lying on the ground, "I have to get this finished."

"Yes, sure. I'm sure I'll find it." Becky hoisted her bag onto her shoulder. "Well, see you tonight, I guess."

"Ja." He had dropped down onto the floor again. Becky gave a quick smile and walked out. Her face was still burning. She wasn't used to such confrontations. Although there was something very enjoyable about the way the two of them had sized each other up like opponents. She couldn't say why but she had the feeling Godson Marimba had deemed her worthy. Arrogant prick. She grinned as she threaded her way along the dusty street towards the main road. Children skipped along beside her, shouting, *"Mzungu! Mzungu!"* as she walked. She smiled and waved at them. She was in a good mood. Suddenly, the future seemed quite bright. She reached into her bag for her sunglasses, smiling to herself.

She met Godson and his friend Thomas at the club that evening. It was the first time she'd seen a mixed crowd; black and white Zimbabweans and tourists sitting around as they would in a bar in London or New York, swapping stories, beers, dances . . . she looked around in ill-concealed amazement.

"What are you staring at?" Godson shouted above the music.

She took a swig of beer. "This . . . it's the first time . . . it's just a very mixed crowd, that's all."

"Where did you say you live?" Thomas asked her.

"On a farm. Near Chinhoyi." The two men looked at each other.

"What the hell you doing out there?" Godson asked.

"I . . . well, my boyfriend helps on a farm, with tourists . . . they run safaris and stuff."

Godson's face broke into a grin. "See? I wasn't so wrong."

Becky grimaced. "It's a job," she said apologetically. "That's why I've been thinking about doing something else."

"Let's dance." Godson got up suddenly. "It's too loud here. Let's dance and talk." Becky looked at him nervously. "Come on. I'm not going to bite you.

I have a wife." He held out a hand. After a moment's hesitation, Becky took it and followed him onto the crowded dance floor. It was surreal, she thought to herself as they threaded their way through the crowd. She felt like Alice, stumbling upon a secret world hidden beneath her own. Zimbabwe was like one giant onion, peeling and shedding layer upon layer; Henry and the Fairfields on a farm in a part of the country that could be the Cotswolds, where the proprietors staked everything they had in making it so; Nadège and her friends and the ridiculously old-fashioned, colonial lifestyle to which they clung; and now this—Godson and his world of young, trendy urbanites. Where did she belong?

"Whose house was it, this morning?" she asked, as they began to dance. "Where I found you?"

"Ah, that's my aunt. She had a sink installed in one of the rooms and it's been leaking for days. I promised to fix it for her."

"And where do you live?"

"Chitungwiza. It's about twelve miles south of here. You should come there. That's where I have my studio."

"You have a studio?" Becky was surprised.

"Of course. How do you think I paint?"

"Yes, of course . . . sorry. I . . . I didn't think." They danced in silence for a few moments.

"What you said this morning . . . a gallery. Are you serious?" Godson asked after a while.

Becky nodded. "Yes. I've even found a place. It's an old café, on Albion Road, just by the Tube Night Club."

"You mean the old Ndebele café?" Godson broke in excitedly.

"You know it?"

"Man, it's a fantastic space. But . . . you have the money to do something like that? I heard it's an Indian who owns the building. They always want to make money."

"Well, *I* don't, not personally. But I think it might be possible to get some."

"Have you gone quite mad?" Henry looked at her, bewildered. She was sitting on the edge of the bed in her white strapless summer dress that he liked so much, swinging her legs and telling him, quite calmly, that she was thinking of moving to Harare.

"I hate it here," she said, picking at a loose thread from her hem. Henry stared at her.

"Since when?" he said finally.

"Oh, since forever. I mean, it was fine when we first got here but I hate living out in the middle of fucking nowhere and I especially hate the Fairfields. I just don't see the point."

"The point of what?"

"The point of pretending you're still in Rhodesia and that nothing's changed. Godson says—"

"And who the fuck is Godson?"

"Godson Marimba. He's the artist I told you about. He's been helping me."

"Helping you do what?" Henry felt his world suddenly sliding out from under him again. Marimba? An African? Oh, God . . . no . . . not again.

"Oh, for God's sake, Henry. It's not like that. He's *married*."

"So? That never stopped any of them, I'm telling you. You haven't got a clue what they're like. I can just—" he stopped suddenly. Becky was looking at him with something dangerously like pity. "Becky, don't do this," he said suddenly, pleading. "You don't know what you're getting into. It'll just be like the other crowd, the Baynes and the Baxters. You used to be so keen on them . . . now look, you hardly go to visit any more. You've always been like that, flitting around all over the place. This is just another one of your fads. It'll pass. I know it will."

"This isn't a fad, Henry," Becky said coldly. "This is what I do. I've been stuck here for two years helping *you* do what *you* do—now I want to do something for me. And besides, I still go round to Nadège's. I've just been busy with this other stuff."

"But where are you going to find the money? Who's going to employ you to run a gallery? This is nonsense, Becky. It's crazy."

"I'll find the money. Anyhow, it's none of your business. You've made pretty clear what you think of it. Why do you care whether it works or not?"

"Because. Because . . . I *love* you," Henry blurted out. He was beginning to whine—he hated the sound of his voice. He ran a hand through his hair in agitation. "Okay. I admit . . . in the beginning, it was more about me wanting to get back at Amber, you know . . . and you were there . . . I dunno . . . it just sort of happened. But now it's changed—" he broke off. Becky was looking at him strangely.

"Revenge? Is that what this is about?"

"Only in the beginning," Henry said, suddenly wondering if he'd made a huge mistake.

"Oh, really? And when did it change? When did you stop thinking about revenge?"

"Shit, I don't know, Becky . . . it doesn't matter. The point is, I love you and I don't want you to go."

"Oh, but that *is* the point, Henry." Becky was calm. "I would say, actually, that's the whole point."

She left. There was nothing he could do or say. She packed her things into the Land Rover that Nadège had sent for her—*the bitch!*—and drove away from the farm without even bothering to say goodbye to the Fairfields. Henry was left standing in the middle of the driveway with the three gardeners looking discreetly over the top of the hedge as she tossed her suitcases and bags into the back, gave him a hug and climbed in. There was a rustle in the bushes and the sound of suppressed laughter. He glowered at them, unable to even shout. He felt completely numb.

It wasn't going to be easy. She knew that straight away. She moved into a spare room at Nadège's— *stay as long as you want, darling*—and tried to think about what to do next. She phoned Godson Marimba and they met again in a café near Africa Unity Square. She had a clear idea of what she wanted; could she get him interested too?

"The thing is," she said, stirring her coffee, "you're absolutely right. Most gallery owners would swoop in here, pick up a few pieces and head out again. I don't want to do that, but not because I don't want to be called a 'fucking vulture,' " she grinned. "It's because I don't think it'll work. Not in the long run."

"Why's that?" Godson asked.

"Well, because it's too difficult. Look, the only two places in the world that really count in the art market are London and New York. Both places are hellishly expensive in terms of setting up a gallery. I should know—the woman I used to work for nearly went bankrupt over some poxy little place in the East End that no one ever came to. So . . . that makes them both impractical. Secondly, there's almost no market for African art—contemporary art, that is. Masks and all the other stuff that Europeans and Americans like to think are 'ethnic' are just about the extent of it. Anything else and it's encroaching on their territory."

"Shit, Becky—you know a lot more about this stuff than I thought."

"What did you think? I told you I used to work in a gallery."

"Sure . . . like I used to work in a car shop. I don't know the first thing about fixing cars." He laughed. "Go on."

"Okay. The thing that keeps a gallery alive are the buyers, and there's only a handful of those. Each gallery has a client list—the buyers, not the artists— and it's worth its weight in gold. Morag, the woman I used to work for, only had two real buyers on her list and the fact that she's still around is due to them. It's a really hard business. Of course, if you get the right buyers you can make a fortune but with the stuff I'm interested in—your paintings and some of the other things I've seen here—it would be almost impossible."

"Sounds pretty gloomy. What's your answer?"

Becky drew a deep breath. "Well, since I've been here I've met all kinds of people, Godson. I mean, *all* kinds. From farmhands to Cape Town lunching ladies. I don't know what it is about this place . . . but it's fantastic. And one of the things I've noticed, especially since I've met you and some of your friends, is that there's a huge great hole in the market somewhere between the primitive masks the carvers turn out for the tourists and the type of stuff you do. I meet people in the northern suburbs who think they have to go to London to buy art. If it were marketed in the right way, they'd buy it here. I know they would."

"So . . . ?"

"I'd like us to fill that hole."

"Us?"

"Aldridge Marimba. A shop, gallery, cooperative, café . . . call it what you want. I want to turn that space downtown into the biggest and best space selling contemporary and antique African art. I want us to sell everything: art, carvings, furniture, sculpture, textiles . . . you name it. I want us to put on events, shows, openings, private views, to create a place where artists can show their work properly, not just in the fucking lobby of the Holiday Inn. We could plow back some of the profits into getting more space, set up studios for rent—"

"Whoa . . . easy, lady! You're running ahead of yourself. Godson held up his hands, laughing. There was a fire in his eyes she hadn't seen before. "South Africa's ahead of us, you know. They already have the major galleries and museums. We're just lagging behind, man. If anyone here wants to sell their work, that's where they have to go."

"Yes, but the problem is, the gallery owners and dealers in South Africa think they're in London or New York. How many African artists do any of them carry?" Godson shook his head. She was right. "Come on, let's do it *here*. Let's just *do* it. There are enough tourists passing through Harare every day, plus there's all the expat crowd and the rich whites . . . and then there are all the banks and corporate offices. D'you know how many cheap reproduction Turners I've seen in Standard Chartered Bank? Even in bloody Chinhoyi!" Godson looked at her. He let out a sigh.

"Man, Becky . . . this could be fantastic. But why d'you need me? You could do this on your own. I've got absolutely no capital to put into something like this."

Becky shook her head. "No . . . I'll find the money. Look, I'll be totally honest. You're the link I need to the artists. I don't know anyone here. I'm good at the marketing and organizing bit—you find the talent. We'll have so much more credibility if we work together."

"Ah, the whole black-white thing. Ja, that's always good PR. Okay." Godson drained his coffee. "Enough.

I'm in." Becky could barely contain her smile. It would work. She *knew* it would work. With Godson interested, the first big hurdle had been taken. She could now move onto the next.

≋82≋

Amber found Max just before he left the house. He listened to her for a few minutes then agreed to meet her the following day in Bamako. He would have to fly up to Téghaza that afternoon but they could spend the morning together. He sounded tired. Putting the phone down, Amber was assailed by a sudden wave of guilt. She hoped she hadn't sounded too—what? Like an officious attorney summoning his witness to the stand? *I need to talk to you. Not over the phone.* Max's voice had been noncommittal.

She spent the day going over her notes, checking dates and figures as best she could. Tendé was at a government meeting in Sikasso, in the south of the country. There had been some border trouble with Côte d'Ivoire and he wasn't due back until the weekend. In some ways, it was better he wouldn't be around when Max came.

The next day she waited anxiously for Max to arrive. She'd asked Lameen to prepare something nice for lunch—and to tidy the house for the fifth time.

"Your father . . . he's coming here?" he asked softly as he dusted the table yet again. Amber nodded. "Please don't to worry. It will be very clean, madame." He moved purposefully through the living room. She smiled. Of course it would. Lameen would have put Max's army of staff back in London to shame. She left him to it and walked upstairs to the room she used as a study.

He arrived just after 11 a.m. He looked tired, she noticed worriedly as he got out of the car. He carried only his briefcase—his cases were in the back of the car waiting to be flown up to Téghaza that afternoon. She hurried to the front door.

"Max," she said, moving forward to give him a kiss. He gripped her upper arm. "Are you tired?" she asked solicitously.

He nodded. "A little. There's still a lot of detail to be sorted out. Where's Tendé?"

"He's in the south. He'll join you at the plant tomorrow. Are you hungry?"

Max shook his head. "So what's this all about? Why the secrecy?" As usual, he wasted no time in getting right down to business. Amber hesitated.

"Let's go upstairs. It's cooler up there and there's . . . something I need to ask you."

Max shrugged. "Sure. Lead the way."

"Look," Amber said as soon as she'd closed the door, "this isn't easy for me to ask you. I'm not supposed to do this—you're not supposed to know I'm working on it but . . ."

"What are you talking about?" Max sat down in one of the easy chairs by the window, next to her desk. He looked over at her cuttings and notes, spread across its dusty surface. She gave a small start—she should have put them away. "What's this?" he reached over and picked up the *FD. Sall Strikes Again! Max Sall, the wealthy financier-turned-environmental crusader intends to put the obscure West African state of Mali firmly on the map.* "What're you working on? A new story?" He let the paper drop. "Is that what you wanted to talk about?"

"Well, yes. Max . . . have you been seeing Galli?" She blurted the question out.

Max looked at her for a second, his eyes narrowing. "What makes you say that?" he asked, his voice dangerously quiet. Amber sighed.

"There are . . . rumors, Max. I've been asked . . ." she hesitated. It wasn't quite the truth. "I asked to be put on the story. Max . . . does Tendé know?" As soon as she said it, she realized it was the wrong thing to say. Max's face closed up immediately. He stood up.

"What the hell are you trying to do, Amber?" he asked, his voice tight with rage. "Ruin this before it's even got off the ground?"

"No. I'm just . . ."

"And what kind of question is that? Does Tendé know? No, your precious little boyfriend doesn't know. You want to know why? Because your *boy*friend—"

"Don't talk about him like that," Amber broke in,

her own temper beginning to rise. "He's not my 'little boyfriend.' He's *your* partner. And besides, we're engaged. He's my fiancé, if you want the proper term." There was a sudden silence. Amber closed her eyes. It wasn't the way she wanted to tell him.

"Really?" Max sneered. "Your fiancé, is it? This is the way you go about things? Sneaking around behind my back for months . . ."

"We did *not*! I asked him not to say anything because . . . well, because . . ."

"Go on, defend him. Typical bloody female. The first man that comes along and you—"

"He is *not* the first man who came along," Amber shouted, tears springing to her eyes. "And there's nothing typical about it! I love him, Max. Can't you get that through your head? What's wrong with him? *You* like him. Christ, you like him better than you like your own son!" she screamed.

"Leave Kieran out of this," Max yelled at her. "If you think I'm going to stand by and watch you sign your life away to that Moslem nigger . . ." he stopped. There was a shocked, horrible silence. Amber stared at him, her heart hammering.

"What did you just call him?" she breathed, shaking her head as if to rid herself of his words. Max said nothing. He looked at her, a strange look of fear and anger on his face. Then he turned and walked out, slamming the door behind him. For a few seconds, she remained where she was in the middle of the room, too shocked and angry to move. The silence was suddenly overwhelming after the shouting and raised voices of the past few minutes. She could hear the sound of her own breathing—a harsh, ugly sound, punctuated only by the gentle whirring of the fan above her head. She swallowed and recognized the salty traces at the edges of her mouth as belonging to her, to her tears. Minutes passed as she struggled to regain control of herself. *Calm down*, she told herself furiously. *Calm down*. The door on the other side of the room was open— anyone could walk right in. She walked over and closed it, not wanting to be seen like this. She quickly wiped her eyes, angry at herself as well as at him. How could he say such things? How *dare* he? She walked a little unsteadily to the desk. Her papers were spread across its dusty surface. She glanced at them—scores of loose, yellow sheets covered in her barely legible scrawl, newspaper cuttings, magazine articles, carefully typed notes. She picked up one of the articles and crumpled it angrily in her fist, then looked about her for the carafe of water that Lameen carefully left out for her every day. She pulled her notepad towards her, anything to take her mind off what had just happened. What would she tell Tendé—she knew exactly what he would say. That he had been right about Max all along. Going into business with him was one thing, sleeping with his daughter was an entirely different matter.

Max almost ran from the room. There was a bitter taste in his mouth, bile forcing its way up from his stomach. He stumbled down the stairs into the living room. Majid was sitting in the kitchen talking to

Amber's houseboy. He jumped up as soon as he saw Max.

"Master . . . sir, is everything okay?" he called out, gesturing to Lameen to bring some water, *quick*! Max nodded impatiently.

"Yes, yes . . . no, I don't need anything. I want to go . . . let's go. I'm in a hurry." Majid looked after him, concerned. "*Now*!" Max barked. Majid jumped. He ran to open the door. Max slid inside, his mind racing. Why? He passed a hand over his face. Why the hell had he said it? He'd never . . . it wasn't . . . he'd never thought of Tendé . . . *that way*. What had made him say it? It was Amber. The way she'd attacked him, jumping to Tendé's defense before she'd even asked the question. It had shocked him, taken him by surprise. Amber was *his* girl—the only one in the whole sorry mess of a family who'd inherited anything like his own intelligence and drive. He'd suddenly seen her slipping away from him, belonging to someone else now. And the news of her engagement . . . Tendé should have asked *him*— the proper way. God knows he'd had plenty of opportunity when it was just the two of them up there in the desert. But he'd kept quiet, like a coward— and then it had slipped out like some sort of *fait accompli* that made him look . . . redundant. Washed up. Of no use. And old. It made him feel old.

"Sir . . . do you want me to accompany you?" Majid was staring at him. Max blinked. They were already at the airport.

"No. I'm fine. Just put my bags on the plane, will you? And let the ground staff know I'll be taking off in a few minutes." Majid nodded doubtfully. Max opened the door and walked out. It was still very hot and horribly dusty. He walked quickly to the tiny terminal building to complete the paperwork for his flight. Fifteen minutes later, he was in the cockpit, running through his pre-flight checks. It was good to have something concrete to do. It kept his mind off what had just happened. He radioed the control tower and got his clearance. As he taxied out towards the runway, he noticed that visibility was poor. A fine, reddish haze lay over the horizon—the damned Harmattan winds. He positioned himself, eased the throttle back and felt the familiar surge of the engines. The little plane began its hurtle down the runway; beneath his legs he could feel the thrust and answering roar—there was a moment of suspension and then the plane lifted. He soared directly upwards, the plane shuddering. Each time it was as new—the exhilarating release as he took off, circling the capital, the earth racing away from him as he tilted the stick and headed north. It was very windy; he usually preferred to fly in the early morning. By the afternoon, the ground had heated up sufficiently to release hot air currents and it was those, together with the red, swirling wind, that battered against the plane. His flight path more or less followed the river and normally, he would be able to see his progress by the silvery twists and turns of the Niger as it snaked its way north. Ségou, Mopti, Timbuktu . . . he was used to seeing the towns unfold in their higgledy-piggledy, chaotic jigsaw—but not today. About thirty minutes into the flight, he hit a patch of turbulence; the plane dipped and dropped alarmingly. He radioed the army flight center at Sévaré for permission to ascend. It was granted and he climbed to 29,000 feet. The sky was thankfully clear at that height. He looked down over the swirling, ochre shadow that the Harmattan had thrown over the entire country—beautiful.

Just north of Timbuktu, the turbulence returned and here the dust cloud was thicker. It was four thirty; the sun was beginning its slow descent to his left. As he flew on, the Adrar des Iforhas mountain range began to glow, casting dark, toneless shadows across its surface, disappearing rapidly into the haze. Up there, sliding over the hazy Sahara with only the sound of his own breathing and the steady drone of the aircraft for company, it was possible to think that the argument with Amber would blow over. He would apologize. He had to. What he'd said was unforgivable. He would call as soon as he landed. The plane gave another, unexpected jolt. He frowned. Even at that altitude the winds were strong. He was considering his position, unable to see the telltale wispy clouds that usually signaled a patch of turbulence. In fact, everything was beginning to lose definition around him—the dust was being sucked upwards. He held the joystick in both hands; the plane was beginning to drop and bounce. What had he been told in flight school? Keep a fixed point on the horizon as you try to maneuver around the problem. But he couldn't see the horizon. All of a sudden, he realized he'd lost his balance. The plane was flying into what looked like a sandstorm, a foggy red mist of pulling winds and air pockets. Which way was up? He flew on for a couple of minutes, trying to clamp down on the panic that was beginning to rise in him. *Calm down,* he told himself. *Stay calm. Wait for it to pass.* There was a flash of something—light bouncing off water, just to his left . . . he strained towards it. It was in the wrong position—above him, not below, tilting dangerously. What the . . . ? There was a sound—a slow whooshing of wind and the sound of something hitting the engine, a single, shocked stutter—and then there was silence. *I haven't finished . . .* He felt, rather than heard, the explosion. *No, it's not finished. I've been interrupted—*

≈83≈

There was a tap at the door. Amber looked up impatiently. It was almost dark outside. She looked at the time in surprise—was it really so late? She looked at the door. It was probably Lameen, calling her to supper.

"Go away!" she called out, as gently as she could manage. "I'm fine. I don't need anything. I'll eat later." There was silence for a few seconds. She could almost hear him hesitating. But the tap came again, more urgently. She sighed and put down her pen. She pulled back her hair and ran a quick finger under her eyes, hoping her tears didn't show, then pushed back her chair and walked to the door.

As soon as she opened it and saw Lameen, his usually pleasant face contorted into a mask of distress and agitation, her heart missed a beat. "What is it?" she asked, the cold hand of fear suddenly snaking its way through her body. Lameen could only stand and stare at her. "What's the matter? What is it?"

"Madame . . . *excusez-moi*," the words seemed to stumble out of his mouth. "Please. You must come now." He turned away from her, backing away down the dark corridor. She grabbed his arm and followed him, hearing the women in the courtyard next door beginning to wail as first one door somewhere in the house slammed, then another. She could hear cars pulling up outside in the alleyway and the sound of running feet. Then a police siren. And another. She followed Lameen blindly as they ran together down the hallway. She was aware only of the flap of his bare soles against the tiled floor and the sound of her heart beating wildly inside her chest.

She knew. The chief inspector lowered his eyes in an almost feminine gesture of self-consciousness as soon as she burst into the living room. She backed away from him, turning a face blindly to the wall. Oh, yes . . . she knew.

Amber had read about grief, of course. The loss of a lover, a parent, a child, even. Pain, hurt, sorrow, shock, fear . . . she ran through the adjectives and turned over the stories endlessly in her mind. But none of the accounts she remembered mentioned guilt. The minute the inspector opened his mouth, guilt hit her with such force her legs buckled and she had to be caught before slumping to the floor. Guilt—with her arms pressed tightly against her ears to stop the words coming out of their mouths; in the screaming she recognized later as having come from her own mouth, her own heart . . . guilt and fear—it was *she*. She had caused it, willed it to happen. *She* was to blame. Lameen held her down, grabbed her hands to stop her from slapping her own face. He called out to someone to get a doctor, *quick*! Amber dimly heard the commotion around her but found it impossible to concentrate on anything other than the hard, tight ball of terror in her stomach. She heard doors opening and the sound of Mandia's voice and the quick, sharp intake of breath . . . a child was standing in the doorway heaving huge, deep breaths that became sobs. All around, everywhere, were the sounds of shock and panic. Mandia tried to put her arms around her; she couldn't—she couldn't stand to be touched. She struggled upright, staggering against Mandia and opened her mouth to say something, but nothing came out. Guilt and fear blocked her throat. She allowed herself to be led away, gently . . . Mandia on one side, Lameen on the other. Outside, the lamentations continued as if they would never stop.

There was no body, of course. The explosion had incinerated everything. The inspector's voice came through the walls and the half-open door to the adjoining room. Mandia and several other family members had gathered in the study next to the bedroom. They spoke in French; low, murmuring voices expressing sympathy—and not a little concern. For Max Sall to have crashed his plane and died in *their* country . . . they knew it wouldn't be long before the media spotlight would be turned on them. Whatever happened next the country's police force would be under intense scrutiny. She could hear Mandia making the right noises, calming everyone down sending someone to get Tendé from Sikasso, immediately. There was no body . . . she heard it over and over again. It's not a body, she longed to scream, it's Max you're talking about—but the Valium tablet she'd been given made her drowsy and heavy and the words just wouldn't come. No body, nothing . . . there was nothing left of Max. Nothing to take home. She pushed her head into the pillow and tried to smother her thoughts.

Later, it seemed to her as though weeks had passed before she was sufficiently composed to undertake the journey back to London. Time in that period of shock was altered, suspended. The day it happened; the day after the day . . . two days afterwards . . . she learned another, more awful measure of time than the one she'd come to know in Bamako; days and nights punctured by the muezzin's call and the rhythm of the mosque. In the darkened bedroom where she lay, she was aware only of the ticking of the clock on the dresser and the whir of the fan overhead. Sometimes she heard Tendé arguing with his parents in the corridor outside—*leave her, she needs to be alone . . . no, she'll be fine*. She knew that lying alone in the dark was not their way of dealing with death—the thought brought fresh tears to her eyes—but she could not have borne the wake-keeping and elaborate funeral rituals that were their custom.

There was something else. Something she couldn't bring herself to speak about, not even to Tendé. There was a coldness in her that she knew puzzled him but she couldn't find the words to tell him what had happened just before Max rushed out. She couldn't even explain the overwhelming sense of guilt . . . that would have meant admitting that he'd been right about Max all along. She couldn't face that. So she turned away from the one person who could have brought her some solace and tried to lock him out. She stayed in the room with the shutters closed and the sounds of whispered conversations outside.

* * *

Angela was surprisingly calm over the phone. Tendé broke the news as gently and sympathetically as he could. He understood, almost from the moment she picked up the receiver, that this was not the loss her daughter felt. There was just the one, sudden intake of breath and then the beautifully modulated vowels down the long-distance, crackling line. *I see. Oh dear. And Amber?* She seemed to accept without question the fact that Tendé would fly back to London with Amber in a few days' time. She was ever so grateful for his call. So kind. Angela would see to the memorial arrangements. Yes, she would inform Francesca and Paola. No, there was nothing further he could do. He'd been so kind. Tendé replaced the receiver gently, a pulse beginning to beat at his temple. He stood for a moment in the hallway downstairs, wondering . . . for all his closeness to Max, there was little about his family Tendé understood. So many currents he found impossible to follow. He looked outside at the gardens, now parched by the seasonal lack of water . . . the yellowed, dun-colored grass, the dusty fronds of palm trees . . . from where he stood he could see the faint, white sheen of dust that lay on the car windows; he turned away heavily. Max was dead. In the confusion of the days that followed the accident, his only thoughts were with Amber. Now that he'd spoken to her mother, he recognized relief in her voice, not grief. It was her daughter who was lying upstairs, unable to come to terms with it. He knew enough, too, to understand that there was more. There was something Amber wasn't telling him. He walked upstairs.

"Amber . . . you should eat something." He sat down beside her on the bed. She turned a tear-stained face towards him, shaking her head.

"I . . . I'm not hungry." Her voice was low and hoarse. He winced. She'd been crying for hours.

"I know, but you must. You need to eat. Something. Anything."

"I'm fine."

It was his turn to shake his head. "No, no . . . you're not. That's okay. But you should still eat something. Something small. I'll ask Lameen to bring something up."

"Tendé, please . . . I'm fine." Her voice was strained. He looked at her. She wouldn't—or couldn't—meet his eyes. He put out a hand to touch her, stung by the way she moved away immediately, as though she couldn't bear the contact, slight as it was.

"Amber, what happened?" The question had been on the tip of his tongue for days. There was no response. He folded his hands back in his lap and looked at the huddled figure lying stiffly beside him. "Amber?" he tried again. There was still no response. "Look, *chérie* . . . I know how hard this is but—"

"You don't know anything about this." Amber's voice was cold. She turned her face to the wall, away from him.

"He was my friend, too," Tendé began slowly. There was a movement under the sheets.

"He is . . . was . . . my father," she struggled to say, her voice cracking. "He's *my* father and it's *my* fault."

"It was an accident," Tendé said gently, his hand going out to her again. This time there was no resistance. He pushed the sheet back from her face and tried to pull her towards him.

"No, that's what you don't understand. It *wasn't* an accident . . . it was my fault," she sobbed.

"Amber, tell me what happened. You need to tell me. I can't help you if I don't know what happened."

"I can't."

"You must."

"He said things, Tendé . . . awful things. About you. We argued, and then he said something . . . I can't say it. I won't. But he left just as soon as he said it. He was in a dreadful state . . . and then he got into the plane and . . . he crashed. If we hadn't . . . if *I* hadn't argued with him . . ." she was sobbing, huge, uneven breaths, the words continuing to tumble out. Tendé nodded slowly, his hand going to stroke her tangled hair.

"I know . . . I know." He sighed. He didn't need Amber to spell out what he feared had happened. "It's all right, *chérie*. Listen to me. Look at me." He turned Amber's face towards him, a mask of pain, grief, guilt—and anger, too. His fingers slipped gently under her chin. She was looking at him now, her blue eyes reddened and swollen with tears. "This will pass." She nodded at him uncertainly. "It will pass." He bent his head towards hers, cradling her, offering the temporary shelter of his own arms against the storm of her grief.

≈85≈

The memorial service for Max was held at *Casa Bella*. It was the one thing Angela and Francesca agreed on. Angela wanted to invite the entire world; Francesca wanted only Max's family. In the end, a strange compromise was reached. Amber, Tendé, Kieran and Angela were there; as was Paola, Francesca and Theo, Max's lawyer. Then there were some of Max's friends—two gentlemen from New York; a businessman from St. Petersburg; a rabbi from London; and Jonathan Sainsbury—no one knew why. For someone who had lived such a gregarious life, his funeral was strangely quiet. Protocol demanded that Angela play the leading role in grief. In truth, as Tendé had suspected, she seemed almost relieved. It was Francesca who appeared devastated. Amber, leaning into Tendé, watched the proceedings with a kind of numbness, still too shocked by his death to understand it or participate in his leave-taking. It was an unusually cold winter in Menorca. The guests stood about on the patio outside, awkwardly making conversation as among strangers, trying to ignore the gusts of cold wind that blasted up the hill from the sea. Theo walked among them with a perpetually worried look on his face. Amber came upon him staring into space by the pool. She stood next to him, unable to speak. She'd known Theo for many years. He put an arm round her shoulders.

"I hate to bring it up now," he said quietly. "But there's the matter of his will. I'll make the arrangements for the hearing as soon as I get back to London. Amber, I must tell you . . . you must prepare yourself." Amber looked at him blankly. "I can't say more than that just now but you must be strong. The way Max would have wanted you to be." Amber put a hand on his arm. Her throat was full of tears. She nodded uncomprehendingly. Whatever it was it would have to wait.

The party flew out of Menorca the following day. Tendé left for Paris to catch a flight back home. Paola and Francesca went back to Rome—Paola's wedding plans were now on hold. She and Kieran hadn't so much as looked at one another during the entire stay. He, Angela and Amber boarded the plane for London shortly afterwards.

They met a week later in the lobby at Theo's Park Lane offices. Francesca and Paola were dressed in black, beautifully and stylishly tragic. Angela was in a powder-blue Chanel suit and seemed more worried about ladders in her stockings than putting on the appropriate face of grief.

"Francesca," Amber greeted her. She and Paola

nodded at each other. Even at a time like this, she thought to herself, nothing had changed. Nothing ever would. Angela sat down beside a huge bouquet of lilies and picked up a magazine. Theo appeared in the doorway. He kissed the women, his touch lingering for a second longer on Amber's arms.

"If you'll come this way, ladies, Kieran. I must warn you . . . there are two other young ladies waiting outside my office. You will be familiar with them, Angela, and I must ask for restraint. These are very difficult times." Amber looked at Angela. What was going on? Francesca's face hardened.

"Who are you talking about?" she demanded, lifting her chin. Theo declined to answer.

"Ladies, this way, please. Do come along." He led the way down the plushly carpeted hallway. They turned the corner and Amber gasped. Krystyna was sitting in a chair, holding a young boy . . . of five, six years of age—the spitting image of Max. Opposite her was Siobhân, holding an infant. She put a hand to her mouth and looked at Angela. Behind her, she heard Kieran say, distinctly, "Oh, fuck." There was silence as the six women stared at one another. "This way, please . . . in here." Theo anxiously ushered the stunned party into his office.

The reading of Max's will took less than ten minutes. When it was over and Theo's voice had died away there was silence for a few seconds. Amber closed her eyes briefly. Then all hell broke loose. She remained in her chair while Theo tried to restore some sense of order in his office. Francesca and Paola were on their feet, shouting—no, screaming—and crying at the same time. Krystyna and Siobhân were crying and trying to quiet their children; Kieran stood up, muttering, "Fuck, oh fuck!" and in the midst of it all, sitting across the vast, polished desk from Theo, Angela calmly inspected her nails. She reached into her cream quilted bag and pulled out a packet of cigarettes. There was a tap at the door—Theo's assistant put her head round the corner. *Can I help?* she mouthed to her employer. Theo shook his head. He got up from behind his desk and walked among Max's women, calming this one, a glass of water for that one . . . his soothing voice and calm, authoritative manner slowly began to work. Siobhân was taken next door with her by-now hysterical infant; miraculously, a game was found for Daniel, Krystyna's little boy, and he sat on the floor by the window, happily absorbed, casting a glance every now and then to his mother; Francesca was given a glass of brandy. Paola announced she was going to be sick and left the room. Only Angela and Amber remained where they were; Angela smoking furiously in an effort to remain calm and Amber silenced by the news she'd just received.

Max's estate—what was left of it—passed directly to Amber. His dream of leaving a more fitting tribute to his wealth in the form of his treasured salt project had nearly undone him. It had drained his reserves to the point that there was very little left. He had made his last will some five years earlier,

and despite Theo's constant reminders, hadn't updated it before his death. Everything he owned,
everything he'd ever made was tied to the comple-
tion of the Téghaza mines. Neither Kieran nor
Paola were mentioned; the house in Holland Park
was given to Angela; Francesca kept her Rome
apartment; *Casa Bella* was Amber's to do with it as
she pleased; there were smaller requests—an annual income for Krystyna and the arrangement that
Max had entered into with Siobhân a year or so
earlier was to be upheld. And the last, strangest be-
quest—a packet of three uncut diamonds that Theo
took out of the safe . . . those too were for Amber.
She held the yellowed, fragile paper in the palm of
her hand, unable to look at them or at anyone
around her. *Why, Max?* Unintentionally or otherwise, he'd left her with an unbearable choice to
make. Even now, after his death, he was forcing her
to choose. Téghaza or the family. Between Tendé
and Max's kin. Her eyes burned suddenly; she had
to get out. She jumped to her feet and stumbled out
of the room.

If Amber had thought that the week following Max's
death was the hardest in her life, she quickly realized there was worse to follow. It had taken her almost twenty-four hours to let the true extent of
her—their—situation sink in. The change in everyone's attitudes towards her was swift and immediate. She now had it all—regardless of the fiscal
shape it was now in—and they, Francesca, Paola,
Kieran . . . they had nothing. Worse than none,

Francesca insisted . . . they had been thrown out, cast aside, trampled on . . . *abused*. Amber, her hands shaking, insisted that nothing would be done or decided until she had had time to think over what to do, how best to accommodate everyone. She went to Theo.

A week later, sitting on one of Theo's plush leather sofas, she accepted a small glass of wine and sat back, looking warily at him.

"How are you holding up, my dear?" he asked.

"I don't know. Fine, I guess. I don't know whether to be angry with him for putting me in this position or honored. I just can't work it out. Why me?" She stared into her glass.

"Who else could he trust, Amber?" Theo said quietly. Amber looked up in surprise. She'd never paid much attention to the kindly, portly lawyer Max seemed to have had forever. She vaguely remembered Theo at the odd family event—she even remembered Theo coming round one evening after Angela had tried to kill herself . . . she remembered him rushing upstairs—Max was away, of course—shouting to the housekeeper to get an ambulance, sitting with Angela . . . yes, he'd always been around. She'd just never really thought about him. "Oh, there was a time when he did think Kieran had turned around," he continued quietly, "with the nightclub. It seemed to be going so well. But then, after the whole issue with Paola," he dabbed his mouth delicately and set down his glass, "it all seemed to fall apart again." Amber stared at him. He knew? Theo caught her glance. "I wasn't just Max's lawyer," he said after a moment. "I was his friend. We grew up together." Amber caught her breath. It was the first time she had ever heard anyone refer to Max's childhood.

"He never said . . . I don't know anything about him," she said, almost whispering. "Are you . . . where do you know him from?"

"Have you ever heard of the *Kindertransport?*" Theo said, getting up from behind his desk.

Amber nodded hesitantly. "The . . . children— Jewish children . . . You? And Max?"

"Yes, both of us. We arrived in different years. I came over in thirty-seven, Max in thirty-nine. We had nothing . . . we both came with nothing. But we were placed at the Neasden Lane Orphanage. I didn't know him well there—he was older than me by a couple of years. But we met again by accident a few years later. He was married to your mother by then. He remembered me. I was just starting out as a lawyer, apprenticing at Rosensweig and Gutman, a big, Jewish law firm. We were suing Sainsbury's over the closure of a small, kosher butchers on Commercial Road . . . I remember it well." Theo paused and took a sip of wine. Amber was totally silent. "We lost the case, of course . . . but Max came up to me. We talked for a bit. He asked me to get in touch with him as soon as I'd qualified." He shrugged. "I did. That was thirty years ago." He took a sip of wine. "Max was good to me. Everything I've earned is due to him. He brought me the right clients, gave me capital when I needed it—he's even godfather to my son." Amber felt the familiar hot prick of tears.

"Why did he never tell us?" she asked, her voice catching.

Theo shook his head. "I wish I could tell you. He thought the world of you, Amber. He used to say it all the time. *If only my son were like my daughter. If only he'd had half her brains.* He was terribly proud of you." Amber felt the tears slide down her cheeks. She looked at Theo. His eyes were bright. "I asked him to revise the will, you know . . . after he'd made it and taken Kieran and Paola out. If only to protect you. But he never got round to it. I sometimes wonder . . ." he shook his head. "I sometimes wonder if this isn't the way he wanted it, after all."

"What d'you mean?"

"It was always his dilemma, see. He'd had such a tough life . . . the early part, I mean. But it made him who he was. You don't get anywhere without struggle, he used to say. And I think he was worried you would never have to struggle for anything. It used to worry him, terribly. He always said you were the most like him—you'd fight for whatever you wanted. Like the time you fought to go to university. He regretted what he'd said, you know. Afterwards, after you'd gone to university, he was ashamed he'd said it. He kept thinking Kieran would come round, you see. I think that was the first real sign. Then when you went to Mali. She's just like me, he told me—he was delighted. So . . . yes, I sometimes wonder if it wasn't intentional . . . you know . . . *not* changing his will. I wonder if this is to be your big struggle, Amber."

"We argued, you know," Amber said after a moment, her voice barely a whisper. "Just before he was killed. He said some things . . . *I* said things . . . I don't know, I've been so . . ."

"Don't." Theo's voice stopped her. "Don't torment yourself. Whatever it was you argued about, it had nothing to do with what happened. It was God's will."

"You sound like Tendé," Amber said with a shaky smile. She paused. "It was over him . . . over Tendé. Max said things—"

"He was just being a father, Amber," Theo broke in. "He was worried about you. And a little jealous, too, you know." He smiled quietly. "I have three girls. The oldest two are married . . . and yes, I get jealous sometimes. It's not easy, being replaced."

"But I would never—" Amber started to say.

Theo shook his head. "It's not about you, I'm afraid. It's us . . . our own vanity. And whatever else you can say about Max, he was a vain old bastard." Theo laughed. "I'm not excusing whatever it was he said—and believe me, I can imagine—I'm just saying . . . he was hurt. That's all." Amber looked at him gratefully. The tightness in her chest that she'd been carrying around for a month was slowly beginning to ease. She picked up her glass and raised it.

"Thanks, Uncle Theo," she said quietly. Theo was silent for a moment, stilled by her words. Then he raised his own.

"No, Amber. Thank *you.*" She saw tears in his eyes. The circle was finally beginning to close.

86

That part, she said over the phone to Tendé that evening, was the easy bit, in comparison. The other bit—what to do about their finances, was the real difficulty.

"I mean, I just don't know . . . of *course* we have to continue with Téghaza. How can we not? It's so close, as well. But . . . what about the others?"

"What about them? Your mother has the house, no? Kieran as well . . . and Francesca has the apartment in Rome. They'll be all right."

"But what will they do for money?"

"What everyone else on the planet does, Amber, including yourself. Get a job. Work."

"But—"

"But nothing. You're not doing them any favors, you know."

"I know. It's just that . . . well, I mean . . . Kieran's never worked before. Never."

"Time for him to start then," Tendé said tartly. He had never been overfond of Kieran—or Paola, either, for that matter. Never mind the first time he'd encountered her. Three years had passed since he'd met them and in that time, his admiration for Amber had grown in almost direct proportion to his growing contempt for the other members of her extended family. In the weeks following Max's death, when he'd flown to London with her, it had come to him slowly that these people—Kieran, Paola, Francesca, Angela—these were the people Amber had grown up around; this—the elegant house in Holland Park with its endless stream of house-keepers and servants—was her *home*. She had shown him the bedroom she and Becky and Madeleine had spent almost all their teenage years in; the little en suite bathroom with the same robe she'd worn as a teenager hanging from a gilt-colored hook behind the heavy white oak door . . . this was home to the young woman he had fallen in love with, and whose reservoir of strength he saw now he had never fully understood. He spent a week among her possessions and the life she'd had before she met him . . . and understood that she had *chosen* not to continue. She could so easily have been a Paola, or a Kieran . . . even Angela. She had made a choice in accordance with what? Her beliefs? Her values? It humbled and astounded him. In so many ways, she was braver than he—his options were the same choices his parents had made before him. In his case, at least, life wasn't so much a conscious decision but simply the gentle molding of himself into a position already deter-mined by his race, his religion, his class. Amber's choices were all the harder for being almost com-pletely out of type.

"I suppose so," he heard her say. And sigh. He smiled to himself. Who knew . . . perhaps this would be the making of them?

"I love you," he said quietly. "Really."

"Me too. I wish you were here."

87

Neither Becky nor Madeleine heard about Max's death until several weeks had passed—Madeleine because she was too busy, Becky because she never listened to the news. Madeleine was walking into her offices on 51st Street when she caught sight of Dari rushing down the street. She stopped and waved. Dari came running up, her breath scrolling out before her in the freezing air.

"Hi—you didn't have to wait," she said, rubbing her gloved hands together. "It's so *cold*!"

"It's hard to believe it's the same city from the summer. I was so hot then I thought I'd melt," Madeleine agreed, tucking her scarf more firmly into her collar.

"That's New York for you. Why they couldn't have put this city in California, I don't know," Dari laughed. "Oh, by the way . . . I kept meaning to ask you. Isn't Max Sall's daughter one of your friends?"

Madeleine nodded, surprised. "Yes. Amber. Since we were teenagers."

"I thought so. How awful for them."

Madeleine turned to her. "What's awful?"

"Didn't you hear?" Dari turned a surprised face towards her.

"Hear what?" Madeleine's heart missed a beat.

"He died. In a plane crash a few weeks ago. It was all over the news . . . hey, where are you going?"

she shouted. Madeleine had started running to-wards the office. She had to get to a phone.

"Amber?" Madeleine was crying with relief by the time she finally got through to her. It had taken almost the whole morning of leaving messages, phoning Max's offices, her parents. "Oh, Christ . . . Amber, I'm *so* sorry. I only just heard. Why didn't you call?"

"I did. I called your flat but your answering machine's been full for about a week—I couldn't leave a message. I thought you must have heard." Amber was surprised at how relieved she was to hear from Madeleine.

"Are you okay? Do you need me to come? Shall I come to you now?"

"No . . . no, I'm fine. Honestly. Theo's been here; he's been marvelous. It's fine, I promise."

"Who's Theo? Where's Tendé?"

"Theo's Max's lawyer—he's part of the family, now. I'll tell you more when I see you. Tendé's at home. He'll be here at Christmas."

"And the wedding? What's happening . . . I wondered why I hadn't heard from you—I just assumed you were all busy with it. Oh, Amber . . . I'm so, *so* sorry I wasn't there." Madeleine began to cry.

"Mads . . . it's fine. I'm okay. Really. What time is it over there?" Madeleine looked at her watch.

"It's 11:30 a.m. I've been trying to find you since nine."

"I know, it's been a bit mad. I'll explain things later. And the wedding's been postponed, although

Francesca's pressing for it to happen as soon as possible."

"Look, I was going to come for it anyway . . . I'll come to London on Friday. I can't believe this has happened and I wasn't there for you." It was on the tip of Amber's tongue to tell her not to be so silly, but she stopped. She hadn't seen Madeleine for almost six months. It was true she'd been busy and there had been so much to do that she'd scarcely had time to think . . . but she missed Madeleine—and Becky, too. It had hurt that she hadn't heard from either of them.

"Oh, Madeleine. Are you sure? It would be really nice to see you." She wiped away a tear. It had been over a month since Max died and her skin still felt raw, exposed. It took only a second for her to turn from capable to crying.

"I'll be there. Has . . . have you heard from Becky?"

"No. We haven't spoken in . . . a while." Madeleine said nothing. She felt terrible. Something like this had happened and neither of them knew? She rang off and immediately began preparing to leave.

In Harare, Becky was putting the finishing touches to her business plan. She'd spent three weeks searching, scouting, checking, analyzing . . . she thought her head would burst. She was going to ask her parents for the money to help get the gallery off the ground but first she needed to do her homework. And she'd done it. She had every angle covered. The £10,000 she was going to ask them to lend her had been accounted for, right down to the last detail. She knew her parents would be skeptical. After all, £10,000 wasn't a lot of money if you were talking about opening a business but the money would go far in Zimbabwe and she and Godson had been over the figures again and again—she was convinced it would work. She stared at the little package she'd put together as the last page came off Nadège's printer. It was beautifully done. *Aldrldge Marimba. Gallery of Contcmporary African Art. 27 Albion Road, Harare, Zimbabwe.* She even had an address. She'd even managed to charm the Indian store owner into letting her pay rent six-monthly in advance instead of the usual two years. Everything was ready to go. All she needed now was to convince her father—and her mother, perhaps more importantly—that she could and would make it work. She leafed through the pages. There were photographs of the space, the surroundings, the street; photographs of pieces of Godson's work; sculptures and masks from one of Harare's best-known sculptors; spreadsheets with numbers and figures; a business plan; endorsements . . . there was everything in it to make someone sit up and take notice. Godson and an accountant friend of his, Ella, had worked with her to make sure it all added up and that it looked good and professional. She would send it to her father as soon as they'd spoken. She looked at her watch. It was 10:15 p.m., 8:15 p.m. in London—both her parents would be at home. She picked up the phone and dialed.

"Mum? It's me . . . how are you?"

"Becky? Becky? Is that you? Oh, God . . . Becky, where've you *been*? We've been going out of our *minds* with worry. We've left a hundred messages with Henry. He said he didn't know where you were. Are you all right, darling? Where are you?" Her mother sounded hysterical.

"I'm fine, Mum. I *told* Henry . . . I gave him my new number." She frowned. How spiteful of him. "I'm all right. I've just moved. I'm staying with some friends and . . ."

"Are you coming back? Amber rang the other day. It's dreadful what's happened . . ."

"What? What's happened?"

"Oh, darling . . . haven't you heard the news? Max is dead. He died in a plane crash . . . gosh, it's over a month ago. I can't believe you haven't heard."

"What?" Becky's hand flew over her mouth. "When?"

"About a month ago. He was flying his own plane, somewhere in Africa . . . you know, that project. Oh, it's been dreadful. The papers have been full of it. Are you coming back?"

"Of course. I'll be back as soon as I can." Becky rapidly calculated she had probably just enough money for an air ticket. The funds from the sale of her ring were miraculously almost intact. "I'll ring you as soon as I've found a flight. I'll ring Amber straight away." She put down the phone. Max was dead? *Max*? It seemed impossible. Not Max.

Amber opened the front door. Becky and Madeleine were standing on the steps. There was no need for words. She felt herself enveloped in their arms. Just as it had always been.

"You have to do it now." Francesca looked at Paola with a thinly disguised look of panic on her face. "Before any of this . . . mess . . . gets out."

"But won't he think it a little odd?" Paola asked doubtfully.

"No, no . . . forget that. You need to get that ring on your finger immediately, Paola. This is no time for subtleties. It's an emergency. An *emergency.*" Paola nodded doubtfully. Of course her mother was right. After the shock of hearing Max's will and finding that there was no provision for her other than a monthly stipend that would barely keep her in shoes—*forget Manolos!*—she was all too aware of the acuteness of her own situation. She'd never really given money much consideration before. It had always just been there. Max had often tried to curb her spending as a way of exercising some control over her, but the thought of there being none . . . she couldn't quite grasp that. She'd always spent what she wanted and never spared a thought for where it was actually coming from. And now Francesca was telling her she couldn't use the platinum card she'd had since she was about sixteen and that they both had to think hard and fast about what to do. No money? It wasn't possible. What were they supposed to do? Francesca hadn't worked for many years and Paola never had. What did other people do for money? "They work," Francesca said dryly, lighting her umpteenth cigarette. "But that's absolutely out of the question. I want you to get a date from Otto—and fast. Once it comes out that there isn't actually that much left of Max's wealth . . . well, there's no telling *what* sort of agreements Otto might make you sign. No, I want you to do this quickly. *Quickly*, you hear me?"

"Okay, okay . . . I heard you. I'll call him tonight. I will." Paola reached for one of Francesca's cigarettes. The whole thing was too horrible for words. First Max, then the will . . . now this. She felt a lump form in her throat. She just didn't have enough space or time for each emotion; hurt, loss, fear—she was being pushed towards something, she knew it. It wasn't that she didn't like Otto . . . she did, or at least she thought she did. But to suddenly go from wanting to marry him to having to do it—they'd barely even kissed! Suddenly, it was all looking rather desperate and not at all how she'd imagined it. Max wouldn't be there, either. Her eyes filled with tears. Who would walk her down the aisle? It was supposed to be the happiest day of her life, not the saddest. She would never get all the way down it without thinking of him and bursting into tears. What kind of a way was *that* to start a marriage? Francesca patted her hand and left the room.

She walked into the sitting room and sat down. She was extremely worried. Otto was no fool—the papers had already begun their speculation about Max's wealth. Jesus. She took a deep breath. Max had really done it this time. She looked around at the lovely room, the beautiful furnishings; the art-work . . . he'd left her with somewhere to live but nothing to live on. Paola was her only hope now. She had little expectation of Amber's goodwill.

It was ironic, Amber thought to herself as she walked upstairs to Angela's rooms. Two daughters on the brink of marriage—and neither seemed ready to move. Tendé was on his way back to London. She'd been unable to leave; there was so much to do, so much to sort out . . . he'd offered to spend a week with her and she'd jumped gratefully at the chance. Paola's wedding had been postponed . . . indefinitely, it seemed. Francesca had rung a few days earlier and talked almost non-stop. Amber had had to break in and agree to meet her the following week. Something had to be done, Francesca insisted. Amber declined to comment. She knew exactly what the meeting would be about. Money. It seemed to be the topic of every single meeting in the past two weeks. She tapped on the door.

"Hello, darling." Angela opened the door. Amber looked around the room in surprise. There were suitcases everywhere.

"Are you going somewhere?" she asked.

"Yes, darling. I'm afraid so. I'm going out to Mary Ann's." Amber looked blank. "My sister. You must remember her. She lives in California. She used to visit when you were small." Amber shook her head. She swallowed.

"Do . . . do you have to?" She was alarmed to feel

her eyes welling with tears. Angela stopped folding a pair of silk trousers and looked at her.

"Oh, darling . . . don't cry." Angela immediately walked over. She put an arm round her and to Amber's horror, she felt herself begin to sob. "Here," Angela said, reaching for a box of tissues. "Let's go into the sitting room. Come on. I'll get Daphne to bring us some tea." She led the way.

Angela pulled a face as soon as Daphne left the room. She looked at Amber and smiled. "See? Ugly as all hell."

Amber smiled weakly through her tears. "Did you . . . know?" she asked carefully.

Angela began pouring the tea. "Yes, of course I knew. There were others, too, long before that. Only I don't think there were any children."

"But how . . . why did you put up with it?" Amber was incredulous. Angela held out a cup and saucer.

"I loved him," she said calmly. "I'm not saying it didn't hurt. After Francesca . . . I thought I would die, you know. From the hurt. It was in all the papers. I kept thinking about what my parents would say. They hated him, you know." Amber shook her head. She tried to imagine what she would do if Tendé . . . she gave up. She couldn't. "I thought of leaving once or twice. But . . . I don't know. You learn to live with it, I suppose."

"But I still don't understand why," Amber said. "I mean, what happened to the two of you? Did it just . . . ?"

"Fizzle out? No, I wouldn't say that." Angela bit into a biscuit. "Max was a very complex man, Amber. I don't think he would ever have been satisfied with just one. And he wanted children. Lots of children. After I found out about Francesca. I decided . . . to have my tubes tied, to put an end to it. I couldn't bear the thought of giving him any more. It was a stupid decision, very impulsive. Max hated me for it." She took a sip of tea. Amber sat opposite her, stunned. "And then Francesca couldn't have any more . . . I don't know why exactly. But it hurt Max. Terribly. He was trying to make up for all the love he'd lost. He was quite alone, you know."

"Uncle Theo told me. Why didn't he tell us any of this? Why do we have to find out from strangers?" Amber said bitterly.

"I'm hardly a stranger, Amber," Angela replied tartly. Then she sighed. "Look, I know I haven't always been . . . well, *there*, really. It's too late to make amends and I'm not trying to." She shook her head as Amber opened her mouth. "Let me finish. Max was a very difficult man to live with but he was impossible to live without. I made that choice—to stay with him whatever way I could. And I know what it did to you and to Kieran. Don't think I don't know that. But you're strong, Amber, much stronger than Kieran. You're just like him, you know. Just like Max. And that's why he did what he did. I don't blame him. I've got more than enough to live on for the rest of my life. I wasn't as silly as I looked, you know. Kieran can stay here—I know you'll look after him. Me . . . I want something different. I need a change. Mary Ann has a huge home; she's rattling around in it. Her children are all grown up now. It'll be nice for us to spend some time together. I don't know when I'll be back but I'll write . . . and you must, too." Amber nodded, unable to speak. "And you must introduce me to this man of yours," Angela said, getting up and brushing crumbs from her skirt. "Max was very fond of him, you know."

"I know," Amber whispered.

"Come on, help me finish my packing," Angela said, holding out a hand. Amber allowed herself to be pulled to her feet. She couldn't remember the last time she'd held her mother's hand.

≋88≋

"He is absolutely *divine*," Becky leaned across the table and hissed at Amber. Amber blushed. Madeleine nodded enthusiastically. All three of them watched Tendé make his way towards the restrooms.

"He's just *gorgeous*. Where on earth did you find him again?"

"Max did." Amber smiled. It was April. Max had been gone for five months and it was only now that she felt herself slowly being pulled out of the tunnel of grief. It was also her birthday. Becky and Madeleine had flown to London to be with her and Tendé had surprised the hell out of her by turning up as well. He'd taken them all out to dinner, aware that it was probably the first time Amber had celebrated anything since Max had died.

"So when's the wedding?" they both asked. Amber blushed.

"Soon. We haven't set a date. Maybe in July. It'll be cooler in Bamako then. You're both coming, aren't you?" she asked suddenly. They both nodded.

"As if you could keep us away. What about Angela? And Francesca and Paola?"

"I don't know. Angela's in California. She loves it—says she'll never come back. And Francesca . . . well, we had words the last time we met. I don't know."

"He's coming back." Becky was watching the restaurant floor. "Honestly, Amber . . . you're so lucky. He's great." Amber smiled slowly. She turned as Tendé slipped into the seat beside her. It was the first time he'd met them—she'd been worried they wouldn't like one another, that they'd find him too serious, too stiff; that he would find them awkward, or girlish. But she needn't have worried. He had them eating out of the palm of his hand, as always.

"Ladies," he said, a slow grin breaking across his face. "I have an idea." They leaned forward expectantly. "You all look worn out—not in a bad way," he added hastily, catching Amber's frown, "more in the way of needing a break, a rest. Why don't we—all of us—go down to *Casa Bella* for a week. Just the four of us. Get a little sun, take a few trips round the island . . . enjoy ourselves for a week. What do you say?" They looked at one another in surprise.

"Well . . . I suppose I *could* . . ." Madeleine said slowly. "I'm supposed to be back in New York next week. I could get an extra couple of days . . . you?" She turned to Becky.

"I hate to ask . . . will it be very expensive to get there?" Becky asked, making a pleading face. Her tiny budget was almost exhausted.

"It's my treat," Tendé said, wagging a finger at her. "Don't think about the money."

"Don't you have to get back to Bamako?" Amber asked, hoping that she didn't look quite as adoring of him as she felt.

"Not for a couple of weeks. I can take the time off. You need it. You look all done in. In a good way," he laughed.

"Well, yes . . . it would be great. In fact, it would be fantastic. Will you come?" Amber looked at the others. They nodded, eyes shining. A week-long break in the sun was exactly what they all needed.

"Then it's settled. I'll get tickets tomorrow. We could leave on Saturday." Tendé smiled. "A toast. To Max. And to Amber." They raised their glasses. Amber felt his arm slide around her waist. She leaned against him. Suddenly the fog of the past few months had lifted. She was looking forward to Saturday in a way she hadn't looked forward to anything for ages.

There was a lot of laughter aboard their flight to Menorca. Tendé seemed to attract an enormous amount of attention striding along with Amber, Becky and Madeleine at his side. Several passengers turned their heads at the sight of them. His own private harem, he told the envious flight attendant. Amber could feel her face turning scarlet.

"Stop it," she whispered, digging him in the ribs. "Don't encourage them."

"Encourage what?"

"You know . . . they probably think you're a . . ."

"Pimp?" he supplied helpfully.

Amber blushed again. "No . . . don't be silly. I wasn't thinking of that. More . . ." she stopped. He was laughing at her.

"Who cares what they think? You're supposed to be having fun, Ms. Sall. Remember?"

"Champagne?" The flight attendant suddenly appeared. Amber had to smile. He'd probably organized that as well.

It was the first time she'd been back to *Casa Bella* since Max's memorial. The island was in the middle of spring. She'd forgotten just how glorious it could be—the way the sun intensified the fragrance of fruit and flowers and how intense and vibrant everything looked. Five minutes away from the airport and already the sharp, citrus smell of lemons came to her.

"Amber Sall, I used to feel *sorry* for you, having to come here on holiday," was Becky's first comment as they waited for their rental car.

"Wow," was all Madeleine could say. The blossoms were out—florid pink and white bunches clustered along the spindly branches of the trees that lined the road leading away from the airport; the sky overhead was a sharp, luminous blue against which the odd cloud seemed so solid and white you felt you could reach up and touch it. They gasped as the metallic silver BMW convertible was brought around to the front.

"That's for us?" Becky squealed. Tendé nodded. They stuffed their bags into the trunk and clambered in.

Tendé nosed the car out of the traffic, changing from lane to lane along the sea-front, the sound of their conversation whipping around him as he accelerated and slowed, the dark-blue expanse of white-crested waves on their right. Bursts of laughter and conversations in a foreign language punctured the air as they pulled up beside one convertible after another, all nosing and champing at the red lights like racehorses against the line. They left the town and climbed high into the hills. The stiff black cypress trees waved, unbending, in the breeze. Apricot, pear, lavender, mimosa . . . the scents mingled with the light coming through the new leaves on the olive branches. It was spring; everything bursting with life.

Andréa and Lourdes were on hand to meet them at the villa. Becky and Madeleine were given adjacent rooms; Amber paused for a second outside Max's room. Should she . . . ?

"Let's take the one down the hall," Tendé said to

her, walking down the corridor with their bags. She nodded and followed him, happy to have been relieved of the decision.

"You okay?" he asked her as he closed the door.

"Yes. It feels good to be back here—now, like this." He put the bags down and walked over to her.

"This is where I first saw you," he said, catching hold of her wrist. He pulled her towards him.

"Yes, except you only had eyes for Paola," she said, putting her arms around his neck.

"Not true." He bent his head to kiss her.

"True." His mouth was sweet and warm. "What about the others?" she said as he tugged her backwards onto the bed.

"They're fine. We'll meet in an hour on the patio for a drink. It's all been arranged."

"Is there anything you haven't planned?" Amber laughed, struggling with him.

"Nope." He slipped his hands underneath her shirt. "I hate leaving things to chance. You know that." His hand encountered her bra. He unclipped it efficiently and began to caress her. She looked across the room—the shutters were closed against the heat outside. She sat up suddenly and unpinned her skirt, shrugging off her shirt and loosening her hair from its clasp. She lay on top of him, her face pressed into his shoulder, tasting the traces of salt and cologne on his skin.

"Thank you for suggesting this," she whispered, sliding a leg between his. He was too busy to reply. It had been a while since they'd made love like this—tenderly, lazily, with all the time in the world. He drew pleasure from her skillfully, slowly; the way cigarette smoke curls and dissolves into the air; a drop of tincture in a pool of clear water. She felt satiated and suddenly, finally at peace.

"Amber said you speak Russian," Madeleine said to him the following day. They were lying by the pool while Amber and Becky were floating in the water; Madeleine was afraid of burning. She and Tendé sat on the rattan chairs on the patio, sipping lemonade and watching the other two turn pink.

"Yes, I studied at the State University in Moscow. It's been a while. I'm not so fluent any more."

Madeleine looked at him, impressed. "I studied it too—in school. But much longer ago."

"Would you like another drink?" he asked in Russian.

Madeleine laughed. "Yes, please."

"So . . . you still remember." He got up to pour her another glass.

"What were you studying?"

"Economics. I did my first degree in France. At the time, fifteen years ago, we had a socialist government in Mali. There were a few of us sent abroad on scholarships."

"Did you like it? Russia, I mean."

Tendé shrugged. "The weather was terrible. And the language was hard. It took me a year to pass the proficiency exams before I could even enter the university. It was good, in a way. I saw a bit more of what life must have been like for ordinary Russians, not just the students. There were all sorts of people in the language institute." He swallowed a mouthful of lemonade. "And you? Amber told me your parents are Hungarian."

"Yes, they came to Britain when I was a child."

"So you must have struggled with English yourself."

"Yeah, but when you're young it comes easier, I guess. School was harder. We were so poor—that was more of an issue than the fact that I couldn't speak English that well."

Tendé nodded. "It's not easy being a foreigner. Children can be very cruel."

"What was it like in Russia? Being . . . black?"

"Same as anywhere outside Africa, I expect. Although in Russia, it was a little different. The only blacks around were African—students, mostly. Most of the Russians I met had never seen a black person before and they were too ignorant to be truly racist, if you see what I mean."

"No . . . I thought it was the other way round. Racism *is* ignorance. Isn't it?"

"Not really. You have to know something—or *think* you know something—about the other person. You know . . . black people do this, are like that . . . the usual stereotypes. When you meet people who don't have any opinions, any experience whatsoever, they tend to be curious, not hateful. A little bit of knowledge—or what passes for it, anyway—is often not a good thing."

"It must be strange for you, going in and out of so many worlds, always moving between places."

"No, not strange. You know, when we were little,

my father taught at a university in France, in Bordeaux. We stayed there for four years and we'd go back every summer to Bamako, to stay with my grandparents. I was about five when we went for the first time and the thing I remember—the thing that's stayed with me ever since—was the way a crowd looked, to me. In France, everyone held themselves apart—there was always a lot of space between people. But back home, everyone is always jammed up against one another; there's a lot of touching on a day-to-day basis. You're always in contact with each other's flesh. In France it was the opposite. I touched someone once . . . you know, a kid in the playground. Just on his arm. His mother slapped me and rushed off with her son. I think she was afraid he might catch something. I remember it well."

"Ouch. That sounds painful. But Bamako . . . it sounds amazing . . . Africa. I've never been."

"No. Not amazing. Just like anywhere." He smiled. "But I know what you mean. Amber likes it, I think. She'll manage. And you'll come for the wedding— see it for yourself."

"I can't wait."

"Me neither. It's been one hell of a year."

"But things are going well? With the project and your work?" Madeleine was curious. She found she knew very little about what he did.

"Well . . . things are moving. It takes time, that's all. Nothing in Africa ever gets done overnight. Or over four years, for that matter." He laughed and drained his glass. "We're getting there. That's the main thing. When the salt project is done, then I'll have time to think about other things. And you?" Madeleine smiled. She liked the way he always asked her a question. He was nothing like the rather self-centred African men she'd met at the UN who loved nothing more than the sound of their own voice.

"Oh, I don't know. After Bosnia it feels unbelievably privileged to be working somewhere safe, you know. Where you can walk out of your office at night, buy a coffee on the way in. And the work itself is interesting. I just never thought I'd wind up pushing papers, though. I'm a doctor—it just hasn't turned out quite the way I expected."

"But you're happy?" It was a direct question. Madeleine hesitated. She wasn't sure how to respond.

"I think so. I suppose so." She looked at her empty glass. "Actually, I don't know." She gave a short, embarrassed laugh. "Look at us. It's a beautiful day, we're in Menorca . . . it's not the time to be talking like this."

"Ah, sometimes these are the best times," Tendé said, smiling. "But you're right. It *is* a beautiful day." He got up. Madeleine tried not to stare at the physical perfection in front of her. He pulled off his T-shirt, flung it on the bench behind them and took a flying leap into the pool. His blackness was like a blow in the shimmering blue surface of the pool. She watched as he swam towards Amber. She was lucky. She hoped she realized just how lucky she was. Men like that didn't come around that often. She stood up and unfastened her sundress, frowning at her shockingly white, thin legs. When had *that* happened? She followed Tendé into the pool.

Their time together was perfect. By the end of their second day, the four of them had settled into an easy, comfortable routine. Tendé wasn't in the slightest bit possessive—he shared Amber freely, finding books in Max's study to amuse himself with; spending hours alone on the beach in the afternoon, swimming out to the wooden raft and soaking up the solitude. It was too early in the season for day-trippers and for the most part, they had the sandy beach to themselves. He and Madeleine found themselves drifting into conversation easily; they enjoyed each other's company. His easy-going confidence and generosity reminded her a little of Péter, she said. She reminded him of his eldest sister, he said. Stubborn—she was the only person in the world he was afraid of. They both laughed.

Amber and Becky too found time to be alone and to start to repair the rift that had opened up in their friendship. Neither of them referred to Henry at first. By some unspoken arrangement they agreed to keep him at bay but gradually, as the days floated by and the nights were spent in front of the fireplace with a bottle of wine, Becky found herself talking about him and about the strange circumstances of her life in Zimbabwe.

"It's as if they're stuck in the past," she said, lying

across the rug and talking to the three of them. Amber lay with her head in Tendé's lap—he was reading and paying them sporadic attention. "They so desperately want to be British or American and yet . . . the way they live there . . . they could never live like that here. In London, I mean."

"Expats are the same everywhere," Madeleine chimed in from her supine position on the sofa. "They were like that in Belgrade, too."

"Yes, but I can't stand the way they speak to . . . you know, to the Zimbabweans."

"Blacks, you mean," Tendé said dryly. Becky blushed.

"Okay. Yes. Them."

"Was Henry really like that?" Amber asked after a while. "He seemed to be the opposite. He was always going on about how awful expats were."

"Oh, Henry *wanted* to be the opposite. Desperately. But I don't think he knew how."

"Is that your ex?" Tendé's voice sounded above her ear.

Amber grinned. "Yes. And Becky's." She slid her foot across and kicked Becky's shin gently. She was still blushing.

"Where is he now?"

"Still there. On the farm. I don't think he'll ever leave—I think he's afraid to. At least there things haven't changed much from when he was a kid. It's like Zimbabwe must have been twenty years ago. If he came to Harare and met some of the people I know, he'd be terrified."

"Why do you stay there?" Tendé asked her.

Becky shifted uncomfortably. "Well, I'm working on something. It's still only in the beginning stages. We're doing up this place . . ." she rolled over onto her stomach and smiled. She hadn't really told any of them what her plans were. She looked at them. Why not? She began to explain.

"It sounds brilliant," Madeleine said from the couch when Becky had finished. "I can't believe you just got up and did it. It's so brave of you."

"It's a *great* idea," Tendé said, looking at Becky with renewed respect. "Really. If this Godson fellow is as good as you say . . . you could really start something."

"He's brilliant. And there are lots of guys like him. A couple of women, too . . . but mostly in crafts and stuff like that. There aren't many painters. But that'll change over time, I expect."

"And they'll find other media to work in, presumably," Tendé added. "Not just the traditional oils and paints and so on."

Becky nodded enthusiastically. "Yes, you should see some of the sculptors . . . they use anything they can get their hands on: phone wire, bits of old bicycles, plastic . . . everything. Oh, when the gallery's done you'll all have to come and see for yourselves. It'll be fantastic."

"*I* want to move to Africa," Madeleine wailed from the couch. "You all seem to be having such fun!" The three of them laughed.

"It's a big place," Tendé said, shaking his head.

"You could just as easily wind up somewhere worse than Sarajevo."

"I'll come and live with you, Becky," she said dreamily. "I'll open up a clinic in the garden." She laughed. "Christ, if any of my colleagues were here . . . you can't believe how serious it is where I work." She pulled a cushion to her and sighed. "You have no idea how good this has been."

"Still is," Amber murmured from Tendé's lap. "It's only midnight." The fire crackled and sent out tiny showers of glowing red light over the four of them. It was almost dawn by the time they stumbled reluctantly into bed.

≋89≋

Paola was fretting. It was May and they still hadn't set a date. To add insult to injury, Amber had announced that *she* was getting married—and that the wedding would be held in bloody Bam-wherever-it-was-she-lived. She'd pleaded with Francesca to be excused from going, but Francesca had been adamant. Something to do with a conversation she'd had with Amber earlier on . . . and the news that she and Francesca weren't to be cut off completely although Francesca was decidedly less than happy about the amount Amber had proposed they live on.

"*What*?" she'd screeched, looking at the piece of paper Amber had pushed discreetly across the desk. Max's desk.

"It's perfectly reasonable, Francesca," Amber said, steeling herself for histrionics.

"You can't be serious. On *that*?"

"It's about ten times more than the average person gets, Francesca. And there's a trust set up for any children Paola may have. It's more than adequate. I've been over it with Theo."

"*Adequate*? For whom? I'm not some *fishwife* . . ." Francesca stopped. The precariousness of her situation had suddenly struck her. She swallowed. "It's a *little* less than I would have hoped," she said stiffly, folding up the piece of paper Amber had given her. "But it's very . . . kind of you, in the circumstances." She ground the words out. And then picked up her bag and walked out of the room. Amber almost wept with relief.

But Paola was finding it hard to concentrate on Francesca's incessant moaning. She was worried about being upstaged by Amber yet again. Otto would be in Rome in a few days' time. She would extract a date from him if it was the last thing she did. A date and a ring. That was all she wanted. God, she thought to herself as she inspected her eyebrows, she was getting as bad as Francesca. A date and a ring. *Quick!*

Otto knew exactly what was going on. He was no fool. He'd seen the way Francesca had set her own daughter up and knew that nothing would stop her from achieving what she'd set out to do—marry Paola off to the highest bidder. He wasn't sure how many other men were in the running but his sources had told him the young woman was actually quite a handful and that there were "issues" in the young lady's past that . . . well, merited a certain amount of *discretion*, shall we say? He listened to the report he'd asked his private secretary to compile and decided to wait a little. Although she was a little on the unpredictable side, she was exceptionally pretty, came with all the right connections to make his business ventures in Africa and elsewhere even more appealing and profitable and there was the added bonus of being Max Sall's daughter. Except that when Max died, it became clear pretty soon afterwards that she was really the *illegitimate* daughter and that it was the other one, the clever one, who'd scooped the prize. Rumor had it that the girl and her mother had been left out of his will entirely. No wonder Francesca had started to push. And now Paola was pushing. Unfortunately, it had the opposite effect on him. The harder she tried to extract a commitment, the vaguer he became. He just wasn't sure . . . did it make good business sense? He couldn't yet tell. And if there was one thing most people could say about Otto von Kiepenhauer, he never did anything that didn't make good business sense. The other sister was getting married and he could sense the sibling rivalry there. Although—he still couldn't quite believe it—she was marrying a Negro—*ein Negger*? The thought was repellent to him. He didn't mind having to do business with Africans, or even bedding an exceptionally pretty one once in a while . . . but to marry one? She had brought shame on the whole family. Another reason to proceed with caution. He sat back, held his cards close to his chest and watched Paola and her mother slowly become more desperate. Besides, he rather *liked* having a beautiful young woman pursuing him with such vigor. It flattered him. It was the other thing that was said about him—his ego was as gargantuan as his appetite, like many a short man.

"Who will give her away?" Mandia asked her son, frowning.

"Her brother?" Tendé shrugged. The details of his upcoming marriage were not foremost on his mind. They were in the kitchen at his parents' home—Mandia was cooking and Tendé was trying to read a newspaper.

"Tendé! It's your *wedding*. Show some interest," his mother said crossly. Tendé looked up.

"Maman, you've been waiting for this day for thirty-six years. Enjoy it. I'm leaving you in charge because I know you want to be in charge."

"Don't joke with me, boy," Mandia said, a half-smile playing around her lips. They looked at each other.

"Okay. What else? What do you want to know?" Tendé sighed. He knew he was beaten.

"Who is coming from her side? I've asked you for a guest list now for over a month."

"Okay. I'll ask her. She'll be here next week."

"And besides, her brother can't give her away," Mandia said, turning back to the pot over which she'd been presiding since breakfast.

"Why not?"

"He's not Moslem."

"So?" Tendé looked puzzled.

"Tendé," Mandia said warningly. "We need to sort these things out now."

"Fine. So Papa will give her away."

"Isn't that bad luck?"

"*Maman* . . . will you stop worrying? It'll be fine. We're allowed to marry outside the faith—you know that as well as I do. Now, stop fretting over silly details. Papa will give her away and it'll be fine." He jumped up, kissed her on the cheek and disappeared before she could say anything more.

In London, standing half-naked by the window, Amber was having the last fitting for her dress. She'd spent months thinking about what to wear and in the end she'd decided on a plain white silk dress for the registry ceremony and a white, embroidered traditional robe for the mosque.

"Hold still for a second," the dressmaker instructed. "There. You can breathe now." Amber turned slowly to face the mirror. The dress was simple and elegant—a fitted bodice, no sleeves . . . a flat, very gently flared skirt to the ankles. It was so simple it was almost austere but the luminous, polished quality of the silk softened it, giving a hint of glamour. She loved the *bou-bou*, the long, exquisitely embroidered robe she would wear inside the mosque, with the lacy headscarf draped around her head. Thank God she wouldn't be required to cover her face, she thought to herself as she turned slowly in front of the mirror. Islam as it was practiced in Mali seemed decidedly liberal in its strictures on women and their clothing. None of Tendé's sisters ever seemed to wear the veil.

The dressmaker finished making her adjustments. Amber walked rather awkwardly to the bathroom—she was still full of pins—and carefully took the dress off. She pulled on her jeans and shirt, ran a hand through her untidy curls and opened the door. She would stop by the next day to pick up the final product. She picked up her bag and walked downstairs.

It was gloomy outside. A thick, ominous-looking cloud had been sitting on the horizon all day, threatening rain. She walked quickly down Upper Street and into Canonbury Square. She still had a lot to do before her flight on Wednesday; she'd promised to finalize her guest list, for one thing. It was one advantage of having the wedding so far away—the number of people who would be prepared to fly to West Africa to watch her get married was small, and dwindling by the day. People came up with the *strangest* excuses. It was pretty funny, actually. Mrs. Dewhurst, their erstwhile cook, had looked horrified when Amber presented her with an invitation—flights and accommodation provided, naturally.

"Oh, I couldn't possibly," she'd said, sounding flustered. "There's my health to think about . . ." Amber had rung off, promising to send pictures. Her *health*? She giggled again at the thought as she pushed her front door open.

It was winter again in Harare, not that the weather was anything to complain about. Becky walked along Takawira Street towards Albion Road. Winter in the southern hemisphere was a wonderful time— clear skies, sharp bright light, crisp nights . . . it was her favorite time of the year. Although this year, she thought to herself with a smile, she'd had a lot to smile about throughout. She'd been back from the week-long holiday in Menorca for just over two months and in a few days' time she would be flying back to London and then out to Bamako for Amber's wedding. She felt quite the jet-set film star. And when she got back to Harare, again via a week in London, she and Godson would almost be ready to begin work on Deluxe. It was Godson's idea, picked up from the taxi drivers who loved to put "deluxe" on the back of their beaten-up cars. She loved it immediately. *Deluxe at Aldridge Marimba*. Her father had been behind her from the start. Her mother, predictably, had been a little more apprehensive about Becky starting up a life so far away from them but in the end she'd been slowly won round. She had so many more opportunities out there, she told them. If she stayed in London, she'd wait thirty years before being able to do anything on her own. So she left London with the promise of the money she wanted

and the threat of a visit in the very near future—
excellent terms, she agreed happily, and arrived in
Harare full of enthusiasm and ideas and ready to
go, go, go. Godson found her high spirits infectious.

"I think you're terribly brave," Nadège said to her the
following evening. They were sitting by the pool,
smoking.

"Why d'you say that?" Becky asked, genuinely
surprised.

"Well, setting up on your own, for one thing. And
doing it with an *African*. Are you . . . ?" She gave
Becky a meaningful look. Becky blushed furiously.

"No, of course not. He's married."

"Oh, Becky—don't let *that* little detail get in the
way." Nadège laughed. "He's not bad-looking either,
you know . . . if you don't mind the hair."

"Jesus, Nadège . . . he's not a piece of meat.
We're business partners, that's all. And besides, I
thought you didn't approve of . . . you know, relationships with Africans and all that."

Nadège raised an eyebrow. "Oh my dear, you
have no idea." She leaned forward conspiratorially.
"If I told you how many of the women round here
have had it off with their servants, you'd be
shocked."

"Yes, I would," Becky said primly. She hated these
conversations. "But I'd really rather not know. Godson's my business partner and that's it. Besides,
even if I was, I'd hardly tell you, would I?" It came out
rather rudely, more than she'd intended. She was

Nadège's houseguest after all, but honestly . . . didn't they have anything else to think about?

"Fine. I've seen it all before, you know." Nadège lit a cigarette and shrugged. "Lots of people come out here, just like you, full of good intentions. You wait— I'll give you a year."

"Nadège, *please*. Can't we just enjoy the evening? Why are you lot so bloody cynical about everything? You've got the most amazing lives. Just look at you: pools, servants, tennis courts . . . you don't have to work. It's paradise."

"Oh, don't give me that, Becky. It's hell. You know it is." Nadège stubbed out her cigarette. She got up from her chair and wrapped her arms around her. To Becky's surprise there was a catch in her voice. "None of us want to be here—the women, I mean. We spend all our time watching our husbands' backs . . . if it's not the other wives they're screwing, it's the servants or the prostitutes or the good-time girls in the bars. I can't tell you how many—" She stopped suddenly. "You must think me a terrible ingrate," she said, turning back to Becky, "but I hate it here. I'm trapped."

Becky stared at her, open-mouthed. It was the first time she had ever heard Nadège even so much as admit to a bad mood. "Why don't you leave?" she asked eventually. "You're English, aren't you? You could just go back home."

"On what? I've got two children, Becky. They love it here. Gid would never agree to a divorce. Or to me taking the children. And what would I live on?"

"Get a job. Didn't you say you'd worked before coming here?"

Nadège laughed, a bitter, tight laugh. "I was Gid's secretary, in London. He worked at the London branch office. I can't even type. He found out on my second day and took me for a drink. And now here I am."

"Gid loves you, Nadège, I'm sure he does." Becky couldn't think of anything else to say.

Nadège gave another high-pitched laugh. "Of course he does. He needs someone like me, you know. It gives him a thrill to be able to parade me in front of his friends. I'm Irish and they can't tell from my voice where in the bloody great pecking order I belong. I'm not posh, not like some of them—not like you, Becky—but they can't tell. And I'm better-looking than most of them. He likes that."

Becky listened to her in fascinated awe. She'd known Nadège for over a year and she'd never even so much as hinted that there was this . . . grief and bitterness hiding beneath her beautifully made up, perfectly sculpted surface.

"My name's not even Nadège, you know," she said suddenly. "It's Noreen. Noreen O'Connor. There was a French exchange student in the village when I was a kid. Nadège Gallimard. God, she was ever so pretty." She turned from the pool to face Becky. In the watery light she looked suddenly old. "That's why I envy you, Becky. You've got something of your own, away from all this shit. D'you want to know why all the men out here are married to English girls?" Becky nodded slowly. Nadège was going to tell her anyhow. "It's because all the white girls who had any sense or beauty left the country, you know, years ago. When it fell. The men left too, just like Gid, but they couldn't handle it overseas. They couldn't handle being *just like everyone else*. So they came back—and they had to con a bunch of fuckin' eejits like myself to come back with them." She picked up the remains of her gin and tonic and drained it. "Sorry, love . . . you probably didn't want to hear all that. I'm going to bed. I'll see you in the morning."

She walked off, her heels puncturing the perfect lawn like the tracks of some strange urban animal seen only at night. Becky sat for a few minutes longer under the thatched canopy of the pool house, staring at the water and at the thousands of tiny fireflies that skimmed across its surface, attracted by the light. She was shocked by what she'd heard, not because she didn't believe it or because she didn't feel sorry for them—she did. But what shocked her was the thought that *this* was what Henry had waited for twenty years to return to? *This* was what he longed for? She shook her head. She thought of Amber and of Tendé and the life Amber would have as soon as they were married. She hated to admit it; she was even afraid to think about it, but that old ghost, envy, had just raised its ugly head. Amber had found the "right" Africa to belong to and a way in. Becky, as usual, had not.

For the first time in years Madeleine found it hard to concentrate on her work. The short break in

Menorca had given her a glimpse of another kind of life. She felt as she had done almost fifteen years earlier, watching Amber and Becky walk up the road together, satchels and long hair swinging. They belonged then as they did now to a different world. This time it had nothing to do with money or success or a nice home—those things Madeleine had more or less achieved for herself. This time it was about pleasure. They took pleasure in their lives in a way she'd almost forgotten to do—or had she ever known how? To lie by a pool, slowly watching your skin turn gold, then brown . . . to turn your head and smell the scent of pomegranate trees wafting in from the garden . . . a glass of wine before an evening meal prepared by someone whose name you may have forgotten . . . of course it was another life, so different from hers . . . but she envied it just the same. She had never quite managed to shake off the feeling of not quite fitting in with them. The simple daily pleasures they seemed to take for granted were for her moments to be treasured, played over in her mind and savored.

There was a gentle cough to her right. She looked up, startled. The panel were looking questioningly at her. She'd been daydreaming again. She quickly took up her papers and tried to focus. They were in a meeting with some of the top legal brains at the UN. The recommendations of the legal and medical team, of which they were a part, was to classify rape separately from other, more general crimes against humanity. It was a risky strategy—they wanted to prevent a woman's previous sexual history from being admissible in court as would have happened in a civil case. Jamilla and Dari were adamant that the recommendation should be pushed through as quickly as possible but Madeleine wasn't so sure.

"I'm sorry," she said after a minute, looking apologetically at Jamilla and Dari. "I just don't agree with it.

Jamilla sighed. "What's your objection?" One of the UN lawyers spoke up.

Madeleine looked at him, grateful for the opening. "I think the problem is more complex than we're allowing. It's all very well to tackle it at the legal level, which we're doing, but you have to take into account the legal traditions in terms of the crime itself. Will women come forward? What is the likelihood of any of them ever bringing a charge? How is rape treated in peacetime?"

"But Madeleine," Dari turned to her, "if we don't put the process in place now, then it's pointless arguing or speculating about whether or not they'll come forward. There'll be nothing to come forward *to*."

"I don't agree. We're spending all this time and all this money—I mean, this whole process costs an absolute fortune—and meanwhile, the women we're talking about have had their children, are being forced to deal with not only the rape itself but the consequences. Splitting legal niceties isn't doing a damn thing for them. Look." She stopped suddenly and bent down towards her bag. She rummaged around for a second then pulled out her Filofax. She opened it and pulled something out. The twelve

committee members around the table frowned—
what was she up to? She passed the rather dog-
eared photograph around. It showed Madeleine
standing in front of a badly damaged building with
an arm around a pretty, smiling dark-haired girl of
fourteen, fifteen perhaps? They were both smiling
at the camera. The photograph was passed around
the table. Her point? "That young girl was the
daughter of the couple I stayed with for two years in
Sarajevo. She was raped at thirteen and released
after the birth of her son. She's one of the lucky
ones—she was able to come to someone; both her
parents are still alive. There are *thousands* of girls
not so lucky. For them, the rape is just part of a wider
trauma. Without the right counseling and support after the event, no amount of us wrangling in New
York over whether her past sexual history is relevant
or not is going to help them. These girls are thirteen,
fourteen, fifteen—what kind of sexual history do you
think they can possibly have had?" There was silence when she finished speaking.

An hour later, the recommendation for a wider
package of support, including counseling, not only
for the victims, but for their families, was approved.
Jamilla and Dari congratulated her—she was right.
They'd forgotten the human cost of their ambitions.

"That was very well done." The lawyer who'd
spoken in the meeting came up to her. Madeleine
was packing her bag. She looked up.

"Thanks . . . it's not an easy issue," she said
quickly. He nodded.

"But very well put. I'm James Fournier, by the way."

He held out a hand. His handshake was warm and firm. "Are you rushing off?" he asked. Madeleine hesitated. Jamilla and Dari were busy conferring with the Red Cross Special Envoy.

"No . . . I was just going to get some coffee; there's a Starbucks on the corner."

"Mind if I join you?" She shook her head. His voice—he was Scottish. A lovely, deep, soft burr . . . it was Alasdair, only gentler.

"Not at all." They fell into step down the corridor.

"I sometimes dread these meetings," he said as they stepped into the elevator. "They seem to lose sight of what they're about. The bureaucracy is overwhelming."

Madeleine nodded. "It's all rather new for me, I'm afraid. I'm a doctor. I'm used to things being a little *too* human, not less."

He chuckled. "Yes, law gets to be a bit remote, sometimes. It's easy to lose track. Like today, I suppose."

"You're Scottish?" Madeleine asked as they pushed open the exit door. The air outside was crisp and cool. It was a welcome relief after three hours spent in the air-conditioning upstairs.

"My mother is, yes. My father's Belgian. But I grew up in Scotland. You're English, I take it?"

"Yes."

"How long have you been in New York?" he asked, opening the door for her.

"Almost a year. It seems like an awfully long time."

"You don't like it?"

"Oh, no, I do. It's just . . . you know . . . when you

move somewhere new it takes a while to settle in, make friends, that kind of thing. How about you? How long have you been here?"

"This'll be my fifth year. It was really only supposed to be two but every time my contract runs out another crisis somewhere in the world pops up and they ask me to stay. Constitutional law. That's my specialty," he added, anticipating her question. "What will you have?"

"A . . ." she looked up at the board. "Oh, God . . . just a coffee. I get dizzy reading the different kinds." He smiled and walked to the counter. She stole a quick look as he walked away. Tall, nicely built, brown hair . . . she'd been too shy to look at his face properly . . . glasses, nice smile . . . something along those lines. And that voice. She looked down at her hands as he came back with two cups. He sat down opposite her and took off his glasses, rubbing his eyes. She looked up. His eyes were unusually beautiful—green, with long, thick eyelashes and a spider's web of laughter lines at the corners. He put them back on.

"Where do you live in New York?" he asked, taking a sip of coffee.

"Brooklyn. On Lefferts Place, near Atlantic. And you?"

"Oh, miles away, unfortunately. I'm up in Washington Heights, near the Cloisters. Have you ever been up there?" Madeleine shook her head. What did he mean by "unfortunately"? She was aware of her heart beating ever so slightly faster.

"No, I've hardly been anywhere since I got here,"

she confessed. "I've just been so busy." She hoped she sounded convincing. The truth of the matter was that she came into work on the weekends simply because there wasn't anything else to do. Jamilla and Dari both seemed to have these fantastically complicated and full social lives and besides, she was ten years younger than Dari and twenty than Jamilla . . . it would have seemed a little odd to start hanging out with them after work as well.

"Well, what are you doing on Saturday?" James asked her. Madeleine blushed furiously.

"Oh . . . I wasn't trying . . . I wasn't implying . . . that I wanted to go somewhere," she said quickly.

He laughed. "No, of course not. But, if you're not doing anything, would you like to come out?"

"With you?"

"Well, yes. Unless you'd rather do something else, of course," he added quickly. He seemed almost as nervous as she was.

"No, no . . . that would be . . . very nice." She smiled at him. "I'll really look forward to it." She wrote her number for him on a napkin and hoped her hand wouldn't shake.

On Saturday, as arranged, she met James at Fortinelli's Deli and was a little surprised to learn he'd got tickets for them both to watch a baseball game.

"It's the biggest game of the season—the Yankees versus the Red Sox! I had to bribe someone to get these tickets." Madeleine tried to look thrilled.

"I don't know much about it, I'm afraid," she said

as they took their coffee and hot dogs back to the table.

"Oh, it's easy. Easier than cricket . . . you'll get the hang of it in no time."

"I don't know much about cricket, either," she laughed. She took a bite of her hot dog. It was good. She took another. James leaned forward suddenly and dabbed at the front of her shirt with his tissue. She jumped.

"Ketchup," he said, handing it to her. "Down your front." She looked down and grimaced. It had taken her almost three hours to decide what to wear. She'd finally settled on a crisp white shirt, jeans and a pair of suede boots . . . and now she'd added ketchup and mustard to her outfit. She blushed furiously. "Don't worry about it," James laughed. "Next time I'll bring you a bib." Madeleine's embarrassment was tempered only by the words "next time." Slow down, she cautioned herself sternly. You've been with him for ten whole minutes and you're behaving like a teenager. But it was hard not to. Perhaps it was the fact of being two Brits in New York; perhaps it was his voice which was at once familiar and comforting to her—or perhaps it was his beautiful eyes and the fact that her heart missed a beat when he said "Madeleine" in that sing-song, utterly familiar and sweet way . . . stop, stop, *stop*! "Are you all right?" he asked, looking at her.

"Oh, I'm fine. I always spill stuff down my front. Although it's getting better. I used to have the most *enormous* tits and—" She stopped abruptly, horrified at what had just slipped out. James stared at her, open-mouthed for a second, then burst into laughter.

"Well, you're certainly candid," he said, grinning cheekily. Madeleine put a hand to her burning face.

"I've *no* idea where that came from," she said, shaking her head. "I . . . it just slipped out."

"Did you really?" James said, stealing a glance at her chest.

"Er, yes. I used to be quite . . . big. Fat, actually. Then, when I lost weight . . . especially after Sarajevo, they just seemed to disappear."

"Really? I'd have liked to have seen you then. I somehow can't picture you with—"

"Can we stop talking about this?" Madeleine cried, trying not to squirm. James chuckled.

"Sure. Sorry. I didn't mean to embarrass you."

"No, it's my fault . . . *I* brought it up. Anyway, what time does the game start?" she asked, desperate to change the subject. He looked at his watch.

"In about an hour. We'll have to catch the train to the next stop. We should probably get going." Madeleine took another bite of her hot dog. "Easy now," he chuckled. "Wouldn't want to spill anything else down that . . . er, *enormous* chest of yours."

"James!" Madeleine wailed. He smiled back.

She remembered very little of the baseball game, which she found boring in the extreme. It was worse than cricket—she could barely see the players and she certainly couldn't follow the score. Everyone else around them seemed perfectly in tune with the commentators' voices over the loudspeakers—a lot of roaring and waving of hands . . . all terribly American, she thought to herself. Perhaps you had to be born there.

They went for a beer after the game, Madeleine praying the evening would last just that little bit longer. He said he had to go out for dinner and left her in a paroxysm of doubt—and then lifted her spirits again by asking if she was free during the week. They agreed on Wednesday which, she rapidly calculated, left her with five whole days and nights to worry about what to wear and whether he was just being friendly to another expat in New York. She frowned. In the very short space of about a month, her life had turned itself on its head. Where was the tough, battle-hardened woman who had run the length of Novodny Street with injured women in her arms? Who walked to the university hospital every morning without even stopping to check for snipers? Without warning, *that* woman had been replaced by a nervous, butterflies-in-my-tummy teenager who couldn't concentrate on what her date was saying because she didn't know when she'd see him next. Pathetic, she scolded herself as they walked towards the subway.

"So . . . see you on Wednesday," James said, turning to her at the top of the steps where the routes to their two lines diverged.

"Yes. And thanks for today, it was really nice." They stood smiling at each other. James seemed a little nervous again. She liked that about him—that away from the conference room and the work arena he wasn't quite as confident as he looked.

"I wish I didn't . . . well, anyway . . . see you on Wednesday," he said in a rush. He hesitated for a moment, then gave a quick wave and disappeared down the steps. Madeleine pulled a little face. She'd been hoping for at least a peck on the cheek. She felt mildly deflated but . . . there was Wednesday to look forward to. Although, she reminded herself as she walked along the platform to her train, he had her phone number but she didn't have his. That meant waiting anxiously by the phone until Wednesday, her heart missing a beat each time it rang. James Fournier. She even liked the sound of his name.

As it turned out, she didn't have to wait very long before he rang again. She got into her office on Monday morning after having spent a miserable Sunday indoors, cross with herself for being so indulgent and wallowing in self-pity. Why didn't she have any friends? Because she hadn't made the effort to make any, she told herself sternly. If you had made the effort you wouldn't be sitting around on the sofa watching that intolerable sitcom *Friends* and wondering why your life wasn't as perfect. Buck up, Madeleine Szabo. Get out there and get a life. She was repeating the little mantras to herself when the phone rang. She picked it up without thinking.

"Um . . . is that Madeleine Szabo?"

Her heart almost stopped. He sounded so like Alasdair. "Yes. Is that James?"

"Hi. I hope you don't mind . . . ringing at the office. I just wanted . . . wondered how your weekend was and if you'd like to go out tomorrow night, rather than Wednesday? That's if you're free, of course. It's a bit short notice and I just wasn't—"

"James," Madeleine said, laughing out loud. "Tomorrow would be lovely. I did have something planned but it's easily canceled," she lied, her face breaking into a wide smile.

"Are you sure? I mean, Wednesday's fine, there's no problem at all. It was just that . . . well, it's just a bit long to wait and—" he stopped himself suddenly and chuckled. "I must sound rather mad."

"No, no, tomorrow's fine. How was your dinner?"

"Oh, it was terrible. It was a work thing; it had been planned for ages. The Bar Society of New York. My boss thought I should go. It was *so* boring. I'll tell you all about it tomorrow, shall I?"

"Yes, do," Madeleine said, her heart lifting ridiculously. "Well, I guess I'll see you tomorrow then." James mentioned a restaurant in Brooklyn, despite her protests about it being on the other side of the world from him and they rang off. For the rest of the day she could barely concentrate on her work. Jamilla said she'd never seen her quite so distracted—was she ill? Madeleine shook her head. It was almost summer in New York. A feeling of heat and warmth stole over her. The life of pleasure she'd been so sure was out of her reach was suddenly, tantalizingly near. James Fournier. How was that possible?

If someone had put a gun to her head two days later and asked her to recount exactly what had happened between meeting James Fournier at Consul's on Atlantic Avenue and waking up next to him on Wednesday morning at 16B Lefferts Place, Brooklyn, in all likelihood she would have been shot. She woke at dawn, confused at first by the extra warmth in her bed and then suffused with tenderness and delight at the sight of his tousled brown hair wedged somewhere between her shoulder and the wall. The curve of his arm was just visible above the sheets; she looked at it as glimpses of the night came back to her. The touch and taste of his mouth when they first kissed; the way her back arched as he pulled her towards him; she being the first to break away, for air. She closed her eyes to savor the fragmented memories.

It was almost midnight by the time they left Consul's. He had two options—an expensive cab ride through the city or a night on Madeleine's couch. They both knew by then that the couch was a euphemism but they bravely kept up the pretense all the way back to Lefferts Place.

"D'you want some coffee?" she shouted from the kitchen as James sat down on her couch and tried to look comfortable.

"Yes, just a wee cup."

"I've only got this." She came through the doorway holding a jar of instant.

He nodded. "Yeah, that's fine. Who's that?" he asked, pointing to her framed picture of Péter.

Madeleine hesitated a second before surprising herself by saying, "That's my brother, Péter. He died when I was about ten."

"I'm sorry. He looks a lot like you."

Madeleine smiled. "Everyone says that. I don't see it."

"Is that you?" he picked up another photograph. It was of Amber, Becky and herself, just before they'd gone to university. "Wow. I see what you meant about your . . . er, chest. You look so different. You should grow your hair long again . . . it's beautiful."

Madeleine blushed fiercely. "Milk?" she asked brightly.

"Oh, you've gone all red. I'm sorry . . . I just keep putting my foot in it with you, don't I?" She tried to shake her head and pour milk into his coffee at the same time and of course wound up spilling it all over the table. They both jumped up, he put out a hand to say he'd get the cloth . . . and that was it. God knows how she'd managed to get across the coffee table or how he'd come round the side but before she could blink, his hand had slid down her arm and into her palm and her own arms went up around his neck—and that was the first kiss. It wasn't like Alasdair, it certainly wasn't like Doug. There was almost no time to speak or murmur a faint protest . . . she wanted him as badly as he seemed to want her. An image of him sitting across the boardroom table from her in the meeting where they'd first met came to her, crazily, as she pulled his shirt off and buried her hand in the fine, silky brown hair that covered his chest, narrowing to a single line just below the belt of his trousers. His mouth was warm, like his hands moving up the skin of her stomach to hold her breasts . . . this wasn't the gentle, tenderly surprised lovemaking she'd had with Alasdair, nor was it the comfort kind of sex she and Doug had shared. This was hungry, explosive, urgent. Pleasure, she thought wildly as they moved from the living room to her bedroom—that was what this would bring. They met each other as equals, perfectly matched . . . and in it, she found a surprising freedom. No need for gratitude, with James; he took as much from her as he gave. And as she was only too willing to take.

He stirred once or twice next to her. She ran a bare foot slowly down his calf. There was an easy intimacy between them already. He slowly opened one eye, smiled at her and allowed his hands to resume business where they'd left off a few hours before.

≈91≈

Amber woke up to the faint rumbling of thunder on the horizon. She looked around the room, disoriented. It took her a few seconds to remember where she was and why. It was her wedding day and she was lying in the guest room at Tendé's parents home. She pushed aside the sheets and stumbled to the window in the semi-darkness. There was another, ominous growl. The air was thick and heavy with the promise of rain. She opened the shutters and looked out across the garden. It was 5:15 a.m. The sky was just beginning to lighten. The tall, majestic palms that lined the perimeter wall were swaying to and fro in the rush of cool wind; a cock crowed several times somewhere in the distance. Their home was a sprawling, elegant colonial mansion that Mandia had renovated at some considerable expense and trouble, according to Tendé, situated close to the Presidential Palace on Koulouba Hill, just north of the city. She had lost count of the number of rooms in the house and exactly who lived in it. The term "family" in Africa, as far as she could make out, held a much more elastic meaning than in Europe—there were scores of relatives, extended family members, friends of Mohammed and Mandia Ndiaye whom Tendé addressed as "aunt" and "uncle" although there was no blood relation. Anyone older than you was automatically an aunt or an uncle. At thirty-five, Tendé still referred to his parents' friends that way; she found it oddly endearing.

It was almost light now. She looked across gardens to the view over the low-rise city with its thousands of tin roofs, minarets and shiny glass buildings poking up through the reddened skyline every now and again. Bamako was dusty; the whole country had been waiting for the rains for almost a month—but not just yet, she prayed silently, eyeing the darkening sky. If it started, it would be nothing like the gentle, misty drizzle of an English rainy day. Here the rains, when they did come, were violent, vertical sheets of water that sluiced through the air and left everything sodden and steaming in their wake. Not today, she whispered silently to the angry mass on the horizon, and closed the shutters. It was cool, even without a fan. She walked over to the wardrobe and pulled open the ornate, wooden door. Her outfit lay in its plastic sheath; a snowy-white, gossamer light *bou-bou*, similar to the one Tendé would be wearing, that came to just below her knees. Underneath was a pair of wide, flared trousers of the same material and draped over her head, a scarf of the same material. She slipped a hand underneath the plastic and fingered the delicate fabric. Lassana, Tendé's sister, had spent weeks looking for the right material. The modest neckline and sleeves were embroidered with fine, cream silk. She had found a pair of beautifully embroidered slippers in cream and silver leather—they looked North African with their pointed, slightly upturned toes and delicate heels. She had chosen silver jewelry to match her platinum and diamond engagement ring; against her tanned skin and white clothing, the combination would look good, smoothly beautiful.

The garden and the compound were beginning to come to life. Next door to her, Angela lay sleeping. She had arrived the night before after a twenty-hour flight via Paris, exhausted. She closed the wardrobe door on her dress and turned back towards the window again. What would it look like, to Angela? Bamako. Africa. The Ndiayes' house. The place was full of relatives and wedding guests and there had hardly been time to say anything to Angela, who seemed more bemused than anything by the fuss and the chaos into which the house had been plunged for weeks. And it was hot—Angela's delicate English coloring was definitely not made for such harsh climes. She'd looked ready to faint at dinner, despite the air-conditioning and the gallons of water Mandia kept placing beside her. Amber had insisted she escape to the calm quiet of her room as soon as dinner was over. She'd been longing to do the same, especially since Tendé wasn't with her. Mandia had insisted—it was bad luck for him to see her the night before, regardless of the fact that they'd been living together for ages. She'd practically pushed her son out of the house after he'd dropped Amber off.

There was a tap at the door. She turned from the window. Prayers had begun; she could hear the muezzin calling the faithful to mosque. She tightened her dressing gown and walked to the door. It was Lassana, Tendé's older sister.

"Hi," she said, smiling and holding a cup of coffee. "Thought you might need this."

Amber smiled at her gratefully. "Might need something stronger," she grinned as she took the cup. "I'm nervous as hell."

"I know," Lassana smiled. "My wedding lasted a week. Don't worry, it'll be fine. Tendé will protect you from the worst of the relatives. Poor Werner was left alone with the uncles for an hour on our wedding day. He didn't have a clue what to do." She laughed. "Anyway, Kadi and I will be around in the afternoon. Just come and sit with us if the aunts go on for too long. You probably won't understand what they're saying anyway—once they've seen you, had a good look at your outfit and your shoes, they'll lose interest, I promise."

"I hope so."

"And leave your mother with us. Is your sister here yet? And your brother?"

Amber pulled a face. "No. I don't think they're coming, actually." She was silent for a moment. She hadn't really expected Kieran to show up; he'd been slipping into a lethargic depression of late and seemed unable to rouse himself sufficiently to do anything, let alone fly halfway across the world for his sister's wedding. And Paola wouldn't be coming, of course. Not after their last meeting at the reading of Max's will. Nothing had really been said, but if looks could kill . . . it had taken all of Amber's self-control not to slap her sister.

"So it's just your mother?" Lassana asked incredulously. Amber nodded. Set against the hundred-strong delegation from the Ndiaye family, the Salls—what remained of them—seemed pitifully depleted.

"'Fraid so. And one of my friends. She's arriving later this morning."

"Well, all the more reason for you to stay close to us," Lassana said firmly. "Anyway, I'll leave you in peace. Come and have breakfast with us when you're ready. Kadi and I'll be in the guest house at the bottom of the garden."

"Thanks," Amber said, taking a sip of the strong, hot coffee. "I just hope it doesn't rain."

"Ah. It'll teach you to have a wedding in July. Next time, do it in March."

"Next time? There isn't going to be . . ." but Lassana was gone, shutting the door quietly behind her. Amber frowned. Next time? What did she mean by that? She sighed. Lassana was a hard person to understand. She seemed friendly enough and certainly much easier to get along with than Kadi who was a year younger than Tendé and almost the prickliest person Amber had ever encountered. She'd confessed to Tendé once that she didn't think Kadi liked her. Tendé's response had been simply to shrug and say that Kadi didn't like anyone, not even her own husband. Lassana was warmer, more open, but the friendship she had thought might flourish, hadn't. She was friendly enough but the gulf that had existed between them the first time they met, stayed. Amber couldn't quite understand it. The truth was his sisters intimidated her. Amber, who couldn't remember the last time she'd been afraid of anyone found the three of them, Lassana, Kadi and Amana, sometimes terrifying. They were so poised and assured, so at ease in themselves and the way in which they flitted between Bamako, Paris and Geneva . . . the contradictions that hit Amber in the face every day seemed to sail straight over their heads. They didn't worry about whether or not they'd remembered to say thank you to the watchman who opened the gate whenever their huge, air-conditioned cars pulled up; or whether their morning cappuccino at La Cigale cost the equivalent of a day's wages for the girl serving behind the counter. Amber agonized over the inequities; they simply accepted them as part and parcel of their daily lives. After all, Lassana pointed out to her one evening, *You don't worry in the same way when you walk into McDonald's back at home, do you?* Amber could only shake her head. It was different for them; they were Malian and entitled to their wealth. She wasn't, would never be. They shook their beautifully braided hair at her and laughed indulgently.

She walked over to the wardrobe and pulled out the bag she'd brought with her the day before. She'd brought several of the skirts she'd had made from the beautifully patterned local cloth—simple knee-length skirts with a side zip fastening. She'd spotted the materials the first time she went into the market at Artisanat—rich, boldly geometric patterns of swirls, abstract shapes, lines . . . all in the lightly waxed, soft cotton that was so much more pleasant to wear in the heat than the crumpled linens she'd brought with her from Europe. She'd asked Mandia for the name of a local seamstress and had come home each afternoon with yet another bolt of fabric, much to Tendé's amusement. He was almost never seen without a suit and tie, even on the hottest of days. She had a feeling Kadi and Amana, at least, would sooner be seen dead than in any of the local cloth. Amana looked as though she'd stepped out of the pages of some glossy European magazine every time she made an appearance—long, swinging braids, expensive jewelry and immaculate outfits.

She pulled her hair into a knot on top of her head and fastened her sandals. She would go next door and wake Angela; they could stroll through the gardens together and join the other women for coffee.

"*I ni sògòma*," Amber greeted the housegirls as she and Angela walked across the lawn. They smiled shyly back. The bride and her mother. They were probably wondering where the rest of her family were. It would probably come as quite a shock to them to realize that that was it: her and Angela. And that the peace that had descended on the two of them was actually quite recent. She felt a sudden pang—she missed Max. Terribly.

"Just look at these trees," Angela murmured beside her. "I've never seen so much greenery in all my life." Amber turned to look across the garden. It was true. The rest of Bamako might be dry and dusty but inside the Ndiaye compound it was lush and green, the dark leaves of the avocado trees jostling for space alongside the flat, horizontal flame trees, their bursts of brilliant carmine in outright competition with the cerise, wafer-thin flowers of the bougainvillea and the thick, furry white flowers of the neem trees. Amber had slowly learned the names of most of the plants—jacarandas, neem, acacia, hibiscus, guava . . . these replaced the oak, sycamore and ash trees of Hyde Park and the pretty lilac trees that bloomed around Holland Park in spring.

"It's beautiful, don't you think?" Amber said as they approached the guest house.

Angela shuddered. "No . . . it's too . . . ripe, if you know what I mean. I keep expecting things to slither out of the branches. It all looks too . . . alive."

"But that's what I like about it." Amber smiled at her description. "Everything's so alive."

"I've never liked the tropics," Angela said after a moment. "I couldn't even stand Menorca." They were both quiet. "He liked it here, didn't he?" she asked suddenly.

Amber nodded. "Yes. Very much. He seemed . . . I don't know . . . at home here, somehow."

"He felt terribly out of place, you know, in England. At times." Angela stopped walking. Beads of perspiration dotted her upper lip and brow. "He would have approved of this. And been terribly jealous, too."

"Jealous?" Amber looked at her quizzically.

"Mmn. Yes, of you. Of the choices you've had. You know, if there's one thing I think Max would have been proud of—apart from all the other things he accomplished—it would have been that. He gave you the freedom to choose. He worked so hard to make a place for you; a proper place, somewhere you could call home, no matter what. I think it was the one thing he'd given up trying to make for himself, so he made it for you. And Kieran—and Paola, too, I suppose, but in a rather different way."

Amber was silent. Six months his death and there were still things about Max to be discovered. Deep, meaningful things. "Why did he feel so . . . outside?" she asked after a moment. "I mean, he had everything."

"Everything that money could buy," Angela agreed. "But not a family. At least not his own family. He had to make that, alongside making money. And they never let him forget it, you know. The English. They never let him forget he was an outsider, a German, a Jew. Oh, there were some nasty things said, back then . . . when we first got married. You should have heard my father—your grandfather. Some of the things he said . . ." She laughed to herself. "Shocking, really. Max never forgave him."

It was on the tip of Amber's tongue to retort that he'd obviously passed the lesson along but she stopped herself. "Do you miss him?" she asked instead.

"All the time." Angela sighed, pulling a disparaging face at herself. "He was so difficult, you know. So terribly difficult. When I first met him, I was . . . bowled over, I suppose. I'd never met anyone like him before. I was young enough, and so in love . . . I thought it would be enough. But men like Max . . . I was never going to be enough for him, I knew that almost straight away."

"But you stayed."

"Of course. I mean, what else would I have done? I couldn't imagine life without him."

"And now?" Amber was gently prompting.

"Oh, now. Well, it's a kind of release. I've spent most of my life living under Max's shadow, you know. Now I have time . . . and some space to myself. I couldn't ever have walked away from him, you see. This way, he walked away from me. From us." She stopped and put an arm on Amber's. "But this is your wedding day, darling. We shouldn't spend it like this. It's morbid. Come . . . let's have breakfast. I promised one of Tendé's sisters I'd help her do your hair later." Her words were punctuated by a loud growl—a mass of rainclouds shifted on the horizon followed by a gust of cool, sweet-smelling wind. "I do hope it doesn't rain," she said, looking anxiously at the sky. "Mrs. Ndiaye said something about rain flies coming out. How awful. I find the heat hard enough without insects buzzing around."

Amber laughed. "It won't rain," she said, slipping an arm through Angela's. She glanced at her watch. It was almost eight. Becky would be arriving in an hour. She felt the butterflies begin to start up in her stomach. She wished Madeleine could have joined them but she was away speaking at a conference in Beijing and couldn't get to Bamako in time. There would be one or two foreign journalists . . . not many. Bamako was just too damned far off their usual radar for the wedding to be inundated with unwanted guests although Tendé had warned her the local press would certainly be there in force. A few people from Agence France Presse had contacted them—no doubt *Paris Match* would be running an article or two. Amber shrugged. Who cared? It was probably the only way the rest of her so-called family would get to share her day.

They knocked on the door and a housegirl silently let them in.

≈92≈

Becky's first impression of Bamako was that she was thankful she lived in southern Africa, not west. She'd never seen anywhere so dusty and barren in her life. The airport was small and almost deserted.

A bus was waiting at the foot of the steps to take the arriving passengers on Air France from the plane to the terminal building. She followed the other passengers into the hot, airless hall, stood in line with the few other Europeans under a single, creaking fan and prayed Amber or someone would be waiting outside for her. The heat was intense and the line moved at a snail's pace with much stamping and inspecting of passports. She'd taken the precaution of changing a few pounds for CFA, the local currency, as Amber had suggested but the thought of trying to find a taxi and negotiate her way from the airport to a city she'd never been in before terrified her. The line inched its way forward. Becky's passport was opened, scrutinized, stamped in several places and handed back. Not a word was exchanged between her and the unsmiling immigration official. She wondered if everyone in Mali was as uncommunicative.

An hour later, sitting in the back of an air-conditioned Mercedes, her bags safely stowed in the back, she was beginning to revise her opinion. Majid, the driver who'd met her with a carefully and correctly written sign, *M'lle Rebecca Aldridge*, was cheerful, if quiet, and he drove slowly and carefully along the highway into the city. She looked around her curiously. There was none of the European, colonial charm of Harare or Bulawayo which were the only African cities she knew. Bamako was almost flat. In the distance she could just make out the outline of hills; above them, in stark contrast to the blank face of the sky directly overhead, a mass of clouds were gathered, almost black with unshed rain. Yes, Majid confirmed. It was the rainy season. But . . . no rain. Not yet. The ground was a dry, ochre color, already beginning to shimmer under the silvery white glare of the morning sun. As they drew closer to the city, she could see glass and steel buildings poking up here and there above the tin roofs; square, ugly buildings that looked as though they'd been thrown together in haste, often without windows and doors; needle-sharp aerials thrust skywards that gave the city a lopsided air of chaos. The traffic was thick and fast—scooters seemed to be in the majority, buzzing around the cars and ancient green vans like the mosquitoes she'd been warned about. The pavements were crowded with an assortment of hawkers, shoppers, women in vibrant cloths and stunning headdresses, children, bicycles, dusty, ragged-looking boys pushing spindly wheels along . . . it was bewildering and chaotic, a million miles away from the quiet orderliness of most of Harare's streets. The city was a combination of dusty, sandy earth and deep green trees, and every spot of shade was utilized by someone—a peanut-seller, shoe-mender . . . she caught a whiff of something sharp and sweet as she lowered a window. She pushed the button and watched the scenery disappear behind the tinted pane; a relief to be cocooned again in the car's cool interior. Overhead, laced against the sky were thousands of wires—telephone, electricity, God-knows-what . . . a delicate lattice-work of connections through which the white hot sun stared down on the city. No, nothing like Harare, she thought as the car began to climb the hill. What on earth was Amber doing here?

But from the moment the gates of the Ndiaye house swept silently open and two uniformed guards peered into the car before letting it proceed, Becky realized Amber had moved on into a world where it would not be possible for Becky to follow, ever. Harare and the genteel world in which Becky had somehow found a place was nothing like the circles in which Amber now moved. The car drew up in front of an elegant, sprawling house with gardens that swept down the hillside and a wall so high it was impossible to see out to the street—or anywhere, for that matter. It was a protected, guarded fortress and behind its walls powerful people were living. She fought down a rising sense of panic and envy—familiar enough territory to her in her friendship with Amber—and stepped out of the car. A servant walked forward and took her bags, explaining in heavily accented French which Becky found hard to follow that Madame Amber was in the main house and would be sent for immediately. She followed the young girl into a huge, high-ceilinged hallway; it was dark and cool and a relief after the few minutes spent in the heat outside. She was shown to a seat. One or two barefoot girls glided in and out; there was the sound of a door slamming shut somewhere in the house and the sound of running feet. She looked around her. It was furnished in a combination of old, antique-looking pieces: a heavy, carved chest on which several very beautiful sculptures stood; dark parquet wooden flooring and muted green walls; the doors were dark, carved wood; on one of the walls a stunning piece of cloth hung—Becky recognized it as belonging to Central Africa somewhere. She'd seen pieces similar for sale in London at astronomical prices. Everything was cool, elegant, tasteful. She had never been in an African home like this one, she thought to herself quickly. This was a million miles away from Mbare and Chitungwiza. She suddenly felt quite out of her depth.

"Becky!" A door was flung open. Amber stood in the doorway, pleasure and relief written across her face. "Oh, God . . . am I glad to see you! I'm beginning to feel like little orphan Annie!" She rushed forward and hugged her. Becky immediately felt guilty. Why was she always comparing herself to Amber? She hugged her tightly back.

"You look so beautiful," she said, stepping back to admire her. It was true. Amber was glowing—her skin had turned a deep, rich color in the sun; her hair was lighter and curlier in the humidity . . . she looked older, sleeker. "And your skirt! It's fabulous . . ." she broke off, admiring the material.

Amber laughed. "I'll take you to the market tomorrow, you'd love it. But now . . . let's go upstairs. You've got a whole suite of rooms to yourself. Angela's quite jealous, you know." They linked arms and Amber called out for one of the servants. "*Bè min yan wa*," she said to her. The girl smiled shyly. "*I ni cé.*"

Becky stared at her. "You're learning the language?" she asked as Amber led her upstairs.

"Of course. It's the only way to have anything even approaching a normal conversation with ordinary people here. And it's not that difficult—not half as hard as German. Tendé laughs at my pronunciation but the servants are incredibly patient with me. It's a beautiful language, too. Like singing." Becky said nothing. She couldn't imagine trying to get her tongue around Shona. Besides, everyone in Zimbabwe spoke English. And those that didn't, Becky would probably never have cause to speak to. She followed her down one long corridor after another. "So . . ." Amber opened a door at the end. "This is it. Hope you like it." She walked in.

"It's lovely," Becky said, meaning it. The room was large and airy with smooth whitewashed walls, dark wooden shutters and a polished wooden floor. There was a four-poster bed in the center with a beautifully light, floating mosquito net above it and crisp white sheets. There was a rattan chair and table in the corner—she ran a quick, professional eye over the workmanship—and long white muslin drapes at the window. Like the rest of the house, with the shutters closed it was dark and cool. Two little wrought-iron tables stood on either side of the bed; a carafe of water and a glass on one and a small beaded lampshade and light on the other. The walls were completely bare. It looked calm and restful, an oasis after the long flight and drive from the airport. "It's lovely," she repeated, watching the girl stow away her bags in the huge wardrobe before withdrawing silently from the room.

"Tendé's mother does all of the decoration," Amber said, looking around the room with her. "She's got very good taste. So, will you be all right in here?" she asked anxiously.

"Of course I will. It's beautiful. I'll take a shower, you get on with what you've got to do . . . I'll be fine. I'll come and find you later."

"I'll send someone to fetch you," Amber laughed. "This house is a labyrinth. You'll be lost before you know it. There's a small lunch before the ceremonies begin at 1 p.m." She turned to leave the room; there were obviously a thousand things to do before then. "And thanks for coming, Becks. Really. It means a lot to me to have you here. If only Madeleine could have made it."

"Well, you paid for it," Becky said lightly. "I just got on the plane."

"It's the getting on the plane that counts," Amber said, smiling at her. "The paying bit's easy." She closed the door gently behind her. Becky stood in the middle of the room for a few seconds, admiring the space around her. She looked at her watch. She barely had time to take a thirty-minute nap and a shower before it would all begin. She began to peel off her sticky clothes.

Tendé wasn't allowed to see Amber until the ceremony was already an hour underway. The *nikkah*, the wedding ceremony, was to be performed in the vast living room at his parents' home. He'd arrived there earlier in the morning with his father, uncles,

relatives and colleagues, including several ministers, although the President himself was absent.
Tendé had done his best to play down the importance of the occasion—something quiet, he'd insisted to Mandia in vain . . . not for him the splashy,
drawn-out, three-day-long extravaganza. He didn't
want the President, nor the half-dozen top ministers
she'd wanted to invite; nor did he want the international stars who were his mother's colleagues to be
present—just his parents, a few close relatives . . .
a few people from Amber's side. "Close relatives?"
Mandia had looked at him, alarmed. "There's no
such thing here, my dear. They're *all* close relatives."

"All three hundred of them?" Tendé smiled, shaking his head. "A hundred, Maman. No more. Please."
They'd argued for weeks. In the end, a compromise
had been reached. A few politicians, a couple of
filmmakers, a hundred relatives and a few close
family friends. There were close to three hundred
people in the house. Three hundred more than he'd
hoped for but probably three hundred less than
she'd wanted. The tented marquees in the gardens
were finally up; the ground floor of the house had
been opened, the patios surrounding the house
were decorated with flowers, palm trees, tables,
chairs . . . the trees in the gardens were strung with
fairy lights that Lameen and half a dozen others had
spent days stringing from branch to branch, holding
an extension cable aloft to test each and every
strand. The relatives had started arriving a week before the day. Every morning a fresh load of cars
pulled up with aunts, uncles, cousins—many of

whom he'd never seen before. Accommodation had to be found for them all; the house was bursting at the seams. Mandia was in her element. Her only son was getting married. Tendé had understood early on that there simply wasn't a way to deprive her of this day. Grin and bear it, was Amber's advice. Maybe even enjoy it? He shook his head and laughed.

And now here she was. He straightened up as the door at the far end of the living room opened. He could see his sisters leading the way; Lassana and Kadi were in full Malian dress; Lassana was in a burgundy and gold outfit with huge, puffed sleeves and a tight, narrow, floor-length skirt; her hair was hidden under an enormous, elaborate headscarf which added at least a foot to her already tall, slim frame. Behind her, Kadi wore a vermilion and gold outfit with a similar cut but with long, bell-shaped sleeves and a gently flaring skirt. They both looked stunning. Mandia came through the doors next, wearing, as she often did, a beautiful combination of the best of Malian couture—a long, tight skirt with an elaborate ruffle at the back—and a beautiful silk lace blouse; Dior or one of the other fashion houses she favored. Her hair was also hidden behind a headdress; he could see the gold of her hoop earrings flash as she moved her head from side to side, smiling and welcoming the guests who had stood up to receive the bride and her mother. He was aware of a faint pressure in his temples; a quickening of his pulse. There was a murmur of approval as Angela stepped through the doorway, a slim, elegant figure in grey silk and then Amber . . . He moved a little; she was almost hidden by the women crowding around her.

She was stopped at the doorway; his father moved forward and took her arm, placing it firmly on his. Tendé watched them walk slowly towards him, Amber's cheeks flushed with the pleasure and embarrassment of it all—she hated being the center of so much attention, he knew. He watched her move forward, eyes cast downwards, her arm steadied by Mohammed's. He didn't look at the outfit that Mandia and Lassana had spent a month agonizing over; he wasn't looking at the delicate white shawl covering her head or at the way her *bou-bou* moved fluidly around her; it was at her face he stared. As they drew near and Mohammed held out her arm in the gesture he'd seen countless times before—at Lassana and Kadi's weddings; at the marriages of half a dozen friends . . . the passing of the woman from one man into the safekeeping of another. It should have been Max; he felt it and he knew she did too. The Koran made specific and clear provision: *a man should not marry until he has the means to do so.* Tendé was not a religious man, at least not in the orthodox sense. But the ceremony, performed in his father's house, the house to which he had brought his own bride over forty years earlier, held a special resonance, for him alone. *The means to do so.* Between him and Amber, the words in the sense that the Prophet might have intended were not an issue. That was not the covenant into which they would now enter. Amber could—and always would—take care of herself. But the life into which he would now lead her . . . could she follow? So far, he had asked nothing of her that she could not give—home, language, religion, culture . . . she had embraced everything he'd had to offer, and willingly. As she placed her hand on his and turned to smile at him— the wide, sunny smile he had come to know so well—the question he knew to be in his own eyes as they turned to her, dissolved.

"Ready for this?" she whispered to him as they both turned to face his parents and the waiting imam. And that was his answer.

PART SEVEN

≈93≈
Windhoek, Namibia
1997

Paola watched in petulant silence as one of the many servants she employed—she couldn't remember the name of this one: Estelle, Estella, Estrella . . . something like that—finished slopping water from one pail to another and sauntered out of the room. She stubbed out her cigarette angrily and tried not to call the girl back into the room to shout at her—but for what? For swinging her hips in provocation as she waltzed through the house? For chewing gum while Paola was talking to her? For being so young and beautiful, damnit, when Paola's looks seemed to her to be fading rapidly? It was the weather, she muttered to herself as she heard the dining-room door slam and then the kitchen door . . . and then the back door . . . and Jesus, couldn't the fucking girl do anything without slamming doors? Namibia was dry, dry, *dry*. When she woke in the mornings in the enormous bed in the enormous house that Otto had built for her in the exclusive little suburb of Klein Windhoek—the most boring, provincial, backward little corner of the globe as far as she was concerned—her face, eyes, lips . . . Christ, even her *teeth* felt dry and chapped. She slathered moisturizer all over her each and every morning, and each and every day as she stared anxiously at her reflection in the mirror, the lines and traceries under the surface of her smooth, white skin appeared deeper and stronger. She was afraid to smile, not that there was anything worth smiling about, she thought to herself miserably. She'd been stuck in this dead-end backwater for almost three years as Otto chased after more and more land, dreaming of building the most exclusive, most luxurious, most sought-after lodge in the whole of southern Africa. As far as Paola was concerned, he could build what he liked, where he liked, but *please get me out of here!* It was a cry from the heart. And one Otto steadfastly ignored.

He had purchased a prime piece of land high on the hills overlooking the city—if it could be called that, Paola said to him through clenched teeth—and had set about building a mansion of so many rooms, so many corridors and stairways that seemed to lead nowhere; rooms full of expensive, imported furniture and nothing to do. Finally, after two years, Paola had come to understand the price of her marriage. It was her job to entertain Otto's business and political contacts; it was her job to look

beautiful and gracious at all times, in all circumstances, no matter what. People of all kinds wandered in and out of the house on Lerner Street at all
hours of the day and night. There were those in the
German community in the former German colony
who had blown whatever chance they might have
had at a prosperous and politically influential future
by voting with the former colonial masters, prior to
independence. In Otto, now a personal friend of half
a dozen government ministers, they saw a chance
for financial—if not political—redemption. Paola
was sick of the sight of them. They came to the door
in their great fat Mercedes cars, coarse, reddened
knees showing above stout calves covered in thick,
khaki socks, no matter what the weather. Where did
they think they were? In what century? Their enormous guts spilling over dun-colored shorts and
great, thick beards showed them for what they really
were—peasant farmers, barely out of the Middle
Ages. As her stay in the country lengthened, her
distaste for them grew. And their wives! Not a stylish haircut or dress among them. Paola was a fish
out of water, a European rose among the scrub-
and-bush bedraggled plants clinging, out of desperation with nowhere else to go, to the African soil.
She hated them. And they hated her.

She could hear the damn girl singing to herself as
she emptied the pail of water into the flowerbeds
that lined the driveway. That was another thing. A
country stuffed to the gills with these half-breed
girls; coloreds, they called them . . . delicate, pretty
girls, the color of coffee with long, loose limbs and

morals to match. Paola couldn't prove anything, of course . . . Otto was far too clever for that—his work made it impossible for her to know with any degree of certainty—but it didn't stop her thinking about it. All the time. Estrella-or-whatever-her-name-was was a particular thorn in her side. She couldn't stand the little bitch. Long, shiny hair; small, pert breasts; legs that seemed to go on forever, particularly in those scrappy little cotton dresses she wore. She wanted the girl out of her house, but Otto was adamant. She was a good worker, he'd said the last time he'd been home. I'll bet. It was on the tip of her tongue to throw the words at him but she couldn't bring herself to. It was a mark of just how low she'd sunk—fighting with the servants for her husband's attention.

She turned listlessly away from the door and walked upstairs to the huge bedroom that she shared with Otto. Not that they really shared it. She couldn't remember the last time the two of them had been in it together. Otto spent most of his time away from Windhoek, on sites or at the various lodges he now owned. She pushed open the heavy, carved doors and stood in the entrance, surveying the room and the view out to the hills beyond. Dry, the earth was a sandy, light yellow color, punctured by the darker brown desiccated acacia trees that dotted the landscape. The light was so strong and clear—it didn't charm her, as it seemed to do to others; she detested it. Too harsh, blinding in its intensity, showing up every blemish, every line . . . she longed for the soft, muted light of Rome or the gentle, warm light of Menorca. She longed for Europe with a hunger she hadn't understood she possessed. She went home to Rome two or three times a year to see Francesca but their visits were getting more and more fraught as Francesca began the slow, inexorable slide into middle age and her fear of being left on some unnamed shelf without Amber's generosity to support her claimed more and more of her attention, and obsession. At the thought of Amber, Paola's mouth tightened. *Madame la Présidente.* That was what they were calling her. Although Paola certainly didn't move in the kinds of circles Amber appeared to, back there, wherever she was, news of her sister always seemed to filter through, somehow. Tendé Ndiaye was now Foreign Minister and being groomed for the presidency, so it was claimed. A diplomat's wife had mentioned it, admiringly, at some intolerable cocktail party Paola had been forced to attend. She winced at the memory.

"She's your sister, isn't she? Amazing, how these things happen."

"What things?" Paola had glared at her.

"Oh, you know . . . where she is, such a different life from yours, I expect. They say her husband's going to be president. How utterly glamorous. They make such a lovely couple—the children are absolutely beautiful. You don't have any yourself?" The woman smiled at her—cattily, Paola thought. She shook her head.

"No," she said shortly and turned away. She didn't

need reminding how wonderful Amber's life had turned out to be. She needed no reminder about how dull and predictable her own was, either.

And now, to make matters worse, Otto had informed her that Outjo Lodge was going to be the setting for the next round of peace talks between the two warring factions in Angola—Paola had long since lost count of who was fighting with whom—and that Tendé Ndiaye and his father would be among those hosting the talks on behalf of Mali, the neutral African country chosen to help smooth the way towards peace. Paola had simply stared at Otto, open-mouthed. The less she heard about Amber, the better. *Madame la Présidente* indeed. And now she was coming here? She felt sick at the thought. She flung herself down on the soft, yielding mattress that Otto had insisted they buy and stared blankly at the ceiling.

≈94≈

Becky looked at the note again, her hand trembling slightly. It was the third one that week. She heard the gallery door open and quickly shoved it to the back of the drawer. It was Godson.

"Hey," he said, walking into the office. "What's up? You look like you've seen a ghost, woman."

"Nothing." Becky shook her head. "Nothing. What's going on? Have the boxes arrived from Jo'burg yet?"

"No, I called the store. Should be in around 4 p.m, that's what Steenmarken said." Godson shrugged off his jacket. "You sure you're okay?" he asked again, frowning at her.

"Yeah, I'm fine. I'll just nip round the corner for a coffee. I'm a bit tired. D'you want anything?"

Godson shook his head. "Naw. I've got some paperwork to sort out. We had a big order in from Côte d'Ivoire . . . did you see it? Came in on the e-mail. Some American couple."

Becky nodded absently. "Back in a sec," she said, and got up. She didn't feel up to showing Godson the notes that had been showing up with alarming regularity over the past month. The first one had been pinned to the wooden frame of the gallery door. She'd picked it up and turned it over casually. It was addressed to the owner. She'd slid her finger under the flap and stared at the note for a second, uncomprehending. *Get out our country.* In bold typeface. She'd immediately tossed it in the bin and put it out of her mind. But when the second and third notes turned up—some stuck to the door, others shoved beneath it—the vague, unspecified threat was harder to ignore. She was strangely reluctant to go to Godson with it; she couldn't really have said why. They were doing so well—the gallery was now recognized as one of the best in Zimbabwe, if not in the whole of southern Africa. They still weren't making a huge amount of money—the crippling exchange rates and the slow decline of the Zimbabwean economy precluded profits from being anything other than marginal every time she left the country but money wasn't everything, as she and Godson kept saying to one another. They had carved out a special, unique place in Harare and now that they were finally connected to the rest of the world by internet, they had buyers coming to them from all sorts of places looking for pieces of art or sculpture or crafts that together she and Godson scoured the country to find. It was perhaps not the career she'd envisioned for herself the day she enrolled at art school, but Becky had an eye for things: colors, textures, workmanship. Deluxe was an ever-changing, steadily evolving space and in it, some of the region's most talented artists found a place to show and sell their work. They'd even been featured in an article in the South African *Daily Mail* newspaper. Becky had ordered fifty copies and immediately posted them back to Britain—and one to Bamako, of course. She and Godson made for an unusual partnership, she knew—he, with his waist-length dreadlocks and lively, animated features; she, with her cool red hair and porcelain skin. But against the odds, it had worked. Everyone knew them. Even Henry had stopped by the gallery almost a year back to tell her he was leaving Zimbabwe and going back to England.

"I'm envious," he'd said to her finally, as he was preparing to go. "You've managed here in a way I can't. And I'm *from* here." She looked at him, uncertain as to what to say. She knew just how much it would have cost him to admit it. But she also knew Henry was looking in the wrong places—and in the wrong way—to belong. She'd hugged him, saddened that it hadn't worked out for either of them, and watched him disappear through the doorway and out of her life. She knew what he was thinking when he walked in and saw her and Godson, heads bent together over some catalogue or portfolio of pictures that someone had sent in—but she didn't care. It would have been pointless to explain it to him, anyway. Not that she could entirely understand their relationship herself.

She felt a hand slide round the back of her neck. She looked up. It was Godson. He'd followed her into the coffee shop. She smiled wanly at him.

"Come on, Becky . . . what's wrong? You've been looking down for days." He slipped into the seat beside her. She felt herself tense, then drew a deep breath.

"It's just . . . I've been getting these letters . . . notes, really. They all say the same thing."

"What notes? What thing?" Godson was looking intently at her.

"Oh, I don't know. Just . . . leave the country, get out, that kind of thing." There was a sudden silence between them.

"What are you talking about?"

"I don't know," she repeated. "The first one . . . it was stuck to the door outside. Lately they've been shoved under the door. I found another one this morning." She looked up. Godson was standing up. He ran a hand over his face.

"What have you done with them? Did you throw them away?"

She shook her head, alarmed by the look in his

face. "No. Well, only the first couple of notes. The others I've put in the drawer in my desk. Where are you going?"

"I'll be back in a minute," he called over his shoulder, practically running out of the door. She looked after him, wondering what he was up to and what the look of fear that flitted across his face meant. It wasn't like Godson to be afraid of anything. She felt a cold shiver run suddenly through her. Stop it, she told herself sternly. Probably some disgruntled artist or a former employee . . . she'd sacked one of the cleaners a few weeks earlier, and a security guard the month before that . . . it wasn't anything serious. It couldn't be. She drained her coffee and got up.

Godson didn't come back until later that afternoon. Becky looked up as he came in through the door.

"Where on earth did you go?" she asked. He hung up his jacket.

"I took the notes to someone I know, asked if he thought there was anything to them. You know . . . if he thought they were something to worry about."

"Godson, it's probably someone I gave the sack, or some artist whose work we turned down. It's nothing, I'm sure it's nothing." Becky tried to laugh it off but Godson wasn't laughing.

"Look," he said, coming over to her desk. She looked up at him, worried. She'd never seen him look so scared. "Don't shrug this off, you know. Don't you watch the news? Read the papers?"

"Godson, you're frightening me," Becky said, swiveling around to face him. He leaned over her.

"Sorry." His face was inches from hers. She held her breath. He pulled away. "You should be careful," he said finally. "Don't come here alone any more. Not without me or one of the guards."

"Oh, don't be silly. It's nothing, I promise you. I'll be careful, I will," she added hurriedly, looking at his pained expression. He walked over to his desk.

"I mean it. It's not a joke. We're living in dangerous times," he said. Becky stifled the impulse to laugh. Harare? Dangerous? Oh, she'd heard the horror stories about white farmers being driven off their lands and their farms repossessed but this was Harare . . . calm, peaceful, civilized. Nothing like that could happen here. But she kept quiet, all the same. She and Godson were already entangled in a strange, ambiguous web and she couldn't see how this was going to help matters any. She bent her head and turned back to her computer.

At half past five that evening, just before dusk fell, Godson got up and pulled on his jacket. Becky looked up.

"Come on, let's go and have a drink," he said, switching off his computer. He'd been quiet all afternoon. She hesitated for a second, then nodded. She too felt like a little release from the tension that had been building.

"Okay. Give me a second." She switched hers off, grabbed her bag and walked quickly to the toilet. She touched up her lipstick, ran a brush through her hair and took a shawl off the stand in the hallway. There was no telling where they might end up that evening. It was one of the best things about working with Godson—some Friday nights when Deluxe didn't have some event going on, she and Godson would walk to Régine's, the bar on the corner and from there, anything could happen. An illegal *shebeen* in Mbare; a party of her friends in the northern suburbs; a wild taxi ride across the city to where he lived, in Chitungwiza; to a party held by his friends or an impromptu concert or on one memorable occasion, she, Godson and his cousins had driven from Harare to Bulawayo one evening, flying along the highway to get to a bar where a visiting musician from South Africa was rumored to be playing. Anything could happen. She loved that about being with him. She loved other things, too, she reminded herself as she carefully blotted her lips. She stopped herself just in time. There was no use thinking about it. She snapped off the light and walked back into the office.

"Ready?" he asked her, holding the door open. She picked up her bag and followed him into the cool evening air.

She'd promised herself not to, she told herself sternly, as the table in front of her lurched and swayed. It was wrong, it was silly, it wouldn't lead anywhere—she'd been through all the arguments, both with Godson and by herself. That one little mistake on both their parts . . . well, one mistake was easy enough to recover from. But two? She wasn't going to make another, was she? She hiccupped. She'd had far too much to drink. Godson was on the dance floor with some girl he'd singled out. She'd wondered briefly as she watched the two of them wind their way through the crowd . . . did he know her? Had he . . . ? She tried to look offhand as Steven and Keith, Godson's best friends, watched admiringly from the sidelines as he took his pick of girls and disappeared. The four of them often went out together. There was a warm sense of camaraderie between them that she'd never experienced with men before. She didn't know what it was—the fact that she was white, perhaps?—but they treated her as a sister, almost as one of them. They made an unusual foursome; sometimes, with a sense of mild shock, Becky would look around her and realize she was the only white person in a room or bar full of Africans; somehow, being with Godson and the other two, it ceased to matter. In time, everyone around them got used to the sight of her, drinking as hard as they did; laughing uproariously at the jokes, even when she couldn't understand them. It seemed to her as though the four of them had been around forever, as though she'd known them all her life. It was very different from her friendship with Amber and Madeleine, or even with Nadège, whom she still made an effort to see. She liked the fact that none of her three circles knew one another. Nadège occasionally raised an eyebrow when Godson turned up at one of their parties and if she'd ever seen Becky tipping back her head and allowing Steven to casually pour half a bottle of rum down her throat at four in the morning, she'd have been horrified. Amber would have liked them, she was sure—but then, too, Amber's world was so different, now. Tendé was now the country's youngest Foreign Minister and well on his way to becoming President one day, or so she'd heard. They had two children; Amber was now a wife and mother. Hers was suddenly a much more serious, much more grown-up crowd, Becky thought. And Madeleine too: they hardly ever had the chance to see her these days. She was back in Europe, living in Geneva with James, and a baby on the way. She wondered what they would make of her life, and of Godson. She shook her head. Not that there was anything to be made *of*, she reminded herself.

"Hey, Aldridge!" Keith shouted to her from across the bar. "What're you drinking?"

"Rum and Coke," she shouted back. "Last one."

He waggled a finger at her. "That's what you always say," he mouthed grinning. A couple of minutes later, he slid a glass dripping with condensation across the table. It was hot as hell inside the bar. "What's up with you tonight?" he asked her as he pulled up a chair beside her. She shrugged and tried to keep the table from sliding away.

"Dunno," she said, taking a gulp of her drink. "Well, actually . . . can you keep a secret, Keith?" she asked suddenly. He looked at her warily.

"Depends. What's up?"

"Oh, you know how it is," she said, aware that her words were slurring a little. "The thing is, I really like this—" She stopped. Keith had reached over and put a warning finger against her lips. She pulled back, startled.

"Don't," he said, moving closer to her. "Seriously, Becky. I can see it—we all can. I'm just telling you not to, that's all. It's great what you guys have . . . you know, the gallery and everything. Don't spoil it, okay?"

Becky looked at him uncertainly. "But I haven't *done* anything," she said, stung by his words.

"Not yet maybe. But it's . . . you know, it's pretty obvious. You like him, don't you?" She nodded miserably. "Well, take it from me. I'm his best friend. You're wasting your time there."

"But why? I mean, I know he's married and all that, but I've hardly ever met his wife. It doesn't seem to me to be much of a marriage and—"

"Becky, drop it, okay? Just drop it. I'm telling you. Like a brother, you know . . . it's for your own good. Godson's a great guy and everything but you'll only get hurt."

"But I really *like* him," she said, feeling tears suddenly well in her eyes. "I really do."

"I know." Keith squeezed her arm. "Come on, let's shake a leg." She looked at him, then giggled. At time, his English was hilarious. She wiped her eyes and stood up. The room swayed dangerously. "Come, hold on tight." Keith laughed and pulled her to her feet. She grabbed his hand and was plunged headlong into the crowd.

The following morning she woke up with a splitting headache and fortunately very little recollection of her conversation with Keith. She lay in bed and watched the sunlight dance across the wooden floor, an echo of the painful rhythm in her own head. It was a Saturday morning—what to do? Some breakfast, she thought, swinging her legs gingerly out of bed; then a drive over to Nadège's . . . maybe even a swim if she felt up to it. She wondered briefly what Godson was doing. He was probably with his family, where he ought to be.

She sat on the edge of the bed and thought about him for a moment. When had it started? She couldn't have said when exactly it was that she suddenly became aware of him next to her in the office at the back of the gallery; or smelled the faint tang of his aftershave as he rushed in and out, dreadlocks flying, all animation and energy concentrated in his tight, compact body. They had moved on, moved up. Deluxe was fully booked these days—small private openings, an exhibition almost every week; they had even been approached by the British Council to see about setting up a regular Thursday evening film screening—the Council premises were too small and everyone knew where Deluxe was. Expressing the appropriate regret, they declined the offer. They wanted things kept under their control, small enough for the two of them to manage alone. It must have been just before Christmas when the space was booked night after night and the two of them spent more time in the gallery than they did in their respective homes, that she'd first begun to notice him in that way.

"What're you doing for Christmas?" she'd asked him, a week or so before they were due to close up for the week-long holiday period between Christmas and New Year. He looked up from the box of soapstone sculptures he was packing.

"Oh, home, I guess. To the family. I'll take Adelaide and the kids."

"Where's that?" she asked, suddenly aware she knew very little of his life outside the business they shared.

"Mbizi. It's in the south, near the border with South Africa."

"And who lives there? Your parents?"

"Yeah, my mother."

"Is it just the two of you?"

Godson laughed. "Are you kidding? Since when have you seen an African family with one child? No, there's eight of us. From my father, that is. We're actually twelve."

"Twelve? You've got eleven brothers and sisters . . . well, some of them are half-brothers, of course, but . . . twelve?" Becky was impressed.

"We don't make a distinction, you know, between half and full and quarter and all that nonsense. We don't even really have a word for cousin, either. We're all family. So, if you count it that way, there's over thirty of us!"

"Christ. There's only me at home," she said, cocking her head to look at him. "And whereabouts are you? The eldest?"

"No, I'm the third-born son. I have two older brothers."

"And what do they do? I mean, are you the only one in . . . well, art, or anything like that?"

Godson laughed again. "Man, you people are so

diplomatic! No, my older brother is an economist. He lives in London. There's a few of us outside, you know. I was in England too, for some time."

Becky looked at him in surprise. "You never said! Where in England?"

He was laughing and shaking his head. "You've probably never been there. Liverpool. Nice place. Bit rough, if you know what I mean. I did two years at the Polytechnic there—printing course. Waste of time."

"No, you're right. I've never been to Liverpool. I've never really been anywhere in England, except Scotland—not that that's England—and the Lake District."

"Yeah, I can tell. There weren't many pretty girls like you at Liverpool Poly, I can tell you!" Godson shook his head. "I lived in Toxteth. Rough place. But cheap."

"And why did you come back? Did you think about staying?"

"Ah, papers, you know . . . I didn't have the right connections. I stayed in London for a couple of months, sleeping on someone's floor. But without my degree—and I just wasn't interested in the course, you know—there didn't seem to be much point staying there. No money, nowhere to stay, you know that kind of thing. Well, probably you don't. I thought to myself, it's better to be broke and home-less at home than in someone else's country, you know. Sometimes . . . well, I used to think about it. You know, if I'd done the right thing. My brother Johnson, he's doing well. He sends money home to our mother; he's doing the right thing. But now, the way things are going here, it won't be long before I can start doing the same."

"I can't imagine having to send money home to my parents," Becky said after a moment. "It's always the other way around. Me constantly asking from them."

"That's where we're different. Man, as an African . . . your money is never your own. There's always someone who needs it more; someone to be sent to school—there's the fees, clothes, transport—someone needs a place to live, a small loan . . . it's never your own, never."

She stopped what she was doing and leaned back, resting on her haunches. She looked down at the white skin stretched tight across her knees as if seeing it for the first time. The faint yellow tracery of lines as the skin slid over her bones, registering sharp angles the way a painting registers the play of light and dark. "But things have turned out well, haven't they?" she asked slowly, not looking at the gallery or the office they were in, but at him. He nodded.

"Yeah. Surprised me, you know." He smiled at her. "When I first saw you. Proper little madam with your yellow straw bag and that ridiculous hat . . ."

"I was wearing a hat?" She looked at him in surprise.

"Yeah . . . some big, floppy thing. It was winter, you remember? And the way you talked to me—as though you were afraid I'd bite."

"Well you did look a bit . . . frightening," she said,

smiling in embarrassment at the memory. "I wasn't sure what to expect. The way Gideon talked—"

"Ah, that fool. Well, never mind. You weren't from here, that's what I remember thinking. I don't know . . . it made it okay. All right."

"Really?" She straightened up from her position on the floor. Her knees were dusty. She brushed them quickly and walked over to her desk. Her stomach was fluttering. In three years it was probably the most intimate conversation they'd had. Strange how you could wind up working with and next to someone for three whole years and never really notice them, at least not in the way he'd suddenly become present to her.

"Godson." She turned slowly. "You never talk about your wife, about Adelaide . . . when did you marry?"

He was quiet for a moment. "Some time ago. Before I went to England. I was young. *She* was young."

"And you have children?"

"Two. She wants more, of course, but I don't know . . . I . . . things have changed for me, you know, with the gallery and the art and all that. I don't know if we want the same things any more. You wouldn't understand; she's very different from me."

"That's not exclusive to Africans, you know," Becky said quietly. "You don't have a monopoly on that kind of change. It happens to everyone. All kinds of people. It happened to me."

"You?" He laughed. "You . . . your life . . . it all

seems pretty perfect from where I'm standing. Pretty Becky Aldridge."

"I wish you wouldn't say that," she said, annoyed. He looked up. "What?"

"You know . . . pretty Becky, silly Becky. It . . . it's patronizing." She felt curiously stung by his words.

"You? Silly? You're joking, of course." He stood up suddenly, flexing his knees. He too had been crouched on the floor beside the unfinished boxes.

"No, well . . . maybe *you* are. I don't know. It just sounds . . . like you don't take me seriously or something." She saw the look of astonishment in his face.

"I take you more seriously than I've ever taken *any*one, ever," he said slowly. "How could I not? I mean, there's this . . . the business, the work we do together. It takes a serious person to do this, Becky. You're being—"

"Silly?" she supplied. They both laughed. "Sorry . . . just a little touchy, I suppose." She pulled out the chair at her desk and sat down, fiddling with the buttons on her sleeve, and turned the chair to face the computer, away from him.

"Why? What's eating you?" He was suddenly behind her. She kept herself very still, intensely aware of his presence less than a foot away. She began to say something but his hand on the nape of her neck stopped her. She froze, all feeling concentrated in the small patch of skin in contract with his won. He began to rub her neck very gently, very softly. "You're tense. Has something happened?" She shook her head, not trusting herself to speak. Some part of her waited impatiently for the next, well-known moves . . . for her to turn around, for their mouths to meet . . . the simple playing out of a script she was sure they both knew so well. But it didn't happen. Godson slapped her lightly between the shoulder blades and told her to relax, have a drink, come and listen to some music with him and Steven that evening. She needed to wind down . . . she was working too hard. The business was doing well. She could afford to relax a little.

After that it was almost impossible to concentrate on anything whenever Godson was near, and even when he wasn't. It was Christmas, Christmas in high summer and the heat was intense. She drove home to her two-bedroom bungalow on Sherwood Drive each evening in a fever of longing. The unspoken taboo that had existed between her and Godson for so long had suddenly and inexplicably dissolved. She was puzzled by it. To say she no longer thought of him as black would have been ridiculous, and pa-tronizing in the way she'd accused him of being to-wards her. But it was strangely appropriate. His being—everything about him; his appearance, his accent, his mannerisms . . . he had stopped being the *symbol* of something—a black man—and had simply become Godson. It was as if a layer that had previously existed between them had simply been peeled away, revealing the truer, *real* self. The fact that the revelation, as she thought of it, had oc-curred mostly in his absence—he was gone for almost three weeks—simply made it harder. There were things she could only talk to him about, things she went over and over in her own mind, talking to him in her head while he was gone, assuming, mistakenly perhaps, that her slow fumbling towards a truth about themselves was a process that he shared, was part of.

When he did return from Mbiza, a week into January, she spent almost an entire evening worrying about what to wear, say, do . . . they had arranged to meet at Kipi's, a popular bar for arty white Zimbabweans, liberal South Africans and expats, just around the corner. Godson was well known among the crowd by now . . . he was Becky's "catch," just in the way she was his when they ventured out into the townships and the streets of Chitungwiza that were *his* territory, as this was hers.

She saw immediately that it had been a mistake. Of course she had assumed too much. He was as friendly as ever; cheerful, smiling, generous . . . the same. Nothing had changed. She, on the other hand, was sure her awareness and desire for him was written all over her body and face. They'd seen a film together, *The Pillow Book*—someone had brought the video over from the UK—and she imagined herself to be tattooed with the text of her thoughts the way the Japanese girl in the film had written her own story across the naked white body of her lover. But if it was, Godson didn't notice. He went back and forth between the bar, bringing drinks, chatting to others, to her. They shared stories of how boring/fun/exhausting the break had been. By the time they stepped out into the still-hot evening, Becky's despondency was complete. They walked in silence to her car—she'd offered to drop him off at a friend's, not far from downtown. She was sullenly tipsy as she bent down and fumbled at the lock of the car door. It was an old Golf; she'd bought it from some friends of Nadège's who were leaving in a hurry. The key slid in easily enough but refused to turn.

"Shit," she said under her breath. "It's stuck."

"Here, let me." Godson threw his cigarette onto the ground and stubbed it out with his heel. He bent his head just as hers was coming up, there was a second's confusion, and then it happened. Quickly. Their hunger took them both by surprise.

Later that night, lying tangled in the white sheets of her bed, she laid her head against his smooth, aubergine chest and opened her eyes. Her bedside light was still on—in its golden glow she studied the skin and shape of the man lying underneath her. His hand was lying on the flat of her stomach, not stirring. He seemed asleep. The dark, matte surface of his skin magnified through the fur of her lashes was fascinating to her, and she was afraid and ashamed of it. Hadn't that business ceased, with her? Hadn't she stripped away the last layer of artifice and reached out to the man below? So why did it fascinate her, trouble her? She put out her tongue, caressing the skin that slid over his ribs. A thousand images flooded her mind . . . Kieran,

Charlie, Henry . . . all were nothing compared to the exhilaration of what she had just done. Amber. Her whole body was suffused with a strange, sensuous pride. Amber wasn't the only one to have crossed a line that Becky hadn't even understood existed before now. After more than three years in Africa she saw that everything was shaped by it, centered around its maintenance, despite the rhetoric about the future and the wonderful, marvelous rainbow nation just waiting to be born in the whole of southern Africa. The cruel fact, as she'd discovered immediately, was that there *was* no rainbow nation; that there would never be one as long as the taboo remained, carefully held in place from both sides. But she had done it. She was different from them all—*she* had put out a hand and touched him; touched and walked over the line that everyone around her dared not cross. She, *she*.

≈95≈

Amber folded the letter from Becky and held it loosely in her hand. She chewed her lip. Where had it come from, this desire to do as she had done? To compete with her in everything she did? As far as she could remember, she and Becky had never had a conversation about Tendé's race. Religion, yes . . . at the beginning, when she'd thought about converting and Tendé had talked her out of it, she and

Becky and Madeleine had talked long into the night once on a rare occasion when the three of them were together. Becky, if her memory served her right, hadn't shown much interest or any particularly memorable understanding of the situation. Her comments had been confined largely to practical questions—what Amber would wear and how she would get her favorite magazines. And now this. She glanced down again at the letter in her hand. Oh, Becky. She'd gone and got herself mixed up in something Amber was sure she didn't really under-stand. As if she was the only person ever to have slept with a black man. A *married* black man. She sighed and slipped the letter into a pocket. She walked over to the window and looked outside. The children were thrashing around in the pool with three of their friends; she smiled. Was it possible for five little children to make such noise? Amber stood at the window, looking at them; Bama, their nanny, watched from her usual spot beneath the purple-flowering jacaranda tree; she smiled, indulgently bored as her son Sibi and the girls performed hand-stands and other acrobatic feats and her daughter Liya looked on jealously from the protective circle of Bama's arms.

She turned from the window and walked slowly downstairs. The house was barely a year old. She and Tendé had built it from scratch. Amber, who had never really given much thought to her surroundings other than the stipulation that they be comfortable and not too far out of the reach of public transport had been astonished to find a latent nesting instinct in her that had begun with the casual news that Tendé had been offered several plots of land in a new development in one of the hills surrounding the city; it was half an hour's drive from his parents'—far enough to warrant a telephone call, but not too far. She shook her head unapologetically. In four years she had not grown accustomed to the habit Malians had of dropping in casually on one another with a blithe—and at times charming, she conceded grudgingly—disregard for the schedules or lifestyles of others. After Lassana and Werner had surprised everyone and moved back home, their own home had simply become an extension of their parents'. She could scarcely remember a day when the house wasn't full of siblings, parents, cousins . . . especially after the children were born. Having them, it seemed, had earned Amber a *bona fide* place within the family structure that no amount of Bambara and French lessons, no amount of cooking classes or attempts to engage Mandia or Mohammed in conversation on the rare occasions she actually found herself in the same room, had bestowed. She was an outsider in the family. Oh, everyone was perfectly nice to her but her status stubbornly remained—until Sibi was born. Overnight, it seemed, she had proved something to them with the birth of her first child—a son! She had shocked and scandalized Mandia with the idea that she would give birth at home, in Bamako. Mandia looked at her as though she'd lost her mind. London, at all costs. She was to go to London for the birth. There would be no discussion, no other decision taken. Even Paris was out of the question. Mandia had herself been to the hospitals in France. It was simply unthinkable that her only son's child would be born anywhere other than the hospital in which Princess Diana herself had had her two children. Mandia's unshakable trust in the British health service was misplaced, Amber kept insisting weakly—Diana's children had been born in the private wing of the hospital. Well, that was where she was to go, Mandia retorted briskly.

Amber boarded a plane six months' pregnant and didn't return to Bamako until Sibi was almost three months old. The difficult birth and separation from Tendé nearly killed her, she said. She would never, *ever* do it again.

A year later, when she was pregnant with Liya, she boarded the same plane although this time, Tendé did come to visit and Angela and Madeleine both found time to come to London to be with her for the birth. And true to everyone's stories, the second time it was a little easier. She left Sibi with Tendé and his family and came back to Bamako with a little sister whom Sibi immediately fell passionately in love with. For the first few months he wouldn't let her out of his sight. *Not* the way it had been with Tendé and his sisters, Mandia laughed delightedly.

Unlike Sibi, Liya was a placid, easy-going child; eager and easy to please. She was quick, like her mother, Tendé said, but without any of Amber's bossiness and ambition to rule. Amber protested at this characterization of her—unfair, she kept insisting—but it was true. Sibi was like her; a born leader, always organizing things endlessly, bossing the neighborhood children and his endless stream of cousins around. At two and a half, already fluent in three languages, he was a daily surprise to Amber. Where had he found the time to learn Bambara and a smattering of Peul as well as French and English? He switched languages the way some children switch moods—at will and seemingly unthinkingly. He spoke English with Amber, despite her attempts to join in when he and Tendé spoke Bambara or French; French with his grandmother and Bambara with his grandfather; with the night watchmen at the house he conversed in a mixture of Bambara and Peul. She caught herself staring at him in fascination. He was fearless, too . . . a certain stubborn set of the jaw reminded her of Max.

Liya was quieter, more like her father. Whereas Amber's relationship with Sibi was one of curiosity and endless fascination, with Liya it was joy, pure joy. She was a gorgeous, chocolate-brown bundle of laughter, occasional outbursts of brilliance and determination—and a desire to keep up with her brother in all things, at all costs.

She walked into the living room, struck as always by the beautiful, almost bare simplicity of the home that they—she—had created. In complete contrast to the overblown, ostentatious and inappropriately enormous houses that some of their neighbors in the new development had seen fit to build, theirs was a clas-

sically simple, pared down version of *Casa Bella*—
Amber's idea of a cool, minimal haven in a hot, sunny
climate, complete with pool, wooden-decked patio
and shady awnings that stretched from the living
room to halfway across the gardens. She loved the
house in a way that surprised her; from the high, airy
ceilings to the polished concrete flooring throughout.
Mandia had wrinkled her nose at the rather industrial
feel of the place, insisting that she knew exactly
where to find nice terracotta tiles until Amber had
firmly told her that she didn't want any tiles, that she
liked it as it was and that, with all due respect, it was
her house, not Mandia's, and as such, subject to her
tastes. Mandia had looked at her and pulled the corners of her lovely mouth downwards. A foreigner . . .
who could account for their tastes? But even she had
to concede that once the place had been furnished
and the hard edges softened by the curtains, rugs
and cushions that Amber had sourced locally—to
everyone's surprise, not only Mandia's—it was a
haven of quiet simplicity in a neighborhood of garish,
outlandish tastes. The house opposite them, to Amber's disgust, was painted patriotically red, gold and
green, a flag standing in for a house. Tendé laughed
out loud when he saw it after returning from a
month's stay in New York—there were no planning
authorities to speak of in Bamako; people built pretty
much what they liked, he explained between chuck-
les. It wasn't their taste but no doubt there were those
around them who thought the simple white cube of a
house that he and his wife had built was far too sim-

ple and downmarket for a government minister. *Vous ne voulez pas des arches?* a wandering mason had asked him on the way out one morning. Tendé laughed. No, they didn't want to add any arches. They liked it as it was.

"Sibi! Liya!" Amber called to them from the patio. "Lunchtime. Time to get out of the water, darlings. Enough sun for one day." She watched them turn and look at her resentfully—enough sun? How could one possibly have too much sun? She smiled. She was familiar enough with the parental desire to give children a better life than the one they'd invariably had—more opportunities, better education, more attention, love . . . the list was endless. But in so many ways, Amber wanted the opposite. She wanted to give them *everything* she'd had: a place in the sun; the understanding that the world was a bigger place than one's immediate surroundings; the desire to travel and to see other things, places, people. Whatever else she and Tendé had done, she knew they'd succeeded in that. Sibi and Liya were only too aware that there were other places that figured importantly in the lives of their parents; Grandmère in America, Tante Paola en Afrique du Sud; Tante Madeleine a Genève . . . Londres, Paris, Harare . . . The names of cities halfway across the globe were as familiar to them as the neighborhoods of their own city; Niaréla, where Nana and Papa Ndiaye lived; Hippodrome, which was where they'd lived before moving to their new house; Quinzambougou, where they went to nursery school.

Yes, Amber saw it in her children; the world was a smaller, more easily graspable concept to them than it was to many of their little friends. She saw it and was glad of it. Max would have approved.

≈96≈

Madeleine examined herself anxiously in the bathroom mirror. She was seven months' pregnant and as large as . . . as . . . words failed her. The enormous breasts she'd jokingly boasted to James about—safe in the knowledge that they were gone from her forever—had returned with a vengeance. She could barely see over them to the concave mound of her belly. People looked at her on the tram into work in the mornings, convinced she was about to squat down somewhere between the briefcases and pinstriped trousers and give birth, right there and then. She had eight weeks to go, she wanted to wail at them. She was nowhere near ready to "drop," as James so charmingly put it. She was going to get bigger. And bigger.

She shoved her dress back down over her stomach and waddled to the toilet. Waddled was the right word. She felt, looked, acted like a . . . a . . . duck, she thought to herself miserably. A gross, fat, overstuffed duck. *Foie gras.* That was more like it. She'd finally found the right words to describe herself. A big, fat *foie gras.*

She heard the front door open and close quietly. James was back. He would tiptoe into the room, she knew, waiting to see what sort of mood she was in before deciding how to say hello. Poor man. That was what it had been like ever since she'd discovered she was pregnant. Her mood swings were alarming and unpredictable. Some days she felt on top of the world; on others she could barely rouse herself from her bed for the black despair settling over her like some fine, grey dust. All perfectly *normale*, her French gynaecologist had told her briskly. Madeleine wasn't so sure.

"Hey." She heard his voice behind her. She turned and smiled, reading the quick relief in his eyes.

"Hi." She tried not to let the bleakness with which she'd been studying herself show.

"Good day?" He put his briefcase down on the floor and walked over to her. She nodded slowly.

"Okay. Fine, I guess. I came home early." She moved into the circle of his arms, trying not to think about the way she'd fitted so perfectly only months before. Now he could barely get his arms around her. Stop it, she told herself firmly.

"Anything wrong?"

"No, I was just feeling tired. I thought I could continue with it at home. But when I got here I lay on the couch for a bit and next thing I woke up just before you got here."

"Well, you know what the doctor said. Plenty of rest." He smiled at her and kissed the tip of her nose. "So, what d'you feel like doing tonight? It's Friday . . . fancy going to the pictures?"

She shook her head. "Oh, James, I hate leaving the house. I . . . I just feel so . . . huge and horrible." She bit her lip. She really hadn't meant to sound quite so despairing but it was true. She felt him take a step back from her.

"Okay. Well, I could pop down to the video store and find something we haven't watched . . . maybe get some Chinese takeout on the way back?" She nodded half-guiltily. They were barely in their thirties but she was behaving like her shrill, pinched mother who was two decades older, something she'd sworn never to do. Maja had slowly squeezed the joy out of her and Imre's life. As a child, Madeleine had watched in silent resentment as she'd wrung them all dry and she'd hated her for it at the time even while she recognized the struggles that Maja had endured that made her thus. But what excuse did she, Madeleine, have? A kind and loving boyfriend beyond her wildest expectations; a solid job; good friends, even if they were halfway across the world from her . . . what the hell did she have to complain about?

"See you in a bit," James was saying as he moved back towards the front door. Madeleine sighed. He was probably relieved to have something to do that would take him away from her while she struggled to place herself on a more even keel. She sighed and walked through the apartment to the kitchen. She poured herself a small glass of wine—thank

God for the French, she thought gratefully—no one frowned upon the occasional glass of wine or slice of soft cheese. She sipped it slowly, standing by the kitchen sink and looking out at the neighboring lives strung out across the rooftops of their hillside apartment, the crowded stiff fingers of TV aerials, washing lines, potted plants waving in the evening breeze, a deckchair or two opened out on a tiny balcony for someone to snatch the odd ray of sun. Not that there had been much of that about lately. It was February and Geneva was blanketed in thick fog and freezing rain. Beautiful as the city was under its winter shroud, Madeleine seemed not to notice. She spent each day longing for the pregnancy to be over, for her life to return to normal. Despite James's gently worried hints, she didn't seem to realize that that was the whole point: That life *wouldn't* return to normal—that she was entering into another, different stage, that the frantic travel and late nights of the past three years would be replaced by late nights of another kind. She saw his concern but was blithely confident. Having a child wouldn't change a thing. She hadn't worked this hard and come this far to allow a baby to interrupt and dictate the way things would be from now on. She wasn't going to be one of those mothers . . . she saw the exasperation in his face sometimes and fell silent. The truth was more complex that she dared admit. She was terrified. Absolutely terrified. What if something went wrong? What if . . . what had happened to her all those years ago had done something, caused some damage that only her silent, secretive body knew about? She never let herself think about . . . it . . . she locked it away, the same way she locked her thoughts about Péter away, somewhere deep inside her where the door was permanently closed. But sometimes, when she least expected it, an emotion would slip out from underneath the door— a pang of guilt; a moment of regret; a fleeting question . . . was this how it would have been? . . . and all the control and keeping the past locked up would suddenly unravel. She hated those moments of weakness but in truth, there was nothing she could do. Her memories kept threatening to undo her. It just didn't seem possible that all the things she'd done and seen in the past twenty years wouldn't somehow catch up with her and make it impossible for her to have what every other normal, happy young woman had—women like Amber, for example: a husband, two lovely children, a full and happy life . . . no, more than that, a life that meant something. She'd been to visit Amber and Tendé twice in Bamako over the past few years and each time she'd come away struck by the simple beauty and ease she saw in the way Amber had organized her life. She came away each time confused by the messiness and confusion she felt in her own—*still*. She was thirty-three years old. When would it all fall into place? When?

She heard James opening the door downstairs. She drained the wine glass and turned from the kitchen sink, determined not to let this evening collapse in a pool of all-too-easy tears.

She wasn't sure quite how it had happened, who had made the introductions and then sauntered off, leaving her standing next to the beautiful sixteen-year-old son of one of their neighbors along the tree-lined road but . . . there it was. She was left standing alone with Dieter Velton, just back from boarding school in South Africa, he told her as she tried not to stare at him. They sipped chilled wine and she looked around for his mother to return. Sixteen? Paola swallowed. Dieter Velton, unlike almost every other teenage boy she had ever met, was an almost perfect specimen of a voraciously healthy teenager who had spent his life outdoors, in shorts and in the sun. He wore his unusual beauty lightly. Neither of his parents, whom Paola had met, briefly, over the three years she'd been living, on and off, in Windhoek, had anything like the marks of physical distinction that had somehow combined and settled on their son. Well over six foot, with the agile grace of a born sportsman, dirty-blond hair, deep brown eyes . . . his face was saved from abstracted perfection by one or two odd blemishes—a long, straight nose; full red lips that parted to reveal a slightly crooked front tooth that had obviously defied the attentions of the expensive orthodontist his parents had sent him to, no doubt; a dimple in the left cheek that gave his smile an endearing, almost lopsided appearance. Paola registered these things in a state of mild, animated shock. The fact that he obviously thought her the most beautiful woman at the late afternoon gathering only added to her confusion. She asked him about school; he shrugged and asked her about Rome. He couldn't wait to get out, finish his Matric and go off around the world. Some friends of his had a yacht; they were planning to go up to Maputo and sail on from there. Paola listened to the teenage fantasy without recognizing it as such. She suddenly longed to be sixteen again, to be back in Menorca with Bernadette and Enrico and Pablo . . . sitting at one of the bars in town, drinking Campari and orange juice, flirting with the beautiful men in their twenties and thirties who sat at the bar and stared at them. For a brief, mad moment, she wanted nothing more than the lazy, sensuous security of that time in her life when Max was still around and she and Francesca had nothing more to do than dress up, look beautiful and bask in the reflected glow of his admiration. Standing there in the dry, warm heat of the Namibian summer with the beautiful teenager from across the road, it suddenly felt like yesterday, still possible, still within reach. How else could she have explained the casual invitation to fly up to Outjo with her the following day? He'd never seen the lodge, never sat on the wide, shaded terrace overlooking the dam that Otto had built specifically to bring the animals to drink in the evening under the admiring gaze of his guests. She saw he was flattered by the invitation—and that he was spoiled enough to accept without thinking; sixteen or not, he wasn't the type to run asking his parents for permission to do what he wanted, when he wanted. She recognized immediately the same rebellious arrogance she'd had as a teenager, as though their shared beauty were all the permission needed to take everything on offer around them, whenever it happened their way. Otto was in Germany and wouldn't be back until the following week. She could have a week of . . . what? Fun? With a sixteen year-old?

"See you tomorrow, then, Dieter," she murmured, moving away from him as his mother approached. "I'll send a driver to pick you up. We usually leave from Eros at eight. Can you get up that early?"

"Get up?" He grinned at her. "I'm going out tonight with some friends from school. We're going to a club in the township. We probably won't even go to bed." He turned his beautiful face towards his anxious mother. Paola blinked and walked quickly away.

The following morning, she woke early and lay in bed listening to the non-stop chatter of the birds outside her window. The morning still held the coolness of the night. She flung aside the cover and lay back, wriggling her painted toes and trying not to get excited at the thought of the day ahead. The little gold bedside clock showed it was still early; a quarter to six. She fished in her mind for something to wear—sexy but not too obvious, something pretty . . . she paused. Suddenly, in the cold light of day, the idea of flying up to Outjo with the teenage son of a neighbor struck her as silly—pathetic, even. She rolled over. She ought to call the whole thing off, quickly, before she made a fool of herself. But what else was there to do? she asked herself, hugging one of her pillows to her chest. There wasn't a damn thing of interest, at least not to someone like herself. No shops worth frequenting, no cafés at which she wanted to be seen, no cinemas or theatres to speak of . . . nothing except the vast, unrelenting outdoors that everyone around her seemed to love and in which she had no interest, none whatsoever. So who could blame her for casting her eye around, looking for a little distraction? And Dieter Velton was certainly that.

A halter-neck top in a striking brown, black and white graphic pattern; low-waisted white linen trousers, tight across the hips and flaring prettily at her ankles . . . flat leather sandals, a wide-brimmed straw hat . . . she inspected herself in the mirror while fastening a pair of silver hoop earrings. She'd hit exactly the right note, sophisticated, edgy, sleek . . . with her long brown hair swinging almost to waist level, she saw herself as a sixteen-year-old schoolboy would—perfect. The halter-top peeked open every now and then to reveal a toned, tanned midriff and pale, soft breasts. Her fingers were shaking ever so slightly as she applied lipstick, adjusted the brim of her hat and picked up her bag. She'd sent the driver ahead to pick up Dieter from his parents' home down the road. It would definitely have looked strange for her to be seen in the car as well. She wondered what he'd told his mother. She seemed the neurotic type, Paola mused. She hardly knew the family . . . the father was something in petro-chemicals or mining, Paola couldn't remember which. They were of good German stock—Otto's kind of people. Paola found them peasant-like and boring in the extreme.

On the way out the front door she noticed Estrella looking at her strangely. Where was the missus going on a Saturday morning so early? She could read the question in the stupid little girl's eyes. She ignored her and climbed into her sleek, black Land Cruiser, the must-have vehicle for Windhoek wives. She started the engine, feeling it roar under her feet, and pulled out of the driveway.

Eros Airport was deserted when she swung into the parking lot. She locked the car and walked quickly to the hangar where Otto kept both of his small Cessna planes. Franz, his German pilot, would probably be inside, checking the plane before bringing it round to the front for their short trip. She wondered where Dieter was—there was no sign of the black Mercedes that had been sent to pick him up.

"*Guten Morgen.*" Franz walked out from around the corner, wiping his hands. Paola stopped. She couldn't stand the pompous toad. "There is someone waiting for you, Frau von Kiepenhauer . . . we are taking him along?"

Paola nodded curtly. "How long before we can take off?" she asked, looking around for Dieter.

"Ten minutes, maybe fifteen. The young man is over there, by the coffee machine." He jerked his head in the direction of the offices. "I'll get the engines started." He disappeared. Paola ran a tongue nervously over her lips and sauntered over, her heart thudding. She could see the top of Dieter's tousled head over the Coke machines. She cleared her throat and he looked up and gave her a smile. She felt her stomach contract—he was just so damned beautiful.

"So, did you get any sleep?" she asked, coming up beside him.

He shook his head and took a swig of Coke. "Nope. Stayed out all night."

"What do your parents think?" she asked, hoping she didn't sound too . . . motherly. She gave a short laugh. Motherly? Her?

He shrugged. "They're pretty cool. I don't have to tell them everything I do. Comes with being shoved off to boarding school, you know."

"How so?"

"You know . . . they feel bad, they want to make it up to us when we're back . . . that kind of thing."

"Oh." Paola nodded dubiously. Her own experience of family life had been so unlike everyone else's that she often found herself at a loss when others explained what was going on in their lives and homes. "Well, Franz is almost ready to take us," she said, looking over her shoulder. The Cessna was being pulled out of the hangar slowly.

"Cool." Dieter finished his Coke and stared at the plane. It did look impressive—white and silver with the words "Otto von Kiepenhauer" scrawled across the wings.

"Shall we?" Paola led the way across the tarmac, her heels clipping loudly in the morning quiet.

Ten minutes later, they were rolling down the small runway, shouting to each other above the noise and din of the engines. Paola couldn't believe she was actually doing it—sitting strapped in next to sixteen-year-old Dieter Velton on her way to Outjo for the day. For the *day*, she kept reminding herself sternly. They would be back before nightfall. But there was something so *persuasive* and reckless about him . . . as ridiculous as it seemed, sitting with him, anything seemed suddenly possible. It had been so long since she'd felt so alive and in charge and game for anything. She could have reached across the narrow aisle and hugged him. The little plane lifted into the air; Dieter was looking out of the window, watching the earth recede. Paola stole a look at him—he hadn't been joking; he was wearing the same grey T-shirt and jeans he'd been wearing the day before. There was a night's worth of stubble around his jaw . . . a shadow under the tanned olive color of his skin. Man-child—the words of a song came to her suddenly. The combination was heady, intoxicating. She liked the way he looked up to her; the way his eyes lit up in admiration when she said something funny or sexy, or both. And her outfit hadn't been lost on him, she noticed as soon as she walked up to him in the hangar. It was his age—he was too young to behave with guile and yet he was old enough to understand that she was flirting with him shamelessly. She shook out her heavy curtain of hair and was gratified to see his eyes widening in appreciation.

They landed at Outjo forty-five minutes later. They were met on the tarmac by Dierks, Otto's foreman and general manager. Paola couldn't help but notice the looks exchanged between Dierks and Franz but she couldn't have cared less. They were paid to work for Otto and that meant working for her, too. She ordered an open-top Jeep and a driver to take her and Dieter around to see the animals and practically stamped her pretty little foot when Dierks said he wasn't sure if there was one available . . . she hadn't let them know she was arriving . . . did Herr Otto know?

"Will you just do whatever you have to do and *get me a car!*" she snapped at him. Dieter looked on in admiration. Dierks nodded sullenly. There was little love lost between Otto's vast staff and his wife. He strode off, his enormous belly shuddering over his shorts as he walked towards the garages in search of a vehicle and driver.

"Man, you're one tough lady," Dieter breathed as the two of them watched him disappear.

Paola smiled. "Only when I have to be," she said archly. "He'll be back in ten minutes, I promise you." She was right. Ten minutes later, a silver Jeep pulled up with a young colored driver at the wheel. They climbed into the back seat and roared off, leaving a cloud of red dust and a spluttering Dierks behind.

Looking for animals—of any sort—was certainly

not the way Paola liked to spend her day, but under the pretext of looking for lions, water buffalo and anything else that might cross their path, she was enjoying the lurch and sway of the Jeep as they bounced and flew over ruts and holes on the 2,500 hectare ranch. It wasn't yet eleven and the air was still pleasantly warm; by midday, she knew, it would be impossible to sit out in the sun. She had brought her gingham pink bikini along. On the deck of each chalet was a deliciously cold plunge pool; she and Dieter could spend a very pleasant afternoon semi-submerged in the water or even walk up to the enormous pool at the main lodge. It was all turning out splendidly. Windhoek and the boredom of her life there seemed very far away. At the moment, holding onto the roll bar, allowing herself to loll and bump against Dieter every once in a while, life was looking up. She gripped the bar, admiring her slender, toned arms and noting Dieter's admiring glances.

It took them almost two hours to drive around the vast ranch. They saw hundreds of antelope, a handful of kudu, one or two giraffes and a lone water buffalo—quite enough, from Paola's point of view. She hated animals. At last they drove up to the chalets. She jumped out of the Jeep and strode ahead; she knew exactly which of the twelve luxury little bungalows she wanted—hopefully, it was free.

It was. Half an hour later they were sitting on the wooden deck overlooking the vast Okahandja plains unfolding beneath them, drinks in hand. The air was sweet and dry with the special, crystal-clear sharpness of landscapes at high altitude. The jagged profile of the distant mountains was laid along the horizon, pale blue and purple in the mid-day sun, while overhead the sky was a deep, sapphire blue. Nothing could have been further from the city and the day-to-day reality of being Otto von Kiepenhauer's wife. A moment of awkwardness came over her; without the distraction of looking for game or the thrill of riding around in the open Jeep, the question of what the two of them were doing there, alone, suddenly arose between them. To hide her confusion, Paola began to chatter.

"How long have you lived in Windhoek?" she asked, sipping her ice-cold gin and tonic. Dieter looked at her, surprised by the question. "All my life. I was born here."

"Oh. I thought . . . I thought you were German," she said. He shook his head.

"Naw. My dad came here when he was a kid. My mum was born here. We're Namibians, through and through."

"But you've been to Germany?"

"No. Never."

"Really? But you speak German at home . . . I've heard you."

He shrugged. "So? You speak English. You don't look English to me."

Paola blushed. Her stomach was beginning to tie itself in knots. She looked at him lying in the deckchair, his long legs sprawled out in front of him. His skin was golden, the muscles and tendons sliding just below the surface—he was youth and beauty and sensuality rolled into one, taut teenage male body. She swallowed. "How do I look?" The question hung in the air. He turned his head slowly towards her, his expression suddenly unreadable.

"Good," he said finally. "You look good." She stared at him. He had her. He knew exactly what she wanted from him, and she had no idea how. What experience could this sixteen-year-old boy have had that would make it possible for him to understand what was going through her mind every time she looked at him? How could he possibly know how hungry she was for admiration, appreciation . . . for some of the beauty and recklessness he seemed to carry within himself with such arrogant aplomb.

"I bet you say that to all the girls," she said, regretting the silly words as soon as she'd spoken. He grinned. He looked as though he'd heard the statement a thousand times before. He took a swig of beer and turned his body so that they were facing.

"I think you're beautiful—everyone in Windhoek does." Paola blushed a deep, fiery red. His words thrilled her even as she reeled from the arrogance of his statement. He's sixteen, she kept reminding herself as he continued slowly sipping his beer and looking straight at her. "All my friends. You can't imagine the look on their faces when I said I was coming here with you this morning."

"You *told* them?" Paola was suddenly alarmed.

"Sure. Why not?"

"Shit . . . I wish you hadn't. I mean . . . I'm married, you know."

"I know that. But we haven't done anything . . .

yet," he said slyly, his eyes coming to rest on the deep V-neck of her halter-top.

"Dieter, have you done this before?" Paola asked, feeling suddenly rather helpless. He continued to stare at her.

"Sure. Haven't you?"

"I'm not sure . . . I don't know what you mean." She hesitated.

"You asked the question. What did *you* mean?"

"Well . . . this. Going somewhere with a . . . someone who's married," she said eventually.

"'Course I have." Paola could only stare at him. "Come on, you're living in Windhoek," he grinned. "Everyone's having affairs. Everyone." She was silent for a moment.

"How many times?"

"Why bother counting?" His response was easy. The balance of power between them had shifted suddenly. Paola now found herself in the unusual position of taking her cues from him, rather than the other way around. She wasn't sure she liked it. But then she looked at him again, at the way his blond hair curled around the nape of his neck; at the silky smooth skin on his forearms and the loose, rangy body she suddenly longed to touch. She was assailed by memories—Didier, Prince Georg, half a dozen one-night stands . . . and Kieran, of course. The sharp, terribly masculine scent of his neck as they got up out of their chairs and stood together, not quite touching . . . it was the scent and taste of Kieran. A terrible desolation burned over her. She tilted her head as Dieter began to playfully, almost lazily, kiss and touch her. His own hands were trembling, she was pleased to feel—not so much the cocky teenager now, she thought wildly as he pushed his hands under her top and his mouth came down on hers. She somehow had the presence of mind to maneuver them into the room, kicking the door shut behind them. Everyone at the lodge knew who she was; that would have been all she needed—some disgruntled employee reporting back to Otto what he had seen on a burning hot summer's afternoon when the acacia trees had stopped moving and everything held its breath.

≈98≈

On impulse Becky swung the car around and headed back towards downtown, towards the gallery. After another evening spent at Nadège's, going over in excruciating detail all the myriad reasons why she ought to leave Harare and head back to London with the children, her head was spinning and she felt exhausted with the effort of pretending to listen. Actually, she couldn't have cared less about Nadège and her decision to leave—or stay. *She* was staying put.

She drove down Mugabe Avenue, past the post office and the bank with its shuttered façade. There were security men sleeping on the pavements outside many of the shops, their wrapped-up, mummified bodies huddled into the doorways of the businesses they'd been hired to guard. A few of the stores in the central business district had been looted in the past couple of months; everyone, it seemed, was on edge. She turned left onto Albion Road, looking for a parking space. It was almost 10 p.m. She ought to go home—she could hear God-son's voice in her ear. He'd been quite cross with her the other day; she was working too hard, she should take time off, to rest. But she didn't feel like going back to her empty bungalow to sit and stare at the walls, thinking of him. Might as well make herself useful—there was always plenty to do at Deluxe.

She maneuvered the car into a space at the corner of Albion Road and Market Street, a block away from the gallery. Locking the door, she walked quickly back down Albion, clutching her handbag tightly to her chest. She was more worried about being pickpocketed than anything else. Nadège had been full of horror stories earlier that evening.

The gallery was completely dark. Random power cuts in the city meant it was safer to leave everything off—the last thing they wanted or needed was an electrical fire caused by the frequent voltage surges as the electricity company struggled to keep up with the growing city's demands. She flicked a bank of switches on the side wall and the place was immediately flooded with light. There was a new exhibition on; the delicate basket-weaving of the Shona Women's Collective from the south of the country, together with some haunting black-and-white photography by a visiting Dane. She stood in the doorway for a moment, admiring the contrasting media. Godson had found a blacksmith to make the most beautiful, fragile wrought-iron stands for the baskets; they each stood perched on metalwork like exotic, textured peacocks in partial flight. The colors were stunning—deep crimsons; vermilion, turquoise, saffron yellows . . . not the typical dun and sand colors of reed and twine. Against the smoky, atmospheric landscapes, they looked even richer. The exhibition had been a success, of course. They'd sold out of the photographs within an hour. Becky had just placed an order with a local printer to run enormous prints of the photographs which the gallery could display and sell; another way of promoting themselves while making a reasonable profit.

She dimmed the gallery lights and walked into the back office. She sat down at her desk and switched on her computer. The office was bathed in blue light as it powered up and began its gentle whir. She was expecting confirmation of a couple of orders from the UK, and perhaps an e-mail or two. She'd sent Amber a long, rambling handwritten letter the other week—she wondered what she would make of it. It had been mostly about Godson. She pulled a face—Keith was right; the sooner she managed to put him out of her head, the better. He couldn't have been clearer. There was no future in it, for her.

She opened her e-mails. Nothing yet from Amber; two from her mother; an order confirmation from London and another inquiry . . . what the hell had everyone done before e-mail? she wondered. She answered the most urgent ones mechanically; her mind was already racing ahead, trying to come up with ideas for the spring season at Deluxe. She liked the quiet and solitude of the gallery at night. It was the perfect time to plan. It was too busy during the day, what with Godson running in and out, artists dropping in and suppliers and tradesmen wanting her to look at samples, sign up for one product or another or pay an invoice . . . there was far too much bustle for her to be able to decide on anything. She scrolled through her in-box, no sound in the space other than the faint click and snap of her own fingers on her keyboard.

Half an hour later, something made her look up. There was a sound, a rustle in the corridor leading to the back door. She paused, the hairs on her neck rising. She looked behind her—there was nothing. She lifted her head and was still for a moment—still nothing. She shrugged. Something outside; a small dog or a cat passing in the alleyway, perhaps. She turned back to the screen. A few seconds later, she heard it again. A scrape. Something or someone was in the corridor. She froze, not daring to turn round. Her hand hovered over the phone but she was too frightened to move. Godson's warning came flooding back: he'd told her time and again not to go to the gallery at night, alone. Then she heard the unmistakable bang of the back door hitting the frame. It was open. She tried not to panic.

"Who's there?" she called out, her voice spilling into the quiet. There was no answer, just the swinging to and fro of the door; the hinges needed oiling. Another rustle . . . the scrape of feet along the tiled corridor and suddenly the office was plunged into darkness. Someone had reached around the door and switched off the lights. Becky sat by the icy-blue glow of her computer and felt her stomach turn to jelly. Fear. Ice-cold, liquid fear. She'd never known anything like it.

"Get up." A man's voice broke through the thumping of her heart in her ears. She swallowed, unable even to blink. Was he alone? She could hear something behind him . . . the sound of another pair of feet . . . and then another. Her heart was hammering. There was a smell in the room, an acrid, sweat-soaked whiff of something . . . *dagga*; she caught another whiff as someone else entered the room. She sat with her back to them, her hand still poised above the telephone, her eyelids suddenly heavy with panic and dread. "Hey. Get up." The same man issued a second command. She turned very slightly in her chair, her eyes tightly closed. She couldn't bear to look. How many of them were there? There was a sudden lull—and then someone lunged forward, shoving her chair so hard she immediately fell forwards, clutching out at the telephone and her keyboard as she went down, hitting her chin on the side of her chair. She was momentarily stunned. In the flickering light of the computer screen she'd caught sight of four men, each holding cigarettes, the red-hot glow dissolving into a stream of light as she fell. She curled herself into a ball, half-hidden by the desk and her fallen chair, and watched in ab-

solute dread as one of them—the one who had spoken, she supposed—leaned forwards and carefully
placed his cigarette or joint on the edge of her desk
before thrusting a hand down to grab her and drag
her upwards.

"Please," she gasped as he yanked her roughly to
her feet. "Please . . ." She couldn't even speak—her
voice sounded strangled and hoarse to her ears.
There was a second's delay before all four started
to laugh. They began talking quickly in their own language—arguing, almost. Becky was too terrified to
cry. The one who was holding her by the arm kept
tugging at her, as if to emphasize a point. She was
held between them, waiting for them to finish talking. Everything seemed to her to happen in slow
motion. She heard the sound of tearing . . . it took
her a moment to realize it was her own clothing. Her
pretty pink summer dress was being ripped from
her body in strips. The man holding her laughed en-
couragingly as the others tore the fabric off her,
tossing the scraps across the desk. Rape. She was
about to be raped. The fact ran through her head as
she desperately tried to distance herself from what
she knew was about to happen. It's not happening
to me, she whispered as one of them shoved his
hands underneath her bra and tore the flimsy material off her. *This isn't happening to me. Not to me.*
She felt a savage blow against her back as the four
of them pushed her face down across her own desk,
and the give of her underwear. One of them yanked
her head upwards by her hair and pushed himself
against her mouth, laughing as she began to gag

and retch. *Not to me. No . . . please. Not to me.* Her last conscious thought before one of them put his hands round her throat and began to squeeze was of Godson. How would she explain what had happened? Or admit he'd been right? And then the lights went out. Everything descended rapidly into a terrifying black silence.

≈99≈

Amber put down the receiver and turned to Tendé, her face drained of color. Her skin had suddenly broken out in goosebumps, as though the air around her had suddenly gone cold.

"What's the matter?" He was at her side instantly. He put out an arm to stop her pitching forwards. Across the room, Sibi and Liya were lying on the floor, watching a video for the hundredth time; she could hear the tinny sound of the television coming to her as if from a great distance. She blinked at him, unable to speak. "What?" He turned her to face him. "Has something happened?" She nodded mutely.

"Becky," she croaked out finally. "It's Becky. She's . . . she's in hospital. In Harare." She stopped, unable to continue.

"What's happened? Amber . . . what is it?" The children looked up. There was urgency in Tendé's voice.

"She's . . . she's been hurt. Raped." She saw

Tendé wince. "That was Godson Marimba, her business partner. She's asking for me." Tendé nodded. Of course.

"When? When did it happen?"

Amber shook her head helplessly. "Last night. She went to the gallery alone. There were four of them, apparently." She closed her eyes. "They strangled her and left her for dead. And then they went to a bar and were bragging about it. Someone overheard and knew who they were talking about; he rushed to the gallery and found her, passed out, on the floor. He called the police. Oh, Tendé . . . this . . . this will kill her parents. They haven't been told yet. I'd better go straight away."

"Of course. Don't worry about a thing. I'll sort the children out. My mother can come here for a few days. I'll see about getting you onto a flight. You'd better go via London; it'll be faster." Amber nodded, her mind already racing.

"What time is it?"

"Six. You could probably get on the eleven o'clock flight tonight for Paris, change in the morning. I'll call Salif." He reached over and picked up the phone; one of the perks of being a minister's wife was that she was guaranteed a seat on any flight, no matter how short the notice. She looked across the room; Sibi was watching her carefully. She smiled at him, hoping the panic and sadness in her face didn't show. She walked over to them and bent down next to him. Liya was still absorbed in the flickering screen in front of her.

"Are you going somewhere?" Sibi asked, his little face looking ready to crumple.

Amber nodded gently. "Yes, just for a few days. I'm going to see Auntie Becky . . . you remember her, don't you?" Sibi shook his head. She smiled at him and hugged him to her. She had no time to think about how to make it any easier for them; Becky needed her and at that moment, that was all that mattered. She gave him one last hug and stood up, motioning to Tendé to take over. It was unusual for him to be at home on a weekday evening before eleven; these days, he had so little time to himself. But thank God he was there, she thought to herself as she ran upstairs to pack. She wouldn't have been able to leave that night if he wasn't. She grabbed a small suitcase from the space above the wardrobe where all their cases lay. Between the four of them, there was always one missing. She flung a few clothes in it, trying not to listen to the sound of Liya's wails as Tendé did his best to comfort her. Maman was leaving—it wasn't the end of the world.

She flew to Paris that night; there was no problem getting a seat for Madame Ndiaye; Air France was careful to make sure any eventuality was covered for one of their most frequent fliers. Awake on the flight, her mind in turmoil, she ran over the news as she'd been given it, again and again. Her skin crawled with the horror of it. Godson's disembodied voice on the phone; the few details; the barely suppressed rage in his words . . . she couldn't imagine what Becky was going through. She hadn't stopped to phone Madeleine, or Mrs. Aldridge . . . Godson had said she'd asked only for her. Becky. *My poor, poor girl.* She turned down the champagne and orange juice offered her and drank only water, as if trying to cleanse herself of the dirtying news.

She had a two-hour wait at Charles de Gaulle and a forty-minute flight to Heathrow; then it was a three-hour turnaround before she was heading back in the direction from which she'd come. An absurd legacy of colonial rule—it was easier and cheaper getting from a Francophone to an Anglophone country to fly back to Europe and out again. She slept a thick, dreamless sleep almost all the way from London to Harare.

Amber stared at the bruised and mottled face in front of her in shock. Behind her, Godson stiffened involuntarily. The nurse busied herself around them; the ward matron had recognized Amber's face when she drew up to reception in a ministerial car. Tendé's connections across the continent ran deep and far. Shortly after she arrived, Godson pulled up in a much more modest vehicle, a taxi. The nurses weren't sure of his relationship to the girl who'd been brought into the hospital that night, unconscious and so badly beaten that even they, accustomed to seeing their patients in every permutation between life and death, were horrified. What had the poor child done to deserve this? they asked one another as they deftly peeled what was left of her clothing away, inserted a drip in her arm and slipped an oxygen mask over her mouth. The rest; the swabbing, the sampling, the testing, the questions . . . all could wait until her breathing had stabilized and the doctors were sure she would make it through the night. Her neck was swollen to almost twice its size. *Left for dead*, one of the senior staff nurses murmured to another as they wheeled her straight into a private ward. One of the girl's friends, a wealthy white woman, had come tearing into the hospital an hour or so after she'd arrived, demanding a private room and an immediate audience with the doctor. She'd got it, too. Rebecca Aldridge was moved into a room on the sixth floor, overlooking the golf course and the lake; not that either was of much use . . . the girl's eyelids were sealed shut. Rapes were a common enough occurrence in Harare, and the nurses knew it would be a long time before she would stand at a window admiring the view. Still, they changed the flowers in her room daily, along with the jug of lemon juice and the occasional biscuit eaten by her daily visitor, the African man from whom one of them, Betsy Ngolo, had managed to extract a little more detail. They owned a gallery together in the center of town. No one knew why it should have happened to her. The police had drawn a complete blank. There were no disgruntled employees, no enemies . . . why anyone should have picked on her was a mystery. Wrong place at the wrong time, everyone around her bedside murmured.

A few days after she'd been brought in, a very tall, ashen-faced young white man had come in, asking for her. Betsy showed him into the room and left to bring him a cup of tea. When she came back she was dismayed to find him on his knees by her bedside, a stream of agonized words pouring from his mouth. *I'm so sorry, Becky, I'm so sorry. I didn't mean for this . . . they went too far . . . I'm so sorry.* She'd tapped him on the shoulder—what was he saying? He'd looked up in fright, scrambled to his knees and run out of the room. Just like that. He never came back. *Ter-rible, ter-rible . . . what was happening to the country? Where were they headed?* The nurses chattered in Shona, an African language unfamiliar to Amber, occasionally breaking into English. She listened with half an ear as they changed bedding or checked Becky's pulse and she and Godson sat by her bedside, not speaking, hour after hour. Her Bambara was almost fluent by now; it was unusual for her to be back in incomprehensible silence as those around her talked.

Later, sitting in the hospital canteen on the ground floor, Godson lit a cigarette; after a moment's hesitation, Amber reached across the table and took one.

"I'll take her back to Bamako with me," she said after a moment. Godson looked at her and nodded, blowing a cloud of smoke out of the corner of his mouth. He shrugged helplessly. "For a while, at any rate. The doctor said she hasn't really spoken much. He asked her if she wanted to notify her parents, but she got really upset. I'll take her home with me to rest for a bit." She looked at him quickly. "You know, I always wondered what she was really doing here," she said slowly, holding up her cigarette for one last, final draw. After nearly six years of fastidious *not* smoking, it still felt good. "I don't know . . . I sometimes had the feeling she was running away from something, although I couldn't tell you what. She had that air of desperation about her at times. I feel I should have tried harder to understand what was troubling her, been around more . . ." She stopped, thinking back to the puffy, swollen face of her best friend who now lay silent after an almost unspeakable ordeal. Would she ever recover? What if there were . . . consequences? A pregnancy, disease . . . the thought silenced her . . . AIDS? She closed her eyes. All they could do was wait. Wait for her to come through, come round . . . to open her eyes and talk, and hopefully, to begin to heal. She stubbed out her cigarette and stood up. "I'm sorry, Godson. I know how much the business meant to you, as well. But I can't leave her here, not like this. She needs to be around family, or close friends. We're almost like sisters, Becky and I. We go back a really long way."

Godson nodded heavily. "You're right. Of course you're right. She shouldn't be here." He ground out his cigarette in the saucer in front of him. "But you're wrong about one thing," he said after a moment. Amber looked down at him warily. "You *are* sisters, you and her. That's how she spoke of you. Always." He pushed the table away from him and stood up. Amber turned her head so he wouldn't see the tears that had suddenly brimmed and were now threatening to spill. They walked back to the elevator in silence.

*   *   *

"Becky?" The sleeping figure in the bed moved slightly. Amber hurriedly put down the newspaper she was reading and drew up a chair. "Becks? Can you hear me?" She stared at the face she'd been looking at almost all her life. The color was slowly beginning to return; around her neck and eyes the skin was still a patchy green and yellow in places as the bruises began to heal and the swelling was definitely subsiding. She stroked the limp, thin arm resting on top of the covers. "Are you awake?" she asked. Becky's eyes opened properly for the first time in days. They stared at each other across the white surface of the hospital sheets and the experience that had brought them together; Amber was the first to drop her eyes. She couldn't bear to read what there was to be read in Becky's face. "Come home with me," she said after a moment when the heat in her eyes had been brought under control. "Come with me to Bamako. Just for a bit. You need to get away from here, Becky . . . stay with us for a while." She watched as Becky's head nodded slowly, once, twice. She reached out and gripped her hand.

Madeleine's reaction to the news shocked and dismayed her. She was jealous. She let the receiver drop in its cradle and sat down heavily on the bottom step of the stairs. She was disgusted with herself. Professionally and personally, she was jealous. She had to resist the urge to pick up the phone again and demand to know why it had taken Amber three weeks to tell her what had happened. Wasn't she the expert in the field? Except Becky wasn't a "field," she muttered as she tried to digest what Amber had just told her. She'd taken Becky back to Mali with her as soon as she was well enough to travel. She was staying in the guest house of the home that she and Tendé had built and that Madeleine had never seen. She was quiet and withdrawn; she ate little and said even less. Amber wasn't sure quite how to help her. She'd refused, point blank, to tell her parents what had happened; she spent her days in near-total silence and now Amber was worried. She linked the fingers of her hands together and tried to imagine how they would manage to care for someone who'd just been through what Madeleine had to deal with on an almost daily basis but never so close to home, never.

She argued with James that night, over and over again. She was seven months pregnant; even if she could persuade an airline to let her on the flight, what use would she be in her condition? Amber was more than capable of looking after Becky; what more could she add to the situation? Better to let her rest, regain her equilibrium. Becky could come and stay with them in Geneva later in the summer, after the baby was born. She listened to his objections calmly; the following morning, just as calmly, she walked into a travel agent's office on rue Gallimard and booked herself a Business Class ticket on the next available flight to Bamako. James drove her to the airport in stony silence. The bond between the three women who barely saw one another, as far as he could make out, wasn't something he could understand.

Amber was waiting for her in a car just beneath the aircraft steps. Madeleine was let off the flight first; a young government official took her passport and bags and she was led straight to the waiting Mercedes. The two hugged as tightly as Madeleine's considerable bump would allow and within seconds, they were being driven straight across the tarmac and out of the airport complex. The circumstances were so different from the last time the three of them had been together—that time, in Menorca, Amber and Tendé had shown Madeleine something precious about herself and her own life; this time, she thought, she just might be able to do something for them in return.

"How is she?" she asked as they drove towards the city. It was Madeleine's first time in Africa—the city flew past in snatches; brilliant green, sandy yellow; corrugated tin roofs . . . it was all she could take in as Amber filled in the details. Madeleine nodded as the familiar story unfolded—first the withdrawal into oneself; the slow shutting down of the sensory stimuli—food, conversation, emotion; then the silence and the thick fog of depression; the denial . . . she had observed and reported on the phenomena so many times it was alarmingly predictable in its outcome. Becky had to talk it out; there was no other way forward. Nothing would heal until the pain had run its course. She knew the procedures for making it happen but the professional distance she'd always maintained between the women she'd treated was dangerously close to breaching as she slipped into Becky's shoes and imagined the worst.

"I can't believe you've come," Amber said as the car began to climb the hill towards their house. "I'm so grateful, Madeleine, honestly. It can't be an easy time for you, either."

"Don't be silly," Madeleine said, looking at her. "How could I not? I don't suppose there's much here in the way of counseling or anything like that. If she won't go home to her parents, we have to come to her."

Amber nodded slowly. "She'll be all right, won't she?" she said, suddenly nervous. She was beginning to feel out of her depth. Madeleine's arrival was more welcome than she would ever know.

"Yes." Madeleine's response was brisk. Becky would get better. That was all there was to it. She had no choice *but* to get better—and however long it took, Madeleine would stick around. She hadn't told James that, of course, but there were some things that took priority over everything else. He had to learn that about her.

≈100≈

"Will you be eating out tonight, *mevrouw*?" The question startled her. Paola turned around to face Estrella and suddenly it hit her. She knew. She felt her face darken with color, felt the heat rising in her cheeks and her fingers begin to shake. How? How could she know?

"No. I'm not . . . yes, yes . . . I'm going out." She turned round and almost ran from the room. She fled upstairs to the sanctuary of her bedroom, slammed the door shut and sat down on the edge of the bed. Her legs had turned to jelly. Had she seen her? Fear flooded straight through her; she shivered. Would she say anything? Otto was due back in a week's time . . . it had to be kept from him, no matter what. He would *kill* her if he found out; of that, she was desperately sure. She picked at the bedcover and looked at her watch. It was only five. Dieter would be . . . where? Playing football with his friends? Watching a video at someone's house? Her stomach contracted into a hundred knots of longing and jealousy; it was impossible to know where he was, who he was with, what he was doing. With the arrogant insouciance of youth, he rarely made plans—he dropped in on people, went out, hung out . . . there were hundreds of phrases for the ways he spent his holidays, all of which were unknown and unknowable to a young married woman who had somehow wound up falling in insufferable love with the sixteen-year-old son of her neighbors. Had she been a reader of any sort, Paola would no doubt have found solace in countless fictional accounts of the same. As it was, she suffered in mute silence, in an agony of indecision and insecurity. No man had ever made her feel this way, she told herself a thousand times a day. And he wasn't even a man! A boy! He was a *boy*! It didn't seem to help.

She was totally, utterly lost. She had never felt so alone in her life—except now, it seemed, she wasn't *quite* so alone. How the fuck had the girl found her out? She stood up angrily. She would have to get rid of her. There was no other way.

She couldn't afford to see her smirking little face every time she opened a door—she would go mad. It was bad enough practically having a heart attack every time a car drove past or the phone rang . . . to have Estrella look at her knowingly whenever she walked into the kitchen—*her own kitchen!*—would be more than she could bear.

She walked over to the wardrobe and yanked the door open. She was going for a drive. She would go past the football ground at the end of the street and see if Dieter was there. She wasn't sure how she would maneuver things to talk to him—lately, he'd been acting a little strange if she showed up when his friends were around—but she could always pretend she was on her way somewhere else; she'd just driven past accidentally, stopped to say hello. She pulled one dress after another off the rails. Pink? Too girlish. Yellow with flowers? Too childish. Black and white? Too graphic. She flung one dress after another onto the bed.

Half an hour later she tied the straps on the green and yellow Pucci summer dress she'd bought on her last trip to Paris and turned to check herself in the mirror. The bold swirls of color looked striking against her tan; she pulled her hair back into a twist and secured it with a clasp. She slipped her feet into a pair of high-heeled green sandals and fished her large, tinted Chanel glasses out of her bag. A yellow clutch bag and some bright red lipstick . . . there was no one to match her in sleepy Windhoek for sheer style. Goddamn it, Dieter had no idea just how lucky he was. On that much more cheerful note, she ran lightly down the stairs and out the front door.

She could read the sulkiness in his eyes. She could have kicked herself for driving past. She'd parked the silver BMW at what she thought was a discreet distance from the playing field and got out. She'd walked over the stony ground, cursing her shoes as she stumbled and nearly lost her balance. She'd tried to make the whole thing look like a happy accident . . . and failed. Dieter was indeed playing football with his friends; at the sight of them, she'd almost turned tail and run back. They looked so *young*! Barely out of puberty. Among them, despite his height and size, Dieter vanished into the mists of childhood. They'd seen her; a few of them stopped running after the ball and stared at her, open-mouthed. There was nothing for it but to continue walking across the gravel and hope that Dieter would come to her—there was nowhere else for her to go. She stopped at the edge of the playing field and waited, feeling more and more stupid by the second.

"What are you doing here?" he asked her, his face a study of embarrassment and awkwardness.

"I was just driving past," she began lamely. "I was wondering . . . what are you doing later on?"

He shrugged. "I don't know. I was going to go over to a friend's." Male or female, she longed to ask. She put up a hand to her hair.

"Well, I was just wondering . . . if you wanted to go for a drink or something."

"A *drink*? Where?" He was looking at her strangely. The question was patently ridiculous.

"I don't know. Oh, why are you being so . . . difficult? I want to see you, that's all." He looked away. *Stop it*, Paola told herself immediately. *Stop. Walk off. Make him follow you.* She looked at his dirty-blond hair blowing in the late evening wind, at his strong, muscular legs in shorts and the rivulets of sweat running down his face. The primitive lust that coursed through her at the sight of him obliterated every last scrap of common sense. "How about late tonight? After you get back . . . you could come round. I've given the girl the evening off. There's no one in the house," she lied. She would deal with Estrella when she got back.

"Okay," he said finally. "But it'll be really late. Like *really* late."

"No problem. I go to bed late. We can have a late dinner. I know how hungry you get . . ." She resisted the urge to reach out and touch his arm. He looked away, irritated.

"Okay, okay. Look, I'd better go. We're winning. See ya." He jogged off, ignoring the admiring glances from the boys closest to him. Paola smiled prettily at them, enjoying the look of confused embarrassment on their adolescent faces. They'd probably never seen anyone quite so beautiful in their young lives. The thought suddenly disturbed her. She walked back to her car as quickly as she could without breaking a heel.

By midnight, she was beginning to worry. She had sat upstairs in bed in her lilac silk negligée for over three hours; she'd bathed, washed and dried her hair; made up her face . . . drops of perfume everywhere . . . and she'd waited. And waited. She'd watched the news—something she never did—followed by a terrible South African sitcom, followed by a wildlife documentary, all the while trying not to think about the beautiful boy and what they would do to one another as soon as he arrived. The butterflies in her stomach refused to lie still—all evening they danced, sending little shivers of deliciously cold anticipation running through her every time she turned her attention away from the TV and thought about him. But as the hours slowly ticked by and there was still no sign of him, the butterflies turned to dread. What if he wasn't coming? What if he'd decided he'd had enough? That she no longer fascinated him? She switched off the television angrily and rolled over onto her stomach. Again. It was the same old story, again and again. She just couldn't seem to keep anyone's attention. No matter how beautiful she was, how good she always looked and how stylishly she dressed, it had always been the same. An unbroken, unchanged line all the way from Max to Dieter. It always started so well—men were bowled over by her physical beauty, falling over themselves to be near her, to pursue her. But once they had her, their interest waned, always . . . every single time. There was always some reason— she wasn't rich enough, good enough, interesting enough . . . there was always some little reason why, after a month or two of the most ardent pursuit, everything simply fell apart and she was left in an agony of self-doubt, wondering where and why it had all gone wrong. Except Kieran. Kieran was the only man who had ever made her feel it was *she* he was interested in, *she* who mattered, not what she looked like or what she wore. Kieran saw straight through and beyond the beautiful façade. He didn't tell her he couldn't live without her; it was in his face, his eyes, the way he looked at her and the way he burned when she was gone.

She held up a wrist to the moonlight. It was three o'clock in the morning. He wasn't coming. Her husband would be back in less than a week. There would be no more frantic, hurried hours grabbed whenever and wherever she could find the time or opportunity; no more early morning flights up to Outjo and long, hot afternoons spent bathed in sweat and the sweet wetness that Dieter drew from her at the sight of him. It was over, finished . . . *klar*, as the people here said. She pushed her face into the pillow and tried to hold her heart from slipping out of her chest and crashing to the floor.

Becky took a few mouthfuls of deep orange papaya and carefully put the spoon down. Opposite her, Madeleine sat placidly, her hand resting on the enormous mound of her belly; saying little, just waiting patiently for Becky to speak. Amber was at the water's edge, soothing a dispute between her children. It was strangely restful—Madeleine's eyes held nothing of the agonized distress that she'd seen immediately in Amber's. Madeleine was quiet, watchful but not expectant; she gave Becky the space and time to organize her thoughts in her own mind before putting them into words. As thankful as she'd been for Amber to come and rescue her, as Amber sometimes put it, as soon as she'd seen Madeleine walking awkwardly across the lawn to the small but very comfortable guest house where she was now staying, something inside her had dissolved suddenly, almost the first emotion she'd allowed herself other than fear since the whole thing had happened. Being Madeleine, she said nothing, just held Becky across the barrier of her stomach, the gentle pressure of her fingers on her arms reminding her how much she'd missed her—and Amber, of course. She'd only been there a few days but already, the late afternoon ritual of the three of them sitting under the bamboo and thatch canopy next to the pool when the fierce heat of the day was beginning to ebb, was soothing to her.

Amber's children—beautiful, although it was hard to find resemblances that weren't blotted out by their dark, chocolate-brown skin—splashed about in the pool with the neighborhood children. Liya's sturdy brown legs shuddered as she clambered in and out after her brother and whoever had joined them for the afternoon. Her hair, when wet, was a

sleek black curtain down her back, springing enthusiastically into tight curls as soon as it dried. She
looked suspiciously at her mother and her two
friends—who were these silent women who sat in
easy companionship every afternoon, saying little?
Why were they here?

A servant came to clear away the tray. Becky
watched as he and Amber talked rapidly in whatever
language it was they spoke here—she still couldn't
get over just how easily Amber seemed to slip into
a way of life that in Zimbabwe would have been almost impossible. Here, her whiteness didn't seem
to count in quite the same way. There was none of
the sullen resentfulness on the part of the Africans
and none of the cloying friendliness or insufferable
rudeness—the only two ways of being, as far as
Becky had worked out—on the part of the Europeans. Differences in class remained exactly that: Amber spoke to the servants *as servants*, not as blacks
or members of an inferior race. She watched in silence as dinner plans were being made . . . this or
that *poisson, riz* . . . salad for Madeleine . . . something simple for the children. Her French was rusty
but good enough to follow the conversation. As she
listened, her confusion grew. How had she managed it? What was the secret? And, worse of all,
why hadn't she been able to do the same? Why had
things turned out so badly for her?

"I'd better go." Amber got up from her chair and
turned to follow the servant back up to the house.
"There's about to be a major catastrophe—someone forgot to buy fish from the market this morning.

I'll be back in a sec." Becky watched her long, brown legs disappear across the grass.

"Does it hurt?" she asked Madeleine suddenly.

Madeleine's hand paused its gentle stroking of her own skin. She looked at Becky. She knew what she was being asked. She shook her head. "Have you been tested yet?" Becky shook her head mutely. "Then that's what we'll do tomorrow. I'll find out where." The calm, unhurried way she dealt with the question that had been tormenting Becky for days unlocked the tight knot of tension in which she'd been holding herself. Again, for the first time, she felt something like the urge to speak. She hesitated, then opened her mouth. Once the first words came, the rest could not be stopped. Madeleine sat beside her, saying nothing, but listening, listening— her eyes missed nothing.

"She's on the mend," Madeleine said to Amber a couple of days later. Amber looked up from where she was checking names against some guest list that Tendé had left for her and paused.

"How can you tell?" Apart from the fact that she'd seen Becky speaking to Madeleine, she still ate very little and stayed mostly in the guest room at the bottom of the garden.

"She's talking . . . about all sorts of things, not just the rape. I think . . ." Madeleine paused, wondering how to put it. "I think she's been very lonely out there, despite the gallery and everything. I get the feeling she hardly had any friends." Amber looked at her and frowned.

"But she never said anything . . . I mean, her letters were always so full of life, of positive things. She seemed to be having a whale of a time."

"That's probably what she wanted you to think. She hardly ever wrote to me, you know . . . just the odd postcard, hardly saying anything. I used to wonder."

"But she should have said . . . I mean . . . we're best friends. Why didn't she tell me—or you, either—if things weren't going so well?"

"Have you never noticed?" Madeleine asked mildly. "How she's always competing with you?" Amber frowned and then reddened. Madeleine saw that a nerve had been touched. She felt her way forwards carefully.

"Oh, that . . . Becky's always been like that," Amber said, trying to shrug it off.

"No, but this time . . . even *I* thought it was something different. I knew she was always comparing herself to you . . . we both did, you know—but I can't help feeling there's more to it than just best friend rivalry. I remember when we were teenagers, Becky always wanted to *be* you. Being herself wasn't enough. She didn't feel good enough, or special enough." Amber's face was bright red.

"Why does this always happen?" She looked down at her hands. "Everyone seems to think I live some kind of charmed life. I *don't.*"

"I know. But you're one of those people who just makes things look easy. I used to really envy you, you know . . . great parents, rich, fantastic holidays . . . it looked perfect from where I was standing."

"You have no idea," Amber said, suddenly getting up. "Sometimes it was . . . hell." She crossed the room and looked out of the window. Outside the sun was slowly sinking. Sibi and Liya were still asleep, stunned by an afternoon spent rushing around in the garden. "Living with Max wasn't always easy, you know." Madeleine nodded. They weren't only talking about Becky now, they were talking about themselves. "He was like the sun—blinding. Next to him, I felt I was nothing. My mother *knew* she was nothing. You should see her now. She's alive for the first time in thirty years."

"It wasn't easy to see that from the outside. I always just thought you were the luckiest person alive. To have a father like that . . . and your mum, she was so beautiful. I used to go home after being at yours or Becky's, just hating my own life. But I always had other people . . . Péter . . . my parents. I don't think Becky did, not in that way." Amber turned to look at her. It was the first time in fifteen years she'd heard Madeleine mention Péter's name.

"Madeleine, how did it happen?" she asked gently. Madeleine's eyes lifted to meet hers. She had gone very still. "We've never talked about it . . . you never said."

"It was a long time ago. When we were leaving Hungary." Amber was silent for a moment, struggling to find the right words. "We always wondered what happened to him, Becky and I. We weren't sure. You talked about him as if he was . . ."

"A lover? A boyfriend?" Madeleine's smile was sad. "Sometimes I wasn't sure myself. He was nineteen when he died . . . in front of me. He was shot in the back by a border guard."

"Jesus, Madeleine . . . why . . . why didn't you ever tell us? It's funny, it feels as though we've all been hiding secrets from one another for twenty years . . . why?"

Madeleine shook her head. "Who knows? There are some things that you can't reveal straight away, even to yourself. Dari taught me that . . . the woman I used to work with in New York. She was a psychologist. She always used to say that she thought women in their thirties were the most vulnerable of all—everyone thinks it's the other way round, that you're fragile in your teens and early twenties but by the time you reach thirty-five or so, you've more or less got your life sorted out. She used to say the opposite. She told me when she was in private practice she'd see all these successful women in their thirties coming to her, breaking down. She thought it was because their bodies somehow knew they would cope with a breakdown at that age, that it was safe to let go, so to speak . . . that they'd recover. If they'd let it happen any earlier, they might not come back." Madeleine placed the heel of her hand on her stomach. "It always used to frighten me . . . thinking that there was this great big collapse waiting for me as soon as I turned thirty-five. But I think we're all different. Some people collapse a little bit at a time—like me, I guess. Each time something happens, a little bit of me dies. Péter, then Mark Dorman . . . then Alasdair. But each time, I got just a little bit stronger. So now I don't worry quite so much about the future. Whatever happens will happen. I don't know about Becky. And now, I find I don't know about you." Amber was staring at her.

"Nothing's ever really happened to me," she said slowly. "Not like you. Losing Max was about the worst thing that happened and even that . . . I can say it to you, now . . . I felt free, too. He'd said something just before he left, something awful about Tendé . . . it killed me, I can't tell you. Oh, everyone explained it away . . . he was protective, he was just being a father . . . everyone had some explanation for it. But d'you know something?" She paused for a moment, wondering whether to go on. "When Sibi was born, I was *relieved*. I was relieved Max wasn't there. I didn't know how he would feel about him being black. I was *glad* my father hadn't lived to see him because I didn't want to spend a single day of my life wondering if he minded." There was a catch in her voice. Madeleine looked up at Amber in surprise. In all the years they'd known each other, Madeleine honestly couldn't remember seeing Amber cry. Becky cried at the drop of a hat—but Amber? Never.

"Did you ever tell Tendé?" was Madeleine's question.

Amber shook her head fiercely. "But he knows. We never talk about it, or about Max . . . but I think it was one of Tendé's biggest disappointments. *He* used to tell me that nothing matters more in the world. Race. Blood. I used to think he was just bitter. Now I know it's true."

"D'you think that's what happened to Becky?

That it was because of her . . . being white?" Madeleine bit her lip.

"I suppose so. I mean, you can't ignore it in a place like Zimbabwe. But I think it's more complicated than that."

"What d'you mean?"

"She wrote to me a couple of months ago. She was having an affair. Well, no . . . not quite an affair. She'd slept with her business partner, Godson. He's married, of course, and it seems he wasn't interested in anything more permanent. I met him when I went down to get her. He seemed nice, but the circumstances were a bit strained, obviously. Anyhow, I got this letter . . . she seemed so pleased about the fact that he was African; it was almost racist, in a peculiar way. I didn't know what to make of it."

"She was probably thinking that if you'd done it—"

"But that's just it!" Amber cried, shaking her head. "Done what? I met a man, I fell in love . . . I married him. That's all there is to it. Tendé's no different from anyone else."

"You know that. *I* know that. At least I think I do . . . he's not quite like other men, you know, and that's got nothing to do with his color. But I don't think Becky ever saw that. It's all that envy I was talking about. It's blinded her, in a funny way. All she can see are the signs, the outward signs. *You* married an African; she wants to as well. *You* moved to Africa; so did she. It's all about what she thinks you've done. And that's what the problem is."

"But how . . . I mean, what are we going to do to help her? Now that this has happened, how's she ever going to recover from it? And what happens next?"

Madeleine bit her lip. She shifted uncomfortably in her chair. "I wish I knew what to say. She has to go home, of course. Back to London, to where she's *really* from. She can't go on running away from it, even if she doesn't quite know what she's running away from. She can't go on living someone else's life."

"Henry used to say the opposite," Amber said suddenly. "All the time. He used to go on and on about living someone else's life—it was the thing he most wanted."

"What d'you mean?"

"I don't know . . . he was so disappointed with his own, I suppose. He wanted to be someone else, anyone else." She was quiet for a moment. Then she turned to Madeleine, a look of anguish in her eyes. "You don't think . . . that he . . . that he might have had something to do with it?" she asked fearfully.

"Amber, no . . . no, he couldn't. He wouldn't have . . . ?"

"I hope to God he didn't. But . . . it was just something Becky said, the other day . . . she said Henry warned her something terrible would happen to her if she stayed. I wasn't sure what she meant."

"No, I can't believe it." Madeleine was shocked. "No one could wish that on anyone, no matter *what* they'd done."

"Maybe he didn't mean for it to go that far?"

"No, don't even think it . . . just don't. She's back

and she's safe and that's all that matters." Amber nodded slowly. She wrapped her arms around her waist, hugging herself. Madeleine was right. It was their job to make sure Becky came out of the terrible ordeal as intact as possible. If she so much as *imagined* that Henry had anything to do with it . . . God alone knew what it would do to her. She turned back to Madeleine.

"And you?" her voice was quiet. Madeleine looked at her hands. "Are you happy?" It seemed the right time to ask. Madeleine said nothing. "Things are okay, aren't they? Between you and James?"

"Yeah . . . things are okay. It's not . . . it's not how I thought it would be," she said slowly, twisting a strand of hair around a finger. "It's just . . . okay. Normal. The same." She broke off. "When I see you, the way you and Tendé are . . . I know it'll never be like that. James is very kind, very sweet—he's reliable and dependable and all the things the magazines tell you to look for in a partner. But that's it, that's all."

"And what else do you want?"

"I don't know . . . something more, something bigger . . . to live a fuller life? A more *necessary* life. Does that make sense? We have a lovely flat in Geneva, we both more or less like what we do . . . we have nice friends, we go to wine bars and to the lake on Sundays . . . everything's fine. But sometimes I wake up in the morning, especially now, and I wonder if this is it. I'll have a nice baby," she stroked

her stomach disparagingly, "we'll have a nice wedding, and then no one will ever hear from me again."

"Oh, Madeleine, don't say that. Of course you'll
move on, do other things. You do want this baby,
don't you?"

"I think so. I did at first. But now I feel almost
scared of it. I'm afraid it'll be the end of me." Amber
was quiet. She didn't know what to say. Madeleine
had changed, it was true . . . she now wore chic
clothes and her hair was long and stylish; she took
holidays in the south of France and had bought her
parents a small flat in Budapest to which they went
every summer. She seemed to have found a kind of
peace that she'd never had before . . . and yet,
some of the fire and determination that had made
Madeleine who she was had also disappeared,
subsumed beneath a layer of good living and tran-
quillity that was alien to her.

"And the job?" Madeleine was now a Chief Medical Officer at the ICM HQ in Geneva; her job, in
preparation for her maternity leave, was now
research-based. She prepared and organized sem-
inars and courses for the ICM Psycho-Social Mod-
ule on Migratory Experience—she and Amber had
laughed over the grand-sounding details over the
phone. The truth was she could have done the job
with her eyes closed and the bureaucracy threatened to overwhelm her. She had always been a
"field" person, getting her hands dirty, literally; she'd
trained as a surgeon, for Christ's sake, she yelled at
James one evening—now all she did was sit behind

a desk getting bigger and heavier by the day, setting up training modules and compiling information that she was sure no one would ever read. Was *this* what she'd given up her job in New York for? It was a sore point between them. James's promotion to the Office of Legal Counsel at the UN in Geneva was a necessary and important one for his career. After months of discussion, Madeleine reluctantly agreed that perhaps she could afford to put her own career somewhat on hold; she would follow him to Geneva, maybe even start the family that he seemed so keen to have . . . and then after a few years, she would move onto something more challenging. ICM were only too happy to have her back; her former boss in Belgrade was delighted. The fact that she would be doing something entirely less challenging and interesting than before was beside the point. To everyone, it seemed, except Madeleine. She sighed and turned to Amber.

"Well, there's not much I can do about it now. I mean, the baby's due in six weeks; I can't really make any plans until that's safely out of the way." Amber bit her lip. Madeleine's choice of words was more revealing than she probably realized. "After that . . . well, we'll see. I don't know. It all seems terribly far away at the moment."

"It'll work out, Mads," Amber said, reaching out to squeeze her hand. "You'll work it out. I know you will."

"I hope so."

"It will."

"Oh. I didn't see you sitting there." Becky was star-tled. Tendé half-rose to his feet. He'd been read-ing—a rare hour of peace, for him. He'd snatched the opportunity to sit in the study that he and Amber had planned right down to the last detail and in which he'd barely spent an hour since the house was built. "No, no . . . please don't get up. I'll go. I was just wandering around. I'll . . . disappear."

"How are you, Becky?" Tendé's voice was quiet. Becky hesitated.

"I'm . . . fine. Okay."

"I'm glad." There was no awkwardness. He ges-tured to a chair beside him. "Have a seat," he said, smiling his quiet smile. "I've hardly seen you in the past few weeks. Are they looking after you well?"

"Yes, yes . . . they've been brilliant."

"And the children aren't wearing you out?"

"No. Everything's fine, honestly. I feel much bet-ter." She sat down gingerly on the chair next to him. She'd never managed to get over her awe of Tendé. No matter how kind he was to her, he seemed a creature from another planet, another time. She couldn't quite believe he was her best friend's hus-band. At times he seemed more like a father; more like Max. They shared the same qualities of intensity and drive.

"What are your plans?"

"Plans? I don't know . . . I guess I'd better start thinking about going back."

"Home?"

"Well, yes . . . to Harare. There's the gallery to sort out and—"

"Go home, Becky." Tendé's voice was gentle. She looked at him uncertainly. "I mean to your own home."

"It *is* home," she said, her voice suddenly shaky.

"No. Africa isn't for you."

"How can you say that?" Becky cried, getting to her feet. "I'm fine there, I *am*. I love it. Even after . . . this."

"It's not your home. You should go back, to your parents, to the place you belong. I'm not saying this to hurt you, or to make light of the things you've managed to do out there. Amber tells me the gallery was a great success. But it's not the place for you right now."

"I don't see how you can judge me," Becky said, angry now. "You've no right to—" Her face crumpled suddenly. Tears had come into her eyes, and voice.

"Amber won't say it to you; she doesn't want to hurt you. Me, I don't know you, Becky. I only know what I see. And I see that this isn't the place for you." He stood up. She was weeping openly. He sighed and put an arm round her shaking shoulders. She turned and pressed her face against the starched white shirt. He was right. Of course he was right. She wept against him, her tears blotted by his clothing. The instruction could only have come from him. Her tears were as much for what she was about to lose as for what she'd already lost.

*   *   *

She flew back to London with Madeleine. They arrived at Heathrow on a gloriously bright mid-March morning. After the dense, muggy heat of Bamako, the fresh, crisp air that greeted them as they stepped out of the plane was a welcome relief. Becky drank in the air, the light, the voices . . . everything around her that was at once so familiar, and yet so strange. Back in England. Back home . . . or was it? She walked through Customs clutching Madeleine's hand and saw her mother standing anxiously behind the barrier, scanning the arriving passengers with her heart in her mouth. She'd been told a little of what had happened to her only child. Becky broke free of Madeleine and surged ahead—yes, crushed against her mother, the tears that she'd held back for so many weeks threatening to soak them both . . . yes, she was home. Mrs. Aldridge turned to Madeleine—she was so close to her term that it was difficult to do anything other than kiss on either cheek. In tears, the three women walked unsteadily to the car.

Mrs. Aldridge dropped Madeleine at her parents' flat in Kensal Rise. Just like old times, she said a little tearfully as she and Becky hugged her. Madeleine watched the car turn around and speed down Ladbroke Grove. She looked up at the block of flats; still ugly, still bleak. Despite her offers to help them, Maja and Imre refused to move. The flat she'd bought for them in Budapest after years of protest was their real home, they said, even after twenty years away. Home . . . even now the concept was strange to her. She'd always thought of it as the place in which she lived, regardless of where in the world she was. An address; a physical cluster of spaces which held her possessions. At times, those had been reduced to the barest minimum: a tooth-brush, a passport, a clean pair of clothes. At others, she'd stared around her in awe of the things she'd managed to accumulate. At their flat in Geneva, there wasn't a surface in the whole place that didn't have some possession of hers, some artifact, ob-ject, piece of furniture, a framed photograph . . . *some*thing. And soon, she thought to herself as she pushed open the entrance door, breathing in the oh-so-familiar smell of stale urine and disinfectant, she would have something more meaningful and per-manent than anything she'd ever owned before—a child. A living, breathing child of her own. The thought terrified her. It would tie her to James in a way she feared, although she couldn't have said why. The past few weeks for her, too, had brought about a sense of closure on so many of the things that haunted her. She realized, too late, perhaps, just what it meant to have her closest friends around her. They were a mirror to her true self; through them, she saw herself as they did. Her image, re-flected back to her through their eyes and experi-ences of her, was true and clear. Without them, her sense of herself became murky and clouded, mak-ing her vulnerable and too easily swayed. She won-dered, as she reached the front door and heard Maja's hurried tread on the other side, if she would be where she was if Becky and Amber had been around. She had a feeling . . . nothing more than that, just a feeling . . . she wondered if James had found her not when she was strong and vibrant, which was the way he liked to tell it, but actually, the opposite: when she was weak. It troubled her. He was kind and decent; he loved her without conditions, without wanting to change her in any way. Why wasn't it enough?

As she felt herself pressed against her mother, heard Maja's exclamations over the size and shape of her stomach, of what the child would be called, of how proud they were, how much they longed to be grandparents, she realized it would have to be enough. There could be no turning away from it. James and the life she'd chosen couldn't be exchanged for another. Wasn't that what she'd just spent a month lecturing Becky about? It was enough. It would be enough. She followed her mother into the living room and stood in front of the picture of Péter. Life . . . that was what counted. Becky had come out of her ordeal alive; she now had a chance to rebuild it. *She* was alive, as was the child kicking away inside her. That was enough.

PART EIGHT

The gasp went through the courtroom. Paola stood in the dock, the color draining rapidly from her face. She was beaten. There was no coming back from the blow Otto had just struck. She glanced down at her hands; nothing would have persuaded her to look up, across the semi-sympathetic gaze of the judge over to where Otto was seated between his lawyers, both of whom, she was sure, were congratulating one another—and him—on a successful job. She stared at the large solitaire diamond on her finger. That was all that was left of her marriage. Now that it had been established that Alessandra, thirteen months old and the spitting image of her mother and grandmother was *not* Otto's child; well, now there was nothing left and nothing more to say.

A tear splashed on the back of her hand; she

wiped it away quickly. It wouldn't do to cry. There was a whole scrum of photographers waiting outside the courtroom—she'd practically had to fight her way in that morning. It was indecent, the way they jostled for a shot, intent on parading her all-too-evident unhappiness to the rest of the world. The day the case opened, she'd been only too pleased to see them, already thinking to the day ahead about her outfit and how to make sure she was photographed at her best. But twenty minutes into the court hearing, she'd suddenly realized she'd made the biggest mistake of her life in bringing Otto to court; he was going to use the opportunity she'd so kindly provided to destroy her. She honestly hadn't expected things to go this far. She'd hired a firm of German-Namibian lawyers to represent her; there had been a fee waiver in lieu of her winning her case. After all, she reasoned, it was highly unlikely Otto would want the expense and scandal of taking his wife to court over custody of their child; he'd never been very interested in Alessandra, he wasn't present at the birth and he'd barely spent any time with her subsequently. Perhaps he just wasn't a particularly interested father. And the only person in the whole, wide world who knew that Alessandra wasn't his was Paola. She'd planned everything, right down to the last detail. She'd even managed to bring herself to sleep with Otto a few weeks after Alessandra had been conceived—so what had happened to make the whole plan go so disastrously wrong?

The minute she saw that damned half-caste, Estrella, walking down the aisle to the witness stand, her heart plummeted. What the fuck was she doing here, in a courtroom in southern Bavaria? She realized she'd never really known fear until that point.

From the moment the girl opened her mouth and answered in reasonably clear and precise German—since when did she speak German?—Paola knew that the game was up. Estrella had come to the court in Munich absolutely prepared. Dates, names, right down to times . . . sixteen-year-old schoolboy Dieter Velton was named; as was a mechanic, Helmut Biederman, whom, the truth be told, Paola had all but forgotten; the year-long affair with Heinrich Brandt, the Deputy Minister of Agriculture and one of the few Germans to hold a position in the new government . . . the list went on; even the photographs from almost ten years ago of Paola servicing—yes, that was the word the prosecutor had used—four men; she gazed at them in utter shock— Prince Georg, Günther, Jürgen, Dave—how the *fuck* had he managed to get hold of them? Everything, right down to the last time Stefan Kellber had come to the house at midnight and left just before dawn. From the timing, it could reasonably be established that the young pilot was not only a contender for the position of father of the disputed child in the case, Otto's attorney concluded smoothly, a paternity test would undoubtedly establish this as fact. In fact, he went on to say while every eye in the courtroom was on him, including the open-mouthed judge, it was obvious from the exhibit of photographs that this was not a woman of substance or integrity. Moreover, it could reasonably be asserted that any of the men listed, *including those in the photographs*, had more of a chance of siring a child. For, he smiled to himself briefly, the facts were clear. His client, renowned industrialist, eminent citizen and undoubtedly one of the country's largest investors, Otto von Kiepenhauer, could not be the father of the child. Why? Why could he say that with such authority and certainty? He held the courtroom in the palm of his hand; no one moved. Because the facts were before him. Otto von Kiepenhauer *did not* father the child because Otto von Kiepenhauer *couldn't*. He was sterile. Always had been. It had been the grounds for his previous divorce. The former Mrs. von Kiepenhauer, now Mrs. Silverman-Groult, a resident of the Upper East Side of New York, had testified to the fact. The court records from their case, should anyone care to look, did the same.

Paola looked straight ahead, then lowered her eyes and looked down at her lap. Her hands were clenched; the diamond stared out from between white knuckles. Beaten and destroyed. Just as he'd said he would.

Amber folded the newspaper and put it to one side. She glanced at Angela. They were sitting in the salon at the Ritz Hotel in London, Angela's favorite place. The waiter placed a tray of tea and delicious-looking pastries in front of them. Angela smiled her thanks and helped herself to a miniature éclair.

"Don't you want one, darling?" she asked Amber through a mouthful of cream. "Heavenly. You just

can't get a decent cup of tea and an éclair in L.A."
Amber smiled and shook her head. After the birth of
her last child, Kedé—their *last*, she warned Tendé—
she suddenly found herself in possession of a little
tummy, a gentle swelling of her abdomen that stubbornly refused to disappear. Tendé liked it; he told
her so, many times, but Amber—who had hitherto
never shown any signs of worrying about her figure—wasn't convinced. She took a sip of tea.
"So . . . what're you going to do?" Angela asked.

"I don't know." Amber picked up the paper again.
The grainy photograph showed Paola coming out
of the courtroom in Munich, head bowed, eyes
averted, holding her one-year-old daughter in her
arms, who it had finally been established, wasn't
Otto von Kiepenhauer's child at all but the result of
her affair with one of his staff. A pilot. A young man
he'd hired from Germany to fly him and his guests
to and from his private game lodges around the
country; a sunny clime and spectacular landscape
as compensation for the paltry salary and limited
prospects. Screwing the boss's wife was certainly
not part of the deal. As Paola had found out. Amber
felt a contraction in her heart—much as she disliked
her half-sister, the divorce proceedings must have
been a nightmare. All that digging up of the past. It
was a miracle Kieran hadn't been mentioned. According to the papers, von Kiepenhauer had known
all along; several of the servants in their home had
been keeping tabs on his wife for years. When she
announced triumphantly that she was pregnant, a
whole new side to him emerged, one that Paola,

certainly, had never seen. Otto was sterile—and if Paola had bothered to do her homework, she could have found that little detail out and saved herself both an enormous legal bill—which now had to be paid, somehow—and the humiliation of being paraded through the courts both in Namibia and in Germany. Otto's legal team had kept the stunning news quiet almost until the last moment; the photographs showed a weeping and distraught Paola claiming incessantly that the child was his. And all the while . . . he'd known. He'd sat opposite her, his pink, avuncular face glowing with another kind of satisfaction: revenge. And now Paola was finished, wiped out—no home, no income and with a little girl to support. Of course she had to come to Amber. Francesca had made the necessary overtures through Angela . . . and she had come to London to plead on her behalf. Amber shook her head. It was quite surreal. Her father's wife coming to beg for his mistress's daughter; herself the divorced mother of a bastard child. It would have made a spectacular film, were it not for the fact that it was real, *her* life, *her* family. How long had Max been gone? Eight years? The complications he'd left behind stretched out endlessly, to infinity.

But Amber was the head of the family Max had so carelessly thrown together; the buck, as Angela said, stopped with her. Fortunately for her, by now, there was more than the odd buck to call upon. The Téghaza project had been a success—but only just. It had taken almost everything Max had left behind and all the willpower Amber had not to throw the towel in and call the whole thing off. He'd left her in the most precarious position imaginable—caught between her family and her fiancée, trying desperately to make a decision based on nothing more concrete than instinct. Tendé had insisted it was hers to make and hers alone. She knew enough about the project to know it was worth fighting for but when the full extent of Max's investment was uncovered and she knew just how exposed her own family would be if she threw in her lot with Tendé, she faltered. Strangely enough, it was Angela who had decided things for her. Watching Angela, after so many years spent on the couch or on the floor, actually finding the strength to get up, dust herself down and reinvent herself, Amber had suddenly realized her family *wouldn't* fall apart if they were left to fend for themselves; that it might just be the making of them. Well, it hadn't quite turned out that way. Paola was now destitute and coming to her for help and Kieran was still living at home, but at least he now had a part-time job in a Covent Garden record store which he *seemed* to enjoy . . . it was a start.

"Well, you'll have to do *some*thing," Angela said eventually, licking the last of the cream from her fingertips. She dabbed at her lips with the linen napkin.

"I know. Look, I'll set up a meeting. She can come to me, to London. Francesca might as well come too. They can stay in Holland Park . . . if you're gone by then, of course."

Angela nodded. "I'm off in a week's time. Mary Ann wants to go to Menorca for a couple of weeks. Now, there's an idea . . . why don't you give *Casa*

Bella to Paola? That's probably what she needs most of all right now: a home." Amber nodded slowly. It would be the humane thing to do. She and Tendé and the children hardly ever used it; Angela and her sister came down once a year . . . for the rest of the time it sat empty. At considerable expense. She nodded again and picked up her tea cup.

"I'll think about it. Good idea, Mum." They both smiled. Amber was nearly forty and it seemed strange after all this time to call Angela "Mum"—but somehow, it seemed to work. That was another thing she'd learned after Max's death . . . other relationships came slowly into her orbit, often unannounced. She and Angela had never been close; for most of her life, theirs had been a relationship in reverse— Amber mothering Angela. But after Max was gone, Angela seemed to emerge into a life of her own. She'd managed to give up drinking—that alone was a miracle—but she'd seemed to really enjoy life in a way that she'd never done living under Max's thumb. Theirs would never be the close, codependent relationship between mother and daughter that Becky and Madeleine had with their mothers . . . but perhaps that wasn't such a bad thing. There was such a thing as being too close, as both Becky and Madeleine complained. Both of them had returned to live in London; Becky was still with her parents although it was clear it was high time she moved on and Madeleine had surprised everyone by leaving James after two years of marriage with a four-year-old son and was now living around the corner from her parents in a one-bedroom flat . . . and doing brilliantly, everyone said. Her son, Peter, was adorable. They had twice been out to Bamako to stay with Amber and the kids; he was inordinately proud of his "African" cousins, Madeleine said to Amber . . . not that it made him any different from the other children in his kindergarten group. Madeleine sometimes looked at her son and his surroundings and marveled at the difference between his and her own childhood. To have dark-brown or red hair was about as "different" as anyone got back then, in Budapest . . . now among the Samirs, Pollyannas, Leylas and Yen-Yens in his little class, brown-haired, blue-eyed Peter Fournier was the exception, not the rule.

"Okay, darling, I'd better go." Angela was signaling for the bill. Amber was brought back to the present. "I've still got a ton of shopping to do. I promised your cousin I'd bring her back something from Harrods."

"We'll see you for dinner?" Amber asked as they both got up to leave.

"Maybe. I don't know. Kieran wanted to go somewhere. I'll phone you later," Angela said, picking up her bags. "You know what he's like—can't stand sharing me with anyone else." Amber nodded. For once, she was alone in London; the children were in Geneva with Lassana and their grandmother. She had a few precious days to herself before the three of them would fly back to London to join her. She needed some time to think about Paola and about how to handle the latest crisis in what was left of Max's family.

*   *   *

Madeleine kissed the top of Peter's head and quickly left the room before he had a chance to start crying. Maja bustled through with a tray of freshly baked biscuits and a large stack of books in one hand. Madeleine blew her a kiss as she grabbed her bag and jacket from the stand in the hallway. *Thank you*, she mouthed silently and then opened the front door and dashed out. Without Maja's help, she thought to herself as she ran down the street to catch her bus, there was no way she would have managed. She was now a senior registrar at Guy's Hospital. After almost ten years away from medicine, and from surgery in particular, the fact that she'd managed to land such a senior appointment in a teaching hospital was a miracle. It was bloody hard work and her nerves were tested a hundred times a day . . . but she loved it.

Her bus came trundling around the corner. It was a lovely morning—the birds were singing, the sun was shining and the blue, blue sky was filled with giant cotton wool clouds: A chocolate-box image of a spring morning. Notting Hill was in full spring bloom; fat, pink cherry blossom was just beginning to fall from the trees that lined the more expensive streets; yellow-green buds were poking through gnarled branches and the florist's façade on the corner of Westbourne Park Road was covered in bright yellow and white daffodils. It was the sort of day to make your heart sing . . . the kind that came along so rarely and yet when it did, you remembered just how good the last sunny morning had made you feel, even if it was ages ago. She pushed her way upstairs, swaying as the bus turned a corner. She found a seat near the front. It took her almost forty minutes longer by bus but she hated the dank darkness of the Underground, especially on a morning like this one. She pulled her bag to her knees and took out her surgery notes. It looked like it'd be a busy morning. She let the notepad slide onto the empty seat next to her and turned to look out of the window at Hyde Park. She'd been back almost six months; it was hard to believe the time had gone so quickly. It felt like yesterday when she'd stood at the kitchen window in their new flat on Rue Dancet and thought she would surely drown if she didn't do something. She pressed her face against the glass and thought about what had happened in the past year.

There wasn't anything she could put a finger on, that was the hardest thing. James was the same as he always was—considerate, kind, predictable. She didn't know quite when it had happened but she woke up one morning praying he wouldn't wake up and realizing that she would sooner have cut off her own arm than make love to him. She was shocked at herself. She hadn't noticed the steady but slow decline in their physical relationship . . . she was always so tired. Peter, adorable as he was, was a handful. She rarely managed to sleep through the night; James snored as she got up once, twice, sometimes three times to feed him, comfort him, take his temperature when he was ill, soothe him after a nightmare . . . the list of his needs was endless. Slowly she found herself beginning to resent his demands, especially those that dragged her out of sleep in the middle of the night. At first he'd slept in the same bed with them but Madeleine found herself unable to sleep properly, afraid she would roll over and squash him when he was tiny and irritated with the way he sprawled across their space, kicking and moving about endlessly as he grew older. Banishing him to his own room had been difficult at first; but she'd held out until he finally got used to his new room and they were able to settle down for the night alone. Until he woke her up, that was. She began to crave sleep—forget sex—the way she imagined an alcoholic craved drink . . . incessantly. She never seemed to get enough. She was officially on maternity leave from ICM but found herself longing to return. Anything . . . writing reports, reading policy statements, training manuals . . . *anything* was better than sitting at home all afternoon while Peter slept and James was away, outside in the real world, doing real things. She could almost hear the wheels of her mind grinding to a halt.

James tried to be practical, of course. He wasn't angry with her when she couldn't rouse herself to make dinner or when she fell asleep night after night, having fed and bathed Peter together, without so much as a peck on the cheek or even a kiss. He didn't complain when the intervals between lovemaking stretched from six weeks to six months . . . and in the last few months of their relationship, to almost a year. He was just so damned reasonable about everything. Avoid an argument at all costs, was his motto, both at home and at work. It was the same quality that made him a useful, if uninspired member of the legal team and turned him into an equally uninspired and uninspiring husband. Madeleine still wasn't one hundred percent sure why she'd agreed to marry him. Was it Maja and Imre? Maja dropped hints the size of boulders: wasn't it time they tied the knot? Wouldn't Madeleine feel more secure with a ring on her finger, especially now that they had a child? Wouldn't she look lovely in white? Or cream? James was all for it and after some initial hesitation, Madeleine gave in.

Her wedding day passed in a blur. Amber and Becky came, of course; Becky looking wonderful and Amber looking tired and heavily pregnant—*for the last time, I swear!*—but her parents were over the moon, and James certainly seemed pleased. Peter was almost two; he wore a sailor's outfit and cried all the way through the simple ceremony. Madeleine had thought there could be nothing more precious to her parents than her decision to name her son Peter . . . but she was wrong. Maja wept all the way to the church and then threw herself into the role of mother-of-the-bride with such gusto Imre had had to restrain her. After all, James, too, had a mother. And a father.

The day afterwards, on their honeymoon in Mauritius—probably the most romantic spot on the entire planet—Madeleine looked at her husband over the breakfast tray and experienced such a profound sense of alienation and distance that it shocked her into silence for almost the rest of their ten days.

James kept asking her what was wrong—luckily, she was able to use Peter as an excuse. He was staying with Maja and Imre; she missed him, that was all. As the honeymoon wore on, she kept praying for some sort of excitement to return; for some thrill of pleasure at seeing her husband, enjoyment in their conversations, if not in anything else . . . but it didn't happen. She lay next to him at night in pretty much the same way she would have lain next to a piece of furniture, or a dog—except she'd probably have enjoyed stroking a dog just that little bit more. Perhaps it'll come right once we're home, she kept thinking. Once we're back in our flat with Peter and our normal routine . . . of course it would come back. You didn't fall out of love with someone just because they were nice, surely?

But it didn't. They got back to Geneva in May, at the loveliest time of year. The lake was splendid; in the afternoons she and Peter would stroll down to the Quai du Mont Blanc, eat an ice cream and wait for the famous jet to shoot skywards, much to Peter's delight. His little face would light up in pleasure and he would look to her to confirm; it was for him, wasn't it? Specially for him . . . she would ruffle his hair and laugh. Sometimes on the way back to their new flat, she would find herself seeking an excuse to stay out a little bit longer, not wanting to enter into the dry, sterile atmosphere in the flat where she and James no longer had much to talk about except their child.

He hadn't done anything wrong, that was the hardest part. All through the early summer she sat at home during the day watching reruns of *Sex and the City* in French and talking to Amber, whose life, it seemed to Madeleine, was like a married, African version of the same . . . all state banquets, foreign travel and urgent debate. Madeleine wasn't like Becky—she didn't want to *be* like Amber or live her life, though she did want something more. But what? James did his best, but even he was beginning to lose patience with her. They had an argument at the end of June about where to go on holiday. James favored Tuscany; Madeleine was scornful. Chianti-shire, she threw at him. Can't you be a bit more bloody adventurous than that?

"What's wrong with Tuscany?" he demanded, frowning. "It's pleasant, it's safe . . . Peter won't get sunburn. There'll be lots of good wine and food . . . what the hell's wrong with it?"

"You don't get it, do you?" Madeleine looked at him stonily. He shook his head.

"No. No, I don't. I don't understand why you don't want a perfectly nice, enjoyable holiday—"

"I don't *want* a perfectly nice holiday! I don't want to spend three weeks of my life in a perfectly *nice*, perfectly *ordinary* little villa in the middle of bloody Tuscany, drinking perfectly nice wine and listening to your perfectly nice, perfectly boring—" She stopped herself. James had flushed a deep red.

"I'm sorry if I bore you, Madeleine," he said stiffly. "It certainly wasn't my intention. I was simply making a suggestion. If you have a better one, please . . . let's hear it. I'm open to suggestions, you know that."

"I'm sorry, James. I . . . I just wish we could do something . . . I don't know . . . something different?" Madeleine was suddenly contrite. He was right. He didn't deserve to be on the blunt end of her anger. She didn't understand herself why she was angry, so why should he?

"Like what?"

"Oh, I don't know. South America. Hong Kong. Even South Africa would be more interesting than Tuscany."

"South America? But it's so far, Madeleine. And there's all sorts of problems. Colombia, Brazil . . . the economy's collapsing, for goodness' sake. And South Africa? Did you know Johannesburg's now the official murder capital of the world? What kind of a holiday would *that* be?"

Madeleine looked at him. "You're right," she said slowly, turning away. "Of course you're right. Tuscany's fine. You book it. You seem to know all the best spots." She walked out of the room before he could see the tears of frustration in her eyes.

After that, things rapidly began to unravel until the morning she woke up and realized that her husband revolted her, physically as well as mentally. She stared at him over breakfast and wondered if she were losing her mind. How was it possible that the same man she'd spent sleepless nights over back then in New York, had woken up next to the morning after they'd first slept together thinking that now, finally, happiness was about to head her way . . . how was it possible that *this* was the same man? She concentrated on her morning coffee, unwilling or unable to meet his eyes. How could she even think of leaving him? The web tying the two families together—never mind their son—was so dense and so tight she couldn't see how to untangle it. What would her parents say? *His* parents? She took another sip. How did you go about leaving a perfectly nice, perfectly kind, perfectly ordinary husband? Well, she thought to herself grimly, she really hadn't much of a choice. Now that she'd admitted to herself just how much she longed to be free of him, there was no going back. All she had to do now was find the courage—and the means—to do it.

It was easier said than done. There were moments in the months that followed when she thought she had made the biggest mistake of her life. Moments when she saw James and Peter lying together on the sofa, Peter's fat little legs entangled in his, hands loosely entwined; or when James looked up at her from the bed that they still shared and made some comment—touchingly innocuous . . . *that dress suits you, Madeleine . . . you look really nice*. At moments like those, she wondered what on earth she was doing. But just as she was about to change her mind, cursing herself for being so selfish and thinking only of her own happiness, not her son's, there would be a small argument, an exchange of opinions, a comment, and she would realize again and again . . . there was simply no way for her to continue. She wanted so much more out of life. She wanted to feel *alive*; to be with someone who brought out the best in her; who challenged her and pushed her forward. James seemed determined, in his own, sweet way, to keep her exactly where she was; at his side, unchanging and unchanging forever.

She left a note. It was the one thing she wished she'd had the courage to do differently. She'd planned her speech for weeks, arguing with herself in front of the bathroom mirror, going over the words in her mind, sharpening her argument, testing it . . . in the end, she'd waited until he left for work one morning just before they were due to leave on holiday and wrote to him, putting everything she'd been practicing in her head down on paper, unable to face seeing him. It was a long letter; it was her fault, not his; she was to blame. All she could say after so many years was that she couldn't do it any more. She was going back to London for a few weeks, back to her parents, where she hoped she would find the space and time to think about what to do next. She and Peter left the apartment in Geneva at 11 a.m. that morning, took a train to the airport and boarded a flight to London. She left everything behind: furniture, books, clothes, possessions . . . everything. It was only fair, she thought to herself as she gathered up only the items that would be absolutely necessary for herself and Peter—mostly Peter's toys and books—until she'd managed to sort things out properly and decided what to do.

"Holiday?" Peter asked her over and over again. "Where's Daddy?" It almost broke Madeleine's heart. She stroked his blond head and made the appropriate soothing noises. Daddy would be coming later. She had no idea what to tell him.

Maja was disapproving at first, of course. Sitting in their tiny kitchen the evening after they'd arrived, she tried to explain to her mother in halting sentences exactly why she'd decided to run away, as Maja put it, and just what the problem with her marriage was. It wasn't easy. But when Madeleine had finished speaking and looked up at her, her eyes brimming with tears, Maja nodded slowly.

"It's just not *enough*," Madeleine said forcefully. "I can't stand it. It's not for me, that life . . . it's too . . . easy."

"*Igen.* You're right. That's what we all thought we wanted," Maja said softly. "The easy life. It's not for people like us." She got up heavily from the table. Madeleine wanted to say something. She saw that Maja had misunderstood, falling back onto the stereotype of themselves as immigrants for whom nothing would—or could—be easy. But Maja's acceptance of the situation was infinitely more valuable to Madeleine, in her present state, than her understanding. She bit back the words and tried to smile.

After that, things had more or less fallen into place. She had enough money to get a small flat for her and Peter almost halfway between Amber's old family house and her parents' flat in Kensal Rise. It was tiny—barely enough room for the two of them, but it was home. It was warm and comfortable and within a few weeks, even Peter was persuaded into thinking it almost as good as their old flat, where Daddy lived and where Peter would go, to visit, at Christmas. She found a job easily enough on the surgical team at Guy's Hospital and Maja stepped forward to help with looking after Peter. By August, it was almost as if she'd never left London. James had agreed to what he called a trial six-month separation—she would go to Geneva with Peter at Christmas, and then they'd see. Madeleine agreed with him over the phone but in her heart, she knew it was over. Everyone around her, including the nurses on the ward, seemed to think her romantic life was over—thirty-five; separated; with a four-year-old son . . . who would want to take *that* on? But Madeleine simply shook her head and laughed at their concern. She wasn't even thinking about dating another man. For the moment, she was content to feel her life coming back into her own hands and take care of the one man who mattered—her son.

"Next stop Westminster Bridge!" the conductor shouted out, bringing her back to the present with a jolt. She gathered up her notes and her bag and stood up. Just behind her she could hear Big Ben chiming nine o'clock. Her surgical teammates were exceptionally kind to her as a single mother. She never had to work the graveyard or early-morning shifts, except when on call. She made her way downstairs and watched the river disappear as the bridge sloped towards the south bank and she jumped off the bus.

103

"Becky!" Someone called her name. She turned towards the man who had just called out to her and there was a moment of tension . . . surely she recognized him? She gasped—the moment was knocked aside, saved.

"Godson!" She almost dropped her bag. "What the . . . ? How . . . what are you doing here?" She grabbed his arm.

"Becky! I've been here for almost six months. I didn't know where to find you. There are so many Aldridges in the phone book . . . Je-*sus*!" he was grinning from ear to ear. Becky stared at him.

"Your hair . . . what happened . . . you cut it off?"

He ran a hand sheepishly over his almost bald head. "*Ja*, you know, getting the visa and all that. Oh, man, it's so good to see you! Where are you these days? What are you doing?"

"Oh, nothing much. Look, come and have a coffee; there's a café around the corner. Or are you busy? Did you come with the family?" The questions tumbled out of her mouth.

He looked away quickly. "No, I'm here alone. Well, I'm staying at my brother's place. You remember, the economist?"

"Yes, of course I remember. So . . . shall we go somewhere?"

"The thing is . . . I have an interview in half an hour. I'm just on my way. D'you have a phone number? Somewhere I can contact you?"

"Yes, of course. I'm staying at my parents' . . . here, I'll write it down. You will call, won't you?"

"*Ja*, promise. I'll call this evening. Oh, man . . . it's so good to see you." He stood grinning at her. Becky blushed. He looked so different without his trademark dreadlocks—shorn, like a sheep. She giggled.

"This is amazing!" she said, shouldering her bag and passing her number to him. "I can't believe it. I just can't believe it."

"Well, I'd better run. I'll call you later, okay?" He hugged her briefly and then dashed off, dodging through crowds in Covent Garden, and disappeared. Becky watched him go, her mind whirling. Godson . . . she had never expected to see him again in her life, ever. She'd done her best to bury everything that had happened to her back there, in Harare. She taken all the right steps; she'd moved back home; gone to counseling, put it all behind her. The only thing she hadn't quite managed to sort out since she'd been back was what to do with her life, where to go next. Somehow, after the thrill of Deluxe and the success they'd had, working as someone's PA or secretary, which was all she felt she could manage after she'd come back, hadn't managed to hold her attention. But the longer she stayed out of the job market, the harder it was to get back in. What had seemed to her to be an enormous challenge and success story in Zimbabwe barely made a dent in people's impressions over here. *A gallery, you say?*

Where? Where the hell is that? She soon discovered that the art world hadn't grown any larger or geographically more adventurous in her absence. Her brief tenure at EC1 seemed to be the high point of her curatorial career and most people knew she'd been let go. Besides, she hadn't even made it to assistant curator at that point. So she gave up on the "real" jobs and instead concentrated on simply making a bit of money and trying to make ends meet. It wasn't always easy. Living at home again at the age of thirty-four had been hard enough—as thirty-four turned to thirty-five and to thirty-six, she began to despair of ever really getting her life back together again. Amber very generously—as always—offered her the use of the flat that she and Tendé had bought in Holland Park, just a few doors away from the old house where Kieran still lived. But it was their place; these days, Amber spent almost as much time in London as she did in Bamako. It just wasn't the same as having her own flat. But the cost of rent in London was so high, and Becky was still temping after four years, so it seemed to make more sense to stay at home until she'd found something else. And her mother was only too thrilled to have her back. Becky had never revealed to her parents the full horror of what had happened to her; she'd never let on that it was four men, not one, and that the attack had lasted for hours, not minutes. She didn't think she'd be able to stand her mother knowing just what she'd been through.

She turned and walked slowly back up Floral Street towards the Tube station. She felt recharged, her nerve endings suddenly come to life. Godson was here, in London . . . unbelievable. An image of her former self—gutsy and vibrant, not afraid to take a chance—came back to her. The distance between who she had been when she left Britain and who she was now, having come back to it, stretched in front of her. For the first time in four years, a glimpse of how she might cross it came to her, without warning. She followed the crowd into the station, a smile breaking across her face.

They met the following day for coffee. Becky sat and listened in silence to what had happened to Godson after she'd left. It hadn't been easy. Deluxe had been everything for him as well. He'd closed up the gallery, sold off the few remaining items that her attackers had left in there and tried as best as he could to sort out the financial obligations that remained. Not terribly successfully, he grimaced. The Indian store owner had threatened him with everything short of a beating—but the news of what had happened to the English girl who'd owned it soon got around and people began to avoid him, thinking that perhaps he'd had something to do with it. Mr. Ahmed, the owner, soon gave up chasing him for the balance of the two-year lease and Godson quickly found himself unemployed again, only this time with an appetite for a better way of life that he soon realized he couldn't possibly feed.

He worked in a series of jobs over the next couple of years, wondering what had become of her; wondering how and if he should try to make contact. Her friend Nadège had met him in the street one morning, almost two years after it had happened. Yes, Becky was doing fine, she reported. No, she wasn't coming back. Zimbabwe had been a failed experiment for her. The sooner everyone forgot her, the better. Becky's eyebrows rose in indignation.

"How could she have known? I never spoke to her again. Ever. How *dare* she—"

"*Ag*, she was only doing what she thought was right. There were some who didn't think you . . . we . . . should have done it, you know. The gallery. Some people thought you'd got your comeuppance. Funny . . . the whole thing brought out the worst in people, in everyone."

Becky nodded slowly. "So what made you come over here?"

"Things are bad at home, you know. The whole place is a mess. I just got fed up. Adelaide took the kids back to her mother's, to the village. It just got so lonely, you know. Then Johnson, my brother, wrote to me . . . we have a relative working at the British High Commission who said he could get me papers. It cost quite a bit, but here I am. I'm working here and there . . . I don't have a permit. But there's plenty of work around. And I send back what I can. That's it. That's life."

"What sort of work?"

"Oh, man . . . different things. Everything. Cleaning. Carwash. Laborer. Anything, I'm not fussy."

"Oh, Godson. It just seems so far away . . . from before." She stared miserably into her coffee cup.

"Yeah, I know. But that's life, Becky. Sometimes you're up, sometimes you're not."

"I sometimes wonder if I dreamed the whole thing."

"What are you doing? Running another gallery?"

"Are you kidding? I'm a secretary—at the best of times. Most of the time I just make tea." She laughed shortly. "I'm working for a property developer at the moment. Been there all of what, six weeks. That's a record for me."

"How come? I thought . . . I was sure you'd find something else, another gallery, a shop. Man, I used to think of you up here in London, living it up. What happened?"

"Dunno. Lost my confidence, I guess. When I got back, there wasn't anything even remotely like what we'd been doing on offer. And I needed to make some money. I couldn't go on living off my parents forever. I still live with them and that's bad enough."

He nodded. "Sure. I understand."

"It's hard to believe, isn't it?"

"Man, that's just life. You'll find something soon. Something will turn up."

"Will it? I used to think that. I'm not so sure any more. Everything that's happened to me—I've done it, I've set it up myself. Nothing's ever just turned up."

"So . . . why don't you set something up again? Do it yourself?" There was a sudden silence. Becky lifted her eyes, as if considering. There was a smile playing around the corners of her mouth.

"You know, that's exactly what I've been thinking ever since we bumped into each other yesterday. It's been on my mind for almost twenty-four hours." She looked down at her cup again. "Would you?"

"What?"

"Do it again?"

"*Ag*, Becky, man . . . this time it's different. I don't know anyone here. I'm illegal, for Christ's sake."

"Well, *that* can be sorted out. No, I'm serious. It's all I've been thinking about."

"But where would we get the money? I mean . . . where, how, when? It's impossible."

"No, it's not. I know where to get the backing we need. All *I* need is for you to say you'll do it. Again." Becky's eyes were shining. Godson pushed back his chair and looked at her. She could see it in his eyes; admiration, for her. It was what she'd been waiting for almost four years to see . . . that some-body thought she was capable of something, that she was brave and not a quitter.

"Jesus, Becky . . . it's so tempting. What . . . well, where would we start?" She had him, she saw that. He pulled his chair forward again. "Are you being serious? Don't joke with me, girl . . ."

"I'm not! I promise. I don't know why I didn't think of it before. I've been sitting here in some kind of . . . of . . . dream. It's so simple. We can do this, God-son. We've done it once before, we can do it again. Oh, God . . . I *knew* there was a reason we ran into each other yesterday. I just knew it!" She jumped up, swallowing her coffee in one gulp and reaching for her bag. "Come on, let's start. Here's what we need to do . . ."

* * *

It was to Amber she went. This time, as before, with a detailed business plan: careful calculations; photographs of locations and premises; cash flow projections; graphic design costs . . . everything, right down to the last detail. Amber looked briefly at the figures and back at Becky. They were sitting in Amber's office on Montagu Place, the office that had been Max's for so long. Sunlight filtered in through the heavy damask curtains; in all the years since Max's death, Amber hadn't wanted to change it. It was still the solemn, rather regal place it had been when he was alive.

"You're sure about this?" Amber asked her as she reached into a drawer. Becky watched her pull out a checkbook. She took a deep breath and nodded.

"About as sure as I'll ever be," she said. "If I don't make it happen, it won't. That much I do know."

"Then it's yours," Amber said simply, and began writing out a check. Becky watched her in silence.

"Thank you," she said, as Amber handed it over. "I can't thank you enough. You'll get it back, Amber . . . I hope you know that."

Amber shook her head, smiling. "I don't want it back. It's a gift. Max taught me that much. Don't lend money to your friends. Give it. When the gallery's up and running, give us a piece of art." There were tears in Becky's eyes as she folded the little slip of paper—such a tiny thing to hold such significance—and slipped it in her bag.

"Thanks, Amber. Really."

"My pleasure."

104

The thought of sitting across her father's desk from her sister, having to beg her for money and somewhere to live, was enough to make Paola physically sick. Francesca, long accustomed to having to make unpleasant compromises, was less than sympathetic.

"You have a child, Paola. And that's all there is to it. You have to do whatever it takes to make sure Alessandra is taken care of. *Basta.*" She pushed a box of tissues across the table and eyed her daughter warily. The last thing she wanted was for Paola and her grandchild—*her, a grandmother!*—camping out in her apartment for months on end. She still couldn't understand how Paola had managed to get herself into such a mess. She hadn't known her husband was sterile? Honestly.

"I can't, Mama," Paola wailed, shredding the tissue with nervous fingers.

"You will. Now, dry your eyes. What are you going to wear to London?" Francesca was brisk and practical. "Nothing too expensive, hmm?" Paola sighed and looked away. She couldn't believe she was back where she'd started, almost five years earlier. She'd married Otto precisely because she never wanted to be in the situation of having to beg from Amber again, ever . . . and now, here she was, with a small child to support, exactly where she'd been before. It was too much to bear. A fresh wave of angry tears threatened to spill down her cheeks. And her mother was being anything but sympathetic. In fact, Francesca had been downright rude ever since Paola had rung her from Munich and warned her that the papers would be full of her defeat in the morning. Lectures and sermons on how silly she'd been and how difficult her life was going to be from now on were not what she needed, thank you very much. Support, kindness, someone to take Alessandra off her hands for a while . . . *that* was what she wanted. But Francesca was a surprisingly reluctant grandmother. In fact, she seemed to abhor the role. "How about the black Armani suit, from last year? It's practical, simple . . . not too flashy?" Paola stared at her mother in disbelief. How could she sit there calmly discussing clothing when her life was about to fall apart?

"Yeah, whatever," she said dismissively.

Francesca frowned. "Paola," she began crossly. "There's really no need—"

"Jesus, Mama! I can't think about stupid things like that just now! Don't you understand? My whole *life* is falling apart."

"And whose fault is that?" Francesca snapped back at her. "Didn't I teach you anything?"

"No, you taught me nothing!" Paola yelled at her, getting to her feet. She tossed aside the box of tissues. "*Nothing*! D'you hear me? You couldn't even get Max to marry you—and now *you* want to lecture *me* about—"

"Paola!" Francesca gasped. "That's enough!"

"You're damned right it's enough!" She ran from the room, slamming the door behind her. Francesca remained where she was, her cheeks aflame. In the background, she could hear Alessandra beginning to wail. She reached for her cigarettes with a shaking hand. How dare Paola talk to her that way?

In her old room, still with its silk counterpane, pretty dressing table and lace curtains, Paola flung herself on the bed as she had done twenty years earlier, pounding the bedspread with her clenched fists. Only this time, her child wailing down the corridor in the spare bedroom forced her to sit up, smooth down her hair and take a few deep breaths before going out to comfort her. This time, there was someone else to think about; someone whose needs were greater than her own. She hurried to Alessandra's room, cursing herself for having slammed the door and woken her up. She was a nervous, sensitive child—a result, no doubt, of the turmoil of the past year. As she picked her up and tried to stop the tears, she realized she really didn't have any other options. She would sooner have died than let Alessandra suffer, and right now, with no home, no money and no means of earning a living, eating humble pie in front of Amber was about the only chance she had. The black Armani suit. She would ask Francesca to get it out for her.

Across the gleaming expanse of cherrywood and leather, Amber looked at her sister in silence. It was almost four years since she'd seen Paola; she had aged suddenly. Fine lines had appeared around her mouth and eyes; the petite voluptuousness that had so tormented Amber in their teenage years was still there, hidden by the discreet, rather severe outfit Paola had chosen—not her style at all. It was probably Francesca's choice, Amber thought to herself . . . somewhere between sophisticated widow and businesslike efficiency. Neither of which suited her sister. It was also the first time she'd seen Paola without the olive, golden tan she'd worn almost all her life. Paola's appearance had always screamed "money"—tanned, slim, well-dressed, bored . . . Amber remembered with a half-smile a necklace she'd worn once for a few months. "Rich," spelled out in diamante and gold, just in case anyone missed the point. It was Max who'd yanked it off her neck one weekend at *Casa Bella* and tossed it down the hill. But that was then. The woman in front of her was pale and wan, her face drawn. Whatever had happened to her in the past few months had taken its toll. Amber straightened up in her chair. She leaned forwards slightly and opened the folder in front of her.

"Look, Paola, I'm sure this isn't easy for you and I don't mean to make it any harder but . . . these figures just aren't reasonable. I mean, £20,000 a month? Most people don't make that in a year."

"But I have a *child*," Paola said obstinately.

"And I have three. And I can tell you, I don't spend £20,000 a month looking after them."

"You have a husband," Paola said slowly. "I am alone."

"I understand that. But I can't agree to that amount. Five thousand pounds would be nearer the mark—and that's being generous."

"Generous? You?" Paola's voice rose. Amber sighed. They'd been in the same room for less than thirty minutes and the atmosphere was already beginning to show signs of strain.

"Paola, I'm giving you *Casa Bella. Giving* it to you. There will be the usual stipulations—you won't be allowed to sell it, of course, and no renovations to it without the Board's approval—"

"And who sits on the Board? You?"

"Among others, yes." Amber refused to be drawn into an argument with her. She was doing her best to remain calm, but somewhere inside her, a nerve twitched. She'd forgotten just how difficult and exasperating Paola could be.

"Ten thousand pounds then." Paola's expression was sulky.

"I've just told you. I'm going to set up a £5,000 a month allowance, out of which you'll be responsible for your own taxes, pension, whatever else you want to spend your money on. Alessandra's education will come out of another budget, controlled by the Trust. She'll inherit a lump sum on her eighteenth and twenty-first birthdays, just as my children will. It's fair, Paola . . . perfectly fair. It's more than *I* make a month—and I work for it."

"Of course you do, clever little Amber. Well, *I*

would have worked as well, only no one ever thought I was clever enough."

"Paola, that's absolute rubbish, and you know it." Amber's patience was wearing thin.

"It's not rubbish! Max always thought you were the clever one. You got sent to all the best schools . . . *I* just got dumped at *Casa Bella*. No one ever bothered with my homework or asked me what I did in school." Two bright red spots stood out on Paola's cheeks. Whatever the veracity of the statement, it was clear she believed it. Amber shook her head.

"You've got it all wrong. *You* were the pretty one; you were always more interested in clothes and boys than in your books. You got Max on the weekends, we never had him. He was never around." Amber's temper had finally snapped.

"That's bullshit!" Paola was on her feet now, glaring down at Amber. "And so typical. You always think you know everything. How dare you tell me what it was like for me. You don't know a thing about me!"

"And you know even less about me," Amber shouted, pushing her chair back and standing up. She gripped the table with both hands. "You're so fucking selfish, Paola. You've always been that way. Take what you want, when you want . . . you don't give a damn about anyone else—"

"*I* don't give a damn? You're the one who's so wrapped up in yourself you can't even see what's going on around you. D'you know that Kieran hates you? Do you?" Amber had gone pale. "You spent your whole life sucking up to Max, never giving anyone else a chance, always stealing the limelight . . . and now you talk to *me* about being selfish!"

"Stop it." Amber's voice was quiet. "Stop right there."

"Why? Because it's the truth? You never could stand hearing the truth, could you? And you pretended like you were this great big journalist, always looking for the truth. You wouldn't know it if it hit you in the face, you scheming little bitch."

"Get out." Amber raised her head, eyes narrowed, and looked at her. "Get out of my office."

"It's not even your office. It's *Max*'s office, d'you hear me? Max's! Not yours!" Paola was screaming by now. Amber heard her secretary, Janice, scrape back her chair on the other side of the door and hesitate, wondering what the hell was going on.

"This is *my* office, Paola. You came here begging *me* for money, remember? *You* came to *me*. Now get out before I change my mind and send you back to Rome without a penny."

"That's right. You always were such a bully. Well, you can take your fucking money and go to hell, Amber. Alessandra is Max's grandchild too, you know. We'll see what a lawyer has to say about that!" Paola picked up her bag and walked out, almost knocking Janice over and slamming the office front door behind her so hard that a vase toppled over, sending water, lilies and palm fronds crashing to the floor. There was a deadly silence as soon as she'd gone. She left the door to Amber's office open. Through it, Amber could see Janice staring at her, open-mouthed. Confrontations like this just didn't happen in the offices of Sall, Inc. She motioned to Janice to close the door and leave her alone for a moment. She sat down slowly, her chest heaving. She and Paola had never confronted one another like this . . . never. She had always tried to avoid a blow-up . . . and no bloody wonder. Paola was insane. How could *she* be accused of being selfish? She was giving her a home in one of the world's loveliest spots; a monthly allowance; a guarantee of the best education for her child . . . and Paola *still* managed to construe it as being selfish? She shook her head. She was outraged.

"Er . . . are you all right, Mrs. Ndiaye?" Janice stuck her head tentatively around the door. Amber nodded.

"Yes, fine . . . thanks. Could you get Clive for me? Tell him I'd like to go home in about ten minutes, please." Janice nodded sympathetically and closed the door. Amber blew out her cheeks and sat down on the couch. A picture of Max stood on the little side table next to her. She picked it up. *Look what you've left me with*, she whispered to the silent black-and-white photograph. Max's eyes stared back at her, unseeing. It was up to her now. She had to figure out what to do, how to do it . . . it was why he'd entrusted everything to her. Again she felt the weight of his legacy pressing down upon her. More than she would ever admit, Paola's words had hurt her. Kieran hated her? How? And why? Memories of their childhood life together came flooding back. She couldn't remember how or when it had been decided that Kieran was the weak one; as far back as she could remember it had always been that way. Whenever Max and Angela fought, it was Kieran who cried, who couldn't stand it, who had to be comforted as their voices grew. *She* was the strong one—it had always been that way. What had Paola said? She always stole the limelight. It wasn't true! Kieran had never wanted to shine . . . everyone said he was just too damned lazy, including Kieran himself. It had even become something of a family joke: Amber did everything well; Kieran did nothing well. She put the frame down slowly and leaned back against the cushions. Tears were threatening. Well, it was obviously no joke. Paola had unwittingly opened up a nerve; perhaps it was true. All along, she'd been trying so hard for both of them she'd never given Kieran a chance. She'd always struggled to please Max—was it possible she'd taken on the role of trying to make up for his disappointment in Kieran? And in doing just that, had pushed out whatever little chance Kieran had of succeeding himself. No wonder he hated her. Seen from his eyes, she wasn't the strong, determined little sister she'd always imagined herself to be, she was a domineering, selfish competitor, exactly as Paola had said. Tears came suddenly. She burned with shame for Kieran's failures: the nightclub; the affair with Paola; the disappointment he knew he was to his father . . . she put her head in her hands and wept, for herself as well as Kieran. How was she ever going to make things right between them? After so many years, how would she even begin the conversation?

There was another discreet tap at the door. It was Janice. Clive was waiting outside. She said nothing but popped a box of tissues on the sideboard before gently closing the door.

"I still can't get over it," she said to Tendé that night over the phone. She needed to talk to him about what had happened that day, even though Tendé wasn't quite the right person. She could hear him sigh at the other end. He had lost patience with Kieran and Paola almost from the first time he'd met them. He'd always said he couldn't understand how those two had sprung from Max.

"You will. How're the kids?" His voice sounded strained.

"They're fine. Asleep, I hope. Are you all right?"

"Yeah, just . . . tired. It's been a long day. Some problems at the palace. I can't talk now."

"Why? What's going on?" Amber was worried. It wasn't like him to sound so careful. Suddenly, the events of the morning seemed far away, even a little silly.

"Nothing. I'd better go . . . . I'm calling from the office. I'll call you when I get home. *D'accord*?"

"Okay. But call me, won't you? It's really difficult to get through to you these days."

"I know." He hung up the phone. Amber sat on the edge of the bed, biting her lip. What a day. She was certainly in no hurry to repeat the experience. She wondered where Paola had gone. Back to Rome, probably. No doubt she would hear something from her—or her lawyers—in the next few days. She was more worried about how to face Kieran.

She lay back against the pillows and cushions and picked up a book. She was so tired that after a minute or two, the text began to blur and lose its meaning. She laid it down, nestled into the duvet and within minutes, was fast asleep.

She wasn't sure what had woken her up. The telephone? She sat bolt upright in bed, confused. The bedside lamp was still on, the radio was a low whisper at her side. She looked down at herself—fully clothed. She must have dozed off while reading. She glanced at the phone. Had it rung? She peered at her watch. It was almost four in the morning. Five in Bamako. She picked up the phone and dialed. *Le numéro que vous avez demandé n'est pas valable. Veuillez accrocher et répéter. Le numéro . . .* She put the phone down. These days, it was harder and harder to get through to Bamako. She swung her legs out of bed and sat on the edge, wondering whether she ought to walk through and check on the children. Liya was a notoriously light sleeper . . . she was sure to wake up. She reached across the bed and twiddled the dial on the bedside radio until she found Radio France. She liked listening to it; it reminded her of home. The familiar strains of the hourly news program interrupted her. She reached over and turned the volume up a little. *Bonsoir, ici Radio France à Paris. Les nouvelles à quatres heures du matin. À minuit ce soir, il y a quelques heures, il y avait un coup d'état dans l'ancienne colonie francaise, Mali.* Amber stared at the radio. A coup d'état? In Mali? Her heart racing, she picked up the phone again, fingers shaking and started dialing. *God . . . please, no . . .* No wonder Tendé had sounded so worried. *Please God . . . please.* She tried his cellphone, the office, the home phone . . . everywhere and everyone she could think of. After fifteen minutes of fruitless attempts, she grabbed her bag and flipped open her Filofax. Lassana might know something. She heard footsteps coming down the corridor; one of the children had woken up. She swallowed, hoping her face wouldn't betray her inner panic. A coup d'état . . . it was the thing Tendé feared most. She reached out to Liya and Sibi with one hand as she heard the phone ring in Geneva at the other end. *Please, God . . . let him be all right.* She had never felt such fear.

≈105≈

Tendé knew as soon as he heard the tanks rumbling past on Boulevard de la Paix that something was going on—and going wrong. He was in his ministerial car, driving north to the Presidential Palace for an early evening meeting with the President when he became aware of a low, ground-shaking tremor.

"What is it?" he asked Majid as the car swung onto Avenue de la Liberté. Majid shrugged.

"I don't know. There've been soldiers moving around the city all day. A training exercise, n'shallah."

Tendé looked behind him. Three tanks, bearing down on Avenue de l'Independence . . . what the hell was going on? There were never any military exercises in the center of the city. Something was up. He turned back to Majid. He looked at the clock face on the dashboard: quarter to seven. The city was almost dark. People and cars were still moving around, and everything seemed normal.

"Put the radio on, will you?" he asked Majid. He was worried. Although nothing had been leaked to the population at large, the army had uncovered two fairly serious and well-organized plots to overthrow the government in the past few months. Several of the junior officers involved had been jailed but with the government's economic reforms starting to bite, unrest was widespread. All it would take, he knew from the experiences of neighboring countries like Burkina Faso and Ghana, was a charismatic and well-armed leader . . . and then anything could happen. Thank God his parents were abroad. They had taken Kadi and her children to Geneva to visit Lassana a week ago. His other sister and her husband would be safe, he knew. They were not connected to the government in any way. Few people knew, in fact, that Amana Keita was Mohammed Ndiaye's daughter; or that Tendé Ndiaye was her brother.

"I can't find the station, sir." Majid started to flick through the pre-programmed stations: Radio Bamakan, Pulsar FM, Radio Liberté, Radio Kadira.

There was nothing save an ominous static cackle. BBC World and Radio France were broadcasting as normal. It was a bad sign. Tendé didn't wait. It was one of the first classic moves of officers wishing to stage a coup d'état: knock out the communications centers. Fortunately for whoever was behind this, Bamako had only one broadcasting station. He knew exactly what had happened.

"Stop the car, Majid. Now." Majid pulled over. Tendé looked around. He knew he had only a matter of hours before all hell would break loose. If the military had seized control of the radio and television center, the airport was surely closed. Control the airwaves and escape routes . . . he knew the drill. He opened the door. "Majid. Listen to me. Take the car back to the office. If anyone stops you or asks where I am, tell them you dropped me off at the palace. Do you understand? Leave the car at the office and take a taxi. Meet me at the Sanza Bar, on the Koulikoro Road. Give me two hours. We'll need a car and a full tank of petrol. Can you do that?" Majid nodded. He had been with the Ndiaye family for almost all his working life. He too knew what had happened. Tendé straightened up, slapped the hood of the car and watched as Majid sped off. He turned, hailed a taxi and jumped in. As Foreign Minister, the soldiers in support of the coup would be at his house within the hour. There was a phone in the house, a mobile phone with a French number. If he could get to that, he could phone Amber and try to make contact. News of the coup would filter through to France in the early hours of the morning, if it hadn't already. Amber would be going out of her mind with worry.

He had the taxi drop him off at a crossroads near the house. He got out and looked down the street—everything was quiet. He walked down the road, tugging at his tie, watching the houses around him. Mohammed, their watchman, was in his usual position in front of the house. He looked up as Tendé approached, probably wondering what on earth his employer was doing walking around in the dark. Tendé walked up to him. Anyone come to the house in the past few hours? Mohammed shook his head, staring at him. Tendé turned and walked through the gates. He broke into a run. His heart was beating fast. He knew, as did every other democratically elected government official, that situations like this could so easily get out of hand. The army had always been the unpredictable element in Malian society. The country had had its fair share of coups: 1968; an attempt in 1971 followed by another in 1978; and again in 1982 . . . and then all through the nineties, discontent bubbling just below the surface, threatening the stability of the Konaré government for whom Tendé now worked.

He ran into the bedroom, wondering where the hell Amber had put the phone. He picked up the house phone: dead. All communications within the country would have been cut off already. His own cellphone registered no signal. Somehow they must have managed to get to the HQ of the service provider. It showed they were more organized than the last few attempts. He pulled open the bedside drawers. Nothing. There was some money in one of the dressers in the living room—he usually kept a few hundred dollars in there. He ran back into the living room, discarding his clothes as he went. He yanked open another drawer. *Yes!* The manila envelope was there. He pulled it out and tore it open. There was more than a few hundred dollars in it— close to $2,000 in $50 bills. Good. He pulled open a few   more   drawers . . . where   was   the   phone? Where would she have put it? And the charger? It was highly unlikely there would be any battery life left. He'd last used it on a trip to Paris, almost six weeks previously.

He slammed drawer after drawer closed, becoming increasingly agitated. He ran back into the bedroom and yanked open the closet door. He pulled out a long *bou-bou* with a matching cap. He would have to discard the businessman's suit and dress as unobtrusively as possible. He stopped in the bathroom and hurriedly shaved off his trademark goatee. He also picked up a packet of contact lenses from the bathroom cupboard and shoved them into the folds of his robe, together with the envelope containing the money and his passport. He would throw away his glasses as soon as he'd found a lift out of the city.

The phone . . . the phone. Where had she put it? Think, Tendé . . . *think!* Where would she be likely to store it? He stopped . . . his study. She always put his things in one place. He walked through the house. The sight of the sparse, beautifully furnished interior hit him suddenly. The photographs of the children; of Amber; the paintings they had chosen together, hanging in carefully chosen places on the simple white walls. The furniture that she'd had local craftsmen make in replica of European classics sitting comfortably alongside African and Malian pieces; cushions covered in cloth from the Congo; the exquisite *kente* runner that always lay along the pale birch dresser she'd brought back from Spain . . . He swallowed. When would he see it again? In the very short space of an hour, his whole life had been turned upside-down. He knew it was better not to think about it. When it came down to it, all that mattered was getting out of the mess alive. Everything else paled into insignificance beside that one, unavoidable fact. He walked into the study. The phone was sitting in its case, together with its chargers—one for the house, one for the car. He ushered up a prayer of thanks—to Allah and to Amber for her fail-safe organization. Then he stuffed the pouch into his deep pockets and walked away from everything he held dear.

He waited at the Sanza Bar for almost half an hour. There was no sign of Majid. News of the coup was slowly beginning to filter down to the public, although there had been no official announcement. People clustered together on the street corner in small groups, trying to pick up what bits and pieces of news there were coming in. Everyone looked anxious. The radio stations were still eerily silent. Neither Radio France nor BBC World had yet heard or suspected anything. He stood apart from the crowd in his long, pale blue robe, nervously fingering the packages concealed in its voluminous interior.

He was almost on the verge of giving up and hailing a taxi when Majid suddenly pulled up in an ancient Peugeot 504—a relic from the seventies. Tendé looked at it in disbelief. Belching smoke and fumes, it hardly looked like the vehicle to drive them both to the Burkina border, which was where he intended to go. He walked around it dubiously. Majid looked at him through the window.

"It will be fine, sir," he said, noticing Tendé's alarm. "Come. Let's go. There's no time to lose." Tendé pulled open the passenger door and got in. He outlined the route quickly, pulling out the car charger and inserting it immediately into the lighter socket. To his relief, the charger made a little "peep" and began its business. He would wait until they were well out of the city before attempting to put a call through to Amber. There was no telling who might be listening in on the airwaves. Majid slung the car into gear—noisily—and pulled out onto the road. Traffic was heavy; a plus, Tendé noted as they began inching their way out of the city. It made it less likely that he would be spotted by the checkpoints the soldiers would surely have put up around the city's edges. He closed his eyes and tried not to think about what would happen if they were stopped.

They exited the city without too much difficulty. There were indeed checkpoints and barricades along the way. Tendé had chosen one of the longest routes to get out of the country. Burkina Faso was at least two days' drive from Bamako; Majid wondered why they didn't head due south, for Guinea. But Tendé knew there would be others attempting that route. Better to go where it was least expected.

They drove east out of the city towards the town of Koulikoro. From there, they would head to Ségou and then make their way across laterite roads to the border. Once they'd managed to get across, they would head straight for Ouagadougou and from there, he would catch a flight to Paris. At least that was the plan. And he knew that at any minute, it was subject to change.

They took it in turns to drive; Majid for a few hours, then Tendé while Majid slept on the back seat. They drove east through Koulikoro, where they stopped for some food and heard that the news of the coup in Bamako had spread this far. The road was empty for many miles, the dark green scrub vegetation of the countryside around Bamako giving way as they drove north as well as east to a dull, sandy brown. Trees were scarce in this part of the country; his headlights picked out a flattened, empty landscape, with few villages. Every so often he checked the phone; there was no reception this far out of the capital. He would probably have to wait until Ouagadougou before being able to call.

As dawn broke over the district of Ségou, he could see that the land looked lean and insubstantial after the recent drought. That too had brought its own economic woes. In a country where eighty percent of the population were occupied in one way or another farming the land, a particularly bad year of harvests was enough to sow seeds of another kind: unrest. The horizontal layer of rice fields around the city of Ségou were testament to the grand plans of the colonial powers; Tendé couldn't remember the details . . . a French engineer's dreams of turning the desert into rice farms. *La delta morte* was brought to life with the help of a massive dam at Markala, twenty-five miles south of Ségou. Like many of the *grands projets* of its time, bedeviled by management failures and labor shortages, it wound up operating at a fraction of its capacity, but the dream of a productive desert still lingered. Max had fallen prey to the same romanticism. Fortunately for him—and for Tendé—*his* project had worked.

At the small town of Bla, he turned the battered vehicle north again; they would follow the road to Sévaré, then turn east again at Bandiagara and from there a straight run through the legendary Dogon country to the border town of Koro. Quite how they were going to cross the border wasn't yet clear to him; he would find out en route just how heavily the country's borders had been sealed. The drive from the plains just before Bandiagara to the escarpment in which the Dogon built their strangely beautiful, cave-like houses was spectacular in the midday sun. The flat, black road snaked ahead of them; off it, like tributaries leading from a main, mighty river, raw red roads carved by human feet and the occasional vehicle led off through the low-lying bush and scrub. As they passed village after village—Tégourou, Djiguibombo, Teli, Kombolé . . . the names were unfamiliar to him—the pattern was always the same. On the approach to the village, people suddenly appeared, strolling, pushing bicycles, women carrying loads of firewood balanced precariously on their heads; men holding cutlasses and hoes, walking to and from the ragged farms that lay scattered around the fragile human settlements. Women pressed their children against their colorful *pagne* skirts as the car passed; boys jeered and threw small stones and mango pips. There were few cars on the road. Occasionally a small mobylette or motorcycle whistled past, tiny engine protesting, but there were certainly no tanks, no trucks full of soldiers. For the first time since they'd left Bamako, Tendé began to relax.

They left Djiguimbombo at two in the afternoon, just when the sun was directly overhead. The sky was white, bleached of all color by the heat. Huge, ungainly baobab trees sprouted up here and there in the otherwise flat, rocky landscape; the savannah grasslands extended as far as the eye could see. Everything was yellow-white, dry. A mile south of the town, the landscape fell away suddenly to reveal the edge of the plateau and sweeping views over the plains to Burkina Faso below.

"Not long to go," Tendé said quietly to Majid as they stopped to make a switch. Majid nodded. He would drop Tendé off in Ouagadougou and then begin the long, 600-mile drive back to Bamako the following day. Majid had a family in the city and there was no question of him not returning home. They had said very little to one another on the long journey through the night; out of some instinctive delicacy, perhaps, Majid understood the fears running through Tendé's mind. He concentrated instead on pushing the little Peugeot as hard and fast as he could; the sooner they made it across, the better. Every sixty miles or so, he offered up a prayer. *I ni tié*. Thank you.

≈106≈

Madeleine was the first to hear the news. The phone rang at quarter past six. Amber was crying through her words. As she listened, Madeleine was immediately catapulted backwards in time and understood immediately just how frightened Amber was. As Amber talked, she got out of bed and switched on the television in her room, softly—Peter was still fast asleep. There was nothing about Mali on any of the UK channels. Things had obviously not gone badly enough for the BBC to be aware.

"Take it slowly, Amber. Stay calm. I know it's hard. Do the kids know?"

"No . . . Sibi knows there's something wrong. I've just spoken to Tendé's parents; they're in Geneva, with Lassana. His dad's already had a couple of phone calls from Bamako. It's a young army officer, apparently. He's got the junior officers with him. Two people that we know have been shot already. Jesus, Madeleine, I'm going out of my mind."

"I know . . . look, I'll come over with Peter. I'll call

the hospital. You need someone with you. Has your mother gone back?"

"No, she's at home. She'll only start to panic and upset the children. When can you get here?"

"Give me thirty minutes." Madeleine put down the phone and stared at the television screen flickering silently in the corner. Poor Amber. She knew what could—and often did—happen in situations like this: confusion; lack of communication between central command and the outposts; someone losing his head . . . it didn't bear thinking about. She jumped up and threw on a pair of jeans and a shirt. She brushed her teeth quickly and went down the hallway to wake Peter. Fortunately, he adored Sibi and Liya and even little Kedé . . . he was awake in an instant, eyes shining with excitement. She dressed him, gave him something to eat and was out of the house in thirty minutes, as she'd promised. She stood on the doorstep at Amber's London flat and prayed that the next twenty-four hours would go well.

Becky arrived next, out of breath. She'd come as soon as she'd heard from Amber. The news had finally broken on the BBC. Amber led the two of them into the living room, where they grimly watched what little information there was to be had in silent concentration. There was even a mention of Tendé . . . the young, charismatic Foreign Minister married to the daughter of Max Sall, the late billionaire financier . . . A nerve in Amber's face twitched as an image of the two of them flashed up on the screen. Becky turned to her in silent awe. In Amber's study, the phone could be heard ringing—she jumped up at once and disappeared. Becky and Madeleine stared at each other, unable to believe what was happening.

"D'you think he's . . . all right?" Becky voiced what could not be said. Madeleine bit her lip.

"I don't know. I . . . hope so. If there's anyone who could get himself out of something like this it's Tendé, of course. But . . . who knows. Anything can happen."

Becky turned back to the screen. Football results. She stared at it in disbelief.

Amber came back into the room. Her eyes were red. She shook her head: no news. Just a relative, calling from Paris. No one knew what to say. Tendé's mother, who had lived through four different coups, had said there was nothing to be done but to wait. Wait for it to be over. Killing each other's not our style, she said over the phone from Geneva. They're more likely to arrest than kill. Pray for him. Amber had put down the phone, unable to respond. Pray?

The three of them looked at each other. The children were squealing in the playroom; Kedé would soon have to be fed. Some sort of routine would have to assert itself, quickly. Amber ran her hands through her short hair, a gesture of frustration and helplessness. She took a deep breath. If there was a way to contact her, Tendé would find it. Perhaps Mme. Ndiaye was right. Perhaps it *was* all they could do—pray. She opened her mouth to speak and the phone rang again. She rushed out of the room.

They were almost through the small village of Koporo-Kenie-Na. Majid was at the wheel, Tendé dozing fitfully by his side. It was just after three. The sun was beginning its slow, fiery descent from its pinnacle in the center of the white-hot sky. At the horizon, the edges of the vast, cloudless expanse above them were turning a deeper shade of blue. It was Tendé's favorite time of the day: between three and four when the shadows lengthened and the sky acquired color and depth. Out here in the countryside where the red earth lay exposed under farmers' blades and every road was a crimson slash through the rocky scrub, the land began to turn gold. In the village, knots of people gathered here and there; women with their hair in the stiffened plaits and braids that their counterparts in the city no longer wore; men, dignified and surprised at the same time, sitting stiffly upright on ancient bicycles, wavered as the car approached them from behind and overtook in a cloud of dust and fumes. Small thrown-together tables sat in lonely sentinel along the edges of the graveled road; piles of blood-red tomatoes; huge bunches of curved green plantains brought in by road from Burkina, from the south; clusters of dried fish brought by the traders from the Bani River, almost fifty miles away . . . Tendé opened his eyes from time to time, the images imprinting themselves on his eyelids as though he were a tourist driving through the landscape with a different purpose and timescale in mind. The road began to deteriorate; Majid had to slow down. There were larger stones and deep ruts in front of them, as though something heavy had passed through recently, disturbing the track. The road forked to the left; there was an enormous baobab, that ungainly upside-down tree with a trunk so fat and wide the entire car could have passed through . . . and there it was, suddenly. A truck. Full of soldiers. Majid shook Tendé roughly awake. It was too late to do anything other than slow down to a crawl. There were maybe ten or fifteen soldiers lying beside the road; the truck lay lopsided and as Tendé sat up he saw that it had a puncture. There were men lying underneath it, tinkering away. His heart sank. Under his breath, Majid swore, softly.

"Sortez de la voiture!" The commanding officer, a young man, perhaps in his late twenties, strode towards the car, a gun in his hand, waving imperiously. Tendé and Majid hesitated. There was a gun in the battered glove compartment; Tendé had taken it from the desk in his study and placed it there shortly after their journey began. He made a quick calculation—no, there were too many of them. Any sign of aggression on their part would have disastrous consequences. Majid killed the engine and they sat in nervous silence for a second. *"Sortez!"* the command came again. The soldier was almost upon them. Majid opened the door cautiously, his hands going automatically to his head. Tendé pushed open his door, and followed suit. The envelope containing cash flapped against his thigh as he

got out and turned to face the approaching officer. As he raised his hands, he suddenly remembered . . . his glasses. A cold shock ran through him; he had forgotten to remove them and put his lenses in. With the dust in the air, he'd waited. With his glasses on he was instantly recognizable: Tendé Ndiaye, Foreign Minister . . . his trademark wireless frames and goatee. He'd shaved the latter off, but forgotten his glasses. He held his breath. The soldier was frisking Majid with one hand on the other side of the car. Could he risk it? Slide a hand upwards and peel them off? Behind the officer, three more approached, guns slung casually around their shoulders, like handbags.

The officer walked around the car, peering at him intently. He held the car keys dangling from the little finger of his right hand; his gun was held loosely in his left hand. As he walked towards him, Tendé became aware of an extraordinary tension in the man's face. He had recognized him, yes . . . the eyebrows raised, recognition dawning, blindly expectant . . . He flinched and closed his eyes briefly.

"Ndiaye. Minister." The man spoke. Behind him, the soldiers paused, frowning. Tendé opened his eyes. Fear had seeped through his entire body; despite the outside heat, he was cold. "You don't remember me?" The man spoke again, a smile breaking out on his face. Tendé frowned at him. The man lifted a hand; the one holding the car keys. "*Je suis* Boubacar. Boubacar Adama. *Vous ne me souvenez pas*?" He spoke in stiff French. Tendé shook his head. Out of the corner of his eye, he could see

Majid tense involuntarily. The man lowered his hand and began to talk excitedly. Suddenly, it came to him. Boubacar! The driver!

"You. You were the driver!" Tendé gasped. The soldier's head nodded up and down vigorously, his face breaking into a wide smile. He held out a hand. Tendé took it, open-mouthed. The coincidence was almost too great to believe. They had survived that time through the skill of the driver. A skid. He had been taught not to brake in a skid, and that was what had saved them. He had tipped him handsomely when they reached Timbuktu, but that was not his reward. He had confided to Tendé that his ambition was to join the army. Was there perhaps anything Tendé could do . . . a word in the right ear? He would enter at any rank: private, army corps driver, anything would do. Tendé took his name— Boubacar Adama—and promised to see what he could do. He had kept his word. Six months later, he was told by one of the other drivers on another trip that Boubacar Adama had indeed been commissioned into the army. He sent his thanks. Tendé had smiled and put the matter out of his mind.

They switched to Bambara, the soldier leading Tendé through his men to the shade of the baobab tree. They squatted in front of it and Boubacar hurriedly filled him in on the details, as far as he knew them, of the previous night's coup. He was a junior officer in charge of the barracks and munitions depot at Ségou. They had had little choice but to join with the rebels. The army had split down the middle; junior officers against their senior counterparts. He had been posted to keep watch on the road from Ségou to the border. The Burkina army were under strict orders not to allow anyone to cross.

"What are my options?" Tendé asked him, his mind racing.

"Not many. You can try to hide out here for some time until it's clear what's happening in Bamako. But . . . it's not easy around here. People know each other. They talk. I can't hide you at the barracks."

"How much time d'you think I have?" Boubacar shrugged. A day. Maybe two days. Command would be sending troops down to the border towns by the end of the week. They had seized control, as Tendé already knew, of the broadcasting stations and the air and river ports. Some said the President had been shot, others that he had been arrested. It was difficult to know what exactly was going on. "Is there an airfield nearby?" Tendé asked. Boubacar looked at him.

"Yes, at Douentza. It's an old military strip. You . . . what are you thinking?"

"I need a phone. Preferably a mobile phone. There's no reception around here, is there?"

"At Sévaré. There's a transmitter. Come, we'll take you back. You'll be safe in the back of the truck."

"Is it ready? It looked as though you'd broken down."

"Just the tire. Ten, fifteen minutes . . . we'll be on the road." He got to his feet. "I never had the chance to thank you," he said, smiling again. "I do it now." Tendé nodded slowly. If he could get through to Amber, she would do the rest.

* * *

The call came through at five in the afternoon. Amber was calm. She took his instructions, told him to wait there for an hour and that she would find a way to get him a plane. Madeleine and Becky looked at her as she replaced the receiver. Angela was in the next room, alternately pacifying and occupying the children. The whole house had the atmosphere of a war room; no one except the children had eaten anything since breakfast.

Amber put her hands to her face. The afternoon had been the longest of her life. "A plane. He needs a plane. He's in the south of the country, near a place called Douentza. Where the hell am I going to get a plane from?" She looked at them. "Or a pilot. Who's going to fly into a country under a coup?" The three of them looked at each other.

"Wasn't . . . ?" Madeleine started first.

"Isn't . . . ?" Becky looked at Amber hesitantly.

"Paola? Yes, he was a pilot." Amber finished their sentences. She swallowed. Alessandra's father. A pilot. She looked at her hands. "Christ, if there was anyone else . . ." She lifted her head, one eye narrowed, as if in pain. "How am I going to ask Paola for help?"

"You've got no choice," Madeleine said. Amber nodded slowly. Of course. She had absolutely no option—and no time to waste. She flicked open her Filofax and picked up the receiver again. "Paola? It's Amber. Have you got a minute? I need your help."

*   *   *

Paola put down the phone five minutes later, her mind racing. Amber had asked her for help? At first she'd thought her sister was joking.

"You've got some nerve," Paola said bitterly, resentment burning in her as soon as she heard Amber's voice.

"Paola, I wouldn't ask, believe me, if it weren't serious. I don't know anyone else. I've never asked you for anything before, but I'm begging you now." There was silence as Amber's words sank in. For the first time in her life, Paola heard fear in Amber's voice. She struggled with herself. It was strange, the way images flashed through her mind: Amber practically shoving her off Max's knee; the look of scorn on Amber's face when Paola got a word wrong in English; Amber and Kieran giggling behind her back . . . waves of buried anger and petty jealousies rushed through her. And Tendé, of course . . . she couldn't believe he was in danger. *Him*? The sleek confidence with which he moved . . . *that* man was in danger?

"Okay." She heard her voice as if out of nowhere. "I'll call you back." There was a sudden intake of breath, and then the words Paola had never thought she would live to hear, not from Amber. Thank you. She put down the phone, a sudden lump forming in her throat.

It took her twenty minutes to find Stefan. He was at his parents' home just outside Düsseldorf. He listened in silence to her request—and the promise of whatever fees he would charge, *anything, any amount*—and told her he would ring back. She spent another thirty minutes waiting by the phone, biting the sides of her nails, praying that he would come through. He did. There were a couple of possibilities. A 4,000-foot long runway at a small town on the eastern border of Ghana named Wa or the former military 8,000-foot airfield at the northern town of Tamale. He knew a couple of South African pilots who were based in Ghana, flying in and out of the mines. He could catch a commercial flight to Accra the following morning and be met at the airport at around 5 p.m. He would fly straight from Accra to Tamale or Wa and then fly on by himself into Mali. He would arrange a pickup with Tendé at around 8 p.m. With any luck, Tendé would make it onto either the British Airways flight from Accra to London at 11:30 or the Alitalia flight to Rome at midnight. Any good? "I'll call you right back," Paola said and hung up. She phoned Amber. Thirty-seven minutes had passed. Amber couldn't hold back her tears.

Just over twenty-four hours after he'd managed to get through to his wife, Tendé stood at the side of the deserted airstrip in Douentza under the cover of darkness and watched the little plane circle overhead, preparing to land. Amber was as good as her word. He shook hands with Majid, handed him a thick wad of dollar bills and gave the rest over to Boubacar and his men. He ran towards the plane, his long, blue robe billowing out behind him in the rush of wind from the engines. Stefan opened the door, threw down the metal steps and extended a hand to the man his ex-lover had said had to be brought out of Mali alive, at all costs.

"Welcome aboard, sir," he shouted above the noise of the aircraft. Tendé smiled briefly and took the seat indicated. It was a tiny plane—a two-seater. It was all he needed, he thought to himself as he strapped himself in and Stefan taxied back down the bumpy runway. He closed his eyes as the plane gathered speed, its headlights piercing the inky blackness in front and all around them. He'd made it. Or rather, Amber had seen to it that he would. He ran a cautious finger around the shape of his lips and mouth, tracing their outline. Amber. Right from the second time they'd met, out there in the desert, he'd known. She had what it took.

The plane lifted into the night. He leaned back in the seat and thought about the woman who was his wife.

At midnight, the phone in the living room rang. Becky was curled up on the couch, fast asleep. Madeleine had reluctantly taken Peter home that afternoon. Call me as soon as you hear he's safe, she said, embracing Amber on the doorstep.

Amber picked it up on the second ring, her heart hammering. "Hello?"

"I'm here. I'm in Accra. At the airport. I'll be in London tomorrow morning at six. Terminal Four." She put down the phone, tears of relief sliding silently down her cheeks.

EPILOGUE
Bamako, Mali
2004

The last of the distinguished guests were shown through the enormous doors at one end of the great hall at State House. Outside, as Amber and Tendé drove up in the presidential limousine, their motorcade wailing, she saw with a start the hundreds of thousands who had come to witness the swearing in of the country's most popular politician. As the car turned into the sweeping forecourt, she caught sight of the banners waving yellow and white in the midday sun. Tendé's name and face were printed in stark black-and-white relief. Some of the women even wore pagne wraparound skirts with his likeness encircled with garlands and local symbols splashed across their thighs and backsides. She stifled a smile.

Police cordons had been erected the night before

to keep the thronging masses at bay. The country's youngest ever Foreign Minister had been instrumental in the talks with the young army officers who had temporarily overthrown the government two years earlier. When the dust had settled and the country had simmered down, it was Tendé Ndiaye and his father whose efforts made the headlines, both domestically and internationally—as a result, his was the name on the outgoing President's lips as the man to replace him. In 2002, President Konaré had stepped down; in 2004, with a massive majority, Tendé Ndiaye had carried the incumbent party to victory.

Inside the hall, Tendé having been led away immediately, Amber took her place at the empty chair beside his, her eyes scanning the rows of dignitaries and foreign guests in front of her. The children were with their grandparents. She looked to her right and saw Sibi's face, gazing with stiff pride and admiration at the two of them. Liya was reaching around her neck to fiddle with the label she'd complained had been scratching her ever since they'd left the house. She shook her head faintly. Kedé was asleep, of course. He slept through everything. She turned her head to the left. There they were—Becky, Godson, Madeleine and Peter . . . and Paola. Behind them, Francesca, Angela and Kieran, sitting side by side. Her gaze lingered a moment on Kieran. It had been hard but the wounds were beginning to heal. She looked down at her hands, at the newly fashioned wedding ring made out of the three diamonds Max had brought with him to England, more than sixty years ago. It had been Tendé's idea to use them. Mandia had found a jeweler and from the moment Amber took off the ring Tendé had given her and replaced it with Max's stones, she knew it was absolutely, unequivocally, the right thing to do. She looked back up at her family sitting quietly, waiting for the ceremony to begin. She felt a contraction in her heart . . . what would Max have made of it? His family, together in this place and time, Paola sitting beside Angela without so much as a slung handbag or a catty exchange between them? She stifled a smile. He probably wouldn't have believed it. And yet much of what was happening in front of her was in no small measure thanks to Paola. When she had needed her most, Paola had come through for her. And for Tendé. It had taken them almost forty years, but the first, tentative steps towards something approaching friendship had been taken.

There was a movement behind her. The Party Chairman and the ministers who would form Tendé's new government were being led in. Tendé himself would be called in last and sworn in before the television cameras and the assembled international crowd of journalists. She knew that many of those who had flown in from London, Paris, New York and Rome were there because of who *they* were, as a couple, as a family. Interest in Amber Sall and Tendé Ndiaye, which had started in a somewhat offhand manner before their marriage, had reached fever-pitch after Tendé's dramatic escape from Bamako. Now that he was about to become

President, it threatened to overwhelm what should have been a rather low-key event.

She turned her head, conscious of her elaborate headdress of brilliant woven silk—a gift from the wife of the President of Ghana, the country to which Tendé had flown just after leaving his own. She was seated among the many African heads of state and their wives in the long row to her left. Her fitted, narrow skirt and corseted top were made out of the same material. She hadn't wanted to wear traditional dress; ridiculous for a European, she said to Tendé in their bedroom, earlier that week. But the arrival of the headdress and beautiful gold earrings from Madame Kufuor made it impossible to think of wearing anything else. At the last minute, Mandia had found material of similar pattern and color and a spectacular outfit had been run up within a day. Despite her misgivings, she looked stunning. There were not many whites who could carry it off, Mandia said to her, as they tucked and pinned and shaped the outfit—but she could. It was the only stamp of approval needed.

At the far end of the room, preparations were being made for Tendé to walk down the red carpet towards the podium and the guests, who were now being asked to stand. Two blasts of a military bugle, and the distant sound of traditional drummers began to waft through the windows that flanked one side of the building. The old and the new. She saw him, thinner now than he had been when they first met; the late nights of negotiation and the burdens of responsibility placed upon him had taken their toll. He was dressed in white; the long, flowing robe and skullcap that had first caught her eye. Later, as the celebrations wore on into the evening, he would change into the three-piece suit she had bought for him in London only weeks before. The old and the new; Africa and Europe; the West and the Rest, as he liked to joke. Tendé moved as he always did: seamlessly, effortlessly—a study in grace.

She took a deep breath and laced her hands in front of her thighs. As she prepared her face for public exposure—a hint of a smile, a challenging, interested glance around her—she caught Paola's eye. Her smile deepened. And was answered in return.